THE OFFER

Irene could not believe [illegible] king of furs, ruler of a fashion empire, was begging her, a frightened, inexperienced girl, to come back to work for him.

"You want me to grovel? I'll grovel—you have a gift. A real gift. The way you look at a fur and turn it to the light, the way you touch it and know it. I saw it every time you touched a pelt. I had to make mistakes, waste furs, waste time, to learn. But even now, you know things inside that I don't."

"Don't say such things. You will only tempt me—and I won't give in," Irene said.

"Why not, Irene? You want it. I want it. Come back."

Irene knew he was talking about more than simply working for him again. He was talking about the passion her beauty stirred in his aging but still vibrantly virile body. And this time there would be no denying him—not to save her marriage . . . not to save her soul.

Then why, when she knew she should say no, was every fiber within her crying to say yes . . . ?

CROWN SABLE

CROWN SABLE

by

Janice Young Brooks

AN ONYX BOOK

NEW AMERICAN LIBRARY

PUBLISHED BY
THE NEW AMERICAN LIBRARY
OF CANADA LIMITED

With love and gratitude to my
"So-Called Writer Friends,"
Diane, Andy, Barbara, Donna and Virginia

PUBLISHER'S NOTE

This novel is a work of fiction. Names, characters, places, and incidents either are the product of the author's imagination or are used fictitiously, and any resemblance to actual persons, living or dead, events, or locales is entirely coincidental.

NAL BOOKS ARE AVAILABLE AT QUANTITY DISCOUNTS
WHEN USED TO PROMOTE PRODUCTS OR SERVICES.
FOR INFORMATION PLEASE WRITE TO PREMIUM MARKETING DIVISION,
NEW AMERICAN LIBRARY, 1633 BROADWAY,
NEW YORK, NEW YORK 10019.

Onyx is a trademark of The New American Library of Canada Limited.

SIGNET, SIGNET CLASSIC, MENTOR, ONYX, PLUME, MERIDIAN AND NAL BOOKS are published in Canada by The New American Library of Canada, Limited, 81 Mack Avenue, Scarborough, Ontario, Canada M1L 1M8

First Printing, January, 1987

2 3 4 5 6 7 8 9

PRINTED IN CANADA
COVER PRINTED IN U.S.A.

1

January 1901

It was the slap that did it.

The slap and Teo's shoes. They crystalized in Irina's mind just what she was and what she wanted to be. And though she eventually put the incident out of her conscious mind, she never completely forgot that spark that ignited her life. It wasn't until years later that she told a man she loved about that day and the girl she had been at thirteen. And although he wanted to understand her, he couldn't.

"But, Mama, I don't want to wear Teo's shoes," she'd protested. "They're too big."

"Yes, for now," Mama agreed. "That way they will fit for a long time. Your shoes, they are too small now and will fit your sister Agnieszka. This is how it is."

That *was* how it was.

"Here. A rag. Tear it and put in the toes. It will keep the snow out. The eggs are in the basket by the door. Take to the big house. We will have two extra kopecks to give your father and Teo for the Journey."

Irina started to object, but tears had come to her mother's eyes as they always did when she spoke of the Journey. "Yes, Mama," Irina said

The big house, the peasants' name for the manor just outside the village, wasn't far, but the walk up the S-curved, tree-canopied drive seemed miles. Irina tried to walk steadily for the sake of the eggs, but she kept tripping over the stuffed toes of Teo's shoes and slipping on icy patches. Twice she nearly fell. The drive was graveled, but there were bare muddy places where the thin winter sunlight shone and the shoes made slurpy sounds as they sucked free of each step.

The manor house, clearly Russian in style to a more educated eye, sat on a slight rise, physically elevated above the rest of the village. Irina had never been allowed to come so close. Any contact between the Kossok family and the manor fell to Teo. He was the eldest, the only son, the clever one, the pride of the family, and thus their best representative on such errands. But he was in the village with Papa, bidding a final farewell to their friends.

The Journey was to begin in the morning.

Irina avoided the front of the house, sensing instinctively that she shouldn't go to the big double doors with the fancy porch. As she walked around the side, she could see lights from inside. How rich they must be to light their candles before full dark! Against her better judgment, Irina found herself drawn to a window.

Inside there was only one person, a girl of about thirteen, Irina's age. She wore a very grown-up dress with ruffles around the neck and sleeves and even a little gold ornament at her neck. She had glorious hair that fell in shiny ringlets and she was sitting very prim and straight on a bench facing a big polished wooden box on legs. It had a shelf in the front with black and white bars. She moved her fingers in intricate patterns, pushing down the bars, and it made music!

Enthralled, Irina leaned her elbows on the sill and listened in awe. Finally the girl stopped and stood, her glossy curls bobbing. As she turned, she saw Irina at the window. She frowned and gestured imperiously. Irina picked up her basket of eggs and hurried away to the back door. It was opened by a big woman with gray braids wound around her head and flour on her hands. "I . . . I have eggs. To sell . . . ?" Irina said.

"Come in. I will see if we have need of eggs," the woman said, and disappeared into the adjoining pantry. Another door swung open and the girl who'd been playing the piano stood there, her arms crossed and her foot tapping. "Who is this dirty girl who spies on me, Grabarski?"

The cook reappeared, wiping her hands on her apron. "Just a village girl, miss. To sell eggs. Kossok's girl, I think."

"This is what I think of Kossok's girl snooping at windows!" she said, striding quickly across the room and snatching the basket from Irina. With a quick, deliberate motion she lifted it and let it crash to the floor. Egg and shell splattered everywhere.

Irina cried out as if she'd been injured. "My mother's eggs! You've broken them. That was wicked!"

The girl met Irina's gaze with a furious look. "How *dare* you talk to your betters that way, you dirty, common girl!"

She slapped Irina.

"Get down there and clean it up!"

She stood over Irina until her order was carried out. The cook tried once to help, but the girl waved her back and she obeyed the young mistress with a cringing nod.

Irina didn't cry until she was out of sight of the house; then the tears came hot and furious. Slumped miserably in the snow behind a tree where no one could see her, Irina buried her face in her shabby skirts. She could still feel the stinging imprint of the girl's hand on her cheek.

Still, the slap only underlined the real hurt. The wicked girl with the glossy curls had been right. Irina *was* common and dirty. She'd never known it before. Up until today her only standard had been the other villagers. Some, of course, had more than the Kossok family, but the differences were subtle: meat twice a week instead of once, an extra petticoat to wear to Sunday Mass, a few more laying hens in the coop at the back of the house.

But this glimpse of another way of life was astonishing. There were people who lived in enormous houses and had clean, fancy clothing and big boxes that made music. It was an awesome revelation. She'd never known or guessed that such a way of life existed, and the way she'd been treated by the girl with the gold ornament and the bobbing curls was a devastating shock. For the first time, she understood inferiority, and it ate into her like acid.

Finally anger began to cool and was replaced by bitter resolution. Irina stood up and wiped her eyes on her dun-colored shawl. She stared down with loathing at Teo's old shoes. The rag had straggled out the side through a hole. She balled her fists, looked back at the manor house, and vowed, "Someday I will be rich and I will slap her back."

* * *

The whole family was to accompany Pa and Teo on the first part of the Journey. Most people had to walk clear to Hamburg, Germany, to leave, but Pa had gotten tickets on a boat that had undergone repairs and was departing from the shipyards at Gdansk. There the man and boy would board a ship for America and Zofia Kossok would take her daughters home to await the passage money that would enable them all to be reunited in the Golden Land.

An hour before dawn, Zofia woke the family and they went to a special early Mass before piling into the borrowed wagon. Zofia sat at the front between Teo and her husband, Jozef, and cried most of the way. The baby at her breast cried too. The other little girls slept cuddled together for warmth like puppies on the bed of the wagon. Irina wanted to sleep also, for Mama and Pa's coupling the night before had been noisy and weepy and had kept her awake far into the night. But her mind wouldn't rest. She sensed that Mama wasn't crying because she'd miss Pa—Teo she would miss, but not Pa. Zofia was crying because things were changing, and to her way of thinking, change was terrible.

But Irina was obsessed with the flowering fascination of change. Before the previous day, she'd lived, thought, eaten, dressed, prayed, and felt exactly as untold generations of her family had lived, thought, eaten, dressed, prayed, and felt. The comforting eternal sameness of her existence was the spine of her life. Until yesterday.

As Irina had sat weeping in the snow outside the manor house, she had realized something her mother might never know: change not only *could* be better, it *had* to be better, at least for Irina Kossok. Without having ever seen the world outside the village, she was convinced that there were places, people, and challenges out there ready for her . . . destined for her. Watching her handsome brother sitting at the front of the wagon, she wondered how he, who was getting to go away and find the riches of the world could be so . . . so irritable. There was no other word for it. Every time Mama sobbed, he drew away, almost shuddering with revulsion.

They went north from the village to the seaport, stopping at every village church along the way. Later, when Irina thought about her native country, she would remember nothing of the landscape, only the churches. Lichen-crusted stone churches, weathered wood chapels, even small family shrines—Zofia had to pray at each of them. As they entered Gdansk, Zofia spotted the steeple of the Church of the Virgin Mary and insisted over everyone's objections that they stop there. The church, one of the largest and most ornate in Europe, was awesome—full of Gothic sculptures, gravestones, baroque family chapels, and brilliantly colored triptychs. To Zofia it was evidence of God's glory; to Irina it was proof that the world was rich with glorious things beyond all imagining. How could she ever return to the gray-and-brown life of the village after knowing gilt and marble, however fleetingly? How she envied Teo!

Zofia would have visited every church in the city, but Jozef said he'd been prayed over enough and they would miss the boat if they stopped again. Zofia paid slight heed until Teo said the same thing. To please Teo, they made their way to the docks. Once there, the Kossok family was absorbed into a milling crowd of other emigrants. Most, like them, were sending only one or two members of the family, mostly older sons. Zofia Kossok was only another weeping, praying woman here, lost in waves of sobbed farewells.

Teo and his father went off to see when the boat was to leave, while Irina stayed with her mother and the younger girls—Agnieszka, the twins, and the baby. Zofia fell into conversation with a dumpy woman standing by them under a wooden shelter. "Your man is going away too?" the woman asked, looking over the mob of little girls with a pitying eye.

"My husband and my son. But we will go to join them very soon," Zofia answered defensively

"Yes, my son goes also. We feared the army would take him, so we send him away. Better for him in America. He could become rich there."

Zofia looked uncomfortable. This fear of the army was exactly the reason they'd scrimped to send Teo with his father instead of keeping him home to look after his mother and sisters. Poland no longer existed as a map entity, and the Kossoks, though genetically Poles, were geographically Russians and subject to the cruel draft of the Russian Army. Too many young men had been taken into the army and either never returned, or worse, had come back with only a worn-out uniform and brash Russian manners that alienated them from kin and village.

But one didn't admit such fears, certainly not to strangers. "My son, Teo, he is not afraid of the army. He is very brave," Zofia said. "He goes to America to be a scholar. He is very smart, Teo is. Some people in our village have cousins in a village in America called New York. My man and boy will stay with them while they earn the passage for us. They will be rich."

The other woman nodded. "This is good. My son, he also goes to live with friends from home."

Before Zofia could comment on this, Jozef rushed up, wringing his hands frantically. "They won't let me go! My eyes—they say my eyes are bad. Some disease. America won't let me come to their country. The man at the boat said that!"

"What about Teo?" Zofia asked, shoving the baby into Irina's arms and looking at her husband's eyes. Irina crowded closer to peer at her father as well. His eyes *were* red and crusty at the corners, but they were always that way. What did America care about such a thing?

"Teo they will take. Teo has good eyes," Jozef said.

Beside him, Teo stood up a little straighter, as if having good eyes were a sign of physical if not moral superiority.

Zofia began to cry again. So did the baby. Even Agnieszka, who had been happily watching the crowd only moments before, succumbed and grabbed a handful of Irina's shawl to weep into. The twins toddled over and followed her example. "Stop that, Aggie!" Irina said sharply over the sound of her parents' lamentations.

After some moments of confusion, Jozef said, "Teo will go now. We will keep the passage money, and when he sends more, we will all go."

Irina was suddenly overwhelmed at the prospect of the long gray-and-brown vista of eternity in the village. Mama had been the guiding strength in saving the money, and it was for Teo's sake. Once he was safely gone, the rest of them would never go. She knew as surely as she'd ever known anything that returning to the village today meant returning forever.

Forever!

She could not go back! It would be like leaping into an open grave and waiting, perhaps for years, for the moist black earth to be shoveled over her. She disengaged Agnieszka's grip and handed the baby back to Zofia. "I will go with Teo in Pa's place."

The words pounded in her ears. The moment held all the brilliant, joyful agony of birth. The simple words were the first important thing she'd ever said. The instant she spoke them she became an individual, not just a unit of family, village, or church, not a generational marker in an endlessly identical repetition, but a single individual with a private course to plot and navigate.

Jozef turned his rheumy eyes on his eldest daughter. After a long, stunned silence, he said, "Don't be stupid! Girls don't go off to America without their people."

"I'll be with Teo, and as soon as we reach America, I'll be with the Spryzaks."

"No," Pa repeated. "Your mama needs you here."

"But if I were in America helping Teo earn money, the rest of you could come twice as soon."

Teo stood to the side, as if he were an impartial and slightly amused observer. "Let her come," he said. There was no real enthusiasm in his statement, but Irina was grateful.

But the words that turned the tide came from an unexpected quarter. The woman who'd been talking to Mama inserted herself between the adults. "No, you must not let her go. A girl like that? What would happen to her in America? She'd be with child in six months, I tell you. These girls have no brains."

Zofia turned and glared at her. She'd been utterly opposed to the idea of Irina leaving until this busybody spoke up. But she resented the slur on the way she'd brought up her eldest daughter. "My Irina, she is a good Catholic girl. And she is not stupid," she said to the woman who'd dared to meddle in a family matter and impugn Irina's upbringing. "Jozef, Irina *should* go in your place."

Jozef could see that Zofia had a point, but he was sick with disappointment over not getting to go to America now. Besides, he didn't like being told what to do by his wife, especially not in front of the children and other people. "No. She will not go. She has no clothes to wear, no food . . ."

"I have the clothes I'm wearing," Irina said, stung by the injustice of this reason. She was clad in virtually the only garments she had—a skirt and blouse cut down for her when Zofia grew too plump for them, underwear and shawl, also handed down from her mother. And Teo's shoes. What more could she have brought along? She had nothing else.

"No! I said *no!*"

"Pa, I *have* to go!" Irina cried. "I can't go back to the village!" She took a step back, just out of arms's reach. "Pa, if you don't let me go on the boat, I will run away. Now."

Zofia put a hand to her mouth and muffled a cry. The busybody woman gasped in outrage. Jozef drew back his hand to slap his impudent daughter, but Irina stood her ground. "I want to go, Pa. I will help Teo earn the passage for you and Mama and the girls. You will go sooner if you let me go now. If you don't, you will never see me again. I swear it!" She stepped back another pace, looking around for an escape route, should she have to keep her threat. She held up the tiny wooden crucifix at her neck. "I swear by the Virgin, you will never see me again!"

Zofia clutched her husband's arm. "Jozef, please let her take your passage."

"You are a bad, bad girl, Irina Kossok," Jozef snarled.

Irina knew she had won, and it terrified her. The prize for her triumph was the opportunity to throw herself blindly into the yawning unknown future. Be careful what you wish, for it may come true, the villagers were fond of saying, and now Irina understood what it meant.

She hardly allowed herself to hear Agnieszka's wails, Zofia's blessings, Jozef's curses, or Teo's urgings that she hurry up or they would be left behind. Her entire will was concentrated on one simple thought:

I must not cry. It would make my eyes red like Pa's.

Midwives know that the stunning miracle of birth often obscures a minor curiosity of nature: a newborn child has strange and transient skills. For a short time the infant's fragile neck can support the weight of its head; the miniature fists can grasp with exceptional strength; the tiny, bowed legs, still smeared with mother's blood, can make precocious walking motions. Within a few hours these skills ebb, leaving the child helpless. The skills must be slowly relearned, the strengths redeveloped, the instincts reacquired.

It was much the same with Irina's newborn vision of a different life. By the time the ship left port, she was paralyzed with misgivings. She had immediately been separated from Teo, her only link with the life she'd known. She was assigned to a bunk in the cramped and filthy steerage hold. She sat on the edge of the stained, lumpy mattress and clasped her hands in her lap. She was in a virtual trance of horror at the enormity of what she'd done. She'd left everything—everything!—behind. Kin and country, language and landscape, customs and clothes.

But the sharpest pain was her longing for her mother and sisters, especially her favorite sister, Agnieszka. She'd never weighed her love of them before; there had never been a need. Leaving them had been madness. Even now, Mama was returning to the village, her pale round face blotched with weeping, the baby, Stefania, nursing greedily at her generous breast. Agnieszka, only two years younger than Irina, but seeming younger because of her delicate stature and features, would be clinging to Mama instead of Irina. How would Agnieszka, with her adoring dependence on her older sister, get along? They had always been so close, so much in tune with each other's moods and needs. Now an ocean would lie between them—for how long?

The twins, five-year-old Lillie and Cecilia, had each other, but would miss saying their lisped bedtime prayers with their oldest sister. Irina could almost hear their sweet voices through the churning and thumping of the engines. She would miss their exuberance, the odd way they talked to each other in half-sentences, even their arguments.

Irina turned her face to the wall and wept for herself, for them all, and vowed she'd live up to her word. She'd work long and hard. She'd bring them to America. The ties would not be severed, only temporarily stretched. Someday the family would join hands around the table again as the dinner was blessed.

But even as she thought it, Irina envisioned that the table would be finer, their hands less chapped and coarse, the food better and more plentiful. And in the corner of the room there would be a big wooden box that made music. For although the trauma of departure had momentarily displaced the events at the manor, it hadn't eradicated her determination to make a better life. Now she'd drawn her family into her dream.

All but Pa and Teo. They were, as they always had been, a world of their own. Pa was a gaunt, round-shouldered figure to whom they all owed respect and obedience. Irina had never felt any particular affection for him, nor had anyone ever suggested that she should. She feared his temper, heeded his words, and bent to his will as a daughter must, but she didn't know him or love him as she loved Mama.

Early every morning Pa went to the room at the front of the house that served as a shop. He spent the day making shoes and gloves for the villagers. He didn't permit the rest of the family in the shop. At nightfall he closed up the front room and rejoined them for dinner and prayers. Often he gave Irina and Teo work to do before he disappeared; boots for Teo to mend or gloves for Irina to stitch. More often he simply rose from the table and left to spend the evening drinking, talking, and playing cards or dice with his friends.

Sometimes in the last year he'd taken Teo with him on these evenings, and the women left at home enjoyed a vicarious pride in Teo's gradual coming of age. Tall, clever Teo. How Zofia and the girls adored him. He was their hope and pride. There had even been talk once about sending Teo to school. Nothing had come of it because there was no money for such an extravagance, but the mere consideration of such a plan had mantled him with a reputation for scholarship.

Their pride extended beyond the warped wooden door of their own home. The other villagers pointed to him with admiration. The younger boys in the village idolized him, following him in a pack, imitating his confident swagger, performing outrageously for his attention. And at the age of sixteen, he was already attracting the attention of girls as well. They simpered and giggled in his presence and brought gloves that hardly needed mending to Jozef's shop in the hopes of seeing Teo.

I must find Teo. He will take care of me, Irina thought, looking up from the rapt contemplation of her hands. But her view of the crowded hold of the ship was blocked by a young woman of about twenty who was carrying a valise and several bundles.

"Oh, I'm sorry. I didn't mean to tread on your feet," the newcomer said in painfully correct Polish. "I'm supposed to share this bunk with you. We're fortunate to have the lower one. I'd be afraid of falling out of the upper. Aren't there any linens or pillows for this bed except for this?" she asked, examining with a distasteful scowl the single urine- and semen-stained blanket that covered the thin, lumpy mattress.

Irina stared at her, dumbfounded. This young woman was plump and pink and scrubbed-looking with oversize white teeth that gave her open face a pleasantly horsey look. The truly wondrous thing, however, was her clothing. Instead of the customary drab homespun skirt, baggy blouse, and shawl all the other women and girls on board wore, she had on a real dress. A fabric with a squared pattern woven right in. It was slightly faded and puckered a little at the armholes where it had been mended, but to Irina, who had never seen plaid cloth, it was miraculous.

The young woman pushed her belongings under the bed and sat down beside Irina. "My name is Clara. Clara Johnson. What's yours?"

"I am called Irina Kossok. Why is your speech so strange?"

Clara Johnson laughed. "Everyone criticizes my Polish, and I'm so proud of it. It's my English accent."

"English?" Irina asked, trying out the unfamiliar word. "What is this English?"

"That's my native language."

Irina's gaze was so patently uncomprehending that Clara went on. "You see, in other countries people speak different languages. I'm from America, so I speak English."

"They don't talk the same in America as I do?" Irina asked. This was a concept so mammoth in its implications that she could hardly grasp it. Growing up as she had, it had never crossed her mind that there were other ways of communicating. There was Latin in church, of course, but that was merely mystical syllables she'd never regarded as language.

"Not the same as you, no." She smiled and uttered some sounds. "That's English for 'I'm glad to meet you.' "

Irina considered this for a moment. Did they really make different sounds in America and understand each other? Until this moment she'd assumed the words for things were God-given designations. How would she ever know what anybody was saying? Could those strange vowel-heavy sounds Clara had made actually *mean* something? She tore her mind away from the problem, unable to reason it any further. "What are you doing here?"

"On this wretched ship? I'm going home. I took a job with the family of a Polish diplomat in America two years ago as governess to their children. When they returned to Poland I accompanied them, as my parents are both dead and I don't have any brothers and sisters. I never realized I'd be homesick, but I missed America terribly, so I saved my money to go back. Now I'm on my way."

Clara watched as Irina considered this information. Under the grime and confusion, she thought there might be an attractive, reasonably intelligent child. Her hair, what could be seen of it under the dreary, tattered shawl, was quite fair. Her chin was square and determined and her wide-set gray-blue eyes were prettily fringed with surprisingly dark lashes. "Don't you know anything about America?" she asked the girl.

"Nothing. Only it is a country of promise. That's what Pa said."

"Is your father on board?"

"No, America wouldn't let him come. His eyes were not good. So I came in his place," Irina answered respectfully.

"Oh, I see. You know, don't you, that the steamship line has to bring back, at their own cost, anybody who isn't physically fit to enter the United States. That's why they're so choosy."

Irina wasn't interested in talking about this. What was done, was done. Before Clara could question her further, she said, "This English way of talk . . . can you tell me how to do it?"

Clara was a born nurturer and had two long weeks of boredom facing her. "I can teach you some, if you'd like."

"I want it more than anything. What will I do for you in return?"

Clara was disconcerted to feel something very like a sob rise unexpectedly in her throat, but she controlled her voice and said, "Nothing. You need do nothing for me."

"But you cannot give me this American languge and I give you nothing."

In her two-year sojourn in the part of Russia that had once been called Poland, Clara had seen this sort of determination before. The Poles, as they still insisted on thinking of themselves in spite of the treaties that had negated their existence, often demonstrated this heady mixture of childish simplicity and biblical sense of justice. It had little to do with age, education, or circumstance. She patted Irina's thin shoulder. "I will give it to you as a gift," she said briskly. "Someday, perhaps you will make a gift to me in return. Now, to start with, your name—how is it spelled?"

Irina shrugged.

"You can't write? Oh, well, perhaps that's better. Let me get some paper from my valise and I will show you letters."

By the end of the first day, Irina was able to print the English alphabet, though she didn't understand what it meant. "You have a fine hand for a beginner," Clara said, studying the tiny, well-executed letters. The child had the eyes and fingers of a seamstress. The letters marched along with the straight regularity of a strong seam. "As for your name, it is probably spelled I-r-i-n-a, but in English it would be 'Irene.' "

"Irene," Irina repeated, rolling the R slightly and drawing out the long E. She repeated it twice, savoring the sweetness of the sounds. "This is who I will be in America. Show me the letters for my American name, if you please."

The first three days of the journey passed quickly for Irene and Clara. They were so totally absorbed in their lessons that they hardly noticed the wretched conditions surrounding them. It was bitterly cold, but Clara shared some of her woolen clothing with the younger girl. Irene enjoyed this, not only for the warmth but also for the luxurious novelty of Clara's wardrobe. Her clothes all smelled so nice.

Eventually the elements impinged upon their euphoria. The sea became rough and many of the passengers, cramped like cargo into the hold, began to get seasick. The air, though chill, became more fetid and foul. The lines outside the toilet facilities at the far end of the ship grew longer and longer and fewer of the passengers were able to wait. Many vomited on the floor before ever reaching the doorway. The toilets themselves, primitive and dirty at best, became intolerably filthy. The vile odor of sickness and despair became nearly tangible. The women and children began to cry with pain and fear and the sounds of their wailing never seemed to abate.

Irene, though queasy from the smells, wasn't unbalanced by the swells and fared better than most of the others. Clara, too, was fairly immune to the ship's wallowing and the two of them spent most of their time tending to various children whose mothers were incapacitated.

It was, therefore, a shock to Irene to discover that she herself was sick. "I've hurt myself," she announced in a perplexed voice when she came back from the toilets.

"Irene, you're pale," Clara said, setting aside the bit of mending she was attempting to do. "What's wrong?"

"I'm bleeding."

"Bleeding!" Clara looked her over quickly. "Where?"

"Only a little bit. Here. Just like Mama when the babies came. I don't know how I got hurt. I didn't fall down or anything—"

"Oh, Irene, didn't your mother explain to you? You're not hurt; you're just growing up and becoming a woman. Sit down beside me and I'll tell you about it."

Later Clara rummaged in her valise and took Irene back to the toilets, where she explained about the little bundles of sewed-together rags. She showed her how to tie the ends to a fabric belt worn under her clothes. "You may have these. I won't need them again before we reach New York. You must change them often and wash them very thoroughly or you will smell bad."

Irene was relieved to discover that this was a natural process, but she was also glad of the opportunity to extend this exchange of personal information into other fields. "Clara, you always smell nice. Why is that?"

Clara smothered a smile. "Because I wash myself all over, every day."

"Every day? Not just on Saturdays?"

"Every day. And I clean my teeth with a special brush and some tooth powder."

The girl at the big house had called her dirty and common. Common she still was, though now she could write and recite the English alphabet, but here was an escape from dirtiness. "How do you get this brush and powder?"

"You can buy them in New York. I'll take you to a store after we arrive."

Irene saw little of Teo during the crossing. He'd been assigned a bunk with some other young men at the opposite end of the steerage compartment. Once, early in the journey, Irene made her way through the packed masses of humanity to find him, but she wasn't well received. He and several other boys his age were crouched down between two bunks playing dice on the floor. "What do you want, Irina?" he asked curtly. "Is there anything wrong?"

"No, I'm fine, I just—"

"Then get back where you belong," he said, going back to his game without looking at her again. Irene went away feeling very guilty and ashamed for having thrust herself into his activities. Certainly he would interest himself in her if she needed attention, but since she was getting along quite well, she shouldn't have interrupted him.

The day they arrived in America was cold and a dreary Atlantic fog tangled itself around the lumbering ship. "Perhaps we'll be able to see something anyway," Clara said. "Wrap up well and let's go see."

They joined several dozen other heavily bundled immigrants at the rail. A cutter emerged from the fog and the ship's engines slowed as several uniformed men from the cutter came aboard. "I must leave you a moment, Irene," Clara said. "These gentlemen are to check the papers of the cabin and first-class people as well as the returning Americans. I will come back to you."

The ship lolled uselessly for thirty minutes while these formalities were completed. More and more passengers came on deck as the word of imminent landing spread. When the uniformed men left the ship and sped away in their small craft, Clara rejoined Irene. "Now we're on our way."

Irene stared at her friend with admiration. "Weren't you afraid of those soldiers? I think you are very brave."

"They aren't soldiers, only immigration officers. Besides, you don't have to be afraid of soldiers in this country. America is free. The army can't steal people or take things from you like the Russians could in your village. Ah, we're starting up again. We'll pass through the Narrows in a few minutes and come into Upper New York Bay. Look over there. You can just barely see Staten Island."

The ship held fifteen hundred people and fully a quarter of them were crowded on deck by the time the fog began to clear. It was almost nine o'clock in the morning when a vast gray shape loomed up in front of them. Irene clutched at Clara's arm. "What is *that*?"

"That's the Statue of Liberty. Isn't she beautiful?"

Irene stared in fascination at the huge figure with the flowing robes, upraised torch, and lovely, inscrutable face. Irene had never seen a figure any larger than the chipped plaster statues of the Virgin in the village church except during the brief visit to the church in Gdansk. But this statue was a different matter entirely. She wasn't the pious, simpering saintly sort. She was handsome, defiant, and unadorned with anything but dreadful dignity. And the scale was so enormous as to be frightening. "Is everything in America so big?" she asked.

"Wait until you see the buildings," Clara replied in a whisper.

It was only then that Irene realized that the crowd on deck had fallen silent. Hundreds of other foreign eyes were focused on the beautiful behemoth that represented the tangible realization of their dreams. It was a potent, heart-stopping silence, punctuated only by the quiet, joyous weeping of dozens of the immigrants, men and women alike. One by one, many of them fell to their knees and began to pray. Hebrew and Latin mingled with German, Polish, and a few grateful American words. The reverent, mixed mumble became a soft blanket of sound.

Irene felt tears spilling down her face. This, at last, was the country where she would make a good life for herself and her family; the country where they could be clean and rich and well fed; the land where the Russian landowners had no hold and the czar's soldiers cast no shadow. This was the Golden Land where she wouldn't be common and dirty anymore.

Kamenets. The reverse [illegible] mixed rhythmic became a soft blanket of sound.

[illegible] thinking [illegible] country where she would make a good life for herself and [illegible] country where they could be clean and rich and well fed, the land where the Russian soldiers had no [illegible] [illegible] Land [illegible]

2

Suddenly the praying stopped and was replaced with nearly hysterical shouting and cheering. Irene and Clara were swept into the crowd that surged to the other side of the ship, where the skyline of Manhattan Island was visible. Over the heads of the crowd, Irene could see only strange rectangular mountaintops. "What are those?" she asked, suddenly frightened by this eerily alien landscape.

"Buildings," Clara answered. "That's lower Manhattan, the financial district. Some of those buildings are as much as thirty stories high."

"Stories?"

"Yes. Floors. Didn't anyone in your village have a second floor? Rooms above the others?"

"Maybe at the manor house," Irene answered, remembering the one time she'd seen that miraculous and despised edifice. It had windows above windows. "Do you mean thirty rooms on top of each other? Why don't they fall down when the wind blows?"

Clara hugged her. "I have no idea, but they don't. Come. We must pack our things. We'll dock soon."

By the time the ship nudged into the pier, they were on deck again. Teo had joined his sister at last. They stood together, the three of them, Clara with her suitcases, the Polish youngsters with all their belongings wrapped in bulging bundles at their feet. "What will happen now, Teo?" Irene asked.

Clara had been watching Irene's elusive older brother. She didn't like what she saw. Irene had bragged about what a fine, admired young man he was, how he was looked on as a scholar, the brightest light in the village, but Clara saw only a cocksure boy, tall and well-formed and looking several years older than his actual age. His face was angular, his dark gold hair was glossy and thick, and he would undoubtedly have broken a dozen hearts before he was twenty. But Clara thought his chin was weak, his eyes secretive, and there was a swagger about him, even though he was standing perfectly still. He made her think of a Polish saying, "*Modli sie pod figura, a diabla ma za skóra*—beads about the neck and the devil in the heart."

He was ignoring Irene's questions as he studied the skyline with a distinctly calculating gaze. Clara was seized by a sudden anxiety for Irene.

"In a moment we'll all disembark," she said because Teo was ignoring his sister. "The cabin and first class first. Then the returning Americans from steerage like me . . ."

"You will leave me?" Irene asked, taking the older girl's hand. "*Pozegnac*, Clara."

"No, not good-bye. We'll see each other. I wrote down the Spryzak's address and I'll come visit you very soon. I'm at the end of this journey. You and your brother must still pass through the immigration inspection at Ellis Island. Don't look so worried. You won't have any trouble. All they do is make sure you're healthy and see that your papers are in good order. The steamship people made sure of that at the beginning of the trip. You see, if the immigrants are rejected, the steamship company has to bear the cost of taking them back, and they're careful that doesn't happen very often."

"But you promise we will be friends in this country?" Irene insisted.

"We will be friends for a long, long time," Clara assured her.

Tilly Spry would have been a very pretty woman if it hadn't been for the birthmark. She had fluffy yellow hair, as curly and fine as a child's. Her eyes were deep blue and fringed with naturally dark, thick lashes. Her figure was as plump and compact as a pet pigeon. Even at thirty-five, with four children, Tilly could have passed for being in her early twenties.

Except for the birthmark. It was a port-wine stain that covered most of the right side of her face in a shape roughly like a map of Africa and it had ruined her life. She'd been the beloved only daughter of a poor Warsaw peddler and his wife who had come to New York before her birth. At first sight of their marred baby, they knew they would have to save to buy her a good husband someday. They scrimped for years, niggling and nagging over every penny, making her childhood a hell of pinching poverty. And when she was eighteen, they had made her a match.

Granted, he was expensive. Andrzey Spryzak was a cousin of a cousin of a cousin in the old country. A second son, he was reputed to be ambitious and eager to come to America to make his fortune. Tilly's parents reached deep into their hoard of coins and sent him the passage money and he agreed to marry their daughter when he arrived. They also paid dearly for him to be employed as assistant manager in a factory that made ladies' coats.

Tilly sat beside Andy now in the waiting room at Ellis Island and remembered bitterly the only other time she'd been here. It was the day the young, handsome Andrzey Spryzak, soon to Americanize himself into Andy Spry, had arrived. Big, bull-necked, ham-fisted, and bursting with ego, virility, and anticipation, he strode through the doorway. And as Tilly and her parents stood to greet him, he looked at her with undisguised revulsion. All Tilly's spirits and hopes, all her innocence, had died that instant. Her blue eyes hardened, her small pointed chin jutted out defiantly.

He'd stuck to the bargain and so had she. They were married at St. Stanislas a week after his arrival. Andy wore the new suit her parents bought him. Tilly wore a white dress with a very heavy veil. Within a year Tilly had a baby, Andy had advanced to manager at the coat factory, but since then little had changed except that Tilly had three more daughters. Andy had advanced no further. His waist and face had thickened and become coarse. He gambled, drank, and seduced the young girls from the factory.

And for all those years Tilly struggled daily to keep up the illusion of having made a good marriage. If she couldn't fool herself, at least she could deceive the rest of the world. Every month was a furious balancing act to pay the rent on the two-bedroom apartment—tiny, but impressive in a section of society where a single bedroom apart from the main room was an incredible luxury. In addition, there were the weekly payments on the furniture, and the expense of keeping the girls well-dressed so that they might snare better husbands than Tilly had.

Now financial necessity had forced her to take in boarders. Everyone on the Lower East Side did so, of course. That part of Manhattan was a virtual rabbit warren of overcrowding, whole families often sharing a single unheated room with several strangers. But Tilly had never been reduced to taking anyone else in and now was busy pretending to her friends that Jozef Kossok and his son were merely coming as guests, not as boarders.

But where on earth were they? she wondered, surveying the crowd. There was a man of the right age, but he had two boys with him. Another had a wife and daughters. Most, in fact, were part of entire family groups. Finally she spotted a pair she thought might be Jozef Kossok and his son. Threading her way through the crowd in a careful manner so none of the newcomers could dirty her dress, she approached a tall gentleman who was standing next to a boy of fourteen or so. "Are you Jozef Kossok?" she asked.

Irene and Teo were standing a few feet away. Irene had been frankly eavesdropping on an argument between two families. Apparently the girl and her parents had been brought over at the American family's expense on the condition that the girl would be a bride for their son. But on board the ship, the girl had fallen in love with a fellow immigrant and now she was trying to extricate herself from the previous arrangement. Both families were upbraiding her loudly. The would-be husband was hovering at the edge of the dispute, his heavy, lumpy face sad and slow to comprehend what had happened. The bride-to-be was fiery and had a tight grip on the hand of the young man she wanted to marry. He looked as miserable as the rejected suitor.

Irene watched and listened, wondering why the girl preferred the scared, skinny young man when the lumpy one looked so kind and gentle. Just as the girl's mother was beginning to slap and berate her, Irene heard the name Kossok spoken. She quickly turned and saw a pretty, plump little woman with fuzzy blond hair speaking to a man who was shaking his head in denial. Seen this way, from the good side, Tilly Spry looked like a little motherly angel.

Irene stepped forward and said, "Mrs. Spryzak? We are the Kossoks."

Tilly turned and Irene involuntarily gasped with surprise at the dark birthmark that covered the side of her face. Tilly's eyes flamed with humiliation and hatred. "You? You are not Jozef Kossok."

"We are his children." Teo stepped forward and explained in Polish, "Our father couldn't come and my sister came in his place."

"That won't do!" Tilly nearly wept. She'd counted on adding an adult wage earner to the household, a skilled glover and shoemaker. She couldn't afford to be stuck with two useless children, even if the boy was old enough to earn his keep. "You can come with us," she said, stabbing a finger toward Teo, "but you? What would I do with you?" she accused Irene.

Irene was stunned. What had gone wrong? She hadn't meant to offend this woman by her surprised reaction a moment earlier. Could she be turned out in the world for that? Suddenly Tilly didn't look anything like an angel.

Before Irene could speak, Andy Spry joined them. "What's wrong here?" he asked his wife.

"The father didn't come. Only these two children!" she wailed. "The boy can go to work, but the girl! The girl will just be an added cost. You could get her a job in the factory, but it don't pay nothing. She couldn't hardly buy her own food with those wages, and think how much she'll eat!"

Andy Spry looked them over. The boy could be put to work, and if he showed promise, might even be matched up with one of the Spry girls. He dismissed Teo from his thoughts and studied the girl. Compared to his own daughters, who were shrill strangers to him, she might be a pleasant addition to the household. "We'll make room for 'em," he told his wife firmly. "You're always bitchin' about the housework and the sewing. She can help you and the girls and he can bring in some money, maybe."

Irene wanted to protest that she couldn't help earn the money to bring the rest of her family over that way, but she recognized shaky ground when she stood on it. This woman would gladly walk away and leave them alone if crossed, so Irene kept her objections to herself.

The trip to the Spry's apartment was hideous. Tilly was pretending to her friends that these visitors were guests. She made no such pretense to herself or them. There would be no touring about, pointing out sights for the Kossok children in her plans. They took the boat back to the docks on the West Side and walked clear across town. Irene and Teo were left to gawk, uninstructed, as they passed block after block of buildings.

There were so many impressions struggling for dominance that Irene felt dizzy. While their small homes had been clustered closely together in the village she'd come from, there had been only several dozen residences, each distinct with little more than a winding dirt path connecting them. Had an outsider come to the village—which almost never happened—it was easy to give directions. "Kossok the bootmaker? Follow the path to the right after the big tree, go up the hill to the house with the glove painted on the front door," one would say.

But how did anyone find the way here? The buildings were enormous, anonymous, indistinguishable to an unpracticed eye. They bore no resemblance to homes or to anything Irene had ever seen before. They loomed straight and geometrical over paved streets, creating dark crowded canyons where a few trees reached spindly winter-naked branches toward the feeble light.

And the people! So many of them it was overwhelming. These city streets through which they were walking were the most heavily concentrated population anywhere in the world. Most of the people moved hurriedly through the busy streets with mysterious, frantic purpose. Shopfronts spilled their wares out into the streets, and vendors of food, clothing, and utensils vied for space with carriages and a few motorized vehicles. Noisy, brash children played tag and hide-and-seek, dodging adults and horses. There was a cacophony of language and an almost tangible city stink. Nature didn't exist here: there were few trees, no grass grew, no fresh air penetrated these alleys of packed people. Even the sky seemed too far away to be real.

Irene found herself searching faces for familiarity. Until she'd left the village, she'd virtually never seen a strange face. Everyone, friend and foe, was known to her. Even on the ship, the people had come to look familiar. Now the only person she knew in this frightening world was her brother, and she clung to him to keep from drowning.

They had to climb five flights of stairs to the Spry apartment. Tilly and Andy made no offer to help Irene and Teo carry their bundles, nor to introduce them to the people they passed in the halls. Irene was at least relieved to hear Polish being spoken again. When forced to address the Kossoks directly, Tilly and Andy had used their native language, but to each other they spoke only English, which sounded completely unlike the words Clara had taught her on the ship.

To anyone from farther uptown, or in the view of any American living in the countryside, the Sprys' apartment would have been a terrible shock, a living nightmare. Minuscule, shabby, roach- and rat-infested, without any plumbing or privacy, it was dark, and reeked of coal fumes, dirty laundry, and stale cabbage. But to the Sprys it was luxury. There were actually three separate rooms inhabited by a single family, a rarity on the East Side.

The main room, about ten feet by fifteen, looked like a second-hand-furniture store. There was a table covered with a much-patched and none-too-clean cloth and crowded around by six chairs, four of which almost matched each other. Against the wall there was an upholstered sofa. Irene had never seen or even considered the existence of such a thing. Straw-filled cushions on wood were the greatest comfort she'd ever known.

"That's genuine horsehair," Tilly said proudly when she noticed Irene staring at the sofa.

Irene nodded as if she understood. Did she mean the funny long chair was covered with the skin of a dead horse? Or did someone shave the animal and somehow weave the hairs together? In a country that cared so much about red eyes, anything was possible.

A small grimy window on the far wall let in what little light there was, but the view was only of a sooty brick wall of the next building a few feet away. Beneath the window there was a small stove and makeshift cabinets where Irene supposed the dishes and food were kept. The rest of the room was crammed with boxes and crates, some covered with garish, flimsy scarves in an attempt to disguise them as tables. An ironing board leaned drunkenly against the doorjamb, and nails driven in the flaking, unpainted walls served as coat hooks. It was impossible to walk through the room without having to edge past something or someone.

The second room was even smaller and was virtually filled by the two unmade beds that left only a narrow aisle between them and at the foot. This was obviously the daughters' room. There were dresses, petticoats, combs, mirrors, shoes, stockings, and cheap fashion magazines strewn everywhere. It looked as if some natural disaster had happened there.

"You'll share this room with the girls," Tilly said in English; then, realizing Irene didn't understand, she reverted to Polish. "There's hardly space as it is, but it will have to do. I don't know *what* they'll say when I tell them."

"Your daughters have pretty things, Mrs. Spryzak," Irene said, sensing instinctively that it would please the older woman. And in Irene's eyes, it was true. She had no way of knowing that the clothes flung about so carelessly were cheap and flimsily made. Compared to her own coarse, ugly garments, they were elegant.

Tilly allowed herself a moment of preening. "Yes, they're real fashionable girls. They'll all make fine matches. But you shouldn't call me Mrs. Spryzak. We call ourselves Spry. What did you say your name was, child?" For a seond there was a hint of kindness in her voice.

"My name is Irina, but my friend on the ship said it was Irene in America."

Tilly nodded approval. This girl might not be too terrible to have around after all. Since her first startled gasp at the sight of the birthmark, she had virtually ignored it. Tilly was accustomed, if not resigned, to people studying it when they spoke to her. Often they stopped and pointed to her. Sometimes she imagined she could actually feel their eyes probing, tracing the outline of the hated stain. But this soft-spoken child seemed genuinely not to notice it anymore.

If, in addition, she admired Tilly's daughters, even in their absence, it would make it easier to have her around. Tilly began to form a plan. Instead of saying this immigrant girl was a visiting relative, which she had originally intended when she thought Jozef was coming, she could say Irene was a maid! It would be a brilliant coup. None of her friends, even those a step above her, had a maid. Yes, she might make up in social credit for the financial loss the girl represented. And if trained well enough, she might be able to hire her out and make some money after all—not that Tilly had the faintest idea what a maid actually did.

"Put your things under the bed," Tilly said, preoccupied with her thoughts.

"I have no things. Those were my brother's clothes I carried."

Without bothering to show Irene the third room, which was really only an oversize cupboard that served as bedroom for the adults, Tilly put Irene to work. "Take off that awful droopy shawl and set the table. Then you can peel the potatoes. Andy, take the boy and show him where to fetch the water."

Teo hadn't uttered a word since leaving Ellis Island, nor had any remarks been addressed to him. Now he drew himself up, raked Andy Spry with an insolent glare, and said, "I won't fetch water. I didn't come here to be a servant."

Irene nearly dropped the plates Tilly had handed her. How could Teo say such a thing! Before anyone could speak, Andy Spry wheeled around and struck the boy on the side of the head with a hammy fist. Teo crashed back against the horsehair sofa, bringing down a chunk of gray-brown plaster from the wall. Andy lunged at him, dragging him back up by the front of his shirt. "I don't need no goddamn lazy Polack bastard talking to me that way in my own house!" he screamed, spittle misting the air and Teo's face.

Teo didn't answer, but his eyes narrowed and glittered with

a defiance and hatred Irene had never seen. With a sudden movement of his arms upward and between Andy's, he freed himself from the older man's grasp. He bent and picked up his bundles that still sat in the middle of the room.

"Leaving, are you?" Andy shouted, massaging his forearm and clenching his fist. "Then get the hell out before I throw you out, you no-good son-of-a-bitch!"

"Teo! *No!*" Irene screamed, throwing herself at him. "Say you're sorry. He didn't mean it, Mr. Spry."

"I *did* mean it, Irina," he said, his voice trembling with fury. He shook free of her and straightened his shoulders. "I'll come back for you when I have a place to stay and some money."

With that, he slung his bundles over his shoulder and stomped out the door without a backward glance. Everyone stood perfectly still for a long moment; then Tilly burst out, "Andy, you fool! Why did you run him off? He could have earned some money for us. You should have thrown *her* out!"

"You got it all figured out, huh? Just remember, this whole thing was your damned idea to begin with. I never wanted no stupid immigrants living with us. Plenty of people right here would be glad for the room and board. You wanted these people, Tilly. Now you got this girl. You're gonna keep her!"

The rest of Tilly's face was almost as red as the birthmark. Sputtering furiously, she took a step forward. "You've forgot that you're a stupid immigrant yourself, Andrzey Spryzak!" She sneered as she said his name. "If it wasn't for me, you'd be digging potatoes for some Russian landlord—"

"I wouldn't have no goddamn purple-faced shrew of a wife!"

"No, and you couldn't afford one! If you earned a decent living, I wouldn't have to take in no boarders."

"You're a peddler's brat, Tilly. Don't try to lord it over me like you was some lady come down in the world."

He raised his arm and would have struck her if Irene hadn't shouted, "Tell *me* where to fetch the water! I'll get it. *Please!*"

The marital dispute, which had a sort of weary familiarity,

as if it had been replayed many times over the years, was aborted. But the anger that permeated the very walls of the room simmered all evening, breaking out sporadically in resentful looks, staccato words, slammed plates, and muttered invectives. Irene's family had argued occasionally, and of course Pa had beaten the children and even Zofia whenever they needed it, but there had never been this pervasive miasma of hatred in her home.

The Sprys' daughters came home while Irene was lugging the second pail of water up the stairs. Three of them were fair, chattery duplicates of their mother without the birthmark. They were all heavier than Tilly, however, and in their frilled shirtwaists and cinch-waisted skirts they looked like overstuffed pillows. The fourth girl, apparently the youngest, was plump and sloppy like the others, but had straight mouse-brown hair and an angular face. When Irene came in, all four daughters had already joined in the bickering and ignored her. Nor did Tilly make any attempt to introduce the new boarder to them. Since there were only six chairs at the table, Irene ate her potatoes and cabbage sitting on a box in the corner.

Only when the meal was done and she'd washed the plates did Irene dare make the inquiry that was becoming desperately important to her. Tilly told her the toilet was at the end of the hall on the floor below, but no one offered to accompany her.

Irene made her way down the stairs, pitch dark now that night had fallen. Roaches crunched under her feet. She found the door Tilly had described and was surprised that such a foul-smelling thing was *inside* the building, but had little inclination to marvel because her attention was fully engaged in simply getting to use the facilities. She knocked timidly at the door. There was no answer, so she tried to turn the knob. The door wouldn't open. A woman's voice called out, "Get away from here, I'll be out when I'm good and ready!"

This was spoken in English and Irene didn't understand. "Please hurry," she said, using two of the words Clara had taught her on the ship.

There was no answer and Irene waited, pacing the bare floor outside the stinking toilet. Her bladder was so full she was in pain. She walked back and forth, trying to distract her thoughts from her discomfort, but it didn't help. She tapped on the door again and got a screaming tirade back from the woman inside. She considered going outdoors and squatting down behind a bush, but there were no bushes out there that she remembered, only pavement and people, and she might get lost trying to find a private place.

She bent over, resting her hands on her knees, hoping to relieve some of the internal pressure. It didn't help. She sat down on the floor for a minute, but that was even worse. She was getting frantic. She got back up, paced stiffly, then knocked on the door once more.

This time it was flung open. An old woman with gaudy circles of rouge on her cheeks stood there, hands on hips. "Who in hell do you think you are to bother me this way? I got my rights. I'm entitled to use this room, same like anyone else. I pay my rent and I'd like to see anyone say I ain't got rights . . ."

She went on and on, but without getting out of the doorway. Irene nodded, apologized, and tried to edge past her. But as the woman reached out and shoved at Irene's shoulder to emphasize her point, Irene's control failed. She felt a hot gush down the insides of her legs. She tried desperately to hold it back, but it kept coming. The woman in the doorway looked down at the puddle of urine growing around Irene's feet. "Filthy foreigner!" she said, walking off.

Irene stood for a moment looking down at her feet, still in Teo's cast-off boots and now soaking wet. "Oh, Teo," she whimpered in the darkened hallway, "please come back. Take me away from this place."

Then she slowly went back upstairs to the apartment that was her new home in the Golden Land.

3

Teo didn't come back to rescue her and it took nearly a year for Irene to fully recognize that he never would. It wasn't a sudden comprehension, but a gradual, demoralizing understanding. At first she saw him occasionally in the streets around the Sprys' building. "Teo! Please take me away with you," she said.

"I can't, Irina. I don't have a place to live yet. But soon . . ."

That time and the next and the next, she believed him. Then she ceased to. "Come back to the Sprys, Teo," Irene begged him at one of their chance meetings. "If you told Mr. Spry you were sorry, he would take you back, I think. We could be together and he could get you a job at the coat factory."

"Never, Irina. I didn't come to this country to be a servant. I don't think you should be either, but you're a girl and that's different. Still, I'd think you'd have some pride."

Stung, Irene replied, "I'll have time for pride when we've sent the passage money to the family."

Eventually the ugly foreign city simply swallowed him up and she didn't see him anymore.

When Tilly discovered Irene's skill with the needle, she set her to work making dresses for her daughters. Though Irene shared a room with them, sleeping on the floor at the foot of one bed like a family dog, she never felt she knew them by anything but name and dimensions. Though she knew to the half-inch the difference between Mary's waist and Kitty's, Elsa's bust and Charlotte's, and could soon sort out their shrill voices, she never guessed what, if anything, they thought or believed that distinguished them from each other.

Nor did they make any attempt to include Irene in their

sisterly circle or even their bickering. They let her wait on them, sew for them, run their errands, and sometimes braid their hair because her nimble, clever fingers were useful. But aside from these services, they ignored her utterly. She became valuable to them in the same impersonal way that a stove or bed is valuable to a household—a necessity, deserving of neither affection nor contempt.

At first, Tilly proceeded with her plan to pass Irene off as a personal maid, even going so far as to have Irene make a black dress and white apron to wear while serving, but soon had second thoughts. Producing a maid was very likely a pretension that would earn her laughter and contempt rather than envy from her friends. She had, however, been impressed with how quickly and resourcefully the girl had repieced the worn black mourning dress into a pert, new-looking uniform, and how even and strong and straight and regular the stitches were. Tilly set her to work sewing for her daughters. Irene, fresh from the village and transplanted to the Lower East Side, knew nothing of style, but she studied the clothes the girls already had and imitated them faithfully.

By spring the Spry daughters were the best-dressed women in the building and even their father was forced to notice the change in their attire. His reaction, however, was not pride, but anger. "Whaddya spend on that cloth, Tilly?" he roared as Elsa and Mary modeled their newest outfits. "You coulda put some decent food on the table for what you spent on them dresses."

"But Irene did all the sewing. It don't cost us nothing," Tilly objected.

"Cost nothing, hell! We gotta feed her, don't we? And that fabric ain't free."

Tilly developed a new plan. She hired out Irene's skills; taking the girls around as a walking advertisement for Irene's sewing, she solicited orders. Most of her neighbors did their own sewing when necessary, and more often wore hand-me-downs until they disintegrated, but there were still enough special occasions, weddings in particular, that demanded a special dress, to keep Irene constantly busy.

Tilly, of course, handled all the orders *and* the money. But for all her greed and dissatisfaction, she wasn't an evil woman.

Nor could she bring herself to permanently hate Irene for not being Jozef. Andy said the girls in the factory made between three and four dollars a week for their work. Tilly figured most of them would have to pay for their rent and food from this and have possibly a dollar a week left, at best. Certainly giving Irene half that, fifty cents a week, was fair, and Tilly did want to be fair to Irene, so long as it didn't cost her much. After all, Irene had her food and rent free and didn't have the additional trouble of walking clear to the factory every day. Nor did she have to endure what Tilly knew were hideous conditions in the airless lofts that housed most of the garment industry.

That conditions in the Spry household were almost equally repugnant didn't occur to Tilly. Compared to a pushcart and a tent, this was a good life. Nor did she consider that the girls in the factory worked ten hours a day and Irene worked twelve or fourteen. And her calculation didn't take into consideration that, at half a dollar a week, it would take Irene over twelve years to save enough money to bring over her family—and only if she never spent a single cent on herself and the steamship fares didn't go up.

Irene realized all this, but she made no objection because she also recognized that Tilly could have made a slave rather than a servant of her and she had no illusions about her range of alternatives. She was an uneducated thirteen-year-old girl in a foreign country. Her choices, *for now*, were nonexistent. Besides, fifty cents a week was fifty cents more than nothing. Moreover, she didn't want to go to work at the factory. She'd quickly observed what happened to the girls who took that route. Many of them lived in the Sprys' building.

These sweatshop girls were afflicted with scurvy and malnutrition from their wretched, meager diets. Lungs full of cotton lint, desperately tired and overworked, most of them were hollow-eyed old women by the time they were twenty. They were dull-witted with the oppressive boredom of their jobs and broken-spirited from the personal indignities they suffered. A month hardly passed that one or more of the girls in the building didn't die, and Irene couldn't afford to die. She had to get her family to America. Then and only then could she get on with making something of herself.

In the meantime, she considered herself fortunate in comparison to the other girls in the building because she lived with a family. The Sprys weren't a model family, nor was Irene invited to consider herself one of them, but they *were* a family—mother, father, and children living together, creating, however unwillingly, a small barrier against the rest of the world. And whether they liked it or not, Irene was an auxiliary part of the unit.

She found vicarious comfort in the private jokes that families share, the traditions and habits. She was comforted when Tilly— not *her* mother, but *a* mother—complimented a job well done. She even felt a vague pride in the girls' appearance when they went out into the world wearing the dresses she'd made for them. Though they had little love for each other and none for her, they still compensated in a small way for Irene's separation from her own sisters. And Andy Spry, though usually taciturn and occasionally violent, had an affectionate streak that showed at odd moments. He would sometimes pat her shoulder as he walked past her, or just stare at her as if he were really seeing *her*, not just another part of the clutter. And if these moments made Irene vaguely uneasy, she assumed it was because they were so rare. Irene watched the factory girls, rootless and alone in the world, starved physically and emotionally, and she pitied them.

There were two other factors that helped her survive the years with the Sprys without succumbing to the epidemic despair of tenement life. The first was her craving to learn. She had everything to learn—and wanted to. To Irene, like many others, the old country was just that—the past and done with. In America there were new kinds of buildings, different clothes, a new language to master, and an exciting, alien way of life to fit into. While it was sometimes frightening, it was always stimulating. Her childhood had left her starved for information and impressions, and she absorbed them all greedily.

The other element that made life bearable for Irene was a person; her friend from the ship, Clara Johnson. She came to visit Irene, as she'd promised, three weeks after their arrival. "We can't be gone long," Clara said. "I have a job interview at five o'clock."

"What kind of job?" Irene asked in Polish as they threaded their way through the packed street in search of a place to sit down and talk privately. A hopeless quest, they soon discovered.

"I'm looking for a job like I had before, as a governess."

"What is this governess? What sort of work?"

"A governess lives with a wealthy family and takes care of their children. Teaching them manners and lessons like reading and language and music."

"But if you do that, what does the mother do?"

"Not very much of anything usually," Clara said. "Tell me about yourself, Irene. Do you like it here? Are the Sprys good to you? How is your brother?"

Irene, desperately eager to share what she'd learned and experienced, confided at length while Clara listened and nodded. "Do you think Teo will come back for you?" she asked when Irene recounted his abrupt departure.

"Of course he will. As soon as he can."

Clara sensed the defensiveness in this and didn't pursue the subject. "Have you been to a candy shop yet?"

"No, I haven't been outside very much since I got here. Are you sure you can find my building again? I don't want to be lost."

"I'm sure. But let me make you a map so you can go a few places by yourself," Clara said, taking a stub of a pencil out of her capacious handbag.

They visited the candy shop, one of dozens scattered throughout the area, then went on a short, exploratory walk, Irene assiduously consulting her map at every corner. She was curious about everything.

"That man over there selling ducks and geese . . . where does he get them? Does he catch them himself? How could animals live around here? There are no woods."

"What is that long yellow thing that people peel the skin off and eat the white inside?"

"That man singing on the corner . . . do people pay him for it?"

"What language were those people talking?"

"What is that smell?"

"Those women on the steps there with the painted faces are calling to men who pass by. Why?"

"How does that cart go without a horse or a man to pull it?"

And for every answer Clara produced, Irene had three more questions. When their allotted time was up, both were nearly hoarse with talking. "Come back soon, Clara," Irene begged.

Clara was busy for the next several months. Her search for a job was more protracted than she had anticipated and her reserve of money was quite low by the time she acquired a new position. But it was with a kind family who paid her well and let her have every other Sunday off. On her first free day she went back to the Sprys' apartment. Irene was delighted to see her again. "I thought you had gone away or something bad had happened to you. I was so worried!"

Clara was touched. She looked at the lanky, overworked child with the pin-pricked fingers and thought: When do you find time or energy to worry about anyone else? "Can you go with me today? I have some surprises for you," Clara said, indicating the paper-wrapped parcels she carried. "But there's someplace special I want to take you before I show you."

Irene's eyes sparkled with anticipation. "Wait, I must get my map. I've been adding things to it." She produced a sheet of brown butcher paper onto which she'd transferred the information from Clara's hastily jotted sketch of the neighborhood.

Clara studied it with the attention it deserved. The lettering wasn't all correct, but it was meticulous. The streets and buildings were numbered, and many were labeled, as well. Since Irene couldn't write many words in English and none in Polish, she'd indicated the function of shops with symbols. A little shirt indicated a clothing shop, a lollipop stood for a candy store, and a carrot represented a grocer. Clara complimented her and made some spelling suggestions. "Now, here is Canal Street, running east and west. Your map goes only as far east as Eldridge, but several blocks beyond that is Essex. That's where we're going."

When they reached their destination, she said, "There's a wonderful place in the basement of this building. Come along."

As they descended a steep flight of steps, a strange odor

wafted up, the combined scents of soap and steam, lightly overlaid with mildew and sweat. Clara glanced at Irene and noticed that the child's eyes were getting wider and she had her head up sniffing the air like a wild animal might do in unfamiliar territory. "This is a free public shower," she explained, leading her to a hallway lined with doors. She chose an open one and gestured for Irene to enter.

Irene looked around the tiny space in wonder. The room they had entered had marble walls and a short marble bench across one wall. Beyond that, there was a canvas curtain and another space with nothing but a circular metal grille on the floor, two porcelain knobs on the wall, and higher up, a shower head. Clara unwrapped the smaller paper parcel. Inside were a bar of cheap fragrant soap, a threadbare towel and washcloth, an inexpensive wood-handled toothbrush, and a small metal canister of tooth powder. "Scrub this cake of soap all over yourself, including your hair. While the soap is still on, you wet this little brush, sprinkle a bit of powder on it, and scrub your teeth. Don't swallow it; spit it out. Then stand under the water until the soap is all gone. When you're done, I have something else for you."

Irene followed all the directions, reveling in the sweet floral fragrance of the soap and the feeling of the shower buffeting her skin. Baths at home had been a weekly occurrence, taking place in a big tin tub of tepid water in which Pa and Teo had already bathed. At the Sprys' house, bathing had meant merely dipping water from a bowl that had to be filled and carried up from the ground floor to the fifth. A hot shower was a miracle to Irene. She loved the way the individual streams stung her skin, and the astringent taste of the tooth powder added a clean, bright edge to the sensation. For the first time in her life, her hair was so clean it actually squeaked when she pulled a strand.

She wasn't aware of how long she was taking until Clara rustled the canvas curtain and asked if she was all right. With terrible reluctance Irene turned the flow of water off and wrapped herself in the towel. Clara brought another package out of her enormous purse. She looked at Irene, clad only in the skimpy piece of toweling, and thought what a pretty girl she could become with proper clothing, diet, and instruction in cleanliness. She said, "I brought you something else, but I don't think it's going to fit. You've grown so much."

The "something else" was a pink blouse and navy-blue skirt with matching pink braid around the hemline. Irene gasped at the sight. "You got *this* for me?"

"It's not new, dear. It belonged to the little girl I take care of. She's only ten, but terribly tall for her age, and she outgrew this. I thought it might fit you, but it's too small."

The sleeves were too short, the shoulders too narrow, the skirt fell barely below her knees, and the fabric stretched too tightly across Irene's developing breasts, but once she had it on, nothing would persuade her to reject it and let Clara get rid of it. "I can make it fit," she said. "Oh, Clara, this is the best thing I have had—the dress and the soap and the tooth things. Thank you. You are such a good friend!"

She flung herself into Clara's arms and hugged her tightly. Clara's eyes began to fill as she embraced the strong young body and smelled her damp, clean hair. She sensed that moments like these must be what motherhood was like. She sniffed once, then drew away, holding Irene's shoulders and looking into her bright eyes. "You can thank me by staying clean and curious and becoming the very best person you can be," she said.

Irene grew serious as well. "I will be the best person I can for myself and my family anyway. Clara, what can I do for *you*?"

"You can let me help you," Clara said. "Let me teach you what I know."

During the years Irene lived with the Sprys, she visited the public showers twice every week. Few of the immigrants felt the need to bathe in such an extravagant manner, and in the winter months the public showers were nearly deserted. In the summer, however, they were a good place to get cool, and Irene often had to stand in long lines and endure the sweaty squabbling of those who wanted the relief of fresh water. But regardless of the competition, Irene went regularly. Being clean became more than a pleasure. It was a religion, an obsession. She found herself judging new acquaintances not on speech or dress as much as on hygiene.

The only money she ever spent on herself was on soaps—for her hair, teeth, skin and clothing. Never overindulgent, she tried all the products within her meager price range. Otherwise, she bought nothing for herself. The only person in the family who noticed her bathing habits was Andy. "Makes your hair soft, puttin' that stuff on it," he said one day, running his big hammy hand over a long braid. "Smells good, too." He leaned down and kept his head next to hers for a little too long. Irene felt a strange mix of gratitude and something like panic. She edged away. He was finding more frequent excuses for touching her lately. She considered talking to Tilly about it, but some primitive warning in the back of her mind told her not to.

Her twice-monthly Sunday afternoon jaunts with Clara were the pegs on which the rest of Irene's days were strung. "What shall we do today?" Irene would ask, putting her destiny temporarily in the older woman's hands.

"Today we are going to the Brooklyn Bridge and I will tell you all about how it came to be built," Clara would say; or: "There is an automobile exhibition at Madison Square Garden and we will go learn about gasoline-powered vehicles."

More often they'd simply find a relatively quiet place to talk and Clara would instruct her in one subject or another. "You've mastered English the way the Sprys speak it," she said one day during the second winter of Irene's life in America, "but that is poor English, tenement English, heavily accented and grammatically incorrect. From now on, you and I will not speak in Polish. We will converse only in English so that you may improve."

They spoke infrequently about Clara's background and only then at Irene's insistence. "Do you have a mother and father now?" Irene asked, strugging for the right words.

"No. They have both passed on. My father when I was three years old and my mother a few years ago."

"You have brother? Sister?"

"Only a few cousins, and I don't know where they are. You see, my mother was thought to have married beneath herself. Her family wasn't wealthy, but they were well off and she'd gone to college for a year to learn to be a teacher before she married my father. He hadn't any money and was in poor health and her family disowned her for insisting on making such a bad match. When my father died, she tried to go back to her parents, but they'd moved and hadn't left any word of where they had gone. She got a job as a governess and educated me while she worked to support us."

"She must have been very sad."

Clara considered. "Not sad. Angry sometimes, but I believe she always felt it was worth it for those few years with my father. They were very much in love."

"I make sorry . . . I *am* sorry," she corrected herself, "that your father passed away. But I am glad, too. If not, you might not go to Poland and come back when I do so I know you."

Clara sorted this out and smiled. "God's will," she said.

Her initial fondness for the shy, grubby child on the ship grew to affection and then love as the years passed. At first she told herself it was merely a motherly feeling in spite of the fact that they were only seven years apart. For a while she even worried that it was a crush—Clara had heard nasty stories about women who loved women the way they should love men. But she eventually realized it was something far different. Her love of Irene was neither maternal nor lesbian, it was the passion of a born teacher for the one promising student of a lifetime. Irene's mind was a wide-mouthed, almost bottomless vessel. Clara realized early on that everything she knew or could learn would only partially fill that container. Other people in Irene's life would have to do the rest, but for now Clara was her only source of intellectual sustenance. She took this responsibility very seriously.

Not all their conversations were instructional. "Do you know what I am most missing from my home?" Irene asked one spring day. She was still struggling with idiomatic English.

"Your family?"

"Of course, but also I miss the seasons. It gets hot here in the summertime and cold in the wintertime but that is only temperature. We put on more clothes or take them off, and it is then the same. I am lonely for seeing trees get green in the spring and yellow and red in the fall. The snow here gets dirty most fast and it doesn't look like snow. Today there is the smell on the air of food and people, but it should smell like spring. I never see no birds . . ." She paused, thinking. "I mean, *any* birds building nests except the dirty old pigeons. I never thought, when I was a small girl, that I would miss birds."

The next time they got together, Clara had a bird-identification book with her. They went to Castle Gardens at the tip of Manhattan and studied seagulls.

Sometimes they talked about the Sprys, but not very often. "Mrs. Spry is liking me, I think," Irene said. "She is sometimes nice."

"And Mr. Spry?"

Irene squinted into the sun, considering. "He is liking me sometimes too, but it makes me feel strange." How to describe the little pats and pinches and strokes that appealed to her deep need for affection and at the same time made her feel soiled and frightened? She had gotten into the habit of keeping physical distance from him, but occasionally she sensed that he knew she was doing so deliberately and it made him angry.

"Strange? How?"

Irene shrugged. She hadn't the comprehension or the vocabulary in any language to describe it. "It is nothing."

No, it is something. Clara thought. Something awful that I would give anything to save you from—if only I had it in my power. But what could she, a spinster on the brink of poverty herself, do? Get Irene out? Where? How?

Once they discussed Teo. "Have you ever told your mother about Teo disappearing?" Clara asked.

"I tell my Mama I write for Teo also and that he does well. It would break her heart to know the truth. Poor Mama."

"Someday she will have to know."

"Someday . . ." Irene said softly. "I say that word often, Clara. Someday things will be better. Someday I will save enough to get my family here. Someday I will have a better life. When is this someday, Clara?"

"Things change in their proper time, Irene. All you can do is prepare yourself to be ready when that time comes."

"I *will* be ready."

4

In the spring of 1904, when Irene was seventeen, Andy Spry brought Piotr Gieryk home to dinner. "I have to go back early to help with dinner," Irene told Clara, explaining why they had to cut their Sunday afternoon short. "Mr. Spry hopes this man will like Elsa or Charlotte."

"The other Spry girls have married already, haven't they?"

"Yes, last fall."

"Who's the man?" Clara asked.

"I do not know. Some worker from the factory. A cutter of furs, I think perhaps. Mr. Spry says he makes a good wage. Very good, more than Mr. Spry maybe even."

Clara shuddered at the sentence construction, so typically "Sprysian," but didn't attempt to delay Irene for a correction. "Perhaps he would make a good husband for you, Irene."

Irene stared at her with astonishment, then laughed. "Me? I want no husband. You sound like my mama. The first time she wrote me a letter in this country, she sent my baptismal certificate, so I would have it to marry."

But when the young man arrived for dinner, she found herself remembering Clara's comment and she viewed the visitor speculatively. He was a man in his early twenties, light of frame, but tall and by no means frail or delicate. The straight hair that fell into his eyes in an appealingly boyish sweep was almost as fair as Irene's own and his eyes were of a peculiarly intense blue and very observant. Irene's first impression was that he looked intelligent, like a teacher, though she knew no teacher but Clara. Still, teachers should look like this man. Besides his apparent intelligence, there was something else about him that attracted her, something she couldn't pin down and label quite so easily. There was a curiosity, an intensity in those blue eyes, and a hint of . . . what?—anger? zeal? ambition?—that struck a responding chord in her.

It was apparent from the moment of introduction that Andy Spry's hope of Piotr Gieryk, the fur cutter, forming an attachment to either Elsa or Charlotte was doomed. They were great pillowy-billowy girls with booming voices and hearty gestures. He seemed at first amused, then disgusted in the face of their onslaught. Sensing rejection, they became all the more boisterous and the visitor retreated behind a carapace of cool courtesy. Why in the world had he done this? he wondered wildly. For the home-cooked food, of course. But could it possibly be worth it?

Almost as an afterthought, Irene was introduced to him. "I'm pleased to meet you, Mr. Gieryk," Irene said shyly, then asked, "Have you been a teacher, sir?"

"No," he said, surprised and pleased. In this wretched place and among these despicable people, as he was loathing himself for so stupidly accepting a dinner invitation, this soft-spoken girl with the lovely eyes had immediately guessed his dearest, most secret dream.

"What do you do at the factory?" Tilly asked, noting sourly that he was watching Irene, not her daughters.

"I cut the furs for the collars of the coats," he replied, glancing back at Irene, who was sitting quietly, hands folded in her lap.

"What a good job!" Tilly exclaimed.

"It pays well, but it is extremely boring," he replied in English as proper and exact as Irene's friend Clara's.

"Boring? How could handling *furs* be boring?" Elsa asked, and emitted a high-pitched shriek that was meant to pass as a girlish giggle. It was a sound to set teeth on edge. Tilly cringed and glared at her daughter. Where had she gone wrong with Elsa and Charlotte? These girls of hers suddenly appeared as what they were—hysterical cows, clumping about like noisy fools while that damned Irene sat there cool and ladylike as you please.

Staring at the Kossok girl, Tilly seemed to really see her

for the first time in years. Her blond hair was as straight and golden as wheat stems; her high cheekbones and slightly tilted eyes gave her that oddly half-Oriental look sometimes seen in Russian faces; her figure was that of a woman, generous in breast and hip, slim of waist and throat. This wasn't the same skinny, drab, cowering child she'd taken into her home three years ago and Tilly just now noticed the changes that had been going on.

She darted a look at Andy. If he hadn't noticed the transformation yet, he soon would. And then where would she be? Knowing he was seducing girls at the factory was one thing; harboring a desirable girl in her own home was quite another. This thought canceled for the moment the fondness she'd grown to feel for Irene over the years.

Tucking the worry away like a partially darned sock in a sewing basket, she turned her attention back to Piotr Gieryk. "Where are you from?"

"Warsaw," he answered shortly. "I came to this country five years ago and served a three-year apprenticeship. I have worked at the factory for two years." His tone was mechanical. He'd been through this sort of interrogation by overeager mothers of marriageable girls before. He knew what she wanted to know and wasn't going to give it to her, but fed her secondary facts instead. Sometimes he was tempted to spout his salary, address, and personal habits just to have it done. Alternatively, he'd considered telling some outrageous story about an idiot sister and Siamese-twin brothers, just to see what would happen. But as yet he hadn't given in to that urge. If the pretty girl who thought he looked like a teacher weren't here, he might have tried it out on the Sprys.

His reserve did nothing to deter Tilly or her daughters. Throughout the meal Tilly prodded at his prospects and the girls showed off. Their demands for his attention gave Irene a chance to study him. She was impressed with what she saw and heard. He had a deep, powerful voice, modulated as if by deliberate effort. She liked his speech, recognizing in it the carefully correct inflections that Clara used. Moreover, he spoke at an even, considered pace, not allowing his sentences to be startled into a gallop by Tilly's conversational pressure.

His appearance was also much in his favor. He was clean,

young, vibrantly male. He was fresh and vigorous, like a newly minted silver coin inexplicably come to rest in the Sprys' shabby home. And every now and then he'd smile at her for no reason and it seemed like they were sharing a happy secret. She found herself thinking again of what Clara had said about a husband. Were she to want a husband, this man would probably be the right kind. Courteous and handsome, but with an underlying aura of power and strength—or was it simply self-assurance? Irene didn't know, she only sensed that there was something very special about Piotr Gieryk. Very special and very attractive.

But as soon as Irene considered the thought, she rejected it. Marriage was of no interest to her. Not now, possibly not ever. Since Teo's defection, she'd purged herself of the concept of man as protector and provider. She was determined to provide for herself and her family, if ever she could save enough to bring them to America.

Still, for all her intellectual resolve, Irene was ripe for change, craving an alteration of the horrible sameness of the days and weeks. Her maturity had not yet manifested itself in sexual awareness, but only in a sort of indefinable restlessness. It was like a toothache—unsettling, shifting focus, ebbing and flowing in intensity. She had no idea of the cause nor the cure of the edginess, the almost frantic misery that sometimes engulfed her. But she did wonder, as Tilly plied Piotr Gieryk with pork jowls and pickled cabbage, if he might be the person who could take away the pain. And she found herself wondering what his hands felt like and how that rich voice would sound whispering in her ear.

Piotr accepted another invitation to dinner a month later. Irene was perplexed; it didn't seem likely that he could be drawn to one of the Spry daughters, but perhaps she'd misinterpreted him all along. After all, what did she know about the relationships between the sexes? Next to nothing. Of the two marriages she'd witnessed at close hand, her parents' and the Sprys', there was little if any affection, but could they have started that way? And could Mr. Gieryk possibly be drawn to one of the Spry girls?

It didn't occur to her that Piotr was interested in her, not

Elsa or Charlotte, but it did cross Tilly's mind and she made sure Irene's tenuous connection with the family was known, thinking this would somehow dampen any interest the highly paid young fur cutter might have. "Of course, Irene is no relation to us," she said as they ate. She had a piece of potato skin stuck to her front tooth.

"Is that so?" He addressed Irene rather than Tilly. He didn't bother to hide the relief he felt that Spry blood didn't run in her veins.

His broad smile made Irene want to laugh for sheer pleasure. "No, my family is in the old country. I'm saving to send them money to come over here. My father is working hard for the same reason. He is a glover and bootmaker."

Tilly sucked the potato skin loose with a loud smack and said, "Irene! I'm sure our guest isn't interested—"

"Oh, but I am, Mrs. Spry," Piotr said. "I think it's most admirable of Miss Kossok."

"Miss Kossok?" Tilly said, offended. "You don't need to call her that. She's just Irene. That's what we all call her."

"Yes, but I'm not one of you," Piotr said firmly. Tilly sensed this was an insult, but couldn't quite figure out why. Puzzling on it, she subsided. Irene was struck by the remark, too. No, he most certainly *wasn't* one of them. Nothing about him was like them.

Piotr went on, asking Irene, "You're in touch with your family, then?"

"I write to my mama," she said, suddenly shy of being the center of attention this way. Tilly and the girls were all staring at her as if she were something they'd found in an apple, and even Andy had an odd, speculative expression. "Well, I don't actually write—not by myself, but they can't read anyway," she finished hurriedly.

At this, Piotr laughed—a rich, booming sound as heady as wine after a long fast. Irene noticed how white his teeth were.

"Irene, serve the dessert!" Tilly barked, cutting short the sound.

"Yes, ma'am," Irene said, knowing she'd inadvertently provoked Tilly's wrath. She got up quickly and took down the apple cobbler she'd made earlier in the day and set up to cool. It was a sad, gummy thing, mostly flour she'd had to pick the weevils out of. The old, sour apples could have used more sugar, had there been any.

Piotr watched her, admiring the way that she, like he, had learned the hard rule of obedience, yet she managed to do as she was told briskly and respectfully without any sign of subservience. And did he see in her fleeting glance a reflection of his own anger at the injustice of it, or did he only imagine it? She maintained her dignity and made it seem she was serving the dessert as if she were hostess, not servant. He noticed, too, that she gave him a piece that was marginally larger than the others—not enough to be obvious, but enough to be flattering.

Tilly sent Irene down to the sink on the ground floor to wash the dishes as soon as they were through eating. Irene wasn't present when Piotr left, so she had no idea whether Tilly had invited him back or whether he had accepted. And she knew better than to ask.

Piotr Gieryk went home thinking about her. He'd only gone back because he'd come to think of her as so beautiful and gracious after the first visit that he'd meant to prove his memory wrong. But she was all he remembered. How was it that she said he looked like a teacher that first time he'd been there? A special perception, or mere chance conversation? If he'd been born at another time, in different circumstances, he might have already become a college professor. As it was, he had started life in Warsaw in poverty so abject and city-bound that it made Irene's early years in the village seem luxurious by comparison. But that was a life he tried not to remember, a past he never talked about or even thought about if he could help it.

Abandoned as a toddler, Piotr Gieryk had only a hazy notion of a mother and no memory of a father or siblings. He had lived for several days in the garbage-strewn alley where his mother left him, slapping with dimpled baby hands at the cats and rats who fought him for scraps. Then a girl found him. She was fifteen and simpleminded. Hardly recognizing that the half-starved, cat-clawed, rat-nibbled child was a human being and not a doll, she dragged him home with her.

Her family, desperate to keep her entertained and out of

their way, let her keep him as a plaything. Fortunately, her favorite pastime was feeding "dolly," and incidentally she saved Piotr's life. But as he regained his tenuous grasp on existence, strengthened by the oat porridge and cabbage she stuffed down his gullet, he began to cry for his lost mother. The girl's parents, burdened with eight of their own children and fond of none of them, refused to tolerate another noise-maker in the single windowless room they all shared. They, like his mother, disposed of him, leaving him in a slightly better neighborhood.

This time he was found by an elderly couple who foisted him off on the local butcher and his childless wife. The wife, of whom Piotr had virtually no memory whatsoever, was happy to take the little boy, but her husband beat him nearly senseless the first time he woke in the night and cried for his mother. Few people remember anything of their early childhood: in Piotr's mind it was as vivid as a fresh wound, never fully healed, sometimes still oozing blood. Before he was three years old, Piotr learned that crying brought pain and upheaval; being quiet and obeying meant food and a chance to sleep in the same place every night. Though he could not, or would not, speak yet, his most primitive survival instincts served him well.

He lived with the butcher's family until he was eight, taking their family name, Gieryk, and the first name they arbitrarily assigned him. Then one night the butcher came home drunk and beat Piotr so severely that he nearly died. This beating was without any provocation whatsoever and when Piotr became well enough to walk, he realized that he was unable to face such capriciously inflicted pain again. He'd learned the rules and played by them; the butcher hadn't. It was a hard lesson, one that left deep scars crisscrossing his back that would last all his life.

Burning with a repressed fury that had never entirely cooled, Piotr ran away. With nothing but a loaf of bread, the rind of a round of cheese, and the clothes he wore, he set out. Chance took him westward to Włocławek, where he lived for two years in a tent under a bridge with another, slightly older orphan. They stole and begged and occasionally ran errands for people who could afford to pay a filthy urchin to save themselves a little trouble. The older boy, who called himself Mateusz, reinforced all that Piotr had learned on his own. "You act real meek, see? The rich folk like that. Don't never talk loud or say more than you got to," he instructed his protégé.

But Piotr needed little coaching. He was remarkably attractive now, and for all the dirt, was a pretty child, with an innate innocence that showed in his enormous blue eyes. The store of anger that was building behind those eyes didn't yet show. He learned that hunching his thin shoulders and bobbing his head eagerly when he was spoken to also helped. Even on the one occasion he was caught stealing, he got away with it because the man whose watch he'd taken could hardly believe that such a sweet-looking child could have known what he was doing. He got off with a stern lecture.

Mateusz also provided Piotr with a good explanation of what had become of his, Piotr's, mother. The story was one that Mateusz had made up about his own parents.

"We was going to America, see. It's a place across the ocean to the west where everybody lives in houses and has cows of their own. But when we was ready to go, these Gypsies stole me."

Piotr knew the story was a lie, but what a wonderful lie! "Me too, Mateusz! A whole band of Gypsies! Only I didn't have a father. Only my mother."

"There wasn't nothing my family could do but go on without me," Mateusz went on, momentarily jealous of having his story stolen. " 'Course, they knew I was smart and I'd get away from the Gypsies and follow them. And someday I will, when I get the passage money."

"Was your mother beautiful?" Piotr asked. "Mine was. She had pretty hair and soft hands." And in his heart he was sure this was true.

"I guess so, yeah. Anyway, I gotta go to America."

"Me too. As soon as I can. So my mother won't worry that I'm not coming to be with her."

"My folks'll have a house—"

"My mother will have a whole mansion because she's so pretty and good . . ." Piotr said.

Piotr adopted it as his own story and after a while managed

to forget it was another orphan's fabrication to account for abandonment. Mateusz got over his resentment at the theft and they spent many hours embroidering the tale. When Mateusz developed a cough and fever that worsened until one morning he was cold and stiff, Piotr put him in a shallow grave and left Włocławek to head west, where he planned to find his mother. Like Mateusz's parents, she'd gone to America. She must have. Everyone wanted to go there.

For several years he traveled, finding shelter from October to March wherever he could and moving slowly westward during the warm months. He saw other people living what seemed fairy-tale lives—in homes with kitchen gardens, with laughing children and revered elders and warm, safe hearths to come to at the end of the day. And he wanted that life with a longing more constant and painful than the hunger that was his ever-present companion.

He lived in Poznań under a bridge, in a cave outside Berlin, in a cowshed a few miles from Brandenburg, and for almost five years in an actual house in Salzgitter. There in Salzgitter, in the cottage of Herr Schmitt, a reclusive old gentleman with severe arthritis, Piotr very nearly found a real home. Herr Schmitt liked the scrawny blond waif with the big, innocent eyes and took Piotr in to keep him company and to do the reaching and lifting that his frozen joints no longer allowed him to do. He cleaned Piotr up and had the village seamstress come in and cut down some of his old coats and trousers for the boy.

He also put Piotr into the village school for lessons every morning, which Piotr hated, but accepted as part of the price he must pay for the security of a real home. All the children were younger than he, making him feel large and stupid. They made fun of his Polish accent and hand-me-down clothes. But he went every morning and learned all he could, as much to spite them as for his own benefit. And at noon he'd gratefully escape to take up his chores at Herr Schmitt's.

The old man liked Piotr's quiet manner because it gave him full scope to talk, explain, lecture, and elaborate. He was a supremely intelligent and altogether unworldly man who'd never found anyone willing to listen to his dry discourses.

And Piotr did listen, at first simply because it was novel to have an adult speak to him in terms that were not abusive. Nor did Herr Schmitt do as the schoolteacher did and demand responses. Piotr had learned a little gutter German, enough phrases to enable him to beg, and was learning basic German in school, but this man spoke a different language, an educated, precise language that Piotr soon learned to interpret. And as the novelty of letting the fine, guttural words wash over him passed, he stopped listening to the glottal stops and began to pay attention to the meaning of the words.

Every night after dinner, Herr Schmitt would open the subject he'd been contemplating all day while Piotr had been doing household chores. "Tonight, boy, I will tell you about the Copernican view of the universe—" he would say. Or: "I shall now recount the death of Caesar Augustus at Nola. Sit down and listen carefully."

One night it would be an obscure aspect of mathematics or an analysis of a chemical formula. He talked about Descartes and Socrates. He read the Declaration of Independence aloud, a poor German translation that bastardized both the elegant language and idealistic thoughts of that document. He explained a theory that Henry VIII's fifth wife, Catherine Howard, was actually a religious martyr, and he described the geography of the Holy Land.

Herr Schmitt loved facts as other men loved butterflies or stamps. The collecting and reexamining of them was a pleasure unto itself. But his was a cold, color-blind intellect: he could talk about the mathematical precision of Bach's music without ever wondering what the music said about the man and his times or noticing that it affected the heart as well as the brain. He could discourse on John Donne's essays one night and Shakespeare's sonnets the next without ever contemplating a comparison. His facts, of which he had an astonishing collection, were cool, remote, separate entities that bore no relation to each other or to daily life.

Herr Schmitt made no effort to simplify; Piotr understood very little of what was told him, but he comprehended the detachment, and for the time being, it suited him perfectly. Until that first summer at Herr Schmitt's house, everything Piotr had learned had come crated in splintered emotion. If you cry, you are beaten. To ease the ache of starvation, one must learn to steal and beg. A shelter with a southern exposure is better than one with a northern exposure. Understand this or suffer the consequences; figure that out or go hungry; learn or die.

Herr Schmitt's facts were safe, comfortable, inoffensive. One didn't have to remember them or put them to practical use. One could simply enjoy them to satiety like the hard, sour candies the old man kept in a bowl by his chair. The intellectual atmosphere of the cottage was untouched by the winds of danger, anxiety, or hunger.

But before long, Piotr began to feel a vague dissatisfaction that made him feel guilty. To collect facts was a pleasure, but Piotr, almost from the beginning, wanted a finer, more specialized collection, not just everything that came his way. And he wanted to know what the facts meant.

Besides the love of a certain dry, remote sort of learning, Herr Schmitt gave Piotr something else:

Religion.

Schmitt was a devout Catholic and one of Piotr's duties was to accompany the old man to Mass. There they both found the emotional outlet other men might have found in books or women or war. The Church was stability—a stone-and-stained-glass womb where one could experience an exalted and impersonal passion.

For Piotr, the Church filled a terrible need. It gave him a mother in the Blessed Virgin. "Holy Mary, Mother of God . . ." he would pray softly, and in a remote corner of his consciousness he could sense the feel of her soft hair in his baby hands, the yielding warmth of her nurturing breast, the remembrance of her thin arms holding him tightly. Piotr got in the habit of going to church every day, not to worship Christ, but to express his adoration of His Mother. Mary became Piotr's own mother, the unknown woman who had gone to America. Herr Schmitt gave him a rosary and Piotr got calluses on his fingers working the beads. The Our Fathers he skimmed through by rote, but the Hail Marys were heartfelt, each word coming from his soul.

As an adult, Piotr was known to others as a deeply religious man, an intellectually religious man. One acquaintance even said he should have been a Jesuit. And Piotr, though he appreciated the compliment implied in such remarks, knew deep in his heart that his bond to the Church was not one of pure piety, nor even intellect. It was that the Church had given him a mother when that was the single thing he needed most. And for that he was eternally grateful, even after the need had passed and been forgotten.

Religion gave him something else as well: it was the crumbly earth in which he dug a deep hole to bury his anger. To that grave he attempted to consign his fury at the butcher who'd scarred his back and his heart. Into it also went the aching injustice of Mateusz's death and the resentment for all those nights shivering under bridges and starving in caves. The Church told him the meek were blessed, that suffering was God's will. He tried desperately to believe this. And if the anger—not eliminated, merely made subterranean—grew and flourished underground, there were always more prayers to throw onto its grave.

At the end of four years' sojourn, Herr Schmitt, in spite of his physical infirmities, made a journey and took Piotr along. They went to visit the university the old man had attended as a youth. A professor friend of his invited young Piotr to sit in on a lecture and Piotr later looked back at that day as one of the most important in his life. It was a small class, only a dozen or so young men, and the professor spoke little—unlike Herr Schmitt and the bossy teacher at the village school. Instead, he drew from the boys, with gentle prodding, the ideas he meant to impart. They asked questions, and he sometimes answered with facts, but more often he rebutted with other questions. This was so utterly unlike what Piotr had come to regard as education that he was astonished. He couldn't imagine either Herr Schmitt or the village teacher *ever* asking a question sincerely. The schoolteacher asked only questions that were to be answered by rote, not imagination.

This was like the sun coming out for the first time. It was *fun*—an entirely new concept in life for Piotr Gieryk. It was as if the professor had taken Herr Schmitt's dry facts and juggled them with the apparently happy abandon of a circus performer. The boys in the class, not more than a few years older than Piotr, laughed and it was the brightest, brassiest sound in the world. These weren't little, mean village boys who found their greatest joy in tormenting an orphan Pole. Piotr had virtually never heard laughter before, not like this, not laughter that grew from the sheer joy of intellectual stimulation. Here was the joy God must surely have intended when he gave man a brain.

This was the life Piotr wanted—this was the kind of challenge and laughter he craved of life. For those few sparkling hours the buried fury withered and fizzled like a punctured pig's bladder. In that chalk-dusty room, Piotr first thought of a future beyond tomorrow's chores.

When they returned to Salzgitter, Piotr suddenly felt like a caged animal. He prayed over it until his knees were bruised, but God would give him no sign, no absolution for the sin of wanting something else—something more. It had been easy to run away from the butcher who beat him, but Herr Schmitt didn't beat him. He had given his protégé facts and food and God. Why did Piotr feel the same intense need to escape? This was a good life, but he finally admitted that he wanted the life he had seen and tasted at the university. It would not happen here—here in Germany he would always be a poor Pole, an object of scorn and derision—but it might be possible in America. After all, everyone said anything was possible there. It never crossed his mind to wonder if there would be prejudice against foreigners in America.

He finally had to tell Herr Schmitt he was leaving. The old man was heartbroken, rejected, but had long ago forgotten how to express tenderness. Piotr felt guilty, but had never learned how to speak of love or gratitude. And so, early in the spring, Piotr Gieryk left the snug little house full of books and dust and hard, sour candy. "You must take this," Herr Schmitt said as Piotr packed his few possessions. "This is the passage money to America, and something more—to get you to Hamburg."

Piotr continued his interrupted journey across Germany with his pocket full of Herr Schmitt's precious gift and his mind full of useless facts upon which he was to build a firmer mental edifice.

* * *

But that was five years before he met Irene. He'd discovered quickly that America was a land full of books and learned people, particularly in the Church. He'd dipped his toes into the revolutionary crowd first, the discontented young immigrants who had great pretensions to intellect, but emotional viewpoints that he felt defied logic. He attended a few meetings and political rallies, hoping to meet someone with whom he could talk seriously, exchange ideas freely, and learn from. But there was no joy in them, only anger, and their arguments, when closely analyzed, were always a bit hysterical. In the end, he found the only men with whom he could enjoy conversing were priests.

There was no money for him to attend a real college, nor was he ready until he learned the requisite subjects and knew the language thoroughly, for it was the tool upon which all the rest was based. He attended night school for several years, learning and polishing his English and getting an introduction to a number of other subjects. By the time he allowed himself to be coerced into dinner at the Sprys', he knew every free library and second-hand bookstore in New York. He'd also had the good fortune to get and keep a good job, one that kept him comfortably above the subsistence level at which most immigrants lived.

The one thing lacking in his life was women—no, not women, a woman. He was attractive, physically and financially, and there was no shortage of factory girls to throw themselves at him. But there had never been anyone who'd captured both his brain and his heart. Nor did he see any place in his life for a woman until he'd fulfilled his dream of becoming educated.

That night, as she got ready for bed, Irene found herself thinking, not about Piotr Gieryk, but about Tilly. The older woman had done what she could to humiliate Irene during dinner, to put her in her place and discourage the guest's interest in her. But Irene felt no anger; Tilly could have behaved in a far uglier manner than she had.

In the years she'd lived with the Sprys, Irene had come to have a grudging respect for Tilly that approached affection. Tilly had a hard path to follow and trod it with a fairly good heart. Or perhaps it was Irene's heart that was good. She'd matured enough to realize that a woman's appearance counted for a lot. A man could be less than handsome—even ugly—without sacrificing success and happiness. But a woman *had* to be pretty. And Tilly's almost-beauty was negated by the mark on the side of her face, which she bravely ignored, or at least never referred to. Irene respected her for the pretense.

Moreover, Tilly labored under the added disadvantage of having made a bad marriage. The very things that were admirable about her were wasted on Andy Spry. Her ambitions for her daughters, her desire to make their tiny apartment as nice as possible, her devotion to her old parents—all meant nothing to him. Tilly even had the ability to be lighthearted sometimes, a rare commodity in the tenement. She liked games and could get giddy over a round of cards or charades. And on those occasions, Andy always told her to stop acting like a damned fool. It was a wonder Tilly had any laughter left. Irene envied that deep resource of occasional good cheer, even though it included Irene only infrequently.

But Tilly's attitude toward Irene had undergone a subtle change since that first time Piotr had come to dinner. Irene could understand part of the change. After all, Tilly's responsibility, if not her primary reason to live, was to marry her daughters off as well as she could. And she perceived Irene's presence as a threat. While she had been rude to Irene at dinner and many other times over the years, there was another side to that coin that couldn't be ignored.

Though life around them was coarse and often violent, Tilly had never struck Irene, and there had even been flashes of friendliness from time to time. Once last year when Irene was having a particularly bad day with menstrual cramps, Tilly had brought her a cup of hot tea with some sugar in it. And sometimes when Tilly went shopping or visiting, she took Irene along to give her a chance to get out of the apartment. There were even rare instances of Tilly asking Irene's advice on some trivial matter. Irene was always careful to give the opinion she knew Tilly wanted to hear. This created a fragile bond between them.

Yes, Tilly could have treated her much worse than she did. She could have added physical abuse to the sharp words—no one would have questioned it—but she never stooped to that. She could have been stingier, more critical, or perpetually cruel to the child who'd come without invitation and stayed for years. Life on the Lower East Side was designed to bring out the very worst of human nature, but Tilly hadn't totally given in to the denigration of her soul.

Irene plumped her pillow and closed her eyes. On the whole, she thought, she and Tilly were even. Debts owed, debts paid on both sides balanced. No matter how pleasant and attractive Piotr Gieryk might be, how flattering his interest and warm, rumbling laughter, Irene could not encourage him and spoil whatever slim opportunity Tilly's daughters might have of catching him in a marriage net. She wouldn't think about him anymore.

Still, her thoughts kept coming back to him and his face appeared to her at the most unexpected times. It was the face of a saint, but a militant saint: a man who might accept God's will, but not man's. There was an alluring strength in Piotr Gieryk and she couldn't get him out of her mind.

5

Irene woke sweating and gasping and couldn't remember for a moment where she was. Was this still the woods or was she back on the boat? No, she was in bed. The dream had been more vivid by far than reality. It had started on an excursion boat like the one she and Clara had taken a ride on once up the Hudson on a picnic.

But Clara wasn't with her. A man was. A faceless, nameless man with fair hair and very pale eyes and a secret smile. He'd stood next to the rail with her holding her hand. Then he was holding both her hands and a wind made the boat rock. Somebody was singing a soft song and fish jumped up out of the water in patterns, as if dancing. She fell—or drifted—into the circle of his arms. And his hands were touching her. Her face, her arms, and her breasts. And she'd leaned into him, drinking in the feeling like a parched land drinks the first autumn rain. And a strength in him flowed into her, refreshing her.

Somehow she'd been in the dream, and watching the dream at once, seeing the unfamiliar sight of her own body with surprise and pleasure. How pretty it was. Then they were on the shore, laughing together in a wooded place, like a spot she remembered near the river outside the village. It was warm and her clothes were gone and the man was pulling her toward his own unclothed body. Leaves reached out from the trees and caressed her. Grass grew up sensuously between her toes as she stood there. A butterfly landed on her breast and smiled up at her. And then . . .

She didn't have waking words for the feelings, the gripping surge of hot tension that filled her from thighs to chest, the prickling sensation in her breasts and between her legs, the gasps that escaped her lips.

She went over and over the dream in her mind, and her hands, as if they were beings apart from her, began to explore her body. Suddenly she came full awake, her drowsing Catholic conscience on full alert. She leapt from the bed as though it were a sheet of flame. She crept, knees trembling, hands shaking, to the window in the main room and stuck her head out, sucking in what passed for fresh air.

It was sinful, she was sure of that. She crossed herself fervently. Why had she dreamed such immoral things? First thing in the morning she'd go to church, but her mission was more to chide God than to appeal to him. She was a good girl, a virtuous girl. Why had God allowed the devil to put such thoughts and feelings into her sleep, against her will?

No one mentioned Piotr again for weeks. Then, one afternoon in June, Tilly said to Irene, "Mr. Spry has invited Mr. Gieryk over on Sunday."

Irene was prepared. "Oh, dear! I promised Clara I would meet her Sunday. But I can change my plan if you want my help."

Tilly almost sighed with relief. "No, you go on. I can manage."

It was nicely done. Tilly was able to clear the apartment of a dangerous element and save face at the same time by appearing to be generous and considerate.

The Sunday in question wasn't really Clara's day off, so Irene planned to spend it alone, leaving the apartment a full hour before the guest was expected. It was an unusually hot day for June, with humid air like a blanket in the tunnellike streets. Irene was going to go to the free showers, her usual leisure activity, but it was too hot to think about it yet. There would be many people today and a long line to wait in. Instead, she walked briskly to St. Stanislas.

The church was nearly empty but still warm from the packed bodies present at the morning service. There was the scent of humanity—perfume, sweat, and a whiff of the fishmonger—mingling with the distinctly church smell of incense and plaster saints and furniture polish. Someday, Irene thought,

Mama and the other girls would attend this church wih her. They would sit together near the front, Mama, Irene, Agnieszka, the twins, Lillie and Cecilia, and baby Stefania. Oh, and Papa too, she added as an afterthought. But while she could picture Mama and the girls, hair shining and sweet smiles in place, Papa was a dim image.

After kneeling and crossing herself in a somewhat perfunctory manner, she settled into a back pew. Irene liked St. Stanislas for many reasons, few of them strictly religious in nature. The quiet babble of Polish while people were being seated and after the services made her think of her family. She found it difficult to think of them at the Sprys', for the world there was so different from the world they were in, but here she could remember the many Masses she'd attended with Zofia and her little sisters.

Second, the Church marked the seasons, even if the city did not. When it was Easter and the priest spoke of Christ's agony and resurrection, Irene remembered that flowers would soon follow back home, even though she would probably see none in New York. Easter meant the land was thawing, the stream was beginning to run, gurgling, behind the house, birds would start looking for nesting materials. At Christmas she remembered the village celebrations, the lung-pinching cold of the river where they fetched water, the excitement of climbing onto the sagging roof of the house and making snow angels. All Saints' Day meant the big harvest market with multitudes of pumpkins and squash and freshly butchered pork, the breathtaking sight of whole hillsides vibrating with color.

St. Stanislas gave Irene the seasons back.

Most important, the church was a refuge, a place of peace in a frantic world of work and often uncontrollable discord. Nobody shouted in church—not even Andy Spry. No one was angry or jealous or fearful in here. And if they were exhausted and nodded off, it was a gentle rest, unlike the tortured nightmare-ridden sleep she sometimes heard people suffering through the thin walls of the apartment.

Though Irene attended Mass almost every Sunday morning, she preferred the church as it was now, full of the aura of people without the actual people. She felt she had more of

God's attention as an individual than as part of a throng. But after years of prayers, none of which appeared to have been answered, she was beginning to wonder if God could hear her at all. He certainly hadn't heeded her plea to spare her the sort of dream she had the night Piotr Gieryk came to dinner. Only last week . . .

She knelt again for a few minutes, not really praying, but letting her mind drift, thoughtless. As usual, a sense of tranquillity began to come over her, temporarily blocking out the anxieties of everyday life in the tenement—the squalling underfed children, the shrill disappointed wives, the men with defeat etched into their once-young features. Here, for a short time, her neighbors didn't exist. There were no thwarted ambitions, starved hopes, rail-ribbed factory workers.

Piotr was in the confessional. He pulled the curtain open, thinking wryly that his life had become too uneventful even to provide him with any interesting sins to confess. When he was younger he'd been able to admit to the fury that burned a hole in his heart, and after absolution he'd feel the temporary dampening down of it. Eventually he managed to put it aside, or at least out of mind, for long periods of time. Later, when he got to America, he'd confessed to some casual fornication through the years. And from time to time he'd admitted to greed, although that wasn't precisely accurate. It wasn't greed for tangible objects that he felt, but a lust for knowledge.

But he'd grown rather self-satisfied. Now that his job provided him with basic needs and the few luxuries that interested him—books, mainly—he was seldom afflicted with greed. He had all he needed, all that he *should* need. And there were few women in his daily circle of contact who inspired him to bother with all the tedious preliminaries of seduction. The factory girls were all so dreary and stupid and pitifully eager to snare a husband to save them from their jobs that encouraging them in any way seemed a serious sin. On the occasions when he'd asked one of them out, he'd always had the feeling that she would have flung herself into virtually any danger or degradation if he'd given the slightest sign of desiring it.

No, any sort of social life with the women he knew was

impossible. He seldom even had sexual longings for them anymore.

Until lately.

But the overeager factory girls weren't on his mind. It was the beautiful young woman at the Sprys' who kept invading his thoughts and sent his blood pumping. He'd started to confess to the longings he'd felt these last few weeks, then changed his mind. He wasn't trying to keep any secrets from God, only from the priest. In spite of the theoretical anonymity of the confessional, he knew Father Strzelecki would recognize his distinctive voice and a confession of sexual longing might lead his friend to believe that he had, at long last, formed a romantic attachment—just what the priest had been trying to urge him into for years. "You need a real woman in your life, Piotr," Father Strzelecki had said so often.

Piotr knew it was true; it was what had kept him from ever seriously considering the priesthood. The Church very nearly satisfied his intellectual needs, but he had other needs, requirements of the heart and body that that philosophy couldn't touch or alter. He wasn't meant for celibacy. He ached for domesticity, yearned for a woman and a family that was his and whole and safe.

While he had met women he thought attractive, occasionally intelligent, or often sexually exciting, he'd never met all three in one and he was too demanding to accept less. The girl at the Sprys' house was certainly attractive and had stirred his dreams in a way the priest would find downright encouraging. But she had shown no interest in him and he'd almost managed to convince himself that her apparent shyness was probably only common stupidity. He'd go along to the horrible Sprys' apartment one more time to confirm this suspicion.

So today, as usual when he went to confession, he'd been able only to admit to doubt, a pallid sin in his view. Who, given normal human intelligence, didn't doubt? In fact, he'd come to believe that God had given the ability to doubt as a virtue, not a vice. Without questioning, there could be no confirmation of belief.

As he stepped through the curtain, slipping the rosary Herr

Schmitt had given him so many years ago, so many prayers ago, into his jacket pocket, he saw Irene. She was kneeling, her hands folded, her forehead resting on them as her lips moved silently. ". . . who art in heaven . . ." he silently mouthed with her. There was a statue of the Virgin against the far wall in almost precisely the same attitude. Seen in profile, Irene looked like a living version of Mary. What a fortunate coincidence. If he'd been an artist, he'd have wanted to paint the scene. As it was, he only closed his eyes for a moment, smiling as he impressed it on his memory. Good God, he was really going *too* far! he chided himself. She might not be as pitiful as those poor wretches at the factory, but that wasn't any reason to cast her as a saint!

After a moment Irene rose, refreshed. Sighing with satisfaction, she gathered her bundle of clothing and prepared to leave. But as she neared the confessional, Piotr Gieryk stepped directly into her path. "Miss Kossok, I didn't know you attended St. Stanislas. I don't remember seeing you here before." Why did he feel tongue-tied? She was just another ordinary girl. No, of course she wasn't. She was the cause for which he was about to subject himself to another gruesome few hours with that ass Andy Spry and his lumpy wife and daughters.

"Nor I, you," Irene answered, employing a phrase Clara used and which she thought sounded very elegant. They moved toward the doors. "I thought you were having dinner with the Sprys."

"I am, in a quarter of an hour. Just time for us to get there.'

"No, not me. I am spending the day with my friend Clara."

"You won't be there?" he asked. And Irene knew then, for certain, that she alone was the reason he'd agreed to endure the Sprys' company. The thought made her giddy, an altogether unfamiliar emotion.

He held the door open for her. "Are you in a hurry or can you walk part of the way with me?" he asked. Damn, was he really going to have to spend hours with those barbarians without Irene present?

"I . . ." Irene hesitated, weighing her debt to Tilly against the lure of that rich voice and the blue eyes that seemed to reflect such fascinating secrets. "I have time to go just one block."

"I'm sorry I laughed at you last time," he said as they skirted a group of ragged boys playing marbles.

It took her only a second to remember. He'd thought it was funny when she said she didn't write very well, but her family couldn't read anyway. "You did not offend me." She smiled.

"I am curious how you *do* communicate with your family." He was smiling too.

"I can write some English. My friend Clara teached . . . taught me. She brings me books and gives me lessons on many things. So, I make my letter, then a girl who lives in the Sprys' building makes my English into Polish—"

"Translates. That's what that's called."

"Thank you. That is a nice word. I will remember it. She translates my letters, then I send them along with money to the village priest. He reads the letters to my family and gives them the money and my mother tells him what to write back to me and I take that letter downstairs and the girl . . translates it back to English. It isn't all good."

"No? Why not?"

"Because it takes so long. Many months before I have a letter back, and I don't think Mama likes telling things to the priest. Bad or naughty things he might not like. She almost never speaks of my father because he and the priest are not . . . well, Papa doesn't like going to Mass." They'd been walking briskly and were almost to the building where the Sprys lived. "I must go now or my friend Clara will worry about me."

"May I see you again?"

"I don't know," Irene answered, bewildered by his interest in her and her own eager response to his questions.

Piotr watched her hurry away, thinking how touched he was by what anyone else would have considered a perfectly ordinary, mundane conversation. He liked the fact that she liked words, liked learning, appreciated her friend Clara, and had carefully tried out and put away for safekeeping the word he'd just taught her. He respected and even slightly envied her obvious devotion to her family. This young woman was clearly somebody very special—not to mention quite extraordinarily beautiful. More beautiful than ever now that he knew she had a brain behind that lovely face.

He glanced down the street to the Sprys' building, squaring his shoulders.

Though Irene didn't realize it at the time, a letter from Zofia was already in transit, a letter that dealt almost exclusively with Jozef. Irene got it two mornings after her visit with Piotr and took it upstairs to have it translated. She came back an hour later. The girl who translated for her always made a written copy so that Irene might have the illusion of reading her mail privately even though two other people were already familiar with the contents. This time the girl looked stricken and said, "I'm sorry," as she handed Irene the original and the copy.

Irene knew the news was bad and couldn't bring herself to read the letter. Instead, she carried it around all day in her pocket, touching it from time to time but not taking it out. She wished she could go see Clara, read the awful news, whatever it might be, in the presence of her trusted friend. But Clara wasn't allowed to receive visitors.

But Irene couldn't bear to read her mother's letter there, in the Sprys' apartment. It was still enemy territory. By evening she'd worked herself into a condition of frantic misery. There was only one place where she could be alone. She waited until the Sprys went to bed; then, packing the letter inside a bundle of clothes, she crept out and made her way along the nearly deserted black streets to the public showers. The hour gave her complete privacy. Entering a room at the far back end of the basement, she turned on the water and sat down, fully dressed, on the bench in the outer half of the cubicle.

When the room was steamy, she took out the letter, looking first at the original for some hope or comfort and finding none in the oddly spiky script of the village priest. She unfolded the translation and read:

Dearest daughter Irina,

I am asking Father Szukalski to write to you of terrible news. Your father is dead.

Irene leaned back against the wall and took a deep breath. Thank God! It was not Mama or Agnieszka. That was, she now realized, the fear that had eaten at her heart all day. She went back to reading, but her hands were rattling the page so badly she had to smooth it out on her lap to make the letters stop jumping.

> It was a sickness of his bowels. He had suffered the misery of it for two years and feared he was dying. This is why I did not speak of him for so long. So I would not worry you and Teo without cause. But now you must know the truth. I am sorry, too, that there is more sadness in this than you know. Your papa, may God protect his soul, went to see a cousin in Gdansk before he died, to make peace for an old family quarrel. The cousin, he took your papa to a horse-racing contest where men bet on which would run the fastest. Papa, he bet all the money Teo sent, but the horse did not win and the money was lost.
>
> I do not know how to tell Teo this terrible thing, that we have lost all the money he gave you to send. Daughter, help me. Make your brother understand and forgive us. We have no man to look after us now with Jozef in his grave. I plead with Our Lord and his Merciful Mother every day that we might come to America. Please help us, Irina. Make Teo forgive our weakness and bring us to America. Soon.
>
> Your mother,
Zofia Kossok

Irene crumpled the letter into a soggy ball and bent double, as if in excruciating pain. A great heart-stopping sob rose from her guts to her chest, gathering in her throat until it exploded in a terrible animal sound of agony. She flung herself up, back against the sweating marble wall of the dressing cubicle.

All for nothing!

All the years of enduring the slavery/charity of the Sprys. All the thousands of stitches in hundreds of dresses for other women. All the quiet acceptance when she was nearly bursting with pent-up defiance. The endless nights on the floor at the foot of the bed. The thousands of trips up and down the steps balancing dirty dishes. All for nothing!

Nothing!

Damn her father! Damn Jozef Kossok for dying. Damn him for caring more for an old quarrel than his wife and daughters, for using her hard-earned money to gamble and carouse with an old cousin. Damn him for throwing away everything she'd worked for.

She twisted around, leaning her head against the wall, banging on it with her fists, screaming, howling wordlessly like a creature in a steel-jawed trap.

Damn Zofia for not telling her sooner. For letting this happen. For being so grateful to Teo.

Irene fell to the floor, rolling forward into a tight human knot of hatred. Her hair had come undone and she jerked loose a hank, relishing the pain.

Most of all, damn Teo. Damn him for having their love and respect and gratitude. Damn him for abandoning them. Her. For not being here when she needed him so desperately.

Damn them all!

Damn God!

She huddled on the floor sobbing until the sobs turned to gags. Crawling forward joint by joint, she let the warm water from the shower drench her head. Bile rose in her throat and she vomited and watched the meager, starchy dinner she'd choked down earlier swirl down the drain.

Only then, only when she'd physically disgorged the anger, was she able to start feeling sorrow.

She put her cheek against the smooth floor and let the water strike her face, pooling her hair. Her nose was running; her swollen eyes were gritty and hot; her chest and stomach ached from the violence of her sobs; her hands were bruised and raw from her thrashing. She thought:

All for nothing.

6

September 1904

"Nearly four years. I've been in America almost four years, Clara, and I have done nothing."

"You've done a great deal," Clara said briskly. "You've learned so much, you're hardly the same person."

"Learning has not helped me."

"It's furnished your mind."

"That is of no use. I have not brought my family to America. That is what I must do."

Clara was hurt; the learning was her gift to Irene, but she tried not to show her feelings because she sympathized with Irene's deep despair. "Then you must put what you have learned to use."

"How? How can knowing English help me get my family to America? My baby sister Stefania is five years old. I would not recognize her. Even my Agnieszka is fifteen, two years older than me when I come here. She is of age to marry. If she don't come soon, she might never come."

Clara had been on the verge of suggesting that Irene attempt to get a job as a governess. Her manners and appearance were nice enough. Her natural reticence was indistinguishable from refinement; her features suggested aristocratic breeding. Simply to see her, one might judge her to be of the upper classes. But her English was still the great barrier. Clara's influence wasn't enough to overcome the contagion of the Sprys' ignorance. "If she *don't* come soon" indeed! "You must learn more. You must speak well."

"You tell me I speak good already."

"You've learned a great deal, but there's much, much more you must know. You still speak *zargon angielsko chiński*—Pidgin English. You should go to school. There are night classes at Cooper Union for immigrants. It's only a few blocks away at Astor Place and Eighth. And it's free. All you have to do is prove you are of sound mind and body and want to learn. You must have a recommendation from someone of stature in the community. I'm sure the priest at St. Stanislas will write you a letter."

"Oh, but Clara, it won't help. I must find a way to make some money."

"You better find a husband, then. A man who makes a good salary." Clara said it with an astringent edge of sarcasm.

"I would not do that," Irene replied. "I do not want to marry and have babies with someone I do not like. And if I did like a man, I would not marry to him just to take his money."

"Isn't there a man you like? That fur cutter you told me about?"

"Mr. Gieryk. I like him, yes." In fact, her feelings for Piotr Gieryk had grown to be much stronger than her words indicated, but she was shy about admitting it. Even as close as she and Clara were, there were personal feelings so mysterious and intense they couldn't be spoken of.

"And he makes good money?" Clara was serious now. It was a way out of difficulties, a way many good women had taken; a way Clara herself might have succumbed to had the opportunity presented itself. Though she considered herself a confirmed spinster, Clara didn't scorn marriage. It simply hadn't been offered to her.

"Tilly says so. But I would not take from him his money. Especially not him. My family is *my* family. When I have my mother and my sisters here, then I can think of nice men like Piotr Gieryk and marrying."

Her voice trailed off. She was thinking ahead to that day. Supposing she could somehow make enough for their passage? What would happen to them here? She'd always imagined them living in a real house together, with a yard with trees and plentiful food on the table and warm clothes. How could she give them that? It was unthinkable that her sisters turn into the pitiful factory drudges she saw every day. But she couldn't even support herself, so how in God's name would she support all of them—Mama, Agnieszka, Lillie and Cecilia, and Stefania?

Her mind had gone around this a hundred times in the month since she'd received her mother's letter. And every time she came back to this same point and said to herself: "Somehow I must do it!" And then the voice that spoke from a dark doorway in her head said grimly, "How?"

And there was no answer. No answer. Perhaps Clara was right, however. School. Maybe some very wise person at a school could teach her the answer. Maybe some word in English would give her the vital clue. "Tell me more about this Cooper Union, Clara."

She went to St. Stanislas the day before her first class, to thank Father Strzelecki for the glowing letter of recommendation he'd written for her and to pray that she would get the answer from her classes. She wasn't at all sure God was listening and went more from a sort of superstition than genuine piety, but she was desperate for a solution.

As she left the church, Piotr Gieryk was coming in with an armload of books he'd borrowed from Father Strzelecki. He stopped dead in his tracks when he saw her. "Is there something wrong?" he asked. "You're so pale."

His concern undid her. All her resolve to keep her woes a secret crumbled. She'd resolved not to speak to anyone but Clara of her problems with getting her family to America, and most especially not Piotr Gieryk, but the words bubbled up, poured out. "I was praying for help," she said, and she told him everything in a torrent she was helpless to stop.

He listened patiently, not letting her see how sick it made him feel to hear how desperately hard she'd worked without coming close to her goals. But he felt that same surge of fury he'd felt as a child when he was beaten and abused. Only this time it was on her behalf, not his. And that made it even worse. In his mind's eye, Jozef Kossok and the butcher Gieryk were versions of the same man—the same evil man.

"Come, you're trembling. You need to sit down," he said, gesturing to a nearby candy shop. They went in and sat down at a tiny wrought-iron table at the front. He set his books on the floor under the table and got them each a long strap of licorice.

When he rejoined her at the table, she said, "I'm sorry I act this way and tell you all these things." Then, before he could respond, she went on with a confident smile. "I am starting at a school tomorrow night. My friend Clara says if I learn English more, I can get a good job and make money for Mama faster."

"Where are you going to school?"

"Cooper Union."

"That's wonderful. Father Strzelecki has been helping me get a position there as a teacher—to Poles just learning English. I was taking back some books he'd loaned me to study verb forms. I'll go with you."

"No," Irene said quickly, thinking of Tilly. "But maybe I will see you there and we can talk sometimes."

"I'd like that," he said, perplexed by her reaction.

Irene looked at him for a long moment and then smiled. The intense way he was looking at her made her feel shy. She hurriedly changed the subject. "You are Polish too? Do you have family there?"

"I guess I must. I've often wondered if I have uncles and aunts and cousins, maybe even brothers and sisters somewhere. I was a foundling . . ." he paused at her questioning look. "My mother abandoned me. I don't know who she was. I don't even know my real name."

"How sad and terrible!"

"It was terrible when I was a child, but that was a long time ago. As if all my misfortune had been given me at the beginning of my life instead of spread out over the years. I had the excellent luck to have been taken in by a kind old man who taught me a great deal. Much like your friend Clara has taken an interest in you and taught you things. We're very fortunate, both of us."

"Did he bring you to this country with him?"

"No, but he gave me the money. When I got to Hamburg, another fortunate thing happened purely by accident—or because God willed it. While I was waiting to board the ship, a man in front of me in line fell over a coil of rope and broke his leg. He was a manservant to an elderly couple who were emigrating. They were very upset. They were fond of their man and very dependent on him. The old gentleman reminded me of Herr Schmitt—the man in Germany who'd given me the money to make the trip—and so I went to them and asked if I could help while their servant was recovering. They were grateful for my offer and I was extremely glad to escape from steerage. I kept on with them for a month or two after I got to America."

"How did you become a fur cutter?"

"The woman's brother had a coat factory and she got me on as an apprentice." He spoke mechanically, still wondering with one part of his mind why she'd so firmly rejected his offer to accompany her to school. He'd recognized that they had so much in common, not least of which was physical attraction. But why, then, was she turning away? Could he be wrong? Reading signals that weren't there at all?

"Do you like your job?"

"It is a job," Piotr said simply.

"What would you rather do?" she asked.

"Teach," he said without even stopping to consider. And just as she had poured out her innermost feelings, he found himself telling her about the day years ago when Herr Schmitt had taken him to the university. "It was thrilling! I felt that until then my brain had been simply a place to store things, some sort of would-be machine that was merely an assembly of parts, but that day it began to work for the first time. I knew from then on that it was the life I wanted to be part of, even though it was impossible for someone of my background. But then last week I had a talk with Father Strzelecki—" He stopped suddenly.

"Yes, a talk . . . ?"

"It's nothing. Of interest only to me."

"Please tell me. I've told you so much."

He needed little more encouragement to share the idea that had taken such firm and outrageous root in his mind. "Well, I was saying to Father that I wanted to start taking more difficult courses and perhaps find a way to go to a real college someday and he said I should be a teacher—not just this job at Cooper Union, but someday a real professor. It was an absurd idea, but he seemed to think it was actually possible. And after a week of thinking of almost nothing else, I've come to believe it might be."

Irene was perplexed. "But why should it not? You are a smart man, well-spoken. This is America. You can be anything."

"That's what they say," he replied with a grin. "But it takes more than just being smarter than the average immigrant. It takes years of grueling study, and even then. . . well, I'd just never even dared dream anything so ambitious. To be educated, to learn as much as I could, that seemed enough—more than enough. And then, when Father mentioned greater possibilities, I—" Again he stopped. "It sounds ridiculous, but I felt like a new person suddenly looking out of the same old eyes and seeing a new world. Does that make any sense?"

"Oh yes, I felt that way once, too. When I said to my papa that I would take his place on the ship and come to America. It was exciting, but for me frightening, too. You, though, have nothing to fear. To teach—my friend Clara, she is a teacher. To me. But she likes to teach me because I'm her friend. Why do you want to teach people you don't know?"

She was staring at him with those beautiful tip-tilted eyes, waiting for an answer. He'd never consciously considered it before, but realized that he knew the answer nevertheless. The priest had introduced the possibility to his conscious mind a short time ago, but perhaps in some deep, secret part of his mind he'd been thinking about it for years. Yes, he must have been. "To accumulate knowledge is worthless, unless it is either used or passed on to someone else who can use it."

"Used for what?"

"I'm not sure. To help the world, ideally. To help a few people in the world at least. Of course, I know nothing of earth-shaking value to pass on. What are you smiling about? Have I said something funny?"

Irene was embarrassed. "No, I just like to hear your words. You talk like Clara."

He grinned. "I like to hear yours, too, Miss Kossok."

"You will do this . . . this teaching?"

"Someday, I hope. But it requires years and years of schooling to be qualified. I've spent the time I've been in this country getting what education I could get free—from reading mainly. But I will start as soon as I save the money."

"It is expensive, education?"

"Fairly. Father says there are scholarships that could help, but I will need to save everything I can. Until now, I just used what I needed of my salary and gave the rest to the Church. But I believe I may ultimately give more of myself to the Church by obtaining a good education, and I think I've learned English well enough so that it's possible. Education in Europe is for the upper classes; here, I now think, it's for anyone who wants it enough to get it."

"Is that true of other things, do you think?"

"What other things?"

"Oh, success. Other ambitions."

"I think so."

"I must go now. Thank you for the candy. No, you must not come with me. Mr. Gieryk, will you forget, please, what I said? At church? I didn't mean to talk about . . . about everything."

"I'll forget. If you want me to," he promised. "Here, don't leave your licorice."

But he didn't forget what she'd said. He thought about her for days. Without some radical change in her life, she'd never accomplish what she so desperately wanted to do. He knew, of course, what the radical change could be. He could give her the money—not now, of course, but in time. If he worked hard enough, if he got some scholarship money like Father had mentioned, there could be some extra. That would mean marriage, because it was damned certain she wasn't one to accept anything smacking of charity. Would she consider marrying him? He didn't even have to wonder whether it was what he wanted. He wanted her. She stirred him as no woman ever had and touched a part of his heart he hadn't known existed. He found himself wanting to shake her hand, salute her, and embrace her all at once. He pitied her circumstances, but not her. And while he was telling himself he hardly knew her, he realized he knew everything he needed to. He wanted to caress her, comfort her, talk to her, and make love to her. He wanted to tell her things he'd never told anyone, and listen to her secrets. He wanted to grow old with her.

But how, when she wouldn't even let him walk her to class, was he ever going to convince her this was meant to be? And how could he have her and become a teacher? For as much as he wanted both, he wasn't willing to give up either for the other. There had to be a way!

While he brooded over this, Irene was studying English. With a voracious greed she absorbed everything she was told. She had read and very nearly memorized her grammar book before the first month was up, and by the second month the overworked teacher was relying on her to help the slower students. Clara was enormously pleased and impressed, and her compliments bolstered Irene.

Piotr was impressed too, and told her so often. Each evening he walked her home, stopping, as she insisted, a block away from the tenement where she lived. She continued to be amazed at his interest in her. He could have anyone he wanted, she'd soon realized. All the girls at school admired him. She'd seen them dallying after classes, dropping books in his path, playing tricks to capture his attention. But while he was courteous to them, he never succumbed and he always walked Irene home as if there were no one else in the world he wanted to be with.

She knew she should tell him to leave her alone. Her unspoken bargain with Tilly forbade her encouraging his interest. But as the weeks went by, her resolve weakened. For one thing, the Sprys seemed to have given up any hope of snaring him for their daughters and were working diligently on impressing the sewing-machine repairman and his brother on the next block instead.

Much more important, she positively bloomed in his company. When she was with him, she felt pretty and free and light-footed and refreshed. If she had consciously set out to define what she wanted in a man, he could not have come closer to her ideal. His speech was clear and correct, his manners polite and neat without seeming the least bit prim, his interests were wide and erudite. He was funny and learned and understanding, a remarkable combination. And he was more attractive than she'd imagined she'd ever consider anyone. She found herself wanting to touch his thick fair hair; she wondered if his lips were as warm as they looked.

She balked at this thought, because it often conjured up

feelings that frightened her. Several times, when he'd taken her hand or let his arm linger around her shoulder while helping her with her coat, she'd felt that "dream feeling," as she called it in her own mind, that she was certain was sinful for a nice girl to feel.

In spite of herself, she was falling in love, too. But she carried more emotional freight—in the form of responsibility for her mother and sisters—and was more cautious than Piotr. She couldn't afford to lose her heart to someone for fear that her determination might somehow be undermined.

She took progressively greater pleasure in Piotr's company after classes and more and more often found herself watching the clock, thinking about how much longer it would be before she saw him again. He was taking more advanced classes than she and she had enormous respect for his scholarship. She felt their love of learning was a great and rare bond between them, much like her relationship with Clara, but with an added dimension, the potency of which half-frightened her.

He didn't mention marriage until the next spring, sensing by some instinct he hadn't known he possessed that she must not be pushed or pressured. But when he did propose, she turned him down flatly. "I'm sorry, Piotr, but I cannot marry. I must first bring my family to this country before I can think of myself."

"I'll pay their passage," he blurted out. He'd meant to lead up to this with a series of carefully reasoned strings of logic that would leave her no intelligent alternative but to accept. Why was it he could hold his own in the most scholarly arguments with the men he talked with at church and yet couldn't even put words together coherently with Irene?

"You cannot do that. I wouldn't allow it. I must pay for them. They're my people."

"But if you marry me, they'll be my family too."

"That is very kind, Piotr."

"It isn't kind. It's the worst sort of selfishness!" he said, thoroughly rattled by her determination and beginning to get damned mad at being thwarted in what was so obviously the right, the inevitable course.

"This is good of you to say, but, no. It would not be right for you to spend your money."

"Irene, I've thought this all out very carefully. I make a good salary. I could support both of us and still save enough to send them all five passages in a year, perhaps a year and a half."

"It is impossible," she said. "You have told me of your desire to go to college, to become a teacher. You must do that."

"I'll do it later. It can wait. I won't get stupid in the meantime. Irene, we're young and healthy and have our lives before us. I want us to live them together. There's no reason we can't both have what we want—we can work to bring your family over and then I'll go to school."

"No! I cannot let you sacrifice for me!"

Piotr was quiet for half a block as they walked along. If she felt half what he did, she couldn't have rejected him so firmly. "I'm sorry. I misjudged," he said.

"Misjudged what?"

"The way you felt. You see, I thought because I had fallen in love, so had you."

He noticed her pace falter for a second and then she said very softly, "You didn't misjudge that, Piotr. But," she hurried on, "you deserve a better wife."

"Better wife! How could anyone be a better woman than you?"

"Well, a less expensive wife, then," she said, trying to lighten the conversation.

He wanted to grab her and give her a good shake. "We've both suffered so much in life, and what I'm proposing is the solution. Why can't you grasp it? You're bright and practical. We love each other and this is the way we can both have what we want and need!"

"Please, Piotr, we will not talk about this."

But they did. He brought it up often, slowly wearing her down and nearly convincing her that he would feel privileged to help her family. He took her bicycling on rented vehicles; they collided with each other, both fell off, and Irene laughed until she had hiccups. They tested the underground train, the subway, which both of them hated and vowed never to go into again. They went for Sunday picnics in Central Park, where Irene was fascinated to the point of near-stupor by the ladies of fashion she saw. They went for boat rides and long walks and danced the polka in the basement of a neighborhood hall. Through the spring and summer, he worked at winning her over, never understanding how thoroughly he'd already conquered her heart. It was her pride and her terrible sense of rightness he was up against.

As often as possible, they took Clara along with them. Piotr and Clara became immediate friends. Their ties to Irene were powerful incentives, of course, and they would each have pretended friendship anyway, but their intellect drew them as well. Clara was on his side in his campaign to marry Irene. "It sounds as if he really means what he says—that he wants to help you," she said one day when just she and Irene had taken a walk to look at the East River.

"Yes, I think he does," Irene said, staring at a small tug that was darting between the larger vessels.

"Then why don't you marry him? He's a good man who loves you." It was hard for Clara to encourage her to marry Piotr. She had been Irene's only friend for a long time and felt a twinge of jealousy when she contemplated Irene's life being legally and emotionally linked to someone else. But she cared more for Irene's welfare that her own selfish dreams, and Piotr Gieryk was obviously the best thing for her. Not only was he good-looking, not a necessary asset but certainly a pleasant side benefit, but his clear blue eyes never left Irene. He was obviously in love with her. He was also clearly bright and had his feet on the ground. Clara particularly appreciated his wry sense of humor, a leavening influence that Irene, who took life so seriously, needed. Most important, Clara detected in Piotr Gieryk a moral strength and determination to match Irene's own. The one time he'd told her about his determination to get a college degree, he'd had that same fierceness—almost fanaticism—in his voice and face that Irene had when she talked about succeeding in life. Yes, they would be ideal mates.

"I cannot marry Piotr so he will help me. I must do this myself."

"You wouldn't have minded if Teo had helped with their passage. In fact, you expected it and counted on it."

'Teo is family."

"And so would your husband be your family. A better family than Teo," she added,

Irene bridled at this. She still couldn't bear criticism of her wayward brother, even from Clara. "You are my good friend, my teacher. I love you and wish to do what you say, but in this I cannot. I must not marry Piotr."

"But why not?" Clara persisted.

"I have said why. I cannot take away from him what he wants in life for the sake of what I want," Irene said in a tone that clearly closed the discussion for the time being.

"The family I work for is going to take an extended vacation and I must go along," Clara said one July afternoon.

"Oh, no! Clara, you can't leave!"

"I must, Irene. Their daughter will be of marriageable age in a few years, you know. They want to take her all over Europe and to stay with some relatives in England. They're scouting the marriage market."

"That sounds like a very long trip."

"Two years."

"Two years What will I do without you?" Irene said. Then: "I'm sorry to be so selfish. Is this something you wish to do?"

"If it didn't mean missing you, yes. It will be a very interesting opportunity to see a world I might not otherwise have the chance to experience."

"Then I am happy for you," Irene said, but try as she might to sound happy, she was obviously distraught.

"Irene, that's one of the reasons I think you should consider marrying Piotr."

"No, Clara. I don't want to talk about that again."

7

As the Christmas decorations began to go up in 1905, Piotr's desire to marry Irene assumed a new urgency. He couldn't understand why, with the sight of tinsel and evergreen in the city, it had become so much more important except that it was the end of yet another year and he was afflicted with a sense of mortality, a sense of time slithering away unused, unmarked by accomplishment.

If they were to get on with the life he imagined for them, it must be soon. Delay was gaining them nothing. Irene wasn't coming any closer to getting her mother and sisters to America, and instead of saving the money himself, he was spending it on seeing her: bus fares, candy, bicycle rentals, excursion-boat fares. Not that he regretted a penny, for every moment, every cent spent on seeing her face light up was worth a fortune, but still, it wasn't getting them anywhere. For over a year now he'd courted her, drawing deeply from the well of patience and courtesy that had been instilled in him in youth.

But his patience had run out. He'd waited as long as he could, and longer than there was any need. He was passing his days in an agony of frustration at time passing so pointlessly and his nights were beginning to be disturbed by angry dreams. The time had come for a decision and he knew she wouldn't make a decision unless pushed to the wall. He had a respect amounting to awe of the nobility of her refusal to let him put aside his own dreams to forward hers, but it was foolish just the same. He told her so. "Still, that is how it must be," she said.

"For how much longer?" he demanded.

They were walking home from school and Irene was brought up short by the new harshness in his voice. "For as long as it takes," she answered.

He took a deep breath and plunged into the conversation he'd been planning for days. He was as tense as an over-tightened violin string, but was determined to keep his temper, thin and frazzled as it was. "No, Irene. It's time to face facts. You're never going to have the passage money for your family."

"But if I work hard enough—"

"No, determination isn't enough. It never has been."

"Piotr, it has to be enough. It's all I've got!"

"That's wrong too. You've got me—if you'll just have me. Listen to me, Irene. I'm going to start tomorrow saving everything I can to bring your family over."

"But they're my—"

"Be quiet! I don't care whose family they are. I'm going to send them the passage fare. That's it! That's how it's going to be and I don't care whether you agree or not. It isn't up to you. I could send Queen Victoria my wages if I wanted, and you couldn't stop me. Do you understand?"

"But, Piotr—"

"*Do* you understand?"

"Yes, but I don't see why."

"Of course you do. Don't be coy. Now, listen to the rest of this and know I mean it as I've never meant anything before. I want to marry you, Irene, but I'm tired of waiting. I've proposed to you until I'm blue in the face. And I'm proposing again tonight—but this is the *last time*. I'll wait until the first of the year for your decision, and it's up to you, but know this, Irene. If you turn me down, I won't ever ask you again and I'm still going to bring your family over!"

"But you couldn't—"

He gripped her by the shoulders so hard that she had to force herself not to wince. This was unlike the Piotr she'd thought she'd known the last year. "I can. You don't seem to be really listening to me yet. I believe you love me, but I could be wrong—"

"No—"

"Will you stop interrupting? I believe you love me and

intend to marry me someday. Well, I'm telling you tonight that the someday must be soon or it won't be at all. So what's it to be?"

"Piotr, I must think—"

"I would have thought you'd have had plenty of time for thinking, but I'll wait for a week more. Just one week. This is Friday. By next Friday you must make a decision."

The rush of adrenaline this speech had caused lasted him until he was home; then it suddenly ran out and he flopped across his bed thinking he might have thrown away any chance of having the only woman he'd ever wanted. But even then, he didn't doubt he'd done what had to be done.

To Irene, trying to sleep in the lumpy bed she'd inherited the right to use when the next-to-last Spry girl left home, there was no question of her decision. She couldn't let Piotr go and she believed he'd meant his ultimatum. She was also quite certain that he'd meant every word about sending her family passage money whether she married him or not. But understanding and accepting the logic and necessity of it weren't enough. She had to have at least a day (she would never take his week) to readjust her thinking. She would tell him tomorrow night—no, she couldn't get away tomorrow night—the next day, then.

The next day was taken up with what Irene now regarded as the last job she ever did for the Sprys. She was working on a wedding dress for Charlotte Spry, the last of the daughters to wed. Elsa had managed to capture the sewing-machine repairman two months earlier and was already pregnant. Charlotte was marrying a candy-store owner the next week and had already made Irene alter her dress twice.

As she worked, she found herself thinking often of Clara, who'd gone away with her employers months earlier. But today Irene missed Clara more than ever. She longed to tell her of the important decision she'd made. Clara would approve, that was certain, but Irene wanted to see the pleasure in her face.

There were new sewing machines being installed in the factory where Andy Spry worked and so he had two days off work during the time when Irene was making the wedding dress. He'd hung about getting in the way the whole time and Irene was wishing there was somewhere—anywhere!—else she could go to work. He was seldom in the apartment for such an extended time. She'd never realized how truly awful he smelled. Every time she'd open the small window a crack, either he or Tilly would close it.

She was turning a sleeve and trying to breathe through her mouth when Tilly announced that she was going out to shop. "Will you come along, Andy?" she asked brightly.

"Naw."

As soon as she'd gone, Irene went over to open the window again. She had to lean over a pile of boxes to reach it and as she was straightening back up, she felt a touch on her back near her waist. "You've gotten to be pretty, Irene," Andy said.

She held her breath and wriggled away from his grasp. Without replying, she crossed the room and went back to her stitching.

"Didn't you hear me?"

"I heard you."

He was still standing by the window. Now he advanced on her. Irene held her sewing needle up like a miniature sword—a warning she hoped he'd understand. She suddenly felt smothered, by his smell, by his very presence. He stopped and grinned. "Well, what you got to say about it? Man says you're pretty and you don't say thank you or nothing."

"I have nothing to say," she replied, biting the words off coldly.

" 'I have nothing to say,' " he replied with mincing mockery. "Well, I got plenty to say. I been watching you, girl. Yessir, I been watching you and I seen the way you look at me when you think Tilly ain't looking."

Irene was afraid to say anything. She carefully folded the dress, moving as slowly as a cat faced with a stranger. Her muscles bunched, ready for flight. If he tried to touch her again, she would run.

He lurched forward with a funny gargling sound, and as Irene sprang for the door and jerked it open, she found herself facing Tilly. They stared at each other for a long moment; then Tilly peered past Irene at Andy, standing red-faced in the center of the room. "What's going on here?" Tilly asked.

She knows, Irene realized, and in the same second realized she must not speak of it openly. "I was just going to see if I could catch up with you. Buttons. We need two more buttons for the wrists of the dress."

Tilly looked back at her, gathering her wits. Then she slid her gaze back to Andy. "You will come with me, Irene, to pick them out."

"Yes. Rounded buttons, I think."

Andy turned and slammed the window shut, pretending that he didn't notice that both women were staring at him. "Get the hell on out of here, the both of you. Man can't get no peace with all this blabbering. Get your goddamn buttons."

Tilly and Irene didn't refer to what had happened. But everything had changed and they both knew it. Tilly had expected it for years, but still felt shocked and betrayed, and though she knew Irene wasn't to blame, she blamed her anyway. She was young and beautiful and unblemished, and that was enough reason to resent anyone.

Irene, however, had been shocked and was still shaken hours later. Tomorrow morning, first thing, she'd leave, even though the dress wasn't done. She'd paid her dues and made her decisions and she must act immediately. She went to sleep thinking over how to pack her few possessions, and what, if anything, she would say to Tilly when she left.

She'd barely gotten to sleep when there was a light tap on the door of the room she shared with Charlotte. Andy poked his head around and whispered, "Tilly ain't feeling so good. She wants you to make her some tea."

Irene dragged herself out of bed and threw a flannel wrapper over the hand-me-down slip she slept in. But as she stepped out of the room and closed the door softly, Andy grabbed her arm, and before she could comprehend what had happened, he had flung her onto the horsehair sofa. "This'll be our little secret, you and me, girl," he said, and his terrible weight came down on her.

She felt her bones were crushed and the wind was knocked out of her. She fought to draw breath to scream, and he clamped a hammy hand over her mouth. "Don't you go making no noise, girl. Ain't no call for that. It'll be good. You'll see." With his other hand, he was pulling her slip up. Irene could feel something hard and hot being shoved between her legs. She twisted, trying to fight free of suffocation. She was dying, drowning in horror. Her fear and his terrible body odor made her gag.

"You're a fighter, ain't ya? I like it that way," he whispered.

Irene managed to get her mouth open a little and bit down savagely. The flesh of his palm gave and she felt a gush of blood in her mouth. He jerked his hand away and shrieked, an injured animal cry, and she scrambled away. He had rolled onto the floor and with his bleeding hand he grabbed her ankle and she fell forward, crashing into the table. She screamed as her forearm struck the edge.

The room seemed to be suddenly full of people. Tilly and Charlotte, blinking stupidly and asking incoherent questions, Andy hunched in front of the sofa, swearing hideously and wrapping some fabric around his hand, and Irene herself huddled on the floor, weeping and nursing her throbbing arm.

"What's going on here!" Tilly demanded, shaking her shoulder.

But Andy answered, "I got up to go to the toilet and this bitch was out here. She tripped me in the dark, then bit my hand. Look at that! I'm damn near bleedin' to death."

It had become barely light enough for Tilly to identify his makeshift bandage. "My God, Andy! That's the wedding dress! You've ruined it."

"I think my arm is broken," Irene said softly. She could hardly draw in enough air to speak.

"It's covered with blood!" Tilly went on as she hauled the rumpled dress away from Andy. "Maybe if we soak it in cold water right away—"

"Ain't my fault. Don't go givin' me no ugly looks. That bitch did it. I knew we shoulda never taken her in."

Irene crawled forward and by putting her weight on a chair managed to stand. She flexed her fingers. It hurt, but they moved. She gingerly bent her arm at the elbow. Pain shot clear to her stomach, but she could bend it.

"If you could keep your filthy hands off the girls—"

"There isn't time to make a new dress, Mama—"

"Run down and get a bucket of water—"

"Stupid bitch just tripped me for no reason—"

Irene staggered to the tiny bedroom and started pulling on

her clothes. Her head was pounding, her arm felt swollen, and she kept bumping it into things. With her good hand she dragged a small battered suitcase out from under the bed and dumped Charlotte's belongings out, then started cramming in her own few things: her baptismal certificate that Mama had sent so long ago; the bird book and several others that Clara had given her; her pencils for school; her mother's letters, and some clothing.

The Sprys were still yelling at each other when she came back out. Andy, Tilly, and Charlotte were squabbling over the wedding dress the way dogs fight over a dead squirrel in the woods, yapping, snarling, and ripping it apart. Carrying the suitcase with her good arm, Irene went to the door of the apartment, opened it, and without looking back, walked out.

She never saw the Sprys again.

Piotr arranged for Irene to stay with Father Strzelecki's housekeeper. She'd turned up at his door, faint with pain, bruised-lipped, and shivering. She didn't even have a coat on. After taking her to the hospital to ascertain that her arm wasn't broken, he'd roused the priest, explained what had happened, and turned her over to the motherly woman who ran Strzelecki's household. "Don't let her go off and do anything foolish," he'd said. "It's Saturday and I have to work until noon. I'll be back as soon as I'm off."

Having done all that with admirable, impossible calm, Piotr went off in a silent, gut-wrenching fury. Never—never in all his life—not even when he was beaten nearly to death or faint with hunger in a ditch, had he felt the soul-destroying anger he was in the grip of now. He walked the streets the rest of the night. In the morning, he found himself at the wretched tenement where the Sprys lived. His head was pounding with rage and he intended to climb the dark stairs and beat the life out of Andy Spry. He flexed his fingers, aching for the sheer thrill of throttling the life out of the man. As a student of philosophy, he was convinced there was never justification for taking another human life: as a man, he wanted to murder Andy Spry and could have done so without a qualm of conscience.

He didn't even pause at their door, but pushed at it violently. To his surprise, it didn't open. Locked? He balled his fist and pounded, shouting, "Andy, you bastard, open this door!" But there was no response. He stepped back, turned sideways, and threw himself at the door, which splintered with the impact. He stood there in the shattered ruin and realized with impotent fury that the apartment was empty. "Damn!" he said. "Damn, damn, damn!" For a moment he was almost overcome with the desire to tear the place completely apart, but a faint voice in the back of his mind warned that Tilly, not Andy, would ultimately be the real victim of such an act.

He went away more angry than ever, but reason was beginning to reassert itself. He couldn't have made a dent in Andy, physically or mentally. Piotr knew, even through the red haze of his rage, that he was a scholar, not a fighter. If he'd burst into the shabby apartment to vindicate Irene and actually met up with Andy, he'd have just gotten himself crumpled up and tossed back down five flights. Piotr wasn't a coward and would gladly have endured the pain and humiliation if there was anything to be gained by it, but there clearly wasn't. He couldn't be much practical use to Irene if Andy Spry reduced him to a pile of kindling. He wouldn't ever go back to get his revenge, but still, what an ungodly pleasure it would be to land at least one good solid blow in that porky lecher's gut.

He still hadn't calmed down when he arrived at Father Strzelecki's at two that afternoon. His stomach was churning. Irene was in the kitchen helping the housekeeper stuff sausages, stirring the spices into the meat with her good arm. The smell of food nearly made him gag.

"Now, you young people run off and get out of my way," the older woman said, flapping her apron at them as if shooing chickens.

Irene was pale and very quiet, still seriously shaken and in pain. She couldn't put her arm in the sleeve of her coat, so Piotr put a shawl around her shoulders and draped his own coat over that. They went out the back door and sat down on a wooden bench under the kitchen window. "We will get married," Piotr said. "I've talked to Father Strzelecki about it and he says you may stay here until the banns are read and we can be married right after Christmas. Then you'll be Mrs. Gieryk."

She raised her head and looked at him very seriously. "Piotr . . . ?"

"What?"

"No, no. It's stupid. I have no right to ask—"

"You have the right to ask anything of me, Irene."

She still hesitated; then, grasping his hand tightly, she plunged in. "Could we have an American name?"

"An American name?"

"Yes, Clara says that people who want to get ahead in America need to have American names."

"Get ahead?"

"Your name in American would be Peter Garrick. See, you're angry. I shouldn't have asked. I'm sorry—"

"No, I'm not angry at all. I don't see why it matters to you, but I don't suppose I care. Piotr Gieryk is just a name someone else gave me—someone I hated. There's no reason not to change it if it would please you. Then I would have a name given me by someone I love. That's much better. Peter Garrick . . ." He tested the name. "Yes, that sounds nice enough. Peter and Irene Garrick. A new year, a new life, and new names. Yes, we'll do it. In three weeks you'll be Mrs. Garrick."

He didn't realize until later that he hadn't asked Irene for her decision, and that small failure, the oversight of a moment, was to haunt him for years.

Peter had quit his job—it was either that or get fired the next time he saw Andy at work, for he knew he wouldn't be able to control himself if he ever met up with the man again. Fortunately, his skill was a worthwhile one and he had no trouble finding the same position at another coat factory. Two of his acquaintances from his previous job, another fur cutter and a woman who stitched the facing to collars, stood up with them as witnesses at the small wedding. Irene noticed the way the woman looked at Peter and surmised from her disappointed appearance that she'd have far rather been bride than bridesmaid. Irene's only regret was that Clara wasn't present.

After the ceremony, they had iced cakes and hot, sweet tea

with the priest and his housekeeper; then Peter took Irene to her new home on East Second between First and Second avenues. It was a tiny, bare rear apartment on the fourth floor. The furniture was shabby and mismatched, the sort to expect a bachelor more interested in reading than surroundings to have. But there were, in honor of Irene's coming, three new pieces: a cheap but pretty dressing screen with printed paisley-design paper panels, a small chest of drawers in which he'd put his own belongings to allow Irene the old but larger chest, and a big double bed with a real feather mattress.

"It's crowded now with the bigger bed," he said, involuntarily lowering his voice on the word "bed" and feeling like a fool for doing so. "You can put all your things here. I'm sorry about all the books in the way. I tried to get them organized, but . . ."

There were books everywhere, in piles under the bed, on the top of the small chest, tottering in corners and along the walls. Many had slips of paper marking his place sticking out of them. They'd even taken over half the space meant for plates in the tiny doorless closet that served as a kitchen. The small room had the old-paper smell of a library.

Irene put her pitifully few belongings away and fixed them a dinner of sliced sausage, potato salad, and bread that Peter had gone out in the cold to buy. Finally the light faded and Irene began to get nervous. It was time to go to bed. She was in the grip of powerful but conflicting feelings. A country girl, she knew in general terms what was expected of her, and while she had no reason to look forward to it, neither did she fear it. But as a Catholic she'd been taught that intercourse was a terrible sin until there was a marriage ceremony to sanctify it. Somehow that ceremony hadn't seemed grand enough to have made such a significant change. How did the few minutes standing before Father Strzelecki and two strangers make this morning's vice tonight's virtue?

Peter invented an errand after dinner, leaving her alone to undress. When he came back, she was sitting up in bed wearing the nightdress she'd made during the three weeks she'd stayed with the priest's housekeeper. She was also "wearing" something else the housekeeper had told her about.

"Not going to have babies right away, are you, dear?" the older woman had asked.

"I . . . I don't know. I hope not until I can get the rest of my family to this country." She didn't know this woman well enough to confess, as she would have to Clara, how dreadful the thought of children was at the moment. She wanted babies, lots and lots of them, but not until she'd gotten her mother and sisters to America and settled.

"Hoping won't do it. Never a good idea to start out with babies anyway. Me and my husband, God rest his soul, had a parcel of them before I hardly knew what I was doing. What about *świadome macierzyństwo*—not having babies? You do know what to do about that, don't you?" she asked.

Irene blushed, admitting she had no idea. It had never occurred to her that there *was* a choice. Marriage meant babies, if God wished it.

The housekeeper, who had left blushes with her youth, showed Irene how to get sponges, cut them up just so, soak them in vinegar, and then with an awkward verbal description she told Irene how and where to insert one each time she and Peter made love.

"And it just stays there forever?" Irene asked.

"Lord, no! I forgot to tell you about the ribbon you tie on. That's how you take it back out and clean it."

"And if I do this I won't have babies?" Irene asked, astonished at the concept.

"There's no promise. But a lot of women use it." She lowered her voice. "Now, not so sure I should be telling you this. I imagine Father wouldn't approve. I know the Bible says 'be fruitful and multiply,' but I figure it doesn't mean all the time and certainly not when you're first learning your way around a new marriage."

So Irene had followed the advice, hating the vinegar smell and cold, nasty feel of the sponge, but hoping desperately that it would work. By the time Peter came back, she'd all but forgotten it was in place.

He turned off the lights, undressed, and shivering with cold and nerves, slipped in beside her. The new bed linens he'd bought and put on this morning felt raw and scratchy. He was perplexed at first at the faint odor of vinegar in the room until he remembered another time he'd noticed the smell and asked the woman he was with what it was. How did Irene know about such a thing, though? he wondered fleetingly. And less fleetingly: why was she using prophylactic methods? Didn't she want children? He'd never even asked her opinion on it, so sure he'd been that they would be in agreement. He put the thought aside. Time enough to discuss it later.

He was as nervous as she and had been remembering all day that her last—and certainly only—physical experience had been Andy Spry's lustful attack on her. If he frightened her, it might never be set right. "Irene, getting married changes people's lives in a lot of ways. You don't have to make all the changes in one day. What I mean is . . . ah, we don't need to . . . to 'do' anything tonight." He heard her exhale and knew she'd been holding her breath. "Let me just hold you. That will be enough."

He raised the arm nearest to her and was gratified that she moved closer without any further urging. Dear God, she was so soft and clean and warm. By no means inexperienced, Peter had never been in a bed with a woman he loved because there had never *been* a woman he loved until Irene. This was, in that sense, as new to him as to her. She was neither a cool, smooth plaster saint nor a painted whore. She was a real woman—his wife. Astonishingly, his wife!

"It was nice of your friends to come be our witnesses," she said softly.

They talked then, aimless, inconsequential chatter about the wedding, about the witnesses, a little about his job. Gradually her voice grew slower and slurred and he kept quiet so she could go to sleep. But he lay awake for a long time, wanting her so much it was a physical pain, but still content merely to hold her. That alone, in this dingy room, was a miracle. That he should have her trust and love, he—Peter Garrick, Piotr Gieryk, whoever he was—was more than he'd ever imagined attaining.

She mumbled something in her sleep, moved a little, snuggling closer, and he felt his blood stir and surge. His muscles tensed, longing to crush her to him. His arm, under her head, was numb and tingling, but he'd have sooner cut if off than move it. He turned a little and with his other hand picked up a tress of her long, soft hair. She moved again, putting her hand on his chest. Suddenly her eyes flew open in surprise; then she smiled. "I didn't know where I was. I forgot," she said sleepily.

But she didn't remove her hand; instead she moved her fingers slightly, testing his flesh, assuring herself that it and he were here and hers. She turned her face up, eyes closed again. "Peter, would you kiss me?"

Agonizing as it was for him, he was slow and tender with her, learning her body and teaching her his, one cautious step at a time. His long-fingered scholar's hands caressed her lightly, learning the swell of her full breasts, the hollow of her throat, the curve of hip and thigh. He kissed her lips, her shoulders, and sucked gently on her arousal-hardened nipples. Finally, when he felt the light sweat of anticipation spring up on her soft skin, he lowered himself on her and joined them. She cried out once, a kitten-mew of pain and pleasure.

When it was done, when she'd become truly his wife, she lay curled in his arms, wide-awake with the wonder of it. She hadn't known what to expect, but it wasn't this. She had respected him, admired him, found his company refreshing, stimulating, and relaxing and exciting in turns, and she'd believed that was love. But now she knew better. That had been only the first stage of love. This was the culmination, this knowing a person in the dark, not by sight or intellect, but by sound and sensation and taste. How could this sort of human experience have been available without her even suspecting? It was a wonder to her and she felt a sudden regret for the time they'd wasted and lost when they could have been together.

It had been, at separate instants, a little embarrassing, slightly silly, and very moving. "I liked that—" she admitted shyly.

She could feel his lips smile as they touched hers. "In time, I hope you'll like it better," he said, knowing something she didn't.

"Oh, I don't think I could!"

"Mmmmm, want to bet?"

She giggled. "How much time will it take?"

He cupped his hand on her breast and nibbled at her earlobe. "Not so much—if we start now."

"Again?" she asked, hugging him so quickly and tightly that he exhaled in a surprised huff.

"Again . . . and again . . . and again."

At dawn, as the watery winter light came into the room, Peter turned away for a moment and Irene first saw the scars on his back. She gasped, not at their appearance, for the raw redness had long since faded, but at the meaning. "Who did this to you, Peter?" she demanded.

"I'd forgotten," he said with wonder and amazement. "For the first time in my life, I'd forgotten about it. That's what you've done for me."

"But I must know. What happened?"

So Peter told her. All of it. The butcher who'd nearly killed him with the strop he used to sharpen knives. The years of living outside. Burying his friend Mateusz under a railway bridge. The years with Herr Schmitt. The Church, the books, the years of wondering and studying. "And to think, I didn't understand why it was all happening," he finished.

"What do you mean?"

"It was just God's way of bringing me step by step closer to finding you. There's a purpose in everything, I believe. And that was the purpose. You're the reason, the goal. That you love me is the vindication and balance of it all."

8

1907

Freezing air swirled around corners at every intersection, buffeting Irene as she hurried along. The frigid wind jerked at her skirts and hair, but she was impervious to the weather as she pulled Clara's letter from her pocket and checked the address again, ducking her head against the granular snow. 1430 Broadway, the Empire Theater. It ought to be at about 40th, another two blocks. She was terribly excited to be seeing Clara again after her long absence, but she was nervous and shy about it as well. So much had happened; they had hours of talk ahead. Of course they'd corresponded in the interval, but letters were unsatisfactory. One couldn't smile in a letter, or pat a hand encouragingly when something became too difficult to say.

Ah, there it was. A poster in front said "THE GREAT ELLEN TERRY starring in *Captain Brassbound's Conversion*, by George Bernard Shaw—opening January 28."

Before she even read the rest, someone touched her arm. She spun around and flung herself into Clara's arms, crying, "Oh, Clara! It's been so long. I'm so glad to see you again. You must tell me everything that's happened to you."

Clara had tears in her eyes. "You've grown up, Irene. When I left you were a pretty girl, and now, a year and a half later, you're a beautiful woman. How old are you now? No, let me think. You're nineteen . . . twenty next April—is that right? How are you, my dear girl?"

"I'm fine, Clara, but please tell me everything you've done. Everywhere you've been. And why are we meeting here?"

"This is where I'm going to work. Let's go inside, I'll show you, and we can sit and talk. I've so much to tell you!"

They went down a side alley and through the backstage door. Clara had a cubbyhole room with a cot in the basement next to the boiler room. There was even a minuscule kitchen area where Clara made a pot of tea while Irene looked around. Clara talked as she bustled. "Miss Terry offered to engage a room for me in the hotel where she stays, but once I saw this room, I knew it was for me. So private and quiet! And warm—I haven't been warm since I left America."

Through a curtain, Irene caught a glimpse of another, larger room hung with beautiful dresses on hangers and all the paraphernalia for ironing and sewing. What a strange place this was, and how very interesting!

"I didn't expect you back until summer. I'm glad you're here sooner," Irene said, taking a sip of the tea and selecting a bakery cookie from the plate Clara offered.

"I'm sorry to say it was for a tragic reason. The little girl I took care of was struck by an automobile just outside London. It was at a race and the vehicle went out of control and ran through a barricade."

"How awful!"

"It was. Her parents were quite distraught. She was their baby, their youngest. They buried her in England. They had family there. There was no need for me anymore and frankly they were anxious to get me out of their sight, as I was a constant reminder of their loss. I stayed on only a week to pack up her things."

"It wasn't kind of them to have you go away so quickly."

"Oh, it was all right. I understood and they were really very nice. They made me a very generous payment and in fact got me this job. They know Mr. Shaw, the playwright, and he wired his friend Miss Terry, who employed me as her dresser. She was getting ready to make an American tour with this play and her usual dresser wanted to stay in England with her family. So I got the job. It was a wonderful way for me to earn money and get free passage back to America as well."

"What is a dresser?"

"A dresser takes care of an actress's clothes. It's quite a big job. Everything must be kept clean and mended and ready for her to change into quickly between scenes. And then I do other things as well—answer some of her correspondence, act as a personal maid sometimes when people call on her at the theater. I wouldn't have to do those things, but I don't mind because Miss Terry is a lovely lady to work for. So thoughtful and down-to-earth. I can't wait for you to see her perform."

"But I can't afford to go to the theater. It's very expensive, isn't it?"

"You can watch from backstage if you stay out of the way."

"Could I really!" Irene had never seen a play before.

"We open in two days. But I'm afraid it won't be for long. The play is scheduled to run for only a few months; then it will tour the United States."

"And you will go away again?"

"If I'm fortunate enough to please Miss Terry and be kept on, yes. First to Chicago and then—"

"Oh, Clara, I wish you didn't have to go!"

"I wish it too. But it's a very good job. I'm fortunate to have gotten it. My mother used to love the theater, and when I was growing up she took me to plays whenever she was able. It wasn't often, but enough to make me love it too. But enough of me. Tell me all about yourself. You're happily married? Yes, I know from your letters that you are."

Irene felt a flush warm her cheeks. How could she even answer? Happiness? She'd never had any idea what it meant until she married. Peter was like the other part of herself she hadn't even known she was missing until she moved into the little apartment with him the day of their wedding. It had been a year now, but she still thrilled with anticipation every day when it was still hours before he'd be home from work. And far from becoming accustomed or apathetic to his gentle kisses and embraces, she found his physical presence more exciting every week that passed. In fact, she had a quite shameful desire to be near him, touching him—but oddly enough, there was no shame to it; rather, their intimacy was an exultation.

Before her marriage, Irene had thought she'd known what men and women who were married did in bed alone, and when she thought about it at all, she had merely regarded it as a matter of some inexplicable hunger for men and a duty for women. The most stunning revelation of her marriage had been that it was not only a hunger for her as well but also an absolute banquet of sensations. She couldn't talk about such things to Clara, of course. She could hardly bring herself to say them out loud to Peter for fear they might become ordinary if subjected to anything so common as language.

All she could say was, "Yes, I am happy, Clara."

"And your English has improved. I notice that you sign yourself 'Garrick' instead of 'Gieryk.' Was that Piotr's idea or yours?"

"Mine. I told him what we had talked about, you and I. How you cannot get ahead in America with a foreign name. He calls himself Peter now."

"Peter Garrick—it sounds very nice. Very American. Very distinguished. Have you sent for your family yet?" Clara asked.

Irene's face brightened. "Yes, almost! It is so exciting. We have four passage tickets now and most of the money for the fifth. I have written to Mama and told her that we will send them in another two or three months. And then they will have to make all their plans. I think they will be here with us by autumn. Actually, we have enough money for the last ticket, but we must use part of it to take larger rooms so they will have a place to stay when they come. Clara, it has been so many years, I almost cry when I think how happy we will all be together. Imagine! Mama and all the girls here with me!"

"What about your brother, Teo?"

Irene drew herself very straight and proud. "I will never see Teo again. Even if he came back to the Sprys', they don't know where I went and couldn't tell him. It's just as well. He would not have come back."

Clara knew what it cost her to say this. "But what have you told your mother?"

"I've told her nothing yet. I don't wish to make sorrow for her sooner than I have to. When she gets here I will explain somehow. May I have one more cookie? I didn't eat any breakfast before I came. I was so nervous and excited to see you."

"You may have all of them. I don't need them," Clara said, laughing and patting her plump thigh.

"No, just one more, thank you."

Clara refilled their teacups and they sat sipping in companionable silence for a few moments. Then Clara asked, "What do you do with yourself now? Do you work? Do you still sew for people?"

"No, Peter doesn't want me to work. He says it is his job to work doubly hard so I will not have to go to the factory. It is good of him and I don't want to become one of those pitiful girls, but, Clara, I don't like this. It isn't right. It isn't fair. He should not have to be so tired for me. I'm not lazy, and I would like to have things to do." Irene stopped, thinking.

The burning ambition that had been sown that day the Russian girl broke the eggs and slapped her had lain dormant for many years. It was like a fertile plot of land that had been covered with a sheet of ice for a long winter. Then Peter had shone his bright, loving light on her life. With marriage and freedom the ice had begun a slow thaw, melting away and leaving the ground warm and fertile once again. For five years she had been so overwhelmed with the hard work of getting from one day to the next that she hadn't let herself dream of the life she wanted. But now, in the last year she had time, too much time, to think and dream.

"What kind of things would you like to do?" Clara asked.

"I don't know, Clara. But I want to do something well, something that will make a better life for me and for my family."

"And Piotr . . . I mean, Peter?"

"Peter . . ." she said, trying to gather her observations into a coherent pattern. "Peter wants me to be happy. He knows I've had a hard time—not as hard as his life, but bad enough. Because he loves me, he wants to make everything easy for me. He works terribly hard, Clara. After his job, he goes to the library and reads and studies. He's determined to be ready for college as soon as we have the money put aside to bring my family over. But he won't let me help!"

"And what do you do?"

"I keep the apartment clean—it's very easy. And I cook. Peter likes a lot of food on the table. He doesn't eat that much, but he gets nervous if he thinks there isn't enough food. I get books for him and I copy his notes. He says my handwriting is so much better than his. I'm glad I can at least do that for him, but . . ."

"You want something more?" Clara asked. In her own heart, she appreciated and admired Peter's desire to take care of Irene and make her life easy, but she knew there was a hunger in Irene she could perceive only indirectly.

"Oh, Clara, I couldn't say such a thing to anyone else. It sounds mean and ungrateful, but no . . . I'm not content. I'm happy when I'm with Peter, and even happy when I'm not, because I'm thinking of him, but I think of other things, too. I don't *just* want to bring my family here. I want my little sisters to live in a real house with bedrooms of their own and a yard. I want to have good food that Mama will not need to work to cook. I don't want Peter to have to give up his college for these things. I want to work for them myself. Other people have such things. It's not impossible, but to Peter what's important is having love and education."

"You think he's wrong?" Clara didn't need to ask. She knew Irene well enough to recognize the eagerness, the drive, in her eyes. It had been there the first time she met her on the boat, the day she had explained to the ragged waif of a child about different languages. Over the years she'd seen flashes of it, but less and less frequently, the longer Irene lived with the Sprys. It was back now, a powerful force, and Clara was both glad and frightened for her friend. But wanting a thing and getting it were often quite different. If she did what her heart told her and encouraged Irene's dreams, might she not be contributing to the girl's eventual disappointment?

"I think he's right—but wrong, too. There's nothing wrong with wanting life to be better even if it is good. Do you agree, Clara?"

The older woman paused only a moment. If you can't count on your friends to share your dreams, then why have friends? "I agree with you. Such things are possible, if you want them badly enough."

"I think perhaps I want too much. I wanted to come to this country and bring my family. Soon I will have both, and already I want more."

"What about a family of your own? Babies—I thought surely you've have one by now."

Irene stood up suddenly. "I will put the cookie plate back for you, Clara. I'm sorry I ate so many."

"Irene, what's wrong?"

"Nothing is wrong, but I must go."

Clara was stricken. "What have I said to make you run away like this? No, put that plate down," she added in a deliberately schoolmistressy voice that Irene reluctantly heeded. "Was it babies? Am I not allowed to speak to you of children? I thought we were friends . . ."

Irene wanted to confide in Clara, but hesitated. It was the one thing she and Peter disagreed about, and while she felt she was justified in her opinion, she was fearful of subjecting it to Clara's scrutiny. What if Clara told her she was wrong? Well, it would come up sooner or later—I might as well get it over with now, she told herself. "I don't want any babies yet."

"What's wrong with that?" Clara asked, genuinely perplexed.

"Peter doesn't want to wait. He wants to have a great many children very soon. He's disappointed in me, but he doesn't ever say so. But, Clara, there is so much time still to have babies, and I want other things first. Things for Mama and the girls. And things for Peter and me, too, and for the babies when they come."

Clara realized now that she had strayed into an area where she had no business and didn't know the terrain. Clara had a good grasp of her own limitations. What kind of advice could a twenty-seven-year-old spinster give a bride? None worth anything. She stood up and said, "Well, I wouldn't worry about it if I were you. You're so young. You have all the time in the world to think about having babies. I'm sure Peter understands. Look, I brought you something from France. Help me pull this suitcase from under the bed."

Peter didn't come with Irene to the play. He had no objection to her going and even accompanied her to the theater and agreed to meet her when the play was over, but he had no interest in seeing it. "But it will cost nothing, Peter. You might enjoy it," Irene said as they neared Fortieth Street.

"George Bernard Shaw is a godless man," he said with a smile as though he were half-joking. "I've read his work at the library, where I can close the book when I've had enough, but I can't bring myself to attend a play of his. It would be like being locked in a cage with a maniac. An entertaining maniac, to be sure, but a maniac just the same. Besides, I've attended a few plays and they make me feel rushed. A play dashes by without giving you time to think about what you're hearing until later. I'd rather read them at my own pace."

"Then you don't want me to go?"

He smiled at her fondly. "Not even Shaw can corrupt you, Irene. No, you go. You'll enjoy going to the theater. You might like it better than I do."

Clara was waiting at the stage door, as she'd promised. "I've got a hem to stitch up," she said hurriedly. "Look around all you want, but don't get in anyone's way, then come down to my room. Hello, Peter. I'm sorry I can't stop and talk to you now."

"You'll be all right?" Peter asked Irene.

"Fine. Are you sure you won't stay with me?"

He shook his head. "No, I'll be back at eleven-thirty. Irene, is there something wrong?"

"No," she said. How to explain the eerie feeling she had? The feeling that something was changing, or about to change, or had already changed without her recognizing it yet? Something important. No, he'd think it silly of her—and he'd be right. "No, nothing is wrong. I'll wait here for you."

She watched him walk away down the narrow alley and once again the feeling came over her. She had to watch him out of sight and remember everything about this evening, for things would never be the same again. She shivered and tried to mentally scold herself into sensibility. Then, as if her legs worked independently of her mind, she ran down the alley and caught up with Peter around the corner. "Peter—"

"What's wrong?"

"I . . . No, nothing's wrong." She flung her arms around him and hugged tightly.

He drew back, grinning. "Clara will think you've gotten

lost, Reenee,'' he said, using the pet name he never used outside the apartment. ''I'll be back for you in a couple hours.''

''Promise?''

''Promise.''

She went directly to Clara's room. ''I've just finished,'' Clara said. ''It's good you're early. I got you a ticket, or rather Miss Terry did. I told her my friend wanted to see the performance and she said that you could watch backstage anytime you wanted, but you must see your first play from the proper perspective.''

''Oh, that's very kind of her. I shall pay her back as soon as I can,'' Irene said, worried about how she'd explain to Peter that his hard-earned money had to go, however indirectly, into Mr. Shaw's pocket.

''No, she gets some tickets free to do with as she wishes, Irene. She's giving you the ticket.''

''But she doesn't even know me.''

''She knows you're my friend and she's a lovely lady. She'll be needing me in a moment to help her dress for the first act. Let me show you where you're to sit.''

Irene, being so early, was the first member of the audience to take her seat and sat in cowed silence as other people eventually began to arrive. The houselights were up and it was Irene's first opportunity to observe the sort of people who lived in the ''other'' New York, the truly American New York. Irene had seldom been beyond the borders of the immigrant sections of the city.

Everyone seemed so much more beautiful here. The men were immaculately attired in sharp blacks and whites, though none of them were half as handsome as Peter. The women's clothes were in bright colors and their very flesh seemed more vivid and alive. These ladies had whiter skin, bluer eyes, and pinker cheeks that anyone she knew. Their dresses were glossy or gauzy or artfully draped—the textures made her fingers itch to touch the unfamiliar fabrics to see if they felt as they looked. These ladies wore long spotless white gloves with dozens of buttons and their shiny hair was arranged in elaborate upsweeps entwined with ribbons and feathers and sparkling jewels. Their voices, too, were different. Money had dampened the shrillness. They trilled like birds.

Something stirred in her. This is what I want, she thought. She wanted to be one of these women. She wanted Mama to have gloves like that. How she would love them! How wonderful Peter would look, with his blond hair, in a perfectly tailored black coat. She wanted those pretty dresses for her sisters, she wanted . . . She wanted . . .

Suddenly the lights dimmed, the voices stopped, and the curtain rose. The first scene meant nothing to Irene. It was simply two men, one with a thick cockney accent, the other with an equally thick Scottish accent, talking endlessly about something. Irene paid scant attention for she couldn't understand a word they said. Instead, she watched the audience.

After a few moments everyone around her burst into applause and Irene looked at the stage to see why. Ellen Terry had made her entrance. She was a woman of middle age, with a handsome figure and an erect British carriage. She paused, not exactly acknowledging the applause, but gracefully allowing it to run its course before she spoke.

She spoke to one of the men on the stage, pitching her voice to the audience while looking at the actor. Her voice was like crackers spread with soft cheese—crisp but soothing and gentle. It was, to Irene, the voice of an angel. Every vowel, every consonant was clearly enunciated, but with a graciousness and humanity that removed it from simple elocution.

Irene was smitten by the sound of her voice.

For the rest of the play, she never took her eyes off Miss Terry, and in scenes when she was offstage, Irene tapped her foot impatiently, wishing all those idiotic men would talk faster so Miss Terry—or Lady Cecily Waynflete, as she was called in the play—would come back. Irene had very little idea what the play was about and cared less. There were a great many men and a good deal of shouting between them about uncles and inheritances and talk about the law of England and morality.

And then it was over. Everyone clapped, the actors came out and bowed, somebody handed Miss Terry an armload of flowers, and then people started leaving. Irene just sat there, stunned. She was still in the same place, deep in thought, when Clara came out and got her. "I thought you'd come straight back when it was over. How did you like the play, Irene?"

"Miss Terry is wonderful—the way she talks, and the way she moves. Did you see how gracefully she used that fan? And how she walks! Why, it's amazing!"

"Would you like to come back and meet her? She was just leaving, but we might catch her—"

"Oh, I couldn't. I'd be so clumsy and stupid!"

"Irene! You're neither clumsy nor stupid. What's come over you?" Clara asked, half-amused, half-irritated.

Irene took her elbow and whispered, "I want to be like that, Clara. I want to be a lady and walk and talk that way! May I come watch again?"

"Anytime you want," Clara said, awed and almost frightened by the intensity of Irene's words.

When Irene told Peter the same thing later, he said, "I'm glad you enjoyed yourself, but why would you want to be like anyone else? You're wonderful the way you are."

He put his arm around her and she cuddled into his embrace, thinking how to explain herself. "Peter, I didn't say it right. I don't want to be like anyone else. I want to be everything I can be. You want to be better, too. You read all the time, learning and studying. Isn't that why you do it? To make yourself better in some way?"

"I guess so," he admitted. But he sensed there was something very different in their motivations, something he didn't understand. And it worried him.

The next day there was a matinee performance and Irene was backstage this time. She managed to dodge everyone, keeping out of the way as Clara had instructed, so well that even Clara forgot she was there until the performance was over. Once again, Irene's full attention was on Ellen Terry. She listened carefully to the way she pronounced her words, and watched her every gesture as intently as a hunter observing rare prey. But as Clara discovered later, when she attempted to discuss the content of the play with Irene, she still had no idea what it was about.

So she wasn't stagestruck, Clara decided. That had worried her at first. Nor was she developing a crush on Miss Terry herself. It was her manners, the life she represented, that had captured Irene. It wasn't until Irene had left the theater, again without meeting the famous actress, that Clara realized that several times Irene had pronounced words differently than she usually did, pronounced them in quite a refined manner. And upon reflection, Clara realized that they were all words that Miss Terry happened to use in the play.

Irene attended the play three more times in the next two weeks before finally meeting Miss Terry. Clara tricked her into it. Irene had been coming to the theater early, helping Clara with the wardrobe preparations. "Come along, we'll just leave these clothes hanging in her dressing room. She's not here yet."

Irene followed along, carrying the freshly pressed apron that was to be worn halfway through the play. Clara knocked at the door and the now-familiar voice called out, "Come in."

Irene froze, but Clara gestured imperiously and she obediently followed. "Miss Terry, I'd like you to meet my friend Irene Garrick. It was she who fixed that glove you caught on the scenery last week."

"And she did such a lovely job. Come in, my dear. I don't bite, only nibble! Why, how lovely you are!"

Ellen Terry was older than she appeared onstage, in her fifties and truly in her prime. Never a great beauty, she was, nevertheless, a stunning "presence." Somewhat heavier now than was usual for her, she still carried herself as if gravity simply didn't pertain to her.

"I'm glad to meet you, Miss Terry," Irene said, somewhat surprised that the words came out.

"I'm happy to have the opportunity to thank you for fixing that silly old glove. How did you ever learn to work on leather so expertly?"

"My father taught me. He was a glover and bootmaker in the old country."

"Oh, yes. I remember now, Clara told me how she met you, coming over on the boat. Do you like the play? I think it's quite ridiculous, really. I told Mr. Shaw that I was totally unsuitable to play a woman so relentlessly cheerful and bossy, but he claims to have modeled Lady Cecily on *me*! Such nonsense, but he is sweet to say it. He's a dear old bear, you know."

A dear old bear? Irene thought, wondering how Peter would react to such a remark.

"You look puzzled, my dear," Ellen Terry said. "Have I said something to offend you?"

"No, it's just that my husband says Mr. Shaw is wicked," Irene said, then wished she could take the words back. Whatever had made her be so tactless?

But Ellen Terry just laughed. "Mr. Shaw would be delighted to hear that. He loves having people think he's wicked, absolutely thrives on it. So you have a husband? You look too young to be married."

"I'm not young. I'm nineteen."

"Nineteen! So old! My dear, there will come a day when you think forty-year-olds are positively childish! Well, I hope you'll bring your husband to meet me, too. I should like that."

"I thank you for letting me come to your play, Miss Terry. I would like to do something for you in return."

To her credit, the older woman didn't smile or indicate that such a child had nothing in her power with which to repay even the most trivial kindness. Instead she paused and considered seriously. "I can't think of anything I need done at the moment, but if I do, I shall call upon you for help. Now, I really must pull myself together and dress for dinner. I'm holding up the whole party, I'm afraid.

"Clara, where is that hideous little muff? You know, the one that makes me look like I'm carrying a mangy dog? Monsieur Neptune keeps promising to bring me a new one, but he forgets unless I nag, and I don't think he'll be back in town until next week. My admirers don't seem to take me very seriously. I really should get out and do some shopping, but it's so tiresome. Perhaps if you'd prod me to a shop at the point of a dagger—would you remember to do that, Clara?" she added with a laugh.

* * *

The next day, a Sunday, Irene asked Peter an important question. "Are there ever scraps of fur left from the collars and cuffs you make at the factory?"

"Pounds and pounds of it. Mostly rabbit."

"What do they do with it?"

"The big scraps are resold for glove linings. The medium ones are shaved and the fiber is used for a number of things."

"What about the littlest pieces?"

"They go in a barrel and are thrown away. Why?"

"Could you bring me some little pieces?"

"Do you know, Reenee, I think that's the first time you've ever asked me for anything. Odd way to start, but yes, I'll be happy to bring you as many scraps as you want."

9

It took Irene a full two weeks to make the muff for Ellen Terry. She'd used light and dark strips of rabbit fur, none of which were more than a half-inch wide and most not more than two inches long. She considered for a full day the pitiful scraps she had to work with, then pieced them into strips and stitched them in a bargello pattern. Then she clipped the fur off the remaining scraps to make a fluffy filling. The lining was a square of satin from a petticoat she purchased from a second-hand clothing vendor. It was a work of art; a work of devotion.

Even Peter, who maintained that a muff was the most useless thing in the world—"Why not just wear a pair of decent gloves that you can put in your pocket when you're indoors, instead of carrying around a fuzzy barrel?"—was impressed when she was done. More than the muff itself, he was pleased with the change working on it had wrought in her. She'd been busy and happy all week. Before that, he'd begun to see disconcerting hints of impatience, if not to say downright crankiness, in her. He began to reevaluate grudgingly some of the precepts he'd held dear. Perhaps his urge to protect her *had* gone too far. She was both energetic and intelligent—those were the traits that had first attracted him to her and they were a part of why he loved her, but was it possible those were the traits that he might very well be stifling in his determination to look after her?

The day she finished the muff, she wrapped it in a clean sheet of brown butcher paper and took it to the theater. "I have a present for Miss Terry," she confided in Clara before the play began. "Would you give it to her?"

"Why don't you give it to her yourself?"

"I don't want to take up her time," Irene said.

"Irene, it's perfectly acceptable to impose on people's time to give them gifts!" Clara said. "I'll go with you after the performance."

But Clara was busy mending a torn sleeve on her employer's evening coat when the play was over and Irene screwed up her courage and approached Miss Terry by herself. When she entered the room, however, the actress had a guest. "I'm sorry, Miss Terry. I didn't mean to disturb you," she said, starting to back out.

"You didn't disturb me, Irene. Come in." She turned to the man who was standing next to the dressing table. In his early fifties, he had thick wavy hair that was just turning from blond to gray and was worn fractionally longer than was strictly fashionable. It gave him a rebellious, somewhat artistic look that was countered by his fine clothing and distinctive features. His face was thin, almost beaky, but intensely masculine, and his fierce eyebrows increased his resemblance to a bird of prey. At first glance, he had the sleek, handsome look of a man of consequence and breeding, but there was about him a barely concealed underlayer of toughness. "Jacques, this is my dresser's friend, Mrs. Garrick. Irene, this is Jacques Neptune. You've probably heard of him."

"No," Irene blurted out. "I mean, I'm pleased to meet you, sir."

Ellen Terry giggled. Neptune laughed, but it was a forced sound and Irene was sick at having offended such an obvious gentleman.

"I see you have a package with you," Miss Terry said in an obvious attempt to smooth his ruffled feathers by changing the subject.

"I brought you a present. It's nothing, really. I can bring it another time—"

"A present for me? How sweet of you, Irene. May I open it now? I adore gifts," she said, tearing open the butcher paper as if she were accustomed to presents coming to her this way. "Oh, Irene! It's just lovely. How very thoughtful of you! Jacques, this is what *you've* been promising me. A new muff."

"I know it's late in the season," Irene said softly, "but you'll be able to use it next winter—if you want."

Ellen Terry held the muff up to her cheek and rubbed it gently on her face, then held it back out at arm's length and admired it. "Such a remarkable pattern. Whatever sort of animal is it made of?"

"Let me see that!" Jacques Neptune said, and all but snatched it from her grasp in a single swooping motion like a hawk diving for a rabbit. He held it nearer the dressing-table lights and blew into the fur in several spots. He ran his fingers over the stitching lines between the strips. "Good work . . . where did you get this?" he asked Irene in an accusatory tone. He had a slight accent, a bit guttural on the R's and ominously sibilant on the final S.

"I . . . I made it. From scraps."

"Don't lie to me, child. Where did you get it?"

"I do not lie!"

"Jacques! What a way to behave," the actress said, taking a symbolic step nearer Irene. I'm on your side, she seemed to be saying.

"So sorry," he said with a mocking bow. "Now, where did you really get this?"

Irene took a deep breath and stood up as tall as she could. She had no idea what this man was so upset about, but she wouldn't behave like a craven in front of Miss Terry, even though she wanted more than anything in the world to run and hide. "I told you, I made it myself. That is the truth."

Neptune sat down at the dressing table and took a silver-embossed penknife from his trouser pocket. Before either of the women could move, he'd sliced through the seam holding the slightly shabby satin lining to the fur outer layer. "Jacques!" Ellen said, lunging for the muff and missing. "You mustn't do that! Irene made that for me and you're ruining it. This is really too, too naughty of you!"

"Don't carry on, my beauty. It's just an inch of seam. It can be put right in a moment. Fur stuffing? No, no, no. All wrong. It would mat in a few weeks. But the joining of the scraps is superb. Junk fur, of course. Shell-y. Hear how it rattles when you shake it? This cheap rabbit would be bald in a season. Good only for a stage prop, not real use—still, the stitching is the finest I think I've ever seen, and the design . . . What did you copy this from?'' he asked Irene suddenly.

''I didn't copy it.''

''Where did you get the idea for the pattern?''

Irene stared at him. What an extraordinary question. ''I don't know. It just seemed like a nice idea, as I had the little strips of two different colors of fur.''

''Come now, I didn't mean to frighten you before, my dear child,'' he said. The tone and the look on his hawkish face belied the words. ''But you must be honest with me now. Where have you seen a muff made this way before?''

Irene felt anger bubbling up, and barely managed to contain it. ''I have never seen a muff like this. I thought it up by myself!''

He heard the anger and apparently took it to indicate her truthfulness. He leaned back in the chair again and crossed his long elegant legs at the ankle. He studied Irene for a long moment, his face relaxing. ''Hmmmm. What did you say your name was?''

''Irene Garrick. And what did you say yours was?''

Ellen Terry burst into laughter. ''I'm sorry,'' she gasped, ''but you had that coming. You really did!''

He didn't look amused, but stood up again and offered Irene a perfectly manicured hand. ''I'm Jacques Neptune, Miss Garrick, and I think you may have talent. *May*. You come here tomorrow night and I will have some decent pelts for you to choose from. I want you to select whichever one or ones you want to make a hat for Miss Terry. Do you understand?''

''What kind of hat?''

''You must decide for yourself. Whatever you think would be useful and flattering to her. You may take as long as you want to complete it.''

''And if I don't?''

He shrugged in an exaggeratedly Gallic manner. ''It matters nothing to me. I will be out the cost of a pelt. That's all. But you may be out a great deal more.''

''What do you mean?''

''We shall see. This little muff might just be a fluke. Or you might be lying to me about designing it yourself. You might have even bought it at some dingy place downtown, though I'd like to have the stitcher's name if that's true. I don't know anybody in New York who does this quality of work who doesn't already work for me."

There was a knock on the door and Clara came in. "I've got your coat ready . . . Oh, Monsieur Neptune, I didn't know you were here yet. I hope I haven't held you up."

"Not at all, Clara," the actress said, crossing the room and slipping her arms into the sleeves that Clara held in place. "We've been having a most interesting conversation with Irene. Now, where have I put my evening bag? Oh, there. And my gloves? Look, Jacques, these are the gloves Irene repaired for me. I'll bet you can't even find the tear."

He took the glove and studied it, spotting the tear immediately. He glanced at Irene again in a clearly speculative way before wordlessly handing the glove back.

In a moment they were ready to go. Neptune held the door open and Miss Terry paused to take Irene's hands in hers. She pitched her voice low so that Neptune couldn't hear her. "Do as he says, my girl. Come back tomorrow and make the hat." And without further advice or explanation, she was gone.

A moment later, Clara dashed out of the room calling, "Miss Terry, you've forgotten your other earring!"

Irene stood in the center of the room looking at the dressing table. The muff lay there, bits of stuffing spilled out. She went to the table, sat down in Miss Terry's chair, and picked up the muff. It would, as he said, be only a few moments' work to put it back together. When Clara came back, she said, "Who is that man?"

"Oh, I thought you knew. He's Monsieur Jacques Neptune, the most famous furrier in New York, possibly the most famous in the world. He designs the coats that the richest, most important women in the world wear. There are actually European princesses who come to America just to see him. The only ones *he* calls on are reigning queens, or so they say."

Irene went back to the theater the next afternoon as Neptune had told her to do. She had debated with herself all night as to whether she should tell Peter about her meeting with the overbearing furrier, and in the end decided against it. After all, what was there to say: An important man is putting me to a test, and if I pass . . . ? She had no idea what he had in mind as the prize. Probably a job sewing furs in his company, a high-class factory, but a factory nevertheless. And if she failed, there would be no disappointment to explain to Peter if he knew nothing of it to begin with. Better to say nothing now.

Neptune wasn't at the theater, but Clara had a bulky package in her room. "Monsieur Neptune sent this over this morning. Your name is on it," she said when Irene came to her tiny, warm room. "What is it?"

"Pelts," Irene explained, sitting down and cutting through the twine holding the package together. It was tightly packed, and when the string was cut, the paper burst open, spilling furs onto her lap. "Oh, my!" she said with amazement. "Aren't they beautiful?" But the words were almost inaudible as she found herself scooping up the furs and burying her face in them. She'd never seen anything like this, and more important, never felt anything so luxurious. They smelled clean and rich and gave her own breath back to her warm and soft. She closed her eyes, blocking out other sensations to give herself to the furs. Clara was saying something to her, but the words were without meaning. For a long, magic moment, there was nothing on earth but her and the furs.

Finally Clara put her hand on Irene's shoulder and shook her gently. "Are you crying, dear? What's the matter?"

Irene raised her head, opened her eyes. She was almost drunk with sensory indulgence. "What? No, I was just smelling them."

She sounded silly in her own ears and must have sounded even sillier to Clara, who cocked an eyebrow. "I was telling you, there's a note here. It says the large ones are plucked beaver 'blankets' and the small ones are Mongolian squirrel peltries. You are to use as much or as little of either or both as you want. Irene, what *is* this all about? Why is Monsieur Neptune giving you these furs?"

Irene gathered the peltries and put them on another chair, the better to concentrate. "Clara, I'm not sure. Yesterday when I gave Miss Terry the muff, he took it and examined it and said I might have talent—he was rude about it, but that's what he said. He told me to come back today for those furs and make a hat to show him."

"Why?"

"I don't know. He said the stitching was good. Maybe he's going to give me a job in his factory."

"Would Peter allow that?"

Irene shook her head sadly. "No, I think he would not."

"Then why are you doing this?"

"Because it's important. I don't know why, but I must do what he says. How can I explain?"

Clara was silent for a moment. She'd waited for years for some sign that her own life might miraculously change for the better. She was attuned to the faintest hint, which had never come. Wasn't that what Irene was saying? That this might be the chance? The thin edge of the wedge that might open some marvelous door to another world? "I think I understand," she said softly.

Irene fashioned the hat in a mannish style with a softly rolled brim of the light squirrel pelts and a crown that was slightly larger at the top, causing the soft structure to topple forward gently. By cutting the beaver into strips and restitching it diagonally, she managed to create a swirling effect. She purchased a length of two-inch-wide charcoal-gray grosgrain ribbon and used it as a band that joined in a large bow at the back. She wished the trailing streamers could have been longer, but she couldn't afford any more ribbon. It took her a week, and when she was done she modeled it herself for Peter. "What do you think?"

He studied her for a long moment. "I think it's odd. You aren't going to wear it, are you?"

"Odd? Oh, Peter!"

"I mean odd for here. Among our own kind. I know ladies uptown wear fancy things like that, but then, they are the sort of impractical women who actually carry muffs instead of sensible gloves."

He said it with a laugh and she smiled back, but she cringed inwardly at his words: "our own kind." She wanted to cry: "I don't want to belong here. I want to belong uptown with the ladies." But instead she said, "It's not for me. It's for Miss Terry. A friend of hers wanted me to make it for her."

"The man who gave you the furs. I know. I hope they like it."

"I hope so too," she said fervently.

She took the hat to the theater the next morning, knowing Miss Terry wouldn't be there. "Would you give Monsieur Neptune these packages, Clara? This one is the hat, and this is the fur that was left."

"You're not going to do it yourself?"

"I can't. I'm afraid to. Maybe he will think this hat is ugly and terrible."

"And you can't stand to hear him say so? Well, I wouldn't worry if I were you, but yes, if you want me to, I'll give it to him. Will you stay and have some tea?"

"I . . . no, I can't," Irene said, fidgeting uncharacteristically with a button on her blouse.

For a moment she looked like the child Clara had first met years ago on the boat, nervous, frightened, alien. But for all Irene's seeming innocence, there was something fierce and complex in the girl that cried out for satisfaction. She was a bundle of undischarged energy and ambition that would someday burn her to a cinder without a proper outlet. Clara felt a wave of tenderness sweep over her and reached out. Irene responded by throwing herself into Clara's arms and hugging her tightly for a moment before pulling away. "I'm sorry, Clara, to be so—"

"You have nothing to be sorry for," Clara said firmly, once again the teacher. She missed being Irene's primary source of information and instruction. If only they could go back to those years . . . No, there was no going back. Not for either of them. "Now, I have work to do and I can't bear to have you around as jumpy as you are. Go home and try to forget about the hat for a while."

Irene smiled. "Yes, ma'am," she said with sweet mockery.

But she didn't forget about the hat.

That evening she paced until Peter said, "You're going to

wear a path in the floor. If you must keep walking about, let's do it outdoors. Why in the world are you so nervous? I'm sure Miss Terry is pleased with the hat. And even if she doesn't like it, she likes you and will be pleased with the gift."

"Yes, but what about Monsieur Neptune?"

"Who's that? The man who asked you to make the hat? What about him?" Peter asked.

Irene could sense that Peter was becoming irritated with her and she quickly changed the subject. "Yes, I'd like to take a walk. Are you sure you're not too tired?"

He smiled at her. "I *would* rather go to bed."

She slipped her arms around him. "So would I."

But for once, their lovemaking failed to completely clear her mind of everything else in the world. She only pretended to sleep until she was sure Peter had dropped off; then she got up and paced for another hour.

Neptune had hated the hat. She was sure of it now. It was a terrible hat. Casting her mind back to the play audience, she realized that not one single woman had worn anything remotely like it. They'd all had sweeping, frilly hats with wide brims and masses of ribbons and lace and feathers. Her hat would be a freak in that group. She'd never hear from Monsieur Neptune again, she wouldn't dare ever go back to the theater for fear of running into him. Miss Terry would be disappointed in her for failing so miserably. Clara would be embarrassed for her.

She shouldn't have made the hat in the first place. Peter was right—they had a happy life. They had love and each other and plenty to eat; she shouldn't be longing for more. Besides, she was only a common immigrant, a foreigner in this country who had no right to expect more. She must work at learning to accept that. She would go back to being who she really was—Irina Gieryk.

Irina. . . .

It didn't even sound like her own name anymore, though. No one had called her that since she left the old country. Irina had been an ignorant, dirty girl who wore her brother's handed-down shoes and whose one burning desire had been to improve herself. Well, she wasn't ignorant or dirty anymore, but she still ached to better herself. She couldn't change that. She still dreamed of the life she wanted for herself and Mama and the girls.

No, it wasn't an ugly hat. It *was* odd, as Peter had said, but it was attractive and well made and would look beautiful on Miss Terry. And if Monsieur Neptune didn't like it, that was simply too bad!

The summons came the next afternoon. A man in a chauffeur's uniform came to the door of the little apartment. "Are you Miss Irene Garrick?" he said, glancing around with obvious distaste. "Monsieur Neptune says you are to be at the theater at five o'clock promptly."

Apparently accustomed to people taking Neptune's word as law, he didn't even wait for a reply, but turned on his heel and walked off. Irene went to the window and watched him come out the door of the building and get in the fancy open car which had been surrounded by a cloud of curious children in his brief absence. He did his best to shoo them off, but two were still clinging to the running board shrieking with glee as he pulled away.

The weather had improved and Irene decided to walk all the way. It would use up time and energy, both of which weighed heavily on her. Three hours until five o'clock. She wound her fair hair into a severe knot at the back of her head, put on her best dress, left Peter a note explaining where she'd gone, and started out.

By five o'clock, however, she was no less tightly wound and was nearly sick with anxiety. She walked up and down Fortieth Street three times before straightening her back, tilting her chin up with assumed assurance, and climbing the short flight of steps to the stage door.

Clara, Miss Terry, and Monsieur Neptune were all assembled in the actress's dressing room, waiting for her. Clara tried to smile her reassurance, but it was a stilted sort of grin. The hat was sitting on the dressing table like a prisoner on the witness stand. Irene felt her heart lift for a moment. It *was* a handsome hat. "You asked me to come?" she said to Neptune.

"Sit down, this may take some time," he said coldly.

She pulled forward the remaining chair and sat down rigidly.

"Miss Terry tells me I have been mistaken in addressing you as 'Miss' Garrick. You are a married woman?" Irene nodded. "What does your husband do?"

"He's a fur cutter now, but he's going to be a college teacher someday."

"That's where you got those awful rabbit scraps? I see. You don't have children, do you?"

Irene's joints felt as if they'd locked, including her jaw. "No, we do not," she said stiffly.

He nodded and handed the hat to Ellen Terry. "Put it on, would you?" he asked her.

They all stared, mesmerized, as the actress donned the hat, adjusted it in front of the mirror, and sat back down, smiling at Irene.

"Now, Mrs. Garrick, let me ask you some questions: you returned the fur scraps along with the hat. Why?"

It was the last thing she expected. "They were not mine. They were yours."

"You took the parts you used from the center of the beaver blanket instead of the edges. You could have left a more usable remnant. Why did you take the center part?"

"There was a faint stripe down the center. I wanted to use it in the pattern. Besides, the fur wasn't as thick at the sides of the peltry. You told me to use whatever I wanted . . ." Her voice sounded defensive on the last sentence, and she hadn't meant to.

Apparently it was the right answer, however, for he merely nodded. "The term is 'dense,' not 'thick.' Why did you use the squirrel pelts for the brim?"

"For contrast and because they look better next to Miss Terry's hair. The color of the beaver wasn't as good for her."

"Quite right. I wondered if you'd know that."

Irene took a deep breath, but her relief was short-lived.

He gestured to the actress. "Do you think, child, that any woman who follows fashion would wear that hat in public?"

Irene stood up slowly. "No. It's not fussy enough."

"Sit down!"

Irene all but fell back into the chair.

"Do you like that hat?"

Irene cleared her throat. "Yes."

"Do you think it looks good on Miss Terry?"

"Yes."

He nodded again. "You must remember this: women like Miss Terry are style-setters, not style-followers. Do you like the hat, Ellen?"

"I love it!"

They all smiled, all except Irene, who was too terrified.

"Now, tell me about yourself—where are you from?"

For a brief, terrible moment Irene could see the village, brown and gray, packed-earth streets, sagging roofs, chickens in yards and houses. She could see herself in Teo's boots carrying the eggs up the hill. "What does it matter?" she asked.

Instead of being angry at her nonanswer, he said, "What, indeed! I'm told Polish is your native language. Where did you learn to speak English?"

"From Clara and at Cooper Union."

"No, that accent of yours isn't Clara's and it certainly isn't those poor souls who teach in the miserable immigrant schools." Irene noticed that as he spoke, his own accent was almost entirely gone. "No, there's something else there. Something in the precise clip to the vowels. I think I hear Miss Terry in your voice."

"I have studied the way Miss Terry speaks—yes," Irene admitted.

"You could study no better example. That's how she's kept that awful semantic snob Shaw enthralled all these years."

Ellen laughed. "How dreadful of you to say that Mr. Shaw loves me only for my pronunciation!"

The tension eased again for a moment, but then Neptune turned his attention back to Irene. "What do you want?"

"I beg your pardon?"

"What do you want? Of life . . . of yourself?"

She hesitated only a moment before saying, "Everything."

The room was silent. Everyone was staring at her. Neptune rose and so did Irene. He took her hand in a firm grasp. His hand was large and strong. "Thank you, Mrs. Garrick. That will be all."

"All?"

"Yes."

Irene pulled her hand away. Her face was burning with shame. She'd thought she'd passed the tests, whatever they were, and now she was being dismissed. Dismissed. She went to the door, but before leaving she turned back to him. "Monsieur Neptune, do *you* like the hat?"

His fierce eyebrows came together as if the question truly angered him. "Yes, I like the hat."

Ellen Terry waited until Irene and Clara had gone, then turned to Neptune. "Jacques, what in the world was that all about? You were unforgivably rude to that nice girl."

He had his back to her, pretending to examine a framed picture of her daughter that she kept on the dressing table. At her words, he slowly turned. "It was about nothing. It was simply the irritability of an aging man. To be so young and have talent—I think I'm a little jealous."

"Age again. Why does everyone around me talk about age? It's bad enough with women, but you? You're in your best years, Jacques. You're rich and successful. Women all over the world would tear each other to bits for your favors and would kill for the honor of wearing your fur coats—how dare you complain to me about age!" She said it fiercely, but there was an affectionate smile to go with the words.

"You're quite right, as always. I'm sorry I drew you into my idiocy."

Ellen gazed at him for a long moment, knowing he was suffering some sorrow she really couldn't comprehend and which he didn't want to explain. "Very well. Why don't you try to draw me into a good meal instead?" she said brightly.

10

In April 1907, six years after Irina Kossok took her father's place and came to America, Peter and Irene Garrick went to the steamship ticket office and purchased five tickets. Remembering the fear and confusion she'd felt going through immigration at Ellis Island, Irene insisted, with Peter's full agreement, on buying second-class tickets for Zofia and the girls, even though it was a considerable additional expense. She also included money for them to make the trip to Hamburg. Her own passage had begun in Gdansk because the ship she traveled on had been there for repairs, but there were few such opportunities.

It would still be several months before they arrived, but Irene had the panicky feeling she would be seeing them any moment once the tickets were dispatched. And she realized that after all the years of looking forward to their arrival, she wasn't ready. Getting second-class tickets had used all their money and there was nothing left with which to rent a larger apartment. They were going to be packed in like passengers in steerage, and not just for a short trip, but possibly for a very long time.

Peter wasn't as upset by this as Irene was. "We have two rooms. That'll be enough space and it won't matter if we're a little crowded for a while. Later we'll get a larger place," he said.

But he hadn't lived with a family for years, nor had he ever lived in a house full of women. Irene worried that the high, constant voices of the youngest girls would disturb his life more than he imagined. He was an orderly, scholarly person and theirs was a tranquil life. A houseful of children would alter all that, she feared. No, she didn't fear it, she hoped for it, but was unsure how well Peter would adjust to the change. She mentioned this to him and he laughed. "That's sweet of you, my dear, but I can assure you," he said, thinking back to his past, "I've made greater adjustments and had worse things happen to me than a bit of noise and giggling."

There was something else undone: she'd never told her mother about Teo's disappearance.

She'd meant to with every letter, but as the years had gone by, it had become easier and easier to maintain the fantasy that she was writing on behalf of Teo. Zofia never questioned it (how could she not wonder? Irene sometimes thought), and Irene never found the words to explain that Teo, the pride of the family, had walked away and forgotten all of them. Or perhaps he hadn't *walked* away. Perhaps he was carried away to some unknown grave. But the time was coming when Zofia would have to know. She would expect Teo to meet them when they arrived in America. How could Irene explain all the years of deception? And how could she make up to Zofia for the crushing disappointment she was going to feel when she realized she'd truly lost her only son?

Through all the years she'd been in America, Irene had anticipated feeling euphoric on that long-desired day when she finally could send the passage to Zofia, but instead she was so worried and preoccupied on the way home that Peter had to jiggle her arm to get her attention. "What? I'm sorry . . ."

"I was asking you how old all the girls are," he said.

"Agnieszka will be eighteen next month; the twins, Lillie and Cecilia, are eleven, and Stefania, the baby, is almost eight. I hardly knew her. She was just learning to walk when I left."

"And Agnieszka is your favorite?" he asked.

Irene smiled. He'd been questioning her about them for weeks. Peter Garrick, the most calm, sober, scholarly of men, was almost giddy with anticipation of getting a ready-made family. "Yes, Aggie's my favorite. We're the closest in age, but mostly I loved her because she was so cheerful. She sang a lot. Sometimes she even sang in her sleep. And she could make noises to imitate all sorts of animals. Especially ducks. Oh, Peter, I can't wait to see her. To see all of them."

It had started to rain, a cold dreary drizzle, before they got home, and as they turned the last corner onto their street, a nasty wind slapped against them. Irene pulled up her coat collar. "You should have kept that fur hat for yourself," Peter said, ducking his head against the onslaught.

I might as well have, for all the good it did me, Irene thought. It had been over a month since her stormy interview with Monsieur Neptune and she'd heard nothing more. As impressed as he seemed to be with her stitching abilities, she'd hoped that he'd let her do minor repair work for his company. It would have been a very helpful extra income—not much, but useful. And with the family arriving so soon, every added dollar would help.

But of course Peter probably wouldn't have approved of her taking a job unless she could bring the work home to do, and nobody was very likely to hand over valuable fur garments and accessories to her to cart all over town. Why on earth had Neptune put her through all that agony for nothing? Why had she let her dreams get the better of her head and suppose that something great was going to befall her?

As they climbed the four steep flights of steps to their apartment, Irene found her thoughts returning to her family again. How would Mama manage these steps?—Mama, whose whole life had been on one level, whose bad knee buckled when she had to climb even a short ladder, whose greatest pride was her tiny garden. Oh dear, what would they all think of New York? Irene had been here so long that she'd nearly forgotten her first impression; now they swept back over her.

All the people and the noise and the peculiar city smell—all so foreign to them, so frightening. There would be so little that was familiar and comforting to Mama. There was no open land, no open sky, no quiet nights when the only sound was the shush of the wind in the trees outside and the birdsong at dawn. Her sisters would adjust easily, by virtue of youth's resiliency—hadn't she proved that herself? But Mama . . . ?

"Look, a letter," Peter said as he pushed open the door to the apartment.

A small envelope of heavy cream paper as thick and pebbly as eggshells lay on the floor. "To Mr. and Mrs. Peter Garrick," it said. Peter opened it, scanned the spiky handwriting, and handed it to her.

> Dear Mr. and Mrs. Garrick,
> I would very much appreciate the pleasure of your company for dinner tomorrow night at eight at my home. If this is inconvenient, please tell me a date you prefer.
>
> Yours most sincerely,
> Jacques Neptune

"That's the man who gave you the furs to make the hat for Miss Terry, isn't it? Why would he invite us to dinner? I guess to thank you for doing him a favor. Look at the address. Fifth Avenue. That's a very fine neighborhood," Peter said.

Irene was glad to see that he seemed to be at least a little bit impressed. While Peter's ambitions didn't match hers, his curiosity about how other people lived did. "I don't know exactly why he's inviting us." It was time to tell him the truth about the hat, that it wasn't a simple favor as she had represented it, but a test of some sort. "Peter, about the fur hat . . ." she began.

He listened while she repeated the gist of her interview—or inquisition—with Neptune. "So what does this dinner invitation mean?" he asked again when she'd finished.

"Maybe it means he has work for me," Irene said hesitantly.

He frowned. "I don't want you to work in a factory, Irene. That's a miserable life. Animals are treated better than those girls."

"I know that, Peter. But maybe he'll have piecework I can do at home. That's not so bad. I'm used to sewing at home. I did it for years at the Sprys'. May we go to dinner with him? It would be very interesting to see his house, and if he has a proposal that is unacceptable, we'll tell him so. There's nothing to lose, is there?"

Peter, say yes, she was thinking. For if you say no, you will destroy me.

He took her face in his hands. "If you want it, we'll do it. I could never deprive you of anything it was in my power to give. But, Irene—don't let yourself think this means anything. This man may be just slumming, giving you a nice evening in gratitude for your making his lady friend a hat. Don't get any foolish hopes up. All right?"

"Yes, Peter," she said, but it was too late for the warning.

"Mr. Chandler Moffat," the butler announced.

Jacques Neptune put aside the book he'd been reading. Damn Chandler anyway. How did he always manage to turn up at the wrong time? A God-given gift, he supposed. All the Moffats seemed to have had it. Chandler's parents, for example, had been standing at a ship's rail watching the waves during a storm when an unusually large one had washed over the deck and taken them with it. Chandler was seventeen at the time. Neptune's late wife, Roberta, whose sister was Chandler's mother, had insisted that they take in the orphaned boy. Neptune, frustrated for lack of an heir of his own body, was agreeable—then. But now Chandler was the unofficial junior partner and heir apparent of Neptune et Cie. "Send him in, Evans," Neptune said.

Chandler entered Neptune's normally inviolate den a moment later. He was only in his late twenties, but he had the portly, self-important look that often comes to men with money in their forties. In his case, it was a disguise of sorts. He had little money of his own, his father having had more charm than cash to leave his only son, and Chandler made an effective business of going through all that Neptune gave him for his work.

Nor was Chandler as important as his dress and manner suggested. It wasn't, Neptune believed, that he was stupid; Neptune suspected that Chandler might actually be canny if pressed, but he'd never had any particular need to be good at anything. He halfheartedly managed the fur-processing operation at work (under Neptune's frequently exasperated guidance), handled the bookkeeping (also under his uncle's eagle eye), and did all the social things associated with a high-fashion house. *That* he was good at. He'd mastered the art of flattery, amusing conversation, supercilious artistic patronage, and light flirtation. Anyone who had a crying need for an amiable clubman to head up a charitable committee or for a moderately attractive and thoroughly safe escort for a virginal visiting sister could do no better than to call on Chandler Moffat.

"Well, well, well, Uncle Jacques. Having a spot of reading? Just what I like too. A good book. Especially the racy bits, eh?"

Jacques sighed. "I'm reading Dickens. There aren't very many 'racy bits.' You weren't in today."

"No, didn't I tell you? Bunny Wiler's looking over a racehorse she wanted me to take a peek at upstate. Nice-looking beast, but legs like toothpicks. Told her not to waste her money, but I don't imagine Bunny'll listen. She never does. Thought I might go to the club for a spot of brandy and a bit of dinner. Would you like to trot along with me?"

That meant he hadn't the money to buy a meal outright and was probably behind in his fees to the club. "No, thanks," Neptune said, making a mental note to make a deposit to Chandler's account tomorrow. "I'm having people in."

"Anybody I know?"

"No, I'm certain you don't. A young person I think I might add to the design staff, actually."

Chandler sharpened up slightly. While his interest in the company that provided his daily brioche was sporadic, he was alert to anything that could be viewed, however obliquely, as a threat to his own status there. He liked mediocre employees; they made him look good. "I've never known you to have job interviews here at your house."

"It's an unusual case."

"Is this man pretty good, you think?"

Neptune almost corrected the gender error, then decided against it. Better to be sure in his own mind before having to explain to Chandler about hiring a woman designer. He was having trouble enough accepting the possibility himself. Not that he needed, nor really cared about, Chandler's approval, but he could be a bloody nuisance. "The work I've seen is exceptional, but I'm a bit curious about the . . . let us say, 'social' aspect of the individual."

"Not quite up to snuff, eh? Shouldn't think there'd be much taste where there's no breeding."

"Maybe not. That's what I'm trying to find out."

Chandler sat down. "I see. Bring him in and see if he steals the silver. Good thinking."

"I wasn't exactly anticipating theft—"

"Don't see what we need another designer for. We've already got two, besides you, of course."

Neptune shook his head. "We've got one, including myself. Delman and Hadley couldn't design their way out of a closet. They're calculators, executors—capable only of figuring out the means of putting together a garment, not inventing one."

"I didn't think they were bad," Chandler said.

"They're not bad—at what they do. They're excellent draftsmen. That's why I need them, but I need somebody with genuine talent, inspiration, call it what you will."

Neptune suddenly felt old and tired, a feeling he usually managed to keep safely at bay. But now and then Chandler drove him dangerously close to the crumbling edge of despair. The man really didn't understand a word of what Neptune was saying. And someday the company into which the older man had poured all his youth, talent, and ambition would belong to this good-natured dolt who was studying his fingernails as if they were truly interesting. What would become of Neptune et Cie when the talent and force behind it were gone? Oh well, why should he care? He wouldn't be around to know the answer. He'd told himself that dozens of times, and yet he still had a mental image of himself in angelic garb, looking down through the clouds and trying to hurl thunderbolts at Chandler.

Evans tapped lightly on the door before entering. "Will you be wanting sherry, sir, when your dinner guests arrive?" he asked in what Neptune knew was an attempt to help dislodge Chandler before he invited himself to the meal.

"Yes, I believe so. Thank you for reminding me of the time, Evans. I must change. Chandler, so nice of you to drop by," he said, his voice crusted with irony. "Perhaps you'll drop in at work tomorrow." For a moment he almost relented and gave him some cash then and there, but decided against it. It would do Chandler good to have to be poor for a day. In fact, Neptune sometimes thought guiltily that the best thing he could have done for his nephew would have been to cut him off years ago. If he'd been forced to make something worthwhile of himself, he might not be so useless now.

Chandler stood up quickly, almost upsetting a flower arrangement on the table next to his chair, and said, "I'll be there bright and early."

They were right on time, just as he expected. "Mr. and Mrs. Garrick," Evans announced, just barely managing to keep the sneer in his voice at bay.

Neptune rose from the chair before the fire and with a quick acknowledging nod to Irene, approached Peter. He would be the crux of the matter. Though Irene had talent and drive, she would almost certainly abide by decisions made by her husband.

"So you're Mr. Garrick. I'm so glad to meet you at last," Neptune said. He wasn't sure what he'd expected, but this wasn't it. Peter Garrick didn't look like the usual immigrant clod with a shuffling walk, dirty nails, and an onion in the pocket. There was an air of quiet reserve about this young man, maybe intellect, maybe not. He was poorly but very neatly dressed. There was a patch on his jacket that most people wouldn't notice, but Neptune's sharp eye recognized it as Irene's careful work. Peter Garrick was undeniably a very good-looking man, and Jacques recognized that Peter would be extremely attractive to women. Jacques himself had once possessed that sort of young, healthy, raw appeal and felt a sharp twinge of jealousy. Why should his own youth have slipped away while this beautiful young couple probably didn't appreciate that they were in their prime?

Irene was visible only in his peripheral vision. He sensed that she was working at resisting the temptation to gawk at the room and stood instead with her hands demurely folded and her gaze level. That was good. He didn't want somebody who was obviously stunned in the presence of money and taste. Neptune steered them to the sofa in front of the fire. She had on the same deep green dress he'd seen her in before—it must be her best dress. But she'd done something with the line of the sleeve and put a different collar and cuffs on it. To an unpracticed eye it would have appeared to be a different garment altogether. Her fair hair was pulled gently into a simple knot at the back of her neck, making her look like a child playing at grown-up. Was it instinctive style or lack of it that made her wear it that simple and yet stunning way?

"It's unusually cold for this time of year, isn't it?" Neptune said as the butler offered tiny crystal glasses of sherry. "I hope you were not inconvenienced by having to come out tonight . . . ?" He'd thought of sending the car for them. They might have enjoyed it, but until he'd taken the measure of Peter Garrick, he didn't want to risk appearing too powerful and beneficent.

"Not at all. The rain has stopped and it seemed to be warmer today," Peter said warily.

Aha. He spoke well. Very good thing. Nice pronunciation. Precise in an attractive way. But was there something a little prickly in the tone, or was Neptune only expecting to perceive some degree of antagonism?

Irene, sipping the sherry (did people really *like* this fiery liquid?) and watching Neptune over the rim of the tiny glass, saw the approval in his face. Peter was being tested now and was acquitting himself well. Did the man put everyone who worked for him through this? she wondered. They continued to chat about the weather for some moments, neither of them appearing to be aware of her presence, which suited her quite well. When the butler came and took back the glasses, Neptune's empty, Irene's hardly diminished, and Peter's untouched, Neptune said, "Is dinner ready, Evans?"

"Yes, sir."

"Then let us go in. Mrs. Garrick?" he said, offering his arm.

It was a huge dining table, the sort Irene had sometimes pictured in her mind, but all three settings were at one end. Neptune seated her at his right, Peter at his left, and took his place at the end. "Rather unbalanced, but I hate shouting down the length of the room when dining intimately," he said. "This table was made for a man with a large family and I, sadly, have neither wife nor children."

Why is he being so friendly? Irene wondered. This gracious man might as well be someone entirely different from the ogre who questioned her in Miss Terry's dressing room. The only similarity was in appearance, and even that was disconcertingly altered. When she'd seen him before, he'd been richly dressed, but now he wore a simple suit, well made and no doubt expensive, but of ordinary cut. Nor was the glittering diamond ring he'd worn before in evidence. His hands were bare.

A waiter appeared with salads made of apples and oranges and nuts in a creamy dressing. When he'd departed, Neptune said, "Mr. Garrick, am I correct in assuming you're a well-read man?"

Peter smiled again, and Irene thought she saw in his expression both suspicion and genuine amusement. "I have read a few books, yes," he said dryly. They discussed early Greek culture in a cool, disinterested way. Neptune directed just enough remarks to Irene to avoid being rude to her. Peter still seemed oddly wary. Though Irene knew very little about what they were talking about, it was obvious to her that Peter was holding his own in the conversation quite nicely. He certainly knew as much as, and possibly more than, Neptune. She felt a great pride in his learning.

The dinner was excellent. Simple fare superbly prepared—roast beef, potatoes with cheese-and-parsley sauce, asparagus, crusty bread with real butter. Irene had never tasted such delicious food. Though she was intensely nervous tonight, and normally a sparse eater in any case, she filled her stomach as if she were filling her soul for a life of memories of this meal. This food, these delicate china plates with the elaborate gold border—a different plate for each course!—this large, warm room, and the silent man who discreetly placed and removed the plates and silver and glasses: this was the fantasy she'd dreamed for so long but never had the material to imagine adequately. She wished she could take a picture of it so that she could study it and remember it for years to come. The silver salt and pepper shakers, individual sets at each place, were enough to provide spiritual nourishment for hours.

Finally, when the dessert was served, Neptune said, "I

understand from Clara that you have sent for your mother and sisters, Mrs. Garrick."

"You talked to Clara about me?" she asked.

Peter frowned.

"Only in passing. To get your address," Neptune said smoothly. "How many sisters have you?"

"Four," Peter answered, as if they were his own. He went on to name them and tell their ages. Irene was relieved to be spared another questioning.

"I wonder if they are all as lovely as your wife?" Neptune said.

"They couldn't be," Peter said simply.

They both stared at her for a long moment. Neptune finally broke the spell. "If we are finished, I'd suggest we go into the study, where we can be more comfortable."

They arranged themselves again in front of the fire, Irene and Peter side by side on the sofa, their host in a deep chair at right angles to them. He settled into the chair as the Garricks expressed their appreciation of dinner. "Well, now," he said. And with those words, Irene felt the very air in the room become charged. She forced herself to look at Neptune calmly in spite of the fact that she wanted to fling herself at him and demand, "Why are we here? What is this about?"

Again Neptune addressed himself to Peter, looking past Irene as if she were nothing more than another lovely ornament in the room, a china shepherdess inexplicably come to life. "I have asked you here tonight for a reason. If you would be so kind as to hear me out, I would appreciate it." The words were as gracious and polite as anything he'd said all evening, but there was a hint of arrogance in them now. This, Irene sensed, was the man she'd met before.

"Mr. Garrick, has your wife told you about the muff she made for Miss Terry? Of course, she must have. You acquired the fur scraps for her. Has she also told you about the assignment I gave her?"

"The hat? Yes. I was not aware that you or she considered it an 'assignment.' "

"And did you see the finished product?"

"I did. It was, as I told her, very odd, but well-made."

"I know your opinion of its construction is valid. I'm told

you're a fur cutter and I went so far as to speak with the man you work for. He speaks highly of your work—"

"You spoke to Mr. Fromann about me?" Irene heard the hiss of surprised anger in Peter's voice, but apparently Neptune didn't, for he went on:

"—but I assure you, I speak from an expertise in fashion. The hat your wife made was utterly out of fashion, as fashion is today, but it was beautifully styled. It was perfect for Miss Terry, the customer. The color she chose for the brim was exactly right, as was the pattern, the size, the way it sat on Miss Terry's coiffure. The bow at the back was precisely the correct finishing touch, a bit of a frill, but controlled, dignified, suitable to a very great lady. Just as important, your wife didn't scrimp. She instinctively took the section of the pelt she needed to do the hat as it should be done and then she gave me back virtually every hair she didn't use. She proved her talent and her honor."

Peter looked at Irene, then back at Monsieur Neptune. "Was my wife's integrity being tested as well as her abilities?"

"It was, as a matter of fact. No, don't become angry about this. I do not know her as you do. She was a stranger to me. An apparently talented stranger—but I had to know more about her."

"Why?" Peter demanded.

"Because I think she may possess an extraordinary talent. Totally undeveloped, of course. It will take years of training before she can rival me, but I would like to teach her, to see if my initial impression is correct. I would like to give her that training."

Irene held her breath. Peter said coldly, "What do you mean? Irene go to work in your factory?"

"No, Mr. Garrick, I don't want to put your wife to work in a factory. I want to train her as a designer of fur garments. I have two such assistants now who have been through the course of study I've developed, and while they are competent . . . well, they aren't exactly beacons of inspiration. Your wife might be better than they are. I cannot know until I've trained her."

"You want to be her mentor," Peter said, thinking of Herr Schmitt.

Neptune sighed, almost smiled. "Yes, I want to be her mentor. Let us talk business. Or rather, I shall talk and you may consider at your leisure." His voice was as cold as frozen steel now, all efforts to jolly Peter along forgotten. "You make forty dollars a week. I checked with Fromann. I propose to pay Irene seventy-five dollars to start and will also give you a job cutting for me at the same rate. That's a total of almost four times as much as you make now. If Irene proves to be a good student, I will keep her on and raise her salary. If I have misjudged and she is unsatisfactory, you will keep your job at the same rate for as long as your work is good—"

"It's not the money," Peter said.

Irene couldn't keep quiet. "Peter, think! We could get enough room for Mama and the girls." One hundred and fifty dollars a week was, to her, an incomprehensible amount of money.

Neptune cut in. "These are the things you two must discuss privately. Let me say the rest of what I have to offer. I propose to make Mrs. Garrick work very hard. Very hard. But not factory sort of work. She will be treated with the utmost of respect by everyone . . ."

He could sense the change in Peter's attitude immediately. No, the money really didn't mean anything to him, but the way his wife was treated meant a great deal. "She would have a decent, modest wardrobe provided without expense, she would be called 'Mrs. Garrick,' But . . ." He let the word hang in the air for a long time before going on. "But there would be things you would have to agree to."

"What things?" Peter asked.

"There would be many very long days, work she would have to bring home and study, possibly some travel. There is a fur auction in Saint Louis, attendance at which is a vital part of the training. This would mean you would have to come along, or send her mother or one of her sisters for decency's sake. You don't have to decide now. And do not forget, I might be wrong. I may find that the muff and the hat were freaks. That she really hasn't any extraordinary talent. If so, it is over. I will have taught her enough that the two of you can start a small neighborhood fur business of your own if you're frugal and have saved enough for the initial investment. You have nothing to lose, and possibly everything too gain."

Everything, Irene thought.

Everything!

Peter started to speak, but Neptune stood up quickly, as if he were suddenly in a great hurry to get rid of them. "That's what I propose. You must think about it. If you have any questions, you may write or call on me here at any time. Otherwise, I will expect your answer a week from tomorrow. You may call in person, and if you don't, I shall assume you have rejected the offer and nothing more will be said. Now, if you will excuse me, I have to be up early in the morning. My butler will get your things and show you out. Good night, Mr. Garrick, Mrs. Garrick."

When he stood, his eyes met Irene's briefly. He hadn't addressed any of his remarks to her directly. He'd not sought her opinion, nor tempered his remarks to please her. But she knew, in that moment when they looked at each other, that it was because he understood her.

They took one of the new gasoline-powered taximeter cabs home. It was the first time Irene had ridden in an automobile, and normally she would have reveled in the experience, but tonight she hardly noticed where she was. Neither she nor Peter spoke until they were home, and even then they were silent while they took off their coats. Each was waiting for the other to speak. Finally Peter gave in.

"Do you want to do this, Irene?"

She hung her coat on the hook behind the door and turned to him slowly. "More than anything."

"But why?"

Irene sat down by the window. "Peter, just before I came to this country, something happened—it wasn't anything important. Not to anyone else, but I've never forgotten. Mama sent me to the big house outside the village to sell some eggs. It was a huge house. I'd never been there before or even seen it except from a distance. I looked in the window and there was a girl with beautiful clean hair and a fancy dress playing a piano . . ."

Memory flooded back and for a moment she wasn't in a cold-water flat in New York, she was that cold filthy child peering through the window again. "I went around to the back door with the eggs, and the pretty girl came to the kitchen. She'd seen me looking at her and she was angry. She took my basket of eggs and deliberately broke them on the floor, then made me clean it up. I said she was wicked to break the eggs and she slapped me and said I was dirty and common."

Irene looked up at Peter to see if he sensed what it all meant. He was listening attentively, apparently waiting for her to get to the important part of the story.

"Don't you see? It was the first time I realized I was dirty and common. I'd never known it before. I made a vow then that someday I'd be rich and slap her back. You have to be rich to be somebody in this world—"

"Irene, that's ridiculous."

It was as if he'd slapped her too, but she'd half-expected it. "Maybe it is, but I can't ever forget it."

"No, maybe not forget. But why couldn't you forgive it? She was, you said, a mere girl. A spoiled, thoughtless girl. How can you let a person like that influence your life after all these years?"

While he was talking, Peter had taken off his jacket, and as he turned to hang it over a chair, Irene could see, through the fabric of his shirt, the shadow of the scars that crisscrossed his back. "Oh, Peter," she said, getting up and coming to him, "I know you're right. It's stupid of me. You have endured so much more. So much worse. But you're a better person. You've forgiven the people who mistreated you."

"I've only tried, Reenee. I haven't succeeded yet. But I decided a long time ago that what they did to me already was bad enough. I wouldn't let them or the memory of them interfere with my life."

That sounded good, he thought. Too bad it wasn't true. Even tonight, the impotent hatred he'd felt for the butcher who nearly killed him had surfaced in Monsieur Neptune's elegant house. Would he never overcome the fury that ran just beneath the surface of his mind? Wasn't he letting that old devil's fists beat him throughout the interview with Neptune?

"But I'm not letting the girl interfere," Irene said. "I'm just telling you when and why I realized that I wanted more of life than was naturally going to come to me. That's why I took Papa's place on the boat. To get away. To be somebody."

"You *are* somebody. Do you think this man's job will make you something else? If so, I don't want you to take it. I love you like you are, Reenee."

He didn't understand. She knew he wanted to, but how could she convey what it all meant when she'd never really comprehended it herself? "I want to do this so that we can afford to live well when Mama and my sisters come. I want the girls to have decent clothes and food and beds of their own. I don't want them to drag themselves to a factory and be treated like dumb animals twelve hours a day. I want them to have time to read and go to church and take baths and meet good men like you, Peter."

Peter shook his head. Of course she wanted a decent life for her family, but so did he, and he was more than willing and able to provide for them. While he knew the reason she had just given was truthful, he also knew it wasn't her primary concern. He recognized in her an elusive sense of purpose, a burning drive for something he couldn't grasp. He burned, too—for knowledge. But could she have the same slow fire inside, which required, instead, "things" to keep it fueled? How could a thoughtlessly autocratic child so far away, so long ago, have made an impression so deep and compelling? For the first time, it occurred to Peter that, love her as he did, he had no idea what sort of internal mechanism really made Irene who and what she was.

"He's a hard man, Irene. He says himself that he'll make it difficult for you, with no promise whatsoever. He could work you half to death and then send you home with nothing."

"I'm not afraid of work. I like it."

He *could* stop her. There was no doubt about that. If he told her how uneasy he was about this slick gentleman with the expensive clothes and furniture and sardonic, hungry look, she'd accede to his wishes. She'd give up whatever she was hoping for because she loved and respected him. She wouldn't argue or nag, or even cry at times when he might catch her at it, but still he feared that if he denied her this opportunity, one or both of them would be crushed in the smoking debris of her disappointment.

"Irene, I want you to be happy. How on earth this could please you is beyond me, but if it's what you want to do, I want you to do it."

"And you'll go to work for him too?"

Peter had almost forgotten that part of it. "I don't think so. I'm content with my job."

"Oh, Peter, please reconsider. I want you to be near me."

If she'd mentioned the increased wages, he'd have stuck to his position. It had made him furious when Neptune revealed that he'd consulted Peter's boss and knew all about his current wages. But if she wanted him near, that was a different matter. He mentally gritted his teeth and said, "If you want me to, I will. I have no particular fondness for the job I've got."

At four in the morning, Irene woke with a start. She'd been dreaming. Dreaming of failure. It had never crossed her mind before, but now the concept washed over her with full force.

What if she failed!

Neptune had expressed some doubts, and now they rose like ghosts before her. What if the hat and the muff *were* freaks? He was offering her an opportunity to be trained in a good job because he believed she had some mysterious potential talent; what if he was mistaken? If she disappointed him, all was lost. Everything she wanted would have come as close as her fingertips and then would be torn away from her. This, she knew, was her only chance. Opportunities for a better life seldom came once in a life; they never came twice.

She'd always believed that achievement of her goals lay in hard work and ambition, and she'd even recognized the element of luck, but she'd never realized that success might ultimately hinge on something as illusive and intangible as this mysterious potential talent Neptune claimed to discern in a hat and a muff.

Irene huddled down on her side of the bed, wrapping her arms around herself and shivering with fear. She realized for the first time that it wasn't simply her dreams for bettering her life that were at stake—it was the underlying pride that was the foundation of those dreams, the foundation of her being. She wasn't being *given* anything; she was being asked to *risk* everything.

She'd thought the road to success would be a wide thoroughfare paved with golden bricks. Now she saw that it was a dark, dangerous path that sloped down into a dense and terrifying unknown land. At least she wasn't alone. She had Peter—thank God! She lay back down, pulled the covers around them like a cocoon, and held him tightly. She moved her lips lightly over the scars on his back, the scars he wore outside instead of inside, like hers.

He didn't move or say anything, but she sensed he'd awakened. A subtle change in his breathing alerted her. "Peter," she whispered. "I know you don't understand this—I don't either. But I know I'd die if I didn't get to try."

He grasped the hand that circled around his chest and raised it to his lips. "I know, I know. I came to this country for the same kind of reason. I left behind safety and security because I simply *had* to. But, Reenee, I left behind someone who loved me. I'm afraid you might be doing the same thing."

She grabbed his shoulder and forced him to turn over. "Never, Peter! Never. Nothing will ever come between us. I promise you that!"

11

Peter went by himself to see Jacques Neptune the next day. When he returned he said nothing about what had transpired between them except for instructions he had been given: he was to report to the main offices of Neptune et Cie on Thirty-fifth between Fifth and Sixth at eight o'clock the next Thursday; Irene was to present herself at Neptune's office in the same building the following Monday. In the meantime she had the job of turning three yards of black fabric into a skirt and two yards of white into a high-necked shirtwaist. The fabric, the sketches of the pattern, and a pair of sensible shoes were in a bundle Neptune had sent along. There was no other communication.

Irene went into a frenzy of sewing. For all her questioning of Peter after his first two days, he said little about his new job when he came home, only that the people he worked with appeared to be amiable and the conditions were noticeably better than the other factory where he had worked. The labor itself, however, was going to be a challenge. Instead of cutting the same collar or cuff pattern from cheap furs day in and day out, at Neptune et Cie each garment was different and the furs were far more valuable. "It will be more interesting," Peter admitted, "but part of what I liked about my old job was the boredom."

"What do you mean?"

"It didn't require much attention, once the skills were mastered for each type of garment. That left my mind entirely free to think about whatever I'd been reading or studying. There's something to be said for a dull job."

Clad in her new uniform, Irene went to work with Peter on

Monday. She never even saw the front of the building because Peter guided her to the employees' entrance in an alley at the side. He delivered her to Neptune's outer office and reluctantly abandoned her. "Irene, if for any reason you want to leave, just come down to the cutting area and we'll walk out," he said before opening the door for her.

She was so nervous her stomach was knotting. She clutched at his arm and took a long, deliberate breath. "Thank you, Peter. I'll be all right, just knowing you're near."

Neptune's secretary was a woman of imposing girth with spectacles that pinched into the bridge of her nose and graying hair that was pulled into a tight bun. "Sit down, Mrs. Garrick," she barked, pointing to a chair. "Monsieur is busy just now. He will see you in a few moments. I am Miss Troutwhite." And with that, she went back to filing a stack of papers. Eventually there was a buzz from her desk and without even glancing up from her work she said, "you can go in now."

Neptune's large office was like a combination museum and library. Two walls were lined with bookshelves, while the wall opposite the window held an artfully arranged bank of glass cases containing stuffed animals so lifelike that Irene almost thought she caught glimpses of them moving from the corner of her eye. Neptune himself sat behind a wide expanse of desk and studied her as she studied the room. Finally he cleared his throat and gestured for her to sit down across from him.

"You will follow the same course of study as my other designers. There is only one teacher—me. And only one student—you. You will have the use of my library and will work at that table," he said, indicating a long antique table on the west side of the room. "I will assign you several animals a day to study. You will have pelts to examine as examples, and you will be responsible for finding out all you can, in a strictly academic sense, about them before going on to more practical areas of study. You do read, don't you?" Dear Lord, why hadn't he asked her that before!

"Yes, Clara taught me," Irene said proudly.

Neptune sighed with relief. "Good. Now, a few basic concepts before you begin. Furs were intended by nature to keep animals warm. Therefore, the colder the climate where the animal lives, the more dense the fur. This is why you must constantly refer to the stack of atlases I've set out for you. In a few years, if you are both studious and intuitive, you will be able to pick up a strange pelt, examine it, and tell where it came from to within a few miles. You may be able to tell the name of the trapper who caught it, even though the man is thousands of miles away, and you will be able to tell me to within a week the date upon which the animal was caught."

He paused for a moment and leaned back in his chair. She was taking this well enough. At least she looked like she was listening and comprehending. "The fur of a given animal changes throughout the year. In the fall the animal is sleek and fat, full of the abundant food that is available then, but its fur, while well-nourished, isn't yet thick. By midwinter the fur is dense and still in good condition. If the animal is young, but not too young, and in good health, this is the best time to take a prime pelt. By late winter the pelt is starting to deteriorate. Generally it's less glossy, the skin is thicker and harder to treat. It is called 'springy' or 'bucky.' Moreover, it is the mating season and many of the male pelts are chewed and bitten, especially those of minks, which are fierce, cruel animals. And in the summer the pelt is virtually useless. It is thin because of the warmer weather, and the nursing females are undernourished. It is vital to know as much as you can learn about world geography, climatic conditons, biology—"

"I see—"

"No, you don't yet, but you will. Now, there are two things that are basic to understanding the qualities of any fur." He turned around and pulled several pelts from a cabinet set under the windows. He tossed them on the desk between them.

"This is raccoon," he said, pushing one toward her. "Notice the long straight hairs—those are the guard hairs. Now, part the fur. Blow into it to separate it. The soft, woolly underfur is the fur fiber. That's what provides the density and warmth of a fur. Each hair is wavy or crinkled, and it holds the guard hairs apart. When the guard hairs stand up well, the fur is said to have 'life.' The proportion differs in types of animals and in individual animals. In a horse, for instance, there is less fur fiber and the guard hairs lie down sleekly. In a good beaver there is a large proportion of fur fiber and coarse guard hairs that are removed. The pelt is then referred to as 'plucked.' In a few weeks, if you stay, you will see all these processes."

If you stay. He wasn't going to let her forget for an instant that she was there on trial. Irene was overwhelmed with impressions—the information he was pouring forth, the grandeur of the room, and even her bemused awareness that his accent was almost nonexistent as he lectured.

"There are two other terms you'll come across frequently in your studies. I'll explain these and then leave you on your own to discover what you can. Furs are taken and transported either cased-handled or open-handled. Do you know what this means?"

"I have no idea," Irene admitted. "May I take notes?"

"I was wondering if and when you would ask!" Neptune said. He pulled a leather-covered notebook from the top drawer of his desk and shoved it across to her. It had her name embossed in gold on the lower-right corner of the front. Irene touched the lettering and glanced up at him, but his fierce expression warned her not to say anything.

"Now, have you ever skinned an animal?"

"Yes, in the village when I was a child. Rabbits and squirrels and such."

"How did you skin them?"

"My mother taught me to cut lengthwise along the front of the animal, then peel the skin back."

"Very good. The fur was then open-handled, cut open and laid out flat. That's the most common way to do it, though a few animals whose belly fur is the most useful are opened down the back, not the front. Beaver, wolf, badger, raccoon, and wolverine are all open-handled. But if you were to make your initial cut around the neck area and take the skin off like removing a sock, the pelt would be called cased-handled. Mink, fox, marten, weasel, and skunk are cased-handled, sometimes skin side out, sometimes pelt-side-out. You will learn the distinctions and reasons for them in time. For now I simply want you to know what the terms mean."

He stood up and walked to a bank of cases in the corner. Irene followed him. "Do you know what these animals are?"

Irene answered promptly. "The top is a skunk, the middle is a fisher, the bottom one is an otter."

He whirled around and stared at her, both impressed and angry. "You are better-informed than I was led to believe. How did you know them?"

She kept her expression bland. "I read the labels on the cases."

He glared at her for a moment, then suddenly laughed out loud. "Very good, Mrs. Garrick. Very good. Now, you will spend the day learning everything you can find out about the skunk, the fisher, and the otter. You may open the cases to study the animals and you may help yourself to any book in the room. This afternoon I will question you closely."

Without any further explanation, he left the room. Irene hardly knew where to start, but after a moment's reflection decided the first thing was to find out what the books were. Going shelf by shelf, occasionally taking one down to glance through when the title wasn't explanatory, she discovered that the library included many of the subjects Neptune had mentioned. Instead of merely books strictly about furs—of which there were relatively few—there were volumes on geography, history, natural science, weather, and even poetry. Irene perused the shelves for nearly an hour, certain that an initial familiarity with the collection would help her in the long run.

Neptune hadn't returned when she finished her first inspection, and she turned her attention to the three cases she was to study. The taxidermist had done a magnificent job. The skunk was posed backed up to a piece of log, tail upraised and fluffy, teeth exposed in a warning grin. The fisher was surrounded by reeds, and Irene assumed they were meant to indicate a wet natural habitat. The otter, too, looked like it must live near water. It had webbed feet, small ears, and a smooth pelt. Irene wrote down the names, one per page in her notebook, and went back to the bookshelves. She'd never seen any of these animals at home in the village and had certainly not come across them in the streets of New York. She was daunted by how much she had to learn.

There was still no sign of Neptune by one o'clock. Miss

Troutwhite had been in and out of the inner office several times, removing or leaving letters and papers. She hadn't spoken to Irene or even acknowledged her presence. Finally Irene set aside her notes, stretched and rubbed her eyes, then approached the formidable secretary. "The ladies' is down the hall and to the right," Miss Troutwhite said before Irene could even ask. "And your luncheon is on the table in the room to your left."

Irene followed her directions and found a small room with a tiny table crammed in among shelves of old files. There was a paper bag on the table and her name written on the outside. It contained a roast-beef sandwich with the crusts cut off (What was wrong with the crusts? Irene wondered), a square of cheese, and an apple. There was a kettle of water sitting on a gas ring behind the door and a tin of tea on a shelf above.

She ate hurriedly, immensely grateful for the food, since she'd been too nervous this morning to remember to bring a packed lunch. When she returned, Neptune was back in his office, busy with letters. He glanced up when she came in, but made no other acknowledgment of her presence. She noticed, however, that her notebook was not exactly where she'd left it. He must have looked at it to see what she was writing.

Shortly after she went back to work, Neptune had a visitor, a customer who was arranging to have a coat made for his wife as a surprise birthday present. It was as much a social call as a business one, however, and they chatted for some moments about mutual acquaintances. At one point Irene accidentally dropped her pencil and the visitor glanced at her questioningly. "My assistant, Miss . . ." Neptune snapped his fingers as if trying to remember a name. "She's doing some research for me."

Irene concealed a smile. He was really a fine actor. What's more, his accent, almost nonexistent when he spoke to her privately, was much more in evidence now. When the guest had gone, Neptune said, "Mrs. Garrick, come here for a moment. No, leave your notebook there. Who was that man?"

"Miss Troutwhite announced him as Mr. Jenkins. To judge by the conversation, he is a banker."

"Yes. What is the name of the hotel he is attempting to get me to invest in?"

"The Plaza. It was completed two years ago, he said."

"What is the range of the skunk?" he asked quickly, hoping to catch her off guard. For some perverse reason, he wanted to shake her calm efficiency.

But it didn't work. "North America from the Hudson Bay to Panama," she replied almost instantly, giving no indication of surprise at the sudden shift of subject.

He nodded. "How is assortment of skunk pelts determined, aside from the qualities of the individual pelts?"

"By the length and width of the white stripes," she answered quickly. "They are classed as blacks, shortstripes, longstripes, western longstripe, and . . ." She thought for a second. What *was* the other one! ". . . and southern broadstripes. The white fur takes dye satisfactorily but still won't match the rest of the pelt because the white hair is longer."

"You didn't have that in your notes before Mr. Jenkins was here."

"No, I was reading it while he was talking to you."

"And you still determined that he was a banker?"

"I couldn't help but hear. He has a very loud voice."

"Quite. I shall have to remember how very good you are at listening," he said. "Can you be as good at *not* listening?"

"If that's what you want."

He questioned her again at the end of the afternoon. She was prepared for almost all his queries, but it was dry, academic material that she rattled off. When she'd made her reports on the skunk, otter, and fisher, Neptune told her more about them. His lecture was lively and showed both the breadth of his knowledge and the depth of his love for the subject. Irene felt she'd learned more in those few minutes than she had all day. When he had covered each animal, he opened a large box he'd brought in and pulled out pelt after pelt. Otter, fisher, and skunk in several shades and conditions. He let her examine them carefully, explaining the origins and differences between them. "The otter is a water animal, the only weasel besides the mink that is aquatic. What do you suppose that means in regard to season?"

Irene looked at him blankly. "Season?"

"Have you observed that when the air and land warm in the spring—"

"—the water doesn't!" she finished, remembering how long they had to wait after the weather had become warm before they could bathe in the river at home in the village. "So the otter is living in cold conditions later into the spring than land animals."

He nodded, obviously pleased at how quickly she'd realized what he was getting at. "The otter has thick fur fiber and the pelt doesn't turn bucky, but a spring-taken otter pelt is identified in a different way. Look at this one. Look closely."

Irene took the pelt to the window, ran her fingers through the thick fiber, and blew into it to see the skin, as he'd taught her. "The guard hairs are strange at the ends. Some of the tips bend over."

"Yes, it's called 'singeing.' This undesirable condition usually occurs because of poor treatment of the pelt after it's taken, or in the chemical processing. In the otter, however, it indicates it was taken late in the spring. What would you do with this pelt?"

"I don't know. It would be a shame to discard it. It's very thick and soft, and the skin seems nice. Could you somehow cut off the tips of the guard hairs. Shave it?"

"Then they would look like the rest but feel prickly when you ran your hand against the growth."

"Yes, I see. Then how could you use this pelt?" she asked.

Neptune took the pelt back, pulled a dull knife from the desk drawer, and slipped a rubber protector on his thumb. Running the knife against the fur, he grasped the singed guard hairs and jerked sharply, pulling them out in one section. After doing this several times, he handed the pelt back for her inspection. "This is called plucking or unhairing. Of course, it's normally done at the beginning of the processing, not at the end. You'll see all this done in a few weeks when you've studied the basics of the furs."

After a few more comments about the pelts, he gathered them up and put them back into the box. "It's later that I realized. Your husband must be waiting for you. Run along, Mrs. Garrick."

"May I take one book with me? I promise to bring it back in the morning. I wasn't quite through reading the fisher section."

"You may take any of the books you want without asking."

He stood at the desk and watched as she gathered her coat, the book in question, and her notebook. He discovered, to his immense irritation, that his hands were shaking with nerves and excitement. She really was extraordinarily bright and fast. She'd learned more in a day than he would have expected anyone to learn in a week. And in addition to the ability to study a subject, she had a quick, intuitive mind.

But he must not let himself get his hopes up too much. She had to have much more than intelligence—she had to have enormous drive, which he'd suspected from the beginning that she possessed. But there was also the matter of talent. That, in fact, was the key to everything. Without talent, the most brilliant, driven person could attain only a high level of competency in anything. The other designers he employed, Hadley and Delman, were living proof of that. Talent was the magic ingredient. But he couldn't even hope to test her for that until he'd instilled a tremendous amount of knowledge into that very pretty head.

Just as well he would have to wait awhile. He was frightened of the terrible disappointment in store for both of them—himself just as much as her—if it turned out she was lacking the magic. For now he could enjoy her presence, her brains, her golden beauty, and the ambition that made her seem to vibrate and shimmer, without facing the possibility that it was all for nothing.

She was obviously intimidated by his gruff manner. That had been quite deliberate on his part. If he could bully her into running away, then she wasn't fit to deal with the sometimes rude capriciousness of the customers she might someday be in contact with. She was also going to have to cope with the fact that she was entering a business that served primarily women but was run almost exclusively by men. If she took a place on the staff at the end of her study, there would be resentment that she'd have to be strong enough to ignore. So far she'd stood up well to his tests, but time might prove she didn't have the necessary backbone.

"Mrs. Garrick," he said as she opened the door to leave, "you've done quite well today." She smiled then, the first real smile he'd gotten from her. "Good night, Mrs. Garrick."

She talked all the way home and found a willing, interested audience in Peter. It was he, in fact, who suggested a trip to the Astor Free Library on Lafayette Street. They'd gone there often while attending classes at Cooper Union, and Irene expected to get more information, though that facility, they found, had nothing on the subject that wasn't in Neptune's private collection.

"Peter, did you know the skunk is beautiful only when it's fresh?" Irene asked, hanging on his arm as they walked the rest of the way home and talking a mile a minute. "If it's not cared for it loses its luster. In fact, the only good pelts are the ones that are put on ice as soon as they're taken and kept that way until they're treated. Neptune et Cie does little business in skunks and it's a shame. They're a lovely pelt, but Monsieur says people expect them to smell bad. They don't, but women especially are afraid the first time they get caught in the rain their friends will hold their noses. Now, the otter . . ."

He smiled at her bubbling chatter. It was good to see her so happy and enthusiastic. Maybe he'd been wrong to worry about this job. He hoped so.

Irene could hardly sleep that night; her brain was too full of new and fascinating information, her heart too full of hope. In the morning she was awake and alert early and was ready to go to work a full half-hour before Peter.

For the rest of the first week, Irene continued as she had the first day, studying the most commonly used furs. One whole day was given over to rabbits. Although Neptune's company had little use for that fur, it was the most commonly used in the world and she could not know the business without knowing about it. There was also a whole day of study of sheep and all their variations—karakul, Persian lamb, broadtail. She studied mink, badger, possum, beaver, fitch, squirrel, fox, raccoon, mole, seal, and muskrat. The next week she was instructed to investigate the lesser-used furs—

civet, goat, hamster, leopard, nutria, pahmi, suslik, wolverine, ocelot, hare, cat, vicacha, and a dozen others.

Then on Friday morning of the second week Neptune changed the routine. "Mrs. Garrick, sit down," he said as she came in. "I want to tell you about our most valuable fur—the *crème de la crème*, the sable."

"What does that mean, *crème de la crème*?"

"The best of the best."

He summoned Miss Troutwhite and gave her a note. "In the cold safe in the basement," he said.

"Very well, monsieur."

He stood up, the better to lecture on an important subject. "The sable is the most desirable fur in the world. It is a species of marten, a high-strung, vicious animal that lives in Siberia, northern Canada, and China. But the Siberian pelts are the only ones of any quality. What do you know of Siberia?"

"I know where it is on the map," Irene said.

"It is a vast, trackless area. The cruelest part of a cruel land. The weather is frigid and devastating, the distances beyond comprehension, and many hundreds of people who have gone there in search of the sable—or the sobol, as the Russians call it—have never returned. The best pelts come from an area northeast of Lake Baikal in the Muiski Mountains. Look that up on your maps later."

Irene scribbled furiously in her notebook, wondering if her spelling was correct enough to find it later, but she knew better than to interrupt him now to ask anything so mundane.

"The sable cannot be shot," Neptune went on, "because that would damage the precious pelt. Instead, it is hunted with dogs who are trained to tree the animal, which is then trapped in nets that are thrown into the trees. It can take hours in the frigid temperatures for a man, using long poles, to force a single creature into the net. As far as anyone knows, there is no way to persuade the animals to breed in captivity, though someday that may be done.

"The inferiors pelts—which are only inferior in a relative sense—come onto the market in the usual way, through China or Japan or in European markets. But the best pelts, the *crème de la crème*, are all, by law, turned over to the Romanoffs. Do you know who they are?''

Irene shook her head, ''I'm sorry—no.''

''The Russian ruling family. The Tzars select what they wish for their own use and derive a large part of their income from the sale of the rest. These precious furs the Romanoffs sell are known as crown sables. Ah, Miss Troutwhite, I was beginning to be afraid someone had locked you up in the safe.''

The secretary came in carrying, at respectful arm's length, a group of furs. Unlike most pelts Irene had seen, these were the skins of the entire animals with a leather thong through their noses tying them together. Her first thought was that they were short, stocky creatures, not the long, sinuous weasel shape she'd expected. She commented on this as Neptune untied the leather thong.

''That's very perceptive of you, Mrs. Garrick. When the sable is skinned, the trapper turns it flesh-side-out and stretches the wet, cleaned skin as wide as possible. This is because it is so tremendously valuable that he must hide it under his clothes in order to transport it. If it were stretched to its natural length, it would hang out of his shirt or coat and be seen. It is turned fur-side-out when it gets to market. You see these pelts even have the tails, which are valuable themselves.''

''For ornamentation?''

''Occasionally, but usually for artists' brushes. The finest, most expensive artists' brushes, as you might suppose.''

He had finished untying the pelts as he spoke, and came around to show them to Irene at close range. He handed them to her, one at a time.

Irene laid them across her lap and ran her hands lightly over them. They were all a deep blue-black color and incredibly soft, with dense fur fiber and fine, glossy guard hairs that stood erect. She had expected the fur to look and feel like mink, since the animal was similar to the mink. But it was in a different class entirely. This fur made the best mink seem coarse.

Still cold from storage, the pelts warmed immediately at her touch. They were the most exquisitely beautiful objects she had ever seen or felt, and the mere act of touching them very nearly took her breath away. Even if Neptune had not told her about them, the difficulties of finding, trapping, and selling them, the romantic association with the rulers of Russia—even without that information, she would have known immediately that these were the most valuable, the most beautiful pelts in the world. "Crown sables," she said softly as she held one up to her face to feel it against the sensitive skin of her cheek.

Neptune watched her and felt a deep excitement—partly intellectual, and, to his surprise, partly sexual—at her obvious appreciation of the treasured pelts. He turned away and went back to the concealing safety of his desk for fear she would notice. But there was little chance of that. Her whole attention was concentrated on the pelts. It was as if she'd forgotten his existence. She'd put one over her shoulder and, tilting her head, was caressing her own face in its luxurious silkiness. How breathtakingly lovely the dark fur was against her fair hair.

"Mrs. Garrick, put the furs back on the desk," he said finally, sensing that he'd never regain her attention without removing them from her grasp.

"Oh . . . yes, of course," she said in a soft voice. She sounded almost hypnotized. She laid the furs between them, one at a time as he'd given them to her. As she put each one down, she touched it in a lingering way.

"It can take years to accumulate enough pelts for a coat," he said, resuming his lecture with some reluctance. "Not only are they rare and expensive, but you must get an absolutely perfect match and sometimes the pelts that are available are not right for what you're collecting. A furrier can have an enormous amount of money tied up in a collection for a very long time before he can make up and sell a coat. A sable coat can cost up to twenty thousand dollars."

This almost brought her out of her trance. "Twenty thousand dollars?"

"Over the years I have collected and made up six sable coats and have partial matches for three more in cold storage."

As he was speaking to her, he noticed that her hand kept reaching out, as if by its own volition rather than conscious thought, and lightly stroking the pelts. "Mrs. Garrick!"

"Yes?" She took her hand back.

"I believe you'd better get back to your studies." He pushed a button to summon Miss Troutwhite, who took away the furs while Irene went back to her own long table and started taking down books for the day's work. He watched her, being careful not to appear to be paying any attention. She'd escaped the spell of the sables and was moving as briskly and efficiently as ever, but every now and then he would notice her lay her pencil aside and stare at the wall for a moment or two.

He had a luncheon appointment which he'd looked forward to, but it seemed to go on forever. He hardly tasted the food and found the conversation of these friends, normally highly stimulating, to be boring and trivial today. He started thinking up reasons why he must return to the office, avoiding the real reason, that he wanted to know how Irene was getting along. Was she still thinking about the sables? Still touching her finger lightly to her cheek at intervals as if recalling the silky touch of the furs?

When he finally escaped, it was late afternoon. Returning to the office and surprising Miss Troutwhite, who hadn't expected him back at all, he found Irene preparing to go home. She had tidied up her table and put back all the books she'd been using. She had on her coat and had tucked her notebook under her arm to take home and study. "Good night, Mrs. Garrick," he said.

As she left, she paused at the door as if to say something.

"What is it?" he asked.

Still she hesitated. "Nothing. Good night, Monsieur Neptune."

He stayed at the desk for some moments. Odd how empty this room seemed without her. It had always been a very comfortable place to be by himself. A sort of den, like any cautious animal might retreat to. But now it seemed large and vaguely untenanted after she left. He was deep in this thought when there was a light tap on the door. "Come in, Miss Troutwhite," he said irritably.

"It's not Miss Troutwhite," Irene said. "I came back to tell you something."

"What?"

"Monsieur Neptune, someday I will be what you said, *crème de la crème*. And I will have one of those coats. A crown sable."

He waited for her to go on, but she had said it all.

12

"Are you happy, Irene?" Clara asked her when they had a late supper together after the final New York performance of *Captain Brassbound's Conversion*.

"I'm happy, Clara."

"I didn't really need to ask. I could see it in your face. "What are you doing now with Monsieur Neptune?"

This opened the floodgates. Irene told how she'd been assigned to learn firsthand every stage of fur processing, how scraped pelts were salted and then soaked in solutions of borax or formic acid to cure them; how different pelts were dried, some in vast tumbling drums of sawdust, others hung in heated rooms so the air could circulate; how the pelts were placed in a tramping machine to soften them. She rattled off to Clara all the different types of dyeing and bleaching and shearing. "You see, most pelts have the ability to shed water, and so they also shed dye. You have to remove this oil with an alkaline solution before you can top-blend or saturate the pelt. Mostly the alkali is soda ash or ammonia, but they used to use urine. Can you imagine? Urine!" She suddenly stopped, stricken. "Oh, Clara! I've been talking for ages. You didn't want to know all this. I'm sorry. I've become very boring."

Clara laughed. "I don't understand a fraction of it, but I don't mind your telling me. Your eyes sparkle like stars when you explain. You are really fascinated with all this, aren't you?"

"Yes, I am," Irene said, taking Clara's hands in a childish gesture of enthusiasm.

"And Monsieur Neptune? Are you as fascinated with him?"

Clara said. She wished she didn't sound so old-maidish and priggish, but she had to ask.

Irene didn't hear the warning tone. "Oh, he's wonderful, Clara. He knows so much. It's amazing. And he explains everything so I can understand immediately. I don't know why his head doesn't just burst with all that knowledge stored up."

"Then you like him?"

"Like him? He's probably the smartest man in the world. Next to Peter, of course."

"I mean, as a man."

"As a man? What . . . ? Oh, Clara, it's not like that at all!"

"Are you sure?"

Irene let go of her hands and drew herself up. "Clara, what do you think of me to ask that?"

"Irene, my dear, I'm not questioning your morals or intentions, I'm inquiring into his."

Placated, Irene said, "Oh, no. Monsieur thinks of me only as a student. I don't imagine he's even noticed that I'm a woman at all. He just enjoys teaching me."

For a moment her naiveté annoyed Clara. "Irene, why do you suppose he's doing all this for you? Don't you see? Someday, some way, he'll expect to be reimbursed for all the time and expense he's investing in you. Nobody does all that for a stranger for nothing!"

Irene looked at her for a long moment and said, "You did, Clara."

"Yes, I did. And gladly. But I had no ulterior motive, but a love of teaching and a recognition that you had the mind and personality to absorb and appreciate what I had to offer."

"Can't Monsieur Neptune feel the same way?"

"There isn't a man alive who could look at you and miss the fact that you're a woman—and an increasingly beautiful one, at that. But perhaps I'm merely getting cynical in my outlook," she said. She felt guilty about casting a shadow on Irene's happiness. Changing the subject abruptly, she said, "I'm sorry you won't be able to come see our train leave tomorrow. It should be quite an exciting event. Miss Terry has completely captured the hearts of New Yorkers, especially the newspaper reporters. There will be a band and a big crowd to see her off to Chicago."

"I'm sorry you're leaving, Clara. I always feel terribly lonely when you aren't near."

"And I get lonely for you, too. But it will be for only a few months. Then Miss Terry will go back to England—"

"Oh, Clara, you wouldn't go with her, would you?"

"No, she has a dresser there. I'll return to New York. I always expected to go back to being a governess, and there are things about teaching I miss, but I've become very spoiled about having so much of my time free to do as I choose. All in all, this job suits me much better. After having served with Miss Terry, I shouldn't have any trouble getting another job with another production. By then you'll be too busy for me anyway. Your family will be here."

"I'd never be too busy for you, even if I had six families. But I am looking forward to the day they arrive. Only a short time now. It will be grand, being with Mama and the girls!"

"Don't expect them to be as you remember," Clara warned.

"Oh, I know. They will be older. Stefania and the twins aren't babies anymore, but that will be even better."

"I hope so," Clara said, surprised at how gloomy she sounded to herself. She hoped Irene didn't notice.

Irene glanced at the small watch pinned at her bosom. "I had no idea how late it was. Peter must be waiting outside for me. I must go. Clara, I'll miss you."

You won't *miss* me as much as you once did, but you *need* me more than ever, Clara thought. As Irene's goals took a step closer to attainment, she was in more danger than ever. Not physical, or even financial, but emotional. Her mind might be full of new and valuable information, her manner might have changed, but her heart was still fragile and untried and terribly, terribly delicate.

Clara hugged her and said, "Be careful, Irene."

"Be careful of what, Clara?"

"I don't know, dear. I don't know."

September already, Neptune thought. Where had the time gone? In a few months it would be time to start making the decision as to whether to keep Irene on and add her to the staff, he thought as he sat in his office waiting for her to arrive. He'd mapped out her course of study in a satisfactory manner. Of course, they'd barely scratched the surface, but she was a quick learner and would continue to master information. He had anticipated that it would take at least two and a half years to teach her all she must know. The usual apprenticeship was four years. But she had learned at an amazing rate, and maybe in a year and a half—two years at the most—she would be armed with all the mental and artistic ammunition she needed to be a valuable and trusted designer.

The next stage, of course, would be to install her as a genuine employee. He'd heard mutterings about her: who was the young blond who was in his office all the time? Miss Troutwhite reported that the gossip favored the theory that Irene was being trained as a new secretary to replace Troutwhite herself. She, the only employee besides Peter who knew better, found it amusing. This was what Chandler thought, and Neptune hadn't bothered to disabuse him of the idea.

Irene was, as usual, a few minutes early. Her notes had outgrown the original notebook and she now had three, whose pages were covered with her tiny, neat handwriting. She took off her coat, put her notes on her own desk, and came to stand before his to get her daily assignment. "Good morning, monsieur," she said, pert as a well-prepared schoolgirl.

"Irene, today you're going to see the salesroom." There, he'd said it. There was no turning back. By this evening he might know if all his hopes for her had been in vain. Now that he'd filled her mind with information, he had to see what sort of taste she really had.

"Very good," she said calmly. Either she didn't sense the import of this or she was concealing her feelings.

He led her downstairs through a sort of vast closet. Racks and racks of coats, stoles, wraps, and throws were lined down the center. To the sides were banks of compartments containing hats, muffs, and even fur-trimmed purses. "These are the garments and accessories that are already made up for showing or for purchase. Many ladies will find something that suits and fits them without having any custom work done. Others prefer to see examples of different styles and furs and place a specific order," he explained. "These lovely butterflies fluttering about are the models," he said, smiling at an extremely attractive blond with hair pulled into a loose chignon on top of her head.

"Out there are the customers," he said, putting his hand to the knob of a large door. "You will open your notebook and appear to be making a diagram of the furniture groupings. Do not look like you are with me, but stay near enough to hear and observe nevertheless. Do you understand?"

"Yes, monsieur," Irene said, opening her notebook. This was the beginning of the real testing, she sensed. Though it was warm in the storeroom, Irene felt such a strong attack of nerves that she shivered, but quickly covered the involuntary motion by brushing at some imaginary lint on her skirt. Monsieur Neptune was still largely a mystery to her, but she had learned some things about him. One was that he admired self-assurance and so she was always careful to exhibit this trait even when, like now, she was far from feeling it.

Neptune opened the door and she followed him into the large ground-level area that fronted the street. It was furnished like a large living room or hotel lobby, though Irene, never having been in a hotel, didn't make the comparison. Clusters of exquisite furniture huddled in intimate little groups. Ornamental screens, artfully placed, set each group apart without appearing to be actual barriers. And they weren't. A good deal of visiting was going on between several groups.

"Jacques, you naughty man!" a birdlike woman wearing muted violet silk and festooned in pearls shrieked, all but flying at him. Irene looked down at her notebook, up at the ceiling as if measuring it, and moved a few feet away.

"Florence, you've not been here for many months," he replied, his accent silky and debonair. "I was afraid you had abandoned me for Revillon Frères."

She let him kiss her hand before tittering. "Would I do such a thing to my oldest and dearest friend?"

"I hear you've been in the country, lucky you," he said, guiding her to an Empire sofa covered in rose-striped taffeta and sitting down beside her. Irene moved around behind them.

"And I'm going right back, my darling. How anyone can bear to remain in the city all the time, I can't imagine. I braved the elements today, however, because I must throw myself on your mercy."

"Ah? Well, I shall endeavor to be merciful, lovely lady."

"Reg and I are going to Finland or Sweden or one of those awful cold places later in the autumn. Some sort of embassy affair, bankers and dull people like that from all over the globe. We'll be there for simply ages and ages. A month at least. And I simply must have a few respectable coats."

Neptune nodded as he listened to this spate of snobbery. "You require warmth and style both."

"So divine of you to understand, darling. Reg, of course, must never know what it costs, even if it is all his fault. Dragging me away like that, just at the beginning of the season. I'm afraid all my friends will forget who I am."

"How could anyone forget anyone like you?" Neptune said smoothly.

Irene smiled to herself. She didn't know him well by any means, but she knew him well enough to recognize sarcasm. Apparently he knew his customer wouldn't, however.

"I think something in fox," Neptune was saying. "Let me get some sketches together for you. Can you come back tomorrow? Or better, let me take you to the St. Regis for luncheon and we can talk about it more after I've given it some thought."

When she'd gone, Neptune summoned Irene. "What do you think?"

"Of her? She's a very silly woman."

He laughed. "Of course she is. She's also very, very rich and doesn't care what she spends as long as she gets something that other women admire and envy. Come back to my office and we'll talk about what she needs."

When they were back on either side of his big desk, Miss Troutwhite came in with tea. Up until now this had been a service only to Neptune. When Irene wanted tea, she went into the little closet down the hall and prepared it herself. Today there were two cups and saucers. So, she thought, Miss Troutwhite recognizes that this is a turning point as well. For some reason, this scared her more than ever. She swallowed hard.

"Will you be mother?" Neptune asked.

"What?"

"That means, will you pour? No, put the cup on the saucer first, then hand it to me with the handle pointing toward me. That's right. Now find out if I want one lump or two."

Irene was completely confused. "Lumps?"

"Of sugar. In that little silver pot."

Irene opened the top and stared at the neat cubes. "How wonderful! How do they make it stay that way in little squares?"

He smiled fondly at her enthusiasm. There was a certain joy in ignorance that he'd almost forgotten. How charming it was to see someone get such pleasure out of the discovery of something so common as a sugar cube. "I have no idea how they stay that way, Irene."

She finished serving the tea according to his instructions, and after staring into her cup with fascination as the cubes dissolved, and then taking the first sip of her own, said shyly, "I like knowing these things, monsieur. Thank you."

Neptune looked down into the depths of his cup. There was something so unaffected, so genuine in her words that he felt an odd warmth in his chest. It was, he was afraid, the beginnings of love—if he remembered what real love was. What a fool he'd be to fall in love with her!

"I'm glad of that, Mrs. Garrick," he said gruffly. "Now let's see what you've really learned. What about Florence—the customer you saw me with. What shall we make for her?"

"I heard you mention fox. I think that's a good idea. It's warm and she's slim enough to wear it well. But not red fox. Silver, I think."

"Why?"

"Because red fox would make her look sallow. Her coloring isn't very good and red would make her eyes look bloodshot and a dark fur of any glossy sort would make her hair appear even duller than it is."

"You have the makings of a vicious critic."

"I didn't mean to be unkind."

"I know you didn't, and you're absolutely correct. Her coloring is the first consideration. The most lovely fur in the world could make her look like a hag if it's not the right one for her. What style?"

Irene had some ideas already, but was hesitant about revealing them for fear he would find fault. And yet, to him, hesitancy was itself a fault. "Are Finland and Sweden as cold as she thinks?"

"Yes."

She took a deep breath and plunged in. "Then the coats should be long, with a collar that can turn up against the wind if necessary."

This was a glimpse into the remainder of her education with him—if he kept her. Her common sense and artistic sense (if she in fact proved to have any) were going to have to be tempered with social sense, of which she had none. "That would be true if she were going to be out-of-doors. But I don't imagine Florence will set foot outside except to get in and out of rather elegant conveyances."

Wrong! The first thing she ventured to say was wrong, but she instantly understood why. "Then a little shorter, so she will not be stepping on it, and a cowled collar that will not disturb her hair. Sleeves like this"—she held out one arm and indicated a sleeve line—"so that any style dress can be worn underneath. A slight flare—"

"No, don't tell me. Sketch it," he said, pushing a blank pad of paper toward her.

Irene looked at it as if she'd never seen paper before. "Sketch it? I'm not an artist. I can't draw things."

Neptune felt his heart sink. Could this be it, the beginning of the end? He stared at her wordlessly. How could she possibly convey what she had in mind if she couldn't sketch? No, no, it wasn't the definitive obstacle, only another hurdle to be overcome. He hoped!

She realized something was terribly wrong. "I'm . . . I'm sorry. I didn't know. Monsieur! I can make it. I know in my mind exactly what I mean. Let me make it!"

"Turn you loose with a thousand dollars' worth of silver fox—just to see what's on your mind?"

"No, not the fox. Rabbit. Fabric. Paper. Anything. Just let me show you. Yes, paper. I'll make you a pattern. Please, monsieur."

"Troutwhite! Bring some large sheets of paper and a pair of shears!" he bellowed.

The secretary all but ran away and was back in a remarkably short time with a roll of tissue. Irene rolled it out and got down on the floor on her hands and knees. Without pause, she started folding and snipping. Scraps were everywhere, but in fifteen minutes she was standing up with an armload of cut tissue. "Miss Troutwhite, have you any pins?"

The secretary, confused by the hectic activity and the rather frantic looks on the faces of both her employer and the girl, hurried away to find pins.

Irene plopped back onto the floor and started jabbing pins into the tissue. Neptune sat down, bemused and perplexed, where he couldn't see what she was doing, only hear the busy rustling. Moments later her head appeared over the edge of the desk. "May I show you, monsieur?"

"Please do."

She stood and gingerly slipped her arms into the flimsy, rattling mock-coat. He was astonished. Even executed in tissue paper, it was recognizably a coat with potential. The collar, in fur, would drape beautifully, exposing Florence's neck, which was one of her best features. The sleeves were full at the armhole, but tapered gracefully to snug wrists. The body of the coat began a gentle flare just below the waist that would make the skirt sway nicely with movement.

He glanced at his secretary, who had remained to watch. "Miss Troutwhite, send these pattern pieces downstairs to be made up immediately in possum. That will approximate the appearance well enough to judge the lines of the pattern."

"No," Irene said. "I made it to fit myself to show you. It needs to be longer in the hem and shorter in the sleeve for the other lady."

Neptune stared at her. "How did you know Florence's sleeves always have to be shortened?"

Irene was surprised at the question. "I could see her arms," she said matter-of-factly.

"Very well. Don't make the changes. I want to see how it will look on someone without dragging in Florence as a model. Let's talk about other coats for her."

* * *

Neptune left his office that night a happy man. It had been a busy day, indeed. Irene had made up patterns for two other garments, one a short cape with a clever diagonal cut that would send Florence into ecstasies, and a cross-over stole with scalloped finishing at the short ends. He'd pulled in Hadley, who had no taste but an excellent eye and a talent for drawing, to instruct Irene how to convey her ideas with pencil and paper instead of tissue and scissors. Hadley had been clearly confused and alarmed by this and stood around shuffling his feet and waiting for further explanations, but Neptune had given him none. He'd explain it all to the man tomorrow.

Toward late afternoon the unlined, unfinished possum coat had been brought to him. Even with ragged edges, no ornamentation, in cheap fur, it was lovely. "Put it on, Mrs. Garrick," he said.

"Do you like it?" she asked, turning so he could see how the back hung.

"Very much. Do you?"

"Yes."

"Then it's yours."

"Mine? Oh, monsieur, I couldn't take it!"

"Why not? It's the fruit of your imagination. Throughout your life you will pour out your thoughts and watch other women walk away wearing them. It's only right that this—your first—should belong to you."

Irene pulled the coat around her and sat down slowly. "My first. Does this mean there will be more? Have I passed your test?"

He reached across and took her small hand. "How could you ask? You are everything I hoped."

"Oh, monsieur!" She clutched his hand.

"But this is only the beginning, you understand. You have only begun to learn what you must know."

"Yes! Yes, I want you to teach me everything."

13

Irene hardly slept for the next month. Both her nerves and the hours in the day were strung taut. In addition to the increased workload Neptune had put on her willing shoulders, she had to prepare for her family's arrival. It hardly seemed possible that the long-awaited event was finally going to happen.

Irene's own most earnest desire was to get an apartment away from the Polish section of the Lower East Side, but she knew Mama and the girls would need to be near their own people and language for a short time until they adjusted and became Americanized. After hours and hours of diligent searching, she and Peter found two second-floor apartments on St. Mark's Place just east of Second Avenue. The location, on the very edge of the Polish community, was ideal for them, as it was only a four-block walk to get the Fifth Avenue bus uptown to work.

The two apartments were not connected, but Irene persuaded the landlord to let them make a doorway through one wall. This made the two small apartments much more like a single home. Mama and the twins could have the bedroom in one apartment and Aggie and Stefania could use the main room there as their own. The tiny kitchen area would be left as it was. In the other apartment, Peter and Irene would have the small bedroom, and the main room could be used as a sitting room and dining room for everybody. The kitchen there, hardly more than five by five, would be Irene and Peter's study. The toilet was just down the hall and they had to share it with only two other families, a real luxury.

Had Irene never seen the inside of Monsieur Neptune's home, this apartment would have seemed palatial to her. It was much more space than they'd had back home in the village where Mama and Papa had slept in a curtained-off area of the single main room and all the children slept in the low-ceilinged loft above. But Irene *had* seen another sort of home, however fleetingly, the sort that had a whole room just for eating, another just for sitting and reading, and a space as large as her new bedroom just for coming in the door and taking off coats.

She couldn't make the apartment bigger or more elegant, but she could certainly make it clean, and she scrubbed until the skin on her fingertips looked like white raisins and her knees ached from kneeling. After her long hours at Neptune et Cie, she came home and stayed up half the night making curtains, mopping the floors, or cleaning the second-hand furniture she was getting piece by piece from street vendors.

For the first time when Peter took her in his arms at night, she only wanted to sleep. "You're working too hard," he said, half-concerned, half-insulted.

"Only until Mama and the girls come," she reassured him.

Even Neptune noticed the change in her. "You look like you're fighting to stay awake," he commented one day. "Are you ill?"

"Oh, no. I've just been working hard at getting ready for my family to come."

"Family! Your family is actually coming here?" he asked.

"Yes, we have sent the passage money to my mother and my four sisters. My father is dead and my brother disappeared many years ago when he and I first came to this country. My husband and I have been saving since we were married to bring them to America."

"Then you must take a few days off to show them around."

"May I really?" Irene had considered asking for half a day, but had decided against it. She was determined to find time for both her work and her family and didn't want to give Neptune the impression that the two were in conflict, since they wouldn't be.

By Tuesday night Irene was in such a state of excitement that she couldn't eat or sleep. The ship was due to dock at seven in the morning. At five she was cleaning the kitchen one more time. "Let's go early," she said when Peter was awakened by the clatter of pans and came to see what she was doing.

"Very well, we can stop in church on the way," he said.

She would never understand about Peter and religion. He went to church frequently, but not with the same motivation other good Catholics seemed to have. Like her, he preferred not to attend formal services, but went to refresh some private need of his own. Most often, at least one evening a week, he went to St. Stanislas to talk to the priest. He'd invited her along when they were first married, and she'd accepted the invitation, but although these evenings had left her more impressed and proud of his erudition than ever, she'd been bored by their philosophical conversations. They could go on for hours about church history and dogma and sometimes even laugh at each other's remarks. It was a mystery to her how he could so thoroughly enjoy these evenings.

But perhaps he was right about going to church today. Her Catholic conscience told her she ought to thank God for bringing her family back together, but in the back of her mind she felt a resentful conviction that it was not God, but she and Peter who'd worked this miracle by their own determination and diligence.

They were at the docks at a quarter to seven, just in time to see the ship appear out of the morning mist and nudge its way into place. "Oh, Peter! It's really happening!" Irene said. She was laughing and crying and had an almost uncontrollable urge to break into a wild dance of some sort. "After all these years, only a few more minutes! I'm so glad we spent the extra money to send them second-class tickets. I'd hate to think of Mama and the girls having to go through Ellis Island like I did. I was so frightened that day."

She searched for faces in the crowd leaning on the rails, but didn't see her family. The gangplank was let down and people started disembarking. There were cries of recognition, tears, hugging, and a babble of languages, but Irene still didn't see them. Had they missed the boat? Was this God's way of punishing her for not giving him full credit?

"There! Is that them?" Peter asked, pointing at a group just coming across the gangplank.

"No, I don't think . . . Yes! Yes, that's Mama!"

She looked so little and dumpy and gray that Irene hardly recognized her. Had she always been this way? Irene pushed her way through the crowd and hugged the little woman as she stepped onto the pier. "Mama! It's me, Irene!" she said as Zofia cringed away from her. *"Przywitać, Mama. Przywitać!"* Welcome!

Her eyes were red. She was weeping and cowering. "Irina? Is that you?"

"Yes, Mama, it's me. Oh, Mama, I'm so happy to see you."

"Where's Teo?"

"He couldn't be here. I'll explain all about it when we get you to your new home."

"Are you sure you're Irina? You don't look like my daughter and you don't talk like my daughter . . ."

Irene knew her Polish was rusty; she hadn't used it for years. She and Peter always spoke English. And she knew her appearance had changed, but how could Mama doubt it was her? "I've just grown up, Mama. I'm Irina."

"Then where is my son? Where is Teo?"

"I'll explain all about Teo later," she said, turning her attention to the girls. "Aggie, is this you?" she said, putting her arm around a tall girl standing next to Zofia.

"Yes, I am Agnieszka," the girl answered. Her eyes, too, were red with crying. Her coloring was much like Irene's, fair hair, pale eyes, but she was too pale, pasty really, and too thin. She must have found the ocean crossing very difficult. Once on dry land she'd feel better.

Irene threw her arms around her favorite sister. "Oh, Aggie, you're going to be so happy here. We can have fun together, just like when we were girls."

"Yes . . . ?" Agnieszka said dully.

Irene had expected Aggie to be as exuberant and excited as she herself was. After all, they'd been very close and this day was the culmination of a long-held dream. But she needed to rest first, naturally. She must have been sick on the voyage—so many people were. When she felt better, she'd be her old cheerful self.

"And you are Lillie and Cecilia. I'll bet you don't remember me at all," she said to the twins. Two pairs of frightened and vaguely sullen eyes in identical thin faces stared back at her. "I'm your sister Irene—Irina. You're going to live with me and my husband now."

They said nothing, just looked at her like a pair of scrappy owls. Irene resolved that the first thing she must do is buy them all some new clothes. Theirs were a disgrace, all of them. Dark, shabby, and not very clean. "And you are Stefania," she said to the youngest girl. "I know you don't remember me. You were a baby when I came here."

"Hello, sister," Stefania said. She was a young duplicate of Zofia, plump and untidy, but without her mother's animation. As polite as her reply was, her voice was dull and her manner wooden.

"Well, it's wonderful that you're all here. Oh, here is my husband. Peter, I'm sorry I ran off that way. These are my mother and my sisters Aggie and Lillie and Cecilia and Stefania. This is my husband, Peter Garrick."

Zofia, who had been occupied with weeping into a gray handkerchief, looked up. "You said you married Piotr Gieryk."

"I did, Mama. But Peter Garrick is his American name. Just like my American name is Irene."

"Irene? What is this? You didn't like the name I gave you? You were baptized Irina. How will God know you on your grave marker?"

"God will understand, Mama. Now, let's find your things—"

"Where is Teo? I'm not going anywhere without my son."

"Mama, just help me find your things and we'll talk about Teo when we get home."

"When are we going home, Mama?" Stefania suddenly asked, clutching at Zofia's shawl.

"We're never going home, baby. I told you that."

Stefania burst into tears, and as if it were a signal, the twins followed suit. They all clustered around Zofia, their wails rising in pitch and volume. Aggie stood beside them, tears coursing down her pale cheeks.

The last time they'd seen each other it had been like this, standing in a crowd of strangers at a dock, all of them crying. But that was different; the family was being split up. Now they were all together. There should have been nothing but rejoicing. Tears of joy, perhaps, but not this heartbroken sobbing.

"Now, now! Stop it," Irene said briskly. "All of you. Of course you're going home. You're going to your new home in America. It's much nicer and you'll have lots of new things and meet nice new people—"

"I don't want new things!" Stefania sobbed.

"Of course you do. Look, you're just upset because everything's different and strange and you've had a long, terrible trip. I remember I felt the same way when I got here, but I didn't have anybody with me but . . ." Oops, she'd brought it up herself.

"Where *is*—?" Mama began.

"Aggie, come with me to find your things you brought along. Peter, would you stay here with Mama?"

When they had rounded up the pitiful mound of dirty bundles that had served as luggage, they faced the problem of transporting them all. It was much too far to walk carrying everything, and Irene was afraid they'd lose track of something if they took a bus. Peter agreed. "I'll find one of those taximeter cabs to drive us. That will be an exciting thing for your mother."

It was more than exciting. Zofia was terrified when the monster chugged up. "*Aieee!* The devil!" she shrieked.

"No, Mama, a gasoline-propelled automobile. Don't be frightened."

"It goes without a horse or a man pulling it! This is against God's will!"

"You don't know how God feels about automobiles!" Irene said rather sharply. Peter put his arm around her. She looked up and he smiled reassuringly. She consciously softened her tone. "You don't have to be afraid, Mama. It's safe. It's just a machine that you ride in."

"*Ride inside!* No, it would kill us, and the devil would take us all to hell!"

"No, Peter and I have ridden in one and we're still here." She meant to reassure them, but it only made them look at her with greater distrust. "God gave me two feet!" Zofia said.

"Irene," Peter said, taking her aside quietly, "I'll take

their things to the apartment in the vehicle and you can walk with them. They don't know the ways of this country yet. It's all scaring them. Especially your mother. Just stay calm yourself and everything will be fine when we get them home."

"Thank you, Peter." Irene forced herself to cast her mind back to the day she arrived, but it was difficult. She'd never been one for dwelling on the past, and so much had happened since then. "Mama, Peter will take our things and we will walk home."

It was a hideous trip. Zofia and the girls cried most of the way. Every new sight, every new sound frightened them. Zofia hated the tall buildings, the twins apparently felt claustrophobic from the nearness of the strange people and clung to each other like Siamese twins. Stefania attached herself to Zofia and kept sobbing that she wanted to go home. Aggie kept her streaming eyes straight ahead, not even responding when Irene pointed out sights she'd been waiting years to show her. By the time they got to St. Mark's Place, Irene was nearly in tears herself.

"This is the street where we live, Aggie. We got a new place because you were coming—"

Aggie finally deigned to reply. She turned a furious gaze on Irene. "Why did you make us do this?"

"Make you . . . ? What do you mean?"

"Ah, there you are!" Peter said, coming toward them. "I've got everything put away, and Irene has a nice pot of stew on the stove for you. She's a good cook, your daughter."

"I don't eat in this country until I've been to Mass," Zofia declared. "I haven't seen a single church! Heathen place!"

"We've passed lots of churches, Mama." She was tempted to add: "if you hadn't been looking at your feet and crying, you'd have seen them."

"I'll take you to church," Peter said. "We'll all go."

"But wouldn't you like to see the apartment first?" Irene asked. "It's all cleaned and ready. We could rest a minute and then go—"

"I must pray for Teo," Zofia said, casting her a baleful look.

Irene's feet hurt, her feelings were bruised raw, and she wanted nothing more than to sit down with a big bowl of stew, but she trailed back south with them to St. Stanislas. Peter, normally undemonstrative in public, held her hand the whole time and whispered several times, "It'll be all right, Reenee. Just be patient."

"Why do you live so far from God?" Zofia asked on the way back. "Why don't you live near that beautiful church? We will move there."

"Mama, we have a nice home for you. You'll see. It's not so far, and after you've gotten settled you can take a bus. It won't seem so far. Peter goes on the bus to church all the time."

"Peter goes? And what about you, Irina? Have you become as godless as this America?"

Peter intervened. "Irene is very religious, Mrs. Kossok. Very pious."

Irene glanced at him with gratitude.

As soon as they were all herded into the apartment, Irene stood back smiling, waiting for their reaction. "Your room is right through there, Mama, and—"

"Where is my son?"

"Oh, Mama . . . Very well, sit down here and I will explain."

Zofia perched on the edge of a chair, the other girls clustered around her. They stared at Irene like a tearful jury.

"Mama, when we got here so long ago, Teo left me and went off on his own—"

"No! Teo wouldn't do a thing like that for no reason. What did you do to make him go away?"

"Mama! I didn't do anything. He got angry with the people we were going to stay with. He and the man got in a fight because Teo talked back to him."

"No, my Teo wouldn't do such a thing. Teo is a good boy."

Irene felt her throat tightening and the words clogging up, but she doggedly went on. "I saw him for a while, but he made bad friends and after a few months he disappeared. I haven't seen him for years."

"But he wrote me letters!"

"No, Mama. I wrote the letters. I pretended they were from Teo so you wouldn't worry."

"But he said he was going to school and had a fine job . . ."

"That was about me, Mama. I'm sorry about Teo, but he's gone. I'm afraid you won't see him again. None of us will."

"He's dead? My Teo dead?"

"I don't know, but it's possible. Mama, I'm sorry—"

"*Aieee!* My son, my son!" Zofia burst into a high-pitched wail. Somebody in the apartment next door banged on the wall. "Who will take care of us? We are helpless and in this godless country without a man!"

"Mama, Peter and I will take care of you. We brought you here and got you this place to live. Wouldn't you like to look at your room?"

"My son is lost! My only son," she kept sobbing.

Irene reached across the table and pulled her mother's hands away from her face. "Mama, you have *me*!"

"You are only a daughter. I have many daughters, but only one son."

"Peter is your son now. He is better than Teo."

Zofia freed a hand and swung a wide arc. She missed, but Irene recoiled in shock. It had been years since anyone had attempted to touch her in anger. "Nobody is better than Teo, you bad, bad girl. To say such a thing of your brother. Teo is good. You made him leave and you're lying to me."

Peter has been standing behind Irene, listening and watching, but at this, he intervened. "*Zachowuj się przyzwoichi!*—Behave yourself, old woman! You must not strike Irene. Your daughter is a good woman. Irene, come with me and leave your mother and sisters to get settled."

"So now you leave us!" Zofia cried.

"Only for a short time," Peter said, all but dragging Irene to her feet and out the door.

Once on the street, he handed her a handkerchief. "She's grief-stricken, Irene. She spoke only in anger and surprise. You've known your brother was lost to you for years, but for her he died just five minutes ago."

"I should have told her before. It was wrong of me to pretend."

"No, if you'd told her the truth, she probably wouldn't have come and brought your sisters. It was better this way, but you must give her some time to get used to the idea. He was her only son.''

''Oh, Peter,'' Irene said, taking his arm and leaning her head on his shoulder. ''You are so good to me.'' She'd known him as a rescuer, a husband and lover, but she hadn't realized until today what a good friend he was to her.

''Let's go down to the candy store and get the girls something special.''

When they returned to the apartment, things were indeed a little calmer. Zofia had worked out an attitude that she was to adhere to from that moment on. Teo, she explained, was not dead, but had merely taken offense at something Irina had done. He would come back in good time. She had prayed over it and God had told her so. Well, not in so many words, perhaps, but she knew it to be true. She would wait. They would all wait, and Teo would come back to take care of them.

Irene, who knew this to be utter nonsense, went along with it to keep the peace. Zofia in patient error was better company that Zofia in full spate of grief, and who could say? Teo might actually be alive, although the chances of his finding them in this teeming city were remote and the possibility of his *wanting* to find them even more unlikely. Still, if it made Zofia happy, it was no more harmful and certainly no more a falsehood than Irene had been perpetrating in her letters home all these years.

The twins were placated with the candy, which they devoured only slightly less greedily than Stefania. Agnieszka politely declined hers and the three others got into a rancorous dispute over her share. Zofia, calmer now about Teo, went to examine the kitchen and nearly went to pieces when Irene turned on the tap. The water gushed out, terrifying her mother into renewed crying. This, too, she declared evidence of the devil, but condescended to make use of it anyway. Irene decided to get all the plumbing terrors over with at once and took them all down the hall to learn about the toilet. This, Zofia flatly refused to consider using. It would suck a person down into hell. She would keep pots under the beds as always, and if Irene wanted to dispose of the contents in that horrible machine, that was up to her.

They sat down, finally, to the stew Irene had made the night before, and during the lull in conversation, Irene had her first opportunity to consider the reality as opposed to the long-nurtured dream of the arrival. For one thing, she was having difficulty talking to them. Her Polish was not only creaky from disuse but also the limited language of an ignorant village girl. She had no words in her resurrected vocabulary for any complex or sophisticated concepts because she'd never known or needed them as a girl. In Polish she had to speak as a child—almost think as a child—because that was all her knowledge of the language allowed for. She would have to make sure they were all offered the opportunity to learn English as soon as possible.

"More, Irina?" Stefania asked, holding out her empty bowl.

Irene got up and refilled the bowl, taking care to give Stefania a healthy proportion of meat and carrots without too many potatoes. She'd have to watch what the youngest girl ate. She was definitely on the dumpy side, too fat by far for one so young. Stefania, as the baby, fatherless for a great part of her life, was evidently Mama's pampered one. She stuck close to Zofia, who had already taken several opportunities to overfeed her.

The twins, on the other hand, were more than self-sufficient, now that they were recovering from their initial fright and disorientation. They had been such sweet little girls; why was Irene having such a hard time liking them now? They were pretty children, aside from their shabby clothing, tangled hair, and dirty faces, but there was something just the slightest bit sly about them. They seemed able to converse with each other almost silently. One would say just a word or two and the other would nod her understanding. Nor did they seem very much interested in extending their conversation to anyone else.

"Lillie, it is more polite to talk with everyone at the table, not just one person," Irene said at one point.

"Polite?" Lillie said as though it were a completely foreign term, as indeed it was, to her.

"Yes, now that you are in America, you will learn American manners and words. Start with names. In this country I am Irene. Your name is the same and so is Cecilia's, but Stefania will be Stephanie and Mama's name is Sophia."

"You are trying to take my name?" Zofia said angrily, spitting a piece of carrot on the table as she spoke.

"No, Mama, not *take* your name. Just tell you what it is in English. That is what we speak here in this country."

For some reason this set them all off into tears again. Irene was perplexed. She could remember vividly the day, the very moment, when Clara had introduced her to the concept of languages. It had been a thrilling revelation and she had enjoyed the challenge. If she had been light-minded, she would have even seen it as a game, learning all the new words. Why were her mother and sisters acting like English was some sort of threat? This was one of the gifts she had most looked forward to bestowing on them.

She got up and started clearing the table and noticed that Aggie hadn't eaten more than a few bites. "Don't you like stew?" she asked her sister.

"I like it. I'm not hungry," she replied, not meeting Irene's eyes.

What was the matter with her? Irene wondered. Was she ill? She must be. Certainly no one could change so completely as Aggie appeared to have changed. She'd been such a happy, loving girl, so full of jokes and songs and a dancing spirit. But this Aggie was a drab bag of bones. And that remark she'd made earlier—something about Irene "making" them come over. What on earth did she mean by that? That she hadn't *wanted* to come? That was impossible to believe. How could anyone prefer the drab existence in a dreary, cold village that hadn't changed in centuries to the unlimited possibilities of improvement here in America? If Mama had been reluctant, Irene could have understood. Mama was old and set in her ways and had never liked anything new and different. But Aggie hadn't been like that. Aggie had always been the first one to succumb to a dare or plot a practical joke or make up a new verse to an old song.

For all the disappointments the day had served up, Aggie was the greatest. Irene had anticipated that they would fall into one another's arms and resume the close sisterly friendship they'd had before. In fact, Aggie had been the only one she'd really looked forward to seeing in any sort of selfish way. The rest she was morally obligated to bring over, but Aggie she had genuinely wanted to have near.

Irene reminded herself that she must not rush things. Aggie had probably suffered seasickness on the journey and would be herself again as soon as she rested for a few days. They had all the time in the world to patch up the missing years. "Tomorrow I will take you to see the markets, Mama. And when Peter and I have to go to work, I will make a map for you and the girls so you may go for walks if you like. I can show Aggie how to make maps like my friend showed me when I came here."

Zofia had no interest in maps. Nor, apparently, had Aggie, who didn't even look up. "What kind of work do you do, Piotr?" Zofia asked.

"Irene and I work for a furrier uptown," he said

"A furrier? You sew pelts, like my husband did when he made gloves?"

"Peter doesn't sew pelts, Mama. He's a cutter. It's a very skilled job and he's very good," Irene said. "I'm studying . . ." She wanted to say "designing," but she had no Polish word for it. "I'm studying making patterns for fur coats." That wasn't quite right, but it was as close as she could get. When they learned English, she could clarify it.

"Studying? Studying isn't for women," Zofia declared.

"Studying *is* for women in this country, Mama."

"No daughter of mine is going to go among men at schools! It isn't decent!"

"Mama, here people of both sexes go to school together. All the girls will have to go to school to learn English."

Zofia was shaking her head emphatically. "No, it is against the will of God. Boys go to schools. Girls stay with their mothers. You will stay home now, not study."

She was serious, Irene realized with a shock. "Mama, things are different here. You must understand that. This isn't the old country. You've left the village. And, Mama . . ." She had to tread gently here. "I'm not a child anymore. You cannot tell me what I must do."

Zofia stared at her in amazement, then, tears coursing down her cheeks again, crossed herself. "Such wickedness. I should never have let you go. Your papa, may he rest in Jesus's arms, was right. You should have stayed home with me. You have lost all respect—"

"No, Mama, don't say that. I respect you. I love you, Mama. But things are different here. Not wicked, just different. I've grown up. I'm not that little girl you put on the boat. I've learned about this country and I just want to help you learn. There is so much here that is good. Really there is! You'll see, I promise."

But as she spoke, she realized she might as well have been explaining something to a tree, so stolid and uncomprehending was her mother. Time, she reminded herself. It takes time. They'd been here only a few hours and she was trying to compress and explain all her years of experience. They couldn't be expected to understand so soon. She must not push them so hard. Their hearts and minds were still in the village and they must be led to forget it slowly.

She caught Peter's eye as he watched her with sympathy. He smiled and it made her feel better. "Everybody is tired, I think," he said in English.

"Yes, that's it," she replied, then in Polish to her family: "It's early, but you should rest. I will show you where all your beds are. Tomorrow everybody will feel better and I will show you the city."

She got everyone settled and went to her room to talk to Peter. "It will be better tomorrow," he said. "You don't know how much you've changed over the years, and so have they. You let yourself believe that everybody would be just the same as on the day you last saw them. Don't worry, Reenee, it will all be fine in a few days."

As she slid into her bed a few minutes later, she could hear muffled sobbing from all the other rooms. Her head ached fiercely, her tongue felt furry with talk, her feet throbbed with all the walking, and she felt bruised all over. She started crying too, and Peter cradled her in his arms like a child.

"Tomorrow *has* to be better," she said fervently in the darkness.

Irene had planned an extensive tour of the city for her family's second day in America, but changed her mind.

Instead, she took them to morning Mass and then conducted them on a short tour of the neighborhood around St. Stanislas. One of the first people they saw on leaving the church was an old neighbor of the Sprys', a woman of about Zofia's age and circumstance named Apolonia Jedrychowski. Irene had made her a dress for her second wedding, but she'd been widowed again and now was raising two daughters and a sickly son on the modest inheritance her second husband had left her.

Mrs. Jedrychowski and Zofia took one look at each other and were immediate soulmates. Irene was glad Mama had so quickly found a friend, but wished it were a different friend. Mrs. Jedrychowski, having been in this country for ten years, was still living in the past. She knew no English and was nearly as suspicious as Zofia of anything unlike what she'd known in the old country. She would hold back Zofia's Americanization, but Irene recognized how much her mother needed someone of her own generation and background, so trailed along contentedly as Mrs. Jedrychowski introduced Zofia to the best markets, the most honest pushcart salesmen, and most of her other friends. She even came back to the apartment and showed Zofia how to cope with the godless gas stove that Irene had paid so much for.

"There is no wood in this country," Mrs. Jedrychowski said. "None. No trees at all. It's been years since I've seen anything but a spindly twig of green."

"But there are trees uptown. Central Park has acres and acres of trees, and there are other small parks," Irene explained.

Mrs. Jedrychowski said, "Such places aren't for the likes of us. All rich overlords, like home. The trees belong to them."

"No, Mrs. Jedrychowski, the trees belong to the city, to everybody."

Both women looked at her pityingly, as if she were an idealistic child.

Irene went back to work Friday; Mrs. Jedrychowski was coming over at noon to take them shopping again. "They'll enjoy themselves. Don't worry about them," Peter said as they got off the bus.

"I'm not worried about their safety or happiness," Irene explained. "I'm worried about what she'll tell them."

"What do you mean?" Peter asked.

"Oh, things like Central Park belongs to the 'overlords,' that sort of thing."

"It might as well, as far as she's concerned," Peter said. He'd had a good laugh out of the story when Irene repeated it to him. He still couldn't understand why she didn't see the humor in it.

"Peter, they'll never become Americanized if they're influenced by someone like her."

"What difference does that make, if they're happy?"

She looked at him with genuine astonishment. "What difference does it make? I don't want them to stay ignorant peasants now that they're here. There's so much to learn, so much to enjoy in America if you just work at improving yourself."

"Why should they improve if they don't want to? Irene, not everyone wants what you want."

They'd arrived at the employees' entrance of Neptune et Cie and didn't continue the conversation further, nor did Irene have time to give it much thought that day. But when she and Peter walked into the apartment that evening, it all came to the forefront of her mind again. She took only a single step in the door before she slipped and nearly fell. "What in the wor . . . ?" She looked down at the mess on her shoe.

At that, Zofia came from the kitchen, holding a flapping chicken by the neck. Two other birds were running in front of her, squawking hysterically. "Finally, you come back!"

"Mama, what are these birds doing loose in the house?"

Zofia looked at her as if it pained her to have to state the obvious. "There is no coop."

"But, Mama, you can't have chickens running around the house!"

"Why not?"

Irene had a vivid flash of memory. Mama had always had chickens in the house in the village. Everybody did. Mostly they lived in the yard and nested on the thatched roof, but she often had a favorite or two inside—those she was afraid might be stolen if left out, or sick ones she was nursing back to health. There was, one whole winter, a foul-tempered rooster who would perch at the foot of the bed Irina shared with Aggie, and peck at their toes between crows in the morning.

"Mama, this is different now. In America people don't keep chickens in the house. Look what they've done to my clean floors!"

"What do you eat, then?"

"We eat chickens, but you buy one when you need it at the market and bring it home already dead and plucked."

"Am I too old and stupid to pluck a chicken now that I am in America?" Zofia said. "I wouldn't eat some stranger's chicken. Nobody raises a chicken like I do!"

"I know, Mama, but . . . Oh well. I'll see if Peter can make a cage of some sort for these three, but that's all. You will have to keep them in the cage. And no roosters!"

Zofia shrugged her failure to comprehend and shambled back to the kitchen, wiping her nose on her sleeve as she went.

Irene looked at Peter and was shocked to find that he was sitting in a chair by the window, grinning like a child at the circus.

"Peter!"

"Chickens!" he sputtered. "I'm sorry, Reenee, don't look so mad. The look on your face when that chicken ran through—it might as well have been a *dragon*!"

"It's *not* funny!"

14

June 1908

Clara returned that winter and immediately found another job as a dresser in a New York play. Unfortunately, she and Irene found few opportunities to get together. Clara's work was in the evenings and Irene's was during the day. But they still met occasionally to catch up on each other's lives. Clara sometimes dropped in and visited with Zofia and the girls, who had taken to her as quickly and affectionately as Peter had. Clara found it immensely frustrating to know of Irene's life only at second or third hand. She'd lost her position as primary provider of learning. Of course, she'd always known that would eventually be the case, but she found herself longing to have a greater role in Irene's life, if only as a closer observer.

The next June, after a mere thirteen months of apprenticeship, Irene took her place on the design staff at Neptune et Cie. The announcement, as unofficial and low-key as it was, caused upheaval on several fronts. Jacques Neptune took her to an office down the hall from his own, where large north-facing windows illuminated a bank of drawing tables. Two men sat on tall stools, bent over their work. At the sound of Neptune's voice, they climbed down and greeted him..

"Mrs. Garrick, you've met Ronald Hadley before. And this is Elmer Delman."

"How do you do, Mr. Delman. I'm glad to see you again, Mr. Hadley," she said, nodding.

She wasn't glad at all to see Hadley; she'd been dreading this confrontation, for confrontation she felt it would be. On Neptune's orders he'd given her some basic instructions in sketching several months ago, before Irene started her classes at Cooper Union's School of Design for Women, but had done so with very little grace. He hadn't been openly rude, merely snappish and truculent. He was a tubby, effeminate little man in his forties with a sharp eye, a weak chin, and thinning reddish hair that swept from above one ear over the top of his head to the other. Elmer Delman was as nearly opposite as possible. Storklike in physique, he was swarthy and had an abundant head of dark hair worn long, à la Oscar Wilde.

"Mrs. Garrick will be taking her place alongside you gentlemen," Neptune said.

"I beg your pardon?" Delman said, folding his arms.

"I believe you heard me," Neptune said firmly. "Mrs. Garrick is possessed of a rare talent for design and we are honored by her acceptance of a position here."

But Delman wasn't having any. "With all due respect, sir, you may be honored. I am not. Do you mean to suggest that this . . . *woman* will be employed as a designer?"

"Not will be. Has been."

"I've never worked with a woman," Delman said.

"Elmer . . ." Ronald Hadley warned in a quiet little whimper.

"Then you have a rare treat in store, haven't you?" Neptune said with a wolfish smile.

"I'm afraid it won't do," Delman insisted.

"Whatever can you mean by that?" Neptune asked.

Neptune's tone was poisonous, and for a moment Irene felt sorry for Mr. Delman. It was like watching a man blindfold himself and walk off a cliff. Irene wanted to say something to stop this, but knew she dared not interfere in Neptune's conversation even though it concerned her.

"I mean I won't work with her," Delman said.

"That's a pity," Neptune said. "One wonders where else you'll get employment."

"Do you mean to say you're firing me?" Delman asked, drawing himself up, his face reddening.

"Not at all. You're entirely welcome to stay on and help Mrs. Garrick learn the ropes. But the choice is up to you."

"I'll go to Revillon Frères," Delman said threateningly.

"I doubt that. I keep a close eye on their operation and I

understand they're already overstaffed. Of course, they enjoy feeling they've stolen people from me. You might be able to make them believe that's the case. So, is that your decision?"

"It certainly is!"

"Elmer, please . . ." Hadley tried again.

Neptune quelled him with a look. "Mr. Delman, you'll get your personal belongings out of here within the hour. And you may take with you anything in your head, but nothing on paper. You will be searched as you leave." He turned his attention back to Ronald Hadley. "Now, Mr. Hadley, are we to repeat this conversation or do you think you can find it in your heart to work with Mrs. Garrick?"

Hadley looked wildly at his friend for direction, but Delman was angrily stuffing extra hard collars and cuffs into a small box and didn't look up. "I . . . I suppose I can work with the lady," he said.

"You suppose?"

"I'm . . . I'm certain of it, sir," Hadley said.

"Very good. I'm going to take Mrs. Garrick on a brief tour of the plant, just to reacquaint her with the general layout. She's studied the dressing process in books, but this week I want her to watch it all firsthand."

Without any further conversation, he turned on his heel. Irene wanted to pause and try to make friends with Hadley, but there wasn't time. Neptune was halfway down the stairs before she caught up. She expected him to refer to the events just preceding, but instead he launched into a lecture. "As you know, the preliminary dressing of the pelts takes place long before it reaches us here. The pelts have been dried or salted as soon as they're taken. They are later scraped of fat and thoroughly wet. How?"

The student in her answered immediately. "Some with brush and water; some, like rabbit, are soaked in a water, salt-water, or borax solution. The best are put in a revolving drum with wet sawdust to prevent oversoaking."

"Very good, Mrs. Garrick. Then what?"

"The fur is dried while the skin side is kept damp. Then the pelts are softened by a tramping machine before being put into another drum with dry sawdust. Next they go to the . . ." She paused, trying to remember the term.

"The flesher. Aside from the hunter who takes the pelt and the designer who makes it into a work of art, the flesher is the most important part of the process. He removes the last of the fat and membrane. He works with a razor-sharp knife, and if he cuts even a fraction too deeply, the hair bulbs and roots will be sheared off and the fur side will develop bald spots."

"Monsieur, about Mr. Hadley and Mr. Delman—"

He went on as if he hadn't heard her, "The pelts then go into a tanning fluid—you've studied the formulas for salt-acid pickling, mineral tanning, chamois tanning, and vegetable tanning. As I say, this has all been done before the pelts reach us, and as you will remember, these processes result in some shrinkage in most cases . . ."

They'd been descending the staircase while he talked. Now he opened a heavy door to a large basement room. "This is where we begin. The pelts are dampened again, very slightly, and stretched to their working size. Most of this is done in our warehouse upstate, but the most valuable pelts are done here."

Under your watchful eye, Irene thought.

Wooden boards stood around the walls. To them were nailed hundreds of pelts, some skin-side-out, some fur-side-out. A dozen men worked feverishly. Some were bent over pelts with their mouths full of tiny sharp nails with which they carefully tacked the edges of the pelts. Others were constantly walking around the perimeter of the room, lightly touching the pelts with the backs of their hands, testing for dryness. The room was warm, but not hot, from the steam-heat pipes that ran down the center. Large fans created cross-currents of air. Every now and then the men would move a fan, move a board, or take down a pelt and turn it over to be retacked.

Irene and Neptune stood out of the way, watching this activity for a few minutes. Finally she said, "Monsieur, about Mr. Delman leaving—"

"Mr. Delman's status doesn't concern you, Mrs. Garrick. He made his own choice."

"But he left because of me."

"No, he left because of his own blindness and personal

inadequacies. It was, let us be frank, you or him. I prefer to employ you. I assumed that was your preference as well."

There was nothing she could say in the face of this blunt reasoning. Nor, it was clear, was she being invited to say anything. "Will he get another job?"

"Naturally. He's skilled in his own way."

That relieved her mind somewhat. At least she'd not put a man out of work entirely.

"You'll come back here later and study in detail everything that's being done," Neptune said, opening the heavy door. "The manager of each department will be given instructions to cooperate with you. The word of Delman's termination will have spread through the building within another hour and I don't anticipate that you'll have any trouble getting all your questions answered."

Irene understood now why Delman had been treated as he had. She'd believed she was at the center of the storm and now knew she was wrong. The dispute wasn't really about her at all, it was about Monsieur Neptune's power. Delman was to set an example to anyone else who thought he could bully Neptune out of hiring a woman—or doing anything else he chose to do. She would have thought that anyone with a grain of common sense would know that Neptune couldn't be bullied, but apparently he felt it was important to emphasize the point.

They spent the rest of the morning touring the company. Neptune took her through the rooms in which the dyeing and plucking were done. "The compounds used here are highly flammable," he said. "That's why anyone who is found to have matches or any smoking materials in his possession is instantly fired. The whole building could go up in minutes if a single flame were to start." They then passed through the vast room where cutters, including Peter, worked at big scarred oak tables. As they neared Peter, he glanced up from his work. For a second there was anger in his gaze; then he forced a smile and gave her a supportive wink. It was the first time Irene had sensed the inherent awkwardness in their situation.

They spent a short time in the sewing room—a large, well-lighted loft—where a dozen men and women labored over patterns and fur. "Look at the back of this mink pelt," Neptune said, picking up one and handing it to Irene.

The pelt had been "let out," by a tedious process of cutting it into squat V shapes only an eighth of an inch apart. The inside point of the V was then pinched slightly and the next strip above sewed back on with tiny, strong stitches. The V then was a long, narrow shape. The result was that an individual pelt that had been between two and three feet long and a foot wide turned into a strip five feet long and seven inches wide, but with the pattern preserved exactly. "This is why mink is so expensive," Neptune explained. "The fur is durable and attractive, which is part of its value, but it's not so terribly rare as sable, for example. The work hours that are put into a coat make the cost. There are several thousand expert stitches per pelt. How long does it take you to let out a pelt?" he asked the woman who was bent over her work.

She looked up, her needle poised. "Two days a pelt, sir," she answered.

"And she's our best," Neptune said to Irene. The woman beamed briefly, then immediately went back to work.

They were about to leave this area when Chandler Moffat caught up with them. "Ah, there you are, Uncle Jacques," he exclaimed. "I've been looking all over for you," he said, glaring at Irene.

"Yes, I imagine you have been," Neptune said dryly. "You know Mrs. Garrick, I believe?"

"I've seen her in your office, of course. I assumed she was training to help Miss Troutwhite. Now I'm hearing the most outrageous stories—"

Neptune sighed. "I suppose you mean the story that I've hired Mrs. Garrick as a designer?"

Chandler laughed. "Yes, isn't it ridiculous the things the staff will gossip up!"

"It's not gossip. It's true."

"Now, Uncle Jacques, I must say—"

"We will talk in my office," Neptune said firmly. "Mrs. Garrick, you may take an hour for lunch today. Afterward I want you to visit the storage rooms, and I will show you the showrooms myself another day."

Irene very nearly let out an audible sigh of relief. She'd

been afraid of having to witness another dispute over her sex and job. "Thank you, monsieur," she said, all but fleeing.

She made her way back down to the cutting room, where Peter was just putting away his tools. "May I share your lunch?" she asked him.

"I don't mind at all, but what happened to yours? You brought it along today, didn't you?"

"Yes, but it's up with my other things in Monsieur's office— "

"And he's holding it hostage?" Peter asked with a grin.

"In a manner of speaking. He's having a talk with Mr. Moffat about me."

"Ahhh, I see. Everybody's been whispering since you and Mr. Neptune came through this morning. Of course nobody will tell *me* what it's about."

As they sat over sausage sandwiches on the doorstep of an empty building down the block, Irene explained what had gone on earlier with Mr. Delman. She expected Peter to be supportive and was shocked when he merely said, "Why do you want to subject yourself to this? Everybody in the building is talking about you.'"

"Does that embarrass you?" she asked angrily.

"Me? No, of course it doesn't. But I'd think it would upset you. Obviously it has. So why go on courting trouble?"

"Because the job is important to me!"

"Irene, I can take good care of you. Why won't you just stay home and let me?"

"You sound like Mama! Women should not know anything or study anything or be anyone." She handed him back her uneaten half of his sandwich.

"Don't fly off like that. You know I don't feel that way. I love you for being bright and interested in things. If I'd wanted a stupid wife I'd have married one. But why put yourself in a position to become upset?"

"Oh, Peter, you don't understand!"

"No, I don't."

She got up and started to walk away, then stopped for a long moment and returned. "I'm sorry," she said, sitting back down beside him. She did feel contrition for her own behavior, but she was sorry, too, to have discovered that they didn't think as much alike as she used to believe.

Neptune's nephew was no more supportive than Irene's husband. "A woman designer! Uncle Jacques, you must be mad!" Chandler Moffat was saying. "The whole staff will quit."

Neptune was trying to remain calm, remembering how much his late wife, Roberta, had doted on this boy. Of course, in many ways Roberta had been a fool. "They will do no such thing."

"Delman quit already."

"Delman will be the only one. He made himself an example of the idiocy of defying my wishes."

"Uncle Jacques, you can't do this!" Chandler realized he was being completely unreasonable, but for reasons he didn't understand, he was vaguely frightened by the idea. Not so much by the woman designer herself, but by the fact that his uncle was so determined to hire her.

Neptune leaned forward, glaring at Chandler with an intensity that surprised the younger man. "I *can't* do this? Is that what you said? Chandler, listen to me very carefully. I wouldn't like to have to repeat it. Neptune et Cie is my business. It always has been and as long as I live it always will be. I have tolerated you on sufferance because of the family connection. But be warned: my tolerance is wearing thin. When you attempt to become overbearing, it tends to point out to me your basic uselessness."

"Useless! Me?" He was genuinely hurt. Through all these years, he'd come to think of Neptune as the ultimate kindly uncle, providing nicely for him without criticizing or interfering in his life. He'd naturally come to believe that the older man thought very well of him. To be called useless was a tremendously unhappy surprise.

"I could walk out the front door and in five minutes find someone on the street who can do everything you do. And I warn you, it's a temptation."

Chandler was shocked. Though Neptune had on occasion terrorized nearly everyone in his employ, he'd never turned his talons on his nephew. Chandler's life was easy and placid;

he seldom faced a conflict more vital than deciding which card to play at whist. He wasn't used to handling basic emotions and consequently didn't handle them well. The only explanation that sprang to his mind was the woman herself. She must have really put some sort of pressure on Neptune. "What is it about this woman?" he asked nastily.

"She's extraordinarily talented."

"You've just gone gaga about her," Chandler went on, ignoring the fury in his uncle's gaze. "I never thought I'd see the day when you'd bring your trollops to the office—"

Neptune rose from behind his desk. He was white around the lips and trembling with the effort of keeping his self-control. "Chandler, you need a vacation. Starting this instant. I don't want to see you again for at least a month, and then you had better be groveling. Get out of *my* office."

"You're firing me? *Me*?"

"God help me, I ought to be! And if you ever have the effrontery to criticize my personal life or my business decisions again, I will. Understand this, Chandler: Mrs. Garrick is an employee of *my* company, and if you can't accept that, you're on your own. I think you'll appreciate what that means after you've had a month to think it over—without that allowance we call your salary."

"Without—?"

"Chandler, get out of here. *Now.*"

He opened the door, and Chandler, dumbfounded and seething, stomped out. Neptune went back to his desk and sat down heavily. This was what he should have done long ago. In the long run, it would be good for Chandler. Or would it? No, he hadn't acted for Chandler's benefit; he'd thrown him out from sheer anger, anger ignited by the younger man's remark about Irene Garrick being his "trollop." Fighting to be reasonable, Neptune grudgingly admitted to himself that it wasn't an entirely unlikely assumption. After all, she was a great beauty with her fair hair, exotic eyes, and wonderfully proportioned figure.

He allowed himself the luxury of reflecting on that figure for long moments. Too bad she was what she was—an apparently happily married woman. Irene was so very attractive. And he'd never known a woman with a body like that who didn't know how to enjoy all that it promised. She'd be a fascinating mistress. Was she really that happily married? he found himself wondering, and as he thought about it, he realized it had been an unconscious query for some weeks. He drummed his fingers on the desk, lost momentarily in a haze of sensual speculation.

He'd forgotten all about Chandler.

That summer the Olympics were held in London, and society, needing little excuse to flock anywhere, converged on England. Those who counted on furs to identify their financial and social status flocked to Neptune et Cie. "Of course I know it's summer, Jacques darling, but it's cool in England," they said.

Neptune et Cie did a booming business in fur-trimmed garments suitable for evening wear. Irene designed a dress with narrow bands of white fox that resembled maribou around the neck and wide sleeves for a style-setting young woman. It was, she heard, the hit of the season. That Monsieur Neptune got all the credit didn't bother her in the least. That was how an apprenticeship worked. He gave her a hundred-dollar bonus, which she used to purchase some new furniture for the apartment.

"I had hoped you'd buy something pretty for yourself," Neptune said when she mentioned what she'd done with the money.

"My mother is having back trouble and it was important to get more comfortable furniture," she said.

For the rest of the summer and fall Irene left the designing room with the tall drawing boards and clean north light for a sojourn in the bowels of the building. "To learn from books what is done to a fur isn't enough," Neptune said. "A good furrier should actually be able to do every step from skinning the animal right on through the process."

"Clara, there isn't time enough for everything I want to do," she said when her friend commented that she was looking tired. "I have my classes to attend, my work, and Mama and the girls to try to teach things to."

"And time for Peter?"

"Of course, but Peter understands why I must work so hard."

"Are you certain of that, Irene?" Clara asked. She now had a more or less permanent job managing the wardrobe department at a large theater and sometimes had an evening off when she could have dinner with them. She had begun to think she sensed a tension in Peter she'd never seen before. It wasn't anything she could label, just a sense of unease when Irene went on too long about whom she was designing things for and where they would be wearing them. Once he had said, "Don't these women have anything worthwhile to do?" and there had been a hint of genuine sharpness in his normally mellow voice.

"Oh, Peter understands. He's busy too. He's going to go to school this winter, you know. A priest friend of his arranged for him to take some sort of test and he did so well he got a certificate that lets him go to college classes at night."

"What's he studying?"

"Philosophy," Irene said, obviously perplexed at the choice.

One day early in November Irene came to Neptune's office to ask a question. Turning to leave in a rush, she failed to notice a packing crate containing a new file cabinet that was sitting by the door. She smacked into it, bumping her head sharply.

Neptune leapt to his feet. "Are you hurt?"

"No, it was nothing," Irene said, but the words were slurred and there was a dark haze closing in her vision. She didn't quite faint, but she staggered and Neptune caught her.

He scooped her up, wondering even in his alarm that she was so slight. "I'll have a doctor called," he said.

"No, please. I'm fine. Really," she said, struggling against his grasp.

Her full breasts pressed against him as she moved, and Neptune caught his breath. He'd forced himself to suppress the attraction he felt for her all these months, and suddenly it all swept back, stronger than ever. The feel of her body in his embrace was as stunning as a physical blow. He had to exert all his willpower to set her down and release her. "Are you sure you're not hurt?" he said, his own voice less steady than hers. "You must see a doctor. Take the rest of the day off."

She put her hands to her head, feeling for a lump. A hairpin fell out and a long ripe-wheat-colored loop of hair came loose. She tucked it back up, but not before Neptune had a moment of imagining what it must all look like loose and flowing down over that luscious body. "I'm sorry I alarmed you," Irene said briskly, and before he could say anything more, she scooped up the pencil she had dropped and was gone.

Jacques Neptune was left to spend a lonely afternoon with his imagination, which became more fevered the longer he thought about her. Wasn't it just possible that she might be as drawn to him as he was to her and was too innately proper to show it? She wasn't one to wear her emotions on her sleeve. She liked him, didn't she? Of course she did. If there had been an animosity in her regard for him, he'd have sensed it long since. Perhaps in the skilled, sensitive hands of an older man that liking might turn into a warmer feeling. That young man she was married to appeared to be nice enough—young and good-looking. But those were the only two points in his favor. Neptune himself had far better ammunition; he was no longer young but he was a handsome man for his age, and he had talent, money, social power. And he did know Irene well enough to realize that those were things that mattered to her.

He stood gazing out the window entirely unaware of what was going on before his eyes, because Irene Garrick's image filled his mind's eye. It was possible that their relationship might ripen to a new, exciting level, to the benefit of both of them. But how would he ever know without putting his desire to the test?

The next morning he asked, "Did you visit the doctor as I asked?"

"Of course not. There was no need," she said, folding her hands and preparing to answer whatever other questions he might ask her.

He realized she'd never fawned or cringed before him. Most people did one or the other. But never Irene Garrick. Did she realize how appealing that particular stance was? Calm, but expectant. Was it deliberate or instinctive? What did he really know about her aside from recognizing her beauty, talent, and intelligence? What did she think of him? Of life? "I wish you to accompany me on an appointment at noon, Mrs. Garrick. It may take the rest of the day. Perhaps into the evening."

"Yes, monsieur," she replied placidly. There was an inquiry in her eyes, but she asked nothing.

"You may tell your husband that I will see you home safely. He need not wait for you here."

"Yes, sir."

Peter didn't like it. "Isn't it enough that you spend your days here, without being expected to work all the time? Where are you going with him?"

"He didn't say. I expect he has some customer he has to visit at her home. Miss Troutwhite tells me he does that sometimes, but only for the most important kinds of people. Peter, maybe this is a princess or something! Wouldn't that be exciting?"

Peter had been on the point of putting his foot down and insisting that she not go off with Neptune, but in the face of her enthusiasm he hadn't the heart to make her unhappy. Besides, in a far corner of his mind there was a nagging fear that she might not accept such an ultimatum with docility. "I'll ask your mother to keep your dinner warm then," he said.

At noon Neptune handed her into his motorcar. They went up Fifth Avenue and turned the corner at Fifty-fifth. The motorcar stopped in front of the St. Regis hotel. Their client must be a visitor to New York, Irene thought. Visiting royalty, perhaps. Neptune took her arm and escorted her into the lobby. She thought that was strange—more courtesy than her role as tag-along assistant warranted—but the thought was quickly lost as she took in the oddly cozy magnificence of the hotel lobby. What an extraordinary place, she thought as he guided her toward the ornate elevator doors.

They emerged on the sixth floor and went down a hallway to a door that was opened by a waiter as they approached. "Monsieur," he said softly as he bowed them through the doorway.

"Were you able to get the vintage I requested?" Neptune asked him.

"Yes, monsieur," the waiter replied, indicating a bottle that was swathed in white linen and reposing in a bucket of ice chips.

They fell into a conversation full of dates and French-sounding words and Irene took the opportunity to look around. It was a corner room—a suite, actually. The main room was lavishly appointed with heavily draped windows on two walls. In front of one set of windows, a table was set for luncheon for two. Neptune and his client would dine and she would presumably be sent away until they had finished. She was sorry she hadn't thought to bring her packed lunch along.

The door to the adjoining room was open, revealing an enormous bed covered with a luxurious lavender spread. Though she couldn't see it, there must be a dressing room and bath beyond, where their hostess was preparing to receive them. Who could she be?

The waiter left with much bowing and Neptune said, "Put your things down, Irene, and make yourself comfortable."

Irene? She couldn't recall that he'd ever called her by her first name before. But then, except for their brief, stormy interviews in Miss Terry's dressing room, they had never been together outside the confines of Neptune et Cie. She wanted to ask a dozen questions of protocol. Whom are we meeting? Exactly what should I do when she comes in? Will I be introduced, and should I bow or shake her hand? Where should I sit while you and she talk? Should I have my notebook out, or should I simply try to remember everything?

Neptune drew out one of the chairs at the table by the window. "Please, Irene, sit down."

"Here? Me?" she asked.

He looked at her as though that were a truly gauche question, and Irene vowed not to ask any more. She sat as directed. She was wishing she'd paid attention to his conversation with the waiter. Perhaps the client was gone, still out shopping or something, and she was to have lunch with Monsieur while waiting for her to return. Another explanation briefly flitted through her mind, but she rejected it as both distasteful and impossible. Monsieur Neptune was her employer and a gentleman, and if Clara hadn't once asked all those silly questions about him, the suspicion would never have entered her mind. She was ashamed of herself for having even thought it.

They had a lovely meal of crab salad with tiny peas still in the pods, a frothy chocolate dessert, and thick, sweet coffee. As they ate, Neptune chatted about various places they could see from the windows. The houses of some of the richest people in New York were along this stretch of Fifth Avenue. He pointed out several homes and told her stories about the backgrounds and habits of their owners. It was very interesting and should have been a pleasant interlude, but Irene was uneasy. She glanced at the watch pinned to the bodice of her dress as the waiter returned and cleared away all but the champagne and goblets. Two-thirty and still no sign of the woman they were here to see.

Neptune said, "Perhaps you'd like to . . . freshen up? The door is just to your left beyond the bedroom."

Irene felt uncomfortable making free with someone else's room, but the fact was, she needed to use the toilet. Ever since that horrible long-ago day when she arrived in America, she'd made it a habit to relieve herself whenever she had the chance so she'd never be caught in a desperate situation again. "Thank you, monsieur," she said, and followed his directions.

The bathroom was larger than the main room of the apartment she and Peter and Mama and the girls shared. She'd never seen anything like it. A huge porcelain tub had claw feet that clutched polished marble balls with brass talons. The ornate taps were brass as well. Irene almost forgot the purpose of her visit in her awed study of her surroundings. There was no sign of the suite's inhabitant except a frilly pink dressing gown in some gossamer fabric hung over the dressing-table chair. She felt the soft fabric and imagined for a moment how grand it would be to have such a garment. Too bad she couldn't show this room to Aggie. That might cheer her up, make her realize how lucky she was to be in a country where such things existed.

When she came out of the bathroom, Neptune was standing in the bedroom, looking out the window at the traffic below.

he turned and looked at her. His eyes questioned, skipped momentarily to the pink dressing gown visible behind her, and came back to rest on her face.

And then she knew.

How stupid of her. How stupid and naive. But still, knowing, she had to ask. "Whom did we come her to see, monsieur?"

"I came to see you, Irene," he said, crossing the room and putting his hands lightly on her shoulders.

She stepped back slowly. "No . . ."

"Your innocence is very attractive, my dear, but do not take it to the point of tedium."

"No, monsieur, I didn't realize . . ."

She should have. Hadn't she learned anything from living with the Sprys? Had the horror of Andy's attack on her faded so entirely from her consciousness that it left no warning traces? Of course, but she'd assumed such base motives didn't apply to men like Monsieur Jacques Neptune. How very wrong of her to have been so trusting!

"Of course you did. You're not stupid. But you are very lovely, very lovely." He touched her again, this time putting his hand gently to the side of her face and rubbing his thumb lightly on her cheek.

Irene's heart was pounding. She despised her own blindness. But that was merely a subsidiary emotion at the moment. Her future, all her hopes, had collapsed with a sickening slither. She could almost imagine them lying broken at her feet, crunching under her feet as she backed up again. Was there, she was wondering frantically, some way to reject his advances without giving up all her opportunities? No, she knew there wasn't. She had been so utterly stupid!

Neptune watched, saw the self-disgust cross her face, and thought it was revulsion of himself. "Irene!" he said firmly.

She put her arms up as if to ward off a blow. "No, no, monsieur. Please, don't."

"Don't what? Force myself on you? Don't be ridiculous!"

She lowered her hands, tried to get a grip on herself, regain some shred of dignity. "I'm very sorry, I misunderstood . . . all this," she said, gesturing to include the suite, the luncheon, the champagne, the pink dressing gown.

Neptune's head was pounding and there was an ache of frustration in his groin that matched the hurt in his pride. "You couldn't have misunderstood. No woman could. Certainly not you!"

"I cannot be your . . . your mistress." Her Catholic conscience coated the word with venom.

"Of course you can. Why not? Believe me, Irene, I can make you very happy. I'm not a raw, groping boy. I'll make you happier than you knew you could be."

"*No!*" She had backed almost to the bathroom door and considered ducking inside and locking herself in, but even in her panicked state, common sense prevailed. There was no exit; she'd ultimately have to come out.

He saw the hunted look in her eyes and it both injured and angered him. What right did this girl have to make him feel so rejected, so inferior? So *old*. "After all I've done for you . . ." he blurted out.

She was crushed by the words, interpreting them to mean far more than he intended. "Is that why you took me into your company? To get my hopes up, to flatter me into thinking I was of value, when all you wanted was to seduce me? How dare you do that to me!"

His self-control had slipped completely; his emotions were a free-wheeling gear, spinning wildly. "To you? You say that as if you were somebody! You're nobody. Nobody! Some common peasant girl come to this country to get what you can of anybody you can. I don't even know your real name!"

"My name's Irene Garrick!" she shouted. He was cutting dangerously near the quick and she reacted violently. "Irene Garrick!"

"No, it's some unpronounceable Baltic mouthful of consonants—I'd bet anything on it. You've learned to speak English and dress decently, but it's all a facade. Underneath you're just foreign trash." He heard his own words, appalled, but was powerless to stop their flow. Her rejection had wounded him deeply, and some primitive urge made him need to hurt her as badly. And he knew how. Oh, he knew how. "You're nobody, Irene Garrick, but I could have made you somebody! I could have made you a respectable lady. I could have given you a good job, a good income—"

"But I won't pay your price!" Irene sobbed. She lunged past him, through the door to the sitting room. Grabbing her handbag and notebook, she threw open the door and ran down the hall. She couldn't wait for the elevator and started running down the narrow twisting stairway. As she reached the bottom, she stopped. There was no sound of footsteps behind no whir and clank of the elevator. She drew a long breath, trying to compose herself, and walked through the lobby with her head held as high as she could manage.

It was over. The hopes and dreams were dead. One of the desk clerks glanced at her, nudged his companion, and whispered something. She could almost imagine a voice behind her saying, "There goes Irina Kossok, back to where she belongs."

15

Irene's impulse was to run to Peter for comfort, but Peter was still at work—at Neptune et Cie, the last place in the world she dared go just now. Then Clara. No, Clara was out of town. Irene didn't know what to do or where to go. In her distress, she got turned around and started walking up Fifth Avenue, not down. When she realized she was nearly to Central Park, she stopped and looked around, trying to get her bearings. Glancing back toward Fifty-fifth, she saw Neptune and his chauffeur standing at that corner, hands shading eyes, searching for her. She hurried along north a few blocks, hugging the sides of buildings for concealment, then joined a crowd of people crossing the street into the park.

It was peaceful here, a quiet, wooded refuge. There was a light wind blowing the last of the autumn leaves off the trees. It was a warm day for November which was good, because Irene hadn't dressed for being outdoors. She meant to sit down in a normal fashion, but it was more of a collapse on the first park bench she came to. A little boy in short pants and long wool socks ran by, rolling a hoop, his nanny close behind trying to keep up without losing her dignity. A little farther away two men stood talking as their wives tossed bread to the ducks scrambling greedily in the lake.

As Irene gradually stopped shaking and calmed down slightly, she realized it was a very good thing she'd been unable to flee to Peter. He must never know what had happened today—for a great many reasons. For one thing, he'd said over and over how much he loved and admired her for her intelligence and good judgment. If he found out that she'd allowed herself to be lured into a hotel suite with Neptune—no, not allowed herself, she'd gone dancing in with a smile on her lips and blinders on her eyes—he'd be gravely disappointed in her. It was all so obvious, now that she knew the truth. The table set for two, Neptune's acquaintance with the waiter, the champagne, the gorgeous dressing gown—a fool would have recognized the situation for what it was. *She* had recognized it but refused to acknowledge her impression. She didn't want Peter to know she was a fool.

There were other reasons he must not know. He would be furious, of course. She remembered his clench-jawed fury that night Andy Spry had attacked her and she'd fled to Peter for safety. If he knew that Monsieur Neptune had made similar, if more sophisticated and less violent, advances, he'd never set foot back in Neptune et Cie. That must not happen. If he gave up his job and salary now that she had none, they would starve. With his skills, he'd get another job, but not one that paid half so well. They'd saved some money, but it would be quickly absorbed in taking care of her family, who'd proved to be more expensive than either she or Peter had imagined. Clothes, food, the nice little extras the younger girls enjoyed—all of it added up. No, Peter must not suspect that his wife's and therefore his own honor had been nearly compromised.

She got up, brushed leaves from her skirt, and looked into her handbag for bus fare. She had none. She'd have to walk home, and she'd better get moving if she was to arrive at a reasonable time. She walked briskly, to keep herself from dwelling on the most upsetting aspect of the afternoon, but it didn't stop her mind from circling and diving at the heart of her distress. Her dreams had proved to be as illusory and insubstantial as the painted flats at the theater where she first met Neptune. She'd believed in the long vistas of happiness and success and they'd been a sham all along. Worse than that—so was she. She'd learned an enormous amount and slaved at making herself better, and yet Neptune in his anger had seen through it all. He'd called her a peasant. That was the very worst. He'd located her greatest fear and held it up, flapping it in her face like soiled laundry.

Was she condemned to remain what she was born? Would she forever be the dirty peasant girl who'd been slapped and made to kneel and clean up the eggs? Was there no escape from her heritage? Did she have some indelible mark that could never be concealed, that would eternally identify her as Irina Kossok?

Finally, feet aching, she neared home. She slowed, knowing she had to get herself under control. The family, and especially Peter, must never suspect the trauma of this day. She must be an actress, more convincing even than Miss Terry. She walked in the door, a false smile on her face. Peter had come in only moments before and was standing in the tiny kitchen sampling something from a steaming pot and complimenting Zofia in Polish. "Ah, Irene, you're in time for dinner. You look tired. Did you have an interesting day?"

"Not particularly," she said brightly, putting down her handbag and notebook. "The client was a foolish woman who wasn't willing to pay for the goods."

Suspecting irony, he glanced at her questioningly, but was reassured by her bland expression as she passed him to change her clothes before dinner. "Mmmm," she said. "That smells good, mama. I'm starving."

The thought of food nearly made her gag.

She told him later that evening when she'd worked out in her own mind how to present it: "I've decided to quit, Peter. I told Monsieur Neptune this afternoon that I won't be back to work."

Now he was suspicious. "What happened today?"

"Today?" she said lightly, glancing up from a blouse she was setting a new sleeve into. "Nothing in particular. I just realized that you're right. I should be here at home, helping Mama and the girls settle in and learn their way around."

He wanted to accept this at face value, but found it difficult to rectify her bubbling enthusiasm this morning—every morning since she'd started her apprenticeship—with this offhand withdrawal from the field. Could she have changed so much in the course of a few hours? Apparently she had. But why? Peter wondered briefy if something—something?—had happened between her and their employer, but quickly dismissed the idea. Certainly she'd tell him if she'd been mistreated or offended. They always shared their feelings even if they didn't always understand each other. A nagging perception nibbled at him, but he ignored it because he wanted to. He longed to believe she'd abandoned that fierce ambition that he'd never comprehended. He wanted to believe that his reasoning had finally penetrated her thoughts and taken root. And he wanted her to be home. It would seem to be tempting fate to question her further.

Maybe now she'd think more favorably about having children. They hadn't talked about it since she started working at Neptune et Cie. He'd realized that to ask her to put aside the enormous pleasure she'd been taking in her work to start a family was unfair and probably doomed. But now? He wouldn't say anything just yet. Certainly it would occur to her.

Chandler came back a week sooner than he was supposed to from a hunting trip to North Carolina. He'd apparently heard through the grapevine that Mrs. Garrick was no longer employed by his uncle. Neither of them made any reference to her, but Neptune hadn't been faring well. He was haggard and the sharp edge of his tongue was blurred a little. "You looked tired, Uncle Jacques," Chandler said, leaning back and lighting a cigar.

"Put that thing out! You know there's no smoking allowed in the building," Neptune snapped.

"Sorry, forgot. That's what being away can do. Things slip your mind. Well, I'm back in the saddle, as they say in the wild west. You ought to take a bit of time off yourself. Just rest up and not think about anything at all." Chandler was beaming. He didn't know just where and when the battle had taken place, but without even participating, he'd won.

"Nonsense!" Neptune barked, and plucked the cigar from his nephew's fingers. "This is our busiest season. I can't afford to go running off to rot someplace even if you can." The last thing he needed was to leave the business now and let his mind be free to think—especially about Irene Garrick.

It was hardly even a real college, just a city institution housed in an old apartment building and providing night classes for the poor but bright and determined. It was nothing like the university Peter had once visited with Herr Schmitt—but nothing like the cutting floor at the factory either. Peter glanced around at the European history class as the students closed their books and prepared to go home. These young men didn't look so very unlike some of those he worked with, and yet there was a world of difference under those shabby clothes and kitchen-table haircuts. These young men, like himself, were obsessed with expanding their minds, and Peter found himself suddenly feeling outright affection for them, even though they were still virtually strangers.

"And will you be after joining us tonight?" a red-headed boy named Michael asked.

"I've got to get home," Peter replied. "My wife's expecting me."

"And can't she do without you for an hour?" Two of the others came to gather around Peter and Michael. "We've got this exam breathing down our very necks and we—"

"We need your help," one of the others cut in. He was an enormous, almost brutish-looking man named Pat who delivered ice in the daytime. "Michael's just got too much damned Irish pride to say so."

"My help? Why me?" Peter asked, rising and slipping his bus fare back into his jacket pocket.

"Because you're the only one of us who seems to be after knowing who all these Yorks and Lancasters are. To us they're just all Englishmen tearing about the countryside," Michael said soberly.

Peter laughed at this, for it was apparent from comments he'd made in class that Michael was more than competent to understand anything he set his mind to.

"I only wish it had kept on for a couple hundred more years," Michael was continuing. "It would have kept the limeys from having time to mess about with Ireland. Come on, just take half an hour for a beer and a bit of talk."

Peter ended up staying and talking with them for three hours and came home both satisfied and stimulated. They'd taken sides, Peter and Pat for the Yorks, Michael and another student for Lancaster, and they'd thoroughly enjoyed thrashing out their respective viewpoints on the politics and morality of the Wars of the Roses.

"Henry VI was a boy king—an infant king, in fact. That's

always a political disaster. His father's brothers had twenty years to squabble among themselves—''

''You're overlooking the entire theory of Divine Right—''

''Divine, my eye! The man was a lunatic!''

Halfway through, their teacher had come in and taken the Tudor position and they'd all ganged up on him.

''A clerk. Henry Tudor was nothing but a cold-blooded clerk,'' Michael said indignantly.

''Isn't that what you are in the daytime?'' Pat asked him.

''Damn right, but I'm not trying to be King of England!''

Peter was guiltily relieved when he came into a silent apartment and realized that everyone was asleep. He wasn't ready to break the spell and return to the real and mundane. Instead he slipped into bed next to Irene and fell asleep thinking of additional arguments he wished he'd thought of in time. And in the morning, instead of being tired from lack of sleep, he was eager to get through the day and get back to class.

Going to college, even just night classes at a poor man's college, was turning out to be everything he had dreamed and hoped it would be. He felt that he'd ''found his own kind.'' He was among people who respected what he knew and would cheerfully correct him when he was wrong without creating any sort of personal pain. And someday he'd be able to pass along this same joy in learning to others. It would be a long time yet, but it was a possibility that was beginning to fill his horizon.

Irene was devastated.

But she was determined that no one would know it. She woke every morning determined to make a better day of this than the one before had been, but it never worked out. She hadn't realized until she stayed home from Neptune et Cie that her home wasn't hers anymore. It was Mama's. In the year since her arrival in America, Zofia had stopped crying and lamenting and had stepped gingerly into her new life, but not in the ways that Irene had hoped. During the day, Irene discovered that endless winter, the apartment was chaos. Zofia's new friends were in and out all the time. Apolonia Jedrychowski and other old ladies wearing dark shawls and muttering in Polish about "the old days" sat around the kitchen table like malignant crows. They treated Irene like they treated all the rest of the girls—as another of Zofia's children and nothing else.

Lillie and Cecilia were becoming adapted to life in America, too, and also in ways Irene didn't like. They had terrific energy, and most of Cecilia's was spent on the front steps of the apartment building, laughing and flirting shrilly with any young men who happened to pass. Irene spent half her time dragging her back inside. "But, Irina, it's so stuffy and crowded in there," Cecilia said. "It's much nicer outside, even if it is cold."

"Why don't we go to the free showers. That will make you feel better."

"The showers!" Cecilia whined. "We went there day before yesterday. And we almost froze on the way home. Mama don't like us to go out with our hair wet."

"Then come in and I'll help you study the English books I got you," Irene urged. "You haven't studied at all today. You have to have some English before you can even start in American school. You've been here long enough now that you ought to be ready."

"Mama says it's ungodly for girls to go to school," Cecilia said. "Besides, nobody we know talks English except you and Peter, and you can both talk to us in Polish, so what's the use?"

She'd tried to explain it to them before, but made no impression. She kept telling herself what Peter said—that it would take time. They were still new to America. When the strangeness wore off, they'd be more interested in what there was to learn. But time was passing and they didn't seem to be changing except in bad ways.

Oh, perhaps that wasn't entirely fair, she reminded herself. Lillie occasionally showed some promise. She took more interest in some of the superficial aspects of success that Irene was trying to impart. No student, she still took an interest in clothing and fashion and was, in appearance, the most Americanized of them. And she'd learned a great deal more English than the rest, although it was Lower East Side English, on a par with Tilly Spry and the like. Still, it was a start and Irene would have to work with what was available in the way of encouraging her.

Aggie had adjusted better. She no longer cried and she suffered Irene's presence with better grace, but no enthusiasm. She never had regained her cheerful personality, however. "Let's walk down to Castle Gardens and look at the ships," Irene would say to her, and Aggie would shrug and answer, "I have some mending to do. Maybe another time."

Finally it became apparent to Irene that Aggie didn't want to talk to her or be friends with her, even though they had been as close and loving as the twins when they were younger. This rejection of her affections hurt more every day and Irene was resolved to get to the bottom of it. She adroitly managed to sit with Aggie in church one Sunday in February, apart from the rest of the family. As soon as the service was under way, she whispered urgently to her sister, "Come with me!" trying to make it sound as though she were ill.

She walked quickly and unobtrusively up the side aisle just as everyone stood for a hymn, glancing back only once to make sure that Aggie was behind her. Once outside, Aggie took her arm. "What is the matter, Irina?"

"Nothing. I'm sorry, but I needed to talk to you—without everybody around. We've never really been alone together since you came to live with us. They won't miss us. Let's walk."

Aggie was reluctant, but allowed Irene to take her arm.

"Aggie, you have to tell me what's wrong. I love you and I waited such a long time to see you, and now you don't even seem to like me. I don't know why. Can't we please go back to being sisters like we used to be? I need that, Aggie. Especially now."

She half-expected Agneiszka to get angry and pull away from such a direct appeal, but instead she walked along in complete silence for several paces. Then she gently disengaged her arm and slipped it around Irene's waist. "Oh, Irina, I have been mean. I know it and I'm sorry. It's just so awful . . ."

"Don't cry. Just tell me what's so awful. We're sisters; maybe I can help." Silly thing to say, really, considering what a mess she'd made of her own life.

"No, you can't help. You are the one who made it awful." The words were an accusation, but she hugged Irene tighter as she said them, as if forgiving as she spoke.

"I've meant nothing but good for you. What have I done?"

"You made us come here."

"I didn't *make* you come. I thought you wanted to."

Aggie stared at her with genuine surprise. "Wanted to? Why should we want to come here? We wanted to be with you, but it would have been better if you and Peter had come back to the village."

"*We?* You mean nobody wanted to come?" Irene had pulled away, completely stunned. "Not even Mama?"

"Mama less than anybody. She had to leave behind her friends and her chickens and her furniture and the house we were all born in, and Papa before us. We picked up *sakum-pakum* and came because we had to. There was no man to take care of her there with Papa dead and Teo gone and your husband here."

"But I thought . . . Peter and I have worked so hard . . ." The words clotted and stuck.

"Oh, Irina. Don't feel bad. I should not have said the truth. I am making you sad. And Mama and the twins are liking this country now. They no longer talk about going home. Even Stefania is coming to like America because there is good candy."

Irene couldn't speak for some moments. She must not be properly understanding what Aggie really meant. After all the years and years of work, of hope, of anticipation—to think they all regarded it as some sort of prison sentence, not the joy she always expected. No, it couldn't be, even if Aggie thought so now. They'd been here only a short time and everything was so different, still so frightening. In a few more weeks, maybe months, they'd realize what a wonderful thing it was to be in America. She blinked back tears, almost having convinced herself that Aggie's words were a mistake on her part.

Aggie leaned her head against Irene's. "I'm sorry I said anything."

"No, I asked you to. I need to know. But, Aggie, you

always liked new things. Why do you think you're so sorry to be here?"

"Irina, you think I am still a little girl, like when you and Teo went away. I am a grown woman. There was a man—"

"A man?"

"Yes, Olbracht Chalupiec. We were going to marry, but—"

"Oh, Aggie, I never thought! I would have been sorry if you hadn't come, but I would have rejoiced if you'd married your Olbracht. Why didn't you do that and let Mama come ahead with the others?"

"Olbracht didn't have the money to marry yet."

"What does Olbracht do? Is he a farmer? A merchant?"

"He is a peddler. Boar bristles and brushes."

"A peddler! Oh, Aggie, you couldn't marry a peddler!"

Aggie looked at her with surprise. "Why not?"

Irene cast her mind back, with difficulty, to that life. To marry a mere peddler was no disgrace for them in that world. Neither she nor her sisters could have aspired to any better match. "Aggie, you can make a better match here. It's not like the old country, where everybody has to stay what they are for generations. I'll find you a good husband—"

"No. I have lost Olbracht, coming here. But I will not have a husband of any other man."

"You'll get over him," Irene assured her.

"You know nothing!" Aggie said. "I will never marry."

"I'm sorry, Aggie. I didn't mean to sound like it isn't important. I know you must care about him a great deal. But the village is a long way and things are different here. People change. You will change. I have."

"I know you have." The words had a brittle edge, but Irene didn't notice.

"Why didn't you tell me this sooner? We've lived in the same house all these months and you didn't say a word—"

"Oh, Irene, when would you have listened? You had your study that you talked about all the time, and then when you stopped studying with that fur person a couple of months ago, you stopped talking to anybody in the house. You're unhappy too. I didn't want to pile my troubles on yours."

They walked along in silence for a while, each deep in her own thoughts, wondering how to keep the fragile bridge that had been built between them from collapsing again. Aggie was the first to speak. "Irina, you can write . . ."

"Yes."

"Can you show me how to write to Olbracht?"

"I'm sorry, Aggie. I can't read or write Polish. Only English."

"That would do. Olbracht has some English. His father had a rich patron when Olbracht was a boy. He and his brothers went to school. Then his father died and they had to leave and work to take care of their mother. I found a man at church who's been writing my letters for me, but I can't say what I really mean when I have to say it to someone else."

Irene's opinion of Olbracht went up a notch. Not enough to make any difference, but at least her mental image of him didn't include broken teeth and a wheelbarrow stoop anymore. If Aggie didn't soon stop pining for her peddler, Irene would have to think about finding a way to get her back to him. But even as she considered this, she was certain that she and America would win this silent battle. Aggie just needed some time. Irene had lost her chance to succeed in this country, but Aggie still might become somebody and forget the man she'd left behind. She'd be happier, Irene was sure of it. America had so much to offer.

"I will be very happy to show you how to speak and write English. I wanted to teach you along with the twins, but I didn't think you were interested. Clara taught me and it was exciting. Let's start today. It will be fun!"

Aggie half-shrugged. She didn't want to learn for the theoretical excitement of it, but for the simple pragmatic means of communicating personally with the man she'd left behind.

They were walking past a clock shop and Irene was reminded of the time. Glancing at her watch, she said, "Oh, dear! Mass will be over in five minutes. We must hurry back so they don't know we were gone."

Aggie smiled, the first real smile Irene had seen on her since her arrival. "Mama will think some godless American thing has gobbled us up. Yum, yum, yum, delicious Polish girls!"

They turned and, holding hands, hurried back down the street. It wasn't quite the same as dashing across a field at home, giggling with girlish abandon as they'd once done, but it made Irene just as happy. She had her sister back.

As for the shocking and incomprehensible news that her family hadn't wanted to come to America—well, it was only because they didn't know what the country had to offer. When they'd been here for a while longer they'd be glad.

And yet, when the joy of Aggie's finally opening her heart began to wear off, Irene wasn't so sure. She was still trying desperately to convince her family that this country was a land of opportunities. She heard herself saying, "In America anybody can become anything he wants!" but her own conviction was damaged. She had believed it, had tried to make herself into a real lady, but Monsieur Neptune had thrown her back into the sea of common immigrants. He'd told her that day at the hotel about people named Astor and Strauss and Belmont who'd started life as starving Europeans and had risen to positions of wealth and power in America, and within the hour, he'd torn that chance from her grasp.

She tried not to dwell on the heartbreaking catastrophe of it. Full of energy and ambition that no longer had a satisfying outlet, she threw herself into cleaning and cooking. All that winter and spring she tried to be a good wife, the only thing left for her to excel at. Trying to exert control as "the woman of the house" over Zofia's sloppy tyranny was a full-time occupation, but Irene always attempted to appear cheerful when Peter came home at night. He must never know how unhappy she was.

But he did know, in spite of himself. There wasn't anything he could put his finger on and say, "This is how she has changed," but he saw it all the time in the way she stood and walked—not stooped, certainly, but not as tall and proud. And the fire had gone out in her eyes. Something that used to glitter in her face was missing, replaced by a placid misery that sometimes showed through for bleak instants when she didn't know he was looking at her.

It was apparent, too, when they made love. She wasn't reluctant, she even initiated it sometimes, but there wasn't any more giggling and tickling or gasping moans of pleasure.

There was, instead, a desperation, a frantic edge to their intimacy. He tried to tell himself it was because their privacy was so restricted with the rest of the family in the next room, and indeed, that was part of it. Irene remembered the nights when she heard Jozef and Zofia having sex in the little curtained-off area of their house in the village and she didn't want to feel that her sisters were now listening to her and wondering exactly what was happening behind the door.

She explained this to him and he understood, but he still felt there was more to the change in her. She didn't smile the same way she used to. Her speech wasn't as brisk and she wasn't as alert as before. Something was broken and hurt inside her and he couldn't find it to fix it.

In some ways he was as miserable as she was. He cared more, he was discovering, for her happiness than his own. In fact, he couldn't be happy unless she was. And when he was in class or happily engrossed in his books, he felt a heavy guilt at the very enjoyment. All those years before he'd known her had started with misery and worked up to a plateau of bored contentment but he'd never known real joy until she became a part of his life. And now he'd found even more contentment in life, while some vital spark in her was flickering and dying, and he couldn't fan it back to life.

He tried; how he tried! He gave up his weekly visits with the priest in order to have a few more hours with her. He even missed some classes and passed up the opportunity to take a course in medieval French history because it met on Saturday afternoons and he wouldn't consider giving up that time with her. He took her for walks, took her for a ferry ride to the Statue of Liberty (a disaster—she'd read Emma Lazarus' lines, "give me your tired your poor, your huddled masses," and started crying), and bought her things, mostly books he thought she'd like. She thanked him brightly and read the books, but he sensed something counterfeit in her enthusiasm.

He was confused, unhappy, and vaguely angry—not at Irene, but at himself, his own apparent failing. Why couldn't he make her happy and fill that miserable void she seemed to be floundering in? He felt guilty for the deep satisfaction he felt in starting up the ladder to his own goal while she was so distressed. He'd never truly understood her deepest needs, so how in the world was he to fill them? Could it be that a child might be the answer, or was that only his own wishful thinking? He brought it up only once.

"Reenee," he asked casually one night as she sat on the edge of their bed brushing out her long fair hair, "have you thought about starting a family?"

"Family?" she said bitterly. "It seems I've got more family now than I should. Peter, I can't even seem to do anything for Mama and the girls. How could I possibly be a good mother?"

"What do you mean you can't do anything for them? We provide for them very well."

"*You* provide for them, Peter. But I can't give them anything, no matter how hard I try. The twins aren't learning any English, no matter how hard I try to teach them. Aggie wants to go back to the village. Stephanie is getting fatter and I can't convince her to stop eating so much candy and bread, and Mama . . . Mama! I tried to get her to buy fabric for a new dress today. I said I'd make it for her. It was dark green cloth. It was pretty and would have looked so nice on her, and she said it was ungodly because it wasn't black or brown. Oh, Peter, I'm failing you and I'm failing them . . ."

He could see he'd picked the worst possible time to initiate this talk, but tried to reason with her anyway. "Irene, you couldn't possibly fail me. Never say such a thing again, and you don't have to change your mother and sisters to be good to them. If the girls want to speak Polish and your mother wants to wear black and Stefanie wants to be fat—well, let them. Why not?"

"Because life can be better than that!"

"Maybe not for them, Irene," he said.

She didn't answer, and after a moment he could see her shoulders rise jerkily as if in silent crying. He crawled across the bed, smoothed down her hair around her face, and looked into her eyes. "Be happy, my love. Please be happy."

She dropped the hairbrush with a clatter and burrowed against his chest. "Oh, Peter . . ." she sobbed.

He rocked her like a child until the crying subsided. "Reenee, what can I do for you? What do you want? I'll get it, whatever it is."

She looked up then, a heart-wrenching attempt at a smile hovering on her lips. "Peter, I don't want anything in the world but you."

She thought she meant it.

He wanted to believe it.

16

July 1909

Zofia needed some fresh onions from the market. "I'll get them for you on the way back from the showers," Irene said, eager to escape the sweltering July heat of the apartment, even though she knew the crowded pavements outside were even hotter. The showers would be refreshing, but she'd be just as hot and sticky by the time she walked back. Still, she needed to get out. Eight months had passed since she left Neptune et Cie and nothing had changed but the seasons. "Aggie, do you want to come along?"

She was dicing turnips for the stew. "No, thank you, Irene," she said in English. She was the only one who called her sister by her American name. Was Aggie adjusting to life here? Irene wondered as she folded her small, worn towel and started out on the long walk. Or was she herself simply so miserable that Aggie's misery seemed less poignant in comparison? She wanted to believe that Aggie was accepting the idea of staying in America, but she had a growing conviction that her sister would never stop wanting to go back to her Olbracht. It wasn't anything she said, just her faraway look and faint smile when she labored over her weekly letter to him, and the resignation in her voice whenever Irene mentioned the future.

But that didn't happen often. Irene didn't want to think about the future—it stretched before her in endless gray sameness. Perhaps Peter was right: she should create her own bright spot on that bleak horizon by having a child. As she stood in the long line outside the showers, she thought about it as she had so often before.

She was young and healthy, and a maternal ache was

growing in her. Sometimes in the night she'd lay her hands on her flat abdomen and imagine it growing and swelling with life. Seeing other young mothers sitting on front stoops, nursing infants, she felt her own breasts throb momentarily. She wanted a baby, or she *would* if circumstances were different. But every time she imagined herself holding and cuddling an infant, she inevitably put the picture in its realistic context. A baby in their crowded apartment? Zofia would take it over as she'd taken over everything else. Virtually the only words it would hear and learn would be village Polish; the attitudes it would absorb would be those of the tenement. Irene had an absolute horror of a child of hers becoming one of the army of ragged urchins who roamed the busy streets, dodging pushcarts and playing stickball in the alleys.

She wanted a child, but she wanted an American child. How could she and Peter hope to influence even their own child in these surroundings? It would be difficult to convince a child that cleanliness was valuable and worthwhile when it meant this long, wrangling wait to take a shower in the summer. It would be equally hard to teach a child proper English in a household and neighborhood that spoke another language entirely. What little boy would want to be a scholar like his father when his cohorts were playing marbles in front of a candy store? What girl would care for courteous manners when her young aunts belched at the table and picked their teeth with their forks?

Finally, it was her turn in the showers. She undressed hurriedly and stood under the lethargic stream of lukewarm water which was all that came out in the summers. Someone started pounding on the door and nagging her to hurry before she'd even begun to wash her hair. "Wait your turn!" she shouted, and was sickened at the tenement shrillness of her own voice and the fact that she'd automatically spoken in Polish.

It frightened her into immobility. She'd feared how the tenement life would influence any child she might have, but now she realized it was slithering its tendrils around her like a voracious vine. In ten years, maybe five, she'd be one of them. One of the women with the untended teeth and sagging breasts and the stink of hopelessness that stayed in the room after they were gone. Those women of beaten spirit whose knees were knobby from kneeling and scrubbing, whose eyes squinted from poor light and little sleep, whose ears were no longer attuned to love . . . or suffering. The girl Peter loved would become an apprentice crone and his love would turn to indifference and finally dislike.

She scrubbed her hair, digging her nails into her scalp, trying to neutralize the mental pain with physical discomfort. Her ambition, her belief that things could and would be better, was what had fueled her days. Without it, she was sinking . . . sinking. Without it she was dull, numb, rootless. Without purpose, without hope, she would lose Peter and she would have nothing.

She rinsed her hair, not sure she was getting all the soap out and not caring very much. Someone was banging on the door again and a child was crying someplace in a wail-hiccup-wail pattern like a primitive timekeeping device. She refused to hurry consciously, but claustrophobia started to come over her and she ended up rushing in spite of herself.

She must make a point of visiting with Clara soon, she told herself as she threw on her clothes. Something had come between them since Irene left Neptune et Cie, and while she knew it was her own fault, she was helpless to do anything about it. Their bond had rested on their mutual belief that Irene could be "somebody." With the collapse of her dreams for a future, that bond had weakened. It wasn't that Clara had abandoned her—she had abandoned herself. Irene had withdrawn from the relationship, feeling that Clara's belief in her only underscored her misery. She hadn't even confided in her oldest and best friend the reason why she'd left her job, although she felt sure Clara, being so perceptive, must know. It was, after all, Clara who had warned her early on of Monsieur's possible intentions. Dear Clara would never have said "I told you so," but Irene sensed that the phrase would be in her head and both of them would hear it. It had been more than two months since they'd gotten together, and Irene couldn't quite bring herself, for all her good intentions, to seek her out and make plans for a day together.

She came out of the showers feeling worse than when she

went in. As she came up the steps from the basement, she found herself face to face with Jacques Neptune.

Monsieur! No, that couldn't be. Before she could think, a rush of pride galvanized her and she instinctively turned to flee, but he grabbed her elbow. "Don't run. I want to talk to you."

"No."

"Only for a few minutes."

"What are you doing here?"

"You mentioned once that you came here. I've been waiting to catch you alone. It's been a long time, Irene. I've missed you."

She should have felt alarmed, but wasn't. She was angry and at the same time oddly glad to see him. Standing in the midst of chaos and dirt, he looked calm and clean, an alien image in these surroundings. But even as she thought this, a renewed surge of outrage coursed through her. It wasn't the attempted seduction she was remembering, much as it had offended her. It was his accusations when she thwarted him that lingered in her mind as if it had been only moments before. "You threw me back," she said. "Now leave me alone. Go away. This is where I belong now. You don't."

His grip on her elbow was firmer. "We will talk."

"You've said everything there is to say. I'm nobody!" she repeated his words to her, mimicking his accent perfectly. "A woman whose name is a mouthful of Baltic consonants!"

She'd remembered every word, every intonation. It had been eight long, hellish months and she still remembered every word. He felt his breath catch for a moment before he could speak. She'd looked so crushed when he said the words to her. That look, preserved as permanently as a fossil fern, had haunted his days ever since. But now she was the living embodiment of defiance. "Come with me for five minutes. Please, give me that much time."

She hesitated only a second, but that was all he needed to steer her toward the vacant storefront two doors down the street. He jerked the door open. He must have made arrangements in advance, for it was unlocked and the shop was empty of all but dusty counters and a few packing crates.

Neptune slammed the door and pulled down the tattered green shade.

Neighborhood children came up and started knocking on the windows and darting away. The temperature inside the closed shop was stifling. But neither Irene nor Neptune noticed. He motioned for her to sit in a rickety chair by the door. "Irene, I want you to come back to Neptune et Cie."

"As what? Your paid whore?"

He almost flinched. It wasn't a word she would have used before. "No, as an employee."

"Never."

"Why not?"

She grasped a tattered end of her former dignity and dragged out her best English, miraculously undimmed by disuse. "I should think that was obvious. I don't care to talk about it." She made a movement, her hand started toward the doorknob.

He almost touched her again, but caught himself and spoke instead. "I was wrong. Very wrong. I had no right to expect . . . what I expected of you. We had a business arrangement. Nothing more. I've thought about it for a long time and I'm sorry for what happened. It shouldn't have."

She paused before answering. "I'm glad you see that, but it's too late. It makes no difference. I can't come back."

"Why? Because of your husband? Did you tell him?"

"Tell him and degrade myself all over again? Tell him how you insulted his wife? No, I didn't. And I won't."

"Thank you."

"Don't thank me. I didn't hide it for your sake, but for mine and his."

"Irene, why didn't you go to work for Revillon Frères?"

"They wouldn't have a woman designer." She answered quickly.

Too quickly, he thought. "Is that the only reason?"

"No."

"Why not, then?"

She'd been looking out through a tear in the door shade. Now she turned to him and spoke venomously, "Because of loyalty to you. I didn't owe you my body for what you did for me, but I did owe you professional loyalty."

He nearly smiled at this admission. "Irene," he said in a

soft voice, "please come back. It will never happen again. I promise you that. I swear to it on everything that means anything to me. I'll never touch you again. Come back and we'll be just like we were before. Teacher and student."

She met his look directly. "No, nothing would be the same. I can never go back to being innocent and trusting and stupid. I learned a great deal in that hotel room, monsieur. More than I learned during my apprenticeship—and I learned it from you!"

He hadn't cried since he was a child, but now he could feel a sob rising in his chest and had to fight it back. Dear God, what he had done to her! He kept remembering a moment he thought he'd forgotten—the day she served tea in his office and was so entranced with the sugar cubes. Her eyes had been wide with wonder and delight at those simple shapes. But the delight was gone, her eyes were cold, and there was a hard edge in her voice. And he—goddammit!—had done this to her. He had destroyed something precious.

She started to move her hand toward the door again, and he said, "No, this won't do. You *must* come back."

"Why? Why me? Find someone else to teach. Leave me alone. Stay out of my life!"

"I can't find anyone else. Not like you, Irene. You're too talented to rot away down here. You could be the best." He hadn't fully realized how sincerely he meant this until he heard himself saying it. "The best," he repeated. "Better . . . better, perhaps, than I am."

"Than you?" she asked, stunned.

"Yes, dammit! Do you want me to grovel? I'll grovel. You have a gift. A real gift. The way you look at a fur and turn it in the light to assess the gloss, the way you touch it and know the density, the look in your eyes when you hold it up to your face, the way you know how it will hang when made up. I had to learn all of that and it took me far longer. You knew it instinctively and I saw that talent and affinity every time you touched a pelt. I had to make mistakes, waste furs, waste time, to learn. You know things inside that I don't. And you know things I didn't have to teach you."

"Don't," she said. "Don't say such things. You will only

tempt me, and I can't give in to the temptation. I won't give in!"

"Why not, Irene? You want it. I want it. Come back."

She crossed her arms and stared straight ahead. Her jaw was clenched and a bead of sweat was running down the side of her face just in front of her ear. "Don't you know fear when you see it? Can't you tell how terrified I am?"

"Of what? Me?"

"Of what you can do to me. I didn't know until that day in the hotel room that the only reason I had anything was that someone gave it to me. Clara gave me manners and books and English. My husband gave me a home and his love. You gave me knowledge and a place in life—but you took it away. On a whim. A whim! Not because I didn't do my job, not because I lacked talent or wouldn't work hard enough, but because I wouldn't play the whore. You had the power to take it back! I didn't know that could happen!"

Tears filled her eyes, but her posture was still rigid. "*I didn't know it could happen!* That's a horrifying thing, Monsieur Neptune. To realize that these things can be taken away. I thought I was earning something that was mine to keep because I was good at it. Yes, I know I'm good. I didn't need you to tell me. But I learned that my job, my place in life was only temporarily in my keeping until you decided to withdraw it. I can't let that happen again. Ever. *Ever*, do you understand? That's why things can't ever be as they were—because I won't accept that. I won't give you that power over me."

Without giving him any opportunity to reply, she stood up, opened the door, and stepped out onto the sidewalk. "Don't ever come back to my neighborhood, Monsieur Neptune. We have nothing else to talk about."

"But, Irene—"

"Good-bye."

Neptune leaned back against the dusty counter, sucking in deep drafts of air. He felt cold and sick. He'd intended a rather routine seduction, nothing more, but he might as well have raped her that afternoon at the St. Regis. He *had* raped her, in a sense. He'd violated her soul, defiled her innocence.

* * *

That night she said to Peter, "Do we have enough money to pay Aggie's passage back to the village?"

He looked up from the shoes he was polishing. "I think so. Do you want her to go?"

"No, but it's the only thing she wants. She must have it Peter. She's never going to be happy here. She'll never be happy anywhere without Olbracht. She'll never stop thinking of him and wishing . . ."

"You'll miss her."

"Yes, but that isn't what matters."

He smiled and went back to what he was doing. "We'll buy the ticket Saturday afternoon."

"Peter . . . put those shoes down and come to bed. Please."

"Haven't you made this unnecessarily complicated?" Jacques Neptune said, sorting through the stack of papers.

"I've only done as you asked," Edwin Ellis replied. He could hardly disguise the disapproval he felt. As a lawyer, he felt a sincere obligation to protect his client's interest. But what was there to do when the client was insistent on a self-destructive course like this?

"There is no way it can be rescinded?"

"I'd like to meet the lawyer who can find a chink in it," Ellis answered with bitter pride.

"Very good," Neptune said, setting the stack on end and tapping it on the desk. "I'll return my copies to you as soon as I can."

"Jacques, we're old friends, and on the strength of that, I beg you to reconsider this. It's the sort of thing that can be taken care of later in a will—if you still feel the same way."

"I plan to live a long time, and by then it would be too late. No, Edwin, it has to be done now."

"But suppose you change your mind?"

"I won't. I've asked you to make it so I can't."

"What about your nephew?"

"It doesn't concern Chandler."

"Of course it concerns Chandler."

"He's made his own bed—"

"Dammit, Jacques, why don't you just set the chit up in a nice house and give her an allowance!"

Neptune put the papers in a drawer of his desk and slammed the drawer. "You are under the wrong impression, Edwin. I'll forgive your vulgarity because of your ignorance, but don't make the error again. She's not my mistress and she never will be."

Ellis had witnessed a number of Neptune's dramatic rages, but he'd never seen genuine anger in the man, and it was frightening. "I'm sorry, Jacques—I assumed you were in love with the girl."

Neptune softened slightly. "That's immaterial to the matter at hand."

Ellis rose, the better to escape before Neptune made any more embarrassing admissions. "I'll come back later this week about those other contracts you asked me to look into."

Neptune waved him away. "No hurry."

He sat for a long time sorting through the papers. There was still time to change his mind. He could crumple them right now and no one but stuffy old Edwin Ellis would ever known the madness he'd considered. Surely it *was* madness. But it was the only way, the only right way to do what he had to do. He'd racked his brains for an alternative, but there wasn't one. There never had been one.

No, of course that wasn't true. There was a logical alternative—to forget this whole foolish idea as Edwin suggested. It was madness. And yet, he'd worked all his life, given up his youth, for this company. If he wanted to treat it recklessly, it was his right. It didn't have to be sensible or logical. It only had to be right, and what he was going to do was right—for him. He didn't owe explanations to anyone, even himself.

He *was* in love with her. He'd tried to talk himself out of the absurd notion for endless months. And then one night a month earlier he'd awakened in the middle of the night with a pain in his chest. It had passed quickly, but it had frightened him into facing the truth. He was getting older. He'd spent a lonely lifetime building up this business and had no one to appreciate it properly.

Worse, in all those years there'd never been a woman he'd felt this way about. Face-to-face with himself that night, he'd admitted that it didn't matter that she was married to a man she apparently loved and would remain utterly faithful to. Nor did it matter that he could never tell her what he felt or possess her body. In fact, as beautiful and alluring as she was, it was her talent and ambition that acted as such a strong aphrodisiac. It was that sense of like calling to like that had first caught his attention and had now wrapped its tendrils around his aching heart.

What difference did it make if his actions didn't make any sense to anyone else? He owed no explanation to anyone. Not even Irene. Especially not Irene.

He pushed the desk buzzer and Miss Troutwhite appeared. "Send for Peter Garrick, Troutwhite. He's a cutter down on the second floor. When he arrives, send him straight in and do not allow any interruptions."

Peter arrived in ten minutes. "Come in, Mr. Garrick," he said, and pretending to fuss over lighting a cigar, he surreptitiously studied the young man. He was as he remembered him: lanky, fair-haired like Irene, with that same clear, cautious look in the eyes that she had. But what else was there? What made her so attached to this man that she could turn down all Neptune could offer in order to be faithful to him? Ridiculous query. This man was young. Youth would win every time.

He didn't know where to start. Reaching in the drawer, he ran his hand over the top sheet of the papers Ellis had prepared. He cleared his throat, but Peter didn't wait for him to begin. "If you've called me up here to fire me, I can save you the trouble. I realize you only offered me this job because of my wife—that was the only reason I took it, frankly. So with her gone, I'll understand—"

"No, no. Nothing like that. But it was your wife I wanted to talk to you about."

Peter sat a little straighter, ready to be offended.

This was it, Neptune realized. His last chance to withdraw. Once he set this in motion, it couldn't be stopped. Nor should it. He reached into the drawer again, took the papers out. "Mr. Garrick, your wife is tremendously talented. I don't mean merely clever. She's remarkable."

Peter smiled wryly. "You called me up here to tell me that? I don't need to be told."

"I'm sure you don't. But I'm not talking in a personal sense in regard to her beauty or charm or any of her domestic virtues. I'm talking about furs. Mr. Garrick, I want her back here."

"Why are you telling me this? Tell her."

"I've tried, but she wouldn't listen to me."

"And you want me to plead your case?"

"Not exactly plead. I have an offer to make. I'd like to explain it to you first."

"Then explain," Peter said, leaning back comfortably in the chair and crossing his arms.

Damn! Where did these two get their arrogance? Garrick was sitting there for all the world as if this were *his* office. Though, to be fair, it was *his* wife they were talking about, and that did place him in a position of some superiority at the moment. Neptune shoved the papers forward, but Peter made no effort to pick them up. Neptune rather liked him for that, in spite of himself. "I have no children, no heirs. I've spent my life building up this business; the years are gaining on me and I have no one to pass it on to."

"There's Mr. Moffat, your nephew."

"He's a fool."

Peter merely nodded his agreement. "What has this to do with my wife?"

"I want to share Neptune et Cie with someone who can appreciate it and help build it. I don't want to wait until I'm dead and won't see the results. I want to give your wife half of Neptune et Cie."

There! It was done. And it had stunned Garrick.

Peter sat forward. "You want to what!"

"I want to give your wife—you and your wife, legally—half of my business. Now. Today if possible."

"You must be insane. Either that or you're making some sort of horrible attempt at a joke. Why on earth would you do that?"

"Because she's good. Because she deserves it."

Peter shook his head. "No, that's not why."

"Because it's the only way I can get her back! And I must have her back. No, don't get up. Don't get that look. I'm not making any sort of indecent proposal. Would I make it of you if I were? Think! I want the best there is for Neptune et Cie. It's all I have. It's my sons and daughters, my past and present and future. This company is my blood and my soul. Would *you* give all that to someone like Chandler Moffat? I believe she's the most talented individual I've ever met in the fur trade. I've trained dozens of apprentices, always hoping the next one would be the one with the magic, and they never are. A talent like that can't be wasted, Mr. Garrick. Here, this is the paperwork to make it legal. Read it, take it to my lawyer or to any lawyer you want."

Peter picked up the papers but didn't look at them. "And what do you want in return?"

"Nothing."

"Don't take me for a fool! Nobody gives away half his life's work for nothing."

"All I want is your wife back here. That's all."

"That's a great deal."

"But it's what she wants. Or didn't you know that?"

Peter had no reply.

"Look it over. Take the offer and the papers to her. I'm not asking you to do this or anything else for me. Do it for her."

"Peter, you're late. I was getting worried," Irene said. She was waiting for him on the front steps of the apartment building.

"I was seeing a lawyer."

"A lawyer? What in the world for?"

"It's a long story. Go tell your mother we're going for a walk so she won't worry about you."

"Peter, what's wrong?"

He ran his hand through his hair distractedly. She'd never seen him make that gesture, and it, more than his words, frightened her. "I'll be right back," she said, running up the steps.

She was back in a moment and linked her arm in his. She waited patiently for him to speak, even though questions were clawing their way up her throat. Finally he started explaining. "Monsieur Neptune called me in today. We had an extraordinary conversation. If I didn't have the papers to prove it happened, I'd be thinking I was mad and had imagined it all."

"Conversation about what?"

"About you. I don't know where to start," he said, pulling the folded sheaf of papers from his jacket pocket. He handed it to her. "If you sign these papers, you will be given half of Neptune et Cie. Irrevocably. For life. Half the company, half the stock, half the warehouses, half of everything."

She dropped the papers, stooped and picked them up slowly. When she'd gathered them, she handed them back to Peter. "Why?"

He repeated the conversation to her as well as he could remember it. Several times he doubled back on himself and had to say, "No, he said that after he said . . ."

She listened to the whole thing without a word of response.

"I took off the afternoon. I saw two different lawyers. They both said the papers are in legal order."

Still she said nothing. She took his arm again and they began to walk slowly. A child playing hide-and-seek ran into them. They veered around a portion of sidewalk where some girls were playing hopscotch. The sun was down now and people were visible in lighted windows. People eating, people laughing and arguing, women crooning cranky babies to sleep and sitting in the window to catch any errant breeze that might come along. A young couple sat on their stoop kissing; an older couple was playing cards on a tiny table they'd set up in the street because it was too hot indoors. An ice-cream vendor made his way lethargically down the street, not bothering to hawk his wares, but merely letting customers notice his passage.

"What shall we do?" she said finally.

Peter shrugged. "It's up to you, Irene."

"No, it's not. You keep promising you can take care of me, and you do—very well. Take care of me now, Peter. Tell me what to do."

He'd suspected it might come to this and had been thinking for hours of what to say. He didn't want her to do it. He wanted her to himself, his alone. He despised the idea of her being part of someone else's sphere. It meant hours apart, it almost certainly meant putting aside any thoughts of children of their own—at least for a long time yet. But all of that was purely selfish and he knew it.

It also meant her happiness. Neptune had been right, and Peter had known it all along. She wanted this. Already there was an almost imperceptible spring in her step that hadn't been there for months, and a briskness in her voice that he'd missed. This would put life back into her eyes. He wanted to clutch at her and say, "Don't do this! Don't ask this of me! Of us! Of the children we might have had by now!" and yet if he did, he'd kill something essential in her. Her spirit would wilt and die before his eyes. It would be the same as her telling him he could never read another book, never talk to another learned person. Never take another class. He would do that for her, if she asked, just as she would abide by what he said. But she'd never ask such a sacrifice of him. Nor could he expect it of her.

He turned to her and said, "Do it, Irene. I want you to."

She looked for a moment as if she hadn't understood the words; then she flung herself at him. "Oh, Peter! My wonderful, wonderful, beloved Peter. I was so afraid . . . Oh, thank you, Peter. Thank you for understanding."

They walked home with their arms around each other's waists like newlyweds, but to Peter it was a death march.

17

August 1909

"I wish I could go home to Olbracht *and* stay with you, Irene," Aggie said.

"I wish it too, but don't let Mama hear you say that," Irene replied, glancing over her shoulder to make sure Zofia hadn't been listening. The ship was due to leave as soon as all the passengers had boarded, and Aggie was only one of dozens hanging back for a few last words. Zofia was busy weeping on Peter at the moment. He gave Irene a look, rolled his eyes to heaven, and went on patting her mother on the shoulder.

Zofia had behaved horribly ever since Irene and Peter told Aggie that they'd purchased her return passage. "What did I do to deserve such daughters?" she'd cried repeatedly. "Girls who leave their mother and go off around the world without a backward glance—*aieee!*" But she never offered to go back with Aggie, Irene noticed. For all the wailing and lamenting she'd done when she arrived almost two years ago, Zofia Kossok had taken firm root in America, in New York, and in Peter and Irene's home. She was both as feeble and as tenacious as the weeds that occasionally sprang up in cracks in the sidewalks.

Irene had found another girl going back to Poland for Aggie to travel with, so that she wouldn't be on her own. But as the day for departure drew nearer, Irene wondered if that had been necessary. Her sister became the old Aggie she'd remembered from childhood—cheerful, competent, and self-assured. What a pity it happened only because she was getting to leave.

"I'll miss you, Aggie," she said.

"And I'll miss you—everybody, but most especially you, Irene. You're the only one who understands how much it means to me to go back to Olbracht. Now, I must let Mama weep on me one more time," she said with a sympathetic smile. They hugged long and tightly, then Aggie asked, "Do you think we'll ever see each other again, Irene?"

"Oh, I hope so, Aggie. I hope so!"

Irene had brushed and aired the black dress she'd worn before as an employee and presented herself to Miss Troutwhite. "I am to see Monsieur this morning," she said.

"I know, Mrs. Garrick, and may I say, I'm glad to see you back. We've missed you here."

"Thank you, Miss Troutwhite. Oh, Monsieur . . ."

Neptune had come out to greet her instead of having her ushered in. She hadn't seen him since that day outside the showers several weeks earlier. All the legal work leading her here today had been done through his lawyer, Edwin Ellis. She'd wondered at first why he hadn't contacted her himself, but soon realized it was his way of making clear that this was a business, not a personal arrangement.

His manner now supported that theory, and no one but himself would ever know at what tremendous cost in self-control. "Mrs. Garrick, please come in. Troutwhite, have our other visitor wait until I buzz you."

They took their customary places, Neptune behind the wide desk, Irene across from him and perched forward on one of the leather visitors' chairs. "I am, needless to say, gratified to have you here," he began stiffly. His accent was prominent today. "There are many things we must discuss, however, before you actually begin work. As you must realize, there will be substantial resistance in several quarters to the announcement that you have become a full partner in Neptune et Cie."

"From your nephew?"

"From him and from many employees. Only Troutwhite knows so far. I will, if you wish it, make the announcement this morning and we shall face the whirlwind as best we can. I don't mind a bit, of course."

Irene smiled. How much they were alike in many ways.

This was something she had thought long and hard about. "I do mind, monsieur. That's why I asked your lawyer to request that you not reveal our arrangement to anyone before my return. I know that I am legally your partner now. But I'm not morally entitled to that distinction until I know as much about Neptune et Cie as you do. I don't want to 'face the whirlwind,' as you say, until I'm in a position to take over your place if it became necessary. For now I would rather be a silent partner. There's so much I don't know yet . . ."

He leaned back, his stuffiness of a few moments ago gone. "You are, without doubt, the most sensible woman I've ever known. No, the most sensible *person*."

"I'm not being sensible, I'm being a coward, monsieur. I'm not ready to defend my position, and I know I'm going to have to defend it. I presume you have an alternative plan in mind?"

"You see through me, Mrs. Garrick. Of course I do. I propose that we present your position as a further stage of your training, which in fact it is. But only a few will know exactly what you are training *for*. Then, when we are both agreed that you are ready for the consequences, we will make the announcement. Is that agreeable?"

"Yes. It's what I hoped for. There is one thing I didn't talk to the lawyer about . . ." She paused, thinking back to the day stuffy old Edwin Ellis had reluctantly laid out the financial outlook to them. Irene had actually felt faint at the sight of the numbers on the balance sheets he showed her. If she understood correctly—and she was sure she did—the income from her half of the profits of Neptune et Cie would be in the neighborhood of seventy-five thousand dollars a year. It was such a staggering amount, so much more than even her most grandiose dreams, that she felt almost guilty. There was someone else, besides her and Peter, who deserved part of it.

"Is there something wrong?" Neptune asked.

"No, but I want to have a secretary of my own."

"That's certainly up to you. What do you need a secretary for right now? Certainly Troutwhite can handle—"

"I'm sure she can. But I want my friend Clara to have a secure job, and she'll also be very good."

"I understand perfectly," he said, and he did. "Very

well." He sat forward, crossing his arms on the desk. "We shall begin. Let me explain something to you . . ." Where to start? he wondered, with something he'd always understood to the core of his being but had never put into words before. Could he make anyone else grasp it? Perhaps no one but Irene Garrick, who seemed to have been born with the same instinctive ambition.

"Mrs. Garrick, the people we deal with are the rich, the socially prominent, as you know. They buy from us, not necessities, but the luxuries that make them stand apart visibly from the common masses of people. Their money, however, imbues them with no more taste and sense of style than the average person. They wouldn't ever admit this, not even to themselves. But they come to us not only for furs but also for taste. Do you see? Yes, I think you do. Now, the crucial part of this is that they would never ask the advice of those they consider their inferiors—and shopkeepers are inferiors in the eyes of *nouveau riche* railroad barons' wives. So we must not appear to be shopkeepers. We must appear to be their social equals, or even their social superiors, who are merely doing this work as an amusement. We must appear to be of their class."

"I think I see what you mean," Irene said. "It's the difference in the way they speak to you and the way they speak to the fitter who takes their measurements."

"Exactly. The fitter doesn't attend their balls and dinners, nor does she 'know' them socially. I do. I am a man of breeding, education, culture, money—therefore, they may ask my advice without losing face. The moment I appear common, I lose everything. You see how important this is?"

"I do."

"And you must have guessed why I tell you this?" He was treading on thin ice and he knew it.

"Because I am common," Irene said with a bluntness that sliced through her as if she'd flung herself on a sword. "Who is this dirty, common girl?" the rich little Russian girl had said. Neptune had said something very like it. The words echoed in her head as if they'd been spoken that moment. But while she despised the memory of those moments when other people had pointed it out to her, that didn't prevent her from knowing the truth.

"No, you're not common. Your background is common, but you are not. You merely lack the polish you must have."

He rose from his desk and went to the window, hands clasped behind his back as he stared out. "You are quite lovely in a fine-boned way. No, this is not an idle compliment, merely an assessment, Mrs. Garrick. Do not look embarrassed or alarmed. You have none of the heavy, dull peasant about you. You look like you might be a princess—though, truthfully, I've seen real princesses who had all the grace and bearing of kitchen maids. You can certainly 'look the part.' The other thing that I have frequently noticed about you is your speech. Your accent is utterly unplaceable and quite intriguing. It is not American, nor English, and certainly not Polish, but something more mysterious and exotic, or so it would appear to anyone who knew nothing of your background."

Irene stiffened. Was he going to ask her about her background? She had made no secret of her past, of her humble origins, but neither had she ever offered any information that wasn't absolutely necessary. And it was still, in spite of their renewed and quite formal relationship, a touchy subject.

He turned and sensed her wariness. "No, Mrs. Garrick, I do not propose to pry. In fact, I don't want to know exactly where you came from, or why. I prefer to work with a blank slate."

"A blank slate?"

"Since your past is, I assume . . . 'undistinguished,' we shall, before long, invent for you a new past. In the meantime, you must become prepared to play the role that you will adopt— that of a mysterious but highly bred lady."

"And my family? My husband and mother and sisters?"

Neptune paused. "They will play what roles we determine they are capable of playing."

Irene pictured Zofia wailing at the sight of a bus, and lumpy Stefania dipping her bread in her stew and slurping. She had her work cut out for her at home, that was certain.

Neptune came back to his chair, sat down, and leaned forward. "There's much you must learn before you're ready.

On the assumption that you would feel the same way about this, I took the liberty of arranging for you to take lessons in deportment. Instead of coming here every morning, you will be reporting on Mondays, Wednesdays, and Fridays to Mrs. Rumsey at this address." He pushed a card across the desk. "She'll instruct you. She's a very old friend of mine who used to have a school for young girls. She lost her school because of unfortunate circumstances, and now gives private lessons. She's utterly trustworthy. you needn't fear that she'll ever reveal to anyone what she might learn about you in the course of teaching you. Nor, naturally, does she know about our business arrangement."

He pushed the buzzer on his desk and Miss Troutwhite came in. "Is Mrs. Rumsey here yet? Good, send her in."

Mrs. Rumsey was a small woman, as brittle as fish bones. Her hair was white, her face lined, but her manner was that of a young and quite magnificent woman. She took tiny, careful steps, but still seemed to sweep into the room. Irene instinctively stood and offered her chair, although there was another next to it that was its equal.

Mrs. Rumsey inclined her head graciously, sat down in a single fluid motion, and addressed Neptune. "Jacques, it was horrible of you to make me wait out there!"

He bowed his head. "It was indeed. Will you ever forgive me?"

"Possibly. Now, what have we here? Is this the girl?"

She took a pair of glasses on a little gold stick from her small tapestry bag and held them up to study Irene. "Hmmm . . . turn around, child. Yes. Now, walk across the room. No, don't run! Walk. That's better. Let me see you sit down. Oh, dear. That needs work, doesn't it? Watch me. It's all in the feet. Right foot slightly behind the left and sink like a flower petal on a light breeze. Bend only the knees, don't lean forward the slightest bit. Try again. Yes, that's much better."

She turned her attention from Irene and addressed Neptune. "She's quite lovely. Has she any brains?"

He concealed a smile. "Yes, considerable brains. In fact, her intelligence may stand in your way."

Mrs. Rumsey's pale cheeks colored. "Nothing has ever stood in my way, Jacques! Certainly no mere girl!"

"I merely meant that she may question the reason for some of society's sillier rules of which there are a great many."

"She may question all she likes on her own time. I will not waste my time on such matters. I am merely going to teach her what is 'the done thing.' "

"You will find her a willing and apt student, Marie," he said. "Very, very willing and extraordinarily apt."

Mrs. Rumsey cast Irene another appraising look. "We shall see about that."

Irene told Peter she was leaving the company's offices for the day and would meet him later at home. Then she was taken with Mrs. Rumsey in Monsieur's private car to the instructor's shabby-genteel home in Greenwich Village. She learned little the first day. The time was taken up with Mrs. Rumsey's testing her to determine, as she put it, "the exact depth of your ignorance."

Irene failed at French, having never seen or spoken a word of it. "I hope your grasp of English indicates a talent for languages," Mrs. Rumsey sniffed. "I presume English is not your native tongue?"

"No, it is not," Irene said. "I grew up speaking Polish."

The instructor seemed moderately pleased, with reservations, about Irene's general movements. "You can at least walk, when required to," she said. "So many girls never get beyond a modified gallop or some sort of crippled mince. Now, let me see you eat."

Irene came home feeling battered. Mrs. Rumsey gave few compliments, and only when richly deserved; she was more generous with her criticisms. But oddly enough, Irene liked her, or at least respected and admired what she had to offer, and the iron-willed little woman's complaints only served to stiffen Irene's resolve to extract all she could from the lessons.

She walked back to St. Mark's Place holding her head high and pretending she was balancing a book. She met Peter at the front steps. "What went wrong?" he asked. "I kept expecting the company to go into an upheaval when people learned why you were back there."

"We're not telling anyone yet," she said, and went on to explain as they climbed the steps.

"Then I guess I'll stay on awhile longer," Peter said, opening the door of the apartment.

"What do you mean?" Irene asked, but there was no chance for him to answer. Zofia met them at the door with a long list of complaints, starting with her irritation at Irene for going to work at "that fur place" and finishing with a story about a rabbit she'd bought to fix for dinner that was spoiled. She wanted Peter to take it back and tell the butcher off.

He patiently listened, then said in Polish, "No, it'll do no good for me to speak to him. He'll just hush it up. It would be much better if you tell all your friends about it, then they won't go to his stand and his business will suffer."

"Ahh, this is right," she said, going back to the kitchen.

"That was clever of you," Irene whispered.

"Clever? 'Desperate' is a better word. I couldn't see myself stalking the streets carrying a spoiled rabbit. But we may not be safe yet—don't you wonder what she *is* fixing for dinner?"

"Peter, what did you mean before, about staying a little longer?"

"Just that I can't stay on at Neptune et Cie." He'd made up his mind the first time Neptune spoke to him of the arrangement, but had vowed not to discuss this aspect of it until all Irene's decisions had been made. His own plans must not be a factor.

"Why not?"

He looked at her for a minute, tempted to spill out his feelings but knowing he must keep it lighthearted. "A man who's too proud to keep company with a spoiled rabbit is a man who won't be his own wife's employee."

"Oh . . . I see. I hadn't looked at it that way. But of course you'll have to have a much more important job."

"No, Irene. I don't want another job. I'm good at the one I do, but I'm not in love with this business the way you are. It's just a means of earning a living to me. Furs are merely dead animal skins as far as I'm concerned. I'll keep on awhile, just to keep you company on the way back and forth to work, but when you're ready to announce the partnership, I'll quit."

"I wish you wouldn't."

He leaned down and kissed her on the tip of her nose. "Don't waste your time wishing. That's how it's going to be."

She went to visit Clara later that evening at the theater where she was working. Clara knew the moment she saw the blaze of excitement in Irene's eyes that something very important had happened.

"I have many things to tell you, my wonderful friend," Irene said. "Let me help you hang all these dresses up so we can talk."

She explained it all, to Clara's astonishment. To her old friend she confessed what she'd never told Peter—about the day at the St. Regis Hotel. As she'd suspected, Clara had guessed. By the time she'd told the whole account of the partnership, she was out of breath from talking so steadily and intently. "I will soon need a secretary, a trusted assistant, a person who will stay with me forever—a friend. Clara, it must be you."

A dirty blond waif on the ship eight and a half years ago had said, "You cannot give me this American language and I give you nothing," and Clara had replied—she remembered as if it were yesterday— "Someday, perhaps you will make a gift to me in return."

Clara Johnson was a proud woman who would have never accepted anything that smacked of charity, but she knew this wasn't charity, this was the repayment of a debt in Irene's eyes. To turn it down would be egregiously insulting. Besides, she didn't want to turn it down. Irene was her spiritual daughter, all grown up and on her way to apparent success of a magnitude that neither of them could have anticipated, but she was still in need of guidance—more guidance than she might know. She did need Clara. Most important, Clara knew she could indeed be the best person in the world for the job she was being offered.

"Yes, Irene. It shall be me."

They hugged, and cried together for a brief moment, but it was Clara who brought back cold reality. "What about Peter? How does he feel about all this?"

"He's pleased," Irene said confidently. "Why shouldn't

he be? We will have more than enough money now to live well. It's everything we've dreamed of and more. He says he will stop working at Neptune et Cie very soon and he will be able to go to school all the time like he's always wanted. He can be a teacher and he can have his own motorcar and anything else he wants. Oh, Clara, it's going to be wonderful. Peter can have nice clothes and a whole library of books and meet influential, important people."

" '*Przypisywanie zwykłym ludziom nadzwyczajnych właściwości,*' " Clara muttered. "All his geese are swans." Why had the old Polish saying come to her mind? And why was she so sure Peter didn't want a motorcar and a library provided by his wife's money?

Yes, Irene was going to need her.

The next week Irene began her study of French. "You need not learn to speak the language," Mrs. Rumsey explained. "You need know only enough to give the appearance of having studied it when young, as all girls of breeding have done. You must grasp the pronunciation, remember perhaps twenty common phrases, and be able to read a menu."

Irene liked this tart, practical attitude, but found herself actually enjoying the study of another language. "What is the past participle of—" she started to ask one day.

Mrs. Rumsey waved away the question before it was completed. "No need to know, unless you wish to study it on your own time. If so, I can give you a grammar book. But our time is too limited and too precious to stray from our specific goal."

"I can always speak French with Monsieur Neptune when I've learned enough," Irene said.

Mrs. Rumsey allowed herself a smile, an exceedingly rare, lemony expression on her thin face. "You must mention the possibility to him. I would like to be there when you do," she said. She seemed on the brink of saying more, but caught herself up short. "Now, once again, what does 'Florentine' mean in the descriptioin of a main dish?"

In her meager free time Irene made quick shopping forays for treats and ready-made clothes for her youngest sisters. Clara could tell, perhaps even more perceptively than Irene, what a difficult time they were causing and what an embarrassment they still were.

Stefania, who had wanted them all to return with Aggie, wasn't interested in the dresses Irene got for her, and clung to her drab old garments, as though they might magically transport her back to the village, but the twins were thrilled, and though the clothes weren't particularly good quality, they were clean and new and the bright colors looked nice on them. Lillie was especially grateful. "Here's a new soap for each of you to use on your hair, too," Irene said. "You may wash it tonight and I'll braid it for you before bed."

"Wash again?" Lillie wailed. "You made us wash our hair just last week. Mama . . .!"

"You must wash your hair more often. It looks and smells nicer. And don't call for Mama every time I talk to you."

She was like a person standing with one foot on the dock and the other on a boat that was drifting away. During the day she was learning how to recognize good-quality pearls, how to set a table for an eight-course meal, how to select a wine. At night she was trying to convince her baby sister not to pick her nose, at least not while she was helping in the kitchen.

Peter was supportive, but his help was confined primarily to setting a good example. He wanted to back Irene, "But I haven't got any business telling them what to do, and they and I know it," he said.

For the next six months Irene subjected herself to the tutor's tyranny. Mrs. Rumsey used Mrs. Beeton's *Book of Household Management* as her primary study guide. "Terribly middle-class and old-fashioned in a number of ways, of course," she pronounced, but nevertheless made Irene study it from cover to cover.

The emphasis of the huge, heavy book was on food. "I'm not studying to become a cook," Irene commented on one of the rare occasions when she dared express dissatisfaction.

"Society centers around sex and food," Mrs. Rumsey replied with uncharacteristic candor that shocked Irene and made Clara laugh when Irene told her about the remark. "Neither Mrs. Beeton nor I are inclined to teach you the first, so we must concentrate on the second. There is hardly a single social occasion in which food does not play a part. You—or rather the lady you aspire to become—will probably never cook a single dish, but as mistress of a household, every woman must know more about cooking than her cook. The same is true of all household responsibilities. If the maid is not getting the soot off the marble firefront, the mistress must know whether it is the formula of the cleaning material or the integrity of the maid at fault."

The course of study included a long and exceedingly tedious section on the servant. Every possible type and degree of servitor was named and defined, along with their precise duties and the order and method by which they were to be done. Mrs. Rumsey drilled her on the differences between the responsibilities of the valet and butler, the housemaid and footman. She made Irene memorize what to use to clean silk ribbons, to wash hair, to whiten scorched linens and soiled collars. They planned picnic menus for forty guests, formal buffets for twenty, and after-theater suppers for eight.

In between bouts with Mrs. Beeton, Irene studied what amounted to a history of fashion. Mrs. Rumsey resurrected stacks of ladies' magazines, made Irene chart the course of hems, study the evolution of the bustle, learn the names of every current and outmoded style of sleeve, cuff, collar, skirt, belt, hat, necklace, shoe, and petticoat. They spent an entire awkward afternoon discussing—with oppressively restricted vocabulary—the full range of undergarments.

All this information was put to a practical application as a new wardrobe was created for her: two evening gowns to start with, as well as tea dresses, afternoon dresses, modestly anonymous dresses for work. There were also shoes, handbags, hats, umbrellas, and hosiery to be chosen. Two things were *not* made in the orgy of sewing. One was nightwear, for these clothes, the selection of which Mrs. Rumsey was overseeing, were for her professional life, not her personal life. The other item excluded from her wardrobe was furs. She had no need for them; she would always be seen in fur coats, preferably a different one for every occasion, but they would belong to the company. She was to be a walking advertisement for their best wares.

Irene was also expected to read vast piles of books as her

training in literature. She and Mrs. Rumsey had a minor tiff over this when Irene had not completed a five-hundred-page assignment one day. "I've been reading every moment I could," Irene explained. "I just couldn't get through."

"Reading? You mean every word?"

"Naturally."

"No, no! You're only to skim the books. You need only read enough to be decently conversant with the plot and remember the main characters' names. If you can do that well, you will appear to be the most brilliant, well-read woman in New York. Any deeper knowledge would terrify both the men and the women of the circles in which you will be moving." That was the first time Irene suspected that Mrs. Rumsey, far from worshiping the manners she was drumming into Irene, had a deep contempt for them but recognized them as extremely useful social weapons.

There was a month-long study of music, at the end of which time Irene knew the difference between pianissimo and fortissimo, the names and compositions of dozens of composers, and could pick out a few bars of Chopin or Beethoven with an offhand grace. She never managed to sit down at the piano, however, without remembering the first time she had ever seen the extraordinary object that made music, played by the Russian girl with glossy curls. She had to remind herself that that impressionable child had been Irina Kossok, the village girl. She was a different person now—Irene Garrick, apprentice and still-secret partner to the greatest furrier in the world. And if Irina Kossok still lived deep inside her, no one else would ever know.

"What if someone asks me to play the whole piece?" she said with an edge of panic when she reached the end of the eighth bar of one of her half-dozen partial selections.

Mrs. Rumsey acted out her reply. She rose from the piano bench in mid-phrase, waved her hand airily, and said, "Oh, too, too boring. I do get so weary of hearing myself. Won't someone else please play instead. . . ."

Monsieur Neptune never inquired into Irene's progress—at least he never inquired of her on her days at Neptune et Cie. She assumed he consulted with Mrs. Rumsey or with Clara, who was doing her own apprenticeship with Troutwhite. The lessons seemed endless. There was always something more to learn, some new and unexpected avenue of correct behavior unveiled just as Irene began to feel she was getting a grip on the situation. "Oh, Mrs. Rumsey, surely I'm nearly 'finished'?" Irene asked after an especially grueling day of lessons on the various roles servants play in the households of the wealthy. Irina Kossok, who could never have even aspired to belong to the servant class in the village, now had to remember that a lady's maid was responsible for sewing only her mistress's garments, while a housemaid was responsible for hemming and repairing all linens except handkerchiefs.

"My dear Mrs. Garrick," Mrs. Rumsey replied (she never unbent enough for first names), "you are attempting to learn what most women spend twenty years absorbing through their pores. You've been at it only six months. But to reply more directly to your inquiry, yes, I believe you are almost 'finished,' as you put it. In fact, I have so informed Monsieur Neptune, and we have an appointment with him this afternoon."

The appointment was at his home, not at his office, where they might be interrupted or overheard. After a formal tea, during which Neptune and Mrs. Rumsey both watched Irene's behavior like a pair of hawks judging their fledgling's first kill, he dismissed the butler and got down to business. "I've planned a dinner party for a week from Saturday. You will be my hostess, Mrs. Garrick. Mrs. Rumsey will attend as well."

Irene inclined her head graciously. How very well she had learned all that Mrs. Rumsey had taught her, he thought. It was quite astonishing. If he weren't quite certain this was the gauche, timid girl he'd first seen in Ellen Terry's dressing room, he wouldn't believe the change. This Mrs. Garrick—wasn't it about time to start calling her Irene?—was the essential grande dame in the making. It might be all surface, all pretense, but she had the looks, the bearing, and the manners to rival anything Caroline Astor or her like could dish up. At least he thought she did. The dinner party would be the test.

"Will my husband attend?" Irene asked.

He'd anticipated that question and had an answer ready that would delay the inevitable. "It's up to you and him, but I would advise against it. Though he's an intelligent and courteous man, and men are not grilled as ruthlessly by society as women, there will hardly be time to prepare him to participate in the charade."

"The charade?"

"Yes, that's why you and Mrs. Rumsey are here today. We are about to create your past. Marie, if you're agreeable, I'll set out my thoughts first and you may amend or add to them your own considerations."

At her nod, he went on, "I think the best approach would be the opposite of the obvious—that is, I believe Mrs. Garrick should claim to be an absolute nobody. Claim it often and loudly and with exaggerated modesty. It will make people suspicious. No one will believe such an outrageous claim. If the lady doth protest too much the social lions will vie with one another to speculate the most exalted explanation."

"Brilliant!" Mrs. Rumsey said with remarkable animation. "You are absolutely correct."

"I, as her sponsor, will of course be dropping hints like a flower girl strewing rose petals. And it is the tenor of those hints which we must determine. Should Mrs. Garrick be my niece?"

Mrs. Rumsey considered this. "No, I think not. The implication is improper. Every rich man has a 'niece,' which sadly has become something of a euphemism for a less respectable relationship. Your real nephew will undoubtedly dispute it. Moreover, Mr. Peter Garrick, though not physically present, must be constantly alluded to. Perhaps if *he* were a cousin, a second cousin . . .?"

"I believe you're right. Yes. Now, where have they come from?"

"Either the Balkans or Russia," Mrs. Rumsey replied quickly. She'd obviously thought this out before. "I think Russia is a better choice. For one thing, it's more nearly true. If faced with geographical questions such as climate or landscape, Mrs. Garrick, being Polish, could answer more comfortably from personal experience than from study alone."

"It's also much more difficult to check on," Neptune said, nodding. "There are so many mysterious branches to the Romanoff family that almost anyone can claim to be one of them and no one can dispute the claim with real certainty."

Irene had been watching them as though they were conducting a spirited tennis match. But what a match! Her whole persona was the prize at stake. Up until now she had merely tried to remember it all, so that she could repeat it to Clara at the first opportunity, but at the last comment she felt compelled to interfere. "You don't mean to change our name, do you? Not to Romanoff!"

"No, of course not," Neptune replied, somewhat surprised at her remark. He'd gotten so wrapped up in the plan that he'd almost forgotten she was present. "No, and we shall never actually say you are a Romanoff. Merely make clear that you changed your name and that you prefer not to use your husband's 'real' family name. That way there is no outright lie to be caught up in. Why *did* they change their name, Mrs. Rumsey?" he asked.

She was ready. "There are always minor uprisings in Russia. It is, in the opinion of many, a vast tinderbox of revolution. And there have been rumors of eccentric elements of the nobility being involved in some of them."

"Marvelous! Mr. Garrick's father, a second cousin of the tzar, was a generous if slightly dotty landholder who misguidedly allowed himself to get caught in some land-reform movement—" Neptune began.

"—and as a result, had his extensive holdings seized by the tzar, leaving the family to flee the country for their lives," Mrs. Rumsey took up.

"He died en route, leaving his son and daughter-in-law a legacy of nothing but remembered glory and a name that is too dangerous to use for fear the tzar's long arm of wrath might extend even this far!"

"Oh, dear," Mrs. Rumsey said. "If we're giving *you* a cousin who is a cousin of the tzar—"

"No, his wife—Mr. Garrick's mother—was my cousin. A Frenchwoman he met while attending the Sorbonne in his youth," Neptune said.

"Of course. How silly of me not to have remembered!" Mrs. Rumsey said, actually clapping her hands together.

They're having fun! Irene realized. Why shouldn't they? This was the culmination of more dreams than merely her own. Neptune had invested a year of caring and money and hope in her, not to mention half the business he'd worked a lifetime building, and Mrs. Rumsey had spent the last six months with all her thoughts on creating a lady from a Polish peasant. Why should they not be enjoying themselves?

If anyone else had tried to influence her present or her future as high-handedly as they were remaking her past, Irene would have stormed out in a fury. But the truth was, there was nothing on earth she wanted to lose as thoroughly as her real past. She was faced with it day in and day out when she returned home. Her only fear was that Peter would balk for some reason at this cold-blooded fantasy. But on reflection, Peter had even less affection for his youth and the memories it brought up than she did. Why should he mind inventing a new and more pleasant past?

When she told him about it, however, he dismissed the idea. "I'm not making up some entertaining lie about myself."

"But what if people ask you questions at the dinner party?"

"They'll have to ask them very loudly, because I'll be right here at home studying," he answered. He was irritated, but wasn't sure why, so he was trying hard to conceal it.

"You're not coming?"

"Did you think I would? Irene, this is ridiculous and I don't see the necessity. But even so, I don't mind what sort of stories you make up so long as you don't expect me to tell them."

"Oh, Peter, you're angry. I'm sorry."

"I'm not angry, just unconvinced and unwilling to take part. You didn't really expect me to, did you?"

Irene hardly noticed that Christmas came and went. She bought gifts, attended church services, and helped the girls put up a tiny, spindly tree, but her heart wasn't in it. Finally it was over, the new year started, and the last week before the dinner party was taken up with preparing specifically to live up to the history Monsieur Neptune and Mrs. Rumsey had invented. A Russian tutor was engaged to enable Irene to pepper her conversation with Russian phrases. Mrs. Rumsey taught her how to toss them in lightly (". . . like herbs in a salad, ever so judiciously") and then carry on as if unaware that she'd lapsed into her "native" language.

On the day of the party, a spare bedroom was turned over to Irene and Mrs. Rumsey to dress and prepare themselves for her debut. At Neptune's direction, Irene wore her hair swept into a loose chignon at the back of her neck. Her dress was a deep sea-green with a modestly high neck and a bodice cut to be both proper and provocative. She also wore a discreet, inexpensive bracelet that Clara had given her in honor of the occasion. Mrs. Rumsey had protested this item, but Irene had implacably refused to remove it. She took one last look in the long mirror before going to the library to meet Neptune and get his final approval.

"Monsieur . . .?" she said, suddenly shy at the way his gaze went over her.

"Lovely, lovely," he murmured, reaching into his pocket for a small padded satin box. He opened it and took out an exquisite pair of small emerald earrings. "For you, my dear Irene, on your opening night."

Mrs. Rumsey noted that he'd used her first name. She cocked a thin eyebrow and said nothing. Unlike Clara, who had shared virtually everything she knew with Irene for the love of Irene and the addiction to teaching, Marie Rumsey was simply doing what she was hired to do and performing in her usual thorough way. It was her job to give the girl the veneer of a lady and she had done the job. The rest was none of her business.

Irene went to the mirror and put on the earrings, turning her head one way and the other so that the candlelight caught and reflected the mesmerizing green jewels. "They're beautiful, monsieur. I will never be able to thank you enough—for everything!"

Neptune was embarrassed by the intensity of her words and even more by the perception he saw in Marie Rumsey's face. Well, she might perceive that he was in love with Irene, but she'd never understand that he would never act on it. Nor did he owe her any explanation. "It's nothing. Only a bauble. There! Was that the doorbell? Are you ready, Irene?"

For a fraction of a second Irina Kossok was on the floor of the manor kitchen mopping up broken eggs. She could feel the cold stone floor against her knees, the yolks running between her fingers, the slap burning on her cheek.

"Oh, yes, Monsieur Neptune," Irene said, standing very straight. "I've been getting ready for a long, long time."

18

It all went by too quickly. Irene wanted to slow time down so that she could hear, taste, and enjoy everything more intensely. It was a brilliant evening; the very air shimmered with spangles of light; a night to cherish for years to come. She was still too young and too smitten with success to realize that with true and further experience the memory would inevitably fade.

Besides herself, Jacques Neptune, and Mrs. Rumsey, there were only five dinner guests: a bright young couple named Smythe who were newly married and too wrapped up in each other to take any interest in anyone else; a business acquaintance of Monsieur's who started drinking the moment he came in the door and was in a fair stupor most of the evening; a dashing sportsman named Edward VanCleve who was frequently mentioned in the social columns of the best papers; and a widow in her fifties whom Jacques introduced as Mrs. Parker Gillis.

"Dear Jacques, that sounds so stuffy," she said. "Please, you must just call me Lydia," she said, taking Irene's hand and giving her a frankly appraising look. "I will now steal you from the rest of the guests, you lovely child, and you will tell me all about yourself."

She dragged Irene off to a cozy sofa and began her interrogation. It was all done with the utmost courtesy and consideration, but was penetrating in spite of the sugar coating. Was she enjoying New York and, incidentally, where was Irene from? How did she come to be in this country? Such an interesting accent. British? Russian? Where had she learned her impeccable English? So looking forward to meeting Mr.

Garrick, tell all, darling, what was her husband like? Where was he tonight? Such a very lovely frock—who made her dress? Such a lovely pair of earrings—were they a family heirloom?

And Irene gave all the right answers. She knew the dispossessed-Russian-royalty story inside and out and managed to follow all Mrs. Rumsey's instructions about sprinkling in phrases, dropping names, feigning fear of recognition for what she "really" was, without actually saying anything. "Oh, I'm the merest nobody, Mrs. Gillis. An immigrant in this lovely country." . . . "Dear me, I couldn't possibly tell you the name of the town I'm from. It's so insignificant you'll never have heard of it, then I'll be embarrassed! How I wish I could say I was from some lovely civilized place like . . . oh, London or Paris. Where are you from. Mrs. Gillis?"

It was like playing badminton with an invisible birdie.

"Please, you must address me as Lydia if we're to be friends, and we *are* going to be friends. And I cannot believe you are a nobody! Next thing you'll be trying to tell me you came here in steerage."

Irene gave a rippling little laugh and glanced around to see if Mrs. Rumsey or Monsieur was near enough to rescue her from this barrage of questions. Neither of them appeared to be paying the least attention to her.

But Edward VanCleve was. When her gaze met his fleetingly, he used the unintentional contact as an invitation to join the two ladies. "I don't believe we've met before, Mrs. Garrick."

"Possibly not. My husband and I have been in this country a very short time."

"Your husband couldn't join us tonight?" he asked.

"No, unfortunately not. My husband is a scholar, Mr. VanCleve. A very learned and reclusive gentleman. He cares little, I'm sorry to say, for the society of large numbers of people."

"I shall, however, look forward to meeting him sometime," Lydia Gillis said. It was almost a direct threat. *You will produce him.*

"I trust your hopes will not be disappointed," Irene answered sweetly.

"Since your husband can't be with us tonight, I shall be more than happy to escort you home," VanCleve said. "He wouldn't mind, would he?"

"Not in the least, but there is absolutely no need."

"I'm sure there isn't, but it would be my pleasure," VanCleve persisted.

"How gracious of you. But I must decline. Monsieur Neptune has already made arrangements for my transportation." Irene studied him as she spoke. He was certainly good-looking enough to justify his reputation as a playboy. Tall, slim, a little like Peter in coloring, but more sophisticated, more flamboyant. Was it a matter of tailoring alone? Or was it that dry, almost-mocking tone in his voice and the languid, self-assured way he moved? Something that came naturally from being born to old American money, no doubt.

Lydia Gillis had been watching this exchange. "No need for Jacques to send someone with you, my dear Irene. You're probably on my way. I'll be glad to drop you off. Where *do* you live?"

Somehow, in all the planning, they'd all neglected to foresee this question, but Irene was so thoroughly immersed in the character she was playing that she countered immediately, "Oh, I hardly know. Some poky little place south of here—or is it north? I'm so bad about directions. We're looking for a suitable house, of course, but it's such a time-consuming business."

"Why don't you and your husband live with Jacques? After all, you are relatives." Mrs. Gillis wasn't about to let go of the subject.

"He offered, of course. So kind of him. But my husband has all these tons and tons of books—well, there just wasn't a place for us and the books! I'm afraid we should be looking for a warehouse rather than a home!" She laughed brightly, partly at Lydia Gillis' defeated expression at receiving this nonanswer.

"You don't share your husband's interest in study?" VanCleve asked.

Irene wasn't at all sure what the 'right' reply to this was. If she implied that she was a scholar, she would violate all Mrs. Rumsey's teachings about ladies not showing themselves as intelligent. But if she claimed ignorance, she would violate her own principles and jeopardize her future image as Jacques Neptune's capable partner. "I share all my husband's interests, sir," she said rather stiffly.

"I didn't mean to offend you, Mrs. Garrick," VanCleve said contritely.

"I took no offense, I merely find myself a tedious and boring conversational topic," she said with a forgiving smile. "Tell me, Mrs. Gillis, have you lived long in New York?"

"Darling, you simply must call me Lydia!"

"I shall be honored to do so when I feel we know each other better," Irene replied.

Strangely enough, Mrs. Gillis took no offense at the snub, but smiled broadly.

Irene had known that people would be curious about her, but she'd had no idea that strangers would question her so aggressively. Monsieur had warned her, and so had Mrs. Rumsey, but until it actually happened, she'd been unprepared for the intensity of the questioning. But of course it made sense. She was an outsider, an unknown interloper who was expecting to be accepted in their very rarefied inner circle. It was a very exclusive if entirely unofficial club, the requirements for membership in which were high. There were constant hordes of socially ambitious people attempting entry, and the stockades had to be constantly, vigilantly patrolled.

Edward VanCleve insisted on taking her in to dinner on his arm, leaving Lydia to the stuporous businessman who apparently supplied Neptune et Cie with tanning chemicals and wanted to mumble about them to anyone who would listen. Fortunately, the seating arrangement was such that Lydia Gillis was thwarted in her attempt to keep up her interrogation, though VanCleve managed to take up where she'd left off, albeit in a more flattering and less aggressive manner. Apparently Neptune had primed him with the story of the Garricks' flight from Russia and it had piqued his interest. "I understand you speak Russian, Mrs. Garrick? Such a complex language, I'm told."

"I wouldn't know. Mr. VanCleve. I speak nothing but English."

"But surely English isn't your native language."

"It is now," she replied. "Have you tasted the veal? Such unusual seasonings."

"Did you enjoy much veal at home?" he persisted.

"As a matter of fact, we had a lovely cut just last Tuesday," she said, and had to suppress a giggle. It was like a game, she was discovering. There'd never been the time in her life for games, but this one—because the stakes were so high and she was so well prepared—was a delightful challenge. Could this be why Peter enjoyed his chess matches with his friends at St. Stanislas?

Finally the meal was done, the dessert plates cleared, the port and cigars enjoyed by the men while the ladies exchanged trivialities in the drawing room. The Smythes were the first to depart, and the chemical-firm owner was poured into his coat and seen off. When Edward VanCleve made a move to leave, offering once again to take Irene home, Neptune firmly rejected the offer and made no attempt to keep him any later. "Very well, if I can't be any further use, I guess I'll run along," he said, still apparently hoping to be urged to stay.

"So good of you to come, Edward," Neptune said, steering him toward the front hall.

When Neptune returned, he sat down before the fire and spoke to Lydia Gillis, who'd shown no signs whatsoever of leaving. "Well, how did she do?"

"Absolutely superbly, Jacques. I did my nosiest best to catch her out and she sailed through."

Irene looked from one to the other, uncomprehending. They seemed to be talking about her. She glanced at Mrs. Rumsey for enlightenment, but the older lady had taken a little piece of needlepoint from her bag and was assiduously threading a needle with green yarn.

"The accent is perfect," Lydia went on. "Did you teach her that? I thought not. Do you know, darling, she even managed to snub me a bit when I pushed too hard for intimacy. Beautifully done. A bit arrogant, but entirely proper. I doubt you taught her the arrogance. That must come naturally."

Irene was stunned and angry, though she couldn't quite figure out why. Jacques caught the glitter in her eye and the clench-jawed look in her face. "I forget to mention that Lydia and I are old and very good friends, Irene."

"Just an oversight, I imagine," Irene said coldly.

"See!" Lydia crowed. "That's the haughtiness I mean. It's wonderful. So few women can carry it off, but it suits her."

Neptune leaned forward in his chair, fixing Irene with his gaze. "I didn't forget. I deliberately deceived you. Is that the admission you want? I had to know—we *all* had to know—if you could stand up under the most rigorous testing before turning you loose on the world at large. Certainly you see that. It's to your own advantage. And I'm pleased to say that any woman who can keep her head and heed her tongue in the face of Lydia's snooping can face anything."

"Yes, I see," Irene replied. And she did see the reason, but she still felt used and foolish. "Was Mr. VanCleve part of this as well?"

"VanCleve? Of course not. He was just a socially acceptable male I asked to even out the table."

Lydia rose and waved an airy summons to the butler. "My coat, please. I've got to get home. I really am delighted to have met you, my dear," she said, taking Irene's hand. "And I'm sorry to have been a party to anything that might have distressed you. The best of luck. I'm sure we'll meet again."

"Thank you . . . Lydia."

When she'd gone, Irene said to Neptune, "I presume you believe she will not tell anyone else the truth?"

"About you? She doesn't know the truth. I only asked her to see if she could find or create any cracks in the facade. And she's utterly trustworthy. We're very old friends and know all each other's secrets."

"Including mine?"

Mrs. Rumsey rose suddenly. "If you will excuse me a moment, I think I shall repair my hair. Then I will accompany Mrs. Garrick home."

"Thank you, Marie."

They were alone for long moments before Neptune spoke again. "Irene, I was born in Cleveland."

"I beg your pardon?"

"I was born in Cleveland. My name was Jack Fisher."

"But . . . I don't understand."

"Don't tell me you didn't suspect?"

She was genuinely shocked, and laced through her shock was a desire to laugh. "Jack Fisher?"

"You don't think anyone's really named anything so romantic and unreal as Jacques Neptune, do you? I made it up."

"You don't have to tell me this."

"But I do have to. You know why, or you should. My mother was a farmgirl from Kansas who ran off when I was a baby, and my father was a drunk ex-Union soldier. I went through fifth grade, then quit school and worked in the stables of a pork baron and his wife. Eventually I worked my way up and took on odd jobs in the house. I was pleasant and quick to learn and they had no children. When I was sixteen, they were killed in a railway accident and I was astonished to discover that they'd remembered me in their will. It was only a hundred dollars, but it was enough to get me here. The wife had a cousin in the fur business, and I went to see him. I won't bore you with the whole story—it's much like your own. Seeing wealth and wanting it. Shaping myself to fit a different level of society. Choosing a name, creating a murky but interesting past. And a glamorous name."

"And Lydia Gillis knows this?"

"Lydia Gillis and I crossed paths quite early. I can't tell you when or how. Her past is her past. But yes, she knows. And now you know. You're the only two people in the world who do."

"What about your family? Your nephew?"

"Chandler's my wife's nephew, actually, and my wife never knew. It would have distressed her."

Irene was speechless and was spared having to think of anything to say by Mrs. Rumsey's reappearance. Neptune's chauffeur was waiting in front of the house to take the women home. As Neptune handed Irene into the car, she kept his hand for a moment and said, "Monsieur, I thank you for the earrings and . . . and for the other gift."

He smiled at her tact and closed the door.

The secret of his own background was indeed a gift, and a valuable one. Irene sensed, without being told, why he'd shared it. It was an effort to even the score, to hand her a weapon of equal caliber to the weapon he held over her. He had deliberately, knowingly, made her extremely dangerous to him. Such knowledge, given out to the jealous, critical society he moved in, could destroy him. And yet, he'd given it to her, trusting that she would never use it.

And in that there was also the promise that there would never be a repetition of the accusations he'd made against her at the St. Regis that terrible afternoon. He could no longer fling her humble origins in her face without her being able to reciprocate in kind.

"Oh, Peter, you should have been there. It was wonderful," Irene said, hanging the beautiful new dress in the closet. Zofia and the girls were visiting neighbors and Irene had hurried to undress before her mother could see the dress and make any comments. She had grave reservations about the sort of remarks she might come out with.

"Who was there?" Peter asked. He was searching for a reference in a large dusty book and the question had a bored, polite note that Irene didn't notice.

"There was this couple named Smythe. I hardly talked to them—in fact they were too interested in each other to bother with anyone else. Then there was a man who does business with the company. I'll have to get to know him later, of course, but since no one knows yet of my connection with Neptune et Cie, I hardly felt I should show too great an interest in his conversation, though I did overhear him say something to Monsieur about a new process. I'll have to ask about that—"

"Hmmm," Peter said, rustling pages.

"Peter, you're not listening to me."

"Of course I am. New process, ask Neptune."

She closed the closet door and started taking the pins out of her hair, and at this Peter did look up. "I like that," he said.

"What?"

"Watching you take your hair down. It's lovely hair, of course, but more important, it's such an intimate thing. There's no one in the world but me who ever sees you that way. What are those? New earrings? Did you buy them today?"

"No, Monsieur gave them to me to wear tonight."

"You're giving them back tomorrow, I assume."

"No, they're mine to keep."

"I'd rather you didn't."

"Why?"

"I don't like other men giving my wife gifts," Peter said.

A silence fell between them. Both were thinking how foolish a thing that was—to complain about her accepting the earrings when she'd already accepted, with Peter's consent, half of Neptune's business, his lifework.

"I'll give them back tomorrow," she said, quickly removing the jewels and putting them into the handbag she always carried to work. She sat down at the battered second-hand dressing table Peter had found and repainted for her. Brushing out her hair, she tried to recapture the bubbling happiness she'd felt until he'd noticed the earrings. "There was a woman there named Lydia Gillis, Mrs. Parker Gillis. She's an old friend of Monsieur's and she gave me a terrible time—asking me all sorts of questions, trying to catch me in a lie. I learned later that he'd put her up to it. It made me angry at first, but Monsieur explained why he'd done it and then he—"

No, she had no right even to tell Peter. It was a sacred secret Monsieur had entrusted to her. It gave her a traitorous feeling to keep it back, but she would have felt equally terrible betraying Neptune. In fact, she simply couldn't do that. She laid the brush down, staring at herself in the mirror. For a single bleak moment she sensed that her loyalties were, of necessity, divided. It was something she hadn't anticipated and didn't know what to do about.

She turned away from the image in the mirror. Peter had gone back to his book, not even concerned about the sentence she'd dropped halfway through. "There was also a man there named VanCleve. Edward VanCleve. Isn't that distinguished-sounding? He looked a little like you, Peter. Tall and fair. But his eyes were darker and he wore his hair shorter. Yours might look nice that way, in fact. We ought to try it. I could cut it like his. And he was wearing a suit that was sort of slate-gray with blue it in. That would look nice on you, too.

Perhaps we could go out Saturday afternoon and see if we could find one like it. You'd look nice in that color."

Peter didn't look up from his book.

"He asked me lots of questions too, but Monsieur hadn't planned his interrogation, as he had Lydia Gillis.' He was just curious, I think. He kept asking me about Russia, and you should have heard how cleverly I managed to dodge his questions. It made me think of you and your chess games. Planning several moves ahead, trying to outguess your opponent. You'd have been proud of me."

She watched him, waiting for his comment, but there was none. So she went on, determined to interest him in her monologue. "At dinner he talked to Mr. Smythe about his new motorcar. It goes thirty miles an hour, he said. Can you imagine? Wouldn't it be exciting to get out of the city and go that fast, just like a train, but without all the soot and noise? Do you think we ought to consider getting an automobile like Mr. VanCleve's?"

At that Peter slammed the book shut and stood up, towering over her. "No, I don't want an automobile like Mr. VanCleve's! I don't want his automobile, I don't want his haircut, I don't want his suit, and I certainly don't want to play his nosy social games!"

"Peter!"

"Irene, can't you hear yourself? Why would I want to be like this man? I'm me, not some useless fop named Van Cleve."

"He isn't a useless fop. He's a nice man."

"With better looks and clothes and much fancier toys than I have."

"I didn't say that! That isn't at all what I meant. I was just trying to talk to you. Peter, you sound jealous."

"Maybe I am," Peter said, surprised at the concept. "Yes, maybe I am."

"That's ridiculous. I'd have far rather been having dinner with you than with him tonight. You should have come along!"

"I had dinner here. And so could you have if you'd wanted."

"But, Peter, you know how important . . ." Against her will, her eyes were filling with tears.

"Yes! Yes, I know!" Peter said wearily.

They were interrupted by the noise and confusion of Zofia and the girls coming home. The twins were crying over something and Zofia was screaming at them. Peter picked up his book and went out to referee, as had become his habit whenever the noise level got unbearable.

By the time Irene got her hair braided and went out to see what was going on, he'd left. "Where's Peter, Mama?"

"He had some book to take back to a friend." She had hold of Lillie and Cecilia by their braids and was holding them apart. Both girls were shrieking. Stefania was sitting in the corner greedily tearing waxed papers off pieces of taffy and stuffing the candies in her mouth as quickly as she could.

"Girls! Stop that noise. Stefania, pick up those papers. They'll stick to everything. Mama, did Peter say when he'd be back?"

"A man who doesn't tell his wife, doesn't tell his mother-in-law," she said, giving Irene an accusatory look.

Cecilia used this temporary lack of attention to slip out of her mother's grip and fling herself at Stefania. "They're to share, you piggy-pig! Mama bought them for all of us!" She snatched the paper bag, which ripped, sending taffy and candy papers all over the room. Lillie got free and fell on Stefania as well. Stefania wailed and clutched frantically at the candy sack. Zofia dashed across the room and started screaming and slapping at whichever child was closest at hand.

Irene went back to her bedroom and closed the door. Flinging herself on the bed, she wrapped the pillow around her head and let the tears flow. She wanted nothing more at that moment than the peace and elegance of Monsieur's home. Even the intellectual danger of the conversation there was nothing like the chaos of her own house. They were savages, completely uncivilized. She had neglected her duties, letting them go on like this. Something had to be done, and she was the one who would have to do it.

But that wasn't what she was really crying over. It was Peter's attitude that had brought her to this. She'd wanted and needed and expected him to share in her pleasure of this so-important evening in her life. Instead, he'd gotten angry.

Irene shivered in the grip of a cold, nameless fear.

When Neptune came into the office the next morning, he found that his first appointment was with Peter Garrick, who was pacing the outer office. Miss Troutwhite was looking upset. Clara Johnson was there as well, having joined the senior partner's secretary for a morning's initiation in some of the more specialized aspects of the filing system. "I told him you had another appointment, monsieur!" Miss Troutwhite said in her own defense.

Clara pretended to be very busy sorting through invoices, but her attention was really on Peter. She'd never seen him quite so forceful and determined. He hadn't been rude to Miss Troutwhite, but he'd made it very clear that he wasn't to be deterred in his insistence on seeing Neptune as soon as he came in.

"Yes, I recall," Neptune said. "With Mr. Salem. Put him off, Troutwhite."

"He has been put off," Peter replied. "He was here a minute ago and I told him to come back later."

"You told him . . .?" Neptune asked. But his outrage over this high-handedness was eclipsed by the fact that Peter had opened his inner office door and gone in. Dear God, what sort of scene was he in for? He'd been so absorbed in his interest in Irene that he hadn't given her husband a thought for weeks. Lax of him, of course. He should have realized that this might happen. Well, unprepared as he was, he'd just have to handle as smoothly as possible whatever was going on here.

Therefore, he followed Garrick into his own office with no show of anger. "How can I help you, Mr. Garrick?" he asked, seating himself behind the desk and fixing an amiable expression on his face.

"You can't help me at all," Peter said, his voice heavy with irony. "I've come for two things. First, to tell you that I've quit my job here."

"I see. I'll be sorry to lose you. You're good. What will you do?"

"That's not your concern," Peter said.

The statement was brisk and matter-of-fact and brooked no further questions, although Neptune had no intention of allowing it to go unquestioned. What Peter Garrick did with himself *was* his business. But still, he'd see what it was all about before saying anything.

"You had two things to discuss, I believe you said?"

"Yes, the second concerns my wife's money."

Interesting way to put it. "My wife's money," not "the money" or "our money".

"You think she's not getting enough?" Neptune said, beginning to let the anger and bristle into his voice.

"On the contrary, I feel she's getting far too much. More than is good for her. For us. But that's not the matter at hand. I came to discuss what's being done with it."

"What *is* being done with it?"

"Nothing. We live, at my insistence, on my income. Everything that's been paid to her since the institution of the partnership has been put into a savings account. There's a substantial amount there already."

Neptune eyed him narrowly. "You have some investment in mind for it?"

Peter paused, aware of the implied insult and debating whether or not to acknowledge it. Then he leaned forward and spoke very softly, precisely, and menacingly. "I have nothing—absolutely *nothing*—in mind to do with it. I refuse to become involved with it. That's why I'm bothering to discuss this with you. Irene feels the money should be 'handled.' Used to make more money—a concept I must assume she's absorbed through her contct with you. She's been urging me to learn how to invest it. I've told her, and now I'm telling you, that I will not do that."

"Why not?"

"I should think that's obvious, even to you. You've bought my wife, and I—God help me—officiated at the sale. I'm beginning to regret that more than you can imagine. And the money she's accumulating is as abhorrent to me as Judas' silver pieces."

Neptune had a sudden recollection of his own early years of marriage. He'd deliberately—cold-bloodedly, to be truthful—

married into money and had found to his surprise that while he enjoyed the security of having succeeded in his goal, he'd quickly come to despise everything he had that came from his wife's bounty. Rather than being the comfort he'd anticipated, the security itself acted as a spur to his already considerable ambition. He was beginning to think he might have seriously underestimated this usually reserved young man.

"I admire you for that, Mr. Garrick."

"Don't condescend to me!" Peter said. "I don't want or need your admiration. Save it for Irene."

Jacques was shocked. It had been years since anyone had talked to him this way. Who'd have thought this cool, scholarly-looking young man had the nerve? "I wasn't condescending. Merely expressing my respect," he said with deliberate, but strained, mildness.

"A pity I can't reciprocate."

"You don't like me much, do you?"

"I don't like you at all, Monsieur Neptune. Not at all."

Why didn't he throw this nobody out? He was nothing but a jumped-up immigrant fur cutter, a mere employee—ex-employee at that. In spite of his self-assured attitude and his air of intelligence, his youth and vigor, he was merely one of the teeming thousands who lived like ants on the Lower East Side. But he was also Irene's husband. Neptune couldn't afford to get into a tug-of-war with her husband over her loyalties. Not now. He wasn't sure enough of her or their relationship. If this virile, good-looking young man insisted that his wife leave Neptune, would she do it? Very likely she would. She still hadn't tasted the best of what the life she was building could offer. Someday when she knew exactly what she might be called to give up—then maybe he could afford to offend Peter Garrick. Right now he was up against the wall and he suspected that Garrick knew it as well as he.

"What *are* you here for?" he said calmly. "Certainly not to trade insults."

"Merely to inform you that your instructions to Irene should branch out to include how to handle her money."

"I see."

"I wonder if you do," Peter said. "I wonder if any of us sees anything."

"What do you mean by that?"

Peter had managed to submerge his anger. "Merely that I think you honestly believe you're doing something good for Irene. She believes that too. I think you're both utterly, criminally wrong. We can't all be right, can we?"

Neptune spent the rest of the morning trying to get Peter Garrick out of his mind, but with little success. His unease increased when Irene came in a half-hour after his disquieting interview with her husband. She should have been brimming with pleasure over her success the night before, but she was remote, preoccupied. And she looked tired. What had happened after he sent her home from the dinner party? What sort of dispute or crisis had gone on away from his watchful eye? Was her friend Clara still in the outer office, and had she told Irene about her husband's visit earlier? He hoped against reason that Irene might confide in him, but felt certain she wouldn't. He was disappointed but not entirely surprised when she handed him the box he'd given her the night before.

"I must return your gift, monsieur."

"You don't like the earrings?"

"They're lovely. But I must not keep them."

"Why not?"

She seemed to draw into herself, and he could almost hear a gate slam. "It isn't fitting for me to accept such a valuable gift."

"Your husband says so?"

She didn't hesitate. "No. I say so."

So that's how it was. Peter Garrick had made this decision, but she wasn't going to place the blame on him. Neptune congratulated himself on not attempting to make her take sides. It was obvious what side she'd choose.

He took the box and slipped it into his pocket. Smiling as if it were of no consequence, he said briskly, "Very well. We have things to discuss. I propose that we make the announcement very soon now of your partnership. There is no reason to postpone it any longer."

He'd expected some expression of joy, but she merely smiled politely and said, "Very well."

Good God, she and her stiff-necked husband must have had

a terrible row last night! "I think it's only fair to inform my nephew before we make it public."

"I agree. He's going to be upset, isn't he?"

"Very. That's why I thought it would be best to discuss it with him somewhere . . . rather more public than my office."

"So he'll feel obliged to behave with decorum?" Irene said, nodding at the sense of this and quivering inside at the thought of what Chandler Moffat would say. Or do. "What do you have in mind?"

"I thought a luncheon at the Plaza."

"I'll have to go home and change my dress. It isn't appropriate," she said, rising from the chair with that fluid grace that so fascinated him. "And I must tell my . . ." She stopped, realizing she had no idea where Peter was. He hadn't come home last night at all, and she was in a frenzy of worry that she was determined to conceal.

"I don't think your husband is here now," Neptune said, watching her carefully.

"Oh?" Very casual except for that faint tremble in her voice.

"No, he was in to see me this morning to tell me he's quit his job."

"He was? Well, of course, I knew he was going to. I just hadn't realized for certain that he intended to discuss it with you today," she said.

You didn't know it at all, Neptune thought.

"Then he's already left?"

"I think so."

"Very well. I'll run home and be back in an hour."

"Irene . . ."

She paused, her hand on the doorknob. Her fingers were trembling. "Yes?"

He wanted to take her in his arms—not as a lover, but as a friend. She suddenly looked so delicate and frail and hurt. But she wouldn't understand. She'd think he was trying to seduce her again, and he might forfeit everything. "Irene, I never misled you. I never said this would be easy."

"No."

"And it's going to get harder before the day is over."

"I understand."

* * *

Chandler, however, didn't understand. Not at all.

"What in the hell are you saying!"

"Keep your voice down. People are staring at us," Neptune said.

The luncheon patrons at the Palm Court were unused to emotional turmoil over the turbot in lemon butter. Several ladies were craning their necks in an attempt to overhear exactly what was going on at the table where Jacques Neptune, his nephew, and that perfectly lovely young woman were sitting. A mèsalliance? Oh, my dear, do you suppose Chandler Moffat is trying to make an inappropriate marriage? She looks quite suitable, but then, who knows? Who is that plain woman with them—the one the beauty keeps looking at, as if for support? they wondered fruitlessly.

"Staring at me? Good God, Uncle. They're going to throw rocks at you if they hear about this nonsense."

"I very much doubt it. Now, please lower your voice, Chandler. There's no reason to cause a spectacle."

"Uncle, I do believe you've gone quite, quite mad. Do you honestly expect me to believe that you intend to turn over half the business to this . . . this woman?" he sputtered, glaring at Irene. His feeling of alarm when she first became involved in the business had been justified. In fact, she'd proved to be far more of a danger to him than he would ever have imagined. How could the old man do this! To him! Neptune et Cie was his future—to just hand half of it over to a stranger! It was unthinkable. He felt an overwhelming sense of betrayal, not only over what was being said but also because his uncle had brought the woman and her friend along to witness the telling. Why had he felt it necessary to slap his nephew in the face with an audience?

Irene sat bolt upright, a deliberately bland expression set on her face. She would not get into this. It was about her, certainly, but it wasn't her fight. It was between Monsieur and Chandler. Oddly enough, she found herself thoroughly in sympathy with the younger man. For one thing, she also felt it was wrong for her to be here. This should have been a private conversation between the two of them. Neptune should not have used her and Clara as buffers. Moreover, she remembered vividly what it was like to have your prospects jerked away, even in private. The memory of that afternoon at the St. Rgis still burned. The feeling of the floor disappearing, of falling into a void when everything had seemed so safe and certain only moments before. Yes, she knew the feeling, and it was a terrible irony that the same man had done it to both of them. Yet it wasn't really parallel. Chandler wasn't being thrown out into the cold. He was having his prospects halved, not destroyed. And half of Neptune et Cie was more than most of the world ever dreamed of having.

"I don't intend to do so, Chandler," Neptune was saying carefully. 'I have already done so. Months ago."

"But you can't!"

"I have. Chandler, you don't seem to grasp the very important fact that I'm not consulting with you to gain the benefit of your opinion. I'm simply telling you what is a fact," Neptune said. His patience was wearing thin. He knew Chandler would be upset. In a way, he was even sorry about it. He did, for reasons completely beyond his own understanding, rather like his nephew. And of course it was a shock. But hadn't he even the sense to accept the situation?

"Who the hell is this woman anyway?" Chandler said, looking at Irene as if he'd never seen her before. In a way, he hadn't. "Just some insignificant little secretary Troutwhite's been training—"

"No, you know better than that."

"Oh, yes. You stuck her in with the designers and made what's-his-name quit over it. I remember. And you hired Miss . . . ah, Miss . . . to help her."

"Miss Johnson. Clara Johnson," Clara said firmly. They'd been introduced several times before.

"But still—"

Neptune tapped his fork lightly on the edge of his plate, as if subtly calling a meeting to order. Chandler lapsed into an incoherent sputter. "Chandler, listen to me. Mrs. Garrick is a brilliant designer, a brilliant furrier. I know you have difficulty understanding that. You see my business—*my* business—as little more than a source of easy income. But you must understand that aside from the business, it is an art. A very high, very rare art. And Mrs. Garrick is an artist of the first order."

"I don't care—"

"I know you don't, but you must. Listen to me. This is, although I know you'll have trouble grasping it, in your own self-interest. I cannot live forever, much as I would like to. Someday I will be gone, and I *am* Neptune et Cie. Without my presence, my talent, my personality, it would quickly degenerate, within months perhaps, into a second-rate house."

"That's ridiculous!"

"No, it's true. You don't have the talent to keep the standards up. It isn't just a matter of being friends with the right people—though that's a very necessary part of it—but you must be able to supply them with rare and beautiful furs, made in unique and creative ways. If I were to die without having firmly established a creative successor, half our customers would go straight to Revillon Frères without ever stepping foot into our building again." Neptune hated having to state these hard truths, and he was beginning to regret the impulse that had led him to have this conversation with Irene and Clara present. But what had to be said, had to be said.

"That's not true. My friends—"

"Your friends would stay your friends—until you ran out of the money to keep pace with them. They'd still go dinners with you and the races and all those charity events. Yes, they'd eat and gamble and drink and sleep with you still, but they wouldn't come to you to buy their furs. Not more than once, anyway."

"Even supposing that's true—and I don't believe it for a minute—what has this . . . this *girl* got to do with it?"

"That's what I've been telling you, if you'd just listen. Irene Garrick is the talent that will keep you going, keep Neptune et Cie going. This young woman, to whom you are being so abominably rude, is your future, Chandler."

Irene caught her breath. She'd never really understood this before either. She'd thought he was doing it all for her, and she'd wondered from the beginning why on earth he should. And it was, no doubt, partly for her. But now she saw the other side of the coin. It was for Chandler, too, though even that was of minor consequence. Most important, everything

Neptune had given her and taught her was to ensure, not her future in this life, but his in history.

There'd been a clause in the contract between them that under no conditions would the name of the business ever be changed. She hadn't questioned it before, thinking it was a perfectly normal and entirely fair condition, but now she saw that it was a crucial element of the partnership from his viewpoint. She was, in reality, an important investment. A very valuable asset. She was a way for Neptune to keep his name and the memory of all he'd built up alive for him. Irene Garrick was to be Jacques Neptune's immortality. She caught, in the corner of her eye, a movement. It was Clara, nodding to herself. Yes, Clara understood now, too.

Irene had been so deeply immersed in her own thoughts that she had missed what the two men were saying. Chandler had pushed his chair back, preparatory to leaving. "You can't get away with this! I'll see a lawyer, I'll see one of those mental doctors. You've lost your mind."

Neptune's face had drained of color. He put a restraining hand on Chandler's arm and said frigidly, "Take care, Chandler. Take very good care. If I so much as hear a rumor that you have taken either course of action, you'll never see another cent of mine the rest of your life. Not a single cent, do you understand? You have no claim on me—moral or legal. If you stay on at Neptune et Cie, you do so purely because of my own charitable impulse."

Chandler nearly reeled. He was a patron of several charities, and like many patrons felt a sense of superiority if not downright contempt for the recipients. To class him with them was an insult of magnificent proportions. He stared at his uncle in speechless horror.

Neptune, too, sensed that he might have gone too far, in spite of being pushed to it. He forced himself to sound, if not friendly, at least calm and reasonable. "You're intelligent enough, and usually amiable. You're probably capable of earning your keep, Chandler, and I suppose it's partly my fault you haven't been forced to do so. But you must clear your mind of the idea that I owe you anything. I don't owe anybody but myself. I made Neptune et Cie out of nothing but my own skill and gall and damned hard work. It's mine to do with as I choose, and I've chosen to turn over half of it to Irene Garrick. As for the other half—we'll see. We'll see."

The threat couldn't have been clearer if he'd painted it in red letters on the side of a building. Chandler's face had gone a milky color and his chin shook with barely controlled anger as he said, "I understand."

"I plan to call the staff together tomorrow afternoon to make the announcement, and there will be a notice in the papers later in the week to make it known officially," Neptune said. "You must realize—you too, Irene—that you'll be under close scrutiny for several weeks. Our regular customers are going to be surprised and curious and will come in to look over the new partner, and they're all going to be watching you, Chandler, to see how you're handling it. If you're petulant and disagreeable, you will show yourself up very badly indeed. On the other hand, if you're gracious and supportive and even—with my permission—act like it was as much your idea as mine, it will be good for the business. And whatever is good for Neptune et Cie is good for you."

"I hardly need instruction in how to save face," Chandler said coldly.

"I suppose not. Forgive me."

At this, Chandler rose, balled his napkin, and tossed it on the table contemptuously. "If you'll excuse me, I have some things to do."

He walked off without another word or glance at Irene, making clear that he still believed her beneath his notice. She let out a long breath she hadn't realized she was holding. "Oh, dear . . ." was all she could think to say. Even Clara was pale, and the hand she laid over Irene's was cold and shaking.

"Well, the worse is over," Neptune said. "He's planning to quit right now and he'll spend the afternoon going around to all his chums testing the waters, seeing if he can round up another source of income so he can tell me off."

"Will he?"

"Find another job? No, I don't think so. He's well-liked, but I don't suppose anyone mistakes him for an empire builder. No, he won't find anyone as tolerant or generous as I am. And I think he's bright enough to realize that pretty quickly."

He patted her other hand reassuringly. "Don't worry. He'll come around. Everything will be fine in a day or two. Now, how about some dessert while we consider a series of newspaper advertisements featuring your work? Miss Johnson, have you any suggestions?"

Everything will be fine. Irene thought: No it won't. Neptune was probably right that Chandler would come around, find some way to save face and make a public show of getting along with her. It was, as Neptune had pointed out, in his own best interest. But she realized something Neptune seemed to be determinedly overlooking: Chandler would never "come around" in his own mind, and he would remain her enemy forever. No matter what she did, she would always be, in his mind, the woman who stole something that was rightly his. And she didn't know but what he might not be a formidable enemy.

She glanced at Clara, who was folding her napkin and gazing back at Irene with a most peculiar look of concern.

19

By the time Irene got home that afternoon, she felt like she'd been beaten. Not only had she endured the agony of luncheon with Chandler Moffat, but she hadn't seen Peter since he left the apartment the night before and she'd been in a fever of anxiety all day. Clara had finally gotten an opportunity, after they left the Plaza, to tell her about Peter's visit with Neptune, but only that it had occurred. She had no idea what had gone on between them.

Irene took the Fifth Avenue bus home and leapt off before it had come to a full stop, then ran the rest of the way. Peter had to be home. Suddenly she felt panicked, as if she might somehow fade away if she didn't see him immediately.

As she rounded the corner of the block, skirt flying in a most unladylike way, she saw him sitting on the front stoop reading a newspaper. "Peter!" She flew at him, crushing the newspaper between them. "Oh, Peter! I'm so glad you're here."

"Reenee! What's wrong?" he asked, grabbing her shoulders and holding her back to look at as if she were an injured child.

She took a long breath. "Nothing—now. I'm just so glad to see you. I'm sorry I was awful last night. I didn't mean to be, really I didn't. But please, please, don't ever go away like that again."

"No, I won't. I'm sorry too. I missed you today, Reenee."

"And I missed you. Oh, so much! Peter, promise you won't ever go away again."

He was gratified and guilty in enormous and equal measure. "I won't, Reenee. You couldn't get me out of your life if you tried."

"I'd never try! Never."

They'd had a pleasant evening mainly because he and Irene both assiduously avoided discussing what either of them had done that day. He knew she wanted to know where he'd been, and he was anxious to tell her, but not now. It would keep.

But Peter couldn't sleep that night. As he sat at the window watching the sun come up, he wondered if he'd ever sleep again with the sound security he'd felt when he and Irene had first been married. He realized he'd frightened Irene with his fury the night before, but he'd frightened himself more.

He heard someone stirring and quickly recognized Zofia's sure but heavy tread. "Ah, the morning bird," she said, coming into the living room. She spoke quietly, and Peter wondered briefly if that wasn't something of a luxury for her, being able to speak quietly. Normally she had to be louder than all her shrill youngest daughters to exert her authority.

In a moment she was back with two cups of coffee, his so liberally sugared that it was gritty in the bottom of the cup. Just the way he liked it. "Take this chair," he said, starting to rise.

She touched his shoulder. "No, I sit in the hard chair here. Better for my back. Aieee, so bad getting old."

They sat sipping their coffee, Zofia with noisy, appreciative slurps. That drove Irene mad; Peter found it endearing. Did his mother, wherever she was, drink her coffee that way? Peter was startled at the thought. His long-departed mother hadn't crossed his mind in years. Odd, he'd once been obsessed with her.

"Zofia," he said softly, "are you ever angry about things?"

She didn't seem to find the question strange at all. "With such daughters as God has given me? Every day, Piotr."

He smiled. "No, I mean really angry."

He started to explain, but it wasn't necessary. She was nodding. "I used to be furious with my Jozef for dying. The village, my friends, they thought it was grief, so nobody but me and God knew. But, Jesus save me, I was mad at God a little too. And there are some days other things. Things I can't even say what they are. And you, Piotr?"

How could he tell her that last night Irene had roused his irritation—nothing more—and it had suddenly turned into a rage about everything that had *ever* happened to him? It made no sense at all. When he'd shouted at her about VanWhatever, he'd really been raging at the butcher in Warsaw; at his mother for abandoning him; at Herr Schmitt for loving facts without loving knowledge; at everyone and everything that had ever oppressed him. Over the years he'd buried all of it, covered it with a deep, protective layer of scholarship and religion, and it had all burst to the surface. "Yes, Zofia, me too. What do you do about it?"

She shrugged. "I pray. I ignore. I go on."

Peter grinned. In all his years of study, all the hundreds of hours with learned men discussing ethics and morals and religion, he'd probably never heard a more sensible, succinct philosophy of life expressed. He rose, gulped the last sticky-sweet tablespoon of coffee, and bent down to give his mother-in-law a kiss on the forehead. "Zofia, you're a treasure. I'm going to follow your advice. I'll keep praying and ignoring for as long as I can go on."

They didn't talk for several days about Peter's work plans. The subject was as fragile as an eggshell. Irene knew he'd made other arrangements, but fearing another argument, waited for him to bring it up.

Peter shared her fear and felt it even more intensely. The emotional upheaval the night of the dinner party had thoroughly unnerved him. But his own behavior, not Irene's, had shaken him most. His very survival since childhood had been founded on "being good." As a small child he'd learned that crying had brought down the wrath of those upon whom he was unwillingly dependent. To be calm, pleasant, and seemingly pliable had become the key to life. And later, with the old German scholar, when the threat of pain and violence and hunger was gone, there was still the absolute need for learning. And his introduction to the teachings of the Church had reinforced it all. "The meek shall inherit the earth," he was told. Well, he didn't feel meek inside, but he could certainly put on the mask of meekness; he'd been wearing it for years. And eventually he'd accept it inside, he believed.

But for reasons he couldn't understand, the mask had dropped away that night. He'd run out of "goodness" and "meekness," as surely as if he'd been allotted only a limited supply for life and had used it all up in the months since Irene went back to work for Neptune. For a few terrifying minutes he'd been a raging creature, wanting to lash out; a wild animal, trapped, wounded, snarling, fangs bared. And until she started talking about that man, he'd been thinking that life was on an easy path, an easy and exciting path. For both of them.

He'd spent the night at St. Stanislas on his knees in a pew at the back where the light was too dim for anyone to see him. But God had failed him—or he, God. No solution was revealed, no wash of relief or understanding, or even acceptance, had poured over him. Instead, the statue of the Virgin simpered, the stale afterscent of incense nauseated him, the flickering of the candles gave him a headache. He threw off prayers to all the saints, flinging them like gobbets of mud from a fast-spinning wheel. And there was no answer given.

Finally he got off his aching knees and sat back, calmed by sheer exhaustion. God wasn't going to pluck him out of this morass and patiently instruct him—when *had* God, come to think of it? He didn't take this to mean he wasn't being heard, only that once again he must figure out for himself what to do. How was it that he could be so content with virtually every aspect of the schooling he was working so hard for and so miserably discontented with other things? It was as if he were two people, the bright scholar greedily absorbing knowledge and enjoying every minute of it, and also the frustrated husband, jealous and petty and not knowing why or what to do about it.

At least he hadn't given in to the urge to leap across Jacques Neptune's desk the next morning and throttle him. And that in itself was a perfect wonder of self-control. He'd grown to despise that slick, self-satisfied bastard who was doing his best to steal Irene's heart and mind.

The reserve of patience had been restored somewhat by Irene's effusive greeting that afternoon and had finally come back to nearly full measure in that dawn discussion with Zofia. Pray, ignore, go on, the older woman had said. All of those he could do. Though eventually . . . No, he couldn't afford to worry about eventualities.

Neptune's predictions about Chandler's alternative business prospects must have been true, because the next day, when the partnership was announced to the company employees, Chandler was at Irene's side smiling and doing his level best to take credit for her success. Irene wondered if anyone else could see how strained the smile was or hear the unfamiliar coldness in his voice even as he laughed jovially about working with a woman. Or was she reading that into his behavior out of sheer worry? Her wondering ended when she, Chandler, Clara, and Neptune returned to Monsieur's office.

"Am I invited in," he asked at the door, "or would you rather I go back down and see if there's anybody who's missed my groveling? There may be some opportunity for self-humiliation that I've missed."

Neptune started to speak, but Irene cut in, "Mr. Moffat, I have no intention of doing you any damange—financially or personally."

He glared at her, completely unmoved.

"I've never wanted to take anything away from anyone," she continued. "Only to have what I earn and can deserve. I want to work with you, and get along with you."

"What a generous little speech. Did you think it up yourself or did my uncle write it out for you to memorize?" he asked.

"Enough!" Neptune said. "We will not have this discussion all over again every day. Chandler, you must find a way to be courteous to Mrs. Garrick. You must."

"Yes, sir," Chandler said, and Irene feared for a moment that he was about to make a mock salute to match his tone. "Would you mind, just to satisfy my curiosity, telling me who you are, Mrs. Garrick? Who you *really* are?"

In a second Monsieur would jump to her defense and attempt to put Chandler in his place, but Irene realized that she must eventually hold her own with him, and the sooner, the better. "I would mind very much," she said firmly. "I do not choose to discuss my past with anyone.'' She didn't look at Clara as she spoke, but she could sense her friend's approval.

His face went from pale to beet red. ''I take it this story that's floating around about your being some sort of Russian royalty is hogwash.''

''I never made any such claim,'' Irene replied frostily.

''But Uncle Jacques has, apparently to anyone who'll listen.''

''I cannot control what anyone else may choose to say.''

His eyes narrowed and he leaned forward, a curiously sinuous motion for a young man inclining toward portliness. ''Including me, Mrs. Garrick.''

Once again Neptune started to intervene, but Irene held up a hand in his direction and spoke to Chandler. ''I *am* your uncle's partner. There is no changing that. If you choose to undermine me and destroy my reputation, you could grievously harm Neptune et Cie. How could that help you?''

Chandler didn't answer; there was nothing to say. He understood the logic of it as well as any of them. He merely stared at her as if surprised that she could not only talk, but talk bluntly. For a second a fleeting expression almost like respect crossed his soft features. Irene had the feeling that something important had happened, but wasn't sure what it was.

Neptune, who had taken a place at his desk and had half-risen to come to Irene's defense, sank back into the chair. Irene and Chandler stood at the doorway staring at each other.

It was Clara who broke the spell. ''I have a stack of letters to write,'' she said briskly. ''If we're going to get to business, we should proceed.'' She slapped a pile of possible advertisements down on Neptune's desk like a cranky schoolteacher fed up with recalcitrant students.

Irene, whose knees were shaking so badly she was afraid they might give out entirely, turned her back on Chandler and sat down, being careful not to let her anxiety show in her face or posture. Chandler, hesitating at the doorway, finally came in and pulled it shut, depriving Miss Troutwhite (who was busily rearranging perfectly alphabetized files) of any further diversion.

He sat across from Irene, studying her like a zoo exhibit for a long moment, then looked at his uncle. Taking a deep breath, he said, "Very well." And as briskly as Clara, he began to outline a surprisingly well-thought-out campaign of advertising.

"You're not ready for a public announcement. The stage isn't set. It would be like sending out tickets to a play before you've figured out the scenery."

"Chandler, Mrs. Garrick has been preparing for months," Neptune said.

"I'm not talking about her preparation. I'm suggesting that you prepare your customers."

Neptune leaned forward, tenting his fingers in a gesture Irene recognized as meaning he was taking very seriously what was being said. "Explain."

Chandler picked an invisible piece of lint off the knee of his gray wool trousers. "Since you've told the other employees, the news will get out, but in tantalizing bits from sources that your customers won't quite know whether to believe. The news, still considered gossip, will spread by mouth, and curiosity will be aroused."

"They'll ask me, you know," Neptune said.

"Of course they will, and you should fuel the gossip by simply saying that you'll be making an announcement soon. Into certain ears you'll pour the absolute sworn secret of the partnership. Those few will of course tell everybody and feel terribly smug about being able to."

"I see. What then?"

"When you're ready, there should be nothing public, but a discreet announcement in the business section of the city papers. Mainly, you should concentrate on the outlying small papers, the society rags, and the local papers that serve the communities where your customers live when they aren't in New York."

Chandler was in his element now, and for the moment there was no sign of his personal feelings: he was an expert sharing his chosen field with amateurs. "You should have a showing of her designs—just two or three really remarkable pieces. No more than four. And make it a clearly social occasion, with personal invitations. Limited, of course. Caroline Astor's guest lists should be a guide. Don't even let anyone consider placing an order. No selling. Just champagne and caviar and the models wearing the pieces she's designed. I'd suggest you have it at a hotel, not here at the showrooms. The Plaza, perhaps. Maybe make it a combined showing, private introduction of Mrs. Garrick, and charity event. That would add a bit of class. Keep to your theme."

"Theme?" Clara asked.

"Yes, the dispossessed-Russian story." For a moment the resentment showed again in the way he emphasized the word "story," but he quickly went on, "A benefit for some Eastern Orthodox Church or something."

Irene listened, her nerves calming as he spoke. She realized she'd regarded him as a nuisance, a possible danger, and a bit of a buffoon. That had been a mistake. Though he knew little and cared less about the design and production of furs, he knew even more than Jacques did about some aspects of the business. A natural social creature, he had a thorough and sensitive grasp of how "his kind," their customers, thought. She would have to remember this and use it.

"Thank you, Mr. Moffat," she said softly.

He looked at her with astonishment and very nearly smiled.

That evening, as Irene set up her sketching materials in the tiny second kitchen she used as an office, Peter came in with a stack of books under his arm. "I won't be back until morning," he said.

"What?"

"I've got a night job. A fur-storage-and-repair company."

"Nights? But why?"

"So I'm free to go to school during the day. Several months ago I took the examinations to enter Fordham College. I started classes today."

"Peter! You didn't tell me. When did you take these examinations?"

"Some time ago. I didn't tell you because I was afraid I wouldn't score as well as I hoped."

"Peter, how could you doubt it?" She tried to sound cheerful, but she was hurt. He'd been making plans and nursing hopes and hadn't told her. His reason made sense, but it still made her feel she'd been excluded. "I'm delighted, but

I don't understand what the job has to do with it—you'll exhaust yourself for no reason. You ought to have the rest of the day free to study and rest."

"We can't eat study and rest."

She was genuinely perplexed. "No, but we can eat very well on what I'm making. We're just putting it all away, when we might as well use it." She realized even as she was speaking that it was the wrong thing to say.

"You use it however you like. It's my job to support this family, and I intend to go on doing so."

She knew she shouldn't pursue it, but she couldn't help herself. "That isn't reasonable at all! Where is this Fordham?"

"In the Bronx."

"You'll be all day getting there and back. You should be concentrating on your classes, and there's absolutely no need for you to hold a job as well."

Peter set the books down on the corner of her small, battered desk. "Irene, my love, I know in the rational part of my mind that I'm not making sense, but there are some things I feel so strongly that I simply can't overcome them. I want to be a teacher. I've always wanted it, and now I'm finally taking steps to achieve it. But no matter how much I want this, I cannot—*will not*—sacrifice my pride to get it. I'm not an idiot or a child who needs to be supported by a woman."

"But, Peter, I'm not 'a woman,' some stranger who has wandered in off the street. I'm your wife. I want to do things for you. I want to help you. You can certainly let me, can't you?"

"Not in this. Not with money. I didn't marry you to be a kept man. I can't build my own success on yours. I can't take anyone's charity."

"Charity! What's charity got to do with it? I'm talking about sharing what we have. You'd share anything you have with me, why can't I do the same?"

"Reenee, there are some things we don't share. Can't share."

"Like what? Why not?"

"Like our dreams. I can't share yours—I don't even understand what it is you want, or why. I won't stop you from trying to get it, but I can't go galloping along with you in pursuit of it. And I don't think you share my hopes. I'd love to share my learning with you, but you're not interested in philosophy or ethics or Church history—"

"I could learn."

He took her face in his hands, touched by her words. "Reenee, I'm not saying you should be as interested as I am in these things, nor should you try to pretend an interest. And I certainly don't hold it against you that you aren't. I'm just trying to explain. There are things we both want; unfortunately, they're not the same things."

"What are you saying?" she asked.

He heard the fear in her voice, and for a moment it struck coldly at his heart as well. "Don't sound alarmed. I'm just trying to tell you that we can both go after what we want in life. I want my college degree. You want . . . whatever it is you want." He laid a hand on the papers she was sketching. "This is your work. These books are mine."

"But, Peter, that's all very well, but it doesn't help me understand this job you insist on doing. Why bother with it at all? It isn't part of your dream."

"No, but supporting you and Zofia and the girls is my responsibility."

She twisted her hands. "This doesn't make sense to me!"

"No, I'm not sure it does to me either," Peter said. "But it's how things must be. We've always lived on what I earned, and we'll continue to do so. I can and will provide food and clothing and shelter, and if I can't manage that and going to school as well, I'll quit school."

"I'd fight you every inch of the way if you tried that. But, Peter, I need clothes for work—fancy clothes, ball gowns, hats, and—"

"Then buy them. Use your own money."

"And the girls?"

"I can't keep you from buying things for your own sisters, but I don't think you should be extravagant. I've got to go now or I'll be late."

Irene wanted to hold him back and talk him into being reasonable. She *did* understand his feelings—in fact, she'd have been disappointed in him if he hadn't felt the way he did. But once having expressed his opinion, why couldn't he be talked out of it by the logic of what she was saying? Her argument was the logical one. She was certain of it, and fairly sure he agreed. But he was still immovable in his resolve. She sketched aimlessly for a minute or two, pondering one thing in particular he'd said. That remark about giving up what he wanted if he couldn't manage both school and work—that was puzzling to her. How could anyone want something as much as he'd always wanted to go to college and still be willing to give it up?

Chandler's plan was followed to the letter. Irene and Neptune, without prearrangement, both made a point of consulting him frequently, even when it wasn't absolutely necessary. Irene meant to flatter him, in the sincerest way, but realized she'd gone too far one day when she asked him about flower selection for the charity reception they were planning for her official introduction. "Mrs. Garrick, you didn't get where you are by being stupid," he said, "so don't pretend you are. And don't make the error of thinking I am."

She told Clara about this conversation, but she didn't discuss Chandler with Neptune. Sorting out their animosity and coming to terms was up to her and the younger man. Neptune couldn't and shouldn't involve himself. Instead, she limited their conversation to furs. She showed him the preliminary sketches of the designs she had in mind. There were six, of which they would make up three. Neptune spread them out on the desk, nodding. "Very good. Yes, very distinctly you. It's interesting to me where you fit into the scheme of fashion."

"What do you mean?"

"Well, as you know, Revillon Frères became the first name in furs back in the 1800's because they were the first to treat fur as fabric. Rather than making the garment accommodate itself to the size and shape of the furs—capes and blocky coats and stoles—old Revillon made the furs fit the wearer. You take that a step further. You tend to treat furs as patterned fabrics and use the pattern to the best advantage. I saw that even in the muff, and then in the hat I asked you to make. Is this diagonal motif deliberate or instinctive?"

Irene looked at the sketches. Four of the six had indeed

some element of diagonal design. "Instinctive, I suppose. I never realized how often I do that."

"Keep doing it, but don't overdo it. It will be fresh and original now, but if you always use it you will date yourself. Now, let's consider these. This"—he indicated a three-quarter-length jacket with wide sleeves, done with Irene's characteristic swirl pattern—"is a bit young. Childish, almost."

"I meant it to be. Your clients often purchase coats for their daughters when they're really too young for anything but ermine trim, and the girls look like they're wearing their mothers' hand-me-downs. This would be appropriate for a girl of sixteen or seventeen."

"Girls of that age don't have control of their own money yet," Neptune reminded her.

"No, but their mothers do, and it seems to me that many of the women of that class are overeager to start reliving their own youth in their offspring."

"Of that class . . ." Neptune mused. "That's quite right. To grow old is not, for a wealthy woman, an honorable state. Very few manage to age gracefully. I presume you intend to institute a line of youthful fashion for the girls and—"

"—and their mothers will start wearing them. Yes," Irene finished. "But the designs will be subtly altered for them. More flattering collars, less pronounced flare in the sleeves unless their arms are long and slim enough. They won't notice the difference, but it will be more flattering."

Neptune leaned back, smiling. "What difference does it make if it's more flattering, if what they want is the coat their daughters have?"

"Monsieur! How can you ask? If a woman goes out of here looking less than superb, it's our fault. We can't attach a sign to the coat saying, 'Neptune et Cie is not responsible for the way this woman looks.' "

"Quite right," he said. He'd made that his philosophy from the beginning, but lately he'd let down his standards more and more often, sometimes giving in to the nagging and the prospect of the money and allowing a customer to purchase something inappropriate. It was such devilish hard work convincing a woman that a coat was wrong for her without being insulting, and he frequently gave up the attempt. But Irene was young and fresh and had the energy to apply the necessary tact.

"Very good. Let's choose the designs to make up, and check the warehouse for what furs we have available."

"I did that before I did the sketches."

"I see." His approval had a slight edge. Did she really have to be a half-step ahead of him on everything? Yes, of course she did. That's what he'd counted on when he trained her and gave her half-interest in the company. So why was it disconcerting?

The date was set for the first week of March for Irene's "unveiling." It was shorter notice than they might have wished, but necessary. But by the middle of the month the weather might be so warm that no one would have the slightest interest in furs. There was also the annual fur auction to be considered. It took place later in the month in St. Louis, and Neptune was determined that Irene attend with him. Putting together the three garments in time became an obsession with Irene. She chose the models to wear the coats and even made one of them change the color of her hair. "I want her to wear the white fox, but the yellow in her blond hair makes the coat look slightly more blue than I want," she explained when Neptune heard about it and questioned her. "Don't worry. Maizie doesn't mind. I'm paying to have it done."

She insisted on hiring a new model to wear the young-looking coat. "We'll need a few younger models to show the line I have in mind anyway. "I'm training her myself. I don't want her to learn from the others."

"Why?"

"They've learned to move as sophisticated women. I want a girl who looks and walks like a girl. A little mincy, a bit self-conscious. The girl needs to look as if she's just about to spill something and break into giggles. But she won't, of course."

The day arrived, bright but—thank heaven—quite cold. "Even the weather is cooperating with you," Clara said when Irene came in that morning. "I made arrangements for us to have a suite at the Plaza to get dressed. It seemed easier than getting ready at home and having to risk soiling your dress on the way uptown."

"Thank you, Clara. I hadn't thought of that."

"Then it must be the only thing you haven't thought of. Irene, you need to get some rest today."

"Do I look as haggard as I feel?"

"Only to me, dear. But everything's done and you should refresh yourself."

"Do you know what would refresh me?" Irene said, suddenly taking Clara's arm. "A picnic boat trip. Just like we used to do on your Sundays off. Remember? We could take the bird book and some sandwiches—"

"You still have the bird book I gave you?"

Irene held Clara's hand tightly, her eyes shining. "I still have everything you gave me, Clara. Everything you taught me, too. Today's as much your day as mine. Let's go, shall we?"

They took an excursion boat up the Hudson. There was only a handful of others who'd braved the weather that day to see New York from the water. The wind was brisk and cold, but they stood at the rail and let it turn their cheeks pink. Irene wore the opossum coat that was her first design. Clara wore a heavy, practical wool tweed. Though Irene had tried to force a fur coat on her friend, Clara maintained that she wasn't designed for furs.

They reminisced about the old days because it seemed the thing to do, but neither of them really was interested in looking back. Gradually their conversation turned to plans for the evening. "Will Peter be coming?" Clara finally asked, since Irene hadn't yet mentioned him.

"No, he has to work tonight."

"Couldn't he take one night off?"

"Certainly. He could take off entirely. But he won't. Clara, I'm so worried about him. He's tired all the time. He tries to pretend he's not, but I can tell. It's all so silly, and it makes me angry at him sometimes. I hardly ever see him."

"But if it's what he wants . . ."

"What he wants is to go to college, and I think that's wonderful. He took all sorts of tests and wrote papers and things and doesn't even have to take two years of the course because he already knew so much. But keeping the job he has is a terrible waste of his time and energy. It's not even a skilled job and he doesn't pretend to like it, but he keeps on exhausting himself so he can make the money to buy food and pay the rent. Clara, it's infuriating. I'm making more money than I know what to do with, and he won't let us use it."

"But how would you feel about him if he let you support your family without his help?"

"How would I feel? I'd feel glad. That's what I'm doing this for—for the people I love."

Clara doubted this. She knew Irene believed it, and it was part of the truth, but if Irene had no dependents in the world, she would be just as obsessed with success. Maybe as she got older and more accustomed to the life she was now living she'd realize that herself. Clara prayed it wouldn't be too late then.

The boat was making for the dock. Irene shivered as if aware for the first time of the cold. "At least it won't last forever," she said.

"What won't?"

"This work of Peter's. He'll finish school and will teach in college. Then he'll be happy doing what he's always wanted and he won't have to have another job."

"College professors don't make a great deal of money," Clara warned.

"No, but by then we will be able to live on what both of us make," Irene said firmly.

What made Irene believe that? Clara wondered. Was it simply her determination to see a future that was somehow better than the present in every way? Clara didn't pretend to know Peter well. They'd never even had a serious, private discussion, but she felt sure that Peter's determination was the equal of Irene's.

As they disembarked, Clara was deep in thought—and not entirely happy thoughts. She'd helped Irene achieve her goals—not helped as much as she wanted to, but she'd done all in her power to see Irene get ahead. But now she found herself questioning those years, that encouragement. Had she in fact done her friend a disservice? If she hadn't encouraged Irene to believe she could rise above her immigrant origins, would she be living more contentedly without putting her marriage at such risk? For it was at risk, even though Irene didn't seem to realize it. Wasn't the love of a good man like Peter more priceless than the riches Irene was pursuing? Or was that simply the way any old maid would think?

Irene went back to the office feeling better, but Clara was troubled. There were clouds on her friend's horizon and thunder rumbling in the distance. Should she point this out? And would Irene listen if she did? It was, she realized as they reentered Neptune et Cie's offices, a pointless question to pose. Irene was brilliant, the quickest learner Clara had ever met, but her astonishing capabilities seemed to extend only to learning what she wanted to. But in spite of herself, when they'd removed their coats and hats and gloves, Clara said, "Irene, why don't you take off next week? Stay at home, be there when Peter is there? He'd like that."

"Clara, that's impossible. Next week it's vital that I be here. People will be coming in to place orders for the fall. Don't worry. Peter understands."

Does he? Clara wondered. *Do you, Irene?*

20

The small hired orchestra played the final bars hurriedly, because Jacques Neptune was standing near the dais looking impatient, and there was no one who imbued impatience with such fierceness. As the last note faded, he stepped up and looked around the ballroom. Within moments it was silent except for an almost inaudible hum of anticipation.

"My friends . . ." he said, and had a quick thought for the irony of it. Who would have thought poor Jack Fisher could ever have said that to this crowd and had *them* feel flattered by the words? Employing the faintly French accent he used naturally after all these years, he went on, "My friends, we've gathered tonight for several excellent reasons, not the least of which is good fellowship. And with that in mind, I wish to introduce you to someone I dearly hope you will take to your hearts as she's been taken into the hearts of all of us at Neptune et Cie." He paused, looked around the room. Nearly a thousand eyes were on him. They'd started the evening looking for Irene, but on Chandler's advice, she'd not been in the receiving line. "Present her as you would an actress," Chandler had said with undisguised irony. "The lead never makes her first appearance wandering onstage with the crowd."

Quite right, that boy. But everyone had been here a full hour, watching, speculating, gossiping among themselves. He'd even, from pure mischievousness, invited a few attractive and unknown ladies just to confuse things. What fun it had been seeing some of the guests question these ladies, thinking they were Neptune's mysterious surprise. Now they were ripe for the curtain to rise. But let them wait a moment or two longer. "There are, in this world, those rare and precious individuals who are born with a great talent. Many of us nurture a skill into a talent, but few . . ."

Irene, standing behind a curtained door just to the left of the dais, took a deep breath for the third time and smiled shakily at Clara, who'd stayed behind the scenes with her. Would he never stop talking and let her get this over with? If only Peter were here, she kept thinking. She'd never longed quite so strongly for his calm support. If he were here now, he'd be leaning casually against the door frame, his own relaxed presence relaxing her. He'd be reasonable and pleasant, chatting or whistling under his breath. He'd be kind and *human* and she'd feel less like she was undergoing torture.

For a half-second she actually considered bolting. It would be so easy, just down that hallway, out to a cab and home. She and Peter could then play chess or go for a walk—or better yet, persuade Mama and the girls to go somewhere while they made love. Yes, that was what she really wanted to be doing right now, making love to Peter. Between her work and his, it had been two weeks since they'd even been in bed at the same time. Too long. Why had she ever thought she wanted this night? All she wanted in the world was to be with Peter.

". . . and so with affection and hope and respect, I introduce to you my young cousin and full partner . . ." The gasp from the audience was audible; they hadn't expected anything quite that dramatic. ". . . Mrs. Peter Garrick. Irene . . . ?"

One more deep breath. Six steps forward, one step up, his hand holding hers, turn, face them. Dear God! So *many* people. They were the theater audience from that first night of Ellen Terry's play. Handsome men in crisp black and white, beautiful women in pastels. Rustling taffeta and whispering silk, sparkling jewels, Neptune et Cie furs, the whole enveloped in a cloud of scent: jasmine, rose, violets. No the scent wasn't just floral, it was the smell of money and power and success, and it was so heady it made her vision shimmer.

And to them she was many and different things. A slim young woman with extremely fair hair in a thick twist of braids atop her head, she was a reminder of lost beauty to some. Her grey silk dress was simply cut: straight sleeves to the wrist, a modest V neck without collar, and a fitted, gored skirt that flared gently. Up the right side, around the back of the neck, and down the left arm, matching beadwork formed a trellis of roses. To those who noticed clothes first, she seemed to have excellent if tantalizingly restrained taste. No gaudy colors, no elaborate frou-frou ruffles. Without the beads and in a less expensive fabric, it would almost be a uniform.

Some of the ladies, older women who'd missed making quite what they wanted of themselves in their prime, saw in her a possible "cause"—a young woman who might be taken under a withered wing. Think of the admirers she'd attract! But they were uneasy about the firm line of her jaw and the self-possessed tilt of her head. Not, perhaps, as pliable as need be, but certainly a person to watch, perhaps cultivate.

A few younger women, less beautiful if more obviously moneyed, also saw her as a possible drawing card. So beautiful, and married besides. A woman like that would cast off suitors by the dozen, and who could tell what might be picked up on the rebound. Yes, this was a woman to be drawn into social circles and used.

A precious few saw the stark terror in her eyes, sensed the frightened girl behind the self-assured woman, and felt a twinge of pity. They were balanced by those whose instincts told them this vision was not one of them, but a masquerader attempting entry though their well-guarded gates.

The men in the crowd, however, were in nearly universal agreement. They accepted her as a stunning beauty, and if their appreciation was marred by any cynicism, it was in regard to her relationship with Neptune. A man doesn't hand over half his business (Half of Neptune et Cie! My God, a virtual fortune! The old boy raked in cash in buckets, if their wives' bills were any gauge!) unless the prize can't be bought at any smaller price. She was lovely, but could she be worth that?

Only one guest completely escaped the dazzle of her entry. Chandler Moffat, standing at the other side of the dais, gritted his teeth and regarded her with pure loathing. Why hadn't the bitch stayed where she came from, wherever in hell that was!

"A cousin of yours, eh, Chandler," a friend of his said, nudging him in the ribs.

"No, not mine, more's the pity," he said heartily. "She's a connection from Uncle Jacques's side of the family. Actually it's her husband who's related."

"Husband? You mean she's really got one? Why isn't he around tonight?" The leer was still there.

"Very reclusive bloke," Chandler said.

"You know him, then?"

"We've met, of course."

The friend leaned closer, grew conspiratorial. "Say, what's this I hear about Russian royalty? My wife says she heard the girl's an illegitimate daughter of the tzar."

Chandler expressed mock astonishment. "When did you start listening to gossip?"

"Is it true, then?"

Chandler laughed. "I've never quite sorted out Uncle Jacques's family connections in the old country. He could be first cousin to the pope for all I know."

At that moment he was saved from this thoroughly distasteful mendacity by a gesture from Neptune. Chandler stepped up, joined his uncle and the despised protégée, and smiled broadly at his friends. It made his face hurt almost as much as his heart. His life had served up few opportunities to self-loathing, but he was sickened by himself and the situation he was forced into now. He cleared his throat and delivered his prepared speech, which had been carefully worded to suggest that he was not only in complete agreement with his uncle's decision but also had helped influence it in favor of Irene. He hated himself for every word. Neptune smiled benignly. "This isn't the time or place for a showing, of course," Chandler went on, "but I did persuade Uncle Jacques to let me show you just a few examples of what Cousin Irene—Mrs. Garrick—can do with furs. In the fall, of course, you'll all be invited to a proper showing. Gentlemen, you're invited too. You and your pocketbooks!" There was, of course, laughter from his friends.

He stepped down and let Neptune resume control. The first model stepped out of her hiding place behind the curtained doorway. She was a redhead with garnet curls that almost but not quite clashed with the burnished red of the cross-fox fur. The garment was an ankle-length coat with a loose, oversize neckline and wide sleeves. But the effect missed sloppiness because it gathered into a neat hobble at the ankles that was accented by a broad band of matching leather. Halfway up each sleeve, the same band was repeated. It was a lovely coat, but hardly revolutionary.

The blond model, her hair lightened to perfectly complement the cape she wore, came forward next. The body of the cape was white velvet, long and sweeping and full. At the bottom edge and up the front opening there was a lush tuxedo of silver fox. But the collar was the primary feature. Instead of lying flat or cowling slightly, it was huge, boned, and stood fully upright at the back, as high as the model's head. It was the exaggerated fur version of the Elizabethan ruff and created a lovely frame for the model's face.

Now, *this* was something new. Dramatic and tremendously flattering if one happened to have a lovely face to show off and a body with a few flaws to hide. Irene could hear breath drawn in sharply and see women in the audience tilting their heads, studying it and imagining themselves appearing at the theater in such a cape.

The final model was the young girl Irene had hired. She had black hair, fair freckled skin, pink cheeks, and pale blue eyes. Irene had made sure she wore no powder to hide the freckles or the suggestion of blush. She wore a three-quarter-length coat with alternating three-inch strips of raccoon and black velvet, sewn on the diagonal. The velvet emphasized the depth of the fur fiber, and the sharp indentations it caused made her appear even slimmer than she was. With it she wore a hat like a baby's cap, a fitted velvet square with ties under the chin and a rolled, padded raccoon strip around the face. She carried a matching muff, both sporty and girlish, almost childish. Irene, still watching the audience, could almost hear several women thinking: Could I get away with wearing that? Yes, I might just!

The girl all but skipped back to the curtained doorway, and someone said, "More! More!"

Neptune raised his hands in a gesture of apology. "I'm sorry, that's all we brought along tonight. Now, come meet our dear, talented partner!" He and Irene stepped down from the dais and were swallowed by the crowd.

"Beautiful work!"

"Such unusual lines . . ."

". . . that striped raccoon was superb."

"Neptune, I'll have to work fourteen hours a day next year to keep my wife in furs."

". . . the eerie feeling that you design with me in mind, my dear."

". . . making a fitting appointment early this year."

"So young to be so clever . . ."

Irene's head was swimming, with compliments, with names to remember, with the intoxication of success. This, at last, was the real beginning of what she'd dreamed about for so many years. Some of these very same people might have been in the theater audience that night while she huddled, a nondescript immigrant in a cheap cloth coat, watching them with awe. Now they were clustered around her, lavishing compliments on her. If only Mama and the girls could have been here to see it, she thought, forgetting entirely that she hadn't even considered inviting them. If only Peter were here! He'd be so proud of her, so pleased that her hard work was finally paying off in recognition.

Her hand was taken in a firm and somehow intimate grip. "Mrs. Garrick, you may not remember me . . ."

"Of course I do, Mr. VanCleve."

"Please, you positively must call me Edward. My father is *Mr*. VanCleve. Your work is stunning, even to a man who hasn't much of an eye for feminine fashion. I congratulate you."

"Thank you . . . Edward."

"May I get you something to eat, or a drink perhaps?"

"Thank you, no."

"You're sure? You look hungry."

He looked so sincerely concerned that she laughed. "I *am* starving."

Edward disappeared and returned in a remarkably short time from the buffet table with a plate mounded high with food—enough for two men. "You will excuse Mrs. Garrick to have a bite, won't you?" he asked of the ladies who'd surrounded her in his brief absence. Before they could dispute this, he took her elbow and firmly steered her to a chair. "There you are," he said, pulling another chair around in front of her to provide a sort of barrier.

She looked down at her plate with dismay. "You could feed a village from this plate!"

"I didn't know your preferences, so I just got you a lot of everything. I failed to meet your husband. Is he here tonight?"

She was prepared for the question. "No, I'm sorry he couldn't make it. He had some appointments at Fordham College today and was unable to get away in time."

"He's involved with Fordham? A professorship?"

"Possibly. He's considering them, as well as some others." It was—or someday would be—the truth.

"I have a number of friends at Fordham. Perhaps some of them know him."

Careful. "I rather doubt it. His field of study is rather specialized and his work solitary."

"Just what is his field?"

She smiled sweetly and hoped he couldn't hear her heart thrashing against her ribs. "I'm beginning to think you're more interested in my husband than in me," she said with a coyness that tasted bitter in her mouth. But it worked.

"Please forgive me, Mrs. Garrick. Just my natural curiosity getting the best of my tongue. Let's talk instead about your designs, shall we? That white cape was magnificent. The only thing that might have improved it would have been your wearing it instead of the mannequin. Is it, perhaps, your own?"

"I have only one fur, a quite practical and unglamorous one at that. I prefer seeing them on others."

"How fascinating."

"Why?"

"I've never met a woman who didn't want more furs than she already had. Don't you like fur?"

"Sir! How can you ask? I love furs, but there's only one other coat I want," she said, thinking of the crown sable she intended to have someday. Until then, she would remain content with the opossum that Neptune had given her. Nothing between the two could mean as much.

"And what's that?"

His interest was so flattering and persuasive that she was on the point of explaining before she realized what she was doing. She must either avoid this Edward VanCleve or learn to be especially cautious in his presence. His questions were so pointed, yet courteous, that it would be easy to slip and reveal too much. Still, it was nice after having information poured into her for so many years to have someone asking *her* questions and actually seeming vitally interested in the answers.

"What is this other coat you want?" Edward repeated.

"It's a fairy-tale coat and I have to placate the pixies before I can have it," she said with a smile. This manner of light chitchat didn't come naturally to her, but it was getting easier to fall into. Especially around Edward VanCleve.

"Ah, a sacrifice perhaps? Then throw me to them. I'll gladly go live in the boll of a tree or a rabbit hole if it will get you what you want."

"Oh, I don't think so. They'd make you two feet tall and you'd grow a beard to your knees and sit around on mushroom chairs." She laughed. This was getting to be fun.

"Seriously, Mrs. Garrick—may I call you Irene?—what is the coat you want?"

"Seriously, Edward—you *may*—it's a secret."

He reached out and laid his hand lightly on her arm, a gently possessive motion, and said very softly, "I hope someday you'll tell me. We're going to share each other's secrets, you know. I have a premonition, and I'm never wrong."

Irene felt herself beginning to blush and was saved from having to reply by Clara's stern presence. "Mrs. Garrick," she said with a stern expression, "Monsieur wants you to meet someone."

"Thank you, Miss Johnson. Have you met Mr. VanCleve?"

"How do you do?" Clara said.

Irene almost smiled at the look on her friend's face. She might have had a persimmon tucked in her cheek. "Where is Monsieur?"

"I'll show you. Excuse us?" she tossed over her shoulder to Edward, who was watching this performance with a bemused expression.

"He's a man to avoid," she said quietly to Irene as they threaded their way through the crowd.

"How delightful to have fresh young ideas at Neptune et Cie," a dowager said as they passed her.

"Thank you. I hope I'll prove worthy of your good taste, Mrs. Piper," Irene said.

"Ah! You know who I am," the woman said, obviously pleased.

"But of course. Monsieur speaks often of you and the many trend-setting purchases you have made over the years," Irene replied tactfully. What he had said the day he pointed her out (she was shredding a fitter into tiny bits at the time) was, "The rich old dragon has six daughters-in-law who wear what she tells them to. Sell her one coat and you've sold seven."

Irene eased away and asked Clara, still firmly affixed to her elbow, "Why do you say that about Mr. VanCleve?"

Clara almost blurted out the truth—"Because he makes you laugh and blush." But that hardly sounded like a valid reason to be cautious of someone. After all, she wanted Irene to be happy. But the blushing part worried her and she didn't want to embarrass Irene. Their relationship since Clara went to work at Neptune et Cie had undergone a subtle change. Neither of them admitted it, but Clara was no longer the teacher and Irene the student. Irene was now, like it or not, Clara's employer, and although the younger woman never took advantage of her position, Clara couldn't quite forget that their roles were changing. In private, like earlier in the day on the excursion boat, they could be the friends they once had been, but most of the time they had to play their new parts.

"I'm not sure what it is about him," Clara said instead. "He just seems a bit too familiar."

"And too curious," Irene added. "I agree with you, Clara. I must not insult him, but I'll avoid him whenever possible. Now, where *is* Monsieur?"

"I haven't the least idea," Clara said.

"I suspected as much. Clara, let's go to the suite where we dressed. I want to find my coat."

"Should you leave? Monsieur won't like it."

"I have something for you. Monsieur needn't know."

Supposing it was merely a list of things to do the next day or something equally mundane, Clara was astonished when Irene handed her a tiny box. "Before you open it, I must tell you something you already know, but I have to say it anyway, Clara. You are my oldest and best friend. Most important, you are my first teacher and I could not have been here tonight if it weren't for you."

Clara was disconcerted. It had been years since Irene had spoken so openly of her affection. For a moment she felt that she was back in the Sprys' neighborhood, showing the still-waiflike child how to make a map or buy candy. She'd been like this then, clutching her arm unexpectedly and saying, "You are my good friend. Please never stop being." Clara felt tears gathering in her eyes.

"Now, open it," Irene said, her eyes sparkling.

Inside the box there was a small silver ring with two silver hearts attached by loops. "It's a friendship ring. Can you see the writing? The jeweler said it nearly made him blind!"

Clara held the ring closer to the light. On the back of one heart in tiny incised script was the name "Clara," and on the other, "Irina."

The tears poured over. If it had said "Irene" it would have been a lovely gesture, but "Irina" meant more—much, much more. It was an acknowledgment of how far back they went, that Clara knew something secret and vital about Irene that few others in the world knew. And it was an expression of trust.

Irene put her arms around Clara's shaking shoulders and cried a little herself as she said, "I wanted to thank you for giving me English. I promised I would. Remember?"

Clara pulled a handkerchief out of her sleeve and mopped her eyes. "Yes, I remember. Oh, dear, what a blubbery fool I'm acting." In an unconsciously motherly gesture she dabbed at the tears on Irene's cheeks as well. "My dear Irene, make me another promise."

"Anything."

"Stay as happy as you are tonight."

"I will, Clara. Oh, I hope I will."

There was a knock on the door. Irene opened it to face

Neptune. "There are five hundred people down there hoping to meet you. What in the world are you doing?" he demanded.

She returned his glare. "We were just having a nice private cry. Now we are ready to return. Clara?"

The two women went off arm in arm. Neptune stood in the doorway shaking his head.

Peter *was* glad for her stunning success, or if not precisely glad, he did his very best to act like it, because he knew how disappointed she'd be if he didn't share her enthusiasm. But he found himself thinking guiltily that it would be nice if she could condense the telling of it a little. Her recounting was cutting into his precious sleeping time.

She realized it too. "You're slipping farther and farther down into that chair, Peter. Please just go to bed."

"Thanks, Reenee," he said, rising and all but staggering from the living room to the bed.

Irene was prepared to just "stew in her own juices," with all the things she'd wanted to tell him bottled up inside, but was surprised when Lillie, who had been in the room but absorbed in some darning Zofia had insisted on, said, "Irina, did all those people you talk about come to see you?"

"Most of them, yes."

"Weren't you scared?"

"Terrified!"

Lillie grinned at the concept of their very bossy, self-assured oldest sister being frightened of anything. "Did you wear a pretty dress?"

"Yes, I did. As a matter of fact, I have to go uptown to the hotel and get it and some other things out of the room we took. Would you like to come along?" As she spoke, she was wondering what her chances were of getting Lillie cleaned up respectably enough to take her into the Plaza. It was risky, but she had a sudden desire to share something of her victory with someone, and since Lillie was showing an interest . . ."

"This hotel—is this another house you live in when you aren't here?" Lillie had never quite grasped the idea of where Irene went so much of the time.

"No, it's a huge house for people who are traveling to stay in along the way. But we—my friend Clara and I—just rented a room yesterday to change our clothes and get ready for the party. Now I have to remove my things so they can rent the room to someone else tonight.'' It gave Irene an unexpectedly warm feeling to explain these things as Clara had once explained them to her. And Lillie was actually listening.

She considered the child. From their infancy on, she'd regarded the twins as a unit, but now that she thought about it, they had been changing lately, becoming more distinctly individuals, and she just hadn't taken much heed. Never quite identical, now they even looked less alike than before. At fourteen, Cecilia was still a flat-chested little girl, but Lillie was developing a figure and getting a bit plump along with it. That would have to be watched or she'd get as doughy-looking as Stefania.

''Do you have lots of other pretty dresses someplace?'' Lillie was asking, the darning laid aside and forgotten.

''A few, yes. I keep a few at my office so I can change if I have to go out for a luncheon.''

''Why don't you keep them here at our house?''

''Because my work is clear uptown and because . . .'' She'd started to say that Peter didn't like to see all the evidence of her activities at Neptune et Cie, but she changed it. ''Because there isn't very much room here in the closet and I don't want to take up everybody else's space. Now, do you want to come along?''

''Oh, yes.''

''Then put on a clean dress and let me get your hair rebraided neatly.''

She hadn't counted on Zofia coming back from her shopping just as they were leaving. ''Mama, Irina is taking me to a hotel to pick up her pretty dress!'' Lillie said happily.

Zofia dumped her string bag of vegetables on the table. ''Ah, I will go too.''

Irene's heart dropped. Getting Lillie in shape for a trip uptown had been possible—but Mama? What if she saw someone she knew at the hotel? Dear Lord! ''Mama, we're not walking. We're going on a bus,'' she said, certain this would discourage her.

''I ride a bus, just last week with Apolonia Jedrychowski. We sat on the top. At first I just cover my eyes, but then I look and saw all the people looking little. I like buses, I think."

"Oh dear . . ." Irene thought frantically. Nine o'clock on a Saturday morning. What were the chances of seeing anyone? Not too great. Not if they hurried. Thank heaven the room was on the third floor and they could walk up. Imagine the scene Zofia could throw in an elevator! "Very well, but, Mama, this is an American hotel and you must not wear your old-country clothes. We'll stop on the way and I'll buy you a new dress—you, too, Lillie, if you want."

"What kind of dress?" Zofia said suspiciously.

"Something you'll like. I promise." Irene was thinking of a shop she passed every day at Thirty-fourth and Fifth. She'd seen a dark gray dress in the window that she'd felt would be suitable for Zofia, but hadn't thought there was any chance of getting her to wear it. Perhaps now . . .

"I'll look at a dress," Zofia said grudgingly.

It took a good deal of convincing, but Zofia wore the dress. In the end, it wasn't Irene's opinion that swayed her, but Lillie's. "What would the women of the village think to see me in such a thing!" Zofia said.

Irene had been ready to point out irritably that they were highly unlikely to cross paths with anyone from the village, but Lillie spoke first. "They would think you'd gotten rich and happy in America, Mama." She even—wonder of wonders—agreed to leave off the disreputable shawl she always wore draped over her head in public.

Irene's stomach was churning by the time they got to the Plaza, but their entry was apparently unnoticed. She allowed her mother and sister a minimum time for strolling through the lobby gawking and pushed them along to the room. There, in relative safety, she ordered up tea and petits fours. She relaxed then, and smiled at Zofia's interest in the food. "Such tiny cakes!" she exclaimed, picking one apart like a surgeon. "And icing all over. How do they do that?"

Lillie was more interested in the silver service. "It's so shiny and pretty. Irina, do you think someday we could have a pitcher like this?"

"I'll buy it on the way home," Irene said. It was only

hotel-grade silverplate. She'd get them something much better. How exciting that Lillie was becoming interested in nice things. "Would you like a tea service like this, Mama?"

Zofia looked up from her examination of a powdered-sugar-covered lemon biscuit. "Would get spots," she said.

"How practical of you. Mama, I could afford to have a lady come work for you and clean the spots. Won't you let me?"

"Another woman in *my* house? That would be like having a mother-in-law!"

Irene laughed. "You're a mother-in-law and Peter loves you."

"This is good," Zofia said, smiling a little herself. "Piotr, he is a good man."

The waiter returned to ask if there was anything else they needed. When he'd gone, Zofia asked, "Why does that soldier act like a servant?"

"Soldier? He's a waiter, Mama, not a soldier."

"But he has such a fancy uniform."

They all enjoyed themselves enormously. Away from home, Irene felt less like the oppressed daughter, slightly more in control. She discovered, too, that Zofia's utter terror of things different had become merely a vague distrust, and that was encouraging. She'd gotten her into an American dress—albeit an exceedingly dull, frumpy one—and out of her hideous shawl. Her mother was, to Irene's great surprise and pleasure, enjoying this treat. She was overwhelmingly impressed with the bathroom, and for some reason was entranced with the tiny white hexagonal tiles on the floor.

"We could put them in our bathroom if we had one of our own," Irene said, and an idea started clicking over in her mind. Why shouldn't they have their own bathroom, their own apartment somewhere nicer? Zofia had possibly adjusted enough now to accept the idea of a move uptown. She'd think about that this week and look around to see what was available.

Lillie was more interested in the view outside than inside. She kept drifting back to the windows that overlooked the front of the building. Irene watched Lillie watching the well-heeled patrons of the hotel coming and going, and she took heart.

They were getting ready to leave when Clara came in. "I wondered if you might have come straight here instead of to work. Hello, Mrs. Kossok. Lillie, how you're growing!"

How typical of Clara, who had met her family only a few times, to remember immediately which twin this was. Many of their own neighbors didn't bother to distinguish between them. Irene caught herself short: until this morning, *she'd* hardly bothered to consider their differences. Clara settled in for a nice talk—in Polish, also typically considerate. Even Zofia could limp through a conversation now in Pidgin English, but Clara saved her the effort.

When they started gathering up their things to vacate the room, Zofia showed a remarkable appreciation of Irene's dress from the night before, the last thing Irene had expected. Placing the cotton cover over it with loving care, Zofia insisted on carrying it. "You will drag the hem," she chided Irene. "I will be more careful. Girls are so clumsy. See, already some of the beads, they are loose."

Clara smiled behind her hand.

"May I carry that little suitcase with your other things?" Lillie asked. "People will think then that I, too, am a traveler."

Emboldened by success, Irene and Clara took them down in the elevator. Zofia started looking around frantically as they began their descent, but it was a short trip and over before she could say or do anything outrageous. Feeling quite relaxed, almost smug, Irene was suddenly struck with horror as they came onto the sidewalk in front of the building.

A cab had pulled up and Edward VanCleve was climbing out.

Irene tried to herd them in the opposite direction as quickly as possible, but they were caught. "Oh, Irene! Miss Johnson! How nice to see you both. I left my cigarette case here last night and am hoping it has been turned in. I never dreamed I'd run across something so much more valuable!" He hadn't even seemed to notice Zofia and Lillie.

Irene was paralyzed.

Clara stepped in. "Mr. VanCleve, you'll have to excuse us. We're in a terrible rush at the moment."

"Then take my cab. Here! Boy, wait up!" he dashed back and opened the door to the vehicle, which Zofia was the first to climb into. Huffing with the effort of keeping the dress bag from getting crushed, she mumbled something in Polish which Irene hoped Edward would take to be "thank you."

Lillie had wandered away a few steps and was studying a lady in trailing pink skirts. "Lillie!" Irene said sharply. "The cab's waiting."

Edward smiled as Lillie, then Clara, then Irene got in. Pushing aside a fold of her skirt so it wouldn't get caught in the door, he smiled at Lillie and said softly to Irene, "Your maid and her little girl seem to be enjoying their outing."

Irene opened her mouth to correct his error, but all that came out was a single word: "Yes."

Clara leaned across to pull the door. "Thank you, Mr. VanCleve," she said briskly as she pulled the handle.

They were silent all the way back to the apartment. Dropping off Zofia and Lillie, they then headed back uptown to Neptune et Cie. Finally Irene said, "Clara, did you hear what I said! He called Mama my maid and I just let it go!"

"I know, dear. But what else could you do?" Clara tried to sound unconcerned simply because she knew that Irene was tearing herself apart with guilt and she didn't see any reason to add to it. "If you'd told him the truth, he'd have ferreted out all sorts of information that's none of his business."

"That's true, but that wasn't why I did it. I did it because I was ashamed of them. I just didn't want anyone to know that the dumpy little foreign lady with the cake icing on her cheek was my mother. Clara, she came within a hairbreath of spitting on the sidewalk! Imagine if people knew who she was!"

For once in her life, Clara couldn't think of anything to say.

Encouraged by her newfound affinity for Lillie, Irene took her along on the long-promised trip to St. Louis to the fur auction. She expected objections from Peter, just because he seemed so often to object to her ideas lately, but he was wholly in favor. "What a wonderful opportunity for her to get to see the country!" he exclaimed. "And you too." Dragging down a book of maps from the shelf, he started tracing their probable route. "You'll go clear across Pennsylvania. I hear it's beautiful, rich country, both on the surface and beneath. Ohio, Indiana, Illinois—you probably won't go far enough north to see Chicago, that's a pity. I'll check out some American history books so you'll know more about the places you're seeing."

Nothing of this aspect of the trip had crossed Irene's mind. She had imagined only departure and destination points, with a void in between. "Peter, come along. Please. You'd enjoy it so much!"

"You know I can't. But I'd love to."

"You can! You can make up a week of school. That's all the time it will be."

"School, maybe. Work, no," he said, and the last word rang with such authority that she didn't press him with the supremely logical observation that he didn't need to have the job anyway and it would make no difference if he quit to make the trip.

Lillie was so thrilled that she didn't sleep the whole night before they left, and fell asleep as soon as the sun set halfway across Pennsylvania. Neptune carried her to the double compartment the women were sharing. Irene and Clara sat up late, dressed in nightgowns and sitting cross-legged in the dark on Irene's bed. They were fascinated with watching the brilliant red-glowing maws of the iron and steel mills the train passed. A fog had fallen and the red was diffused in an unearthly glow. "That must be what hell looks like!" Irene whispered.

"No, it's much too beautiful and awesome. I wouldn't mind if heaven looked like this," Clara replied.

The next day Lillie was up at dawn, gabbling about every town and cow they passed. She covered the length of the train over and over again, taking enormous pride in getting her "sea legs," as Neptune said, and being able to make it through a whole car without lurching into anyone. He and Lillie ate at least six partial meals in the dining car simply because she loved eating while in motion. Irene was relieved that Neptune had developed an intense grandfatherly (though she wouldn't have phrased it that way to him) interest in Lillie.

"You don't have any children in your family, monsieur?"

Clara asked, and Irene was tickled that she, too, had avoided a generational reference.

"Unfortunately not, but I keep hoping Chandler will marry and provide some."

It was a long day and not nearly as interesting as the evening before. They passed hundreds of miles of rich but boring farmland, broken only by the stands of trees lining creeks. Lillie, however, loved the landscape. "So much more pretty," she told Irene—in English, wonder of wonders! Bless Monsieur's non-Polish presence.

"Prettier than what?"

"Than the city. New York. I would like to be living here. With trees and places to run and think with quietness."

"Oh, but Lillie, it would be so dull. Not very many people, and no interesting places to go."

"Me, I would like not so many people."

"Would you really?" Irene asked, surprised. Why was it she'd lived in such close proximity to this child for several years and had to get hundreds of miles away to get to know her? Maybe if she'd drag each of them off someplace in turn, they'd all get acquainted. No, it wouldn't work with Stefania. She'd have plopped herself down in the dining car and never moved or spoken. Yet, it was odd that Irene still felt closer to Aggie than any of the rest of them, even though Aggie, now married to her beloved Olbracht, was half a world away and touched Irene's life only in the letters she sent.

St. Louis itself was interesting to Irene for only one reason—the fur warehouse they were to visit. Her first impression was that of the odor of the place. It smelled a block away. Neptune noticed her nose wrinkling and said, "The skins and hides have only a preliminary flesh-removal when they get here. That fragrance is, in fact, rotten meat." Irene turned and noticed that Lillie and Clara, walking behind them, were having more trouble accepting this than she was. Lillie was holding her nose and Clara was pretending not to notice, but looking distinctly green and breathing through her mouth in convulsive gulps.

"She'll be sick if you make her come along," Neptune whispered.

She sent them off to shop for the day.

The American Fur Exchange warehouse was more of an education than she'd imagined. Since she'd come to work at Neptune et Cie, she'd come to regard the pelts as clean and well-organized, as they were by that stage. This was chaos on a grand scale. The enormous old brick building sitting only a precarious few hundred feet from the Mississippi was an almost solid mass of men, furs, and stench. "Three times a week during the spring and early summer there are floor sales," Neptune said. "The primary divisions here are by region and animal. There is no assortment for quality whatsoever. Ah, thank you," he said to a clerk who'd handed him a small printed booklet.

He went on, "That corner, for instance, is lot one, which means furs and hides from the Northwestern states. The separate piles are minks, muskrats, coyotes, and so on."

"But if they aren't sorted for quality, how do you buy them? Do you just pick through for what you want?"

"No, you make a bid on the whole lot. Come on over, they're beginning to auction lot four. You'll see. Here, take the book and follow along."

The booklet listed each lot and the types of furs and skins within it, with an approximate number of each. A white space next to each lot was marked "Bid." They pushed their way through a crowd composed largely of extremely rough-looking men, with a few obvious gentlemen like Neptune scattered throughout. Strangely, no one seemed to notice that Irene was the only woman present. They were all far too intent on their business to care.

The auctioneer stepped up on a small crate and started his spiel. "Lot four to commence! Lot four to commence! North Central states and central provinces. Gather around, gentlemen. Prime pelts, first out. Came downriver with the ice floes, direct from the frozen north to you! Now, this first group is minks. Good year for minks, as you all know. Long winter of moderate cold with moderate rainfall. You old hands will recognize that many of these skins are Jack LaBelle's trappings, and I don't have to tell you how good he is at picking the best to ship to us."

As he bellowed on, three clerks were busily flinging the pelts around as if they were engaged in a pillow fight. Pelts were literally flying through the air, being caught, and tossed along. Some were actually being kicked back and forth. Neptune reached out a long arm and snagged several for Irene to examine. One was an excellent pelt, but one was late-caught and already going shelly. A third was fine fur and dense fiber but badly chewed up. "This young knight must have been in a mating fight with every other mink in North Dakota," Neptune said of it.

"Awright, gents, mark your page and turn it in. Gotta move right along." All around, men were scribbling names and figures on the sheets of paper and folding them tightly before handing them to the auctioneer's assistant. The clerks were retrieving the pelts. "Last chance, boys. Last chance. Let's see who gets them." He opened the sheet quickly, perused them, and called out the name and dollar figure of the high bidder. That man nodded to two of his own assistants, who started sorting out the mink pelts that had just been purchased into stacks of number one, two, three and four grades.

"Why would he buy such a mixed lot? How could he know what he's got? Do you—do *we*—buy this way?" God forbid! She'd never get the hang of it.

"He's an old hand, Irene. There's not a fur in that lot he didn't take at least a quick look at, and no, we don't buy at this stage, but watch what happens next. Come here." He grabbed her elbow and pulled her through the crowd to get closer to the man who'd bought the mink. The better-dressed gentlemen in the crowd had all gathered around him and were shouting offers. "Four hundred dollars for all your number-one grades . . ."

"Don't make me laugh, Joe. I could grab some fool off the street and talk him out of three times that."

"Not unless he was mother naked and in a blizzard!"

"Don't bother me."

"There's only sixteen damned number-ones in the lot."

"Nineteen! Get lost."

"Five dollars each for your number-threes. I can trim away the bite marks for collars—"

"Make it ten."

"Seven and a quarter."

"Eight-seventy-five."

"Eight."

"Take them away."

Bit by bit the whole lot was disposed of and the high bidder had made his profit without ever reaching a hand in his pocket to pay. Irene was stunned. Neptune led her away, saying, "That's the best way to make money, of course. It takes a tremendous amount of knowledge and bargaining skill and absolutely no work at all. The man never walks out of the building carrying so much as a single pelt and yet he might buy and sell a hundred thousand dollars' worth in a day or two. Now, I want you to spend the rest of the day here, pretending to bid. Take the book and mark, first of all, what you think you'd bid for the lot if you were bidding, then what you'd pay for the number-ones of that lot. Under each number, write what they actually went for."

"You're not staying?"

"There's no need for me. You'll learn more without me, and nobody will accost you here. Besides, I can't bear the stink of the place. I'll come back at noon to take you to lunch if you can stand the thought of food by then, and we'll look over your book and see how you'd have done."

"Not at all bad," he said later as he studied the neat notations in the booklet. "Not at all bad, but you'd have bankrupted us on that Louisiana muskrat."

"I know, but it was lovely fur. I couldn't believe it came from that far south."

"Yes, but they were hungry pelts."

"Hungry? I don't think I've heard that term."

"It means they'd absorb too much of the chemicals they're treated with as well as the dye. It would weaken the skins in the end."

"Are you going back to buy, monsieur?"

"I don't see anything we could use now. I don't often purchase here, except for beaver, which won't come in with the best until later, and novelties—Mexican ocelot, Canadian timber wolf, that sort of thing. But it's necessary to know your way around this kind of auction. Later in the year when the Asian and European pelts come into New York, I'll take you to an entirely different kind of auction. Terribly civilized—not as much as the Chinese, of course, but then who is?"

Away from the smell and crush of the Fur Exchange, Irene was feeling better and realizing that this was an important area of the business of being a furrier that she'd never even considered. How much she still had to learn! "How do the Chinese do it?"

"The buyers and sellers all wear wide-sleeved kimonos. The bidding takes place when a potential buyer grasps the seller's hand and wrist and presses a number of fingers on the inner side of the seller's wrist. The number of fingers serves as a bid, and successive pressures of all the fingers mean 'times five.' It's the same with counterbidding from the seller. It's all done in absolute silence and secrecy, since no one else can see what's going on under the sleeves."

"Have you ever bid that way?"

"I've never been to China, but we have a representative there. A native Chinese. You've seen his name in the bookkeeping."

"Oh, yes. I've meant to ask you about him, but kept forgetting."

"Never forget to ask anything you don't know," he said, suddenly all business again. "Now, if you're through with your lunch, I'll walk you back—"

"To the hotel?"

"The hotel? No, the fur exchange. You're spending the rest of today and tomorrow there."

"And you?" She bridled at his bossy tone. "What are you doing the rest of the day?"

"I'm taking some lovely ladies of my acquaintance for a ride in the country. Lillie wanted to see an old fort that your husband taught her about."

One the way back, empty-handed and still carrying in her imagination, if not in fact, the smell of the fur exchange, Irene thought about the purpose of the trip. She'd assumed they were going to purchase pelts, though she should have been suspicious, knowing that Neptune et Cie used few domestic furs. But they'd purchased none. Reflecting on it, she realized now that there had been an entirely different reason.

Neptune had implied, without ever speaking the words: You have had some success, but don't let it go to your head. You're still a student with much to learn.

But couldn't he have simply said that to her outright? No, perhaps not. The charity ball at which she was introduced to his customers and his society *had* gone to her head to some extent. She'd begun to feel that at last the learning process was drawing to a close, and this trip had pointed out that it would never stop and that if she ever started thinking she knew all he had to teach her, she'd better think again.

Nemine had [illegible] without ever speaking the words. You are something special, but don't let it go to your head. You're still [illegible] much to learn.

[illegible] said that to her outright. [illegible] perhaps [illegible] which she was introduced to [illegible] And [illegible] to her [illegible] some [illegible] to find that [illegible] was [illegible] and [illegible] that it could never [illegible] and that [illegible] again.

21

1912

Neither of them really believed it was the house that caused the problem, though it did come to symbolize the difficulties between them. It was, as mansions went, rather a modest one. It was farther uptown—Thirty-third—but not far enough to be ostentatious, and Irene had purchased it without consulting any of them shortly after her trip to St. Louis two years earlier. She took her mother and sisters to see it one evening while Peter was at work. Irene had already had the bathroom remodeled to duplicate the one at the Plaza that Zofia had been so taken with. The girls' bedrooms had already been redecorated with fresh wallpaper and they smelled faintly of the rose-petal sachets in the drawers of the wardrobes.

Peter had gone along with the move, despising the house, but deprived of the opportunity to object on Zofia's behalf. She, who hated to leave her friends, had been promised that she might have them visit her anytime she wished and was already happily puttering about in the enormous kitchen with Mrs. Jedrychowski when he first saw the place. "We don't need this much room," he said. "You could feed an army in the dining room, and our bedroom is bigger than the whole apartment we have now."

"We might not actually need this much room, but it certainly can't hurt us," Irene countered. "Look, there's a room next to our bedroom with bookshelves clear to the ceiling. Just think, Peter, a whole room for your studies. A nice southern exposure, and there's this wonderful little elevator thing that goes to the kitchen. When you're working and can't take time for going downstairs, Mama can put your dinner on a tray and send it up. Isn't that wonderful?"

He didn't tell her that one of the things he enjoyed most in life was sitting around the battered kitchen table with Zofia as she slapped plates down and gabbled about her daily round of haggling at the markets. It kept him from forgetting that real life went on no matter how tired he might be or how deeply immersed in *Fourteenth-Century Philosophy* or *Foundations of Church Law*.

"How am I to pay for this?" he asked instead.

"You don't have to!" Irene said brightly.

"We won't live on your income, I've told you that before."

"No, it's not my income paying either. It's the interest on the money we've saved. It's just sitting there in the bank doing nothing but creating more of itself." She didn't mention the stock Neptune had advised her to buy and then sell at a huge profit, with which she had made a substantial down payment. No point in distressing Peter with that aspect of the purchase. Besides, at that stage, the house was already theirs. If he became irritated enough to absolutely refuse to make the move, she'd have all the bother of selling it.

At that point Stefania had rushed in from her explorations and said, "There's a yard in back and I found a little animal hutch in the basement. Mama said I could have a couple pet rabbits if it's all right with you, Irina. Can I? Please! I want a pet of my own so much. Piotr, tell Irina I should have some soft little rabbits!"

So they'd lived in the house on Thirty-third and Peter hated its imposing pretensions and the half-witted flocks of maids Irene insisted they needed to save Zofia the trouble of keeping it clean. He felt a very personal animosity to the increasingly expensive, delicate furniture that seemed to just "appear," unmentioned, at intervals, and to the thick carpets that made his shoes look so shabby when he glanced down. He despised the delicate china that replaced the thick, comforting plates and mugs they left at the old apartment, and he loathed the blanket-size bath towels and the array of expensive shaving paraphernalia in the big bathroom that he and Irene shared.

But he endured the house for two years, and though every new carpet, every new maid and dish and razor strop was like acid eating into his pride, he said nothing because the rest of them seemed so happy. The twins raced up and down the curved staircase and sent each other things through the dumbwaiter. Stefania sprawled contentedly in the big kitchen while her mother showed off the modern utensils to her Polish friends. Much more than they, Irene loved it here. She walked through this big, impersonal house as if it were a palace and she a princess. She loved every wall, every painting, every ornament, and so, loving her, he accepted them with what dignity he could manage.

One night, soon after the move, he'd awakened to find her missing from the bed. Padding quietly down the curved staircase, he'd found her sitting at the piano downstairs—not playing it, just stroking the keys. In her flowing nightdress and robe with her hair loose and hanging like a gold curtain past her hips, she was a vision that burned into his mind's eye. If he lived to be a very, very old man, he would always remember how she looked that moment—so innocent, so vulnerable. How could he begrudge her anything? How utterly selfish of him to resent the things she loved just because he himself had not provided her with them.

"Irene?" he said quietly.

She'd leapt up from the piano bench, guiltily surprised for a moment before smiling. "Oh, Peter, I'm so happy," she said.

They'd sat down together in front of the marble fireplace, where a few embers still glowed, and ended up making love there on the thick cabbage-rose-patterned carpet. "What would the maids think!" Irene laughed.

"They'd think we love each other too much to bother going upstairs," he said.

"And they'd be right!"

No, it wasn't the house that destroyed them, nor was it even the time Irene spent socializing. If she was out at least three evenings a week attending various balls and parties, Peter had no reason to complain. Not really. He was never home himself and she made sure she was always there when he was. Almost always. But the small room that served as a closet to her increasingly rich wardrobe haunted him. There was an aroma of expensive cigars and more expensive perfume that lingered in the clothes. Those gowns, the silks, the taffetas, the sheer hosiery and rich petticoats were a part of her life that had nothing to do with him and were, for reasons he'd never understand, terribly important to her.

At least that life was never allowed to impose on them directly. None of her society friends visited her at home, but Peter wasn't so naive as to believe that it was through any effort to spare her family inconvenience that Irene arranged it this way. He had picked up remarks that indicated that the great Irene Garrick's home address was a well-guarded secret. She didn't want people to visit because the family didn't fit the image of the person she and Neptune had invented for her to be. The dispossessed-Russian-royalty theory could be blown to ribbons by a few words from Zofia. But though he regretted her motives, he approved the results.

Neither was the school the girls attended an important factor in the problems between Irene and Peter. After the trip to St. Louis, Irene had developed an increased affection for Lillie, who had apparently shown an interest in the trappings of success that Irene set such store by, at least that was what Peter assumed to be the motivation for the sisters' newly amiable relationship. Lillie had rather suddenly acquired quite a number of new dresses and hair ribbons and hats, and that fall, just after they moved to the new house, Irene announced that she had arranged for her sisters to attend a private school farther uptown.

Again, Peter questioned the motives, but silently, because the result was to his liking. Unlike many of his colleagues, who felt education for women was either unnecessary or dangerous and often both, Peter felt strongly that everyone capable of digesting knowledge ought to have it made available. An educated person, man or woman, was simply more interesting and had more to contribute to life.

Cecilia hadn't much liked the idea, but went along with it because Lillie was enthusiastic. And between them, the twins convinced Stefania to attend with them. Their speech and manners—at least in the twins' case—started changing almost immediately. Zofia still objected. "How can I raise them good Catholic girls when they go to heathen school like boys?"

"It's a Catholic school, Mama, and there are no boys there. Only girls."

"The teachers, they are nuns?"

"Some," Irene answered. The religion classes *were* taught by sisters.

Zofia managed to undermine the scheme where Stefania was concerned. She lasted only one year, failed all her courses, and gained another ten pounds. She cried every morning when it was time to leave and made them all nearly wild with her sniffling and whining. Irene finally gave up and let her stay home with her mother. But she insisted on a tutor coming in for two hours every afternoon to try to force a respectable grasp of grammatical English on the child.

Cecilia didn't do well in her studies either, nor was she ever eager to don her prim schoolgirl uniform and go off so early in the day, but she couldn't imagine staying home without Lillie, so she continued to attend without any real fight. Maturing more slowly than her twin, she had taken on a slightly subservient role and let Lillie make most of her decisions.

Lillie seemed to enjoy school. Not studying—she had to repeat several courses, in fact. But she liked the girls, she liked the private car Irene arranged to have pick them up every day, and she very much liked Irene's approval.

"I had begun to worry that none of them would ever appreciate what life had to offer," Irene said to Clara one day. "But Lillie is really very much like me."

Over the years Clara had developed a sort of split-personality method of conducting herself. In the office, she was Irene's employee and acted the part. Away from work, she was still the girl's elder and once-mentor and felt free to say frankly what she felt. This was such a time. "She's nothing like you at all, Irene. You've always wanted a great deal but fully expected to have to earn it. She wants and appreciates only what's given to her."

"Clara! That's not true!"

"It certainly is and you know it," Clara said, genuinely surprised that Irene would argue such an obvious point.

"Well, it's only because she's young. As she gets older—"

"She's sixteen years old! A young woman already. Think of yourself at that age, Irene! How long had you been on your own? How hard were you working, not for yourself, but for them? She won't even take the trouble to study and absorb the education you're handing her. You were working your fingers to the bone with those awful Spry people at her age."

"Why should she have to live like that?" Irene said, her voice rising and her face flushed with anger. "I did it so they wouldn't have to! This is what I did it all for, Clara, and you are saying bad things about my sister!"

"No, I'm not saying bad things about her. She's a nice girl, no more spoiled and self-absorbed than most girls her age. What I am saying is that you shouldn't deceive yourself about her. I know you want to believe she's like you, but she's not. She's not, Irene. She enjoys all the benefits you provide, and she appreciates you for providing them—be happy with that and don't try to cast your virtues on her. They are your own."

Irene intended to talk about this to Peter that night, but never had the opportunity. It was nearly eight and she had gone ahead and eaten a light supper with the girls and taken a bath. Coming into the bedroom, her long hair wrapped in a towel, she found him sorting through some papers on the bed. She could tell from the scowl that he was angry about something. "What's wrong?"

He looked up. "When you hire new maids, you really ought to mention to them that you have a husband! That red-headed fool didn't want to let me come in 'madam's boudoir.' "

"Oh, I *am* sorry, Peter. She just started today and doesn't seem to be very bright. She must have thought you were my lover!"

He stared at her. "Reenee, that's not funny, and a few years ago you wouldn't have thought so either."

"I only said it because it was so absurd!" she said, as embarrassed as a child caught saying a dirty word.

Peter stacked the papers he'd been looking at and handed the top sheet to Irene. "I'm sorry, Reenee, that girl just ruffled me the wrong way. Here, take a look at this."

Irene read, her face registering equal measures of pleasure and perplexity. "Peter, that's wonderful. A college offering you a position. I'm so proud of you."

"I'll be paid enough for teaching freshman philosophy to

pay my own tuition in graduate school, plus as much as I've been making at my other job. It's the most generous offer they've ever made, I'm told."

"But . . . what do you mean? You'll *be* paid? You're not taking this position, are you?"

"Of course. How could I turn it down?"

"But, Peter, it's clear upstate. It must be a hundred miles away."

"A hundred and ten—but it's right on the train route."

"But still, you can't take that long a ride every day. You'll have to stay there during the week."

Peter took the letter of acceptance back from her. He was holding himself in such tight control that his movements were stiff to the point of jerkiness. *He'd* have to take a long ride? *He'd* have to stay there? Could he be hearing her right? He didn't trust himself to speak.

Irene went on, heedless of the anger and frustration bubbling in him. "At least when you're home you won't have to be working all the time. Maybe it's best. You can be here on weekends and do some things with me. Some parties. There are people who think I'm not really married, you know. I've heard the whispers that I've just invented you—"

"Irene!"

She jumped, so startled at the fury in his voice that the towel came undone and her wet hair tumbled down in her face.

"Don't you care that this is a wonderful opportunity, a compliment to my abilities that I've been waiting half my life to hear? Is this damned trivial gossip all you care about?"

She shoved her hair back. "Peter! What are you so mad about? Of course I'm thrilled you've been asked to take this position. Even this is far less than you deserve! They should be asking you to be president of the college, not just a teacher—"

"Instructor."

"Instructor, then. I just meant I'll miss you during the week. I wish you could have gotten the same sort of job closer to home."

There aren't a lot of Catholic colleges in the neighborhood needing me. He wanted to say that, but sarcasm didn't come naturally to him, and besides, he was still too stunned to trust himself to say much of anything. Drawing a deep breath, he dared express just one sentence of his thoughts. "I thought we'd all go upstate."

"All of us? We couldn't. How would I work? How would the girls go to school? There aren't boarding facilities. Peter, where are you going? You just came home. I want to talk to you about this."

He was already at the door. "I'm going . . . I don't know where. We'll talk later." He went out, shutting the door so hard he heard an ornament topple and break.

He walked for hours, and when he found himself back at the corner of Thirty-third, he was surprised and somewhat alarmed to realize that he really had no idea where he'd been or how long he'd been gone. The house was completely dark except for a faint light from their bedroom window. He went up the long staircase feeling old and defeated and still angry.

Irene heard his footsteps and ran to the door to greet him. "Peter, I've been so worried! Where have you been?"

"Reenee, sit down, please. We have to talk." He still didn't know where to start. "I'm going to take this position. I have to."

"I understand that, Peter. Really I do."

"But there are things you don't understand. It's as if we can speak a common language about some things, but the important ones require some other tongue that neither of us has. No, you don't see what I'm talking about, do you? Irene, when we got married, I knew you wanted all sorts of things I don't care anything about—social status, money, all the trappings. And I didn't mind. At least I didn't think I did. It seemed easy to say, 'Good, let her have them. It's nothing to me. I'll even give her what I can of them.' It seemed simple. It made you happy to work hard for all this"—he made a gesture that took in the room, the wardbrobe, the whole house—"and if it made you happy, there was nothing else to consider. But I was wrong. I don't know yet why or how, but I was dreadfully wrong—"

"Peter—"

"I do mind, Irene. I mind so much it makes me want to grind my teeth and shout and break things. We aren't separate beings, we are a pair, and what you have, I have, whether I like it or not."

"What do you mean?"

"I hate this house and I can't understand a word those Irish maids say and it embarrasses me to have them popping in and out of rooms making stupid little curtsies and—"

"Peter, you're saying you want to go back? Back to cramped little rooms, and a filthy toilet shared with strangers, and the constant smell of overcooked cabbage in the air? You can't mean that! How can you not love this house? It means so much to me. It's so beautiful. I've put so much thought into making it a beautiful place for us to live—I never knew!" She was trembling like a sapling in a breeze and there were tears tumbling down her face.

Peter sensed that he'd genuinely hurt her and he hadn't meant to. "It isn't having them that I hate. The things are nice enough. If I'd gotten them for you, I'd be happy."

"Peter, it doesn't *matter* who paid for them!"

"It *does*! Can't you see that yet? It does matter. And it matters that you love them so terribly much. Look at this thing!" He picked up a small silver flower basket. "Some poor bastard would have to work for three years to earn what this cost!"

"But no one did! I wouldn't have bought it if we didn't first have enough for our needs. You know that. I think it's pretty. I like looking at it. Why is that such a crime? Why is everything I think so immoral to you lately? I'm just trying to do nice things for my family—all my family. Can that be so wrong? Peter, I feel like there's nothing I can do to please you. The harder I try, the less you love me."

He started to reach out to her, and realized he might crush her to him violently enough to hurt her. Instead he sank into a chair by the window. "The less I love you? How can you say that? If I didn't love you more than myself, I wouldn't mind any of this."

"That's a lie. You love your stupid pride more than you love me or anyone else. 'I can't stand to be in a room with things I haven't paid for,' " she mocked. At that moment she hated the woman who was saying the words, but they'd been dammed up so long she couldn't stop them. "There's nothing wrong with appreciating nice things, Peter. You can't make me feel guilty for that!''

''You don't just appreciate them, you're obsessed with them. You live for them. If there was no other way to force them on us, you'd throw us all in a pit and bury us in them! That's what I feel like. Buried alive in china and crystal and useless expensive knickknacks!''

''What do you want? Should I pretend I care nothing for beauty? Shall we get out some boxes from the basement and load everything up? We could live in this room like monks! Maybe tear the drapes down and hang patched bedsheets. Take up the carpets and see if someone can come in and warp the boards a bit. Import some of the roaches and rats from the old apartment . . .'' She stopped, breathless.

''Irene, you've changed—''

''Yes, I've changed. I've worked hard at it! Do you want back the wretched child I was when we met? I was tired and hungry and oppressed and desperate with anxiety most of the time. Do you want me to be like that again? You liked me better when I was miserable and helpless? Well, I won't do it. Not even for you.''

''No, of course I don't want that! Don't act hysterical and melodramatic! I want you happy and contented. I just want to have something to do with making you that way.''

''You can't!'' she screamed.

He spoke very quietly. ''I think that's true.''

Silence fell like an instant blizzard, blinding and deafening them both.

''No! *No!*'' she cried, flinging herself into his arms as he rose from the chair. ''Peter, I didn't mean that. You know I didn't mean it. Neither did you. We're both just overworked and overwrought. Peter, I'm sorry. Please forgive me!''

''No, you should forgive me, if you can. You're right. It's just my pride, and I'm being insufferably selfish.''

''And you should be. You're wonderful and I shouldn't have been so rude and horrible. Peter, let's take a trip. Just the two of us. We can go somewhere peaceful and make love all day and not think about anything unpleasant.''

''We can't. I can't. I'm required to be at the school in a week. A week from yesterday, in fact.''

"Oh . . . oh, yes, I see. I didn't realize how soon. Of course. Perhaps another time. Later. At Christmas?"

"Maybe. Reenee, I love you."

"I know, Peter. And I love you."

She reached out and turned off the bedside lamp and flung back the covers invitingly. They didn't talk anymore. He was afraid to ask her to give it all up and come with him. She was afraid to ask him to give it all up and stay with her.

They were entering their busiest season, and an important showing had been scheduled for the day Peter had to leave. Irene tried to change the date, but Neptune reacted so scathingly that she abandoned the idea. He was right: the invitations had gone out weeks ago, the public announcements had been made; it would be foolish in the extreme to cancel because one partner wanted the day off to ride the train upstate to a small Catholic college nobody in the city had even heard of.

Peter acted like it didn't matter, but as he boarded the train he concentrated on making sure the porter loaded all his boxes of books so he wouldn't have to talk to Irene.

At the last minute, she almost leapt on the train, and even took a few running steps before realizing she couldn't possibly catch up with it.

"You'll have Christmas dinner with us, won't you, Clara?" Irene asked one day several months later. "Good morning, Mrs. Piper."

Clara waited until the dowager had moved on through the showroom, a partial representation of her flock of daughters-in-law in tow. "I'd love to. Peter will be home, I assume."

Irene nodded to another customer. "You're late for your fitting. I'm not sure there will be time to take care of the hat as well today."

"But I have to have it for the holidays!" the woman exclaimed.

"So I supposed. That's why I was surprised when you weren't here promptly."

As the woman scurried off to the fitting room, Irene said, "I hear she was late for her own wedding, and her first child was two weeks overdue. I'm making it my personal crusade to reform her. What did you ask?"

"Peter—"

"No, he won't be home. There are some foreign students, some English and French boys, who can't go home for the holidays and have to be looked after at school. Peter says as the junior member of the staff it was his responsibility to offer to stay there with them. I begged him to bring them home with him, but apparently there's some rule against that."

"Then you'll be going up there instead, won't you?"

"At Christmas? It's our busiest season. You know that. With Monsieur staying at home with that awful cold, I wouldn't dare leave. Chandler would have the place in a mess—"

"I think you're still underestimating him," Clara said. "Why don't you go off and stay with Peter and see what happens? I'll be here to keep an eye on things for you."

"Clara, I can't do that. I'd be letting Monsieur down."

"But you're letting Peter down."

Irene assumed the haughty expression that she so often used with customers these days, but Clara knew her well enough to see the pain behind the look. "Quite the opposite. He volunteered to stay up there. Lovely, Mrs. Keilor. I knew it would suit you. Now, be quite sure you don't ever wear a red dress with that coat. It would kill the color of both. Promise?"

Clara waited out the exchange of holiday wishes and persisted. "You haven't been up there to visit him once in all these months, have you?"

"What's gotten into you, Clara?" Irene asked in a low, angry voice. "You're as aware as I am that September through January is our busiest time of year. I've told Peter that every time he's asked me up. And he's every bit as able to get on a train and come here—if he didn't have all that private tutoring he arranged to do on the weekends."

Clara subsided into silence. She'd pushed the issue too far, but she could hardly resist the urge to interfere. Irene had worked herself nearly to exhaustion the whole fall. She'd acted as though working harder than ever would somehow get Peter home. She deserved a vacation. And Peter deserved some of her attention.

"Good morning, ladies."

Both women turned quickly. "Monsieur!" Irene exclaimed. "I had no idea you were in this morning. You shouldn't have come out in such weather."

"I'm not an old invalid. A few snowflakes can't do me any harm. Besides, I saw by the appointment book that you have Adelaide McCoy coming in this morning. Her father's an old friend of mine and I haven't seen her since her coming-out ten years ago. She and her husband have been off in Brazil or some exotic clime. Ah, here she is now. Adelaide, my dear child, how wonderful you look!"

Irene's first thought was that Adelaide, though quite pretty, looked exceptionally well-fed. There must have been a lot of starchy food in Brazil, to judge by her double chin. "How do you do, Mrs. McCoy," Irene said when Neptune introduced them. "I think I have just the thing for you. Come sit down here. Monsieur, you will join us? Miss Johnson, will you have the models bring out these coats?" She jotted some names down on the small pad of paper she always carried.

But six coats later, Adelaide wasn't happy. "They're all so . . . so 'plain,' if you'll forgive my saying so, Mrs. Garrick. Lovely, of course, but not quite what I had in mind. My friend has one of your coats from last year . . ." She described the coat.

"I remember it quite well," Irene replied. "But that's not the coat for you."

"Not the exact same, of course. I know you never exactly duplicate a design. But I'd like something like it."

Irene shook her head. "Impossible."

Neptune sat up a little straighter, looking alarmed.

"Whatever can you mean by that?" Adelaide asked.

"Your friend is at least six inches taller than you and considerably slimmer. The tall, thick collar treatment on that coat minimizes her long neck. Very flattering to her, but not to you." She almost added a remark that Adelaide had virtually no neck and her head would sink into the coat like a turtle's in its shell, but refrained.

"Well, perhaps a different collar, yes. But I do like the cut of the coat and the fur. That's what I want."

"I'm terribly sorry, Mrs. McCoy, but I won't make a coat like that for you."

"I beg your pardon!"

"No, I can't do it. Did you say something, monsieur? My mistake, I thought you spoke. Mrs. McCoy, you need a flat fur like mink, and sleek lines."

Adelaide's face had gone alarmingly pink. "Mrs. Garrick, you seem to forget that I'm your customer. It's your job to sell me what I want!"

"And you forget that I'm an artist and it's my job to protect my reputation. If I let you walk out of here in one of my designs looking like a hedgehog, I will suffer as much as you."

Adelaide gasped with outrage and Neptune stared at Irene as if he'd never seen her before. Only Clara, who had rejoined them and was standing behind Irene, showed no concern.

Irene went on, "I'll be delighted to make you a coat like the one you admire if you lose twenty—no, thirty—pounds. You could carry it then, with a different collar, of course. In the meantime, let's take another look at that first coat. If you try it on you'll see—"

But Adelaide was on her feet and flailing about to put on the coat she'd worn in. Neptune was trying to help her and nearly got punched in the face as she rammed her arm into the sleeve. "I have never been treated so shabbily in my life! Monsieur Neptune, you disappoint me gravely. I can see things have certainly changed at Neptune et Cie since I've been gone!" She snapped her fingers for the maid who'd been waiting at the door and stormed out.

"Have you gone insane?" Neptune inquired.

"I was right, wasn't I?" Irene asked calmly.

"Of course you were, but did you have to say it?"

"I saw no other way to convey the situation to her. Ah, there's Mrs. Piper again. Excuse me, I want to show her something."

Neptune turned to Clara. "What have I created? She can't talk to customers that way!"

Clara smiled. "Of course she can. Not many people could, but Irene can. You impress them with masculine charm, she does the same thing with feminine intimidation. They're all afraid of her to some degree, and not one of them suspects that she's more frightened than they are. I'll make you a wager, monsieur. That woman will be back before the season is out and she'll have lost the weight."

He smiled. "No, Miss Johnson. I never make bets I'm not sure of winning."

Clara repeated the conversation to Irene later. They'd gone shopping that afternoon after the showrooms closed and had stopped at a tearoom to have a hot drink and share a tiny slice of chocolate cake before heading their separate ways. "I don't know why he's surprised," Irene said. "He's the one who taught me that I must never, never act like a shopkeeper or social inferior. And couldn't he tell how scared I was?"

"No, men never can, I believe."

"I am afraid, you know," she said very softly.

For a fraction of a second Clara could see her again as the girl she had been on the boat. "Of what?" she asked. "You have everything you wanted of life—more money than you can count, your family with you, a reputation as a lioness of society, the admiration of your peers . . ."

"That's why I'm afraid. I never guessed it would be this way, but the more you have, the more you stand to lose. I'm still terrified sometimes that something or someone is going to come along and tear it all out of my hands. Partly it's because it came to me by coincidence. If Peter hadn't been able to get me the fur scraps to make Miss Terry's muff . . . well, it would never have happened."

"That's quite wrong, dear. If Peter hadn't been a fur cutter, you'd have simply found success in some other way. You've had some luck, I can't deny that, but luck comes only to those who are looking for it and know what to do with it. You have all you have because of drive and taste and ambition. Besides, who would take anything from you? Who *could*?"

"I don't know. It's just a sense. Like the sense I had today that I must speak very firmly and frankly to Mrs. McCoy. I'd never even met the woman, but I knew instinctively that was the proper way to handle her. She's a fluffy, girlish thing who's used to being told what to do. She might not like it, but she expects it. I can't guess how I knew that about her in a few minutes, but I did. It's the same sort of thing."

She pushed a few crumbs of cake around her plate before going on in such a quiet voice Clara could hardly hear her. "I keep having nightmares that I go home some evening and the house is gone. The old apartment building—not ours, but the one I lived in with the Sprys—is on the lot and I'm wearing hand-me-down rags and nobody knows who I am. I keep telling them I'm Irene Garrick and they just stare at me. In the dream I'm afraid to say I'm Irina Kossok because I know they'll recognize the name and all these years will just be wiped out."

Clara reached across the little table and took her hand. "Irene, you're just tired. You must take some time off. Go visit Peter, for God's sake! You aren't yourself anymore."

"No, I'm not. I know that. I should be grateful for everything, not worrying it away. But, Clara, I don't really think Peter wants me with him."

"Nonsense!"

"It's not. He keeps asking me to come visit, yes. But they're formal invitations—all talk about the scenery and the weather. And the rest of his letters are just hurried notes about what a wonderful time he's having. He's so happy there with his books and his new friends. I'm afraid I'd ruin it."

Clara thought: This is what she's afraid of losing. It's not the business, it's Peter. And she's afraid with good cause. But Clara knew there was a difference between being the repository of confidences and being asked for advice. Irene didn't want her opinion now.

Before she could formulate a tactful answer, the moment had passed. Irene had gotten a grip on herself and was gathering her parcels. "Mama will wonder what has become of me. Spend the evening with us, will you, Clara? Lillie's been asking me when you'll visit again. It's been too long."

"I can't, dear. And you can't stay home anyway. Have you forgotten the Leibers' party?"

"Oh, no! Tonight? I can't face it!"

"You must. The girl is engaged to be married in September and is planning a wedding trip to Sweden. There are a lot of coats to be sold in that. You know Monsieur's not up to it, and one of you has to be there."

"You're right. As always," Irene said, taking the money to pay for their treat from her purse. "Would you mind waiting for the bill so I can get home and dress?"

"Not at all."

Irene stood for a moment, then leaned down to exchange parting kisses. "You are a dear friend, my Clara. I don't know why you tolerate me, but I'm glad you do."

Clara smiled. "As long as you don't ever tell me what's wrong with *my* figure, we'll stay friends."

Irene was able to leave with a smile.

22

1913

It happened in February. It was a bitterly cold day and for years afterward Irene associated such weather with personal disaster. Zofia met her at the door. "Peter, he is here," she said. She hadn't been told why he'd come home unexpectedly, but she radiated impending doom.

"Where is he?" Irene asked. She tried to sound calm even though her heart was beating in her throat. It was like sensing death in the house. She should have been eager to see him. She *was* eager—it had been a long, lonely time. But the atmosphere was wrong. The air itself seemed to reek of something gone terribly wrong.

"Upstairs in that library room. Irina . . ." She paused and then decided against whatever she'd been about to say.

When Irene got upstairs, he was sitting calmly on a crate of books as if he no longer had the right to sit on the furniture. He was wearing an elaborately patterned green sweater she'd never seen before. The library was empty. Irene suspected his closet and his drawers were too. She felt like a part of herself had been wrenched away.

"No, Peter." It was all she could say.

He was pale and had the shaken look of a man who has just witnessed a tragedy—or is about to. He stared at her for a long moment, as if memorizing her appearance. "I didn't want to leave without talking to you, without explaining that I don't think it's your fault."

She stood there in the warm room, shivering in her coat and hat and fur-lined gloves. A small, cozy fire glowed and made the pine boughs on the mantel fill the room with their fragrance. The smell made her sick. "Peter, you can't—"

"Irene, you've known this was coming, and so have I. We were right for each other a long time ago. We aren't anymore. I've found a life I love, where I fit in and mean something. So have you. And they're different."

"I can't live without you."

"I think you believe you mean that, but it's not true. You can. You have been. And very nicely." He stood up and started to put on his own coat, which was lying over the back of a chair. He spoke with deliberate calm, as if giving a lecture. But there was an almost imperceptible tremor in his voice and a painful stiffness to his movements. A part of her recognized that he was as anguished as she.

"Irene, when we met you were a child. For all your years of hard work, you were a child wanting a better life. I had it. I was better-educated, had a better job, could give you some—not much, but some—of what you wanted. But I was just a way station—a long and, I hope, pleasant stop on your way someplace else. In your own way—the ways that matter to you, money, social position—you've passed me up and outgrown me. At least that's how it must seem from your viewpoint."

"That's not true!"

"Irene, I'm not accusing you of anything. I'm just speaking the truth in the language we both understand. It's not kind or noble to deny it. Please don't bother. It's sad—no, it's a tragedy, a damned tragedy—that love wasn't enough, but it's true. I simply can't live the life you feel you must live, and you'd hate the life I've found. I live in a small town—a clean, quiet, small town. Everyone there is associated somehow with the college. A big evening out is a walk in the town square and a game of football on somebody's lawn and then maybe a quiet game of cards or chess or just talk with a friend or two. I thrive on that. It's what I want the rest of my life to be, and you'd despise it."

"There's someone else!"

He shook his head. "You know better. I'll never love anyone else. And I'll never stop loving you, Reenee, but we can't go on."

She grabbed the bedpost to keep from sinking to the floor. "Peter, what have we done wrong?"

"Nothing. Everything. There were a thousand mistakes. Half yours, half mine."

"Peter, you're trying to make me choose between my career and you."

"No, I'm not. I've thought about it." He was wrapping a long green scarf around his neck. "I've imagined myself coming in here and saying, 'Me or the goddamn furs, take your pick,' but I was afraid you'd pick the furs. Then I was afraid you'd pick me and be miserable the rest of your life and I'd wither away of guilt for having done that to you. There was no right answer. So I'm not asking you to choose. I've chosen."

"But it's not just your decision to make."

"Nevertheless, I've made it. Irene, I know you must be hating me right now. Maybe you always will. I hope not. I hope you'll see before too long that I'm doing the only thing I can. I care too much for you to be a millstone and, frankly, I care too much about myself to go on being an emasculated fool, hanging on the fringes of your life."

She reached out, but he avoided her touch, leaning over and picking up the last box of books instead. "Peter, this is a nightmare. It isn't happening. How will I live without you?"

"Just like you always have," he said, opening the door. "Irene, I won't divorce you. I don't believe in it and I still hold out a hope that someday we may find a solution. I know it's impossible, but my long suit is faith. But I'm sure that would be most inconvenient for you, so I won't fight you over an annulment. You have all sorts of influential friends. You shouldn't have any trouble with it. Without any children, you can claim nonconsummation and I won't object—"

"That's it! That's what you want! I see now. Children. Peter, stay. We'll have a baby. Right away."

"Yes, I wanted children, but, Irene, you've known that for seven years, ever since we got married. It's too late now, and the reasons would be the wrong ones. Listen to me. I'm leaving you. I'm deserting you. That's the grounds you need to free yourself."

"No! I don't want to be free. I want you! Peter, don't go. Don't leave me."

But before the words were out of her mouth, he was gone

and she was too paralyzed with shock and horror to follow him down the steps. She heard his voice and Zofia's at the bottom landing, only a few sentences, then the sound of the front door closing.

Clara was surprised when Irene wasn't at work before her the next morning. Since coming to Neptune et Cie, Clara had never known Irene to miss a day unless there was some business appointment or social function she had to attend elsewhere, and since Clara was in charge of keeping track of just such things, she knew there wasn't anywhere else Irene was supposed to be. She told herself not to worry, that everyone was entitled to sleep late occasionally and it was a cold, rainy day—the best kind for staying in bed.

But her anxiety turned to genuine alarm when a messenger delivered a note from Mrs. Leiber wondering why neither Monsieur nor Mrs. Garrick had attended her party the evening before. Clara called the house and got Zofia after giving a sharp lecture to the maid who answered and didn't want to let any calls through without knowing the caller's name, business, and life history. "Where is Irene, Mrs. Kossok?"

"Here. She is here. In her bed. She won't let nobody go in her room."

"Is she ill?"

There was a pause. "I don't think so. Piotr was here last night."

It's happened, Clara thought. It was inevitable, but she had prayed her premonition was wrong. No, it wasn't a vaporish premonition, it was pure logic. "I'll come right over."

Zofia was waiting at the door for her. "He gave me an address," Zofia said. "He said if we needed anything to write to him. There was shouting."

Clara nodded as she stripped off her gloves and unpinned her hat. "I'll talk to her."

The bedroom door was locked. "Irene, open this door," she said loudly when there was no response to her knock. When there was still no answer, she pulled out a hairpin and went to work on the lock. Years of being a governess hadn't been entirely wasted. Many a time she'd had to deal with a child locked in a room. Zofia had been looking on, and when the door swung open, she nodded her satisfaction and clumped away, knowing that if anyone could deal with the situation, it was Clara.

The room was dark, all the draperies pulled. Clara sat on the edge of the bed, eyeing the mound of blankets for a long moment. "It's me, Irene. Come out here and talk to me."

There was a slight stirring and Irene's voice, raspy and muffled, saying, "He left me."

"I know." She started pulling gently on the bedclothes and stifled a gasp when Irene emerged. She was a wreck. Had this not been her own bed in her own home, Clara wouldn't have been certain this creature was her friend Irene. Her hair was tangled, her eyes swollen nearly shut, her face blotched. There was blood from a bitten lip and dark purple shadows under her eyes.

"What are you going to do about it?" Clara asked briskly.

"I . . . I don't know!" Her voice was hoarse with crying and she buried her face in her hands and began again, silent sobs shaking the whole bed.

Clara knew better than to encourage this crying, but couldn't help herself. She wrapped her arms around Irene's huddled figure and patted her, saying, "There, there. This won't help a thing, my dear. But get it out of your system. That's right. Everything will be fine. There, there."

After a bit, she pulled away and said more astringently, "You really must stop this now. Get ahold of yourself, Irene, and tell me what happened."

"I don't know. He was here and he took his books and he left."

"Why? Certainly he didn't just march out without saying anything."

"He said all kinds of things. I can't remember what anymore. I feel so stupid and horrible. He . . . he said he hated this house. He wants to give it all up and live somewhere else without me. He said I'd changed. He deserted me. That's what he said, that he was deserting me so I could get a divorce."

"And are you going to get a divorce?" Clara asked, ever the practical voice in Irene's life.

"No! Never! But maybe . . . he hates me. He used to love me, Clara. I know he did and now he hates me."

"I'm sure he didn't say that."

"He didn't have to. He said he hated the house and all the things I've worked so hard for."

"That's not at all the same as hating you."

"Isn't it?"

Clara couldn't answer. The question was too close to the quick. "What do you want?"

"What?"

"What do you want, Irene?"

"Why are you asking? I want Peter back. You know that!"

"Good. So you must now consider what the price of that is and if you're willing to pay it. You must get a grip on yourself and figure out what it is that Peter wants and determine whether you can provide it."

"I don't know what you're talking about."

She was beginning to get irritated and angry. That was, Clara felt, a good sign. An improvement, at any rate, over desperate self-pity. "First you must get your brain working, my dear. Get out of that bed and into a brisk shower. I'll find towels and a robe. While you're in there, think about just what it is that Peter wants of life."

Irene did as she was told, stumbling pitifully to the richly appointed bathroom with Clara dogging her steps. "No, not hot water. Cold. It will wake you up."

By the time she emerged, wrapped in a thick robe, her teeth were chattering with cold and with anger. She still looked a wreck, with bloodshot eyes, swollen lips, and an unsteady gait, but there was color in her face now and energy in her step. "What Peter wants," she announced, "is somebody else. He wants that dreary, hopeless girl I was when we first met. That's who he fell in love with. He just fell out of love, that's all. If I gave up everything, went back to being hopeless and poor, he might love me again. That's what he wants, Clara, and I'm not willing to do that!"

"You're not?" Clara asked mildly. She knew, even if Irene didn't, that this, too, was a stage in accepting the catastrophe that had fallen on her so unexpectedly. Yet, how could it have been unexpected? Clara had seen all the signs, had for years known that this day would come. How could Irene not have known? Or perhaps she had.

They talked all day long. Zofia sent in food at intervals, which was ignored, and Clara made one call to the office to make excuses for herself and Irene, but other than those interruptions, they simply talked. Or rather, Irene talked and Clara listened. At least half of what Irene said was entirely crazy as her moods swung violently. She stormed and cried and raved nonsense interspersed at random with good sense.

She'd sell the house tomorrow, she'd give it all up.

She'd take them all back to Poland, that would show him.

She'd kill herself and he'd be sorry because it would be his fault.

She'd take the whole family to his college today. She'd quit Neptune et Cie and take back her real name.

Since she was such a failure as a woman, she'd cut her hair and dress as a man and nobody would resent her success because men were supposed to be successful.

By noon she was ready to don peasant garb and throw it all away to get Peter back—or Piotr, as she was referring to him. By midday she hated him. Ungrateful, hateful man who had simply deceived her all along. He'd never loved her at all; he just wanted someone to be overbearing to, and she was fed up and despised him.

When darkness fell, she was the most pathetic woman in the world. Everyone, including Clara, hated her for no reason whatsoever, and it was all her own fault for having abandoned the teachings of the church. She'd go to Mass every day the rest of her life and give all she'd acquired to a mission for fallen women.

By ten it was another woman. He'd denied it, but she knew it was true. Some fat cow who was probably already pregnant and would give him a whole houseful of babies. The woman had made that green sweater and he'd worn it deliberately to taunt his wife. At midnight she was back to packing and running to him first thing in the morning, dragging the whole family along. No, nobody else. She'd get tickets for a nice long trip to Europe. They'd have time to themselves and everything would work out. He'd love her again. She was sure of it.

Anyway, the whole thing was a tempest in a teapot. He hadn't meant any of it. He'd be back in a day or two. They'd had their problems before and they'd always solved them. This was no different, it just seemed worse because it was such a dreary time of year.

At a little after two the next morning she fell asleep, finally talked out. Clara, stiff and exhausted and thoroughly sick of the very sound of her friend's voice, turned off the light and closed the door behind herself. Zofia was napping on a chair in the hall. "I'm going to sleep now, Mrs. Kossok. So should you."

"I have hot-water bottle ready for you."

Surprisingly, Clara had trouble getting to sleep even though she was exhausted. Irene's voice kept echoing in her mind. Somewhere in all the nonsense she'd been through that day was the answer, the solution. Irene had been trying on options all day, but she wouldn't find the proper fit anytime soon. It would take time and more rational thought. But Clara felt she herself ought to see some way to fix a marriage that deserved fixing, and she couldn't identify it any more than Irene could. Clara, knowing and loving both of them, could define the conflict better than either Peter or Irene, but that didn't seem to help.

Irene would count on her for advice (which she might or might not follow), and how was Clara to give it? They loved each other, Peter and Irene. They'd both be desolated apart. But Irene's greatest virtue and most devastating vice was her burning ambition that scorched everyone who got near it. Peter had lived in the continual glare of it for seven years; she entirely sympathized with him for not being able to stand it anymore. It wasn't weakness on his part, it was self-preservation. He had every bit as much right to his own dream as Irene did to hers. Truth be told, he was more admirable, more understandable—at least to Clara.

And yet Irene couldn't understand him and she couldn't change. Even if she ultimately decided she would try, she would simply burn to a cinder inside, because a fire like that couldn't be put out. Ever. She'd tried once before, during that long stretch after she quit Neptune the first time. They'd all seen what happened then. She was miserable and so was Peter.

Were all life's tragedies like this? Clara wondered as she dug her toes in under the hot-water bottle. Merely terrible muddles without sense or reason? Surely love and ambition didn't have to poison each other this way. Or did they?

Irene slept the whole next day, rousing only a few times to visit the bathroom or take a bit of the soup Zofia kept hot and ready. She'd not only lost her voice entirely, she didn't seem to want to say anything. Clara didn't try to make her talk anymore. It was, Clara thought in a hungry moment, like making a stew. You run around and gather all the vegetables you can find, you cut them all up in little bits, then throw them together to cook slowly. Irene's alternatives were all in the pot now, examined, peeled, chopped up, and simmering. Who could guess what she might ladle up with the first scoop?

Clara stayed the night again, and early the next morning she woke to discover Irene standing over her. "We'll be late if you don't get stirring quickly," Irene said. She was dressed, with her hair arranged and face powder disguising the worst ravages of the past few days. "I've asked the maid to bring you breakfast. I imagine you'll want to stop at your apartment to get fresh clothes."

Clara sat up. "Irene, are you . . . well?"

The younger woman turned away and started needlessly rearranging the brushes and perfume bottles on the dressing table. "No, I'm so unhappy I could shoot myself if I could lay my hands on a gun. But I won't. And nobody will ever know. Nobody but you, Clara. I'm in your debt—once again."

"Oh, Irene! When will you learn that friendships aren't ledger books! There are no debts between us. Now, get out of here so I can pull myself together. Did you remember to tell the cook I don't like marmalade?"

"Mama fired the cook again. That's three of them now. Or four."

Irene conducted herself from then on as if it were an ordinary morning. Only Clara noticed the way tears kept welling in her eyes at odd moments and her hands shook as she pulled on her fur-lined gloves. They stopped at Clara's apartment and on the last leg of the trip uptown Clara said hesitantly, "Have you . . . have you made any decision?"

Irene nodded. "I've decided *not* to decide anything. Not now. My brain has turned to talcum powder. If I went to Peter now, I'd just start blubbering like a madwoman. That wouldn't do any good. And I'm not sure that's what I should do. Maybe it's truly hopeless, as he said. It might be that I really can't make him happy, that there's some vital part missing in me. I don't know. I just don't know anything. I hardly know who I am."

"Is there anything I can do?"

"Yes, give me a hard slap if I look like I'm going to start crying again."

The next two months seemed to last for years—long, agonizing years. The changes in mood kept occurring, seemingly beyond her control. Sometimes Irene would forget for two or three minutes at a time what had happened, and then she'd remember again and be swept by a wave of panic that nearly suffocated her. That *couldn't* have happened, she'd think. It was a nightmare from which she would awaken.

She was desolated, betrayed, guilty, and furious by turns. Sometimes a sense of indignation carried her away. Didn't he know, didn't he realize that he was the rock of stability upon which she'd rested her whole being? How dare he just leave her this way!

And other times, she'd realize with the force of a hammer blow that she hadn't so much as asked his opinion on anything since they'd made the joint decision for her to accept Neptune's offer. And yet, that was truly his decision as much as hers. She'd put her future, their future, in his hands then. It was his fault she was where she was, what she was. What right had he to stop loving her because of it?

She tried this one out on Clara—who wasn't having any.

"He made that decision so you would be happy. It was never what he wanted, and you know it."

"Whose side are you on?" Irene snapped.

"The Garricks' side. Your side . . . and Peter's!" Clara shot back.

They didn't speak the rest of the day, and worse awaited

Irene at home that evening. Zofia, who had so far stayed out of it, was lonesome for Peter and said so. "Go to him, silly girl. Bring him back."

"I can't do that, Mama. Not now. Maybe not at all."

"Too busy with your job? Too busy with all them other people for your own husband. Parties and fancy dresses mean so much? A woman can get just as old and ugly in a fancy dress as a plain one."

"Mama, I don't want advice."

"*Wypij piwo, któregós sobie nawarzył*," she muttered. "*Drink as you have brewed.*"

"What do you mean by that?"

"I mean you have run around to so many places and left your husband behind, now he leaves you behind."

"Left him behind, Mama? You have no idea what you're talking about. I've begged Peter to be part of the life I've made, and it's not as if I'm a courtesan! I'm away from here because I'm working—working hard at a respectable job! And for all of you, not myself."

Zofia just sniffed.

The one person she wanted to keep Peter's defection a secret from was Neptune. She hated the thought of his knowing that while she was making an apparent success of one area of her life, she'd failed so utterly in another. But it was not to be. One morning in April, two months after Peter had left, Neptune came to her office. "I've been talking to Chandler," he said.

"And he was complaining about me—"

"Of course. But this time I think he's right. I trust him in social matters. It's the only thing he knows anything about."

"What *faux pas* does he accuse me of? Have I slurped my soup or offended someone important?"

Neptune stared at her a moment questioningly. "How brittle a remark from you. No, it's not a question of manners. It's a question of your marital status. Irene, you simply must make your husband come to some of these functions."

"I can't do that."

"I don't mean everywhere, all the time. Just once at a large party would do it. If a number of people saw and met him, it would go a long way toward quashing the rumors.

Chandler says they've gotten particularly vicious in the last few months. Remember that night I was ill and couldn't attend the Leibers' party and you didn't go either? Some idiot started saying she'd seen us at a hotel that evening and now they're all buzzing about your being my mistress. That won't do. It's bad for business. It weakens both of us professionally. Gossip connecting either of us with anyone else in the world does no harm, but—"

"Monsieur, you don't understand. I can't bring my husband with me because he's left me."

She wasn't sure what she expected—shock, sympathy perhaps. She got none. "Why?" he asked in his usual blunt way.

"Can't you guess?" She made a sweeping motion. "This. All of this."

He shrugged. "It was to be expected."

"Expected! Not by me, it wasn't. If I'd known—"

"If you'd known, you'd have done no different."

"I most certainly would have!"

He didn't argue. "It's the price you pay."

"That's insufferably smug of you, monsieur. The price I pay. Did you pay such a price?"

"I'm a man."

"And that makes a difference?"

He shrugged again, a very Gallic gesture. "No one ever promised that life is fair, my dear girl. It's not fair, but that's how it is. A woman has to pay much more for success than a man. You simply outgrew your husband. Face it."

"That's what he said, too. And you're both wrong. Absolutely wrong."

"Oh, we are? How odd, Peter Garrick and Jacques Neptune in agreement on anything!"

"How dare you be amused by this!"

"Believe me, I'm *not* amused. What are you going to do? Divorce him, I hope."

"No."

"That sounds like a very Catholic 'no'—and very foolish besides. It's been bad enough for you, having this ghostly husband who's never seen, but I suppose your private life with him made it worth it to you. But now, with him gone, what's the point, Irene?"

"The point is, I love him."

"I see," Neptune said, trying very hard to keep the disappointment out of his voice. He'd vowed years ago to think of her only as a business partner, and even a friend on occasion, but never as a woman. Still, the news that she might be free of her husband had fired his imagination. Foolish aging man that he was, he still had hopes, and no amount of good sense or willpower could stifle them.

"I have to have him back," Irene said.

She'd spoken softly, and Neptune realized she was talking to herself. A shiver of fear went through him. What if she decided to throw it all over to get her husband back? That's what Peter Garrick would require; Neptune didn't doubt it for a moment. But would she go that far? Could she possibly decide to give up everything for the sake of patching up her marriage? Dear God, what if she *did*! All the years of training and putting all his hopes in her, not to mention giving away half his life's work.

With the sudden stunning and altogether terrifying realization of what this might all mean to him, Neptune felt something very like giddiness. He couldn't just drift along and see what happened. He had to guide it the way he wanted. But how? He stood up quickly. "Mrs. Garrick, life goes on, and so does business. There is work to be done."

"What? Oh, yes, of course," she said, still preoccupied with her thoughts.

April 3, 1913

My dearest Peter,

I should be saying this to you in person, but I'm afraid I'd fall apart and make nonsense of it. I want you back. My life means nothing without you. The days since you left have been torture and the nights unbearable. You're a part of all my thoughts and I don't know how I can live without you.

I've given it a lot of thought. The money I've made and we've saved can be put into any one of several investments. I've talked to a lawyer about it. This money, plus what I can get from the sale of the house and furnishings, will pay dividends to my mother with which she can support my sisters. It wouldn't be the way they've been living, of course, but it would be adequate to keep them comfortably until the girls marry, then Mama would have the income the rest of her life. The girls' school fees are paid through the end of the year, when Lillie and Cecilia graduate. I don't believe there's any chance of persuading Stefania to continue her education under any circumstances.

There are business projects here that have to be finished up, designs I've promised, contracts to be honored, and so forth. Monsieur is not in very good health and it wouldn't be right to leave him suddenly with the full responsibility. I should be able to get free in six weeks to two months. I'm sure Monsieur would keep Clara on as an assistant to Miss Troutwhite, so my oldest friend wouldn't be left without a means of support.

Peter, if I do this will you have me back? Can we live together and love each other like we used to? My feelings haven't changed—you are the most important person in the world to me. Please say yes—and please, please say it soon.

Your loving wife,
Irene

The bell rang, signaling the end of class, but no one seemed to pay any attention. One of Peter's brightest students, John Follette, was in the middle of refuting a point Peter had brought up with the intention of provoking discussion. "We'll have to continue this tomorrow," Peter said.

"Only one more point! That theory, if accepted, would negate nearly everything the medieval philosophers . . ." He plunged on. Other students, having to get to their next classes, were drifting toward the door, but reluctantly.

Peter smiled to himself. There were a great many classes that regarded the bell as a signal to evacuate instantly. It was deeply satisfying that most of his classes emptied slowly, with the discussions spilling out into the hall. "John, you're losing your audience. You're going to have to finish this tomorrow,'' he said.

The young man opened his mouth to say just one more thing, then grinned and shrugged. ''I give up.'' He gathered his books and approached the front desk. ''Mom asked me if you'd come to dinner tomorrow.''

It was tempting. He'd enjoyed many excellent meals at Mrs. Follette's table. And it wasn't just the food that drew him. The big old house at the edge of the campus was a pleasantly untidy structure full of children and laughter. John was the second of six young Follettes, the oldest being his sister Jane. And Jane was why Peter was determined to stop abusing their hospitality. Not that there was anything wrong with her. Quite the contrary. She was a pretty girl with curly garnet-colored hair, a voluptuous figure, and sparkling greenish-blue eyes. She was an excellent cook, a superb seamstress, and a charming companion. And she was in love with him. *That* was the problem.

He hadn't realized it at first. She'd just been one member of a warm, delightful family that had opened its arms to him. But then, during the long Christmas break when he'd been so very lonely, he'd begun to sense Jane's affection. There was the gift—a beautiful sea-green cable-knit sweater that must have taken her hundreds of hours—and a special attentiveness in a dozen small ways. He and his two charges—the foreign students who couldn't go home for the holidays—had been invited to have turkey and dressing and presents with them on Christmas Eve; then they'd attended a Midnight Mass with the family. Walking back through the crisp night, the younger children and the two foreign boys had dashed ahead with John and his parents. Jane, slipping on a patch of ice, had clung to Peter's arm and walked slowly and carefully. Finally, without being quite aware it was happening, he found that they were quite alone.

''It was a lovely service, wasn't it?'' she said, her voice as soft and sweet as a baked apple in the cold night air.

''Very. It was good of your famiy to let me join you.''

''It was good of you to come with us. We love you. All of us. Especially me.'' The last words were said very softly.

''Oh, Jane . . .''

She stopped, and before he could say anything more, she was in his arms, warm and yielding. "Peter, I do love you ever so much!"

"Jane, please don't say that. You know I'm married."

"I know and I don't care! If your wife loved you half as much as I do, she'd be here with you. But she's not. I am."

The worst of it was, he thought she was right. He'd extricated himself from her embrace in as kindly a manner as possible. "Jane, you don't know the situation. You can't understand."

"I don't have to know anything except that I love you. You're wonderful, Peter."

He put his arm around her shoulders in what he hoped was a clearly brotherly manner and started walking, all but dragging her along. "Jane, you're a beautiful girl. If I didn't love my wife, I'd probably be madly in love with you. Any man would be crazy not to be, but the fact is, I *do* love my wife. Even if I didn't, I'm married to her, and I wouldn't dream of compromising someone as good as you."

"I'm sorry I said anything," Jane said, pulling away and increasing her pace. "I'm very embarrassed."

"Don't be. You just let your warm heart get the better of your head for a minute. Nothing more," he said. "We'll both just forget this conversation ever happened. How would that be?"

"Yes."

But they hadn't forgotten it. Nor, he suspected, had she changed her mind, only her frankness of expression. Sensing instinctively his need for the comforts of domesticity and her own need to supply them, she began to provide little niceties, but always in a manner that denied a particular interest or obligation. Via her brother, she sent a long scarf to match the sweater. When Peter thanked her for all the trouble she must have gone to, she merely said, "Oh, I'd miscalculated on the yarn and had some left over. I can't stand waste. It was nothing." Then there was candy. "I forgot most of the children don't like coconut, and there was such a lot of it. I thought you might help me get rid of it. It's sinfully easy to make." And a crocheted afghan: "It was a design I wanted to experiment with, but the colors weren't right for our house."

The afghan smelled faintly of the orange-blossom scent she sometimes wore.

"About dinner tomorrow?" John Follette repeated.

"I don't think so. I've fallen behind on some paper grading. But thank your mother for the offer. And tell the children hello for me."

Peter waited until John was gone, then picked up his lecture notes and a stack of themes that had been turned in that day. He wished he'd accepted the invitation now that it was too late. No, better that he hadn't, he told himself as he walked home. Automatically checking the small mailbox at the front gatepost to his small house, he was surprised to find it contained a letter.

He went in, dropping the books, papers, and jacket on the front-hall table, then sat down at the desk in the small den of the house the college provided him. The house, more of a cottage, was tucked into the edge of a stand of handsome oak woods. Very quiet, very private, and very, very lonely. To have her here, just her, just Irene, had been his dream since he arrived. In a way, she'd lived here with him all along. He'd sit in front of the fire in the evenings, listening to the shush of snow at the windows, and imagine her in the chair across from him. He ate his meals in the tiny kitchen and pictured her at the counter cutting up vegetables while he told her about his day. When he shoveled the walk, he made a wide path, thinking, without consciously realizing it, of her sweeping skirts. And at night . . . oh, the nights were the worst. Such a big, cold bed, like a frigid, barren landscape—and yet there was someone so appealing and so near who would like to share it with him. Did Jane Follette know what a temptation she was?

The coming of spring had made it easier in some ways—the nights were not so long and quiet; and harder in others—the air itself was so full of life, so fecund and stimulating, that his blood stirred violently and he made love to her in his dreams nearly every night. He woke morning after morning sweating and sticky and ashamed at the way his body insisted on betraying his mind. Ashamed, too, that sometimes her features and Jane's seemed to blend.

He shut the windows, determined to shut out the seductive spring-blossom scent while he read the letter. He'd recognized her stationery before he'd even reached into the letter box and had made himself wait until he was calm and alone. He slit the envelope carefully, anxious and yet dreading, wanting to read it and wanting to crumple it unread. He slipped the pages out, opened them slowly.

To Irene it seemed like years before he answered. Several times she started to write to him again, but ended up crumpling the efforts and resolving to see what, if anything, he replied before she said anything more. Then finally the response came:

April 9, 1913

Dear Irene,

I waited to answer your letter to be sure of what I had to say. The delay's been unpleasant, I imagine, and I'm sorry.

I'm sorrier yet to say: it cannot be. While I was moved by your expressions of love, and I return them fully, it won't work. Your letter itself is what finally proved that to me. In the first place, had you wanted with all your heart to do the things you suggest, you would have gone ahead and done them, not asked my opinion. That's not fair of me, I know, telling you you've failed a test you didn't know you were undergoing. But I didn't know it either until I read it. You don't want to give up what you've worked for, and that's what I've been trying to tell you—you shouldn't. I have no right to ask it of you. More than that, I will not accept that sort of sacrifice.

The other thing that struck me about your letter was this: only a few sentences at the beginning and end are about us, did you realize that? No, I'm sure you didn't. That's the crux of it all, Reenee. I'm not sure I even understood that until this week. Your letter is all about your responsibility to your mother, your sisters, Jacques Neptune, the company, your career, and your friend Clara.

Realize right now, that's truly admirable. You've chosen a heavy load and you carry it bravely, relentlessly. You're a good woman, probably a Great Woman. And your extended sense of responsibility is your most stunning virtue. I admire you for it, I love you for it, and no one, man or woman, will ever live up to your standards in my mind.

But, Irene, I can't live with it. I'm simply too selfish. I love you just as you are, but I want you all to myself, and that's impossible. Your ambitions and your sense of duty make you the woman I love. I'd be flattered beyond belief if I thought you really wanted to give them up for me, but if you did, you'd no longer be my beloved Reenee.

None of this is your fault. It's all mine. If I could put aside my own pride and live in your shadow, I would.

Reenee, don't fight this. We both want what we want too much to accommodate each other. You must think, as I try to, that God gave us some good years together. We had happiness and love, days we brightened for each other, and nights we'll never forget. Considering where we both started life, what our prospects were, that's a true gift. We haven't any right to expect more. And who can say—someday, something may change for us. I don't know what, but miracles have happened before.

I'll always love you, Reenee. I told you before, I won't divorce you, but I won't stand in the way of any action you choose to take. How formal and stuffy that sounds. It's not the way I wanted to say good-bye. But, for the life of me, I can't think of a good way. There isn't any.

Good-bye, my love, my Reenee,

Peter

The spring term would be over in a week, then a week of vacation before the summer tutorial duties began. Peter looked over the final-exam questions he was preparing one last time, made an adjustment in wording here and there, and then put them away. In the morning he'd take them to the department secretary to be typed. He stood and was stretching when there was a knock at the door.

He was surprised to find Jane there, her arms wrapped around a basket. "Jane? Come in. Here, let me hold that."

"Thank you. It's for you."

"It's heavy. Did you carry this all the way yourself?"

"No, John brought it most of the way, but he had to get over to the library before it closed. It's jelly. Mother and I are getting ready for the summer canning and discovered that we had a number of jars of cherry preserves left from last year. They're still quite good, but the trees look like it's going to be an awfully good crop again."

"Cherry preserves. My favorite!"

"I've noticed."

Of course she had. It was the sort of thing she did notice. "Then have a cup of tea with me and I'll fix some toast to start using this present."

Peter was uneasy at first. She'd never been to his house and he'd made sure they'd never been alone together since Christmas Eve, but she quickly allayed his fears. While they had their tea-and-toast snack, she chatted brightly and impersonally about the family: little Dan's grade on his arithmetic test, Mrs. Follette's contretemps with the vet over the dog's flea treatment, her sister Laura's preparations for her First Communion. Peter realized he'd almost succeeded in forgetting what pleasant company she was. Too bad he had to be reminded. The kitchen seemed warmer and cozier with her here. The whole cottage took on a friendlier air with the addition of that faint scent of orange blossom.

Finally she rose, rinsed out her teacup, and said, "I guess I ought to get along. I'm probably keeping you from your work."

"Oh, I was done for the night," he said without thinking. And quickly added, "But your family will be worried about you, I imagine."

He offered to walk her home, but she insisted it was unnecessary. After she left, he went through the house turning off lights, but heard another knock at the door. It was Jane again. "I'm sorry, but I forgot I needed to take the basket home. The basket I brought the jelly in . . ."

"Oh, yes, I should have realized. Come in."

He expected she'd wait at the door, and being familiar with the house himself, he didn't bother to turn on lights as he went back to the kitchen for the basket. But as he picked it up and turned, he collided with her and dropped the basket. "Jane! I'm sorry, did I step on your foot?" he said, catching her as she appeared to stumble.

"No, it's nothing," she said. "I was in your way."

He had his hands on her shoulders, and though he knew he should move away, he couldn't seem to manage it. She felt so warm and soft. "Peter . . ." she whispered, slipping her arms around his waist and raising her face to his for a kiss.

He bent, touching her inviting lips with his. She even tasted like orange blossoms. "You're delicious," he said.

She laughed softly. "So are you. Peter, my family goes to bed early. They won't notice when I come home. Please let me stay awhile. Just awhile."

Dear God, why not! She wasn't offering lightly; she wasn't that sort. She was a good, beautiful armful of girl who loved him. What more did any man want or need of life? The bedroom was only a few feet away with that big empty bed where he'd spent so many restless nights.

He had, in fact, taken her hand and made the first move in that direction before his conscience reasserted itself. *Then what?* it said. What about tomorrow and next week and next month? Could he really sleep with her tonight and then go back to being merely a friend of the whole family? Certainly not. This wasn't some tramp of easy morality who would be equally willing and able to forget that anything had ever happened between them. This was a nice Catholic girl who was willing to toss all her ingrained morality aside because she loved him so deeply.

Why couldn't he accept that gift, the most generous anyone ever had offered or ever would offer him?

Because of his conscience? No, because he still loved Irene. It didn't make any sense, it never would. It wasn't a function of mind that could be subjected to logic. It was simply a building block at the core of his being, without which the structure of his life couldn't stand. That the love wasn't reciprocated—at least not in kind—didn't alter anything.

"Jane, you have to go home. Now."

"Peter, please let me have a chance to show you how happy I can make you."

"That's just what I'm afraid of."

"I don't understand."

"I know you'd make me happy. Everything about you pleases me, but I can't do anything but hurt you, Jane. And if you stayed here now, eventually I'd hurt you terribly, because there's a part of me that can't ever belong to anyone."

"Anyone but your wife?"

He nodded, backing away and picking up the basket he'd dropped. "I'm sorry, Jane."

She straightened her shoulders. "I believe we're meant for each other, Peter. I don't mind how much of a fool I have to make of myself to prove that."

The next morning Peter went to see Father Bentley, the priest who taught Hebrew and Greek and who had often advised his young colleague. "Father, do you remember mentioning a college in Chicago to me last fall? You said you thought I might fit in well there."

"I remember. You said you were entirely happy here."

"I'd like the name of that school. Do you think there would be any chance of getting a position there—now?"

"Right away? For the summer?"

"Yes."

"The Follette girl?"

Peter nodded. "How did you know?"

Father Bentley smiled. "When I took my vow of chastity, I didn't suddenly become stupid or blind. I think you're doing the right thing. I have a friend in Chicago I believe can help you. Leave it to me."

23

May 1913

Neptune threw a house party in May for the most select of his customers—"So they don't forget us over the summer," he said.

"Monsieur, I didn't know you had a house on Long Island," Adelaide McCoy said. She'd come in to arrange for summer storage of her furs, including the one Irene had designed for her when she'd lost that thirty pounds.

"Oh, I don't have a house out there," Neptune said. "It belongs to a friend of mine who's almost never in America. He spends most of his time in Europe and drops in only occasionally. A very reclusive man. Here, Mrs. Garrick, this needs to be turned at the cuff before it's stored, don't you think?"

Irene studied the coat. There was a bit of wear on the underside of the sleeve. "Who's your friend?" Adelaide was asking. "Perhaps we know him."

"I'm sure you don't. Nobody does. His name is Jack Fisher."

Irene looked up, catching the glint of the private joke in Neptune's eyes. So that's where he went when he took time off and disappeared. She'd been wondering. He hadn't been well the last few months, and while her own troubles had almost filled her mind, she'd noticed that he'd been gone for several days at a time, presumably for medical treatment and without giving any explanation of his whereabouts. This was the answer to that small mystery. He had a secret house in the country, taken under his real name.

At the last moment, Clara decided not to go. "It's this ingrown toenail," she explained. "Shoes are an absolute torture. I must have it treated, and I'm looking forward to lying about my apartment, reading, eating bonbons, and feeling sorry for myself while you're all gone and I don't have to be at work."

"Then please stay at the house and let Mama take care of you. She'd love it."

Clara sighed. Her discomfort made her irritable. Why did Irene insist on believing that everyone needed to be "taken care of?" Everyone but herself, of course. "No, thank you, dear. I'm treasuring the prospect of being alone."

Irene couldn't understand that. Why would anyone want to be left to the mercy of her own thoughts without any distraction? These days Irene lived for distraction; it was the only thing that kept her from going mad—or reading Peter's last letter for the thousandth time. She still didn't understand it, though she'd been over and over it until the paper was nearly worn out. All she really grasped was that he'd completely rejected her. Sometimes, of course, depending on her mood, bits of it did make sense. His accusation that she hadn't really wanted to do what she planned was true—she could admit that to herself on the days when she was feeling strong-minded. She'd hoped he'd say, "No, I can't let you do that. But I'll come back, since you made the offer."

She hadn't realized at the time she wrote it, but later she was able to see the truth. As much as she wanted him back, she really didn't want to sacrifice everything she'd worked so hard for. She loved the big house, the maids, the beautiful "things" that money could buy. She loved seeing the girls go off to school in the private car she hired, and the closet full of clothes that Irina Kossok couldn't have even imagined. These things were the proof that she wasn't dirty and common, and she couldn't honestly imagine being without them. Nor could she imagine having nothing to fill her day but waiting for Peter to come home from his classes.

Neptune's party would be a superb way of putting it out of her mind for a few more days. And after that? She'd have to find something else to keep her mind busy—and she *would* find something.

* * *

It was a small house by the standards of the neighborhood. Only a master suite and eight guest suites on the second floor. The entire ground floor was designed for entertaining—a ballroom, huge kitchens for the preparation of food enough to feed an army, an enormous powder room for the ladies. It wasn't a house to live in; it was a house to entertain in. And yet Neptune did live in it sometimes. It was, as he said privately to Irene, his "bolt hole." "Everyone needs a secret place where the world can't find him. You're the only person in the world, besides my lawyer, who knows I own the place. Even Chandler believes the story about my friend Jack Fisher."

Neptune and his valet went to the house on Wednesday, Chandler and Irene went to the house on Thursday afternoon, the other houseguests were to arrive Friday, and the dinner and dance for fifty couples was to be held on Saturday. Thursday evening Neptune summoned them to his suite, where they would have an informal dinner on trays and make final plans.

It was the first time in a very long while that Irene had been thrown into Chandler's company. They'd seldom been alone together for more than a minute or two. By mutual unspoken agreement, they avoided each other almost entirely. Chandler's primary duties to Neptune et Cie were social. He oversaw the official schedule of entertainments for the three of them, making certain that the right people were wined and dined at the right intervals. It was his responsibility to discover who was buying furs from the rival Revillon Frères and bring them back into the Neptune et Cie fold. He did it well, and Irene was content to follow his directions in the matter of who should be seen, what parties and dinners she should attend, and which hostess needed a little extra flattery. But she took the advice second-hand. Chandler laid out plans to Neptune, who passed them along to Irene. There was seldom direct contact between them, and never private discussion. When they were together, it was always in the company of customers, and they acted the part of amiable business associates like well-trained actors.

Irene was relieved that Chandler kept up the act on the way to the country, commenting innocuously on the passing countryside and pointing out the country homes of some of their customers as they neared their destination. "Old Mrs. Piper's grandsire built the place up there on the hill. Terribly old money, don't you know," he'd say in the slightly English accent he used. He wasn't friendly; he'd never be friendly to her. But he wasn't nasty either, and Irene had always suspected that he could be very nasty indeed if he set his mind to it. He hated her still, always would, but was willing to disguise it in the cause of Neptune et Cie.

But all that changed that evening.

They had a light supper in the parlor of Neptune's suite and went over the final plans. "I've asked Edward VanCleve to be your escort," Neptune said.

"Oh, no, not him," Irene said, startled. She hadn't seen him since the night of her "unveiling," as she always thought of it. He'd gone for an extended European trip, she'd heard, and since his return they hadn't happened to cross paths.

"Why not?" Chandler asked sharply. Neptune had suggested the pairing, but he'd incorporated it into his plans and didn't intend to have them messed about with at this late date.

"I don't know why, exactly. He asks so many questions."

"I should think you'd have all your answers well in hand by now," Chandler said. "You must have some man designated as your dinner and dancing partner."

"Why not Monsieur?"

Neptune drew himself up. "That's exactly the sort of thing we most want to avoid. Besides, I'm paired with Lydia Gillis. Her husband is off on business in Florida."

"Can't I be your partner, Chandler?"

"Most definitely not! I've invited Miss Clemence. We have an 'understanding.' "

"I see. Very well. Monsieur . . . is there something wrong?"

Neptune had started to rise from the table and sat back down suddenly, his face pinched. "It's nothing. Just a bit of stomach pain. I think I'll lie down for a minute or two. It will pass."

Chandler and Irene each took one of his arms to help him to his bedroom, over his strong objections. Turning on the lights, they both saw the ranks of medicine bottles arrayed on the bedside table. Pills, elixirs, tablets. His ammunition against age and illness. It was embarrassing to all of them, like accidentally happening on someone in underwear. "I'll call a doctor!" Irene said.

"You'll do no such thing," Neptune answered. "All I need is a little rest. It was the olives, that's all. I know better than to touch olives. They always do this to me. Go away, both of you."

They tucked him in with assurances that they could manage the rest of the arrangements and would see him in the morning. Closing the door softly, Irene realized that something vital had changed as surely as if the temperature in the house had dropped twenty degrees. Monsieur's bedroom was the next thing to a hospital room. He was seriously ill, and olives had nothing to do with it. The force of his personality had put him outside the considerations of age in her mind, and now she recognized for the first time that he was as subject to the years as anyone.

Chandler realized it too. He sorted through the guest lists, pretending to study them, but it was a useless pretense. Irene could almost see his thoughts on his full face. Neptune would die someday—not decades from now, but years, maybe months. And death meant a will, which meant the final disbursement of Neptune et Cie. What would become of the older man's remaining half? Would he give it all to Irene? He couldn't. That would be a financial and social death blow to Chandler. Perhaps he intended to leave her a small portion that would give her controlling interest. That would be very nearly as bad. It would mean she could call the tune, that he was working for her! Was it possible Neptune would leave her none of his share and turn it all over to his nephew? Even then, they'd be equal partners. How in the world would they get on?

Chandler knew that Uncle Jacques's arrangement with the woman gave her an equal share in the profits and an equal responsibility for the liabilities, but there was a clause saying in the case of irreconcilable differences of opinion in any business matter, Neptune's opinion took precedence. Chandler had had to invest a whole evening pouring expensive whiskey into Neptune's lawyer to find out that much. Certainly that power wouldn't pass along with Neptune's share—or would it?

Irene saw the fleshy lines of his face harden, and felt a chill. She knew what he was thinking, for she was wondering the same thing. But her thoughts were colored by a good deal more love than his. She was trying, without success, to imagine life without Monsieur in the middle of it, demanding, insulting, managing, directing. It was inconceivable. "If you'll excuse me, Chandler, I'm very tired . . ."

But he was paying no attention. His mind was buzzing. He'd counted on having years yet to further ingratiate himself with his uncle. He'd never doubted that Jacques and Irene would fall out eventually. Two such determined, overbearing souls couldn't get along forever. It was amazing they'd hit it off this long. She must be truly extraordinary in bed to have kept his affections for this long. Terribly discreet, both of them, but there was no question in his mind as to the real nature of their relationship. Why else would any man put up with a hard, haughty woman like Irene Garrick?

Irene rose very early and tiptoed to the door of Neptune's room. Before she could even knock lightly, his valet opened it, having heard her footsteps in the hall. "Did Monsieur sleep well, Iverson?" she whispered.

"Very well, madam. Quite soundly. He's had these little bouts of indigestion before, madam."

"So you think that's all it was?"

"Naturally. Monsieur is in the peak of health."

And you're a loyal liar, she thought.

Her mind was eased somewhat when she returned later. Neptune was having his breakfast and did look entirely well. His color was good, his manner as sharp and energetic as usual. "Why must I be surrounded by fools!" he barked as Irene entered the parlor of his suite. "Sit down and eat something. You look peaked. I hired these caterers on the very best of recommendations and now they tell me they can't get the mushrooms for dinner. Anybody can find mushrooms. And I told the housekeeper months ago to make sure all the chairs in the ballroom were recovered, only to discover this morning that half of them are still at the upholsterer's shop."

He raved on for a while, Irene making soothing noises as she sipped a cup of strong tea. It was as if last night had been a dream. This wasn't a sick old man; this was a belligerent tyrant. She found herself nearly believing Iverson's statement, that it was nothing but a harmless bout of indigestion. She could have convinced herself of this, in fact, if it weren't for the memory of all those medicine bottles.

"I wouldn't have believed you could become more beautiful, Mrs. Garrick," Edward VanCleve said, bowing over her hand. "But you've accomplished the impossible. You should always wear blue; it becomes you enormously."

"How nice to see you again, Mr. VanCleve. It's been a very long time. You've been doing a great deal of traveling, I hear."

"Far more than I wanted. My uncle passed on and I had to take up the reins."

"Oh yes, VanCleve Steel, isn't it?"

"Yes, he was in charge of the rails—railroad rails, that is. We purchase the steel in Germany for the most part and import it for use throughout the western United States. I think I've seen every inch of it now."

"You must have seen a good many interesting things."

"None so interesting as the sight of you, Mrs. Garrick. May I call you Irene? It seems I had just gained your permission to do so the last time I saw you."

"Certainly."

"I've thought of you often," he said, taking her elbow gently and guiding her to an intimate sofa grouping at the far corner of the ballroom.

Irene laughed. "You've done no such thing. That's pure flattery."

"But you liked it, didn't you?" he asked with a smile.

She wished he wouldn't be so gracious and attentive. He was so very good-looking, and in a way that reminded her of Peter too much for comfort. And yet, except for the similarities in coloring and general physique, they weren't at all alike. Peter would never have wasted his time with this sort of frothy, trivial, and altogether delightful exchange. While Peter's brand of conversation was far more intelligent, Edward VanCleve's was more nourishing to the ego—especially to an ego so starved for a handsome man's attention.

Suddenly, after months of depression and unhappiness, Irene felt an overwhelming need for fun and flirtation, something she'd never needed before in her life. "You take me for a light-minded girl, to have my head turned so easily," she said.

"Light-minded, never. I *have* been thinking of you lately. That's the truth. I was in Chicago last week and saw a local paper that had pictures of some function or other in New York. There was a very nice portrait picture of you. 'Mrs. Peter Garrick, of the famous furriers Neptune et Cie,' it said. I realized then it had been far too long since I'd last seen you."

"How nice of you to say that."

"I hope I'll see a great deal more of you now that my wanderings are over. I'm settling in permanently. I won't be dislodged from New York again—except for parties like this—and then only if I know you'll be there."

It was outrageous and she knew it wasn't true, but his empty flattery was like cool lotion on a burn. For the first time in months, she felt relaxed, happy, and, most important, feminine. "I *am* glad you could come this weekend," she said, forgetting flirtation for a moment in favor of honesty.

He recognized the flash of sincerity and returned it in kind. "I'm pleased that you welcome me."

Irene felt herself blushing, something she couldn't remember ever doing before, but was spared any further embarrassing revelations by the intrusion of an elderly cousin of Edward's who wanted to sit down and talk about the family business.

She didn't see Edward again until it was time to go in to the opulent late supper Chandler had planned. It was served buffet style on a series of long tables that groaned under the weight of some of the most elaborate food Irene had ever seen, but she noticed it only in passing, for Edward had once again taken light hold of her arm and she was terribly aware of the warmth of his hand on her flesh. When they reached the end of the serving line, he took a bottle of wine from the huge silver tub of shaved ice, tucked it under his arm, and scooped up two glasses with his free hand. "I think we ought to take this outside and enjoy ourselves a little more privately," he said.

"Don't you think it will be too cold outside?" she asked.

"Do you?" he asked, and she knew what he meant—that neither of them was in any state to notice the temperature. Something was happening between them, and it was frightening and thrilling in equal measure.

Good Lord, what was she doing? she wondered. For once in her life she'd lost all interest in being sensible and rational and ever-so-proper. She just wanted to be in the spring-scented darkness, drinking chilled wine with this handsome man she hardly knew.

There were some wrought-iron tables and chairs outside, but they seemed cold and uninviting. Instead, Edward led her around the corner of the flagstone terrace to where a wide stone ledge overlooked the formal gardens behind the house. They set their plates down and began to nibble in solitary, if ill-lighted, splendor. "I haven't any idea what I'm eating," she said, biting down on something hot, crunchy, and slightly gingery.

"It's more fun that way," Edward said. "There's more excitement in the unknown than in the visible and familiar, isn't there?"

"I'm not sure . . . sometimes," she replied.

Edward abandoned all pretense of eating and walked a few paces away. Staring out over the moonlight-flooded gardens, he asked, "I assume your husband isn't here this weekend, or I wouldn't have been invited to be your dinner partner."

"He isn't here . . . this weekend." She hadn't meant the bitter emphasis on the last words. Or at least she hadn't meant anyone to hear it.

"Is he ever here? Or anywhere?"

"Are you asking me if he exists?" she asked bluntly, going to where he stood and leaning slightly on the stone ledge. "Yes, he exists. But we no longer live together."

Danger! a voice in the back of her mind cried.

"I should say I'm sorry to hear that. It's the polite reply. But I'm not the least bit sorry, Irene. Are you?"

"You ask too many questions."

"Perhaps I do." He turned to face her, putting his hands on her shoulders and slowly pulling her closer.

He didn't have to use even the slightest force. She came to

him easily, eagerly, and while the sensible voice screamed hysterical warnings, she raised her face to his kiss. How luxurious to be kissed! And to be kissed so expertly. Edward was restrained, only lightly brushing his lips against hers, just barely touching her arms, tantalizing her, teasing. His feigned reluctance was more erotic than any force could have been. He bent his head, barely breathing on the sensitive place at the side of her neck just below her ear. She sighed, savoring the expensive scent of his hair. It was she, not he, who initiated the actual embrace. Winding her arms around his waist, she pressed against him and felt his slight—ever so slight—gasp of surprise and pleasure as her full breasts touched his chest.

It had been so long, so terribly long, since she'd felt the hard, hot strength of a man's body against hers. She shivered with pleasure as he placed his hand firmly at the small of her back and pinned her against him. She could feel his excitement now through the thin silk of her skirt and slip, and it was all she could do to keep from thrusting her pelvis even closer. She knew too much; if she'd been an ignorant virgin it would have been a different matter. But she'd been wife and lover and knew precisely what she'd been missing since last fall. This was a hunger she understood much too well for her own good and was powerless to ignore. She wanted him. No, she wanted Peter. No. She wanted love and was only several layers of insignificant fabric away from it.

Too hungry, too lonely, too tortured by the dreams that so often invaded her nights, she abandoned herself. She clung to him, moaning as his lips pressed hers—now with hot intensity. The teasing was over, the pretense abandoned. "I want you, Irene. I've never wanted anyone or anything like I want you," he said, his voice a low growl.

"How very romantic."

They sprang apart, and Irene felt a flash of cold, as if someone had drenched her in ice water.

"Chandler," Edward said furiously. "Somebody ought to put a bell on your collar. I didn't hear you sneak up."

"Obviously," he drawled. "But I wasn't sneaking. I could have driven a coach and four past and you wouldn't have noticed."

Irene turned away, trying to make her eyes focus on the garden beyond. She was mortified to find that her breath was still coming in near-sobs. God in heaven! What *had* she been doing? Had she lost her mind? Her morals? She felt as if she'd looked into the core of her being for the first time and been faced with a slut!

"Well, I suppose I might as well leave you to it," Chandler said, his voice dripping with smugness. His footfalls, jaunty and victorious on the stone flagging, faded away.

Edward put his hand out. Irene stumbled backward so precipitately she nearly fell. "No! Don't touch me."

"You don't mean that. You want me. You need what I need." He sounded smug too.

"I don't!"

"We understand each other, Irene. We both know what we want, and we're going to have it. Sooner or later."

"No!"

"Oh, yes, Irene. Yes."

She turned and fled, terrified that he was right.

It had been a total self-betrayal. For a few mad moments on the terrace she'd let the needs of her body and heart completely overrule her mind. It was a shocking revelation of a weakness she'd never suspected she was subject to. Her behavior had been in defiance of everything she was, everything she believed in. She had, for a few passionate minutes, been ready to throw lifelong morality to the winds. It must never, *never* happen again. And most particularly, it must never happen with Edward VanCleve. Of all the men she might have become involved with, he was one of the most dangerous. She'd been uneasy about him since the first time they met. He was too curious, too eager to ferret out her most important secrets. She'd already given away one piece of vital information—that she and Peter no longer lived together—which she hadn't wanted anyone to know. She shuddered to think what else she might blurt out if she ever let herself get in that situation again!

It wasn't as if she was in love with him—even if that had been a valid excuse for her behavior, which it certainly wasn't. She barely knew the man. She hadn't any idea what he believed in, how he felt about a single issue. Nor did she care. What had attracted her wasn't his character or personality; it was surface aspects of him: his finely bred good looks, his born-to-money manner, his expensive clothes. And something else—an indefinable magnetism that had nothing to do with any of those qualities. He spoke to her and looked at her as if there were only the two of them in the world and they shared a need . . .

No, she must not think about that. It made her feel she was once again teetering on the brink of her self-control. This sense of a private, secret traffic between them was simply the result of a well-developed seduction technique and her own loneliness. Nothing more.

She stayed in her room until the guests started leaving. Only then did she go back down to see them off, and she made very certain to stick close to Neptune and Chandler. She'd allow no more opportunity for private assignations. When VanCleve was ready to go—among the last to depart, she noticed—he took her hand. "I look forward to seeing you again in the city, Irene."

"I think not, Mr. VanCleve," she said coldly.

She'd expected, or at least hoped, that he would understand, or perhaps be insulted, but in any case retire from his pursuit. She was delivering the verbal equivalent of a slap in the face.

But he seemed impervious. He merely smiled a knowing, intimate smile and said, "We'll see."

Damn the man!

Clara's ingrown toenail proved to be more trouble than she anticipated. The initial stages of the treatment caused her more pain than the affliction. And even when the healing process was well under way, she couldn't come to work. "I can hardly travel through the city barefoot!" she complained when Irene came to visit. "I tried cutting part of the toe out of a pair of shoes, but it doesn't do. I just can't walk with anything on that foot. Even hosiery is torture. It makes me so angry. I've never given in to a physical infirmity before, and certainly not something so undignified as this!"

"Clara, don't worry. You've never been willing to take a vacation—"

"Neither have you, allow me to point out!"

"Well, we both deserve one. I'll take mine later. You take yours now. We're going into an easy time of year and Miss Troutwhite can look after me while you're recovering."

"Easy? For you, perhaps. Your concern is creating coats. My primary duty now is seeing that they all get put away. Our summer cold-storage vaults are already bulging, thanks to the increased sales you've generated for the company. The bookkeeping involved is stupefying, and I'm falling further behind every day."

"Clara, don't worry. Please just rest up and try to enjoy having nothing to do."

"Would *you* enjoy idleness?"

"You know I wouldn't. Why are you so angry with me?"

Clara sighed. "I'm not. This just makes me feel old and feeble, and I don't like it. You're right. You and Miss Troutwhite can handle it. She won't be happy about all the extra work, but she'll manage. How was the weekend in the country? You haven't said anything about it."

"It was very nice, of course. Chandler planned things beautifully and the house was a perfect setting."

"But you didn't enjoy yourself."

"Why do you say that?"

"I don't know. You just seem strange. Did something happen?"

"No, nothing happened," Irene said, going to the mirror to adjust her hat so that she didn't have to meet Clara's too-penetrating gaze. "I must get going."

Irene began to understand better the problems that concerned Clara that afternoon when she informed the senior secretary that her additional responsibilities were to go on a little longer. Irene had realized in theory, but never in practice until now, that the storage of furs was as specialized a business as the designing of them. Each garment had to have room to breathe and had to be hung in a cool, dry place, not an easy atmosphere to create in the city in the summer. The main storage vaults were in a subbasement of the New York office, with additional vaults in New Jersey. In addition to the paperwork involved in keeping track of every single hat, coat, cape, muff, and stole, there was a great deal of summer help to be hired, overseen, and paid. The storage vaults not only had to be kept cool and dry, they had to provide protection from moths, which meant either naphthalene or open containers of carbon disulfide in the rooms, the vapor from which was positively explosive. A fur-storage vault had to be regarded as a bomb, always ready to be set off by the slightest spark, and the workers had to be aware of this.

Irene took on a share of Clara's work as well as Neptune's when he took a long weekend off, and found herself an unwilling traveler to New Jersey several times to look over additional space available for rent. It was when she came back from one of those trips that she found Edward VanCleve waiting in her office. "Will you take luncheon with me?" he asked.

"I can't," she said. She'd been dreading seeing him again. But it was inevitable; they moved in the same circles. But oddly enough, his unexpected presence didn't affect her as strongly as she'd feared it might. She was a little breathless, true, but a long morning of arguing with a New Jersey warehouse manager had effectively dampened her appreciation of the softer, subtler emotions. She'd actually been driven to scream at the man, and still carried an edge of anger that helped protect her against Edward VanCleve's insidious influence.

"I suppose you're going to tell me you're too busy," he said with that infuriatingly smug smile.

"As a matter of fact, I am."

"Now, Irene, I know better. You're a designer of furs. Nobody wants to think about fur coats in May."

His condescending attitude made her mad. "I'm not just a designer. I'm a partner in this business that operates year-round. We have no slack season. Right now I'm up to my eyebrows in trying to find places to store half the fur coats in New York, and it's time for us to buy our stock for next fall. That means long days at the fur exchanges in the city, possibly a trip to St. Louis for domestic pelts—"

He raised his hands in a mock defenseless gesture. "I

didn't mean to set you off like a firecracker. I just wanted to take you out for a meal."

"I really haven't time," she said, feeling a little silly about her outburst. "I've got a sandwich in my bag you can share with me on my way to the auction house, if you'd like," she said, and could have bitten her tongue for making the offer. She wasn't going to have anything to do with him. She'd promised herself that, and here she was inviting him to come with her. It was too late now to retract the offer, and what harm could one afternoon do? Besides, she had an urge to show him that she wasn't just a part-time person, that she existed and functioned well even when it wasn't obvious to anyone outside the business. She didn't pause to consider why it was important to impress this upon him.

As she rode along in the cab, eating her sandwich (slightly squashed from a morning in her handbag), Irene told Edward about the fur auction in St. Louis, adding, "This is different, however, since there are a number of auction houses in the city who import from all over the world instead of a single central location where everything that's available is in the same place to be seen. Here the furs are sorted first for type of fur, then within types for quality, and within quality for size. Everything in the lot can then be represented by a single numbered pelt that potential buyers can request for examination. Unlike St. Louis, where the bidders buy a huge mixed lot and then have to dispose of it however they can, a buyer here purchases exactly what's needed."

"What if a seller puts out a better sample pelt than the group actually contains?"

"He wouldn't dare. The word would get out within minutes and he'd lose his business."

They went first into a small room full of elbow-height tables. Clerks circulated, taking orders. "Ah, Mrs. Garrick, we've been expecting you," the floor manager said. "We have some interesting things today. I know you don't buy much rabbit, but I have some prime winter bucks from New Zealand I wish you'd take a look at. I've also got a remarkable lot of black fox, thirty large peltries. There's also some very good Yukon white fox. With your reputation for creating stripes, they might work well together."

Irene felt her tension over both the warehouse man and Edward VanCleve evaporating and being replaced with the healthy thrill she always felt when she was doing business. For all the problems Neptune et Cie might have caused in her private life, it was deeply satisfying to be recognized and respected in her business. This man knew her work and expected her to know his. "What about baum marten? We used more than we anticipated last year. We don't want to be caught short."

"We have some twos, but I know you have no use for them. There is one lot of ones—Kubanels—but they're rather small pelts this year."

"Very good. I'll see all of those, plus whatever ermine you have, and some white fitch for trims."

The manager snapped his fingers for a clerk, gave the order, and retired to let Irene examine the pelts as they were brought out from the storage area in the next room. As she studied them, she told Edward what qualities she was looking for in the pelts, what use she had in mind, and the areas of the world from which they came. Without realizing it, she'd adopted Neptune's instructive tone and mannerisms. Edward listened, nodding and asking an occasional question. She wasn't sure whether he was genuinely interested or merely putting on a good show of seeming so. At the moment, it didn't matter. She was in her element, sharing a small portion of what she knew and thoroughly enjoying herself.

When she was done and had jotted down in a tiny notebook the numbers of the lots she was interested in, she led him to the auction area. It was a beautifully appointed room, with polished wood paneling and rich Turkish rugs. On either side of a center aisle there were rows of single desks, like a classroom. A bell rang somewhere and the rest of the bidders came in and took their places. Irene leaned over to Edward, sitting at the adjoining desk, and said, "It's a silent auction, so no one speaks except the auctioneer and the clerks, but for your own protection, don't move a muscle. They probably wouldn't accept a bid from you because they don't recognize you, but any motion could be interpreted as a bid."

"Good heavens!" he said, grinning. "Do you mean I

could rub my eye and walk out owing for a bale of rabbit fur?''

''Or something more expensive.''

''Taking you to lunch would have been safer,'' he whispered as the auctioneer banged his gavel for silence.

Maybe for you, but not for me, Irene thought.

In the cab on the way back to the office, Edward said, ''I had no idea there were so many fur houses. There's you people and Revillon Frères and . . . and I can't think of any others.''

She laughed, thinking how narrow the horizons of the born-rich really were sometimes. ''There are hundreds of others. Your friends just don't patronize them. There are the glovemakers, for instance. They buy most of the rabbit as linings. There are also small houses that specialize in what's called scarves—narrow stoles. There are factories that mass-produce cheap ready-made coats. They use the lower-grade furs in tremendous volume for the collars and cuffs—'' She caught herself on the verge of saying that's what Peter had been, a cutter for a factory, when she met him. She must be more careful.

''I was surprised to see other women there.''

''There always are. They represent the small family businesses. Their husbands do the cutting and stitching and they usually do the buying and selling. It's a terribly hard life for them. You see, furriers make nearly all their money in the fall, and some in the early winter, up until Christmas. There's no income except what little is made on storage in the spring, and none whatsoever in the summer. But spring and summer, when they're not making much, is when they have to lay out all their money for stock. In a small operation, that calls for extraordinarily careful budgeting, and many small furriers fail because of it.''

The cab pulled up in front of Neptune et Cie and Irene started to get out. Edward stopped her with a hand on her arm. ''I've enjoyed today.''

''So have I.''

''You're a truly fascinating woman, Irene.''

She suddenly felt like an animal out of its environment, her protective coloration lost. All afternoon she'd been the confident Irene Garrick, partner in a thriving and prestigious enterprise, in control and in her own world. In a few words he'd brought her back to being plain Irene, the lonely abandoned wife, girlish and insecure. She simply didn't know how to handle this sort of situation. "Thank you," she said, flustered.

"Am I going to have to wait until the dead of summer to take you to lunch, or will you come out with me tomorrow?"

"I don't know."

"I *will* wait, you know. As long as I have to."

"Don't say things like that. Please."

"It's only the truth. No reason to be afraid of truth, is there?"

Truth is one of the few things I *am* afraid of, she thought.

Miss Troutwhite was at her eternal filing when Irene came back into the office and handed her the invoices for the purchases she had made that afternoon. "Send a truck down there, would you, to pick up the furs?"

"It's already on its way. I knew you wouldn't come back empty-handed. There are some messages on your desk, Mrs. Garrick," she said.

Irene looked them over, decided none of them required immediate attention, and turned her chair around to look out the window for a few minutes. She needed the respite. The work she'd done for Neptune et Cie all day was usual. She'd had longer, busier days than this many times. What had tired her was Edward VanCleve's company, or rather the sense of wariness she felt when he was around. The attraction he exerted over her hadn't diminished in the least, but it was easier to overcome when she was busy and in her own element. But there was still an exhausting feeling of underlying frenzy between them that she couldn't quite manage to ignore, no matter how hard she tried.

For all her intense interest in the auction, she'd never been unaware of exactly where he was, how close his hand was to hers, how near their shoulders were to touching, the occasional hint of the scent of the cigar he must have smoked earlier in the day. And of course there was the fact that twice she had almost called him Peter instead of Edward. Very upsetting.

There was a light tap on the door and Miss Troutwhite came in, frowning. "There's a man to see you, Mrs. Garrick. I told him you weren't taking any appointments this late in the afternoon, but he insists on seeing you today."

"What does he want to see me about?"

"He won't tell me. He says it's personal."

"Did he give a name?"

"Miss Troutwhite looked at the scrap of paper in her hand. "Yes, he says he's Teo Kossok."

Miss Ormerod looked at the strip of paper in her hand.

"Yes, he says he's [illegible]."

24

"Teo?" she whispered. "Show him in, Miss Troutwhite."

Her voice was barely audible, but the secretary understood. In a minute Irene's long-lost brother stood before her. He was taller than she'd remembered, and older, naturally. His golden hair had darkened and his brows seemed heavier, but he was definitely Teo. The eyes, brown, but tilted slightly like hers, were the same. The confident stance was the same as ever. Handsome Teo, the pride of the Kossok family. She couldn't have been more surprised if a corpse had actually risen from a grave and walked in. She stared at him, her emotions in complete turmoil.

"I was right!" he said. "It *is* you. Well, well, well, look how our little Irina has come up in the world."

She stepped around the desk and he embraced her. "Teo . . . how . . . where . . . ?"

"It's been a long time, hasn't it? I've been living in Chicago, Sis, and I saw a picture in the newspaper last week and thought to myself, 'If I'm not crazy, this society dame Irene Garrick is really my little sister.' I came back east to see, and sure enough, here you are. All dolled up and sitting in your own office. How'd you get here? Was that thing in the paper right, about you being a partner in this outfit?"

"You didn't come back for me," she blurted out. "You promised and you didn't come back."

"Well, I couldn't very well, could I? I got into some bad company, real dangerous characters. What did I know then? I was just a dumb kid straight off the boat. This guy uptown named Benny got it in his head I'd crossed him, and had his pals break my leg. I had to leave town. Went to Chicago. But that don't matter. I've come back now. Are you glad to see me, Sis?"

Irene wasn't sure of the answer. In spite of a hundred reasons to resent him, she was happy he was back—at least for Mama's sake. "Teo, I've got Mama and the girls here in America, all but Agnieszka. She came, but she went back to get married. Papa is gone. He died in the old country years ago, before they came. I told Mama you were dead. I thought you were. Your return will be the answer to her prayers." She had to pause to get her breath. She was babbling. "What have you been doing, Teo?"

"Oh, a little of this and a little of that. Let's get out of this place. I'm starving. I just got off the train and came straight here."

"Of course, Teo, you'll have to let me prepare Mama. She might go completely to pieces if we spring you on her without any warning. Oh, Teo, she'll be so happy. I thought you were dead. You never came back, and I told her you were dead. If you just walk in and surprise her, she'll—"

"Sure, if you say so. Say, this is a big operation. This your own office?"

"Yes. Let's go home. Miss Troutwhite, I'm leaving. Will you lock up?"

She felt a tiny shard of guilt for not introducing Teo to the obviously curious secretary, but there would be plenty of time later to explain who her mysterious visitor was—if Troutwhite hadn't been listening at the door and figured it out already.

"This is your place?" Teo asked as they pulled up in front of the house.

"Mine and Mama's and the girls'."

"You got a husband or what?"

"Yes, but he's away now," Irene said shortly. "Now, you wait in the car until I come back to the door and signal."

"Listen, Irina, you're acting like she's some kinda frail old lady."

"Teo, she hasn't seen you for twelve years and she's believed you dead, as I did, for half that time. She's not a young woman anymore."

"All right, but don't make it too long."

Irene found Zofia plucking a chicken in the kitchen. Normally she would have reminded her mother forcefully that plucking chickens was the sort of work she hired people for. But under the circumstances, she just said, "Mama, I need to talk to you. It's very important."

"Piotr, he is coming back?"

"No, Mama, nothing to do with Peter. Sit down, please." She took the older woman's hands, heedless of the chicken gore. "Mama, sometimes we make mistakes—big ones—without meaning to. I made a mistake like that. It wasn't my fault, but now I have to tell you I was wrong. I know I made you unhappy, but now everything's going to be all right. I want you to stay calm, now—"

"Somebody's died! Who!"

"No, Mama. Nobody's died. Just the opposite. Somebody we thought was dead, isn't. Mama . . . Teo's alive."

In spite of her warnings, Zofia nearly swooned. Her eyes got huge and she clutched at her heart with one hand and the table edge with the other. "Teo? My boy, my Teo? He is alive?"

"Yes, Mama. I thought he'd died, and he'd only gone away. But he's back now."

"Here? My Teo is here?" Zofia screamed. Before Irene could stop her, she was on her feet and running through the house, shouting for him.

"Mama! Stop it. I'll get him," Irene said, opening the front door to summon her brother, but he was hardly out of the car before Zofia shot down the steps and threw herself on him. She all but carried him to the house, chattering so fast in Polish that Irene couldn't understand a word and suspected that Teo couldn't either.

In any case, he didn't appear to be listening; he was looking around at the house. "Some place, Sis!" he said.

"My boy, my boy, my dear boy!" Zofia went on. "Come, sit in kitchen and I cook for you. Just like old days when we were in village. I remember all your favorite things. Some nice sausage and cabbage . . . ?"

Irene went to bed that night hating herself for succumbing to self-pity, but succumbing just the same. Zofia hadn't stopped fussing over Teo for a single second. The girls, raised on tales of their legendary big brother, the brilliant, handsome

Teo, were completely taken with him. Well, why shouldn't they be? They were a household of women and he was a gregarious, handsome man dropped into their lives like a belated Christmas present. He told funny stories, talked in a brash way they weren't used to, and was Teo. That was the important thing. He was their Teo, returned miraculously from the dead.

So what right did Irene have to feel pitiful about it? She was, in some ways, as glad to see him as they were. No matter what had happened in between, a small part of her was still Irina Kossok, the simple village girl who adored her dashing big brother. It was petty of her to let her old resentment of his abandonment of her color her thinking. He couldn't help it. He'd explain all about it. He'd been badly hurt, his leg broken, his life in danger. He'd had to leave New York. She understood that. And if he had come back to find her, it might have been after she left the Sprys. He wouldn't have been able to find her if he'd tried.

But he *hadn't* tried.

That wasn't fair, she told herself. He *had* come back eventually. As soon as he saw that picture of her in the Chicago paper, he'd come right away to find her. He'd left his own friends, his home, his business—he never had gotten around to saying exactly what it was—to be reunited with his family.

Still, it hurt that they all acted for all the world like they'd been in some sort of suspended animation, doing nothing in life but waiting in the hope he'd return. Mama sat there at the kitchen table picking her teeth, belching, gushing over Teo just like in the village. Lillie and Cecilia danced and pranced and preened in his presence, and even shy, lumpy Stefania had giggled when he chucked her under her several chins. Irene could hardly remember the child laughing about anything. Did all the years, all the money, all the love she'd spent on them mean nothing now that Teo was back? They didn't laugh for her; Mama didn't dash around like a maniac trying to please Irene's palate.

This was an ugly way to be thinking, she told herself. It was plain old jealousy and she wouldn't let it get the best of her, she resolved.

The resolve lasted a week.

Teo had taken over the best guest room; the house had to be silent until noon so his sleep wouldn't be disturbed; meals were devoted to pleasing him; conversation revolved completely around him; several of the younger, prettier maids had to be reprimanded for neglecting their assigned duties in their efforts to cater to him. The twins graduated from high school with a pretty ceremony three days after his arrival, but completely ignored Irene—who'd made them go and had paid for it. Instead, the evening was spent with them introducing their brother to all their friends. Teo was gone most evenings—"Seeing a few old friends. Catching up on old times, you know. Say, Irina, I'm a little short of cash. You couldn't loan me a ten-spot, could you?"

Irene finally caught him alone one afternoon. Zofia, the victim of near-exhaustion in her efforts to please her son, had given up and taken a nap. The girls were in their rooms. "Teo, I'd like to talk to you," she said.

"Sure. What's up Sis?"

"First, I wish you wouldn't call me 'Sis.' It sounds so . . . so lower-class, somehow. Please call me Irene."

He heard the sharpness in her voice and bristled momentarily, but quickly got it under control. "That's right. We ain't just dumb immigrants anymore, are we? We got class. What's on your mind?"

They went into the music room, Irene closing the door firmly behind them. Seating herself on the piano bench, she said, "I'd like to know a bit about your plans, Teo. How long a visit have you planned in New York?"

"Visit? I'm staying here."

She was pleased. Naturally, she was pleased to hear it. But why did she feel a sinking sensation in her stomach? "I thought you might be. You've left your business in Chicago for good?"

"Yeah, I guess."

"What sort of business was that?"

"I told you. Lotsa things."

"I see. Well, which of those things are you going to do here?"

"What?"

"I mean, what sort of work are you getting? I can't help but notice you seem to be short of cash—"

"Only temporary, Sis. I got a big check coming—"

"In the meantime, I'm sure you'll be happier with work to do. It must be an embarrassment for you to have to keep asking me for money—"

Teo glared, apparently taking this for sarcasm. But it wasn't. Irene was simply going by the tragically hard lesson she'd learned from Peter. Men loathed being the recipients of money earned by women. Peter had made that clear—bitterly clear. She didn't want to continue to put her own brother in such an awkward and unpleasant position.

"What have you got in mind?" he asked.

She ignored the belligerent tone in his voice, thinking he was merely uncomfortable talking about this. "I don't know, Teo. I'll help you in any way I can. You know that. You know what might be very profitable . . . ? Oh, what a good idea—!"

"Profitable? What?"

"Well, we've been having a terrible time finding places for summer fur storage. You could rent some space near here and equip it, and Neptune et Cie could rent your services. I'm sure Monsieur would agree. If your check hasn't come in time, I could loan you the money to get it set up with the refrigeration units and chemicals and so forth. Oh, Teo, say yes, please. I'd enjoy working with you. And by next summer I will have found someone to teach you all about repairing and so forth and you could be well on your way. What do you think?"

"I dunno. I guess I'll have to think about it."

"I'll start looking for a place for you today."

Clara thought it was a terrible idea.

"Let him find his own way, Irene. He's been doing so all these years."

"It will be his own way. I'm just helping him get started."

"You didn't put the idea in his head?" Clara asked disbelievingly.

"I suggested it, yes. But he was very enthusiastic. I think he's eager to settle down and start a business."

Clara thought back to the sullen, arrogant boy she remembered from the boat coming to America and tried to reconcile that memory with the man Irene was talking about—the man who, according to his sister, was just dying to be set up in business so he could work hard at honest labor. It didn't seem possible, but then, people changed. Irene was an entirely different person than she'd been then. So might Teo be. She'd never really known him, only made a judgment on instinct. She might have been very, very wrong.

Not only was it the fair thing to give him the benefit of the doubt, it was the expedient thing. Irene, loyal as always to her family, wouldn't have listened to adverse remarks about him or the ideas she was proposing. Clara considered going to Neptune quietly and voicing her concerns, but decided against it, first because she, too, was a victim of a strong sense of loyalty and second because Monsieur wasn't looking well lately and she didn't want to worry him.

Irene had Teo in business in a remarkably short time. A pair of storefronts on Second Avenue were rented, knocked together, and fitted up as a small warehouse. They had the first floor and basement and there were four floors of apartments above. Perhaps it would be convenient for Teo to rent one of them when he was set up. It wasn't a stylish address, by any means, but it would be convenient for him.

By dint of her usual superhuman persistence, Irene had the cooling equipment, the insulation, the racks, and the chemicals ready in less than two weeks. And if Teo sometimes seemed less than enthusiastic, well, it was to be expected. It was such a new business to him, it must seem a bit daunting, and he was probably worried about paying her back. She kept reassuring him there was no hurry. In fact, it would probably be a year or two before he could clear enough profit to start reimbursing her, but that was perfectly acceptable. Fur storage, in itself, wasn't very profitable. It was the repair work that often resulted from the contact with the customer that brought in the money, and Teo wouldn't be in direct contact with customers until the next year.

She brought in one of the warehouse supervisors from Neptune et Cie to hire a handful of workers and explain to them and Teo all the ins and outs of fur storage, with a special emphasis on the fact that there was never, under any circumstances, to be anything lighted in the building. "No matches, no cigarettes, no pipes, metal that might strike a spark, no hot plate, nothing!" they were told over and over.

When Irene got the final total for the cost, even she was stunned. It wouldn't have cost so much if she hadn't been in such a rush, she thought, so it wasn't fair to expect Teo to pay back the full cost. It wasn't his fault he was starting the business at the end of the peak time of year. If they'd waited even another week or two, it would have been too late to start at all until next spring. She just wouldn't let him know how expensive it had been.

She'd enjoyed herself, getting Teo set up in a good job. Not only was it morally satisfying for the right reasons, it was gratifying for some less admirable reasons. First, this work meant Teo wouldn't be at home all day letting the whole family run around in circles to please him. She expected he would get a place of his own to live as soon as he was adjusted. She tried not to be discouraged when he showed no signs of doing so, even though she mentioned the apartments above the warehouse facilities. It was probably for the best, his staying with Zofia and the girls for a while longer. They enjoyed him so much.

The other side benefit of the hours spent helping Teo was that she honestly had no time at all for Edward VanCleve. After the afternoon at the fur auction, he'd called her nearly every day and sent her flowers with notes several times. "Come out, come out, wherever you are!" one note said. "You must stop work to take food on occasion—take it with me, please," another read. Every time, she sent back a missive turning down the offer, thanking him for the flowers and promising nothing. Clara, back on her feet, had instructions always to say Irene was out when he called, and followed this instruction without any explanation being necessary.

"We're taking the first truckload of furs to Teo's storage today, Clara," Irene said one morning. "I think I'll just go along to see everything gets unloaded properly."

"Good idea," Clara said. And made a mental note to contact the insurance company to increase the coverage on the items being farmed out to Teo's establishment.

* * *

Two weeks later, Irene was taken by surprise as she approached the back entrance of the Neptune et Cie building. "Aha! I caught you. I knew I would sooner or later!" Edward VanCleve said.

"Oh! You startled me. What are you doing, lurking in alleys?"

"I was waiting for you. Do you realize it's been a full six weeks since I last laid eyes on you?"

"Has it? I've been so busy—"

"Yes, so I hear. Well, you're not busy today. I'm being the big bad pirate, stealing the overworked lady furrier. I have a picnic hamper in the car—a very nice open touring car, by the way, equipped with dusters and goggles. We're going out in the country."

"I really can't—"

"Very well. Make all the excuses you want. If you're too busy to come with me, I'll come with you. Think how embarrassing it's going to be, having a man trail along behind you, munching on egg sandwiches and celery sticks. People will stare, they will ask, 'Does she know he's there?' You will be a spectacle!"

Irene started laughing in spite of herself. How could she have regarded him as threatening? He wasn't a danger, he was a ray of sunshine. "Oh, very well. Just to save myself public humiliation. But I really do have to check in with the office and change my clothes."

"I could run you home."

Home. Her warning system, temporarily resting, came back on full alert. No, she didn't want him coming home and meeting Zofia and the girls. One day last week she'd come home to discover that Zofia had spread some wash out on the big bushes that flanked the front door. "Will dry better in the sunshine." With her luck, Zofia would have forgotten all her previous warnings and be beating rugs in the front yard. "No, I keep a few things here. Just wait, you and your hamper, and I'll be back out in fifteen minutes."

It was a lovely day, cool for early July, but sunny and beautiful. A perfect day for a ride in the country, they agreed. They went to Scarsdale, where Edward's parents had built an elegant summer house which had passed to him on their deaths a few years earlier. They had their picnic in the small white-painted ha-ha that overlooked a tiny jewel of a lake. "They had it excavated when I was a boy, and I thought it would never fill up!" he recalled. "For two years it was a huge vat of mud and then the third summer we came up and there must have been a lot of rainfall because it was nearly full."

"It must have been a happy childhood, with a place like this to come to in the summer," Irene said, gazing around at the well-manicured lawns, croquet layouts, and well-groomed trees, perfect for climbing. She had a sudden painful memory of her own childhood. There hadn't been time for playing; there was always work to be done. And if there had been time, there was nothing to play with save what their imaginations could make of sticks and rocks and dirt.

"Happy? I don't know. I never thought about it. It was just here, and come June, my nanny would pack me up and we'd come here," he said. "Was your childhood so different, Irene? I'm sure it was much more elegant, of course. The grapevine has it you grew up in a genuine castle."

You can't imagine how different, she thought. But she'd caught that dangerously curious note in his voice and became cautious. "Not so very much, I suppose. A different climate and customs—"

"Just where are you from? I've never quite understood."

"It doesn't matter," she said, briskly stacking up the plates and silverware.

"It must matter—at least to you," he persisted.

"Not in the least. There are some clouds coming up in the west. Don't you think we should start back?"

He'd turned away to set the dishes in the picnic hamper, and for a second she was struck once again by his fleeting resemblance to Peter. Her heart gave a great lurch and then he moved and the image faded. He was *nothing* like Peter!

"When did you meet Jacques Neptune?" he was asking. "While you were still in Europe? Or did you just get to know him in this country?"

"He's a relative of my husband's. I believe they'd been in touch for many years."

"Ah, yes. The husband."

"What do you mean by that?"

"Come on, Irene. We don't have to indulge in pretense. You don't have to fabricate a husband for me. And I don't care in the least what your relationship to old Jacques has been in the past. You're a full partner now!"

She stood up so quickly she toppled the small table onto his lap. Cake and crackers flew everywhere. Lemonade drenched his shirt. It was an accident that she regretted wasn't deliberate. "How dare you! How *dare* you!" Turning, she lifted her skirts and started running. She had no idea where she was going, but it didn't matter because she didn't get there.

Halfway across the lawn, he caught up with her. Grabbing her by the elbow, he whirled her around. "Am I wrong? Am I? Tell me I'm wrong, Irene. Tell me the truth! Who are you? Where are you from?"

"I don't owe you any explanations. I don't owe you anything! Let go of me!"

"Please, stop fighting me. I'm sorry. Just tell me I was wrong and we'll forget it even happened."

"Oh, we will, will we? Maybe you can forget having all but called me Monsieur's whore, Mr. VanCleve, but I can't!"

"I didn't mean that."

"You certainly did."

"Irene, please . . . I'm sorry. Really sorry. I can see now what an awful mistake I've made. Please forgive me."

"Take me home. Now."

"Yes, yes, of course."

They rode back to town in silence that was punctuated at five-mile intervals with Edward's apologies: his remarks, hideous as they were, reflected a flaw in his own character and she shouldn't put any credence in anything stupid he might say . . . he knew he was utterly, horribly mistaken in his vulgar implications . . . any fool could see at a glance that she was an entirely honorable woman, and the very thought of anyone suggesting otherwise was downright criminal. . . . By the time they crossed the Harlem River, he'd gone so far in his thinking as to be making threats against anyone else who ever had the gall to cast doubt on Irene's character.

Irene was discovering that it was difficult to maintain a

"good mad" for such an extended period, especially when the object of the anger was so humbled and willing to take blame. When they pulled up in front of Neptune et Cie ("Let me drive you home!" "No, thank you, Mr. VanCleve.") she'd reached the point of being almost, but not quite, amused by his verbal contortions.

"I'm going to go on a hunger strike unless you say you'll forgive me," he said, opening the door for her. "I'll tell all my friends it's your fault I'm fading before their very eyes. And when I'm dead, the world will blame you."

"Edward, do me a favor," she said.

"Anything!"

"Stop talking."

"Does this mean I can eat?"

"Yes, and I suggest you start with the piece of cheese stuck to your shoulder."

She watched him drive away, and to her surprise, found that she was smiling. Had she gone mad, or was the world mad and she'd just figured it out? For all the emotional upheaval of the day, hadn't it really been far more interesting than sitting over a pile of ledgers as she'd planned? Of course. She might even consent to see him again, now that he knew the dangers of his prying. Certainly he wouldn't try it again.

Clara was waiting when she returned to her office. "You should have gone home long ago," Irene told her.

"I wanted to talk to you. I had some confusion in the records about Mrs. Rieke's moleskin cape—you know, that wretched thing she nurses along year after year like a child? I marked it to be sent to your brother's warehouse, then Mrs. Rieke decided she wanted to remove it to take along on a summer trip to Toronto. I called and he said it wasn't there, so I went to see if I could figure out what the problem was, but he wouldn't let me take a look at the cold safes."

"He's very sensitive about operating independently of us, Clara. It *is* his own business—even though we contract out to him, we don't own it."

"I'm perfectly aware of that."

"Yes, I'm sure you are, as am I. But he's still wary of anything that seems to place him in an employee position.

I've been over twice, and he wouldn't even let me look around. He'll get over it."

"Still, I wish you'd check for that cape."

"I'll ask him about it when I get home. Clara, you're getting yourself upset over nothing. Either he doesn't recognize it or it's been sent to one of the other storage areas. It'll turn up. We've never lost anything entrusted to us."

"I hope so," Clara said.

Irene paused and studied her old friend for a minute. "What do you mean by that?"

"Mean? Absolutely nothing, my dear, except I'm turning into a worrier. It's my age, I guess."

When Irene had changed her clothes, looked over her messages, and left the office for the day, Clara was still sitting over her ledgers trying to find Mrs. Rieke's moleskin cape. She was positive it had gone to Teo's warehouse.

25

Against all her better judgment, Irene allowed herself to be persuaded to go out with Edward VanCleve several more times. It was always "harmless"—a ride in the country most often, or occasionally dinner in a part of the city not frequented by their friends. Though it wouldn't have hurt his reputation as a dashing young man about town to be seen with a married woman, it would have been very harmful to Irene and he was sensitive to that fact.

Irene felt a strange mixture of guilt and pleasure in his company. Her conscience told her she shouldn't have anything to do with him; she kept thinking with a shudder of what her mother would say if she knew her married daughter was seeing another man. But she was a grown woman; why should she still care what her mother thought? Zofia was a peasant still, her perspective still firmly lodged in the old-fashioned, old-country morality of the village, Irene told herself. And yet, to her irritation, so was Irene herself. She found herself concealing what she was doing even from Clara for fear she would see her own disapproval of herself reflected in her friend's eyes. No matter how far she had come socially and financially, she disliked herself for appearing to be what she would term a "loose woman."

But she wasn't, really. Nothing indecent transpired between them; she made very sure there was no opportunity. She had a vivid—all too vivid—memory of those few moments on the terrace and was absolutely resolved such a moment would never occur again. Still, while she was always ready to dodge any potential embrace, to avoid any contact, Irene was perpetually aware of Edward's physical being: his hand on hers as he helped her into the automobile, his shoulder barely brushing hers when they sat near one another, the lingering warmth of his arm when he draped her summer shawl over her shoulders. And it was all very exciting.

The excitement he brought to her life was both his danger and his appeal. It was never dull or even comfortable to be around him. There was always an aura of tension between them that she found both thrilling and disconcerting—perhaps thrilling *because* it was disconcerting.

He never gave up trying to find out more about her. He took greater care after the day in Scarsdale when he had assumed too much and asked too much, but he didn't quit. "Someday let's go swimming," he said, for instance. "Do you know how to swim?"

"I doubt that I remember," she answered, temporarily off-guard.

"Did you learn in still water or the sea?"

She avoided answering, knowing he was attempting to pin her down geographically. If she'd answered "the sea," he would have worked on finding out which sea. "Why, in my bath, of course!" she replied with a laugh.

There were times when she wished she could tell him the truth; times when something they saw brought the past back so vividly she could barely refrain from commenting. On one ride, they passed through the old neighborhood within a block of the tenement building where she'd lived with the Sprys. She saw a young woman on the street she recognized—a girl she'd made a wedding dress for who was now dispiritedly trailing three grubby children in her wake and carrying a fourth. "She looks so old and tired and she can't be more than twenty-five," she said.

"How do you know?" Edward asked.

"Oh, I don't know. I'm just supposing," Irene said, and fastened her gaze on the road ahead.

That was the day she knew she could never tell Edward the truth about herself or her past. For one thing, he might tell other people, and all the years of subtly convincing her circle of her exciting background would be lost. She'd also lose his interest and affection—of that she had no doubt. He liked believing she was of more impressive birth and background than he. He, like many third and fourth generations of American wealth, had a basic insecurity, an obsession with not appearing parvenu, and inadvertently showed it in a doting interest in European history and titles. It wouldn't have mattered if she'd been poor; to the social ranks in which they moved, there was a certain romantic nobility in being "ruined." Countesses with darned gloves and dukes with holes in their shoes counted for more than wealth without bloodlines to these people whose bloodlines often were traceable for only a century. But it would have mattered enormously that she was nobody.

And even if her background had been as exalted as he wanted to believe, the *not knowing* was a large part of his interest in her. Her mystery intrigued him as much as—perhaps more than—any of her other attributes. It wasn't a flattering realization, but Irene couldn't deceive herself on that point. If ever he solved the riddle of her origins, these pleasant afternoons and evenings would cease. Perhaps not abruptly, but they would cease eventually. And she didn't want that. She liked having a man compliment her, give her gifts, take her arm to support her when she was perfectly able to support herself. It was more than a vain liking, it was a desperate need. Peter, the man she loved, had rejected her, and Edward proved over and over that she wasn't a failure as a woman.

Besides all that, she liked him. She didn't love him, but she liked him very well. His conversations never went beneath a surface level, but they were bright, witty, and entertaining. His manners were gracious and flattering in the extreme, his speech well-bred and pleasant, his tailoring exquisite. And if his witticisms were sometimes repeated and his private-school drawl a little artificial—so what? She could enjoy him when she was with him and forget about him when she wasn't. Well, *almost* forget about him.

"So Mrs. Rieke has her wrap back?" Irene asked Clara. "Teo found it?"

"Yes, he said there was a mix-up in the bookkeeping. Odd, though . . ."

"What's odd?"

"Nothing. Now, about those letters you need to answer . . ."

Clara was quite concerned about the moleskin cape, but wanted to be very sure of herself before making any accusations. It had turned up, all right, but it smelled funny. Not like any chemicals she recognized, but like cooking grease. There was no reason why it should. Clara didn't know a fraction as much about furs as Irene did, but she did know there was no reason why the mothproofing process should make the cape have that odd odor. Even if Mrs. Rieke had brought it in smelling that way, the storage processing should have eliminated the smell.

Irene noticed the worried expression, but knew that prodding Clara for information or opinions was a lost cause. She'd say whatever was on her mind when she was ready. Still, it might be a good idea to stop on her way home and ask Teo about the cape again

The door was locked when she got there. After a few minutes of fruitless pounding, she gave up and went home. Teo was already there. "Why wasn't anyone at the warehouse?" she asked.

"Who would need to be?"

"Any number of people. What about Mr. Waithe and Charley Bonhomme?" These were the Neptune et Cie employees who'd been on loan to him to get him started.

"Oh, I sent them on back to you. No need for them now. I've learned all about the chemicals, and you said yourself there won't be anybody wanting anything out till the end of October. That's two months from now."

"I guess. Still, I'd feel better if you kept at least one of them on. Just in case. Where was the watchman, if nobody else was there?"

"I fired him. Drinker. Got a new man coming in tomorrow."

"Teo! The warehouse should never be unattended. There could be a robbery, or—God forbid—a fire."

"Yeah, yeah. I know. I was just getting ready to go over there myself. Stay the night."

"Oh . . . I assumed you were going out with someone. The way you're dressed . . ." He had on a yellow silk shirt and one of his new suits, a brown with a stripe that was just a bit gaudy. Irene didn't approve of his wardrobe, verging as it did on the flashy. Time enough later to try to influence his taste in clothes, she'd been telling herself. As he turned away to adjust his tie in the mirror in the front hall, she was certain the rectangular bulge in his coat pocket was a deck of cards. "Teo, where are you going tonight?" she asked.

Her thoughts darted along. If he was playing cards with friends, he might be having the game at the warehouse. That, in itself, was odd but within his rights. But she'd never known men to be able to handle cards without smoking—the two seemed to go together.

He turned around very slowly, with a calculating look in his eyes she'd never seen before—or had never been willing to see. "I'm going down to the warehouse like I said." He spoke very slowly. "And where are you going? Out to one of your high-society parties? One of them dinners folks read about in the paper? Maybe you'd rather I'd go with you—you could introduce me to all your high-and-mighty friends, couldn't you? That would be nice. I've heard things about your life, Sis, all about growing up in a castle somewhere in Russia, being a cousin to the czar. I could tell your friends a lot."

There was no mistaking the threat. Teo was actually saying: "Don't question me or I'll blow this story to bits."

"You wouldn't." She whispered the words that caught in her throat.

"Oh, yeah? Try me, Sis." He smiled and patted the deck of cards in his pocket before turning and sauntering out of the house. "Have a good time at your party," he said over his shoulder.

Irene went to her room, shaken to the core. Her own brother had become her most dangerous enemy. He was blackmailing her, and unless something changed, he could hold out his threat for years and years to come. She slumped in the window seat, hoping to catch whatever summer breeze might come her way and cool her fevered thinking. But the air was still and her thoughts continued to race.

"You are eating dinner somewhere, eh?" Zofia asked from the doorway. Since living here she'd reluctantly started speaking English—not very good English, but enough to communicate with the staff and even with her own daughters.

"No, Mama. I'm going to the theater later, but I'll be here

for dinner. Mama, please come sit with me a minute. I must talk to you.''

''I get the cook woman to start food.''

''In a minute, Mama. This is important.''

Zofia settled herself on the bed, sitting gingerly at the edge, as if afraid that it might swallow her up. ''So, there is something wrong?''

''Yes, Mama. It's Teo. Mama, we've been wrong about Teo. We were all so glad to see him that we didn't stop to wonder what kind of man he'd become. He's not nice, Mama.''

Zofia stood up quickly. ''Such a thing to say. Your own brother, Teo is. Is good man.''

''No, he's not a good man. He's a wicked man.''

Zofia took a step forward and her hand came up in the old familiar gesture, ready to administer a slap.

''Stop! Hitting me won't change anything.''

''Why do you say such terrible thing about your own brother! You are a bad girl, Irina Gieryk! Never say such thing again!''

Irene sighed. ''Never mind, Mama.''

Zofia went off shaking her head and muttering to herself in Polish. Irene paced her room for a while. If only Peter were here; she could put her problem before him and he could tell her what to do. Peter was so smart, so sensible . . . No, that was ridiculous. Peter wouldn't have helped her protect her image; he'd never understood why it was so important. And besides, she simply had to stop thinking about him so often. He had left her and she had to learn—*would* learn—to stop thinking of him as the rock of stability and reason in her life.

She picked up the phone. ''Clara? Are you going to be home later this evening?''

''Yes. Is there something wrong? Do you need me for something?''

''I have a terrible problem, Clara. I don't know what to do. I have to go to a theater party tonight, but I'll beg off as early as possible and come over. It's about Teo.''

There was a moment of silence from the phone; then Clara said, ''I see. I'll be waiting.''

Irene didn't hear a word of the play and responded to her friends' comments with short, mechanical replies. ''Are you unwell?'' Edward VanCleve, an inevitable member of the party, finally said to her at the first intermission. ''Shall I take you home?'' She'd never allowed him to know where she lived, but there was always hope.

''I'm well, thank you, Edward. I'm only concerned about a business matter. I think I'll just call my chauffeur to take me to Miss Johnson's apartment. I need to talk to her. Please make my excuses to the others.''

Clara, still dressed as for the office, came to the door. ''I've made your favorite cookies. Now, sit down and tell me what's wrong.''

Irene poured it all out. Clara didn't appear shocked, and neither asked questions nor made comments until Irene was done recounting the incident earlier in the day. She just listened and nodded.

''Why did he change, Clara?'' Irene asked when she'd finished. ''He was such a nice boy, so bright and good—''

''No, he wasn't. You just wanted to believe he was. All of you.''

Irene was stunned. ''Is that true, Clara?''

''I don't know. It was my impression.''

''Why did he come back to us if he doesn't care about our welfare—?''

''Irene, I don't want to hurt you, but isn't it obvious?''

''Because he saw the picture of me and figured out that I was rich? . . . Oh, Clara, can that be all it was?''

''None of that matters. Irene, about the moleskin cape. . .''

Irene looked confused. ''The moleskin cape? Clara, what difference does *that* make? We must talk about Teo.''

''I *am* talking about Teo. The moleskin cape smelled funny when it was finally found—a cooking smell. I was curious, so I went around the neighborhood where the warehouse is. I found a pawnshop that had the same funny smell.''

''A pawnshop!'' Irene's eyes widened with dawning comprehension.

''The owners have an apartment in back and cook their meals there. I described the cape to them and they knew it.''

''Teo pawned the cape?''

Clara stood and went to the hall closet. ''The moleskin cape and two coats.'' She opened the closet door.

Irene joined her, touching the sleeves of the garments and then smelling them. "These are ours—Mrs. DeAngelo's fox and Mrs. Harvey's mink." She went back to the living room and sat down heavily on the sofa, her normally serene features bleak and defeated. "That's why he wouldn't let anyone in. That's why he fired the men, even the watchman—because they worked for me and he was afraid they'd tell me. He must have thought he could redeem them before fall. Or maybe he didn't even care! Oh, Lord, Clara, what's he done with all of the garments we trusted to him—*I* trusted to him! What a fool I've been."

"He's probably distributed them all over town. Do you know how many pawnshops he has to choose from?"

"Hundreds. Clara, we have to find them all. My God, it'll take weeks!"

Clara nodded. "And in the meantime, what do you do about Teo?"

"I don't know. What can I do?"

Clara didn't answer right away. Rather, she poured them each a fresh cup of tea and sat down nibbling on a cookie and thinking. "You have several options, as I see it. None of them good. You could face him with the evidence of his traitorous behavior and hope he'd see the light and mend his ways." She said this with thick sarcasm, half-afraid Irene would take her seriously otherwise.

For a second Irene actually looked as if she were considering it, but finally she said, "He wouldn't change."

Clara relaxed with relief. "Then you must consider just what he wants. He wants unlimited money without working for it. And I see nothing you can do but give it to him. But you must make it conditional on his going as far away as possible."

"But he'll just keep asking for more."

"Probably so. But if you can send him away immediately with enough to keep him happy for a while, maybe some other solution will present itself," she said.

"What other solution?"

Clara shrugged and didn't answer. She couldn't say to Irene what she was really thinking—that a man like Teo was certain to come to a bad end sooner or later, and with any luck at all, it might be sooner. In fact, it was surprising that he hadn't already fallen out with someone who would break his neck instead of merely his leg. "You must buy him off, Irene. And you must do so very quickly. Tomorrow. You could go to the bank first thing in the morning and take out a temptingly big sum, then transfer some to another bank in some remote place that he has to go to in order to claim."

"Where? Out west someplace? California, Nevada?"

"I was thinking more of putting an ocean between you. Perhaps Spain or Italy." In Clara's experience Latins were as hot-tempered as their reputation. He was certain to provoke someone's ire in either of those countries without even trying.

"Yes, that's good. He couldn't come running back for more as easily."

"I'll get the boat tickets in the morning while you go to the bank. As soon as you've given him the cash and the tickets, we'll get to work finding those coats. He must have the claim tickets someplace."

They spent an hour working out the details. A check of the newspaper revealed that a ship was leaving for Barcelona the next afternoon. A few old and trusted employees were selected to take up a post at the warehouse first thing in the morning to guard against Teo's getting back in before a locksmith could be found. Teo might be vindictive enough to try to destroy the claim checks. Another employee, the head of their security staff, would be summoned to come to Irene's house at dawn and take over Teo's room there as soon as she'd confronted him. "Should we call them tonight and make arrangements?" Clara asked.

"No, I don't think so. He never even gets up before noon anyway," Irene said. "Morning is soon enough to tell them. It will leave less time for anything to go wrong from the time I confront him to the time the boat sails."

Clara's admiration for Irene was renewed and refreshed. She knew all too well how devastatingly painful this was to her friend. To have to face the fact that her adored brother was a common crook was horrible enough for anyone, but doubly torturous for someone as fanatically family-minded as Irene. And without Zofia's name ever being brought up, Clara knew that she was on Irene's mind the whole time. But having faced the truth, Irene never hesitated or wavered, never expressed the disappointment and sorrow that must have been tearing her to ribbons. She merely forged ahead, thinking how best to remove Teo from the country with the least damage to everyone concerned.

Clara wanted to say something comforting and affectionate, but refrained. She knew that the least crumb of sympathy might shatter Irene's self-control. So when Irene left the apartment, Clara merely said, "I'll meet you at the office at seven. Do you think you ought to tell Monsieur Neptune? I believe he's back in the city and planning to come into the office tomorrow."

"We'll tell him when we have it all straightened out."

She meant to go straight home, but couldn't resist the temptation to go by the warehouse. There was nothing to be gained from it, of course. And she certainly wouldn't get out of the car and risk seeing or speaking to Teo, but she had to just see if he was, as she suspected, there with his friends—whoever they might be. Her action wasn't reasonable, but it was a compulsion she couldn't resist. She wanted to see a light shining from some window on the ground floor and confirm that her suspicions were correct. She needed to know.

As the car turned onto Second Avenue, traffic slowed. "Some sort of problem ahead, Mrs. Garrick," the chauffeur said. "You want to turn back?"

"No, keep going. It's probably some accident they'll get cleared up in a few minutes."

They crept along another two blocks before coming to a complete stop. "I don't think we're going to get any farther, ma'am. Smell that smoke? There must be a big fire up there."

"Fire?" she said. "A fire?"

"Yes'm. Mrs. Garrick, ma'am, don't get out! It isn't safe—"

But she was gone, leaving the car door standing open as she ran up the street. In spite of a broken heel, an ache in her chest, and a stitch in her side, she didn't stop running until she was close enough to confirm her worst fears.

Teo's warehouse was engulfed in flames.

26

The storefront windows, painted over and heavily barred, had shattered with the heat, and the bars had melted as though no more substantial than chocolate sticks. Flames, acrid with chemicals, billowed out and licked up the outside of the building. Hundreds of people were converging on the scene, which was already chaos. Policemen, firemen, and onlookers dashed about like overexcited bees in a hive. Women were screaming, men shouting, babies crying, and fire equipment clanking and gushing. But all the activity was to no avail at all. Within moments of Irene's arrival, the building was engulfed, its face a shimmering sheet of flame, black clouds of smoke obscuring the night sky. Nearly a block away, she could feel the intense heat through her clothes. A few pitiful streams of water could make no difference, and the firemen seemed aware of this. They were concentrating their efforts on the adjoining buildings, soaking them in an attempt to keep the raging fire from spreading.

As Irene watched, sick and horrified, a figure silhouetted against the blaze inside appeared in an upper window and flung something out. A baby! No one was fast enough, and the blanket-wrapped bundle struck the ground with an appalling little thud that was swallowed in the roar of the fire. A mere warping of perception—she couldn't have heard that pitiful sound, but it seemed, nevertheless, to thunder in her ears. Irene staggered into an alley, sweating and retching. She leaned, shaking violently, against the wall for a moment before rejoining the crowd and pushing her way through. She grabbed the arm of a passing fireman and screamed, "What can I do? How may I help?"

He shoved her away. "Get the hell out of the way, lady. That's what you can do!" he shouted back.

She tried to be useful. "Clear the way! Please move back!" she in turn shouted at others, trying to push them back physically and make more room for the firemen to do their jobs, but it was hopeless. For every one person she moved, four others pushed forward to gawk at the free spectacle. Faces were glazed with sweat, speckled with soot, and glowed with the diabolical orange of reflected flame.

Returning to the car and all but falling through the still-open door, she told the alarmed chauffeur to do what he could to free them from the crowd and take her back to Clara's. "Yes'm," he said, and turned the wheels hard in order to drive up over the sidewalk. Honking a warning at those ahead, he drove the length of the block and reentered traffic. But Clara, when Irene urged her to come back to the scene, refused. "There's no purpose to be served, save upsetting yourself even more. You can't do a thing."

"But, Clara, I've got to do something! All those people in the building . . . It was Teo's fault, and that makes it my fault!"

Clara had to restrain the urge to slap sense into her. Her face was red with anger as she said, "Even if it was Teo's fault, which you don't know, not for certain, it is absolutely *not* your fault. You idiotic girl! Why are you so determined to carry the sins and failings of everyone you know on your own shoulders?"

"But he's my family!"

"So what? That's a mere accident of nature; it doesn't make you responsible for his actions. You didn't cause that fire any more than you pawned the coats or fell in with the wrong people. You not only didn't have any part in doing it, you didn't even know about it in order to prevent it. Now, stop talking this way. What you must do is get home. As soon as the fire's under control, the police will be wanting to talk to the leaseholder, and they may come to your house. Do you want them calling on your mother?"

"Mama! Oh, my God, no! I don't want Mama to know about this until she has to. Clara, will you please at least come with me? I can't stand to be alone. I'll go mad!"

"Of course," Clara said. "I'll just get my things together." That she would go along for a night in the mansion was a measure of her very real concern. Irene had been trying to get Clara to live with them there ever since they first moved into the big house and had been particularly insistent since Peter left nearly a year before. Clara had resisted with all her strength, feeling what little independence she had would be lost if she ever spent a night under that roof. But this was different.

By seven in the morning, after a night of taking turns pacing and speculating on what could have happened, Irene remembered that she'd used her office address on the lease for the building. "If we take a cab and leave my chauffeur outside the front door here to tell anyone who comes that Teo is at the office as well, they'll go there without bothering Mama, won't they?" she asked. "I don't dare speak to anyone here without the possibility of Mama bursting in to see what's going on."

At nine o'clock a police detective came to call at the office, having been sent along as per the plan. "Mrs. Garrick, I presume you know about the tragic fire at your brother's warehouse."

"I do. I saw it."

"How did you happen to be there at that time of night?"

Stupid of her to have volunteered that, she realized. "I thought he might be there and I had some business to discuss with him." She hoped she didn't sound as guilty to his ears as to her own.

"But I understood he lived at your same address. Why couldn't you have waited to discuss your business at home?"

"No particular reason. Just an impulse," she said.

"You had reason to believe you'd find him there?"

"No, no reason. It just seemed a possibility."

"And was he there?"

"I don't know. When I arrived, the building was burning."

"And have you seen him since then?"

"No. I left the message at my home that he was here in order to spare my mother distress."

"What distress might that be, exactly?"

Irene didn't answer right away. She was fully aware of the

antipathy and belligerence in the man's tone. "*Any* distress, sir," she said mildly. "I'm afraid of the obvious, that my brother perished in the fire. My mother has already mourned him once in error. I don't want to risk doing that to her again. What do you really want to know?"

"Well, it's like this, Mrs. Garrick: your brother was seen by the neighbors going into the warehouse with some friends a few hours before the fire. They carried bottles and one of them was smoking a cigar. Nobody saw any of them come out. That doesn't mean they didn't, of course, only that no one saw them."

"I see."

The detective consulted a notebook pulled from his coat pocket. "It's my understanding that the premises were used for the storage of furs and that the processing material is notoriously flammable. Is that correct?"

"It is."

"Fourteen people died in that fire, Mrs. Garrick. Here, don't do that! Put your head down for a minute . . ." When Irene had recovered, he went on, "If your brother and his friends caused that fire and if he survived, he may be guilty of criminal negligence. That's a manslaughter charge. If they caused the fire deliberately—say, to collect insurance or to cover up something—it's murder. So, you see, it's important for us to find out just where he is."

Irene was still feeling shaky and faint. A scheme to collect the insurance? Dear Lord above, she'd never even thought of that, but Teo might have. Yes, it was the sort of thing that might occur to him, she realized now. How could she have been so stupid in her judgment of him?

"He must have died in the fire," she said, and felt awful because it wasn't so much an assumption as a hope.

"Possibly. We'll have people going through it as soon as the ashes cool, but even then it may not be possible to tell. It was an unusually fast, hot fire and you must realize identification will be difficult. You're not going queasy on me again, are you, ma'am? Now, can you think of anything to tell me about your brother's possible whereabouts?"

"I know less than you," Irene said, and then in a burst of candor and bitterness brought about by nerves added, "My brother is very much inclined to come home for help. I think I would have heard from him by now if he'd escaped the fire. Now, If you'll excuse me . . ."

"Are you ill? Do you want help?"

"Please, ask my secretary in the outer office to have a car brought around to take me home. I'm not well."

At this, he became solicitous, apparently feeling he'd shaken her into the state he'd intended. In a few minutes Irene and Clara were on their way home, Irene leaning heavily on her friend. Clara started to ask a question in the car, but Irene gestured at the driver and shook her head. Clara helped Irene up the steps, but once inside the door, Irene threw off her faintness. "Upstairs, quickly!" she said quietly, dragging Clara along. "They want to charge him with manslaughter or murder if he survived. I'm certain he didn't, but just the same, they might come snooping around here. We have to search his room before they do."

They found what they wanted right away. In with an astonishingly large and tasteless collection of silk socks Clara found a packet of pawnshop claim tickets. "Clara, take them to the office. We'll have some calls this morning if the newspaper account mentions that Neptune et Cie stored furs there. Customers will wonder about their coats. Tell anyone who calls that it's too soon to tell—say the ledgers are kept at the bank or something. I'll stay here for now and talk to Mama and the girls. Then I'll come back to the office and we'll get busy reclaiming. Thank heaven we hadn't yet bought Teo's tickets to Barcelona. The police might have found out and assumed we were involved." She shuddered.

She called her mother and sisters together in the music room, wondering how in the world she could break the news to them. When they arrived, she had decided on simple but highly edited honesty. "Mama, I'm afraid I have very bad news. There was a fire in Teo's warehouse last night. The police think he was inside and perished in the fire."

Zofia stared at her for a very long time, tears gathering in her eyes and spilling over soundlessly for a minute before she bent forward and started keening. Lillie and Cecilia fell into each other's arms, weeping as loudly as their mother, and Stefania started great blubbering sobs. Irene went to Zofia and put her arms around her mother. "Mama, I'm sorry. I'm so sorry. I wish there was something I could do." There was, of course, a chance he might still be alive, but it was a slim chance and she was almost afraid to mention it for fear Zofia would cling to the idea hopelessly for years.

"You never liked Teo!" Stefania wailed.

"Of course I did, Stefania. I loved Teo. I'm as much his little sister as you are. Now, stop that carrying on and help Mama. Get her a clean handkerchief, and you, Cecilia, go fix some hot tea with plenty of sugar like Mama likes. Lillie, you call the doctor and ask him to stop by and see Mama. Also the priest."

She was grieving too. For the rest of them, Teo had died as he'd lived in their minds—their handsome, beloved "man of the family." For Irene, he'd died twice in the last day. Once when she'd discovered the truth of his character—or rather, lack of character—and again in the fire. She should have realized what he was like long before; she was generally a good judge of character. But she'd chosen not to because she wanted to believe he was grand and noble. She needed to believe that. Oddly enough, that death of belief was harder for her to accept than the physical removal of him from their lives.

She stayed with them for another hour, until the priest had prayed with them and the doctor had given Zofia a sedative and put her to bed. When she had them settled, she dashed back to the office. "Monsieur Neptune has been asking for you," Clara said.

Irene went into his office, taking Clara along to engage Miss Troutwhite in a loud conversation that prevented her eavesdropping while she explained to Monsieur what had happened. She told him the whole truth. "And you have the pawn tickets?" he asked after listening to the account with apparent calm. "Give me some of them and I'll help."

"I would appreciate that, monsieur, but please keep careful track of what it costs you, and I will assume the expense. Clara insists this isn't my fault, but I realize now that I never got your permission to farm out coats to my brother. I shouldn't have made that decision on my own."

Neptune nodded, pleased that she saw her error. But before

he could comment, Chandler came in. "Uncle! Have you seen the paper? . . . Oh, Mrs. Garrick, you're here. How many of our furs were in that warehouse?"

"We don't know yet," Irene said.

Neptune was on his feet. "Chandler, we're on our way to look into that now. Can you hold the fort here?"

"Without any information? Not very well. The papers implied that there was something questionable about the fire. One even mentioned the possibility of arson. Just where are you dashing off to? The records right here in the office ought to tell you which coats are missing."

Neptune looked questioningly at Irene. After a moment of indecision, she nodded bleakly. "Chandler, there's something you should know," Neptune said.

Irene told him. "Mr. Moffat, my brother—" she began.

"Brother? What has a brother to do with this?"

"Teo Kossok, the man who ran that storage business, is—was—my brother. I set him up, and it now appears that he pawned the coats in his care—"

"Pawned!" Chandler was shocked. "Oh, Christ! That's the lowest trick in the business. Lord, if anyone finds out, we're ruined! Even if we returned the cost of the coats to all of them, imagine if one of their maids or poor relations bought the very same coat in a pawnshop. It could happen, and it will absolutely destroy the trust—"

"Chandler, quit gabbling like a turkey! If you're so concerned, you can help us," Neptune said.

"We have the pawn tickets," Irene explained. "We're going out to try to reclaim the coats. In the meantime, you've got to hold people off. Clara has been telling callers that our records are kept in the bank and we'll know what was lost by tomorrow. And we will, if we can stop talking and get on with our search."

"Did your brother do this on purpose? Start the fire to cover his crime?"

"I don't know. He's missing. Presumably he died in the fire, and I doubt he would have deliberately gone that far to fool anyone," Irene said tartly.

"Oh, I say! I didn't know he was there. The papers didn't mention that," Chandler said, clearly embarrassed at having appeared so unfeeling in front of his uncle. Not that he cared in the least what happened to Teo Kossok; he'd never even met the man. Dammit all! Much as he'd like to see Irene Garrick roast over her own fire, it would be extremely foolish not to cooperate. If there was so much as a hint of hanky-panky on the part of Neptune et Cie, it would severely damage the reputation of the firm, and that would harm him as much as any of them. "I'll take care of it," he said grimly. *And I'll take care of you yet, Mrs. Garrick!* his look added.

She recognized the message, but hadn't the time to deal with it now. Leaving Chandler in charge, she and Clara and Neptune went to her office to split up the pawn tickets and set out.

Miraculously, they located all but three coats, a hat, and a muff. None of the coats was of enormous value. "I'll pay for them myself," Irene told Neptune when they met back in the office that evening. "I don't think it would be wise to attempt to make an insurance claim for them."

"No, we don't want to encourage the insurance company to look too closely into the matter. I'll call them tomorrow and assure them that we had already transferred all the goods to another warehouse before the fire. I'll say we managed to find a building with lower rents and were going to sell this one. Of course, they'll wonder why we didn't insure the other building with them, but I'll think of something."

"Monsieur, I'm grateful for your help. And I'm even more grateful to you for not telling me what a fool I've been."

"I did not think there was a need to," he said with a fond smile. "No, my dear, I understand how it is—family loyalty."

They both knew he was referring to Chandler. Though Chandler was presumably more honest than Teo, he certainly wasn't much more likable—at least not as far as Irene was concerned.

"Monsieur, you look very tired. Let me drop you off on my way home. My driver is waiting."

"I'm not the least tired!" he barked, his mellowness of a moment before gone. "I've got work to do here. Get along!"

She went, but with reluctance. Not only did she dislike

leaving him alone, she didn't relish her own companionship. So far, she'd had mercifully little time to reflect on the loss of her brother. She'd been too busy sorting out the mess his actions had caused. And now she had to go back to the house, to a house of mourning, to a long, silent night.

It was dark when she got home. The chauffeur helped her out of the car. "Go home and take tomorrow off," she told him. "It's been a very long day."

"Thank you, ma'am. I'll see you to the door."

"No need. Good night."

The light above the front door was out, and as she fumbled in her bag for a key, she made a mental note to remind the housekeeper to get it fixed. It was late and she didn't want to rouse anyone to let her in, but she was having trouble finding her key in the dark. She'd just located it when a hand reached out from the big bushes that flanked the front door and clamped over her mouth.

For the first second she was frozen with fear and confusion; then Teo hissed, "Don't make any noise! It's me."

The hand came away and she whirled to look at him. He was a mess, his tie gone, his suit dirty and torn. "Teo! What happened to you?"

"Do you mind if we don't stand here and talk?"

"Oh . . . Oh, yes. Wait."

She went in and took a quick, quiet tour of the house to make sure everyone was asleep. Zofia was tossing restlessly, but the girls were sleeping soundly and there was nothing but peaceful snoring from the servants' quarters. Irene went back and let Teo in, taking him to the kitchen. It was the cook's night off and they wouldn't be heard or disturbed there.

Teo sat at the table, head in hands, while she made them some coffee and fixed him a sandwich. She kept darting glances at him as she worked. The change was awful. All the brash confidence and slick self-assurance were gone. He was tired, hungry, and scared, and it showed in the slump of his shoulders and the slight trembling of his hands. He must have been crouched in those bushes all evening, maybe all day as well.

She was quiet while he gulped down the sandwich, and waited until he was blowing on his coffee to ask, "Teo, did you do it on purpose? Set the fire?"

"Are you crazy? Why would I do that?"

"To cover up the fact that you'd pawned the coats."

"I was gonna get them back. I had a nice run of luck going. It's not a bad idea, Sis, letting the insurance company pay for the stuff, but if I was going to do that, I sure as hell wouldn't let myself get caught in the middle of it. I damned near killed myself crawling out a back window when the place went up. I mean, one minute we was sitting around playing cards, then Louis tossed this cigar and whoosh! Everything turned orange! Scared the shit out of me, I can tell you."

"You'd been warned repeatedly not to have any smoking materials— "

Food and talk were rapidly restoring his brashness. "Yeah, yeah, I know what you're gonna say," he said. "I've heard it till I'm sick of it. Anyway, it didn't really matter. I mean, I'd hocked all the stuff, so its's safe."

"Teo! Fourteen people died! Innocent people *died!* It doesn't matter about the coats, but what about those people?"

"Aww, they were nobodies. Just a bunch of poor immigrants. Nobody'll ever miss them."

Irene's stomach was churning. She edged closer to the sink, afraid she was going to be sick. "Teo, listen to yourself! You don't know what you're saying. I . . . I saw a baby die. Its father threw it out the window to save it."

"That's not my fault!"

"But it is! You caused the fire."

"Not on purpose."

"Oh, Teo . . . how can you? And what about Mama and the girls? I had to tell Mama about it, and I thought you were dead. She's grieving terribly."

"So what? She'll get over it."

"Not if she knew the truth."

"Sure she would. Mama thinks I'm a god."

"*Not anymore*."

"Mama!" Irene cried. "I thought you were asleep!"

Zofia was standing in the doorway, her gray hair in frazzled braids, her face as pale as her white nightdress. She shook a finger at Teo and said, "You are bad boy. Bad man! God forgive me for bringing you into this world to be so wicked. That I should live long enough to atone for being mother to such a man! I hear all you say and I am sick in my heart."

"Now, Mama, you don't mean that," he said cajolingly.

"Yes, this I mean. From this minute, you are dead. I have no son. I never had no son. Go away, Teo!"

His face hardened. "I'm not going away. You think I'm going to give up all I've got here? Our little Irina wouldn't like to have me out roaming around telling what I know about her."

"Teo, what you know about me isn't half as damaging as what we know about you," Irene said. "The police want you for the murder of those people."

"What!"

"You heard me. Murder."

"What am I going to do?" he asked, suddenly deflated.

"Face it, I suppose," Irene said bleakly.

"No!" Teo and Zofia cried together, and Zofia went on, "Irina, you cannot have people know what he has done. All my friends, they will say Zofia is such a bad mother she raised a murderer. Aieee! How could I live? How could I ever show my face in church again? All parishioners will point and pity."

"Mama, he can't just walk away from what he's done."

Zofia stumbled across the room and grasped Irene's shoulders. "My daughter, I have been wrong. I have said bad things to you many times. But you are my best. You are good girl . . . "

Irene felt her breath clog. How long she'd waited, how desperately she'd longed for her mother's love and appreciation. But why did it have to be this way, now?

"But, Irina, don't do this to us. Don't tell the police. They will take pictures and tell people in the papers what a bad man is Teo Kossok."

"Mama, he *is* a bad man!"

"Yes, yes. You are right. But people, they will say we are bad too. Who will marry your sisters if their brother is a murderer? How to make them marriages that way? Irina, nobody should know our shame. Enough that God should know. Let God give the punishment in the next life."

"Oh, Mama, I don't know what to do."

"Then ask Clara, your friend. Clara is of good sense. She will tell you I am right."

"Yes, I'll call Clara!" Irene seized on the suggestion. She was exhausted and sickened by the situation, beyond being able to know what was right or wrong anymore. Clara could tell her, help her sort it out. "Teo, you stay here," she said, and looking at him, realized it was unnecessary. He was still sitting at the table looking stunned.

Though awakened from a sound sleep, Clara understood just from the tone of Irene's voice what had probably happened. Unlike Irene, she'd already speculated on what would occur in the unlikely event that Teo had survived the fire. "I'll be right there," she said, and was at the door in less than twenty minutes.

Irene silently ushered her into the big kitchen. Zofia was rolling out pie dough. Clara glanced at Irene questioningly and Irene whispered, "She does that when she's upset. It calms her nerves, I think."

Teo was still sitting tapping his spoon on the handle of his coffee cup in unwitting rhythm with the thump-thump of the rolling pin. He looked up at Clara with an expression of bored scorn.

"I see you turned up," Clara said coldly. "What are you going to do with him, Irene?"

"That's just it. I say he must turn himself in to the police, and Mama doesn't want him to."

"What would be served by turning him in?" Clara asked as calmly as though she were asking what the pie-pastry recipe was.

"Justice," Irene answered. "He must pay his debt for the death of those innocent people."

"Would that bring them back?" Clara asked.

"No, Clara. Of course not, but you can't just kill people and get away with it. Do you mean you think he should go free?"

"I think so," Clara said.

Teo spoke up. "Thanks."

Clara's calm was shattered. "Don't you thank me! Don't you dare assume I'm concerned about your welfare. I'd love nothing better than to see you hang for what you've done. For you I'd be happy to see burning and disemboweling brought back. I'm concerned only with Irene and your mother and the company."

She stepped back and closed her eyes for a moment to get a grip on her emotions, then turned away from Teo and addressed herself to Irene. "My dear, making public your connection with him would be a disaster, both personally and financially. The family name and the company name would be dragged through the mud. There are a thousand so-called journalists out there who would cheerfully tear you and your family and Monsieur to tiny shreds."

"But those people, Clara. All those people who died!"

"What would putting Teo on trial do for them? How would it help them? It wouldn't bring back the dead, it wouldn't contribute anything to healing the injured. *You* might be able to help some. See that their medical care is paid for, absorb the funeral costs, give the survivors new homes, erect a monument, anything! But don't sacrifice everything you've worked for, everything Monsieur has worked for. That would just be creating more innocent victims."

"But it's not right—"

"Right is relative, Irene. Is it right to shame your mother and sisters? Is it right to create a scandal that will eat at the very foundations of Neptune et Cie? The company is half yours, but it's also half Monsieur's."

"Oh, I wish . . ." Irene began, and then stopped. She wished Peter were here. He would know what was right, and she would happily put her mortal soul in his capable hands. But Peter was gone. He'd removed himself from her life. She must stop longing for his wisdom and love. They were no longer hers to call on. "I must think, Clara. I must have time to consider."

"There isn't time, Irene. The police are probably already watching the house to see if he turns up here. You have to get him out before daylight. They may very well decide to search the house to see what they can find." Clara didn't think this was really likely, but she wanted to force Irene to a decision.

The room was quiet. Zofia had stopped rolling pastry and was standing rigidly with her back to the rest of them, waiting to hear what Irene said. Teo had quit banging his spoon on the cup and was staring at his sister.

"Irene, there is a Polish community in Pittsburgh," Clara said. "He could make a train tonight. I still have two hundred dollars left from the money you gave me to claim the coats. Give him that. It's enough to get started in a new life with a new name."

Irene paced for a moment, then turned to Teo. "I think this is wrong. You should go to prison. For myself, I would make the sacrifice of my reputation to see you pay your debt. But I will do as Clara suggests . . ."

He stood, his hand already coming forward for the money. But Irene wasn't finished. "There are conditions, and I still might change my mind. You must never come back here—"

"Are you kidding? Why would I want to?"

"For money, of course. It's the only reason you came back here in the first place. But it must never happen again. It will never succeed again, that I promise. Also, you must never use your own name. And you must never contact Mama or ask for anything more of us."

"Well—"

"I see. Then I'll phone the police now," Irene said, heading for the telephone.

He caught up with her at the door. "Yes. Yes, all right. I'll do all that."

"Swear!"

"I swear on all that's holy."

Irene laughed bitterly. "Some oath. Nothing's holy to you, Teo. But know this and believe it: if you break your word, I'll come after you. I'll throw away everything—Mama's happiness, my own, Monsieur Neptune's, everything—to see that you get what you deserve."

She spoke with such venom and intensity that Teo's eyes widened with surprise and with the realization that she meant every word of it. As it was, he simply took the money and slunk to the door. "Good-bye, Mama," he said.

There was no answer. Only the renewed thump of the rolling pin on the pie dough. When the door closed and his footsteps echoed away, Zofia said very quietly, "You are a good girl, Irina Kossok. A good girl."

27

August 1913

Zofia's manner didn't change in ways that anyone else noticed. She didn't apply herself to becoming the wealthy, well-bred American mother Irene had always hoped to make her. But there were subtle alterations that only Irene was aware of. For one thing, Zofia all but abandoned Polish. In the past, her speech had been a hodgepodge of both languages, a word of one, a phrase of another, as the whim took her. But after that night in the kitchen with Teo, she spoke only English with Irene, even when it was difficult for her to find the exact word she wanted. More significant and certainly more subtle were the ways in which she deferred, however slightly, to her oldest daughter. Menu items that Irene seemed to enjoy appeared more frequently; Zofia reluctantly abandoned the threadbare shawl Irene despised; she stopped baking cookies every day for Stefania. Small enough things, but Irene noticed and appreciated what they meant.

They never referred to that night again, nor did Zofia ever reiterate her realization that it was Irene, not Teo, who was the best of the lot. But it wasn't necessary. She had said it once and Irene had heard it.

The police came to the house the morning after Teo's disgraceful departure. They asked questions and searched Teo's room for signs of his return or some evidence that the fire was deliberate and premeditated. But aside from having taken the pawn tickets, Irene had left the room just as Teo left it that night when he went out to play cards, so they found nothing. They repeated several times that Irene must report it to them if he returned, and one uniformed officer disappeared during the search—presumably to let the staff know they had an obligation to report anything suspicious. There was no question in Irene's mind that the maids would do exactly that, given any excuse. The Kossok family didn't exactly provoke loyalty in their employees, at least not at home.

Within a week, the worst of it was over. The newspapers lost interest, the victims were buried (at Irene's expense, with the funds disguised as an anonymous charity), the police had made their final report—two unidentified bodies, burned beyond recognition, one of them presumed to be that of Teo Kossok. The priest at St. Stanislas had a short memorial service, with only the family in attendance. Zofia wept bitter tears and Irene realized that to her mother Teo really was as dead as if his body were in a coffin before them. In some ways, it would never really be over for Irene and Zofia, who knew the ugly truth, but at least no one else but Clara and Neptune would ever know that secret.

"You don't think he'll change his mind someday?" Neptune asked when she explained what had happened.

"I don't think so. I've become more dangerous to him than he is to me. He could still hurt me socially and financially, but I could have him imprisoned."

"You wouldn't do that."

"I'm not sure," Irene said. "More important, he's not either."

But for all the confidence she showed to Neptune and Clara, Irene was deeply distraught. Teo's actions had been a devastating betrayal. He was one of them, blood of their blood, the man of the family. She had deliberately blinded herself to his faults, and he had slapped her in the face with them. He'd cared nothing for any of them, not even Mama. He'd used them, just as callously as he'd have used a stranger or an enemy. Except that a stranger or enemy wouldn't have allowed it, and the Kossoks had welcomed the opportunity.

And through that next week, when things were settling back to normal, Irene kept finding herself wishing more and more fervently that she could pour this out to Peter. He would understand her distress, and in the old days he would have cared deeply. He would have made it all right somehow. He would have listened, and then, in a way that would have lessened her despair, explained how such awful things could happen. And eventually they would have made love and laughed together, and the healing would hurry. Irene never quite understood that while she thought she was mourning Teo's perfidy, she was really mourning her loss of Peter. Twice she wrote to him and twice she threw the letters away instead of mailing them. For while she needed him, she knew he wouldn't allow himself to be summoned back, and she couldn't bear to be rejected again.

In late August they had their annual fall planning meeting. Chandler and Irene, who managed to avoid each other almost entirely, spent this day every year in Neptune's office together. Irene's responsibility was the designs they would launch their season with, and this year she was uneasy about her presentation. Not that she hadn't come up with some very good ideas, but she didn't feel there were enough, and they seemed to be just short of the innovative sparkle everyone expected of her. The last month, when she normally would have been giving her whole mind to it, had been taken up with other things. A portion of her creativity had been drained off by emotion.

Chandler's responsibilities were the business and social aspects of the fall showing. When to have it, where, whom to invite, whom to pamper, what to feed them, what parties to give in preparation. It was he who knew which duchesses and countesses and plumbing-fixture factory owners' wives would be in town, and more important, which of them had money, which had influence, and which had both.

"Lady Elizabeth Edgerton is emerging as an important force," he said. "Visiting her cousins at Fifty-eighth and Fifth for the fall and winter. I've arranged for you to be her dinner partner next Tuesday, Uncle Jacques. And on Thursday you're both dining with the VonHeusers. She's a great horsey woman, you'll have the devil of a time fixing her up so she doesn't look like a Clydesdale, Mrs. Garrick, but I think you ought to make an effort. If you can get her looking decent in a fur, you'll win over a lot of other ladies of her dimensions—and political views. They claim they're just visiting, but word is they've taken all their lovely money out of

Germany because they think there's a war coming and they didn't want it gobbled up. Now then, Mrs. Piper's two oldest daughters-in-law are showing signs of rebellion and I think the old lady is going to be working at spending her way back into their good graces this year. Her influence is waning now that there are so many grandchildren to take the family focus off her, but she still has control of the purse strings . . ."

Neptune normally took an intense interest in this process. Usually he was in the middle, arguing with Chandler's assessments, contributing his own opinions, bemoaning the costs, criticizing Irene's design ideas, defending his own, alternately predicting wild success and utter ruin with melodramatic abandon. Next to the first showing itself, this was the high point of the business year to him.

But today was different. He was subdued and seemed preoccupied with something else. He approved Irene's designs with a bland acceptance that was far more upsetting than any criticism could have been. His own contributions seemed conservative, nearly repetitive of the previous year. He didn't even ask what Chandler anticipated the first showing would cost, and once Irene caught him gazing at the stuffed animals in the cases across the room and not even listening to the discussion. Concerned, she grew quiet and Chandler's unease was evident in the increased speed and volume of his talk. The tension in the room mounted until Irene felt she could hardly breathe the thick air.

It was just the heat, she told herself. Late August in the city was no time for sensible people to be cooped up in an office talking about furs. Neptune himself had suggested that they conduct this business at his friend Jack Fisher's house on Long Island, but Chandler had an afternoon appointment in the city that made it impossible. But somehow they got through it and by three o'clock had mapped out most of the major decisions. Irene and Chandler gathered up their paperwork to leave.

She didn't actually see it happen.

She'd turned away toward the door when Jacques Neptune stood, clutched at his heart, and fell forward over his desk. She heard Chandler Moffat yelp, "Oh, I say, Uncle, what's wrong?"

By the time she turned, Neptune had began to slide backward and was making an odd keening sound. Chandler and Irene both dashed around behind the desk and eased him onto the floor. "Troutwhite!" Chandler screamed, his voice high and effeminate with fear. "Get a doctor. Quickly! Uncle's had an attack of some sort."

"Monsieur," Irene whispered . "Monsieur, please hear me. Please don't die. We need you. Please . . ."

He was writhing in pain, still making that terrible noise that would echo through her nightmares for months. Then suddenly he went quite rigid and took a huge rasping breath. His face was as blue-white as thin milk and sweat was pouring off him, drenching his clothes and making the room stink of tragedy and terror.

"Irene . . ." he said. Just that. Her name.

Then he relaxed and there were no more sounds, no words, no breathing, no struggle for life.

When the doctor arrived, Chandler was standing by the window, his eyes red, his hands trembling. Irene was sitting on the floor holding her mentor's lifeless hand and weeping quietly. The doctor knelt beside her and she said, "There's no need. He's gone." She stood slowly and noticed for the first time that Clara and Miss Troutwhite were in the room as well. Both were silently crying. "Miss Troutwhite," Irene said, "I think it would be fitting if the employees were informed of Monsieur's death and given both tomorrow and the day of the funeral off out of respect for his memory. If you will call them together, I will break the news to them in ten minutes."

"I beg your pardon?" Chandler said, coming away from the window. "It's hardly your place to start making company decisions on your own, you know."

"I am . . . was Monsieur's partner in this business," Irene said.

"And now you're mine."

"It's a bit early to be sure of that, isn't it?" Irene asked, ashamed of both of them for even discussing this in the very room where his stricken body still lay between them.

"Do you mean you think my uncle would have left any

part of his half to you? To you! Absurd. That would give you controlling interest in the company, and he'd never do that to me. In any case, he's my relative, not yours, and I'll make the announcement."

Irene hadn't the energy to argue with him. What difference did it really make who gave out the news? "Very well," she said.

Miss Troutwhite went with Chandler. Clara went to call the lawyer and cancel appointments. The doctor went to get a stretcher and some men to carry it. "Come along, Mrs. Garrick."

"No, I'll stay with him. Someone should."

"I can get someone else."

"No, I want to. Please. I'd like to."

When the doctor had gone, she went back to sit down on the floor next to her old friend. The doctor had closed his eyes and he looked at peace. Irene could almost imagine there was a hint of a smile on his lips. She folded her hands and tried to pray, but she couldn't think of the words to say to a God who could strike Jacques Neptune down. This shouldn't have been. He couldn't have just gone so suddenly like that. There hadn't even been time for parting words or last advice. Only her name, and pain and indignity. It shouldn't have happened like this. And not now, not yet. "There should have been more time, monsieur," she whispered. "You had so much more to teach me, and I have so much more to learn. What will I do without you? How will I keep going? You've left me alone. How will I bear it? Peter left me, and Teo betrayed me, and you've died. What will I do? How can I go on?"

The funeral was horrible, and yet it was everything Monsieur would probably have wished. Everyone came. Virtually all the wealth and society of New York was there. All Neptune et Cie's business associates and employees attended at well. The line of automobiles and buses hired for the employees' use stretched in a seemingly endless line. Several of his longtime friends gave short eulogies before Chandler, almost grand in his dignified and genuine grief, tossed a handful of earth onto the coffin.

To his credit, he had asked Irene if she would like to take part in the ceremony. It was a grudging offer, which she turned down. She'd said her good-byes privately and had no need to make a spectacle of herself in public. Besides, she had several good reasons for staying in the background as much as possible. First, she suspected that half the women who attended the services had really come to see her. The rumors that she was Neptune's mistress had never ceased to circulate and she suspected that there was nothing that would please some of these women more than to see her break down and throw herself into the grave—or some such melodrama. Dry-eyed and only lightly veiled, she would make one last attempt at thwarting the gossip.

Her other reason for not taking an active role was Chandler. While she'd never liked him, and heaven knew the antipathy was mutual, she didn't wish to create any more hard feelings than already existed between them. The lawyer had informed them that he wanted their attendance at the reading of Neptune's will that afternoon, and Irene felt quite certain that by evening she would *be* Neptune et Cie. Monsieur would certainly have left Chandler enough interest in the company to provide him with a generous income, but he wouldn't yoke them together equally by leaving Chandler his whole half-share in the business.

That was going to be a severe blow to his nephew and Irene had no wish to make it any worse than necessary. She disliked him mainly because he disliked her, not because of any real faults she could find in him. He was pleasant, at least to other people, could be amusing, and often made downright intelligent and useful observations. She'd promised herself she'd keep him on in whatever capacity he chose to serve the business. He was, after all, very skilled at what he did.

Moreover, she owed it to Monsieur to be as good as she could to his nephew. Monsieur, like her, had a very protective interest in his family—or rather, his wife's family, since he had none of his own. If Jacques Neptune could tolerate Chandler's expenditures and silly pomposity, then so could Irene Garrick for Neptune's sake. After all, Neptune had put up with her involving Teo in their business, when he certainly must have seen the error of it. But family was family. In that, she and Neptune had thought as one.

So she stood aside, nearly faint with the heat and her own sorrow, and let Chandler Moffat bury his uncle with all the considerable ceremony he could muster. And when it was over, she accepted the overflow of condolences in a brisk, businesslike manner that she knew some felt was cold and unfeeling. When she and Clara got back to her car, Edward VanCleve was there holding the door open for her. "Thank you for coming, Edward," she said. "Monsieur would have been pleased to know you were here." It was a line she'd repeated with variations several dozen times that morning.

"I didn't come for his sake. I came for yours," he replied. "Is there anything I can do for you?"

He seemed to really mean it. "No, but thank you for offering, Edward."

"You don't get off that easily," he said with as much of a smile as was acceptable at such an occasion. "I'm going to keep on asking until you think of something for me to do. You might as well apply your mind to it now. A picnic, a ride? I write a marvelous thank-you note if you need help responding to all the flowers."

"That really is nice of you, Edward. I appreciate it, but all I want right now is to put this all behind and get back to normal."

She remembered later having said that and wondered why she didn't sense then that nothing was to be "normal" for a long time to come. In fact, that day was the beginning of a long, slow turn in her life—not a single change, but a series of alterations in the course she thought was to follow. The first came about that afternoon when she and Chandler met with Edwin Ellis, Neptune's lawyer. They sat on the two sofas that flanked the fireplace in Neptune's study, just where she and Peter had been the time Neptune invited them to dinner to look them over before giving her a job. Irene couldn't help thinking how far she'd come from that innocent girl. And she wished she could reach out now and hold Peter's hand as she had then.

Chandler offered her sherry, secure in his role as host in his late uncle's home, soon to be his own, most likely. Though he had expressed an absolute assurance that he would be his uncle's only heir, he was apparently suffering second thoughts. He kept licking his lips, twirling his glass, and tapping his foot. Such little feet on a portly man, Irene thought. The better for dancing around society. She *would* be gracious to him, no matter how badly he might behave over this. She owed that to Neptune's memory.

Mr. Ellis had arranged with the butler to set up a lovely Louis Quatorze desk between the sofas, and on this he laid out several stacks of paperwork. With a sigh he began: "As you see, this is all rather complex. I've had copies made of the will for each of you for your records, and you may look them over or have another attorney look them over at your convenience. In the meantime, I would prefer to merely explain the terms of the will to you in layman's language rather than read all the way through. Is this satisfactory to both of you?"

Irene and Chandler looked at the fat stack of documents he'd handed them and nodded their agreement. They could be here all night if he read them, and might still fail to grasp the essentials.

"First, I have a sealed envelope for Mrs. Garrick. Neither I nor any of my staff know its contents. Monsieur Neptune brought it in several months ago when this most recent will was drawn. I should imagine you would prefer to open it in private, Mrs. Garrick."

She didn't like the implication. His tone seemed to hint at something personal and possibly indecent, but this wasn't the time to get into a verbal duel with him. She accepted the envelope and put it into her handbag. She was dying of curiosity, but wouldn't give Ellis or Chandler the satisfaction of seeing her reaction to whatever it contained.

Ellis shuffled papers and cleared his throat. "Now, this house, which is fully paid for, and all its contents are to be your property, Mr. Moffat. There is a special account set aside which contains the next year's salaries for the domestic staff. Should you terminate anyone's employment before that time, you are required to pay the balance in the account. I am instructed to handle this account until it is paid out. The interest on the balance is yours and I will turn it over to you each quarter—''

''Yes, yes,'' Chandler said impatiently.

''There are several other items listed specifically as going to you, Mr. Moffat. Monsieur's town car, some family jewelry, and so forth. Those items are listed on page seven. As for Neptune et Cie, Monsieur owned an interest equal to Mrs. Garrick's. This equal interest is to go entirely to Mr. Moffat.''

''What?'' Irene gasped.

''Good old boy!'' Chandler crowed. ''I knew he'd do it.''

''Please! Please, allow me to finish. Monsieur knew this might create . . . ah, a difficult situation, and so he's made provisions as to how it may be rectified, should either or both of you feel uncomfortable with the partnership.''

Irene was so stunned she hardly heard him. How could he have done this to her? All he had to do was leave her a single percent of his fifty percent. It would have made a barely perceptible dent in Chandler's income, but would have given her the control she needed. Irene Garrick and Chandler Moffat equal partners? Dear Lord! She disliked him only marginally less than he disliked her.

''The first condition is that neither of you may sell your half without full agreement of the other partner, nor without first offering the same or better terms to the other partner,'' Ellis was going on. Irene forced herself to pay attention. ''As for selling out to each other, either partner may set a price, which is then to be considered either a selling or buying price.''

''I beg your pardon?'' Irene said.

''Allow me to imagine an example. If you should wish to purchase Mr. Moffat's half of the business, for instance, you would ask him to set a price. Let us say, just as an example, that he said he would sell for half a million dollars. You would then be entitled to buy his interest for that amount. If you chose not to purchase, however, you could instead demand that he purchase your share at the price *he* set—the half-million. If, in reverse, you wished to sell your half, you would tell him the price you wanted and offer it to him. He could either pay your price or require that you purchase rather than sell at that amount."

Irene and Chandler looked at each other, each trying to figure out all the implications. Neptune had, it seemed, truly bound them together even more than they had first realized.

"It's a little unusual, but not unheard-of," Edwin Ellis was saying. "In many ways, such an arrangement is very useful. The conditions prevent either party from asking an unrealistically high amount for fear he himself may end up having to pay it. On the other hand, if one party offers to buy at a deflated value, he or she may end up forced to sell short. It is complex, but probably the fairest way to bind a partnership. Naturally, the best way to avoid any problems is for you each to hold your half and work together for the common good. Now, in the case of irreconcilable difference of opinion on business decisions . . ."

They both looked at him sharply. Having absorbed the gist of the previous conditions, they were both already thinking of that very likely possibility.

"Monsieur Neptune has laid out suggested guides for who should make decisions at different areas of operation. This isn't binding, of course, and I believe it reflects what you normally attend to. Mrs. Garrick purchases the furs and provides the designs and manages the design staff. Mr. Moffat arranges for showings and so forth. But should something come up that you simply cannot agree on, you are to apply to me for arbitration."

"You don't know the fur business!" Irene said, more abruptly than she intended.

"I don't. That's true. But I hadn't finished what I was saying. You apply to me for arbitration and I will find a panel of three knowledgeable judges, individuals who do know the fur business, but who no longer have any potential of gain from decisions made by Neptune et Cie."

"In other words, air our dirty linen, should there be any," Chandler said grimly.

"And give away the secrets of any innovations either of us has in mind," Irene added.

"I'm afraid that's what it would amount to. Any specialized business is its own small world. Even retired furriers are in touch with one another and are bound to talk."

Chandler started laughing, a strained, high-pitched laugh. "Well, Irene, he's managed it. He's tied us up in the same sack, thrown us in the river, and forced us to swim or sink together. I wouldn't have thought it was possible, but the old bastard managed it just like he's managed to get everything else he ever wanted. Uncle Jacques, are you up there listening? You've won, old boy. You've accomplished the impossible!"

In spite of her distress, Irene started laughing too—not from amusement, but from pure tension. She felt herself on the brink of full-blown nervous hysteria. Both men stared at her, alarmed as men are around women who are going to pieces. She managed to pull back barely in time.

She took one last look around the room. She'd certainly never be here again, now that it belonged to Chandler. They would work together and they would remain as outwardly amiable as they'd been in Neptune's presence when he was living. In fact, he would always be with them both, watching over them through that damned will. Oh, yes, they'd stay partners and they'd get along so well that nobody but their nearest and dearest would ever suspect their true feelings. But the only thing they would ever really agree on was their resentment for the way Jacques Neptune had bound them to each other.

Why had he done this to her? she kept wondering over and over as she rode home. By the time she arrived at the front door, she was in an unspeakable state of anger and nerves and just plain hurt feelings. He, like Teo, had betrayed her. He hadn't trusted her with control. She had failed as a wife, failed as a sister, and failed as a business partner.

She went to her room and took off the sweat-soaked black dress and lay down on the bed, hoping for a cooling breeze. But there wasn't any breeze and there wasn't any peace. Her mind darted and careened like a bird trapped in a barn. Peter, Teo, Monsieur. All had failed her . . . or had she failed them? Was there something terribly wrong with her that made everything she touched turn bad? She considered herself an honorable person. She always tried to do what was best, even when it meant self-sacrifice. And yet she'd lost the three important men in her life.

Peter. Teo. Neptune.

She sat up in bed. Neptune was dead; Teo might as well be; but Peter—Peter had said he would always love her. She hadn't believed it, but maybe it was true. He'd said there was a chance for them if things changed. Had they? She didn't know what sort of change he meant. Perhaps it had happened and she wasn't aware of it.

She needed Peter. She had needed him ever since the day he'd left, but she suddenly felt she couldn't exist another day without him. Peter would understand. He was stability and good sense and generosity and intelligence. He could make sense of what was happening to her life, where she was going wrong, how to make it right again. At the core of her being there was a vast empty space where he used to be. If only she could wrap her life back around him . . .

She got up and paced the room, trying to sort this out. Was it right? Could it work? What if he sent her back, turned away from her again? He couldn't. God wouldn't let that happen to her. She threw on a fresh dress and dumped some necessities in a small suitcase. She'd go to Peter. Swallow her stupid pride and go to him. Somewhere she had run off the track. She hadn't figured out just where or how, but it would be all right once she was back with Peter. They'd start over. They'd be as happy as they once were, and she wouldn't feel empty and lost anymore.

In the end, she waited until morning to leave, not because she had any doubts, but because she felt it would be extremely inconsiderate to drag the chauffeur out of bed to drive all night. But as early as she could, she summoned him, asking her mother to give Clara a message that she'd be gone for a few days, but not to worry. Zofia guessed her daughter's destination, but she didn't ask for confirmation.

It was a pretty little town, a romantically rural setting. How happy they would be here for the next few days. Irene gave the chauffeur the street address, which she remembered from the letters she'd written and never mailed. "Shall I go to the door, Mrs. Garrick?" he asked.

"No, just wait a moment until I'm sure there's someone home." She went up the walk a bit unsteadily and knocked. Her mouth was dry. What would she say to him first? Would they make love that afternoon or would they have to talk first? She felt a shiver of anticipation and then the warmth of a blush. She waited what seemed like years, then knocked again. In a moment it was opened by a young man she'd never seen before.

"I'm . . . I'm looking for Peter Garrick," she said.

"At this address?" the man said. "Oh, he must have had the house before I did. I moved in at the beginning of summer term. Maybe he moved to a boardinghouse or something here in town."

"Oh dear . . . how could I find him?"

"Well, I'd start at the post office. They must have a forwarding address for him. It's that little brick building just down there at the corner."

She knew then that this was going wrong, but she didn't realize how wrong until she put her question to the large woman behind the counter at the tiny post office. "Peter Garrick? Hmmm. I don't recall having occasion to forward anything, but I must have a record here. Yes, an address in Chicago. Shall I write it down for you, miss?"

"Chicago? Illinois? How long has he been there?"

"This notice is dated last May, end of spring term. I remember him. He was a teacher here, wasn't he? I imagine he got another job. They do that, move around a lot when they're young. Then they settle in someplace and you couldn't get them out with dynamite. We've got some old fellas here who look like they came over on the *Mayflower*, if you ask me."

"Thank you," Irene said weakly.

With a short stop for lunch and to allow the chauffeur to attend to the automobile's needs as well as his own, they turned around and went back. Concerned and perplexed at this seemingly pointless journey, he kept looking back at her in the rearview mirror. Irene held back the tears and gazed unseeingly at the landscape.

That he wasn't there was horribly disappointing, but the fact that he hadn't been there for months was downright shocking. All that time she'd been believing he was only a few hours away if she needed him. And now, when she did need him so terribly, he was gone. She hadn't gotten the address in Chicago. She should have done that. No, she shouldn't. What difference did it make? She'd never, ever put herself through this again. Never. It was too cruel for words. It was as if he'd left her all over again, only this time it was even more painful than the first. She hadn't believed that was possible.

She was nearly back to New York City, rummaging in her handbag for a fresh handkerchief, when she discovered the envelope Edwin Ellis had given her from Neptune. The revelations of the reading of the will and her subsequent insane dash after Peter had caused her to forget about it. Lethargically, no longer caring very much what was in it, she pried open the stiff seal.

Inside were a number of smaller envelopes. Inside the first was a deed of sale on the Long Island house. Seller: Jack Fisher. Buyer: Irene Garrick. Attached to this was a list of the employees, their length and conditions of service and their wages, as well as a key. He'd given her his secret hideaway and he'd done it several months ago, according to the date on the document. In the second envelope there was a bank statement showing an account in her name in a city bank. The balance was $100,000. The third small envelope was a letter:

My dearest Irene,

I'm certain as you read this you're despising me for what I've done to you under the terms of my will. I don't suppose you'll understand my reasoning, but I feel I must explain. I could give you control of the business. I think you are, with good cause, expecting me to do so. I know you would treat Chandler with fairness and run the company to the best of your very considerable abilities.

But doing that would destroy Chandler's personal pride. I can see you raging at that remark! I know he has far too much of that commodity already, but it's important to someone who has nothing *but* pride to fall back on. You and I have talent and arrogance. He hasn't.

We also have ambition, and that's dangerous to everyone near us. We're willing to make sacrifices for what we feel must be done, even if that sacrifice has to be made by others as well as ourselves. But the others sometimes can't afford to give up what we expect them to. I didn't understand this until the last year or so. You probably don't grasp it now. You'd do this to Chandler. You wouldn't mean to, you wouldn't realize you were doing it, but you would.

I can't let that happen to him. God only knows why, but I feel an obligation to him. An obligation to protect him from you. I know that sounds critical and I hope someday you'll understand that I don't mean it to hurt you. I know you'd never deliberately harm anyone—but people like us tend to wreak disaster.

Is this just the nonsensical ramblings of an old man? Perhaps. I prefer to consider it the wisdom of age.

Irene, my dear, I couldn't say this to you in person, but here and now I must: I love you more than I've ever loved anyone. My life has been fulfilled and graced by loving you. A thousand times I've cursed fate that we weren't born closer together in years so that I might have had a chance to have that love returned in kind. I have one more thing to give you that I think will say everything else there is to say. It's in the basement of the house on Long Island.

With love,
J.N.

Irene folded the papers, carefully returned them to the envelope. The chauffeur glanced back. She cleared her throat and put on a strong voice. "Do you remember how to get to the house where Monsieur had the party last spring? . . . Good. Take me there, please. Then you may leave me and take a few days off."

Spent, she leaned back against the lush upholstery and allowed herself the luxury of sleeping the rest of the way.

"Your name is Iverson, isn't it?" she asked the butler who opened the door. "You were at the funeral."

"That's correct, madam. May I take your bags?"

"In a moment, Iverson. We have some matters we must discuss. I understand you've been in charge here for a number of years. Monsieur obviously had great trust and faith in you."

"I was fearful sorry when he died, ma'am."

"I know you were. So were all of us who loved him. I presume you were employed by 'Jack Fisher.' "

"In person, ma'am."

"Then we share that secret. Monsieur has left me this house. I hope you will stay on and honor my own desire to keep my ownership as private as Monsieur did his. Now, I'd like a few days, perhaps a week, to myself, and I imagine you might enjoy a short vacation as well. I've written you a check as a salary bonus which ought to provide for it." She was astonished at herself, managing to act and sound quite normal when her mind was in such turmoil.

Iverson looked at the check. "That's far too generous, ma'am."

"No, it's not. Iverson, I don't wish to be disturbed, but I'm not very much of a cook anymore. I wonder if you could arrange to have someone come in with some simple groceries and set out a cold luncheon once a day. Here is another check for that. Now, if you'll just leave me instructions for who I might call on locally in case of an emergency—plumbing gone wrong or the like—and show me where the entrance is to the basement, you can get on with your preparations for vacation. Oh, yes, I'll want to write letters to my secretary and my mother, if you'd be so kind as to mail them as you go . . . ?"

She went to bed that night without having investigated the

basement. Whatever was down there could wait, and she had a superstitious reluctance to find out. It was to be her last communication from Monsieur and she wanted to wait as long as she could for that oh-so-final act. She was half-afraid of what she might find. Everything she had anticipated lately had gone so terribly sour.

Iverson had done all he was asked and had departed for his sister's home in the Bronx. Not Irene's idea of the ideal vacation, but he seemed eager and grateful for the opportunity. She undressed, put on a light nightgown, and went to bed. It was claustrophobically quiet here. Over the years she'd become thoroughly accustomed to the constant noise of the city, and the utter stillness was disconcerting. It was also extraordinarily dark; no streetlights, no headlights, and tonight not even moonlight. It was like being in a cave with nothing to distract her from her thoughts.

But she was determined not to think, not about herself. What she wanted was a week to vegetate mentally—sleep, eat, breathe fresh air. Nothing else. She needed to clear her mind, and perhaps some understanding just outside her conscious grasp would come to her. Think cool thoughts, she told herself. She fell asleep trying to remember how it used to feel to make snow angels on the roof of the house back in the village when she was a little girl.

She awakened to the sound of birds. Dozens of them. If only she'd brought along that old bird-identification book Clara had given her years ago. It would be relaxing and mindless to just sit outdoors and see how many she could recognize. It would effectively occupy her mind with harmless things, not the despairing memories that kept invading like bats, streaking in, black and silent, when she let down her guard.

She took a bath, then, content that she was alone in the house, roamed around in her underwear from bedroom to bedroom looking for something comfortable to wear to take a walk. As she suspected, Neptune had kept a good supply of extra clothing for guests who might arrive unprepared for country life. She found a pair of boots that were only a little too big, and some riding breeches that just fit. An oversize man's shirt completed the outfit. She went back to her room to do her hair and realized there was no need. After all these years of so rigorously training herself always to be the proper lady, she'd been given a short reprieve. She merely braided it into two long plaits to keep it from blowing in her eyes and set out.

It was a large estate. The deed said twenty acres and Irene hadn't realized how much area that was. She climbed a small rise and lay in the grass for a while watching seagulls wheel overhead, and fell back asleep in the sunshine. When she woke, she was starving and sweating and itched with a dozen bug bites. Irritated, sunburned, and sleep-stupid, she went back to the house. As she'd hoped, the unseen cook had done her job. At least one plan had gone as it was supposed to. There was a minced-ham sandwich, some pickles, hard-boiled eggs, and a thermos flask of hot coffee on the kitchen table.

She ate slowly, trying to concentrate on tasting each bite, but finally she'd finished every last crumb and drop. She had drawn out the time as long as she could. In spite of her deliberate attempts to relax, her tension had merely grown and she found herself chewing on a fingernail, a habit she hadn't indulged since childhood. She cleaned the table, washed her hands, and went slowly down the basement steps.

It was a clean, well-lighted room, and the first thing she was aware of was the mechanical hum from the north corner. There was some sort of machine down here. Turning on another light, she followed the sound. Set in the corner there was a closet-size cold safe, and the hum was the refrigeration unit. She pulled open the heavy door and closed her eyes for a moment at the outrush of cool, dry air. Then she looked. Hanging on hooks around the small room were sables. Dozens of them.

Crown sables.

She took down one bundle and studied it. They were the best pelts she'd ever seen. Lustrous, thick, and a deep, dense brown, almost black. She took down another bundle and another and another. Perfectly matched. Nearly enough of them for a full-length, full-styled coat. It must have taken years, possibly decades, for him to collect such a set. All that time, probably before he even knew her, he was searching out these pelts, caring for them, saving them for someone. For her.

She sat down on the floor, cuddling the pelts like a child, and buried her face in them. The clean fresh smell triggered a flood of memories—the first time she'd touched such pelts, when she was just starting to learn the business. What hopes she had had then. How confident that she would *be* somebody! The future had stretched out gloriously before her then. But this—this absolute misery she was drowning in—this was what she'd made of her future! She had more money than she'd dreamed existed. She had rich, powerful acquaintances who considered her an equal. But she'd lost more than she'd gained.

Suddenly all the sorrow and hurt she'd been damming up burst through and spilled over. "We were wrong, monsieur, both of us. I'm not the *crème de la crème*. I don't deserve crown sables. I'm a f-f-failure. All I've tried so hard to do right has been wrong. Oh, monsieur, monsieur, why did you have t-t-to die? I'm losing everyone. Everything."

She wept herself into exhaustion and fell into a tortured sleep there on the floor. It wasn't so much a sleep as a state of temporary escape. When she woke, it was starting to get dark outside and one of the basement lights had burned out. She was disoriented. Gradually she remembered, and the practical streak in her soul reasserted itself. She got up and put the pelts back, checking the temperature of the cold safe, carefully brushing the dust off the furs and drying those she'd dampened with her tears. Salt was damaging to the fiber. She shouldn't have cried on them. Most irresponsible. She would make a coat of them someday when she'd finished the matches. A few more, six more pelts perhaps, and there would be enough. And she'd never cry again around them. Crown sables deserved better treatment!

She dragged herself upstairs, washed her face, and made a sandwich that tasted like cardboard. She should have felt better, and in a way, she did. Her unhappiness was no longer frantic, but had gone deeper, as if she had swallowed it, absorbed it into her very cells. She knew she should get out of this house. The nice quiet week alone she'd planned would drive her mad. But she'd passed into a state of ennui.

Sleep. That was it. She could sleep some more. Sleep forever. That was an appealing idea. There were sleeping powders people took. She'd never tried them, but certainly with all the medications Monsieur had left in the house, there would be sleeping powders. She'd find them. Take enough that she could sleep for a long, long time. But she hadn't even the mental or physical energy to go look for them. She simply sat in the empty kitchen listening to the breeze that had sprung up, and the light patter of rain.

28

A pearl is a collection of rare material built on a speck of sand. Oftentimes the rare and important events of life trace back to nothing more significant than a speck of sand—a trivial incident, a forgettable moment, a meaningless action. In Irene's case, everything afterward was different because of a cat fight.

If the eerie howling hadn't awakened her at eight o'clock the next morning, she'd wouldn't have been coming down the main stairs at seventeen minutes after eight and she wouldn't have heard the knock at the door. The house was vacant and looked it. A few minutes earlier or later and the visitor would have assumed no one was there and would have gone away.

But the cats did battle outside her bedroom window and she did get up and put on her riding breeches and a fresh man's shirt, and her bare foot had just touched the bottom tread when he tapped on the door. Thinking it was someone local—a gardener, a peddler, the mailman—she opened the door. "Yes?"

"Irene? You look like a different person," Edward VanCleve said, his surprise at her outfit turning to appreciation of her natural if pale beauty. The soft shirt draping over her breasts suggested more about the grace of her figure than the bones and stays of a ball gown. Her hair, loose and tumbling in disorder, was more intimate than the simple knot she always wore. In men's clothing she was excruciatingly feminine.

"Edward, what are you doing here? How did you find me?"

"Instinct. May I come in? Actually, I had six or seven ideas of where you might have disappeared to, and I'd tried the rest of them. This was all that was left. Can you give a starving wayfarer some breakfast?"

Not knowing what else to do with him, she led him to the kitchen. "All I have is some eggs and bread—"

"That's all it takes. What are you doing here? I wasn't aware that you knew the man this place belongs to. I thought he was a friend of Neptune's."

"He is. Or was. But I'd met him too."

"An older man?"

"No, quite young. Fried or scrambled?"

"Scrambled. I'll turn on the oven for the toast. He's an admirer of yours, the owner of this house?"

She turned from the stove. "Have you come to interview me?"

"No. Sorry. Just naturally nosy. And a bit jealous."

"You needn't be." It was a double-sided remark. He could take it to mean that he had no cause for jealousy of Jack Fisher or that he was in no position to be jealous of anyone.

He cut thick slices of bread from the loaf, nursed them along in the oven, and said nothing more until they sat down with their simple meal. "What are you doing here?" Irene asked, buttering her bread.

"Seeing you. I was concerned. You looked half-dead yourself at the funeral. No, I put that badly. You looked ravishing, as always, but under a terrible strain. When I called at your office, your Miss Johnson seemed genuinely not to know where you were and appeared somewhat worried. That worried me. I guessed you might have come here. It was a lucky guess."

"Were you one of the ones waiting to see if I had hysterics at the grave?"

"I beg your pardon?"

"I'm sorry, Edward. My tongue's too sharp these days. I just felt so horribly 'on display' at the cemetery. Never mind. It was kind of you to come, but I'm fine. Really. I just need some time alone."

"Correction. I think you need some time *almost* alone. Isn't anybody here? Why are you answering your own doors and fixing your own food?"

"There's only the butler full-time, and I gave him a vacation,'' she said, and then wondered if that wasn't unwise to admit.

''I'm surprised. I mean that you know how to be alone and take care of yourself.''

She smiled enigmatically. He imagined that she'd been born into the arms of a nursemaid, been graduated to a governess, and then passed to a succession of lady's maids. If only he knew the truth! Thank God he didn't. He would be shocked if he knew that the once Irina Kossok hadn't even been allowed to look in the windows at the rich.

''You're beautiful like this—your hair down, your feet bare, in those clothes. Like someone from another time and place. Finish your eggs. You'll need your energy.''

''Why?''

''Because you're going to have to show me around. The ocean's not far. We'll go walk on a beach, shall we?''

''Yes, why not?'' It was nice to have someone tell her what to do with her day. She'd been planning—if she could be said to have done anything so positive as plan—to sleep the day away, with perhaps a bath and a meal or two for variety between naps. A walk on the beach was a better idea by far. And Edward's company was certainly an improvement over her own.

She shouldn't be doing this; that she knew full well. It was scandalous and dangerous—a day alone, completely unattended, with a man not her husband. Someone might see and recognize them. The gossip would spread faster than fire across a dry field. But in her oddly numbed state, she didn't care. All she knew was that he made her feel less miserable. The way he seemed to be absorbing her with his gaze, warming her with his smile—that was what she needed, like a starving individual needed food.

They took his open car and her hair whipped around in the wind, stinging her face and making her suspect that she was partially alive after all. They walked a crowded beach, drove a few more miles to find a less-crowded one, bought soft pretzels from a vendor, picked up seashells, and talked about nothing at all. Irene realized this last was hardest for him. He was working at suppressing the urge to ask her questions about herself. It was a compulsion with him and she vaguely appreciated the effort he had to make.

As the day wore on, they bought some fried-egg sandwiches and greasy fried potatoes and ate them in the shade of a tree. "I'm going to start clucking with all these eggs," Irene said with a laugh.

She studied the horizon, how the line between sea and sky seemed to shimmer and blend if you stared long enough at a single spot. And the smell! Why had she never appreciated how you could taste the salty tang of the air near the sea? Or the way the sun made the sand sparkle and seem to move? Seaweed was interesting and varied, she discovered, and driftwood came in shapes that were beyond human design and felt so smooth. They looked at clouds, imagining shapes in them. "A map of Selwig Island," she said of one.

He looked at her, impressed. "I have no idea what that looks like. Or where it is."

"Neither have I. I just made it up." She laughed then at her own joke, and it was as if something inside had opened up and let a little life course through her.

They rode around aimlessly for a while, seeing the sights, looking in the shop windows, commenting lazily on the weather, the passersby, a yellow dog trotting down the road. Finally, by late afternoon, Edward pulled up in front of a rural drugstore. "I need some tobacco and . . . and a razor. If I'm to stay over. I *am* going to stay over, aren't I?"

"I think you probably are," she said.

It was that easy. She knew exactly what it meant, but she didn't care. She needed his companionship now more than she needed air to breathe. He was the rope she had to cling to between sanity and despair. And if her conscience would have to pay a heavy price later, then let it. Right now she had no past or future. She had only a shaky, transient present that Edward VanCleve was holding together with his easy chatter, his flattery, his good cheer. Edward VanCleve liked her. He just liked her. He made no demands on her—none that she wasn't prepared to submit to. He made her feel pretty and irresponsible and valuable. Not valuable for what she'd done or become or wanted or worked for or given up, but simply because she existed and today was today and they were together.

They went back to the house at dusk and she showed him to his room. They both pretended without any particular effort at sincerity that he was actually going to sleep there. Separating, they bathed, changed, and met in the kitchen. The unseen cook was on her toes. Instead of a lunch, she'd left a dinner. For two. They filled their plates with cold sliced veal, potato salad, newly baked biscuits, raspberry jam and mushrooms marinated in a spicy wine sauce.

Instead of eating at the kitchen table, they carried their food and tall glasses of iced rosehip tea out onto the flagstone terrace. They'd eaten here once before—the night of Neptune's party—and the memory was with them both.

Irene had become her senses. She could discern every scent—the faint rosemary the veal had cooked with, the bouquet of the wine the mushrooms had soaked in, the heady perfume of the roses in the garden below and the geranium leaf one of them had stepped on, the faint masculine scent of the soap Edward had used. Her vision had sharpened until she saw the darkening sky as a solid blanket of stars. Every pattern of the rock in the flagstones was in high relief, every hair in Edward's eyelashes was distinct. Her perceptions had become both microscopic and telescopic.

So had her sense of touch become acute. The slightest breeze on that warm night was a wind that wrapped itself around her, caressing her bare arms, teasing sinuously through her hair. The stones were cold through her shoes, the potato salad warm through the plate. She could feel the texture of her clothing as it moved against her skin.

Edward set his plate down, turned slowly. She licked her lips, which had unaccountably gone dry. And when he reached out wordlessly and took her hand, she could feel the separate muscles and bones. "Edward!" she whispered, her voice trembling with anticipation. He put his hands on her shoulders. She was wearing a light dress, gathered around a scooped neck. He gently pushed it down over her shoulders and she shuddered with pleasure, making a strange whimpering sound.

He smiled as he slipped his hand slowly under a breast,

lifting it free of the cloth. He looked down at the firm flesh, white in the moonlight, and then slowly, so very slowly, he bent his head and barely touched the nipple with his tongue.

Irene moaned and clutched at his shirt, nearly tearing off his buttons in her need to touch him. "Here, wait. Wait. It will be all the better," he said, his voice amused but tense. He stepped back from her, but her hand stayed on him. She couldn't lose touch. He opened his shirt and she buried her face in the curling blond hair of his chest.

"Irene, how I've wanted you . . ." he whispered.

She was taking off his clothes, he was removing hers. Every new inch of skin savored, explored, kissed. Slowly they knelt, then sat, then stretched out on the cold stones. The contrast of hot, perspiring bodies and hard, dry stone was exquisite. The slight pain of hard edges of rock only intensified the glory of soft flesh. Irene closed her eyes, arched her back, presenting her breasts to his hungry lips: Her fingers found his genitals and she cupped and stroked until she thought her nerves would explode with anticipation.

Suddenly they could wait no longer. She pulled him over on her, guided him, though he needed no guiding. As he penetrated her, she cried out as though she were a virgin losing her maidenhead. But she wasn't a virgin, she was a woman who had known real love, remembered the intense pleasure of intercourse, and had been building up a long, ravenous hunger for this sensual feast. Her whole body was frigid, then searing. She wrapped her arms around him, wound her legs around him, every muscle pulsing and straining.

For those moments, she wasn't Irene Garrick. She wasn't anyone. Only an unraveled being who needed this manifestation of love—this divinely mindless, opulent, sweating, painful, awesome proof that she was fully and entirely a woman. On her, *in* her was a man who was moaning testimony to that. Every thrust, every wet, salty touch of lip to lip was validation of her existence. She was entirely alive and would remain so.

They went to her bed later and made love again, just as urgently and wordlessly as the first time. In the morning they slept late, then went to his room, which faced east, and they lay on the bed bathed in the sunshine that poured in from the balcony doors. Afterward they slept again. Wrapped in a blanket in case she ran into the phantom cook, Irene went downstairs later to bring up lunch. They nibbled more on each other than the food and ended up with crumbs in extraordinary places.

They said very little, at least very little of consequence, nothing of any real meaning. No one mentioned love, only pleasure. "That tickles . . . mmm, what a soft place . . . put your leg here, like this . . ." Such was their conversation. "Don't you have to go back to work?" "Never!" "Me neither."

Eventually it changed, as it had to. Irene's body, sated and sore, ceased to be her sole interest. Edward's curiosity, temporarily locked away, pried open the door and peeked out.

On the evening of the fourth day, she saw a bird with an interesting pattern in its wing and she thought how she could use that subtle line of light and dark in a sleeve. Perhaps sheared beaver . . .

Edward noticed the string of pearls she'd put on and asked if they were family jewels.

She made a few sketches; he remarked that his office must be wondering what had become of him. She glanced at the kitchen calendar; he drove into town to report in. The world was calling to them both, and though neither would have admitted it, both were listening to the summons.

"I have to go back tomorrow. There's a contract that must be signed or we're in danger of losing it," he said that evening. "I'll be back by dinner, though."

"The butler's due to return in the morning," she said. "We wouldn't be alone. And I have to go back too. In spite of Monsieur's death, we have a fall line to show."

"How long will it take to get the season under way?" Edward asked.

She nearly said, "Until spring," but that wouldn't do, even though it was, in a way, the truth. "I'm not sure."

"But we have to make plans," Edward said.

"What plans?"

"Why, to get married, of course. You've got to tell me the truth now. Have you really got a husband somewhere?"

"I . . . I . . . Yes."

"Then I'll get my lawyers busy on finding out the quickest way to get a divorce. They'll talk to you about possible grounds. It shouldn't take more than a couple months. I'll start looking for a house for us in the city and a house out here somewhere. We'll come out every weekend. It'll be just like this week has been. The rest of our life is going to be like this."

He'd turned as he talked, his hand up in a gesture of assurance, and for a second—just the most fleeting second—he'd looked exactly like Peter once looked. Her husband had been talking about a class he was taking. Irene didn't even remember the subject, but her eye had saved the image of Peter in that precise stance.

It was over in a flash, the gesture, the memory. But it was long enough and powerful enough to jar her. During that moment she missed Peter so much it literally took her breath away. "I have to pack," she said hurriedly. "I'll be ready in a half-hour."

But instead of packing, she went up and sat on the bed staring out the window. Divorce? Remarriage? A house in town? Impossible. What had she been doing to herself and to him this last week? She couldn't divorce Peter—Mama would die of shame. Catholic girls didn't get divorces. Ever. Even an annulment was a disgrace—though she could get one. Peter had suggested it himself. And she certainly had enough money and influence that it would present no problem. A few well-placed donations . . . Peter wouldn't care. He'd proved that by leaving her the first time and by going even farther away without even letting her know. Peter had forgotten her by now. Oh, why did that thought make such terrible pain in her heart? Why should she care anymore?

"Irene? Are you ready? I've brought the car around."

She threw her things into the bag and took a long look around the room.

* * *

She hardly spoke all the way back to the city. Edward talked. At first she let the flow of words wash over her; then she started listening and realized he wasn't saying much of anything. That was when she first appreciated the fact that he'd never said much of anything. He was funny, good-natured, and wonderful to her when he wasn't prying and questioning. But search her memory as she would, she couldn't remember a single thing he'd ever said that was of any consequence—nothing to raise questions in her own mind, to illuminate her perceptions, to inspire her. When they'd been together for short intervals earlier, she'd found him exciting and attractively dangerous. And this week, when they'd had complete sexual freedom, she'd blossomed in the light of forbidden pleasures. But what about later? Could she stand his gossipy chatter if she was sick or tired? What would they talk about when they weren't making love?

And how would he react to Zofia? That, of course, opened up a whole new line of thought. She couldn't be married to him and keep her past a secret. It had proved very nearly impossible to keep her family world apart from him. But her past, in the persons of her mother and sisters, lived with her. He'd have to know everything—about the village, the poverty, everything.

She studied his profile, his handsome, square-jawed, old-money face, and knew the expression it would have if he knew that she wasn't a Russian princess, but a common Polish peasant who'd come over in steerage and fought her way out of the Lower East Side. To have been poor, illiterate, and dirty would be, in his eyes, more unforgivable than having been a murderer.

"Why are you staring at me that way?" he asked.

She forced a smile. "No reason."

Perhaps she was being too critical. Was he really as shallow as she was assuming? Possibly. No, it wasn't that he would cease to care for her if he knew she'd been Irina Kossok. It was that he'd cease to care if he really *knew* anything about her!

That was it! She knew it as surely as she lived. He was fascinated with her for two reasons: he couldn't have her (they'd effectively negated *that* this week!) and he couldn't figure her out. She was a mystery, and his real interest was in solving it. His love—had either of them ever used the word? . . . she thought not—his affection for her was based on curiosity. Even if the story of Russian royalty were true, his interest would diminish enormously as soon as she confirmed it. If she sat here now and gave him dates, names, places, and details, by the time they reached the city, the first tendrils of boredom would have wound themselves around his heart.

Why, even making love had begun to pall with him after the first few times. She hadn't quite realized it then, thinking it was she who was losing the hot, sweet edge of her desire, but it had been him, too. Once he knew her body thoroughly, he'd become just the slightest bit perfunctory.

And if he'd tire of Irene Garrick, displaced royal cousin to the czar, think how much more quickly he'd tire of Irina Kossok, daughter of a woman who still put butter on her bread with her fingers in spite of having a thousand dollars' worth of fine silver utensils! It was almost funny, picturing Edward VanCleve and Zofia Kossok at the same table, living in the same house. She tried to imagine him as Zofia's son-in-law and failed.

According to the standards of her time and her society, she was a fallen woman now, but she knew better. She hadn't fallen, she'd risen from the ashes of her own near-fatal sense of defeat. She was ashamed of herself—not for having made love to him, but for having used him so shamelessly to save herself. She didn't love him, and though he might not have realized it yet, he didn't love her either. They didn't even know each other.

Before she formulated what to say to him, they were in town. "Leave me at the office, please," she said. "I don't want to take you out of your way."

"I wouldn't mind, but whatever you want. Shall we have dinner tonight?"

"Oh, Edward. Not tonight. I'll have so much work piled up that I don't expect I'll be able to crawl back out for days."

"All right. I'll call you tomorrow then?" Was there a hint of relief in his voice, or did she only imagine it because she wanted to?

"Tomorrow. Yes."

She went to her office, greeted Clara crisply as she passed through, and started busily sorting through things on her desk. There was even more than she remembered to be done. A note regarding the progress of the work on one of the designs for the fall show informed her that the furs had become singed during dyeing. What did she want to substitute? A company that supplied the satin linings had gone bankrupt and there were competing bids from other firms to weigh. A Revillon Frères advertisement showing a hat very like one they planned to show had been clipped and left for her to deal with. Alongside was a death notice of one of their most loyal customers—a condolence note to write to the family. An employee had been hurt falling down the stairs when the railing gave way; who was to pay the hospital bill?

She'd barely gotten started when Clara appeared at the door, arms crossed. "Where have you been this week?" she asked.

Irene looked up and found she couldn't answer. It wasn't that she didn't want to, she simply couldn't. The silence between them stretched tighter and tighter until Clara said, 'Are you all right?"

"I'm fine, Clara. Really fine."

If they'd gone back to the house on Long Island right away, things might have been very different. In spite of her realizations on the way back to the city, Irene was still—for a while—in the grip of the romantic and sensual web they'd woven together during that week. It was, after all, a delightfully sticky and wide-ranging web. Several times she'd felt herself longing for the sight, and more avidly the feel, of Edward near her. But real life imposed itself. As throughout her life, the world demanded her attention. Decisions had to be made coolly; domestic quarrels had to be settled, business choices had to be weighed, the past had to be consulted and the future guessed at, and the web of romance and sensuality quickly grew tattered in the gusts of everyday life.

That week she'd spent alone with Edward became, with astonishing speed, a memory—a lovely idyll that had no real bearing on the essential Irene Garrick. As if it had occurred years before or in another life, she began to regard it as something that *had* happened, rather than something that *was* happening. It was a fantasy, nothing more, she realized with a deep sense of sadness. It couldn't go on, any more than a colorful soap bubble could last forever simply on its own beauty. She had floated with luscious ease on a summer breeze and had now come back to earth—and it wasn't a bad place to be.

She told Edward the next week. "I can't marry you."

"Why not?"

"Because I'm Catholic. And I'm already married." That wasn't the reason, but after weighing all the alternatives, it was the justification she'd decided to stick to.

"Then what . . . ? What's to become of us?"

He sounded genuinely hurt. She took his hand across the restaurant table. "Nothing, my dear Edward. We'll remain friends, I hope. And we'll both have a lovely memory of a magic week. Think how it will warm us when we're old and gray."

"Irene, you can't mean this!"

"I do mean it."

"But did the time we had together mean nothing to you?"

"Oh, Edward, it meant everything to me. You saved my life. I know that sounds like an overstatement, but it's quite literally true. I'm more grateful to you than you'll ever imagine. I want to give you something in return. Something you won't like now, but you'll appreciate someday."

"Give me something? There's no need. Irene, I—"

"Shhh. This gift isn't in a box. I want to give you the truth, and I trust you not to give it to anyone else. Edward, I grew up in a one-room hut near Gdansk. We had a mud floor and chickens on the roof. I didn't know how to read or write until Clara Johnson taught me. She also taught me not to blow my nose on my skirt and how to wash my hair—"

"Irene, I don't know what you're trying to do, but I don't find this funny!"

"It's not meant to be, Edward. Don't you understand? I'm solving the riddle for you. You don't have to wonder about me anymore. I'm not related to royalty. In my childhood, it would have been grand to have been related to the village butcher. As for Monsieur, I wasn't his mistress. I swear that to you. My husband is a college professor in Chicago and my brother is a petty crook. I have a sister in the old country who's happily married to a boar-bristle peddler—"

"Irene, don't—"

"Edward, you needed to know these things about me. Believe me, you did. You wanted the truth, you've been trying to get a sliver of it out of me since we met. Now it's yours. Nobody outside my family except my friend Clara knows this."

"You can trust me." He spoke very seriously, but there was a hint of a smile at one corner of his mouth.

"Go ahead. Laugh. I'd be glad if you did."

Grinning, he took her hands and kissed her thumb in spite of the odd looks the other patrons of the restaurant gave him. "Irene, I have to believe this, I suppose. I don't think anyone, not even someone as obviously imaginative as you, could make it up."

"Can you stay my friend?"

"Forever and ever," he said, putting a hand to his heart. "And I do promise I'll never tell anyone, but it just might kill me keeping it to myself."

"A bargain, then: you keep my secret and I'll never tell anyone you wanted to marry me."

He realized she was calling him a snob, and for a second he looked offended, but then he realized how true it was and laughed. "A bargain, Irene. A fair bargain."

The fall show was on time. In spite of Monsieur's death, Irene's week-long disappearance, and the strain of working with Chandler, they made it on time. There was a big turnout, especially of their competitors. Everyone was curious to see just what Neptune et Cie would do without Jacques Neptune. Perhaps it wasn't their best effort ever, but neither was it the worst. The day of the show was the hardest. The preparations done, Irene realized how very alone she felt without Monsieur beside her, but she managed. Chandler was more gracious than she'd expected, which was an unforeseen bonus.

The next morning, while Chandler took a day off to bask in their accomplishment, she took a solitary train ride to a small town in New Jersey she'd picked at random from the train schedule. There she saw a doctor under the name Mrs. Irene Smith. He confirmed what she was already certain of.

She was pregnant.

29

She had to tell both Clara and her mother, the two people in the world who would disapprove most strongly. But there simply wasn't any way to keep it from them. She went to her friend first. After a quiet dinner at Clara's apartment, Irene revealed the disastrous news and was astonished that Clara didn't seem particularly shocked. "What are you going to do now?" she asked.

"I don't know."

"Have you told Peter yet?"

"Peter? Good Lord, no!"

"He deserves to know."

"He's the very last person in the world I want to know."

"But it's his right. He's always wanted children. Even I know that. I'm certain the two of you will be able to work something out now."

Irene suddenly realized that they were talking at cross-purposes. "Clara, are you assuming this is Peter's child?"

"Well, of course! You were with him that week you disappeared, weren't you?"

"Oh, Clara . . . no, I wasn't. I went to his college, but he wasn't there. He'd left months before without telling me. I went to Long Island. The house Monsieur used out there was actually his, and he signed it over to me before his death."

"You didn't see Peter at all?"

"No."

"Then who . . . ? Oh, no!"

"Yes, Edward VanCleve."

Clara had gone white. She stood up and walked back and forth across the room several times. "The beast! I knew he was dangerous to you. But I never thought he'd go so far as to force—"

"No, it wasn't force. And, Clara, understand this: it was every bit as much my doing as his."

"Don't *say* such things. You're not that sort of woman!"

"Any woman is 'that sort' under the right circumstances. Or perhaps the wrong—"

"How did this ha . . . I mean . . . Oh dear, how difficult! What I mean is, all those years you were living with Peter, you had no children, and now, one, uh, unfortunate occurrence outside of marriage . . ."

No use in pointing out to her that it was by no means *one* "unfortunate occurrence." "I failed to use any precautions. I just didn't think of it, and maybe that's because I secretly wanted to have a child. I've always wanted to be a mother, but I'd been thinking about it in some vague future time. Of course, I intended it to be Peter's child. I guess that's a small part of it too. I think I was punishing Peter for going off without letting me know."

"That makes no sense at all!"

"I know it doesn't. It doesn't matter anyway, how it happened. What matters is that it has!"

Clara, angry and shocked, heard the distress in Irene's voice and forced herself to put aside her own emotions. "Well, you'll just have to get a divorce, get this man to marry you, and give up the business. You'll be ruined socially, and it's not really fair to Mr. Moffat to let your problem deflate the value of Neptune et Cie."

"Clara, I'm not going to marry Edward VanCleve."

"Do you mean that unspeakable man won't own up to his responsibility? I just never—!"

"He's not unspeakable, Clara. He's a nice man. A friend. And he doesn't know about this and he's never going to. It's not that he wouldn't marry me. Quite the contrary. I'm afraid he'd insist on a wedding, and I don't want to spend my life with him."

"Irene, you don't know what you're saying. The child must have a father, for its own sake, not to mention yours."

"Don't lose patience with me, Clara. I know this is very

upsetting and I'm not trying to be difficult. I just think there has to be some way out of this."

"There's abortion, of course—"

"Abortion! Clara, I never thought I'd hear you say such a thing! Murder my very own child?"

"I'm not suggesting that. Just mentioning it. The thought is every bit as repugnant to me as to you, and I'm not even Catholic. Irene, you're going to have to yield on some point. You're just going to have to marry Edward VanCleve. It will take months, and everyone will know . . . Oh, when I think of the years and the effort you've put into creating a respectable reputation, and then to have it destroyed this way—"

"Clara, you're not being very much comfort!"

"Is that what you want of me? Comfort? I haven't any. I've given you everything else I could. This isn't just your own future, you know. Yours is mine as well."

"Oh, Clara, I know! I'm so sorry. I've wrecked everything. I can't excuse myself. I was stupid, and you and Mama and everybody are going to have to help me pay the price for that stupidity. I just don't know what to say—"

Clara was still pacing the room. "Shhh, let me think awhile. Fix us some fresh tea and keep quiet."

Irene did as she was told. Why not? Clara could think forever and there wouldn't be a solution. The society in which she'd chosen to move was vicious in its condemnation of any woman who broke the rules. Irene was always on shaky ground anyway because her mysterious husband was never seen. Nobody believed he existed, but as long as she behaved with exemplary decorum they were just barely willing to pretend to accept the "Mrs." in front of her name. But if she turned up pregnant and tried to claim it was his child, it would be like slapping them in the face. They'd never accept it. They'd turn on her like rabid dogs. Nor would she consider that anyway. No matter what Peter had done to her, she couldn't risk his finding out she was trying to pass off another man's child as his. He would rightly despise her for such moral cowardice. She no longer had his love, but she would sooner die than incur his hatred.

She really had ruined her life! Clara was right, she'd have to sell Neptune et Cie to Chandler and do so very quickly at whatever price he was willing to pay. If she remained associated with the company, it would fail. So-called respectable women would absolutely refuse to do business with a whore—and that's what she would be labeled. How could she have done such a thing to Monsieur's business—and in the house he gave her, the house with the cold safe full of crown sables, the symbol of his belief that she was the *crème de la crème*! The appalling irony of it!

It was all so unfair. A man could father a child out of marriage and it was seen as nothing but a good healthy sign of his virility. No stigma attached itself; in fact, it was often the contrary. For that matter, a woman could have affairs. Plenty did. It was a constant source of gossip. And she could get away with it if she were circumspect and never, never provided anyone with proof. But a bulging abdomen was proof positive.

She set the hot teapot on the tray and went back to Clara. The older woman had stopped pacing and was staring out the window, tapping her forefinger meditatively against her front tooth. "You've thought of something!" Irene said.

"I don't know . . ."

"Clara, what? Tell me!"

Clara sat down and poured herself a cup of tea. "Do you remember Julianne Astor? Not one of *the* Astors, though she made wonderful capital of the name."

"Julianne Astor . . . yes, I think so. She bought a coat from Monsieur years ago and made all sorts of trouble about the length of the sleeves. She was a widow, I think. Very haughty woman."

"And she had a child."

"Oh, yes. A little boy she adopted after her husband died, wasn't it?"

"Maybe. That's just it. She went off on a long trip to Africa a year or two after her husband's demise, and when she came back, she had a baby. A poor orphaned child of English missionaries, she claimed. It wasn't widely believed. As I recall, there was a lot of gossip about the fact that she'd been very friendly with a married man before this trip."

"You mean it was her own child?"

"Probably. At least that's what everyone thought, but no

one could say with absolute certainty. Her name was tarnished, but not destroyed. She weathered it."

"Clara, do you think I . . ."

"I'm not sure. We'll have to think about it. When are you due?"

"Next May."

"That means you probably won't start showing until December. Possibly January, with the right attention to your clothes. That would be risky, however."

"The height of the season would be past," Irene said. "I could say I'm going to Europe to attend the spring and summer fur auctions. I've never needed to before because Monsieur handled that end of the business. Clara, I think it could be done. I would be back by midsummer."

"But not with the baby. Not right away. That's too much. If, instead, you went, had the baby and came back, then received a communication from some mysterious relative summoning you back—a cousin who was in frail health . . ."

"She'd die before I got there and I'd bring back her baby. That way no one would have grounds to gossip if the child looks like me! And the story would be set up in advance. Why can't I just tell the story about the frail cousin before I go the first time?"

"I suppose you could, but it would be far more convincing the other way."

"I think you're right. Oh, Clara, you are wonderful. It's brilliant! Chandler will be delighted to have me away for months; neither Peter nor Edward will ever know; nobody will be able to say the child is mine."

"Including the child," Clara said.

Irene fell silent. That was true. It would be terrible in some ways. Perhaps when he—or she—grew up, Irene could tell him the truth. But by then it might not matter. "Yes, I see what that means," she said softly.

"And your mother will have to know. You can't very well claim a mysterious cousin with her."

"I know. Mama's going to be crushed, but I couldn't lie to her about something so important. Besides, she deserves to know she's going to have a grandchild. And my sisters can be told the cousin was on my father's side. We were never very close to his people."

Zofia's reaction astonished her. "My poor girl," she said, her eyes filling with tears. "God will forgive you. This I know. You must pray hard . . ." After a long pause she added, ". . . as I did."

"As you . . . ? Mama, what do you mean?"

"Nothing. It is done."

"Mama, you must tell me."

Zofia wrung her hands and wouldn't meet Irene's eyes. "It was long ago, in the old country. It no longer matters."

"Mama . . ."

Zofia was quiet for a while, obviously torn. "Since you tell me, I should tell you. God forgive me!" she said, crossing herself. Tears were trickling down her cheeks. "You remember the big house on the hill?"

"Where I took the eggs to sell?"

"Eggs? I don't remember no eggs."

"Never mind. The manor house . . ."

"Yes, the big house. My papa, he worked in the garden. One day when I was soon to marry your pa, I went there to take a shovel he forget. Such a black day! The lord at the manor, he saw me. He said to me I was pretty. I *was* pretty girl, then. All my teeth they were still good."

"The lord of the manor?"

"Yes, Irina. Today I am still ashamed. Your pa, he never knew. Girls are stupid, but men are more stupid sometimes."

"You were seduced by the lord of the manor and pregnant when you married Papa?"

Zofia nodded.

Irene felt her world had been turned upside down and given a brisk shake. "You mean Teo . . . ? *Teo* . . . ?"

"Your papa, he think till he die that Teo is his. Only I know. Now you, too."

"Teo!" Irene repeated numbly.

Suddenly the full implication of what she'd been told struck her. All these years she'd been artfully pretending she had some vague connection to the Romanoff family, the ruling class of Russia, and all that time Teo . . . ! She'd always believed the people in the big house were some sort of relations of the czar, which meant that Teo, by blood, was the one connected to the Romanoffs. Teo, who had threatened to reveal the truth, and he hadn't even known! "Oh, Mama . . ." she said, and started laughing.

"This is funny? You laugh at your mother's misfortune?"

She hugged her. "No, Mama, never. I'm laughing at myself. At my own silliness. I'm so glad you told me."

Chandler Moffat, that inveterate gossip who could normally be counted on to ferret out any stray gossip, didn't even question Irene's plans for a lengthy trip. He was too thrilled to find himself totally in charge of Neptune et Cie to question his good fortune. Irene Garrick was going to go halfway around the world and stay away half a year—that was all he considered. "You'll be taking along Miss Johnson as your secretary and companion, won't you?" he asked.

"I think not. She'll need to stay here and handle the day-to-day bookkeeping and keep me in touch with the business," Irene said, making clear to him that she was going to keep a finger in the pie in spite of her absence. "I'll just hire a companion."

She'd given this a lot of thought after Clara pointed out the pitfalls to her. "Whoever you take along is going to be the most-sought-after employee in New York when she comes back. All the ladies who are so anxious to know about your connections are going to want to question her as to where you went, what you did, whom you stayed with."

Temporarily escaping from being Irene Garrick was going to be as difficult to accomplish as escaping from being Irina Gieryk had been, she discovered. But it could be done. This time she had money, and money made many things easier. It *would* be done.

The only one who raised objections to her trip was Edward VanCleve. "Why are you leaving for so long?" he asked. They had, oddly enough, become and stayed friends after that week in the country together. Every two or three weeks he took her to dinner, and they sometimes allowed themselves to be paired at theater parties and dinners.

"There's a lot to do, and it's a long way. The fur auctions last for several months in one place and another. Besides, I just want to get away for a while. Visit family . . ."

Edward smiled. "Are you going on the road with your boar-bristle in-laws?"

It occurred to her then that everyone in New York might be forced to accept the story of the child belonging to a cousin of vague but exalted circumstance. Edward knew better and Edward was the one who must not ever notice that this child-to-be had a birthdate nine months after their interlude. "My sister doesn't travel with her husband. She lives in the village with her two children. She's expecting another in the spring and I don't think she's in very good health." She would remind him of this later, when she came back with her "adopted" child.

In time, it was all worked out. The hardest part was keeping her figure concealed. Zofia, the only one of the family or household who knew the situation, helped her lace her corsets every morning, a chore that became increasingly more uncomfortable. In the end, she had to pretend a bad cold over Christmas because there wasn't any dress she could wear to the holiday parties. At the last minute, Stefania decided she wanted to go along. "I want to go back to the village," she said in Polish. "You can take me there and leave me with Aggie."

"Impossible, dear. You'd miss Mama," Irene told her.

"But Mama could come too. She wants to go back."

Fortunately, Zofia overheard this and stepped in. "No, we will not go back until your sisters they are properly married. They are American girls now." Irene realized then that Zofia never intended to go back. In her own way, she had become as thoroughly American as Irene.

She sailed the last week in December, a bleak, bitterly cold midwinter crossing. She didn't mind the weather, however, as it gave a perfect excuse to remain swathed in concealing layers of clothing. She had with her an elderly, prune-faced companion named Inez Huddleston who had been given an extremely detailed and entirely false itinerary including visits to the European fur markets Irene knew she'd probably not visit—not on this trip, anyway. "I'm not accustomed to a great deal of personal attention," Irene informed her when they sailed. "I take care of my own clothing and hair. I simply need a respectable lady to stay in the next cabin and take meals with me."

Mrs. Huddleston, who had accepted some little "gifts"—bribes—from various people, wasn't thrilled with this, but soon discovered that the mysterious Mrs. Garrick meant exactly what she said and wasn't the least inclined to have pleasant heart-to-heart chats about anything.

Irene jettisoned her in London a week after they arrived. "Mrs. Huddleston, I went to dinner with old friends last night," she told her. "They have a family connection in desperate need of employment. I agreed to take her along in your place. I will, naturally, pay you now for the entire amount you were to earn with me, and I've already purchased your return tickets. I'm sorry to disrupt your plans this way, and by way of expressing my regret, I've included a little something more." She gave the woman an envelope that contained an extra fifty dollars in addition to the salary. Clara had warned her against giving too much for fear of appearing suspiciously eager to get rid of her.

That afternoon she wrote notes to all the social acquaintances she'd supposedly planned to visit while in England. "So sorry, but I've received word from a family member who is seriously ill asking me to come immediately. Please allow me to visit at the other end of this long journey. I shall drop you a line as soon as I know my revised schedule."

She left within moments of posting these notes so that no one could get back to her and try to determine just what family member and what country she was going to. Taking the train from London immediately to Dover and then sailing to Calais, she rented a small house and hired a housekeeper. Leaving her wardrobe at the house, her jewels and part of her money in the local bank, she bought new and decidedly comfortable, frumpy-looking clothes for the rest of the journey before the housekeeper arrived to take up residence. At this point she "became" a pregnant widow. "I'll stay here to rest and wait for the weather to improve for a month, then I'll be going to visit relatives near Gdansk and will return shortly before my confinement," she told the housekeeper. "While I'm gone, you will simply keep the house prepared for my return and forward my mail."

The housekeeper, who was being paid generously but not extravagantly by this young widow whom she believed to be Russian, was all too glad for such an undemanding job.

During that month and the next, while Irene was making her way in a leisurely fashion across France and Germany, she began for the first time to think of the burden she carried as a living child. Until her elaborate "escape" plan had been completed, her pregnancy had simply been a medical and social condition to be dealt with. But now, when the baby kicked, it began to seem like another life. And as she had to sit down and walk and sleep in the postures of a pregnant woman, she began to think of motherhood. In spite of all the dangers the child posed to the life she'd worked so hard to attain, she could hardly wait for the time to pass. She wanted a child and had never realized how strong the impulse was until it was about to become a reality.

Unlike most women of her acquaintance, who suffered morning sickness, back pains, constipation, and a host of other annoying complaints, Irene felt superb. Her hair became glossier than ever, her nails stronger, her sleep more sound and satisfying. Food tasted better, air smelled better, music sounded sweeter. The first faint lines of worry and fatigue that had begun to mark her face filled out and disappeared. She found that every time she glanced at her reflection in a mirror or shop window, she was smiling without even realizing it. Pregnancy suited her perfectly.

Which is what Aggie said when she finally reached Gdansk. Aggie and Olbracht had come to meet her. Irene and Aggie clung together in a long embrace before they stood back and studied each other tearfully. "You are more beautiful than ever," Aggie told her in English—quite good English at that.

Irene had been mentally practicing her Polish, which was wretched, and was relieved that Aggie remembered enough English to converse. Olbracht, too, had a fairly good grasp of the language. "We shall welcome you to our humble home.

My wife, she has talked of you for years and I'm honored to meet you."

"It's I who am honored that you accept me as a guest, Olbracht," she said, shaking his hand and then standing on her toes and giving him a peck of a kiss on his cheek. In the mellow state induced by her pregnancy and her joy at being reunited with Aggie, Irene found Olbracht quite acceptable as a brother-in-law. He was devoted to Aggie, treating her like porcelain. No, nothing so delicate and useless; he treated her like she was valuable but sturdy. He was a big man, tall, broad, and somewhat florid under the tan that marked him as an outdoor traveler. For all his size and rough clothing, he had a gentle mouth and radiating laugh lines around his eyes. Aggie, she thought, had done well to go back for him.

Aggie herself had gained a little weight, and it made her prettier than ever. This contented, self-assured young woman was a far cry from the thin, sorry girl who'd left New York five years earlier. She absolutely exuded happiness. She welcomed Irene without questions or reservations.

They stayed in Gdansk overnight, the children having been given into a neighbor's care for the night. "The whole village is anxious to see you," Aggie said.

"What have you told them of me?" Irene asked.

"What you wrote and asked that I say, that you are the widow of a furrier. They think you are very rich and important because you go to America and have enough money to return just to visit me and Olbracht."

Aggie and Olbracht lived with their children, Stefan and Wanda, in a house only four doors away from the house where the Kossok children had grown up. Their house, with three separate rooms, was far grander, however. When Zofia had gone to America with the remaining girls, she'd sold the old house to a bootmaker. One of the first things Irene did was to go look at it. It was even smaller than she remembered (how had they all lived in such a confined space?) and much, much shabbier. But she had to remind herself that thirteen years had passed, half her life, since she last saw it. Zofia must have lost heart for the upkeep when Jozef died, and the bootmaker apparently had neither time nor inclination to make improvements.

Irene shook her head sadly at the sight and went next to the cemetery on a little rise over the river where Jozef was buried. A small gray headstone, set by itself, marked her father's final rest. Jozef Kossok, 1857–1904. Pa had been only forty-seven years old when he died. He must have been only forty-three when she left the village. And he'd seemed such a very old man to her then. Try as she would, however, she couldn't manufacture any sense of regret at his passing. Here in the village with her past forced on her, she couldn't stop remembering what he'd done, the horrible disappointment she'd felt that day when she got Zofia's letter and learned that he'd lost all the travel money she'd worked to send them. She resented him then and resented him still.

Irene had one more place to see. The manor house. She started to walk up the long road that would afford her a view of it, but turned back. She wasn't ready yet. Something held her back, and she told herself it was just her pregnancy and a reluctance to walk so far for such a trivial reason.

As she passed back through the village, she was aware that she was being watched from windows along the way. She was an object of curiosity here, a native come home a stranger. And she *was* a stranger. When she left this village, she had put it out of her mind, and she'd done it so effectively that she had virtually no memory of anyone but her family. There must have been playmates, but she couldn't remember playing very often. Her childhood had been taken up mainly by helping Mama care for the younger children and the house. But even the older people, who must have been customers of Pa and fellow worshipers at church, were strangers to her. "Are these really the same people?" she asked Aggie. "I don't recognize anyone."

"They are the same and they all claim to remember you," Aggie said with a smile. "But it isn't true. They only wish some of your glory to reflect on them. Old Lena Czekala, the midwife, has been repeating every moment of your birth to the village since she learned you were coming back—all invention, I'm sure. And Djoizy Lesniak, the carpenter, talks of nothing but the doll he carved for you. That, I'm certain, is not true. The only doll any of us ever had was a stuffed leather one Pa made for the twins the year you left. You must not hold it against them. It is a small vanity. Everyone wishes to believe in a better life someplace else. You prove it is true. You left here a child no one ever noticed and you come back a fine lady from America.''

There was, to Irene, surprisingly little satisfaction in this. In fact, had it not been for her happiness in Aggie and her family, the visit to the village would have been crushingly depressing. It was as gray and grim as she remembered.

Within a week of Irene's arrival, Olbracht had to go on a selling trip. He took Stefan along. ''But he's just a baby, only four years old,'' Irene said to Aggie. ''Don't you miss him?''

''Yes, I do, but if he and Wanda both stayed with me, Olbracht would be lonesome. And Stefan learns so much from his papa. Already he knows as much English as Polish.''

That left the three of them in the house. Wanda, just turned three years old, was a shy, pretty child who adored her aunt almost as much as she loved her mother. When she wasn't clinging to Aggie, she transferred her grip to Irene, hanging on her skirts just as Aggie had done as a child. Every time Irene sat down, she'd find Wanda in her lap pressing her little hands to Irene's abdomen in the hopes of feeling the baby move. Once in a while the unborn infant would oblige with a hearty kick that made Wanda shriek with delight.

''You're very big,'' Aggie said. ''Are you sure you counted right?''

''Absolutely certain,'' Irene said, and that evening told Aggie an edited version of how she came to be pregnant. She was fully aware for the first time of the irony of the situation. Years before she'd tried to discourage Aggie from returning to the village and her peddler lover. Now Aggie was happily—so *very* happily—married and the mother of two wonderful, legitimate children, while Irene, abandoned by her husband, was carrying an illegitimate child whose father didn't even know of its impending birth.

Telling Aggie was a relief and opened the floodgates. The sisters talked for days, the gentle hum of their voices mingling with the spring bird calls coming in the windows. Irene told Aggie about Peter's departure, about Neptune's death, and at length about Teo and the fire. "Poor Mama," Aggie said. "To get him back and then lose him again in such a terrible way. She always expected so much of him. Because he was the only boy, I guess."

And because he was the son of the lord of the manor, Irene thought, but this was the one thing she didn't share with Aggie. It was Zofia's secret, not hers.

Irene had arrived in the village in the middle of March, intending to stay a week. But a month later she was still with Aggie. The time had passed so quickly she was hardly aware of how long it had been. But Olbracht brought it to her attention when he returned. "You should go," he said bluntly.

"I didn't mean to outstay my welcome," Irene said, hurt.

"It's not that. We would be glad if you stayed forever," Olbracht said. "But it is getting near your time."

"I'm not due for over a month."

"It's more than that, Irina. I hear many things in my travels, and there is talk everywhere of war. I'm not a worldly man, I don't pretend to understand the reasons, but people who do understand are talking of nothing else. Travel could become dangerous, perhaps impossible."

"Then you must all come back with me. Please, Olbracht, you and Aggie and the children come to America with me. I will buy you a farm. You talk often of how you wish to be at home with your family instead of traveling. You could be at home in America."

"That is generous of you, but no, Irina. This is our home. We will stay here."

Irene had finally learned to recognize determination when she saw it. One more sentence and she would offend him. He was a proud man and would not be swayed by anything she could say. "Very well, but I hate to leave."

"I will take my things from the wagon tonight so we can all go with you to Gdansk. This time the children will come and enjoy the trip," Olbracht said.

That afternoon, Irene took the walk up the hill she'd been putting off. She'd convinced herself she didn't need to fear that big house and the memories it would stir up, but still, her feet dragged and she felt bigger and more awkward with each step. Finally she took the last turn in the steep road and saw it. She'd been sure it, like the rest of the village, would be smaller and dingier in reality than in memory. But she was wrong. It was a magnificent house.

She turned away quickly, almost able to hear the tinkle of a piano, but knowing it was in her head, not in the air. There! Was that the tree where she'd leaned weeping into her skirt and hating those shoes of Teo's? Was she perhaps treading in the same mud that had sucked at her feet that day? Without knowing it, she'd started to run and could nearly feel the rough handle of the egg basket in her hand, the empty weight of it against her leg.

She got back to Aggie's house breathless and with a throbbing stitch in her side. What a fool she was being!

Irene and Wanda took a long nap in the afternoon while Aggie fixed a special going-away dinner. Irene woke feeling achy and bleary, the pain in her side still echoing. She wasn't even hungry, but forced herself to eat rather than offend her sister. The thought of the long, bumpy wagon ride in the morning made her squirm. If only she hadn't waited quite so long. It was hundreds of miles back to her cozy little house and the doctor she'd seen in Calais. Hundreds of long, uncomfortable miles with a backache and an unsettled stomach.

Aggie had just set the dessert on the table when the baby gave a lurch and Irene felt an odd sensation. She stood and excused herself, Aggie immediately in her wake. "What's wrong?" Aggie asked.

"Nothing. I think the baby just kicked me in the bladder. I've wet myself," Irene whispered, embarrassed. She'd been having to run outside to the privy every half-hour or so for the last week, and she was worried how she was going to endure the trip back to France this way.

"Good Lord! Don't you know anything about having babies?" Aggie asked. "Your water's broken, Irene. You're going to have the baby here."

"No! It's not time yet."

"Too bad nobody told the baby that. Just lie down. I'll send Olbracht for the midwife."

Irene was rigid with sudden fear and with rage. How could God do this to her? She'd escaped the village; and now her child was going to be born here, just as if she'd never gotten away.

30

The baby was born early in the next morning. "Is it all right?" Irene asked weakly.

Aggie sat down next to her on the bed while the midwife finished cleaning the infant and wrapping it up warmly. "I think so, Irene. It's very tiny. Probably only five pounds or less because it was early. But other than that, it appears to be normal. Listen!"

The baby wailed, a thin, jerky little screech of outrage.

"It? A boy or a girl?"

"A girl."

Irene lay back on the sweat-soaked pillow and smiled. She'd always thought of the child as a boy, expressed to Zofia, Clara, and Aggie her hopes that it would be a boy. But now she realized that secretly she'd been longing desperately for a girl. "Constance."

"That's her name? Why? Is it in honor of someone?"

"No. I've never known anyone by that name. But it's a good word, both in meaning and sound. She can be called Connie. Connie Garrick. Do you like it?"

Aggie laughed. "It's very American-sounding."

"Yes, I want it to be." But when it came time to take the baby to the tiny village church for baptism, the priest asked what her name was to be, and Irene, without pausing to analyze her motives, said, "Konstancya Gieryk."

The baby was delicate, both in constitution and coloring. Like Irene, she had hair so fair it was almost white, although it would probably darken, as Irene's had, to a deep honey color when she grew up. She wasn't sickly, but she was very tiny and easily chilled. Irene spent the first month cuddling and feeding her, reluctant to let her out of her arms. She slept curled around the baby to create a circle of warmth, a circle which benefited Irene as much as the child.

Once the pain and effort of childbirth were forgotten, she was awestruck that she had, from her own ordinary body, brought forth another human being. She had long ago ceased to think of Edward VanCleve as having had anything whatsoever to do with the miracle. "We are one, Connie," she whispered, touching her finger to the baby's strong, soft cheeks. "I am you and you are me. Soon you will start becoming your own person, but not yet." And when the baby nursed, relieving the pressure on her overfull breasts, Irene could feel a sensation that spread to the very core of her body. Her uterus contracted, reminding her anew of how short a time ago they had been physically united.

For that one month, Irene was a mother and nothing else. She was totally absorbed in the child. Furs meant nothing; money and ambition meant nothing; the threat of war didn't exist. She and Connie were the center of the universe, with Aggie and Olbracht and the children as beloved but dimly lighted satellites. Nothing beyond this small circle existed for her.

But after a month, the postpartum bleeding stopped and Connie began to get cranky. "It's your milk, I think," Aggie said. "I believe she's hungry."

"What can I do?" Irene asked.

"Irene, what *are* you going to do? About everything?"

"I don't understand."

"When you came here, you told me you were going to return to France, have the baby, get a wet nurse and return to America, then come back in a few months to 'adopt' the child. I haven't heard you talk about any of that since she was born."

The door had opened a crack and the world started crowding back in. "Yes, I know. I haven't thought about it."

"It's time you do."

"I have to go back. And I cannot leave Connie behind. I know for the sake of making the story convincing, I should, but I just couldn't bear to be parted from her. I was a fool even to consider it."

"The story that this is an adopted child will not be believed if you're nursing it," Aggie pointed out with a grin.

"That would be pushing credulity, wouldn't it? But I hate to give it up."

"I know. But if your milk is failing, you have to anyway. I've been asking around the village and may have an idea to help. The midwife has a niece about ten miles from here. The niece—I think her name is Marya Nowak—has a new infant too. She and her husband want desperately to go to America. All his people are already there. If her milk is adequate and agrees with Connie, you could take them with you."

Marya was a fat, placid girl of sixteen whose milk was not only adequate but so abundant that the front of her dress was always damp from it. It was apparent within days that Connie would thrive on its richness, and while Irene was pleased, she was also a bit sad every time she saw her Connie in Marya's arms, greedily sucking at that round freckled breast. She and Connie were no longer one. The baby had taken the first step away from her, and it was time to go home to America.

Irene made one last attempt to persuade Aggie and Olbracht to come with her, but Olbracht was firm. "This is our home. We will stay. The Poles have endured much and will endure more."

"But that is a race, not individuals. Individuals die and suffer. I can't bear to think of that happening to any of you."

"This war, if it really comes, with be over quickly. Everyone says so."

"Everyone might be wrong."

"Yes, there may not be war at all," he answered, deliberately misunderstanding her.

It was hard to leave them. Aggie cried and Wanda sobbed hysterically and little Stefan, trying to be manly like his father, failed at the end and wept into Irene's skirt. He wouldn't miss her, but he loved the baby and didn't want it taken away. It was, in his mind, *his* little sister. Even Olbracht turned away once or twice and wiped a tear from his eye and gave Irene a beautifully crafted silver-backed hairbrush. "I know she's as bald as a new turnip now that her baby hair had fallen out, but someday you will give her this and tell her about her uncle, won't you?"

At that Irene nearly went to pieces.

Clutching Connie as if she might actually get away and try to stay in the village, Irene departed in the wagon she'd hired to take her little household to the nearest railway station. Marya and her husband, Pawel Nowak, were so thrilled to be on their way to the promised land that they managed to lighten Irene's depression within an hour. Though they had no English, Irene's Polish had improved during her stay and she'd managed to make quite clear to them that their passage to America and salary were dependent on two things: that they remain with her until Connie was weaned and that, as far as anyone was concerned, they had absolutely no idea whose child she was.

Not that there was much danger of anyone in New York questioning them; they showed no interest in learning so much as a syllable of English. Pawel had four older brothers already residing in a Polish community in Detroit, where they intended to live when their job with Irene was over.

Once again, Irene made her way slowly. This time, however, she wasn't sightseeing, but doing some of the business she was allegedly there for. She attended a fur auction in Hamburg and met a number of European dealers who had known Jacques Neptune and were effusive in their condolences. ''Perhaps it's as well he didn't live to see what is apt to happen,'' one outspoken Russian dealer said.

''What do you mean?''

''Do you not read the papers? Are you not aware of the coming conflagration? Maybe this year, maybe next, but it is bound to happen. Europe, all of Europe, has been aligning itself into opposing camps for the last half-century.''

''You think there will be a war?''

''But of course. Germany is set on it. When old men fall in love with their uniforms, young men are certain to die. Countries that have armies feel the need to use them. Have you not seen the soldiers?''

''I have indeed,'' Irene answered. It was the one aspect of traveling in Germany that had penetrated her cocoon of motherhood and business concerns. Everywhere they went there were men in uniforms; arrogant men whose officers took the best seats on the railway cars and looked down long noses at civilians.

"They are costly and handsome, these armies, and anxious to do something besides drill in public squares. The kaiser sees himself as a military leader. Every head of state is the same right now. The Austrians, even the czar. When you see pictures of them in public, they are in their own grand uniforms as if on their way to oversee a battle. And when it comes, this war they are all so anxious for, all the ports of Europe will shut down. Our Siberian furs, the best in the world, they will be locked into Russia, rotting in warehouses. Japan will join Germany, most certainly, then even the eastern ports will be closed. If you are smart, Mrs. Garrick, you will buy everything you can this year, for you may not see anything from us for a long, long time."

"You must have told this to many people," she said. "The prices you are getting reflect it. Besides, everyone says it will be a short war, if it comes."

"Those who say that do not know the Teutonic mind or genetics. The kaiser and the czar are cousins, you know. Grandsons of Queen Victoria. Stubborn, unforgiving men. And the French . . . Tchaa! The French can be counted upon to be brave and tenacious and idiotic in any situation. Throw a plum at a Frenchman and he will build a shrine to his martyrdom around the pit."

Irene went away from this conversation alarmed, but later managed to convince herself it was nothing but melodrama. Still, she bought more than she had originally intended and committed extra money to assuring that her purchases be shipped to New York immediately. Besides the purchases for Neptune et Cie, she bought something important for herself. At one of the markets she found six crown sables that her furrier's mind's eye told her were the perfect matches she lacked. These she wrapped and took with her. That evening, she sat down to sketch some designs that had come to her mind and mailed them off to Clara.

It took her and her party until the middle of June to get back to Calais. Once there, she intended to rest awhile, but became uneasy after three days and, closing up the house and paying off the housekeeper, set out for England.

Once there, she became Irene Garrick again. Taking a house in Mayfair, she sent out a flurry of letters to friends. When the first one called and heard Connie crying upstairs, Irene drew a deep breath and said, "My cousin's child. Poor dear died in childbirth and her husband—a rather weak man, the family never approved of him—killed himself in grief. Such a tragic situation. There was no one to take the child. A nuisance, really, but what else could one do?"

She hated herself.

"Gavrilo Princip," her dinner companion said.

"But why would he shoot Franz Ferdinand and his wife?"

"Because he's a crazy hothead. All the Serbs are."

"He wasn't even a Serb," the gentleman across the table said. "He was Bosnian, part of the Black Hand. That's a group of terrorists dedicated to freeing the Balkans of the Hapsburgs, Mrs. Garrick. The real hotheads are the military men in Vienna. They'd drag us all in if they could."

"Nonsense," the man next to Irene replied. "England isn't going to get involved in Balkan squabbles. They're always shooting each other. It's their national sport."

"Archie! Lawrence!" their hostess trilled. "Enough of that boring political talk. I want to hear something interesting. Mrs. Garrick, tell us what you have in mind for your fall collection."

Clara was asking the same thing repeatedly by transatlantic mail. "Things are going well enough under Chandler's regime," she reported. "I have to admit I'm quite surprised at how well he is managing things. But the company will come to an abrupt halt if there isn't an autumn showing, and Chandler couldn't design a paper box. I believe, if pressed, even he would admit that. The designs you've sent are quite lovely and the first shipment of furs is of superb quality, but you are needed here in person. Some of these items can't be put together without your expertise. My love to Connie."

And a week later: "I heard the first twitterings today about Connie. One of your English hostesses told her sister-in-law all about this mysterious child you're hauling about. She was telling her friend. They closed up like a pair of Egyptian tombs when they realized I could overhear them, but the tone was as catty as you would suppose. Irene, you simply must return and face this down yourself or it will appear that you're hiding from something!"

Reluctantly Irene obeyed the summons. She sailed from Southampton the last week in July. While she was at sea, Austria-Hungary declared war on Serbia. The czar partially mobilized his armies within striking distance of Austria. His cousin the kaiser, an ally of Austria-Hungary, demanded demobilization and the czar refused. There was a flurry of telegrams and troops began to drill in earnest on village squares all over Europe. Before Irene's ship could dock, Germany had declared war on Russia and France and had begun its invasion of neutral Belgium, forcing Britain to honor her pact to defend Belgium's neutrality and declare war on Germany.

Irene was unaware of all this, though it would be forced to her attention soon enough. She was in her stateroom holding Connie up to the tiny porthole through which the Statue of Liberty was visible.

"Isn't she beautiful, Connie?" Irene whispered, tickling the baby's ear with a kiss. "She's welcoming you home, just as she welcomed me once. But you won't have to suffer what I did. You'll never suffer anything if I can help it."

She wasn't alone in failing to realize that the world was about to enter the period of the greatest suffering it had ever known. No one, including Irene and Connie, would be spared.

The War to End All Wars had begun.

If Irene and Connie had arrived in New York at any other time, her circle of acquaintances would have had an enormous interest in the baby's mysterious origins. As it was, however, the newspaper headlines took temporary precedence. Irene, having just returned from the Continent, was cast in the role of expert on foreign affairs. "Did you see any battles?" one fluffy-headed young matron asked, unaware that there had *been* no battles—yet. Another woman, having caught only enough of the gossip that always surrounded Irene like a fog to remember a supposed Russian connection, asked what Rasputin was really like.

"I really couldn't say," Irene replied, surprised and amused by the question.

This was taken to mean she was being diplomatic and didn't want to say, and within a week the story made the rounds and came back with trimmings. Irene, it was widely reported, had met with her cousins Nicky and Alex and tried to convince them to rid their household of the evil monk, but without success. One particularly creative lady even suggested that the child Irene Garrick was said to have brought back with her just might be a secret daughter of the czarina, fathered by Rasputin himself.

The war was looked on by many as a grand lark. "It'll be all over by Christmas and those damned Germans will be put back in their place," people said. "With Russia on one side and France on the other, what chance has the kaiser got?"

"England just needs enough time to tear the epaulettes off those pompous old Viennese and then everything will get back to normal."

"War—especially a short little war like this—will be good for the economy eventually, even if it pinches a little at first. It'll help America, too, in the long run."

"It'll get some young men out in the world and give them a look at what life is really about."

"I've half a mind to dust off my old sword and go over there and show them how to do it."

The New York *Times* carried no alarming news of the war in Europe that first month, helping to lull any fears that might have taken root.

Those who were concerned saw the war in economic terms. European stock exchanges had collapsed and on July 31, the New York exchange closed briefly to retrench and consider the situation. Bankers were frantic and Treasury Secretary William McAdoo came to the city to attempt to sooth ruffled feathers. The city itself had seventy-seven million dollars in bonds and notes held in Europe.

But Irene, even though she had some European investments herself, hardly had time to listen to such talk. Her first concern was spending as much time as she could with her daughter, an almost impossible task with all the other pressures that were being relentlessly applied to her. Fortunately—or so it seemed at the time—Zofia became totally absorbed in the baby's welfare, rocking her when she was fussy at night, taking endless pains to find and mash up foods that would appeal to her infant palate, singing her to sleep, and knitting like a madwoman to provide a tiny wardrobe that was wonderful in intent but ghastly in its tastelessness. Between Zofia and Marya, Irene had to practically fight for the opportunity to worry over Connie.

And it was a good thing. The fall line had to be ready shortly. Irene looked over the sketches she'd been sending back and those she'd brought along with her and realized they all looked vaguely military. "It's all the soldiers I saw and the constant talk of war," she told Clara.

"I think you're worrying needlessly. War has become, at least this year, very chic," Clara replied sardonically. "You need to add four or five items that are purely feminine, though. I like this one—the cossack coat and the tall hat."

Chandler liked the designs too. He thought she'd created the rather martial motif on purpose and actually complimented her. "The ladies will be mad for these. Especially this one with the gold pin. Just the faintest suggestion of a spur about it, isn't there?"

"Why, thank you—" Irene replied, immeasurably flattered even though she seldom put any faith in Chandler's artistic evaluations, only his social judgments. She hadn't meant the gold pin to look like a spur, but he was correct. It did.

By the beginning of October her part of the preparation was done, and it was a good thing, because world events took precedence in her concerns. The Germans, undeterred by public opinion that they couldn't expand both east and west, were doing exactly that. The news from France held very little interest for Irene, but the news from the German eastern front obsessed her. According to the newspaper accounts, which were often garbled and contradictory, there were battles being conducted very near the village she'd come from—the village where Aggie and Olbracht and the children were.

She was frantic for their safety. First she fired off rounds of cables and letters, none of which elicited any reply. Many of the letters came back to her because they were impossible to deliver. "I've got to go back for them," she told Clara.

"Don't be a fool, Irene," her old friend said astringently. "What do you think you can do, march through the lines and ask everybody to please stop the war while you attend to your family? I doubt you have the same power over the German military that you do over New York society."

"How cruel of you!"

"Possibly, but I'm being honest, and so must you."

"But, Clara, the things you hear—"

"Of the German atrocities in Belgium? Yes, I know. But the fact remains, there's nothing you could personally do there. You couldn't get through anyway, and if you did, you'd just be another civilian individual with no power at all. Besides, from what you say, Olbracht is an intelligent man who cares deeply about his family. He may have already gotten them to safety if the village is in danger at all—and you don't even know that it is."

Finally, in desperation, she went to Edward VanCleve. "I'm worried sick about my sister's family. What can I do?"

"The boar-bristle people? You know, I've developed a sort of fondness for them, just from knowing they exist."

"Edward, stop trying to be amusing."

"Sorry. I meant no disrespect for your sister."

"I can't go to anyone else for help, Edward, without having to tell them who these people are and consequently who I really am. You see that, don't you?"

"Of course. Let me see what I can figure out. Write down their names and the village and everything else that might be useful. It may be very expensive—"

"Of course it will. Do you think I'd mind that?"

In the end, his efforts were enthusiastic but not very helpful. He hired a virtual army of European detectives to try to locate Aggie, but they couldn't get through the lines either, and their ranks kept diminishing as they went into the military services of their own countries.

Word of his search got around. Mrs. Piper, she of the many daughters-in-law, told Irene about it. "They say he's trying to find this Polish woman who's a former mistress of his. You know he did a great deal of traveling in France several years back and the Poles and the French are as thick as thieves. Dorothy Evans-Smyth says she met her once when she ran into the VanCleve party in Marseilles. Dorothy says the woman is a perfectly ravishing redhead, but quite common-looking."

"I think this collar might be a little higher, don't you, Mrs. Piper. To conceal a bit more of your neck."

"Well!"

By March 1915, one of Edward's people had actually gotten to the village and back out again. The Germans had moved through, then been forced back. Many houses were burnt, crops trampled, some civilians injured and killed. But the Chalupiec family—mother, father, and both children—had loaded up their goods on Olbracht's peddler's wagon and left before the soldiers came through. No one knew where they were going. They themselves hadn't known when they set out. Nobody had heard from them since. They, like thousands of other Poles, had been swallowed up in the war.

"Irene, I'm sorry," Edward said. "But there's no point in pouring any more money and effort into this search right now. All you can do is wait for the dust to settle—"

"This stupid, pointless war was supposed to be over in a few weeks!"

"When it's over, you can send in a battalion of searchers. Until then, you've just got to hope that your sister will find her way to safety and contact you."

"If she's still alive."

"Yes, if she's still alive."

31

History as studied, and history as lived, are very different matters. A battle may rage in Europe that has the potential to engage historians' interest for centuries. But it may legitimately mean nothing to a man in Nebraska who breaks his leg falling from a horse the same week, or a woman in California whose baby has diphtheria, or the eager young Rhode Island salesman who has lost his sample case on the train. To those hundreds of thousands of individuals who have no immediate personal stake in the outcome and who have problems of their own, the great events of history are merely newspaper headlines, to be read and forgotten in the laborious business of getting from day to day.

So it was with much of America during the first two and a half years of the Great War. For one thing, the United States had soldiers in Cuba, Haiti, and along the Mexican border. That was military involvement enough for any country. Moreover, at first it was considered very much a "European" war, and in a country with a large population of Germans, it wasn't clear until later which side America would join, should it become involved. A good many prominent and respected individuals were speaking out on behalf of the Germans and Austrians.

On May 7, 1915, however, the shape of things to come began to become apparent. As Irene was getting ready to go to St. Louis to the fur auctions, the newspapers screamed about the sinking of the *Lusitania* by the Germans. There were 112 Americans on board in spite of the warnings the German ambassador had placed in the New York papers.

'I think you should reconsider this trip," Clara said. "St.

Louis is a German city, and who knows what kind of situation might exist there if Wilson declares war while you're en route."

"It's also a French city and primarily an American city," Irene said, folding a gray dress and placing it on her small trunk. "And it doesn't matter. I have to go. A furrier can't conduct business without furs, and our supply is going to be seriously depleted this fall if I haven't stocked up on American pelts."

Clara nodded regretfully. It was all very true, but such a shame Chandler wasn't knowledgeable enough about this aspect of the business to take her place. "Are you taking Lillie along again? She enjoyed the trip the other time, remember?"

"That seems a century ago, doesn't it?" Irene said. "No, I invited her, but she didn't seem interested. She's involved in some charity or other that's taking up a lot of her time."

"That doesn't sound like Lillie. What's the charity?"

"I don't believe she's told me."

America didn't enter the war. While Irene conducted her business, a series of telegrams was exchanged between the United States and Germany—policies stated, warnings given, reasons elaborated—but nothing actually done. And by the time Irene returned, all political considerations were put aside for family matters. The exact nature of Lillie's "charity" became clear.

"Mama, what *are* you talking about?" Irene exclaimed. She hadn't even been home long enough to take off her hat.

"Love."

"Nonsense! Who are these men? Where did Lillie and Cecilia meet them?"

"At a dance in the old neighborhood."

"They've been going to dances down there? Why on earth did you allow that? You know how I feel—"

Zofia was angry too. "Yes, everybody know how you feel, Irina. All we hear in this house is how you feel. You want your sisters should be ladies with all them dresses and lessons, but then you don't let them go with your fine friends. You think your sisters not good enough for society people. Where they supposed to go—young girls with high spirits? They like dances and young men."

She had a point, but Irene wasn't about to recognize it. "Who are these men?"

"Aleksy and Max Zoilek. Nice boys from Warsaw. They got a cousin in California who make them partners in business—a factory, makes fish in cans."

"Cannery workers! Oh, Mama—"

"No just workers. Owners, Irina. They have business in Warsaw they sell for good money to buy business here. They take good care of Lillie and Cecilia. Are going to buy big house for all to live in."

"Mama, I forbid it. I can't allow the girls to marry fish canners. They're too young anyway."

Zofia drew herself up. "Not for you to forbid, Irina. This is your house, but I am mother. I give my permission. Your sisters, they are nineteen years old. It is time they marry. Zoileks are nice boys, make good husbands. No drinking, no card playing. Good Catholic boys, go to Mass every morning."

"Mama, please listen. They can make much better marriages. I've worked so hard to give them the best, I can't bear for them to settle for cannery workers. I can introduce them to men of breeding and wealth—"

'No, Irina. You don't do that. You try to make them like you."

"Is that so awful?"

"Irina, now you listen to Mama. You lose husband, have baby from man who don't even know, work all the time, never go to church, have no time for pretty baby. Are you happy woman? Happy as Lillie and Cecilia with nice young men who love them and want to give them houses and babies?"

"Mama, you once said I was the best—"

"The best of my children. Yes, but not the happiest. I want the twins be happy women."

Zofia prevailed. The twins were married in a double wedding with identical gowns at St. Stanislas. The Zoilek brothers weren't twins, but looked more like it than Lillie and Cecilia. They were big men with huge smiles and larger feet, but at the wedding reception in the church hall that night, they danced wonderfully. Irene never heard either of them speak a word of English; in fact, they hardly spoke to her at all. They seemed in awe of her. Irene found, to her surprise, that she rather liked them, or thought she would if ever they'd communicate with her. They seemed very nice and they adored the twins. Even though they weren't what Irene would have chosen for her sisters, they might not be the disaster she'd originally considered them.

Irene found herself wondering what in the world her sisters had told these young men about her. What did Lillie and Cecilia think of their oldest sister? And what, for that matter, did she know about them? It was a pity that she'd never really become close to them, and more of a pity that she hadn't realized it until today, when it was too late. She had a better memory of them as little girls in the old country than she had of them in the last few years. They had shared a house and she had taken responsibility for them, but they were virtually strangers.

She had wanted to give them something spectacular for a wedding gift and had mentioned it to Clara. "I could find out about the area and buy them houses. Have them all furnished and everything when they arrive," she'd told her friend.

"Good Lord, you can't mean it? Irene, you'd destroy those young men if you did that."

"Whatever do you mean?"

"Oh dear," Clara sighed. Odd that she, the spinster, seemed to know more about men than Irene. "From what Zofia says, these boys are desperately anxious to provide for your sisters to the best of their ability. And you'd better let them do it their own way. If they live in fancy houses that you buy, they'll feel like eunuchs."

"That's ridiculous!"

"Believe me, it's not. Just give them a modest cash dowry that won't embarrass anyone."

"How much? Four thousand? Five?"

"Four or five *hundred*. If that much."

Feeling that she'd completely lost her grip on the situation, Irene allowed herself to be directed by Clara. She gave each couple five hundred dollars and gave another five hundred to St. Stanislas. But she came away feeling she'd cheated the girls and that somebody had cheated her as well.

* * *

The wedding was in the middle of July. The next week Irene came home and found Zofia waiting in the hall, bouncing with excitement. "She talk, the baby talk. Come, see!"

Irene dropped her hat and parcels and raced up the steps behind Zofia. She'd started to wonder if Connie was ever going to say anything but baby noises.

Connie was sitting in the middle of the playroom. The nursemaid was rolling a ball back and forth to her, and Connie, all pink ruffles and golden curls, was laughing and throwing herself around with delight. When she saw Zofia, she got to her feet and toddled over to grab her skirts. Zofia lifted her and nuzzled her neck. Connie giggled. Zofia whispered in her ear and jiggled her as if this would jar loose the desired response. Connie just kept giggling. Zofia whispered again and pointed to Irene. Connie took a breath and said something that sounded like "Aughhh aloog mhhm."

Zofia beamed. "See, what I tell you?"

Irene reached out and took the baby's little chubby hand. "But, Mama, what did she say?"

"She said she's hungry."

Irene smiled. "It didn't exactly sound like it."

"Not in English. Polish."

Irene suddenly felt cold. "No more Polish, Mama! She's an American child! She must speak English!"

Connie, alarmed by Irene's tone, jerked her hand back, buried her face in Zofia's neck, and started to cry.

In the dark hours of that night, when she could be honest with herself, Irene faced a number of facts she'd been doggedly ignoring for years. She'd missed the essence of sisterhood with the twins because she was too busy providing for them to get to know them. She wouldn't allow that to happen with Connie. They'd been truly mother and daughter back in Europe, before Irene brought her back and flung herself into her daily round of business activities. But since then, Irene had seen her only in that brief interval between her return from the office and Connie's bedtime. An hour a day at the most to spend together, and then usually with Zofia and the nursemaid both hovering. That sweet, cuddly baby would soon be past cuddling and Irene couldn't bear to lose her love—not even to Zofia.

She vowed that night to do things differently. She couldn't abandon the business; in these difficult times she didn't dare even neglect it. But she would cut out something else and find ways to spend precious moments with her child. She instructed Clara that she was to plan no more than three luncheons a week for her henceforth. The remaining days of the week she'd lunch at home. Even though it meant only a few minutes with Connie, they were important minutes. She also battled Zofia and the nursemaid into rearranging Connie's sleeping schedule so she was sleeping later in the morning and staying up later in the evening when Irene could be with her.

Irene did most of the design for the fall line in the room that had once been Peter's study. With a drawing board attached to the wall and all dangerous objects off the floor, Irene could sketch and plan while Connie played at her feet. She even took her to the office a few times because Connie loved seeing the stuffed animals in the cases in Monsieur's old office.

During the first visit, Chandler happened on them. Never married, he showed an astonishing ability to get along with small children—a trait Irene would never have suspected. He held Connie, allowed her to take liberties with the gold watch fob that spanned his ample girth, and showed her the sights outside the window. The next day he called on Irene in her own office. "I say, Mrs. Garrick, about my uncle's office . . ."

It had been a touchy subject. Both of them had felt Neptune's old office ought to be their own, but neither was ready for the bitterness that would surely follow moving into it. The result was that it had remained empty, just as Neptune had left it. Miss Troutwhite, now officially Chandler's secretary, just as Clara was Irene's, dusted the furniture weekly and swept the floor.

"It's a pity to leave the room vacant, don't you know," Chandler said, resorting to his fake English style of speaking as he frequently did when he was uncomfortable. "I was thinking, since your little girl took such a liking to it, you might like to use the room yourself—for her sake, of course."

"That's very generous of you."

"No, it's nothing. Such a well-lighted space. Shame to see it going to waste. Too small for my needs, don't you see? If you were to use it, the little girl could see the display cases anytime her nanny wanted to bring her down here."

Irene thought the fall line was undistinguished. Last year's vaguely military cut was out, now that so much of the world was engaged in a genuine war that was proving so deadly and so very ugly. One couldn't hear of the atrocities in Belgium and wear anything that looked remotely martial. Instead, Irene deliberately chose to make the theme of the line as feminine as possible, but she was hampered by lack of variety in materials. Since she had begun designing, she'd always had the advantage of being able to choose any fur that was suitable to a particular style. Now her choices were somewhat restricted. She had to think in terms of muskrat, which she despised, and raccoon, which seemed to her too coarse to appear feminine. There was North American mink, which was nearly as good as the European pelts, but mink had limited uses. But in spite of her own reservations, the line was a success. Her buyers found the American furs an interesting novelty.

By December, it appeared that Neptune et Cie, rather than suffering from the war, had made a greater profit than any previous year. Irene studied the figures, recognized that they were correct, and shook her head in wonder.

She had a tiny white rabbit coat with ermine tails on the collar made for Connie for Christmas. "Why don't you have something made for yourself?" Clara asked her. "You've never owned a single fur of your own except that first opossum Monsieur gave you when you designed it."

"I don't need a fur of my own. There must be a dozen in the cold safe downstairs that I wear." Monsieur had instructed her early on that the very best advertisement for a fur was a beautiful woman wearing it, and she had heeded the advice. When the weather was suitable, she always wore furs of her own design. She wore them only two or three times and there had come to be a certain status attached to buying one of the coats Irene Garrick had been seen in.

"Besides, Clara, I have a full set of sables in the safe at the house on Long Island. I bought the last ones in Europe, just before the war started. Someday, when this war is over, I'll have them made up." She didn't mention that she wasn't ready to wear such a coat. It would symbolize success in a way she didn't feel she was entitled to—yet. She couldn't wear the crown sables until she was secure in personal, emotional ways as well as financial and social. How or when she might ever feel that security, she didn't know. Nor did she have time to dwell on it.

The next spring, when business pressures eased somewhat, she packed up the family and went to the house on Long Island for the week of Connie's second birthday. Stefania didn't want to go along, but both Irene and Zofia insisted. At sixteen, Stefania had passed from being a lumpy girl to a downright fat young woman. Having refused to go to school, she could barely read, was shy even with the family, and passed her days in sewing—or rather handwork. She knitted, crocheted, and tatted. Unfortunately, she had no taste whatsoever and even Zofia had trouble finding nice things to say about her work, which was invariably grubby and knotted and off-center.

Irene decided Stefania would learn to ride, which was the main reason she took them to her secret house. She hadn't intended to let anyone know about it, but Stefania needed to be outdoors. Irene had the small stable cleaned up, rented three horses, and hired a young man to look after the animals and teach Stefania. In the back of her mind she knew the plan was doomed to failure, but she had to give it a chance. Stefania wasn't having any of it. She was terrified of the horses, shy of the teacher, and broke out in hives. It seemed she was swelling before their eyes, and given her size, that was particularly alarming.

"I hate them!" Stefania sobbed, her face red and wet and more unattractive than ever. "They are big and ugly and make awful noises."

Irene was very nearly provoked into saying, "Just like you!"

At least Connie enjoyed herself running around outdoors. She was enthralled with the grass and butterflies and birds, and Irene realized what a city child she was raising. Well-chaperoned trips to the park were nothing like free romping in the wild. There weren't nettles and cow pies and bumblebees in the city, nor was there such an expanse of sky or such utter quiet at night. Connie was a little frightened of the quiet and insisted on sleeping with Irene the first few nights. Irene snuggled in with her and told her old Polish fairy stories and made plans. "Next winter we'll come here and I'll show you how to make snow angels," Irene promised her.

The day before they'd planned to go back to the city, they had a visitor. "I thought this was where you'd gone," Edward VanCleve said when she opened the door.

For a moment, both of them were embarrassed, remembering the last time he'd shown up here and what had followed. Irene broke the spell: "You've just missed my mother and sister. The driver took them into town to buy some honey. Mama wanted to make some cookies with it to take back to the city. She doesn't like the honey they sell in town. Let's sit on the terrace . . ." And she found herself blushing. The terrace was where . . .

"You're babbling, Mrs. Garrick. I haven't come to compromise your virtue. Actually, I'm tracking you down for Chandler. I didn't think you'd want me to tell him about this place."

"Chandler? Why? Is something wrong?—a fire!"

"No, no. Nothing like that. It's just that Chandler has something to tell you. And so have I."

"How very mysterious," Irene said. "Come in."

When they were settled with cups of tea, Edward explained. "A few months ago I ran into Chandler at one of those flying displays—you know, airplanes. Have you ever seen one?"

"Good Lord, no!"

"Don't take that attitude, my girl. They're the coming thing. Someday everybody will have one."

"Everybody but me!"

"Anyway, we both got rather interested and started going out and taking lessons in flying them—"

"*No!* Oh, Edward, you couldn't. They must be horribly

dangerous. And Chandler? How could Chandler have ever been held up in the air?''

''Haven't you noticed how much weight he's taken off over the winter?''

''Why, yes . . . I suppose he has, now that you mention it. Is that why?''

''He wouldn't admit it, but yes.''

''Have you come all the way out here to tell me why Chandler Moffat is taking off weight?''

''No, I've come to tell you that Chandler and I are going overseas.''

''This is no time for traveling, Edward. With all those neutral vessels the Germans keep attacking. That's madness!''

''I'm not talking about a vacation, Irene. I mean the war. There's this bunch of French fliers who are forming an elite corps called the Lafayette Escadrille. A flying corps to fight the Germans. Some of us here in the United States have volunteered to go over and help them.''

''Edward, no! You can't do that. This isn't America's war!''

''It's going to be, Irene. Wilson can't keep us out forever, you must realize that.''

''No, don't say that! Edward, this is too dangerous.''

''It's an adventure!''

''An adventure that could get you killed. You have no stake in this.''

'We all have a stake in it, Irene. Like it or not. Even you. Have you heard anything from your sister Aggie?''

''No, you know I haven't or I would have told you. I really think they must all be dead or she would have found some way to contact me. She would know how worried Mama and I are. Still, that's got nothing to do with you risking your neck. It's a damn-fool stupid thing to do!''

''Well, maybe so. But I'm doing it anyway, and so is Chandler.''

''I don't suppose he can be talked out of it either.''

''Do you want to talk him out of it? I thought you'd be delighted to have him out of your hair.''

''I would be, but I don't want him dead! That's taking a good thing too far.'' Irene paused, then added. ''That was a smarty remark. I'm sorry. Chandler's not all that bad. Since Monsieur died, he's taken more of an interest in the business and he's gotten quite good. That whole time I was gone, he ran things."

"Can you get along without him for a while?"

"How long a while? You can't answer that, can you, because the answer might be 'forever.' Edward, if you're right that we'll get into this war eventually, why don't you just wait?"

"I don't know why. Really. It's just something I have to do. Something I want to do. You know, Irene, I've always sensed you had just the slightest bit of contempt for me because I haven't got the sort of drive and purpose and ambition that you do."

She opened her mouth to deny this, but he didn't let her speak. "Now, when there's something I'm set on doing, you're trying to stop me. Well, you can't have it both ways."

They left in the middle of June. Chandler became engaged before he left, which everyone except Irene thought terribly romantic. "It's plain irresponsible!" she told Clara the day of their departure. "The poor girl is going to end up a virtual widow without ever having been a wife. He just wanted her scarf to tie to his sleeve, like a knight in a tournament. It's ridiculous!" Irene didn't add that she didn't like Chandler's choice of bride-to-be. "Poor thing" was a misnomer. She was Old Line Philadelphia, with a brittle, aloof manner that barely disguised what Irene believed to be a strong streak of ordinary greed. Irene hated the idea of Chandler marrying this disruptive individual just when they were beginning to get along with each other. She would be an interferer.

"And you're being cranky," Clara came back. "It'll look bad if you aren't at the docks to see him off and it'll look even worse if you're grousing around like this. Now, get that parasol so you don't get sunburned and let's go!"

Clara still had a mysterious power over Irene which she employed rarely, but to excellent effect. Irene did as she was told and got through all the *bon-voyages* with a smile that was more of a grimace. She was terribly sorry to see Edward leave. He'd turned out to be a true friend. But she could see why he wanted to go. He had so little to fill his days. Money from the family business just seemed to pour in with or without his attention to it. She'd always felt he lacked purpose; now he had it. But did it have to be something so dangerous?

"Stupid war. Stupid men!" she muttered on the way home.

Early the next week, she said to Clara, "I've been reading about flying. They say it's very cold way up in the air. Even when it's warm on the ground."

"Yes, I suppose it might be." Clara said nothing else, but she knew when a furrier started talking about cold weather, it would lead to only one thing.

The next day Irene brought it up again. "We lay off a lot of cutters and stitchers in the summer, and rabbit fur is so cheap right now . . ."

"Yes?"

"Clara, don't you see? We could give some of our people summer employment making fur-lined gloves and jackets for the fliers. We wouldn't need to make a profit—just enough to pay for the labor and materials. I'm sure Chandler wouldn't mind that. He'd be proud of his company helping his efforts."

"You're wanting to do this for Chandler?"

Irene was silent for a long monent, thinking about this. "I guess I'm doing it for Aggie, in a way. I mean, I can't do anything for her. I don't even know if she's alive. But if I can't help her, I feel like I must help someone."

Her thoughts were echoed a month later from a most unexpected source.

The first shipment was ready the third week of July. Using a photograph Edward had sent of himself in his "uniform," Irene had designed a jacket that was sleek and comfortable but had plenty of arm room for ease of movement. The pattern was adapted to a range of sizes and two dozen were made up. Likewise, two dozen pairs of gloves, lined with the best rabbit fur available, were made up in several sizes. A label on each coat and glove identified it as a garment supplied to the Escadrille by Neptune et Cie. In the end, there had been no negotiating for sale. "Just keep track of all the costs. I'll contribute it," she told Clara.

They made quite a ceremony of packing the coats and gloves. All the summer employees were present and helped nail the crate up, and though their work was done, they all stayed on until the carters had come to take it to the docks. Irene went home that evening feeling a warm satisfaction that had nothing to do with the heat of the day. Zofia had taken Connie and Stefania to the country to escape the sweltering city and Irene was sorry they wouldn't be home. She needed to share the sense of pride and well-being that was bubbling over in her. She supposed she'd leave the next morning and join them for a few days.

She had her driver drop her off a few blocks from home. She had extra energy she had to walk off or she would be up all night. She was watching her feet as she walked, humming a tune that had been stuck in her head all day. That's why she didn't see him sitting on the front porch until she was almost there. He was reading a book—naturally. His head was bent and the later-afternoon sun reflected the gold in his hair.

She stopped, staring in amazement. Was there time to turn and run? Was that what she wanted to do? She had no idea.

He looked up, set the book aside, and stood. "Irene," he said.

"Peter."

32

July 1916

Irene's thoughts were like fireflies on a dark night, a light here and a flash there and an unexpected twinkle just on the periphery of her vision elusive and flickering. In her surprised state, she couldn't articulate anything significant. There was so much that needed to be said, but she couldn't think of where to start. In desperation she fell back on the mundane, just to be speaking because it seemed someone should say something. "Didn't anyone come to the door?" she asked.

He'd grown older and it suited him. His hair was darker, and he seemed taller than she remembered, though of course that was imagination. Had his eyes always been such a pale, clear blue?

"Yes, a maid answered. But I didn't think I should go in your house until I knew if I was welcome."

She looked half-scared and younger than he remembered. He shouldn't have taken her by surprise this way. He should have written first. It wasn't fair to her. But then, he'd feared asking her if he could visit; she might have refused to see him.

"It's your house and of course you're welcome."

Three years. Had it only been three years? It seemed a century, so much had happened. She was a different person. A wiser person, she thought.

"Then we're still married?" he asked.

God, but she was even more beautiful in person than in his dreams. He'd have given anything to take the pins out of her hair and once again feel the silky weight of it in his hands.

"Yes."

How could he wonder? Wouldn't there have been thunderbolts from an angry Polish God if she'd gotten a divorce?

"I'd like to talk to you . . . somewhere else. If you're willing."

He shouldn't have done this. How was he going to do what he had to do now that he'd seen her and been caught back up in the spell?

"Shall we walk? There's a park a few blocks away."

What did it all mean? She'd come to accept—almost accept—that she'd never see him again, and yet he'd come here of his own volition. Why?

"Yes, I remember. It hasn't been *that* long."

It seemed suddenly as if they'd never been apart, that they'd had breakfast this morning together. How was he going to keep his hands off her? He didn't dare go in that house. What a fool he'd been to leave, to put himself through the torture of separation. Nothing could really have been that bad? He hardly remembered why it seemed the thing he had to do way back then.

They set out for the park, carefully keeping a safe distance as if they were half-afraid of each other. "Monsieur Neptune died," she said simply because there was a crackling silence between them that had to be muffled with words.

"I know. I saw an article in the paper."

And I came to you for comfort and you weren't there, she thought to herself, remembering that humiliating day.

"Where have you been?" she asked.

She knew, then, that he hadn't stayed at the college upstate. Did that mean she'd inquired after him?

"I've been living in Chicago. Teaching. I have something for you."

She hadn't noticed he was carrying a small package. He handed it to her and she stopped walking to unwrap the brown paper. A book. The cover said *Historical Origins of the Judeo-Christian Ethic*, by Dr. Peter Garrick."

"Dr. Garrick?" she exclaimed.

"Only a scholarly one, not the kind with pills. You don't have to read it. It would probably bore you senseless. I just wanted you to have it."

Irene opened the book, flipped carefully through the pages.

She was in absolute awe of the densely filled pages of print and the sheer bulk of the volume. So much of what she had and knew of life had come from books—she had a tremendous respect for them and their authors. A whole book of Peter Garrick's thoughts and ideas. She was overwhelmed and didn't know what to say. For lack of anything more profound, she asked, "Do you make money writing a book?"

Peter stared at her a minute, then burst into laughter. "Oh, Irene, only you would ask that!"

"What's funny? I only meant that you're so very smart and it must have taken you so much time and thought, I hope you were well paid for your efforts."

He just laughed all the harder. Finally he said, "No, it doesn't pay very well, but fortunately it's regarded as an important work in philosophical circles. It's getting some excellent reviews, I'm glad to say, and will probably continue to sell for some years to come. Over the course of them, it ought to make a respectable amount of money. There have already been several of the largest theological schools in the country inquiring about getting enough copies to use as a standard text." He was smiling.

"Have I said something wrong? You're laughing at me."

He answered her very seriously. "No, Irene. I'd never laugh at you. I'm just surprised that I didn't correctly predict your reaction. I should have, as well as I know you."

"I'm not so sure you do know me anymore. A lot has happened since . . . since you left me."

There it was. The bitterness he'd expected and feared. "Tell me what's happened," he said with deliberate mildness, refusing to rise to the bait of argument.

She didn't want to fight either. Not now. There was so much they had to talk about, but certain facts could be shared first, gotten out of the way before they discussed themselves. Like clearing a table of decorative knickknacks before setting it for a meal. "Teo came back," she said.

"Your brother Teo? You mean he was alive all that time?"

She told him all about it—her brother's return, the business she set him up in, the fire, his midnight departure. She was careful not to say how she felt about it all. He wasn't entitled to her emotions—not yet. Perhaps not at all.

"Have you heard from him since then?" Peter asked.

"Not a word."

"What about your sisters?"

"The twins are married. They married brothers and moved to California."

"And Stefania?"

"Home with Mama and me. Fat. Shy."

"And how is Zofia?"

"Happy as can be, looking after Connie."

She could have bitten her tongue. How stupid could she be! This wasn't the time to spring Connie on him.

"Who's Connie?"

Too late. She didn't dare fumble for an explanation or he'd suspect something. "Connie is my adopted daughter." Damn! She'd almost cured herself of the guilt she once felt about Connie's birth. Why did it flood back over her now?

"Oh? Why is that? I mean, why did you adopt a child?" For a second the word "adopted" hadn't registered with him. Only "daughter" and he'd thought they'd had a child after he left. He felt a pang that was part regret, part relief.

"I went back to the village to see Aggie. One of our cousins died and left the child motherless." Later, if there was to be a "later" for them, she'd tell him the truth. She'd have to. But not now; she couldn't yet trust him with something so heavily freighted in emotion.

"What about the child's father? Why didn't Aggie take it?"

"Why are you questioning me this way?" she asked.

He was taken back by the defensive sharpness in her tone. "I'm sorry. I have no right to ask anything, I guess. What about Clara? How is she?"

They talked awhile longer, filling in some of the more gaping blanks in the missing years, then Irene said, "What about you? What are you doing here? In New York, I mean, if you live in Chicago."

"I'm going to England. To enlist."

He might as well have punched her in the stomach. "You too? I didn't think you'd be susceptible to the romantic lure of a uniform."

"Me too? Who else are we talking about?"

"Oh, just any number of people—Chandler Moffat, for one."

Peter smiled. "I see how you'd find it confusing, then. But I'm not going with any sort of romantic notions. I'm going because I have to."

"I've heard that before, too."

"You're sounding remarkably bitter, you know."

"I guess I am, but I despise it when people think they can avoid rationality by claiming that they just 'have to' do something that there's no sensible reason for."

What a fool I am, she thought, thinking he'd come back to me. I'm just an acquaintance to visit between the train and the ship. A way to kill a few hours of boredom. She found that she was clutching the book he'd given her in a grip so tight her fingers ached.

"Then I'll give you my cause—sensible or not. I'm going because of what's happening to the Poles. They're caught in the middle, getting trampled by both sides of a war that has nothing to do with them. It makes me angry. I tried to ignore that anger for a long time, telling myself like most of us do that it isn't my affair. But my mind and conscience kept coming back to the thought that my people are there."

"Your people? But you don't know who your family is."

"True, but that doesn't mean they aren't there and they aren't suffering. My mother is probably there, if she's still living. All that business about her going to America was just a childish way of dealing with the pain of knowing she . . . she threw me away." He paused, sorry that he'd let that shard of fury come into his voice. With purposeful calm he went on. "I know I don't owe her anything; she abandoned me. But who can know why or what pain that might have caused her. I may have brothers and sisters, cousins, aunts and uncles. I can't call them by name, but they may exist, and if so, they need all the help they can get."

"Like Aggie," she said softly.

"Aggie? You mean she's still there?"

"She wouldn't come back with me. I found out that she and her husband and children left the village, but I've never heard of or from them since."

"I'm sorry, Irene. I feel a fool for making all those 'noble' remarks about theoretical people, when real ones—"

"No, you're quite right. And whether the individual Poles are related to us or not, they do need help."

They sat in silence, watching darkness settle over the park and thinking about the extraordinary situation they were in. Irene's primary emotion was still an embarrassment that she'd misjudged what his sudden appearance meant. How foolish and vain of her to think he'd come back just to see her. She would never forgive herself for falling into such an error. But still, he hadn't needed to. He could have passed through New York without her ever knowing. He'd managed without seeing her for a long time without any apparent ill effects. Why now?

His thoughts were along the same lines. As if reading her mind, he suddenly said, "I may not survive, you know. War doesn't give special treatment to scholars. I had to see you again—in case."

"In case . . . ?"

"I wanted to tell you something—in person."

"What's that?"

"That I love you. That I've never stopped loving you and thinking of you."

"Then why—?"

"Never mind why anything. Irene, I've only got two days before I have to go. Let's don't talk about the whys. Could we . . . could *you* forget the past for that long? Could we spend this time together, not as husband and wife—I've forfeited that right—but just as two people who care about each other? No, don't say anything. You don't have to. I'm not trying to force any issues with you. I've said it, now let's talk about something else. Are you hungry?"

"I think so."

"You don't know?" He grinned.

She smiled too. "I'm still too shocked to know anything. Yes, I'm starving."

"Then let's go have dinner and get to know each other again. Shall we?"

"Yes."

* * *

It was as though the rules had been laid out in advance and both of them had memorized them. No talk of anything in the past that touched on both of them or the way they felt about each other. No references to the future at all, either hers or his. But they filled the evening with talk, just the same. Irene told him interesting things about the business—her trips to the St. Louis and German auction houses, details about the twins' wedding, politics (insofar as they could be kept apart from any reference to the war).

Peter chatted brightly about his studies, making the dullest courses sound marginally interesting. He described the places he'd been, some of the eccentric professors he'd worked with, the stages of getting his book published. Anyone else seeing them or listening in would have been certain they were a friendly brother and sister who hadn't seen each other in a long time. When at last it grew very late, Peter took her home.

"You'll stay here? It's your home too."

"I think not. I've got a room uptown at a hotel. I think it's best I stay there."

She wanted to beg him, but refrained. This evening had been torture, being so close and not daring to touch. Whatever else might have changed, she still wanted him—now more than ever before.

"May I see you tomorrow?" he asked.

"Yes. If you want."

"Don't you have to go to work?"

Was there a hint of criticism in that, or did she just expect there to be? "I was going to work at home anyway. Sketches for next fall's line. But they can wait."

He looked pleased. Was this, too, a test? And had she passed this time? "Good. I'll pick you up at ten."

Irene was still lying awake at two in the morning when a tremendous explosion rocked the house. The first of her many scattered thoughts was that the furnace in the basement had blown up, but that couldn't be it. It was summer. Next, as she scrambled out of bed searching frantically for her robe and slippers, she thought how fortunate it was that Zofia,

Stefania, and Connie were still gone. As frightened as she was, Connie would have been terrified.

She jammed her feet into her slippers and raced downstairs, sniffing for smoke and looking around for flames. The staff, cook and three maids, were in the front hall in their nightwear, shouting fuddled questions at each other. One of the maids had a suitcase—apparently she kept it ready for instant flight, and Irene found herself wondering why. There was glass all over the front hall where the elaborate fanlight above the front door had blown out.

"Stop that hysterical shrieking!" Irene screamed. "If it had been inside the house, it would have blown the glass *out,* not in. It must have been something outside." She wasn't sure this was correct, but it sounded logical and did have the effect of calming the others.

They opened the door and peered out. All up and down the street, people were outside, asking questions at the top of their lungs. "Is it the Germans? Have we been bombed?" Somewhere in the distance there was a rumbling sound like a massive fireworks display run amok. Another loud boom split the air and shook the ground.

Irene's maid started wailing. The cook, having greater presence of mind, slapped the maid briskly and then trotted off around the corner to Fifth Avenue and came back a few minutes later with what little news she could get from a passing cab. "It seems to have been something that blew up downtown. Not near here. That's all anybody seems to know."

"It's the war!" the maid with the suitcase screamed. "They're bombing us. I'm going home." And before anyone could stop her, she hitched up her nightgown, hoisted her suitcase, and disappeared into the night.

While trying to calm the others, Irene was considering the same thing. It just might be a battle. If so, they ought to flee. But where? If the rest of the family had been home, she might have considered it more seriously, but Zofia was with the girls, safe (she hoped!) in the country. If she went to join them as they were trying to come to join her, they might lose track of each other entirely. After a while, however, it occurred to her that the police, who were now patrolling the neighborhood checking for injuries from broken glass, would have alerted them if there was any need to evacuate. She went back in, dressed, and set out looking for an officer.

"Just some munitions dump over by New Jersey, ma'am," he reassured her. "No Huns on the horizon."

It went on for three hours, blast after blast of noise. Sometimes a rocket would soar into the air and light up the southern sky. Eventually they all went back inside and tried to go to sleep. But no one got any rest at all. Even by five, when the noise had subsided to an occasional muffled burst, no one could relax. The feeling of incipient warfare had been planted like a malignant seed. They were vulnerable. All of America was vulnerable. This might not stay a safely distant European war.

Moreover, Irene was struck by the fact that Peter was about to place himself in a situation in which nights like this were normal. He was going to be in the midst of the hysteria, the alarms, the horrible danger of bombs and guns. And for the first time, she felt the maddening frustration of knowing that war is a juggernaut that, once set in motion, cannot be stopped or even slowed by any individual. There was *nothing* to do but somehow try to survive and endure.

Early in the morning the cook went back out for papers and news and reported to Irene. There was, it seemed, a peninsula off the New Jersey shore just behind the Statue of Liberty, called Black Tom Island. It had been used as a munitions dump for millions of pounds of explosives awaiting shipment to the Allies. Something—or, more likely, someone—had blown it up. It was widely assumed, though never proved, that German agents were reponsible. Not only was all the valuable war matériel lost, but the city had sustained expensive damage. All the skylights at the Aquarium were broken, though the fish tanks were miraculously left intact. Every single window in the House of Morgan was gone, and there was over a million dollars in damage to windows throughout the Wall Street Area. In fact, there were windows shattered as far north as Forty-second Street, so powerful was the explosion.

He was there at nine-thirty.

She was ready.

"I thought you might have changed your mind," he said.

"Why would I?"

"A hundred reasons. You have very good cause to hate me." When he realized she wasn't going to reply to this, he went on, "Where shall we go? Would you object terribly to stopping by St. Stanislas for a few minutes?"

She did, but wouldn't have said so for the world.

The farther downtown they went, the more apparent the damage from the explosion the night before. And the more apparent the fear. People seemed to be hurrying, as if eager to get their work or errands done and return to the relative safety of their homes. Even those who stopped to talk seemed to be almost jabbering in their haste. But Peter and Irene didn't talk about it, pretended not to notice. It was part of the war and a forbidden subject.

Peter visited with the priest at St. Stanislas and an old friend who happened to drop by at the same time. He sensed Irene's boredom and impatience and kept it short. She sensed his need to reestablish these old ties that once meant so much to him, and tried not to look bored.

They stayed only a few minutes, then started back uptown. Neither of them even looked out the window of the cab when they passed the block where their first apartment was. They stopped six blocks short of home and got lunch, then, without discussing their destination, started back to Irene's house—which is how Peter thought of it in spite of any legalities of ownership.

"Irene, if I come back from Europe, will you see me again?"

"Yes," she said softly.

"I made an awful mistake, leaving. I see that now. These few hours together have made me realize what I gave up. Is there any way you'll ever be able to forgive me?"

Irene didn't know what to answer. She wanted him back; there was no question of that. She'd felt happier and more alive this last day than for years before. But could she forgive him the pain, the humiliation of the past? She wasn't sure. "Peter, what's changed? What's different now?"

"You are. I am."

"How?"

"You don't seem so driven and I'm not so threatened by . . ." He stopped.

"Threatened by what?"

"I'm not sure. You. Your ambition. Your sense of knowing what you want to do and how you want to do it. I understand that better now because I've had the opportunity to do what I wanted. Does that make any sense?"

"No, not really. I'd have given up anything you asked me to."

"I know you'd have tried, but you'd have been devastated by it. That's why I could never ask. But I don't feel like I need to ask you to give up anything anymore. Do you remember when I said I felt like I was a way station in your life? That you'd caught up with me and then moved ahead, leaving me behind?"

"Oh, I remember. But I didn't agree then and I don't agree now."

"Regardless, I feel like I've caught up again. I guess it doesn't matter whether you understand that as long as I do. I know it's wrong to just throw myself back into your life and expect things to go on. I can't do that anyway. Not now. All I'm asking is that you keep an open mind and open heart until I come back. I *will* come back. I promise that."

You can't promise that, she thought, but it was not something that could be spoken.

"Don't feel you have to say anything now. I don't leave until this evening and if you are still undecided then, I'll understand."

"I have to think. I'm so confused . . ."

They'd been walking and had reached the corner of her street. As they turned, Irene saw the chauffeur driving off from the front of the house. "Mama must be back," she said. "I hope there's nothing wrong."

Zofia was still in the hall when Irene dashed ahead of Peter up the steps. "No, nothing is wrong with us. But we hear a big noise last night and they say it's from the city. I bring the girls back to see what happen. Who's that man . . . ? Piotr! Are my eyes lying to me? Piotr, is that you?"

She flung herself at him and dragged him inside. For a few minutes they exclaimed over each other in Polish, while Irene stood aside thinking how very good it sounded to hear his voice in this house again. It made the colors brighter and the spaces bigger. Zofia screamed for Stefania, who came downstairs and greeted him with the happiest expression Irene had ever seen on her round face. It all seemed irrevocably right, a moment that could be treasured and remembered and referred to as long as it might take for Peter to return. In the months to come, she could tell herself: This is what life will be like.

Finally Peter said, "What about this daughter of yours? Do I get to see her?"

Zofia gave Irene a quick, alarmed look.

"I told Peter about adopting the little girl in Aggie's village, Mama. You didn't leave Connie behind with the nursemaid, did you?"

"Would I leave my darling? No, she's upstairs. I bring her."

She galloped off up the stairs and Peter said, "Zofia looks ten years younger. It's amazing."

They went into the music room to wait for Connie to arrive, and when she did, she ran across the room to Irene and crawled onto her lap. "Peter, this is Connie—obviously!" Irene said, laughing.

Connie put her thumb in her mouth and snuggled closer to Irene, giving Peter shy looks. Finally she climbed down and went back to Zofia, babbling about a doll she'd left upstairs.

"Zofia, I'd like to speak to Irene alone," Peter said, his voice as smooth and metallic as polished copper.

"Piotr—"

"Please, Zofia."

With a hopeless shrug she gathered Connie up and left the room. Irene was frozen in place.

"Why did you lie to me?" he asked.

Irene couldn't speak.

"Did you honestly believe I would be too stupid to see the truth? Do you have so much contempt for me? She's exactly like you, *your* daughter. Who's the father? Anybody I know?"

"Peter, please, let me explain . . ." What did she think she was going to say? What explanation was there?

"It's too late. I don't even want to know. If you'd told me to begin with, Irene, I could have probably accepted anything. After all, I left you. That was my fault. I wouldn't have liked knowing that you had a child by another man, but I could have understood. But you *lied!* You thought you could play the same cheap trick on me that you're no doubt getting away with playing on your society friends. How dare you assume I'm so placid and dull-witted that I'd just believe it!"

"Peter, I had to."

"No, only moral cowards have to lie. And that, apparently, is what you are, Irene. What you have become, rather. Whatever your faults may have been, I'd have never expected that of you. You were always so devastatingly truthful; it was one of the things I most admired and respected about you, even when it hurt both of us. But you've lost that integrity."

She was torn between outrage that he could say such things to her and a terrible sense that he was right. Had she really believed he wouldn't know? She should have told him the truth; she would have, eventually. Why not at first? "You didn't give me a chance to even get my thoughts together," she said. "You just dropped back into my life—I had no idea why; I had no opportunity to think about what I should say or do!"

"And that, my dear wife, is exactly the sort of situation in which people show their true colors," he said stiffly, thinking of that night Jane Follette had brought the basket of jelly to his house. A priggish, superior attitude, he knew, but still he was in the grip of it and was as helpless as Irene at the moment. He stood up. "Well, I came back to see if either of us had changed enough to make the marriage work. Now I see that one of us has changed a great deal. Good-bye, Irene."

She wanted to get up and run after him—whether to try to detain him or scratch his eyes out, she wasn't sure. But she was simply too stunned to move. The music-room door slammed. The front door slammed. And then opened and closed again. Had he come back? She waited a moment, but the house was still. All she could hear was the faint sound of Connie's laughter from the playroom above her.

She got up and slowly went up the stairs, holding the banister in case her legs should give out on her. The nursemaid was putting away some colorful blocks and Connie was sitting cross-legged in the window seat trying to put a dress back on her doll. Irene sat down and helped her and then took Connie in her arms. The little girl smelled faintly of soap and the peppermint candies Zofia sometimes gave her. "Do *you* love me?" Irene whispered miserably.

Connie put her arms around her neck.

The next morning, Zofia woke her. "Irina, get up. There is something here to read."

"Leave me alone, Mama."

"No, get up. A boy from the church, St. Stanislas, bring this letter from the priest for you."

"Peter! It's something about Peter!" Irene said, then remembered *all* of the day before. "Throw it away. I don't want to know what it says."

"I do!" Zofia said, jerking the covers away and sticking the envelope under her nose.

Reluctantly Irene opened it. Inside was a single sheet of paper, a note from the priest. "I'm sorry that I'm indisposed and cannot bring this to you in person. My prayers are with you and your family for good news. Do not hesitate to call on me, should you feel the need."

Folded inside this note was a small, much-folded and very dirty envelope. It was addressed simply to "Irina Gieryk, St. Stanislas, New York, America."

It was in Aggie's handwriting.

"Mama! It's a letter from Aggie." Irene carefully opened the envelope and pulled out a piece of paper, written on in faded pencil. She read aloud:

> Irina, this is the fifth letter I've written you. I do not know if any have reached you. Each time someone here tries to get through the lines, many of us give them letters to take. Most, I fear, are captured. That is why I can't give your address or mine; the Germans should not have such information.
>
> Olbracht was captured by the Russian army and put into a uniform. I saw him last as he marched away at gunpoint. Wanda had been sick, mostly from poor food

and being frightened all the time, but God willing this war ends, she will recover. Stefan broke his foot stepping in a hole in the ground as we fled at night once. He is apt to walk with a limp, but has a good, brave spirit.

I haven't any more paper, so I must simply tell you that we are determined to live and thrive someday. We think of you and Mama and Stefania and the twins and Connie with love. Pray that we may all be together again someday.

God's blessing on you all,
Aggie

33

It was all a matter of bargains and trades, Irene decided in the next months as she struggled to keep the business going in spite of the restrictions on international trade and her own personal worries. God gave things, but they weren't gifts as people like Zofia believed. For everything he gave, he took something else away or inflicted a punishment—sometimes in excess of the boon. Irene had gotten to come to America, but she'd spent year after deadly year with the Sprys. She was given half of Neptune et Cie, a greater ''gift'' than she'd ever dreamed of, but in return, she'd lost Peter, a greater price than she'd dreamed of paying. God had provided her with Connie and deprived her of Monsieur. It was even apparent in the family; she'd finally been granted her mother's love at the same time she lost the love and respect she'd had for her brother. And it had happened again this summer. Within a few hours she'd received the wonderful news that Aggie and the children were alive, but had again lost Peter's love.

That was one thing that would never happen to her again, she vowed over and over as summer faded to fall and dashed into a bitter winter. *Never*. Whether Peter Garrick survived the war or not meant nothing to her; nothing at all. She didn't wish him dead, of course, but neither would she ever see him again. Only a fool let someone destroy her three times. Twice was her limit. After long thought, she'd come to the conclusion that he'd been wrong. Utterly wrong to assess her morality so scathingly. Why had she owed him the truth he demanded? After Neptune's death, when she so desperately needed him—had, in fact, sought him out—he wasn't there. So what earthly right had he to expect her to pour out her most treasured and dangerous secret to him just because he showed up at the door one day?

She couldn't bear for him, of all people, to impugn her morality. She wasn't smart enough to write books; she might not be a doctor of philosophy like he was. She didn't even attend church often anymore. But she was a good person. At least she tried very hard to be. She'd never knowingly cheated anyone of anything. She'd never stolen. She didn't lie. Well, not exactly. The lie she lived about her mysterious past did no one any harm, and the lie about Connie's birth only protected the child from the stigma of illegitimacy. Irene knew she was generous—she gave frequently to charity and more frequently to her family. She was a respectful daughter to Zofia and a true friend to Clara and a loving mother to Connie.

And for all of that, Dr. Peter Garrick had felt free to waltz into her life, disrupt her heart, and then berate her for her morality. Who did he think he was, anyway? To claim he loved her and immediately start hacking at her foundations! What arrogance!

Well, he'd never get the opportunity again. And neither would anybody else. She was fed up with men. They had all, in one way or another, betrayed her. Her father had used her hard-earned money for himself, Teo had done the same. Neptune had died; Edward had gone prancing off to somebody else's war for the sheer glamour of it; and Peter . . .

It was the women in her life who'd stood by her and deserved her loyalty. Her mother, difficult as she could be, was a support; and Clara, who could likewise be sharp-tongued and far too blunt for comfort, was devoted to her, Irene's, welfare. And there was Connie, too. The centerpiece of her life. That and her financial and social success were all she wanted or needed of life.

She went into the winter with that attitude firmly in mind. The economy was booming, or so the papers said every day—several pages into the paper, because the front pages were invariably taken up with war news. And it certainly seemed to be true at Neptune et Cie. The women who bought the coats and muffs and scarves and stoles seemed to be spending as if there were no tomorrow. Unfortunately, skirts had gotten shorter and fuller, and while Irene had always followed Neptune's maxim about being a style-setter rather than a style-follower, she had to take this into consideration. It was difficult to design an attractive coat to go over a short, full skirt. They all ended up looking like shapeless tents. Nor had she ever come to like the coarse American furs that were so popular now. She could, of course, still get European imports, but the price was nearly prohibitive. Still, there were plenty of women happy to pay it, so she found herself making more money than ever before.

The improved economy was also evident in the increased number of charity functions she attended. She had always been assiduous in this duty; it was an absolute prerequisite to women of her social standing. It also, as Neptune had cynically pointed out, gave an excellent opportunity to be seen with the right people wearing the best furs. During the winter of 1916–1917, Irene threw herself wholeheartedly into a half-dozen charities. There were a number of war-relief organizations: funds to be raised for Belgium widows and orphans, French widows and orphans, British widows and orphans. There was also a move on several fronts to help the poor of their own city. A number of prominent ladies had noticed that there were immigrants on the Lower East Side who lived like animals and were determined to help them.

Irene contributed to all these. She attended fund-raising dinners and dances and theater performances. She bought and sold tickets for raffles. But far more quietly, she continued to make regular shipments of jackets and gloves to Edward and Chandler for their men. And she contributed what she could to Mrs. Pankhurst's efforts on behalf of women's rights. She had mixed feelings about this. She herself had acquired a good life by herself, in spite of being a woman. But she'd had to pay what she considered an unfair price. She'd had to pretend a husband, and while she was sure no one bothered to believe in his existence anymore, she had to keep up the pretense or she could still be "cut," which would seriously damage her financial well-being. She was also forced to pretend that her beloved Connie wasn't really her child because society was willing to accept a man's extramarital affairs, but not a woman's.

In spite of the time and work her charities took and the

cash they relieved her of, she still had more energy and money than she quite knew what to do with. By January she was bored and needed a new project to occupy her mind—and keep it off Peter. It was maddening the way she kept thinking about him in spite of her resolve to put him entirely out of her life.

She bought a new house—or rather, an old house farther uptown. A mansion far grander than their house on Thirty-third came up for sale near Fiftieth and Fifth and Irene bought it in spite of an outrageous price. The house they had lived in all these years was not suitable for entertaining; she had never wanted to entertain there anyway, with her unruly and still-unpresentable family around. But the twins had gone and she felt fairly secure than neither Zofia nor Stefania would wish to be a part of any guest list. Besides, they had taken to spending more and more time at the house in the country. She could just plan for company when she knew they would be gone.

She spent a fortune on the house, redecorating its heavy, oppressively Victorian interior to her more subtle, spare tastes. She derived such pleasure from a number of Alphonse Mucha advertising posters that she used them as her guide. Not that they were considered art to be hung, but she adopted the rich but understated color schemes, the flowing lines, the repeating circles and arches, the voluptuous simplicity of his work. The dining room, though no one ever guessed, was based on a Lefèvre-Utile biscuit ad. Her bedroom was Moët et Chandon White Star champagne; the front entryway was Alfred De Musset's *Lorenzaccio;* the ballroom was Nestlé's baby food; and the music room was based on a bicycle ad. This harmless secret joke gave her inordinate pleasure. And in some complicated way, so did the book that had a place of honor above the mantlepiece in the main sitting room—the book by Dr. Peter Garrick.

The decorating helped keep her mind off the war, but there were still reminders everywhere. The city had a large German population, some of whom were reservists in the German Army. They would sometimes stage marches and rallies and as often as not clash with other groups of French and English descent who brandished their own flags as they leapt into the fray. Mayor Mitchel eventually banned the display of all foreign flags, but this didn't stop the conflict.

New York had become the headquarters of a network of underground saboteurs and spies, primarily German. That winter, tempers grew frayed, suspicions exaggerated, and plots seemed to be going on everywhere. At one point, a house on Fifteenth Street was raided—a house where there had been so many men coming and going that the neighbors complained of it as a whorehouse. But rather than ladies of doubtful virtue, it was discovered to be full of bombs and dynamite. Stored in preparation for some attack on the city itself? No one knew for sure.

America was still officially neutral that spring as Irene feverishly went over wallpapers, paints, and fabrics for her new house; but the neutrality was strictly official. Germany announced that it was going to resume unrestricted warfare on the high seas. "Unrestricted? They've been blasting anything they want to out of the water already!" people said.

President Wilson asked Congress to arm merchant ships so that they might defend themselves against attack; the Senate refused; Wilson proceeded with the arming by executive order. It was an informal declaration of war.

When Clara made this observation, Irene just said, "Why not make it official? The city looks like it's under siege already."

"What do you mean?"

"I was running errands yesterday—some fabric swatches and paint samples I wanted to look at. But I saw all kinds of other things I wouldn't ordinarily have noticed. Do you realize there's a cavalry force guarding the water supply? And soldiers all up and down the East River, guarding the bridges? They're hardly even bothering to look discreet anymore."

"What will happen to us all?" Clara asked sadly. "And what will an outright declaration of war do to the business?"

"I can't imagine, but I fear the worst. They say the Allies are losing, you know."

"The maps in the newspaper certainly make it look that way. But they think if we come in, it'll end in victory pretty quickly," Clara said.

"'I hear that too, but I heard it from Edward and Chandler when they went over, and that was nearly a year ago."

"How are they both getting along?" Clara asked, eager for a change of subject. Chandler had burst an eardrum in an early flight and had been serving in an administrative capacity since then. A month earlier Edward's small plane had crashed on takeoff and he'd miraculously suffered nothing worse than a broken leg and a laceration on his left hand.

"Fine, I believe. Edward says he won't come back until it's over. By the way, his last letter said something about Chandler's engagement being broken. Typically, like a man, he didn't bother to mention who broke it off. He also said all sorts of nonsense about joining the ground crew if they wouldn't let him fly again, but he wouldn't last long that way. It's too plebeian for his tastes."

"That sounds very cynical," Clara said.

"I feel cynical. It's as if life's supposed to be moving along to some natural conclusion, or at least in some sort of progression, and this horrible war is . . . is just stirring us around in aimless, terrible circles. Nobody's getting anywhere. I don't mean just me. I mean everybody."

"I think that's why there are so many people who are desperately anxious for an official declaration of war from our own government, don't you? It would at least seem like a specific action, however awful, instead of this standing at the sidelines, being part but not really part."

"I suppose you're right. Most people do seem to want us to get in."

"Don't you? For Aggie's sake?"

"I'm not sure. Our own soldiers could just as well kill her as the Germans. The more soldiers there are running around Europe, the more danger there is to people like her—the innocent noncombatants. Oh, Clara, do you think there's a chance she's alive? Or that I'll ever see her and her family again?"

"Yes, I'm certain of both," Clara said, even though she wasn't at all certain and Irene wasn't fooled by her words. She also found herself wondering just how much of Irene's concern was really for Aggie and how much was for Peter. Irene had told her in the briefest possible terms about his return and subsequent departure in a fury over Connie's parentage. Clara had longed to know more of the details, but had sensed that Irene was hanging on to her self-control by a thread, and hadn't asked anything. And Irene had never brought up his name again. Clara was left wondering about the book she'd seen at Irene's new house—the philosophy book Peter had written, which was displayed so prominently but never mentioned.

The decorating was to be finished the last week in March. Irene planned a party for the second of April. First a small party at the Metropolitan Opera House, then a late supper and dance in the ballroom of her new home. As always, she had the problem of an escort to consider. And as always, she chose a "harmless" man—old Mrs. Piper's elderly bachelor brother, Fenwick Greenston. Unfortunately, Mr. Greenston didn't quite realize he'd reached the harmless stage of life and flirted hideously.

The opera was De Koven's *The Canterbury Pilgrims*, and as they were settling into their places, old Fenwick temporarily abandoned his attempts to find excuses to touch Irene and started pointing out people in the audience to her. ". . . and isn't that James Gerard?" he asked.

"I don't know him," Irene said, anxious for the performance to start so he would settle down and be quiet and stop fondling her hand.

"Of course you do, my dear. He's our ambassador to Germany. Was, I should say. Wilson recalled him. Bad sign, that."

Finally the lights dimmed and Irene was able to relax. She stayed in her place between acts while Greenston went off to get himself a drink. She was feeling very odd, knowing that after tonight there would be that inevitable letdown when a project was finished. By tomorrow, she would need to start thinking of something else to consume her interest. As she was considering this, people started filing back in and there was suddenly a stir behind her. She looked around to see James Gerard, the man Greenston had pointed out earlier, striding down the aisle with a newspaper folded under his arm. People were gathered around him, asking questions. He went to the front of the theater, between the orchestra pit and the front rows, and held his arms up for silence, waving the paper aloft.

"Ladies and gentlemen, your attention, please. I have an announcement of import. President Woodrow Wilson has asked Congress to declare war against Germany!"

Cheers drowned out anything else he might have had to say. The orchestra struck up the national anthem. Everyone stood, many with tears in their eyes, and broke into cheering again when the music stopped. To her own surprise, Irene joined them. She'd never favored the idea of war, but still, it had been a threat hanging over the country for so long now, it was a relief of sorts to have it finally arrive.

When the curtain rose on the last act, a German singer by the name of Margarete Ober, who was singing the part of the Wife of Bath, came onstage, attempted croakingly to continue for a minute or two, and fell into a faint.

Irene's party was a success in most eyes, an utter failure in her own. All the people who had attempted for years to get an invitation to her home, or even find out her address in order to look over her surroundings, were absorbed in the news of the war instead of showing the least interest in the unveiling. This evening had been terribly important to her, a new stage in her life. To the rest it was important for an entirely different reason. She supposed she should be relieved to be spared the sort of questioning she'd grown so wearily accustomed to, but it was still a vague disappointment.

Four days later, Congress voted as Wilson asked. At five o'clock that morning, six hundred customs agents seized the eighteen German ships that were in New York harbor. The Germans on board—twelve hundred sailors and 325 officers—were taken to internment at Ellis Island, the German flags came down, and American ones went up. The Twenty-second U.S. Infantry marched through the Hudson tubes to Hoboken, where they followed their instructions to seize the piers of the North German Lloyd and Hamburg-American lines. The waterfront fell under martial law. These were the first acts of war.

Before very long, a steel net was stretched across the

Narrows and sunk to prevent German U-boats from entering the harbor. Many felt this was an unnecessary and downright overdramatic gesture until some German subs planted mines in the water around Sandy Hook in the path of outgoing troop ships. Tugboats had to be refitted as minesweepers. The World War had really come to New York and it was terrifying.

In May Irene received a chilling communication from a lawyer in St. Louis. A man named Leo Jones had been arrested as a result of a street brawl. He had no funds for his own defense, but asked the lawyer to mention Teo Kossok to Mrs. Garrick. He indicated that she had once been acquainted with him under this name.

She wrote back, enclosing a check, saying that Mr. Kossok was a distant relation and while she didn't know him well, she didn't want any family member, however slightly connected, to be without legal representation. A few weeks later, another letter came explaining that Mr. Kossok had been found guilty, but the judge had not incarcerated him on receiving proof that he would joint the army, thus serving his country rather than disrupting it. Irene hoped this was the end of it, but that proved to be a vain hope. Two months later, she got a telegram from the army stating their regret to inform her that Teo had died in the accidental explosion of a munitions dump in Georgia.

"I have to go down there," Irene told Clara. "Will you come with me?"

"Naturally. But why? There will be a short military funeral, and under the circumstances, you don't really have to attend."

"Oh, yes I do."

"What about Zofia?"

"I haven't told Mama yet."

When they arrived, Clara understood better. "I must see the body before the burial," she told the officer in charge.

"It's not a very pleasant experience, ma'am."

"I don't imagine so. Still, I have to be absolutely certain it's my brother. You see, I've thought he was dead twice before and had to break the news to my mother, only to have him turn up again. The next time I tell her that her only son is dead, I have to be absolutely sure."

The plain pine box did contain what remained of Teo. One side of what had been his face was covered with a bandage, presumably to spare her unnecessary distress, but even in death there was a hint of smirk that identified him unquestionably. Irene stood looking down at him for a long moment, her own face nearly as bloodless as what showed of his. "Bury him wherever you like," she instructed the officer. "But don't put him in with any heroes."

She turned on her heel, leaving the man gaping with surprise. They took the next train back to New York, a train crammed nearly to bursting with soldiers being posted to the city before being shipped out. Clara went home with Irene to tell Zofia. The older woman listened impassively, only the drumming of her gnarled fingers on the arm of the chair giving away anything. When Irene had finished, Zofia said, "My son, he died long ago. Now he is buried at last."

"Yes, Mama," Irene said.

Clara felt a chill crawl down her spine at the stoicism of the two of them. Only she, of all those who were acquainted with them, knew of what very strong stuff they were made.

That same month, Irene read in the paper about the death of the czar and his family. They were distant, unreal figures to her, but when she thought of his daughters, she pictured instead the little Russian girl who had played the piano and broken Mama's precious eggs. What had become of her? she wondered. She tried to feel a decent Christian regret for the grand duchesses, but that other girl kept coming to her mind and it was impossible.

The American Expeditionary Force under Black Jack Pershing didn't set foot on land until late June, the raw young army having been thrown together with strange haste, considering the amount of warning the United States had had. On July 4, 1917, there was a feverishly excited reception in Paris. "*Vive les Teddies!*" the French shouted. "Lafayette, we are here!" the Americans said at the Revolutionary hero's tomb. But for all the cheering, Pershing's men didn't actually see battle until late October—over six months after the declaration of war—and the first of the fifty thousand American soldiers who would die didn't do so until November, because Pershing had no intention of handing his troops over to the European military leaders. He was there to command them, and command them he would. In his own way.

The state of war was evident at every turn in New York. The city was the primary embarkation point and was perpetually mobbed with soldiers. Almost as numerous were those raising money for war bonds. Irene herself gave far more than she intended at one dinner because it was Douglas Fairbanks making the request.

"Well, he kissed my hand and called me 'Irene, dear,' she explained to Clara when they were going over the accounts later that week. "What else could I have done?" She was furious with herself for blushing as she made this explanation.

They had a fall line to show that year and combined the showing with an appeal for war bonds. This time it was Charlie Chaplin who made a guest appearance and Irene found him easier to resist. It was a lovely selection of designs this time, Irene felt. Dresses had gotten sleeker and trimmer, which suited her very well indeed. Less fur to use, a more attractive result. She'd put her whole heart into the designs that summer, fearing with good reason that there might not be a fall line at Neptune et Cie the next few years.

While the economy continued to improve and spirits were infectiously high, so were prejudices, and Irene found herself near tears at some of the results. One of their workers started to bring his little dachshund to work because he feared leaving it at home unattended. The second day he brought it, one of the "patriots" at work kicked it, calling it a "nasty German bitch." The dog died and Irene fired the man who'd killed it. She was astonished to find *her* actions caused more discontented rumbles than the killer's.

All over the country, courts were inundated with Schmitts becoming Smiths. New signs with American names went up on German storefronts. Menus renamed sauerkraut "Liberty cabbage," as if the vegetable itself had nationalistic leanings and was capable of less digestive sabotage under a different title. Even German measles were now called "Liberty measles." Schools were forbidden to teach German. "How stupid can people be!" Irene complained to Clara one day. "We need to know more about the ways of the Germans, not less, if we're to win.'' Banks got new names, statues or plaques showing the imperial eagle were destroyed or altered. Suspicion was rife, no one was exempt.

The Committee on Public Information was formed and placed ads in magazines urging people to report to the Justice Department anyone who spoke pessimistically or asked questions or even expressed a desire for peace. To speak dishearteningly of the war was to ''become a tool of the Hun.'' Those who turned in names would remain anonymous. Irene found it terrifying. It was sharpening the point of patriotism and putting it into the irresponsible hands of the gossips.

Chandler Moffat came home the day after Christmas. Ever since his initial trouble with a burst eardrum, he'd been having recurring problems. An infection in the autumn had left him deaf in one ear, and with the advent of cold weather he finally gave up and came home. Irene was surprised at how glad she was to see him. It had been only slightly more than a year and a half since he and Edward had left, but seemed far, far longer. He had gotten quite thin, which was flattering to him, and brought home an English bride, a fair, shy girl named Gwendolyn who dressed in baggy tweeds and seemed to worship him. All in all, she was a tremendous improvement over the woman he'd been engaged to before.

Irene expected his war experiences would have made him more intolerable than ever, but strangely enough he was ready to resume work the day after he arrived. Bright and early, Clara came in Irene's office and told her Mr. Moffat was in his office and asking to see her in an hour, if it was convenient.

He called on her five minutes earlier than that. ''I was glad you came to meet us yesterday,'' he said stiffly. ''In lieu of family, it was good to see a familiar face.''

''Thank you, Chandler,'' she said, firmly putting them on a first-name basis. ''I'm glad to have you back and I think your wife is charming. Very English, with that fair complexion—''

''And dowdy clothing,'' Chandler added ruefully. ''She doesn't know that, of course. I'm hoping you'll take enough interest in her to help influence her wardrobe. Dear girl, but rather Yorkshire-looking still.''

Irene laughed at his forthrightness. He was quite right, but she'd never have expected him to voice his concerns, especially to her. "What about Edward?" she asked.

"He'll be along home in a few weeks, I think. It's a wearing thing, that duty. Ages a man."

"You've aged well, Chandler. I hope Edward has."

"Thank you, Irene. He's got a limp, you know. And . . ." He looked embarrassed.

"And what?"

"I don't know. Just different. It's been hard on him. Of course, it's beastly for everyone. Now, let's see just where we stand here," he said, suddenly all pompous and prickly like before. The momentary slide into friendliness was corrected.

They talked business for a while; it was mainly a social call, however, and it set a cooperative tone. If they weren't very careful, the mutual respect they'd unwillingly grown to have for each other might turn into friendship. When he'd gone, Irene sat looking at the door. If only you had been here to see this, Monsieur, she thought to herself, smiling. But it probably wouldn't have been this way had Neptune lived. It was his death and the restrictions of that hateful will that had forced them to get along. Perhaps he'd known exactly what he was doing when he handcuffed them together.

A little later, she got a message from Chandler that he was expecting a business caller at two and would be very glad if she would come to his office then. She was a little late arriving and the visitor was already there. A tall, long-legged Wall Street wizard she'd met several times before. "Mrs. Garrick, you know Mr. Baruch?"

"Of course. Hello, Bernard. I read about your presidential appointment. The papers are saying that your position as head of the War Industries Board makes you the most important man in America, next to the President."

"What they don't realize is that I always have been," he said with a charming smile that made it seem a good joke, even though it might well have been true.

"I'm glad to see this isn't going to your head," Irene replied. "You've come to convert us to a war industry, haven't you?"

"Fashion furriers aren't exactly an essential business to a

nation at war," he said. "Chandler's been showing me some of the jackets you've been making for the French fliers. Very nice work."

"Thank you."

"Could you do it a little less nicely?"

"I beg your pardon?"

"Look at this—the labels are hand-sewn, the buttons have heavy waxed thread whipped around the shanks, the seams are triple-sewn—that's part of what makes it so fine, of course, but they're all expensive and time-consuming niceties. We are going to need thousands of jackets that aren't meant to last a lifetime."

"Depends on your lifespan," Chandler muttered to himself.

Baruch heard him. "You've got a point. Let's be frank, Chandler, most of the fliers who will wear these *don't* have a long life expectancy. That's what I mean about the quality. What we need are warm jackets and gloves that are easy to move in. We aren't planning to give men clothes that they'll still be wearing to putter around the farm when they're fifty-five."

This talk of mortality subdued them all. "We can make them less expensively, Bernard," Irene finally said. "But we've got some problems."

"I know. You'll have machinery to convert. The War Finance Corporation will help with that, of course. That's what it's set up for."

"I wasn't thinking of that so much as the manpower. Or womanpower. Our workers are quitting. Several of our most skilled cutters have been drafted. We can train women for the unskilled jobs. We already have quite a few, but it takes years and years to be a good cutter."

"I can get you a few exemptions—essential civilian work. But only a few. Our first considerations are ships, planes and munitions, and food. Most of the exemptions are for these areas. You'll write up a report of exactly what you need? And what you think you can produce?"

"You'll cut the first in half and double the second," Chandler said.

"Probably."

"Will we be able to carry on *any* of our own business?" Irene asked.

"You can do repairs, storage, anything that doesn't take space or manpower away from my needs. By the way, speaking of storage, I'm taking all your warehouses in the city."

Irene gasped. "You can't do that!"

"Of course I can. You're going to have to pack up your ladies' pretty coats and send them to—"

"To Nova Scotia, perhaps?" Irene asked sarcastically.

"Not a bad idea. It's cold there. Don't look so mad, Irene. I'm going to win this war, and while you're a charming and beautiful lady, I'll toss you to the sharks if I have to."

Irene had never met anyone who could say a thing like that to her and make her smile, but his was a powerful personality. "You throw me to the sharks, Bernard, and you'll find I have hold of your coattails as I go over the rail."

"That's the spirit! We really should send women to war, not men. They are much more sensible, and at the same time, much more vicious. Get that report ready for me by . . . let's say, tomorrow morning?"

"Let's say later in the week," Chandler said, rising as Bernard Baruch did to see him out.

He made his good-byes, but paused at the door and said, "Tomorrow morning. At ten."

The report was ready by nine-thirty. By mid-January, all the furs that Neptune et Cie had in storage in the area of the city had been transferred to hastily equipped warehouses in four neighboring states. Irene had even bought a farm upstate with the idea that they could build another warehouse there later if need be. It was a perfect nightmare of logistics and bookkeeping, not to mention the travel both Chandler and Irene had to do finding the facilities. By March the main building had been converted to making jackets and gloves and the leather helmetlike hats the fliers wore.

Irene felt she was always under the threat of some deadline that was about to expire. True to his promise, Baruch had set quotas above what she and Chandler thought they could possibly meet, but they met them anyway. Between the long hours of work, the war-bond drives, and her precious time with Connie, which she wouldn't relinquish, Irene was perpetually exhausted. In April the German forces made a great push and American production was stepped up on all fronts. The worse the headlines—withdrawal from Ypres, Noyon, Reims—the higher the quotas went and the longer the hours got at Neptune et Cie and thousands of other companies contributing to the war effort.

The Kossoks' domestic life reflected changes as well. Zofia became a one-woman knitting factory and turned the small backyard into a garden and with Connie's help—or interference—grew a positively astonishing crop of rutabagas.

"Why rutabagas?" Clara asked.

"I asked her that too," Irene said. "She said, 'Why not?' She likes them and assumes the whole world does."

Cecilia's and Lillie's husbands had left their cannery jobs the previous August and their partings must have been satisfactory, because within a week of each other the next May Cecilia had a baby girl and Lillie had twin boys. But there was no lamenting their husbands' absences because both young men had been posted to noncombat duty in New Orleans, and aside from suffering from the heat and being parted from their wives, were perfectly safe and happy.

Edward VanCleve returned home that summer, later than Chandler had predicted. Irene was surprised at the sight of him. He looked much older and far more tired than she expected and his limp was very pronounced. He had family of his own to greet him, so Irene stayed away from his homecoming, but he turned up within a few days at Neptune et Cie—to see Chandler first, then her.

"I'm insulted, Edward," she said, hugging him and exchanging a quick kiss.

"I had to talk about a job before pleasure. Lord, you've gotten even more beautiful. I wouldn't have thought it was possible!"

"Flatterer! What about a job?"

"You know I turned the operation of the family company over to my cousin when I went overseas. Well, he's doing very nicely, thank you. All but threw me out and told me to go home and be a happy invalid." The words were light and should have carried the usual charm, but there was a discordant note, like a single clarinet being flat in an orchestra. Irene said nothing and Edward went on, "He's right, of course. He can manage quite well without me. But I've got to have something to do."

"I never thought I'd hear you say that!"

"I didn't either. But it's true. I'm more easily bored than before the war. Besides, everyone I used to drink and play cards and go to the theater with is off fighting. Some timing, eh? I'm worn out and sent home just as everyone else starts going."

"Just means you're a man ahead of your time." She said it laughingly, hoping to cheer him up, but she sensed his state of mind was beyond such first-aid techniques. He was being his usual polite, charming self, but there was something missing. Or maybe it was something horrible added.

"Chandler says you've got problems with the fur storage, and if it's all right with you, I'd like to help out. Travel, bookkeeping, whatever you need. Would you mind?"

"Mind? Mind! I've never heard anything that made me happier. Can you start this minute?"

He didn't do a terribly good job, but at least he helped some. Irene knew his involvement would probably stop when it ceased to be new and the sheer tedium of it took over, but in the meantime, any assistance was welcome. Irene found it odd and somewhat comforting that she could work with Edward and regard him as nothing more than a friend. Whatever had happened to the magnetism between them? It had once been so strong that she'd thrown all morality to the wind just for the sake of his touch.

He'd changed, of course. That was part of it. There was a desperate edge to his bonhomie, his pale eyes seemed to reflect some of the horror he'd seen and the devastation he'd inflicted.

But even then, it wasn't him so much as it was her. She'd suffered too, the way women suffer—without being able to do very much about it. When one of Edward's friends had died in what they called a "dogfight," he could leap into an airplane and go chasing off into the blue, swooping, diving, perhaps killing. But Irene had undergone losses and been able to take no revenge at all. In war, someone had said, men fight and women wait, and in that simple statement was the agony. In many ways, waiting was the real horror.

She'd learned from it, she supposed. She had to believe she'd learned something, otherwise all of it was for nothing. Patience, never one of her well-developed traits, had at least begun to seem a virtue, even if it was one she couldn't attain very well. Mostly the experiences of the last two or three years had made her start questioning things—values, beliefs, standards she'd swallowed whole because they were those of the upper class, the exalted realm to which she aspired. But now, at the pinnacle, she was beginning to shade her eyes and look around and wonder.

She and Edward had only one opportunity to talk to each other about anything other than the day-to-day necessities of work. Or perhaps it was that they didn't make the time for more intimacy. It wasn't a happy experience. He'd brought in some paperwork he'd finished late one afternoon and stayed to have a glass of iced lemonade with her. "Would you like a few days off?" she asked.

He bristled. "No, why do you ask?"

"Don't take offense. I just thought you looked tired."

"No, I wish I were. Irene, do you ever have trouble sleeping?"

"My only trouble is not getting the opportunity often enough," she said, and stifled a chuckle when she saw that he was serious. "Edward, what's wrong?"

He shrugged. "I don't know. I wish I did. A year ago I was on top of the world—almost literally. In the skies, cocky as hell, feeling I knew everything and had everything. In spite of all the danger, I'd never been happier. And now—now I'm not worth much. In spite of all I've been through, I can't for the life of me figure out what I've learned from it. A person who faces death a half-dozen times a day ought to get some vast understanding of life out of it, shouldn't he? I'm just surprised and sickened—and not better off than before. In fact, I hardly remember 'before.' What did I do to fill my days? What will I do from now on until . . . until when? Am I going to be an old man someday, still wondering how to get on with life?"

She didn't know what to say. So much of this merciless

self-assessment was close to the truth. For all his sophistication back in the old days, he'd been an innocent about life, having never seen anything but the best and easiest of it. It was, she realized only now, one of the barriers between them, and it was the essence of his charm. But somehow the innocence had been tarnished without augmenting his character. Afraid to attempt denial, more afraid to agree, Irene managed some meaningless but vaguely comforting words and determined that she'd give him some serious thought just as soon as things calmed down a bit and they'd talk again.

There was, however, little time for reflection that summer. She was genuinely worried about Edward, but simply didn't have the leisure to give him much thought. In July the Allies, with the help of the hundreds of thousands of American troops that had been pouring in steadily, finally put a stop to the German offensive that had been sweeping across Europe. It was the beginning of the end, though not many sensed it at the time. By late summer it was more apparent. The Germans were falling back, their lines crumbling, but not without bitter fighting and tremendous loss of life on both sides.

In September the St. Mihiel salient was taken by American forces, and fifteen thousand Germans were taken prisoner. Late in the month the final major battle of the war started between the Argonne Forest and the Meuse while, farther north, the Hindenburg line was broken by the British.

But in Irene's life, these earth-shaking international events were eclipsed by more deadly battles on home ground.

34

Irene was so rushed that morning that she didn't even notice that Edward hadn't come in, until Chandler, pale and grave, came to her office without warning. He was usually very careful to make an appointment to see her. It was part of the game they played. But he came in that morning without even letting Clara announce him. "It's Edward, Irene. I'm afraid you must prepare yourself for a shock."

"Edward? What's wrong? Is he ill?" she asked, but it was a futile question. She knew what he was trying to say. Why delay it?

"I'm sorry, but he's dead."

"Dead! No, Chandler. You must be mistaken. He's a perfectly healthy young man. People like him don't just die!"

"They do when they put guns in their mouths. Sorry. That was a terrible way to put it."

"No!" Irene couldn't take it in, and yet she should have known it was coming. He'd been so depressed, so empty, ever since his return. But who would have imagined he'd see suicide as a solution? How could anyone? And yet, even as the thought went through her mind, she remembered how she'd felt the week before Connie had been conceived. Willing to die. Not eager, but willing. He'd merely gone a step farther.

But the thought of Connie made her wonder: if she'd told him he had a daughter, would it have mattered? Would he have felt a need to live on for the child? For a long time she was sick with guilt, feeling that she might have had Edward's life in her hands and unwittingly let it go. And yet she wasn't positive it would have mattered and she found herself thinking more often of the possible consequences, had he known. She couldn't have confessed the truth, that he had a daughter and was forbidden to acknowledge it. He could have insisted, quite rightly, that they marry. And what would his life—or hers—have been like then? Friendship was important, in or out of marriage, but not basis enough to support the whole emotional structure. Not for her, anyway. And just as surely not for Edward.

In the end, what upset her the most was that her caring wasn't of a different sort. She was sorry, deeply sorry, and would miss him horribly. He was the father of her child, even though he'd never suspected it. She should have been desolated by his death. They had created a human being between them. It should have counted for more. It should have made them love each other.

And yet all she really felt was a sense of guilty, rushed frustration. And somewhere, layers beneath that, an anger at him for not having the strength to overcome whatever it was that drove him to the brink. He's grown up useless. Charming, but utterly without worth. Then he'd become valuable in the war. He'd done worthwhile things under conditions of terrible danger. Shouldn't that have made him more of a person? Couldn't he have used that courage, once he'd learned it was within him? She didn't blame him, or think less of him, but she simply couldn't understand. How could he have spent all that time so skillfully avoiding death and then go seeking it?

She attended the funeral with Clara and Chandler and Gwen and afterward invited them all back to her house. She no longer felt that letting Chandler in on the secret of her family was a danger. The war had taken the edge off their competition by forcing them to respect each other. He might as well know the worst.

He was, she was almost amused to see, rather taken aback by Zofia. "So you work for my Irina?" she said.

He puffed up like an irate porcupine.

"No, Mama. Mr. Moffat is my partner. He and I each own half of the business."

Zofia just nodded. "Good thing you back. Irina, she work too hard. You are war hero, no?" She'd heard Irene mention that Chandler was deaf in one ear and so she was considerately screaming. "You and pretty wife stay for dinner, yes? It's Tuesday, so we have no meat or wheat. This is war rule, you know. But I got nice rutabaga. Plenty for company."

Irene had to admire the way he kept cool under the threat of a meatless, wheatless, rutabaga meal. They stayed and Zofia struck up a conversation with Gwen about crocheting which bored the rest of them nearly senseless, but seemed to please Gwen. She didn't appear to find anything strange about Zofia. Finally Chandler said, "We must be going. Irene, you look tired, if you don't mind my saying so."

"I am. It's been a long day and I've got a bit of a sore throat, too. I'll just turn in early and be bright as a button tomorrow."

"Sore throat?" Chandler said. "I hope it's not that influenza business."

"What influenza?" Irene asked.

"The Spanish influenza," Gwen said. "They say it's sweeping through the city. Mainly in the more crowded parts. Terribly infectious."

Irene had been too busy the last week even to look at a paper, and she knew nothing about the Spanish flu, but by the next morning she had a personal acquaintance with the dread affliction. Zofia had called the doctor, who made the diagnosis. Irene was miserable. She started running a fever during the night and felt like a large hot elephant was sitting on her chest. It was a painful effort to breathe.

"I think you're going to get off easy, Mrs. Garrick," the doctor said. "You're young and in good health and it seems to be a mild case."

"This is mild?" Irene croaked. It was an agony to force the words through her throat.

"The serious cases are dying by the truckload. You're just going to feel awful for a week or so. But I suggest you isolate yourself. It's terribly contagious. Your mother and daughter are in greater danger than you, if they get it."

"My daughter!"

"Children and the elderly are particularly susceptible."

In spite of her condition, Irene managed to issue a string of strongly worded orders. She was to be left entirely alone. No one could come in her room. The cook was to serve her meals on expendable old plates, set in the hall on a tray, and then the plates were to be destroyed, the silverware boiled. Further, Zofia, Stefania, and Connie were not to leave the house except to go into the backyard. Nor was anyone to have guests. Irene felt like the mistress of a castle ordering the oil to be boiled and set on the ramparts.

It was more like the plague than she knew at the time. All over the city people were falling ill. The disease had come from Europe by ship. Among others, young Secretary of the Navy Franklin D. Roosevelt returned from a two-month overseas tour and was carried off the *Leviathan* on a stretcher and taken by ambulance to his mother's home. By the time Irene felt well enough to sit up and read a newspaper, the city had been all but felled. Incoming ships were being fumigated, but it was too late for such measures to do any good. Spanish influenza was ravaging the city and getting ready to sweep across the country.

Within a few days, a handful of cases became a deadly epidemic. Within twenty-four hours more than eight hundred people died in the city. Hospitals filled and had to turn away patients, whom they couldn't have helped much anyway. The doctors and nurses were dropping in their tracks, and in many places prostitutes, whose business was suffering, turned to temporary nursing. The telephones hardly worked because so many operators were sick; all the city services ground nearly to a stop. Garbage collectors didn't collect, firemen were too weak to drag themselves from their beds to fight fires, there weren't enough men alive and well to drive the buses or dig the graves or repair broken water mains.

"We're giving up," Chandler told Irene a week later when she finally got through to him on the telephone. "We have to close down. So many of the women are off sick. I haven't got a man left in the place but myself, and I'm not in very good shape either."

"Oh, Chandler, not you too? I could come down in a day or two. I'm feeling much better. I guess the doctor was right that mine was a mild case."

"There's no need. The war is about to end anyway. We don't need to kill ourselves to keep on making coats nobody is going to wear. I've made Clara and Troutwhite clear out. You stay home and take care of your family. How is everybody? How's Connie?"

"I'm told Connie is fine, but going wild with being kept in. I heard Stefania coughing in the hallway this morning, but she and Mama seem to be fine. I think we're all going to survive it here."

She was quite wrong.

Stefania went suddenly.

The day before, she'd escaped Zofia's watchful eye and gone to a candy store a few blocks away. By morning, when Irene heard her coughing, she was feeling nauseated and weak and complained to Zofia that she had pains in her eyes and back. By noon she was distinctly feverish and Zofia shouted the word in to Irene.

"I'll help, Mama. I'm well enough," Irene said, getting up dizzily and dressing. "Send Connie and the nursemaid to the top floor and lock them in if you have to." She had to stop and lean against something several times before she had herself together, but eventually she staggered into Stefania's room and was appalled at the girl's flushed face and rapid breathing. "Has she been around Connie today?" Irene asked.

"They made fudge," Zofia answered.

Irene groaned. "Probably taking turns licking off the spoon. My God! Mama, you get out of here. I probably can't get it again, but I don't want you sick too."

But there was no budging Zofia. Irene might be her best child, but Stefania was her favorite, and she was not about to abandon her, even for her own safety. By evening Stefania was desperately ill. The doctor, himself a walking wreck, had given them little hope and had nothing to offer but suggestions for making her more comfortable. Connie was resenting her incarceration, and her screams of frustration could be heard echoing from above as Irene and Zofia tended Stefania.

She was gone by dawn. "At least God was merciful and took her quickly," Irene attempted to soothe Zofia.

Zofia started wailing uncontrollably, which woke Connie, whose thin cries were a distant counterpoint. Irene gave her mother the rest of the sleeping draft the doctor had left for

Stefania and spent an hour on the phone trying to get through to the funeral home and Clara. "Do you want me to come over?" Clara asked when Irene finally reached her.

"I'd love to have you here, Clara, but no. You'd be both in danger of infection and a danger yourself. We're just going to have to stay here by ourselves. Please, just tell Chandler. He should know. I'd like to run away to the house in the country, but it's too great a risk. We'd have to be in contact with the chauffeur and the staff there. It's bad enough that we'll have to go out for the funeral."

But they didn't. Stefania was buried by the priest without any family in attendance. Irene was at home nursing her mother.

At that point, Clara insisted on coming over. She turned up without warning or invitation. "I can't give it to you or Zofia, since you've both had it. And I won't get near Connie—dear God, is that her crashing around up there?"

"She's like a caged lion. Poor little thing has no idea why she and the nursemaid are locked up and nobody can come see them. She alternates between calling for me and calling for Mama. It breaks my heart. I'm afraid even to go up on that floor for fear I'll somehow carry the infection."

"And your mother? How is she?"

"Very bad. I'm frantic with frustration. She's lost all sense of time and place and forgotten all her English. I can't understand half of what she's saying. She doesn't even know Stefania was buried this morning. I suppose that's a blessing."

"Irene, go to bed. You look a hundred and five yourself. I'll sit with her."

"I can't let you do that. You'll get it too."

"I think I may have already had it, milder even than you. I didn't tell you, but I was sick all last week. Headache, fever, sore joints."

"Clara, you're lying."

"I most certainly am not!"

In the end, she convinced Irene it was the truth and got her to bed. Irene slept nearly sixteen hours straight. When she returned to the sickroom, however, the news was not good. "She was getting dehydrated. I've been working at getting liquids into her, but it's almost impossible."

"She's stopped thrashing and mumbling. Is that a good sign or a bad one? I'm calling the doctor again."

"I already did. He's dead, Irene. I can't find another who will come."

Zofia barely hung on for the next two days, seeming to die by inches. Irene became numb. The days and nights were a never-ending round of changing bedding, wringing out cold cloths, and trying to force liquid into Zofia, drop by drop.The third morning there was no change, and leaving both Zofia and Clara sleeping, Irene went downstairs, just to force herself to move. As she came down the steps, she noticed a letter had fallen through the slot in the door and slipped under the carpet. Only a corner showed. She stooped, groaning a little. Her breath caught as she looked at the envelope. She hadn't seen that handwriting for a very long time, but she recognized it. Peter's.

Her hands were shaking and she instinctively slipped it into the pocket of her dress. What could he say to her that she would want to read? Nothing. It was done. He wasn't a part of her life anymore. As soon as the war was over, she was going to divorce him. She didn't know what he might be writing to her about.

She got halfway back up the stairs before she took the envelope out and opened it. There were only a few lines of rushed, spiky writing:

Dear Irene,

Only a minute before the mail goes. Have found Aggie and children. All well. Looking for Olbracht. Will get them back with me somehow. More later.

Love,
Peter

She flew up the stairs and into the sickroom, waving the letter and shouting, "Mama, Mama, listen! Aggie's all right. Peter found her and the children. They're coming! Oh, Mama, you must listen to me! Do you understand?"

Zofia mumbled and Irene and Clara nearly bumped their heads together leaning forward to listen. "What did she say, Clara?"

Clara started laughing. "She says she'll fix them some nice rutabaga when they get here!"

Zofia's recovery was slow but sure. She wasn't able to get out of bed for another three weeks. When the first two weeks had passed without anyone else in the household falling sick, Connie was freed. She wasn't supposed to get near her grandmother, but ignored the rules immediately. Eventually Irene gave in to her mother's and daughter's nagging and allowed Connie to play on Zofia's bed, which made them both happy. Connie was furious at first with her mother for having her shut upstairs, but quickly relented. "She's so sweet-natured," Clara said. "I'd have never forgiven you."

The time passed slowly. None of them left the house. The influenza epidemic seemed to be waning, but there were still hundreds and hundreds of new cases every day. By the end of it there would be more than twelve thousand dead in New York City alone, half a million nationwide, and twenty-one million worldwide. Those weeks were important for Irene, though she wasn't exactly conscious of it at the time. No work to go to, no socializing, no callers, no pressure—it was a strange way of life for her, and surprisingly, she took to it rather better than she would have expected. There were long, quiet evenings in front of the fire, soothing games to be played with Connie and her tattered paper dolls, leisurely meals and sound-sleeping nights.

Perhaps because those weeks had been initiated by her own illness, she didn't undergo the pacing frustration she might have otherwise. Occasionally, of course, she would wake "on the run" and for a minute or two wonder hectically what she had to do that day. And as she got better and Zofia demanded less attention, she found herself sometimes itching to get back to work. But for the most part she was able to luxuriate in inertia.

She found herself thinking often of Peter, wondering where he was, how he'd found Aggie and the children and how the search for Olbracht was coming along. There had been no return address on the letter, no indication whatsoever of where it had come from. And another didn't follow for some time. She was eager to hear from him again, but she wasn't anxious anymore. The war was nearly over. Everyone knew it had only weeks or perhaps days to run. She didn't expect to know more until the horror was officially over.

In her relaxed mood, Irene unwillingly began discovering in herself a faint understanding of Peter and a glimmer of what had gone wrong so long ago. If now, as she played with a wooden train set on the floor with Connie, someone had insisted that she throw herself into the world, into business and society, if someone had tried to tear her away from the gentle, contemplative cloud she floated on, she'd have fought it. Just as he'd fought it. And given up the fight.

Of course, she was feeling benevolent toward him because he'd cast himself in the role of Aggie's savior. While it was a good and noble thing for him to have done, it had nothing to do with the two of them and less to do with the horrible pain he'd caused her when he walked out—both times. She tried to remind herself of that frequently, to keep from tumbling headling into a romantic haze that would obscure both the past and the future.

On November 7 United Press reported—wrongly—that the armistice had been signed. New York City went wild with rejoicing. Enrico Caruso came out onto the balcony of the Knickerbocker Hotel and sang "The Star-Spangled Banner" to the crowds assembled in Times Square. Wall Street office workers threw ticker tape out the windows and their bosses gave bonuses. Irene and Connie went outdoors to watch an impromptu parade going along Fifth Avenue. A candy-store owner was giving away candy to any child who asked. Strangers were dancing and hugging in the streets.

Connie came home sick with the excitement of it all and threw up her candy. Irene tucked her into bed with orders that she be kept quiet for the rest of the evening, then fought her way through the crowds to go to the office. She didn't have any real reason, except that she hadn't been there for several weeks and it seemed a good way to privately acknowledge the end of the war. She had some trouble convincing the new night watchman that she was in fact one of the proprietors of the business.

The rooms, normally humming with activity, were empty,

dark, and quiet. There was a skeleton staff at night and Irene chatted briefly with the man who checked and turned the pelts in the drying rooms before going up to her office. She was surprised to see a light under the door of Chandler Moffat's office. She opened the door. "What are you doing here?" she asked.

"I might ask the same," he replied. "I just came down for some paperwork, and it was so peaceful . . ."

"Peace—yes, we're at peace now," Irene said.

He pulled out a chair for her and poured a glass of sherry for each of them. She noticed that he was putting back on the weight he'd lost before he went to war. He certainly looked like a rich man. A bit portly, self-satisfied, self-important. She'd once had such contempt for him, but he'd changed over the years and so had she. They toasted silently and Irene took a sip. "The first time I tasted sherry was at your uncle's house the night he invited me to come to work as an apprentice designer. I wondered how anyone could like it—sherry, I mean."

"And do you?"

"No, but I do like the look and smell of it."

They contemplated their glasses in silence again. Finally Irene spoke. "We're out of the business of making jackets and gloves for the army now, I assume. I've been making some designs for women's coats and accessories. All very feminine. Trim, but not the least military."

"Enough for a full-line showing?"

"No, just a token showing. It's too late in the season for a full line anyway. If we could start next week, I think we could have a Christmas showing. Just a modest affair. Could you do it by then—get out invitations, all the rest?"

"I could if you have the coats ready. Fourteen or fifteen models?"

Part of her wanted to say yes and dash off to spend the night sketching like crazy. It was what she would have done before the war, and she would have enjoyed every hectic minute of it. But things were different now. She was different. The fire of ambition that had fueled her for so long was flickering a bit. It was in no danger of going out—ever—but other sorts of ambitions were vying for her energy. And the tranquillity of her home was beckoning as well. "I can have six, maybe seven."

Chandler nodded his agreement.

She went home both anticipating her return to business and dreading it a little bit too. It had turned cold and she shivered a little, even in the old opossum coat that was still the only fur she owned. She found herself thinking about the sables, still in the cold safe. It was time for that coat. She'd finally earned it. She wasn't sure what barrier she'd passed, what prerequisite she'd finally fulfilled, but she was ready to wear the crown sables.

When she reached the house it was late, but glancing up, she noticed a light on in Connie's room. Her heart was pounding as she turned her key in the lock. Dashing upstairs, she met Zofia in the hallway. "What's wrong with Connie?"

"Nothing. Don't distress yourself," Zofia said, but her voice was pitched a little higher than usual.

"It's the flu, isn't it? Connie has the Spanish flu."

Zofia shrugged miserably. "I don't know. Maybe. Maybe it's just the candy and everything."

It wasn't the candy.

They went through it all again—the medicines, the doctors, the alcohol baths for fever, the ice chips for dehydration, the worry and sleeplessness. And Connie got worse and worse. At first she cried a lot, then only whimpered, and finally just made occasional lethargic peeps. Her blond hair, soaking with sweat, glued itself to her head. Her little limbs trembled and grew weaker and weaker and as her weight dropped, her eyes, miserable and unfocused, seemed to get bigger. Irene was frantic, nearly insane with frustration.

On November 11, the day the war actually ended, the doctor's visit ended in a warning. "There's nothing else to do. You should call a priest."

"You're giving up! How dare you!" Irene said, loathing him.

"I'm not God, Mrs. Garrick. Only he could save her now."

"More medicine . . . more liquid—there must be something!"

"Mrs. Garrick, sometimes all we can do for those we love is let them go in peace. I could put her in a hospital and put tubes down her throat and all the rest, but it probably wouldn't help. It would just be useless torture."

That evening, as the bells of the city started ringing and joyous fireworks lighted the sky, Irene sat in a rocking chair in her darkened room gazing out sightlessly. She had wrapped Connie in her favorite quilt and held the now nearly comatose child in her arms. Connie's breathing was shallow, her skin clammy, and her pulse almost impossible to discern. Irene was afraid her baby's life was slipping away and she couldn't hold on to it. Perhaps the doctor was right to insist that she be allowed to go quietly.

She wiped a tear from her cheek with the corner of the quilt and smoothed Connie's blond hair back from her pale face. "What have I done to deserve losing you? I've lost so much else, so many other people I loved—Monsieur, Peter, your father, Aggie, Stefania. But not you too. What have I done to God that he'd do this to me? I've had you in my life for only four years, but I can't remember who I was without you."

Irene rocked gently, whispering to Connie. "What would I do without you, my darling? How would I look forward to another day if you weren't part of it? I want to see you grow up. What sort of woman will you be? A good one, I'm sure—with your sweet nature and lively mind. I want to see you grow up and fall in love and make your own life and family."

Irene had surprised herself with her own sudden perception. Yes, this was what she wanted for Connie. Happiness, contentment; not things, success, position. Those were the aims Irene had given up everything else for, and hadn't truly realized until now how little they counted when balanced against love and peace of mind. She smiled bitterly at the irony. She'd worked so hard for what she had, turned herself into her own all-too-willing slave to achieve wealth and social power. And only now did she realize what it had truly cost her and those she loved. Nor could the achievement of her goals buy what really did matter. Money couldn't buy better medicines; there weren't any. Social power couldn't make the doctor truthfully give her hope. This big beautiful house was no better place to die than any other. What good were the expensive ornaments, the beautiful clothes, the chauffeur and the car and the jewels? What good was it all? No help, and faint comfort.

A group of revelers staggered along under the window singing "Over There." A skyrocket appeared above the house across the street, turning the sky pink and glittery. Connie stirred, her legs stiffening feebly for a moment, then relaxing.

"Mama?" the child said in a pitiful, croaking voice. It was the first time in two days that she'd spoken a word.

Irene pulled her close, buried her face in the soft blond baby hair, and wept quietly. "You *will* get well, Connie. You will. You have to."

in better place to die than just once. What good were the expensive amusements, beautiful clothes, the chauffeur and the cars and the jewels—what good was it all? No help, and little comfort.

A group of revelers staggered along under the window singing "Over There." A skyrocket appeared above the house across the street, making the sky pink and glittery. Connie stirred, her legs stiffening tautly for a moment, then relaxing.

"Mimmy," the child said in a pitiful, cracking voice. It was the first time in ten days that she'd spoken a word.

Irene pulled her close, buried her face in the soft blond baby hair, and wept quietly. "You will get well, Connie. You will. You have to. . ."

35

Fall 1919

Irene came into the bedroom carrying a large box. "I have something to show you. Something pretty. Want to see?"

Connie was propped up in bed, surrounded by the zoo of stuffed animals her mother, grandmother, and honorary Aunt Clara had provided her with during the last year. It had been a hard time for her. Her initial recovery from the influenza had been agonizingly prolonged, with slow progress and numerous setbacks. For a while there had been repeated ear infections and they'd feared she might lose her hearing. Though the doctor assured them that there was no permanent damage to her ears, it did seem now that she tended to turn her head a little to the left when spoken to, a trait strangers found cute and Irene worried about incessantly. Connie had been seriously weakened, and all through that first winter and spring she'd had a succession of colds. After a while, however, they became less frequent and less severe. Today was the first time in over two months that she'd been out-of-sorts, and Irene wasn't sure the child was even ill, but had put her to bed just in case.

"Is it for me?" Connie said, flinging aside the covers and crawling to the end of the bed to see.

"No, it's for me. But it's very lovely and I thought you'd like to see it first." Irene opened the box and took out the coat.

"Oh, Mama! How pretty. Is it rabbit fur like my coat?"

Irene slipped it on. It was of an extremely simple, classic style, the sort of style that could be worn for years, maybe generations, without looking old-fashioned. "No, honey. It's crown sable."

"'I don't see a crown."

"That's just its name because it's very special fur. It's the best of the best, Connie."

"Is it a present somebody gave you?"

"It's a present I gave myself, honey. Somebody gave me some of the furs and I bought the rest the year you were born, but I didn't have it made into a coat until now."

"'Why not?"

"Because . . . well, remember when Mr. and Mrs. Moffat gave you that very fancy doll when you were sick and you wanted to play with it right then, but we put it up in a case to just look at until you're older and can take good care of it? This coat is like that in a way. I wasn't quite 'grown-up' enough for it until now."

"Oh, Mama, you're being silly!" Connie giggled. "You've always been a grown-up."

"It might seem that way to you, honey," Irene said with a laugh. She sat down on the bed and gave Connie a hug. Until Connie had asked her, she hadn't even questioned herself about why she'd finally had the coat made up, but her first impulse answer was as close as she could get to the truth. All those years she had yearned for the coat and collected the pelts to add to those Neptune had given her, she'd never felt she deserved to wear it. Then finally, that night Connie nearly died, she'd changed her fundamental attitude toward herself. To have weathered so much, to have finally had the wisdom to see the true value of life was the hurdle she'd needed to overcome, without ever knowing what it was. That night had culminated years of struggle for understanding, and having gained the knowledge, she felt she'd finally *earned* the coat. Strange that she'd had to explain it to her daughter before she could grasp it herself.

Connie rubbed her face against the fur collar of the luxurious coat. "I bet this is the best present in the world."

"Mmmm, yes," Irene said absently. It was strange, but wearing the coat didn't seem all that different from wearing any of the hundreds of coats she'd had on in the last few years. It was nice, of course, and she was fully aware of the enormous financial investment it represented—a person could buy a mansion with what this coat would have cost. But it wasn't as special as she'd expected, and that surprised her. Odd that now, finally having it, it meant less than she'd anticipated.

She cuddled Connie a little longer, then said, "Are you feeling all right now?"

"Mama, I'm all well. Really and truly. Can I get up from this stupid bed?"

"Yes, but you have to stay in your room where it's warm. I'll tell you what, I'll ask Gramma if the three of us can have dinner in here tonight together, but only on one condition—you have to go through your toys and pick out what you want to keep for yourself and which ones you're going to share with your cousins when they get here. And there had better be more to share than to keep."

"Have I seen my cousins before? I don't remember."

"You saw Wanda and Stefan—or rather they saw you—when you were a tiny baby. You were born in their house. And you haven't seen your Aunt Lillie's and Aunt Cecilia's babies at all. But you will. Soon now."

It was to be a reunion with as much of the family as possible present. Aggie had written in March to say that Peter had located Olbracht in a German prison camp and he should be well enough to travel by June or July. She also explained that Peter, now out of the army and free to go home, was staying to come with them. During the wait, he was going to search for his old friend Herr Schmitt. In late May there was another letter. Olbracht had been recovering nicely and then had a serious setback, a severe bout of pneumonia. But he was now recovering again and Peter was trying to book passage for all of them in August. Peter had found his old teacher's grave and was relieved to find that the old man had died peacefully before the war broke out.

But again, there was a delay. Vast numbers of Europeans were coming to America, not to mention all the thousands of American soldiers who were gradually being sent home. It was impossible to get all of them together on the same ship until October, and they couldn't even consider being separated again.

Finally the wire came with the name of the ship and the day and time of docking. Irene had sent train tickets to Lillie and Cecilia for them and their children and husbands to come to New York and be present to greet Aggie and Olbracht. They were to arrive the next morning.

Zofia was happy with the idea of a bedroom picnic, and after they'd eaten, Connie got busy going through her things. "This is a baby thing," she said, showing her mother a once-favorite rattle. "We can give it to my cousins."

"Oh, do you really want to?" Irene asked with a catch in her voice, and caught her mother looking at her suspiciously.

"For what would you keep it?" Zofia asked Irene.

"Nothing, of course."

Later, when Connie had gone to bed, Zofia came to the music room, where Irene was reading. "You need another baby," Zofia said.

"Too bad I can't just order one from the shops."

"Don't talk that way to your mother!" Zofia said, easing herself into a chair in front of the fire.

"Mama, I can't get a baby like buying a new hat, and besides, having a baby requires having a husband first."

"You got a husband."

"I won't for long. As soon as the homecoming is over, I'm getting a divorce. It's best for Peter *and* me."

"A divorce!"

"Or an annulment. It comes to the same thing."

"Not in the Church."

"Yes, Mama. But the point is, I won't have a husband anymore."

"Then get a new husband and have babies."

"I don't want a new husband, Mama. I've never met a man I wanted to live with."

"Except Piotr?"

"Except Peter—a long time ago. When we were young and foolish."

"Such an old woman my daughter has become."

"I'm thirty-two, Mama."

"I was thirty-seven when Stefania was born."

Irene was taken aback. That meant Mama was only six years older when Irene left home than Irene was now. She had seemed, even then, to be an old lady. Irene stood up and stretched. "I'm going to bed, Mama. So should you. Tomorrow will be a long day. We have to leave by eight to be at the train station on time, then only an hour after that we must get to the docks."

"Irina, you finish that coat yet?"

"Yes, Mama. The crown sable coat is finished."

"Why don't you wear it tomorrow?" Zofia asked. She knew that coat meant something special to her daughter, though she'd never been able to figure out just what the significance was.

"No, Mama. It's too warm. Later. Someday later I'll wear it."

The next day was full of laughter—and tears. They gathered up the train travelers, dashed home, then left Lillie's two children and Cecilia's three there with the nursemaids Irene had hired to help out during the visit. Only Zofia, Irene, Lillie, and Cecilia went to meet the ship. Before it had even docked, they'd spotted Aggie at the rail. She was thinner than ever and there was already a bit of premature gray in her hair, but her face was radiant. Olbracht stood proudly at her side, with Stefan and Wanda flanking their parents.

But there was no sign of Peter.

The greetings were nearly hysterical. Zofia sobbed with happiness until she got the hiccups. Wanda got passed around until she finally started crying from exhaustion. "Why didn't you bring Connie along?" Aggie asked. "She isn't still taking naps, is she?"

"She's been sick a lot and I was afraid to bring her out to stand in the cold. She's at home playing with her little cousins and watching for us."

Olbracht was charming, but obviously tired and weak, and Irene did what she could to get them herded together and back to the house. She pushed Aggie and Olbracht into a taxi with Zofia; Stefan and Wanda went with Lillie and Cecilia in another taxi. "I'll stay behind to take the luggage in my car," she assured them. As the first taxi was starting up, she said to Aggie, "What about Peter? Didn't he come back with you?"

"Oh, yes. That Peter! We have him to thank for this day. If I didn't know Olbracht, I'd think Peter is the best man on earth. The trouble he took—"

"Yes, but where is he?"

"He said the family meeting was just for us. I told him he was wrong, that he was one of us, but he insisted he'd stay away until we were all settled. He said he would come visit in a few days."

"I see." Why was she so horribly disappointed? Seeing him again was the one thing she'd dreaded about the reunion.

That night they had an enormous dinner that Zofia cooked herself, claiming it would be next door to heresy to let a hired cook provide such an important meal for her family. They talked—all of them—until their throats hurt and jaws ached. Aggie and Olbracht refused to discuss the war. "It's over —thank the Lord God—no use fighting it again," Olbracht said. Wanda curled up in Aggie's lap and went to sleep; Stefan lasted a little longer, but gave up and leaned against his father finally. Cecilia's and Lillie's babies were all put to bed with Connie's dubious help, and still the family talked . . . and talked.

How Peter would have enjoyed this, Irene caught herself thinking. All those years they'd saved to have the family together—the family he wanted so badly to be part of—and here they all were for once. All but Stefania and Teo. And Peter. Teo, however, wasn't missed. He wasn't even mentioned. Peter was. Frequently.

"Remember how Peter took us to the Statue of Liberty?" Cecilia said.

"Peter helped me with my geography. He even made it interesting," Lillie reported.

"Remember how mad he was that time we cut all the pictures out of a book of his?"

"These noodles are wonderful, Mama."

"Yes, they were Piotr's favorite."

"Uncle Peter fixed my jumping rope," Wanda said, stirring from her sleep just long enough to deliver this proof of her kinship.

To their credit, nobody openly blamed Irene for his absence. Perhaps they didn't even think of it as being her fault, but she imagined they did and had an overwhelming urge to apologize. He meant so much to all of them. His faults and virtues were a part of the fabric of their lives. Especially Irene's.

"I'll put the children to bed for you, Aggie," Irene finally said, unable to hear his name mentioned again.

Olbracht carried Stefan up and she carried Wanda. With his help, she got them tucked into the extra beds that had been set up in Connie's room. There had been extra guestrooms, but Connie had insisted and Aggie's children had liked the idea too.

"Olbracht, you should go to sleep too," Irene said in Polish as they closed the door.

He answered in English, "I'm in America now. We will speak English only."

"Good. It will make your life and your children's easier."

She bid him good night and went to her own room. The others wouldn't miss her, she didn't think. Their hearts and minds were full of each other. Only Irene herself had an empty place in her heart tonight.

Everyone else slept late, but Irene was up early. She was getting ready to make a quick dash to the office when Clara came by. "I'm on my way downtown," she said, coming into the room Irene used for her design studio. "I've got a few things for you to look over, and there's no point in your having to come to work to see them. Stay home today with your family. How did it go?"

"Wonderfully. They stayed up half the night talking over old times and babies and plans. I heard Lillie and Cecilia in the hallway about five o'clock. They were giggling. It really took me back."

"And Peter?"

"I haven't seen him. He came on the ship, but not to the house."

Her tone was cool and hurt. Clara dropped the subject. She took some papers out of her case and they went over them. A supplier had overcharged them for some chemicals. "I think it's an honest error," Irene said. "They're really struggling since the father died. Pay it as it is."

A customer was complaining that her coat hadn't been shortened as much as she asked. "She's just trying to keep up with fashion at our expense. I told her hems were going up more, but she wouldn't take my word for it. Offer to take the coat back for the original cost. That'll jar her out of this nonsense."

A property sale upstate had fallen through. "Damn. That was such a foolish move on my part ever to buy it."

"No, at the time it made sense. If the railroad spur had gone through where it was planned, it would have made an excellent warehouse site."

"But I shouldn't have agreed to buy the whole farm just for the five acres I wanted."

"You didn't have any choice. The farmer wouldn't sell it piecemeal, remember. Don't worry. Lots of these soldiers coming back are interested in farming, and it's good farmland. You'll find another buyer. Shall I run another ad?"

"No, not for a while. I want to get my family settled before I get back into that. Is there anything else?"

"Not that Chandler and I can't handle."

"It's good of you to take so much off my hands right now."

Clara shrugged off the gratitude. "It's not good of me at all. It's my job and I enjoy it."

Irene saw her to the door and stood reading the newspaper headlines for a moment before going back upstairs. When there was a knock a few minutes later, she assumed it was Clara back for something she'd forgotten. Waving away the maid who was scurrying to respond, Irene opened the door and said, "Did you leave something—? Oh, Peter."

They stood staring at each other for a long moment and finally Peter said, "May I come in?"

"Of course. I'm sorry. I was just so surprised. I wasn't expecting you. Well, I mean, not just now." Irene closed her mouth to keep from babbling any more.

She led him to the music room and summoned a maid to bring them coffee. In the time this took, she attempted to get her emotions under control. He looked wonderful, she hated to admit. There was something different about him. Of course he was older and the years sat well on him. His hair was as fair as ever and the dark uniform he still wore made it appear lighter than ever. Though he hadn't put on weight, he seemed more substantial somehow, more solid. And the changes weren't only in a physical sense, but in the way he moved, the sound of his voice, the way he looked at her. There was nothing of the haunted, perplexed look so many men, including poor Edward, had brought back from the war. Instead, he wore an assurance as crisp and practical as the uniform. As soon as the maid had gone she said, "I wish you'd come here yesterday. The family missed you at dinner."

"I didn't have any right to be here."

"You had every right. You were responsible for . . . for everything, really. Even Mama and the other girls wouldn't have been here if it hadn't been for your efforts so long ago. Besides, this is your house."

"My house?"

"We own it—you and I."

Peter glanced around, an eyebrow cocked with amusement. "*We* did a nice job of decorating it, didn't we?"

Irene felt a smile trembling on her lips. She fought it. She didn't want to be in love with him again. She'd worked so long and hard at curing herself of that affliction. But love and gratitude were different matters and she certainly felt gratitude. "Peter, I don't know how I can even begin to thank you for all you've done for us."

"I owed it," he said simply.

"'Whatever do you mean?"

He smiled. "You chose me as your husband—well, that's questionable—but it's certain that your family didn't select me, and yet your mother and sisters accepted me as part of their family. I wasn't helping my wife's sister over there. I was helping Aggie—a young woman who had the grace and generosity to love me like a brother."

Irene had hardly registered the last part of what he said. "What do you mean, 'questionable'?"

"It doesn't matter. Just a figure of speech. Irene—"

"Peter, I think it may matter. What did you mean?"

"Irene, it's too long ago to worry about."

"I must know!"

He hesitated, taking out and lighting a cigarette. Irene had never seen him smoke before. "Very well. I've always suspected that you married me from desperation. Andy Spry had attacked you. You had no one to turn to but me, and I'd just made an ultimatum. To find safety, you had to accept my terms and marry me."

At first Irene didn't even remember what he was talking about. Then the memory came back. Andy Spry . . . the midnight flight to Peter . . . the wedding. "Peter, you can't have believed that! I'd already decided I was going to leave them the next morning anyway and tell you I wanted to get married."

He slipped the dented cigarette case back into his pocket. "You never said so."

"You never asked. I didn't know there was a need."

"I see. Well, as I say, it doesn't matter now anyway. But something else does. Irene, the last time I saw you I went out in a fury. But Zofia followed me. She told me off properly—at the top of her lungs and right out on the sidewalk. Thank heaven she was screaming at me in Polish. It cut down on the number of people who understood."

"I don't understand."

"She told me what had happened—about Monsieur dying and leaving half the business to Chandler Moffat. About you coming to the college to find me and discovering I'd disappeared. She told me all of it, even about herself—and your brother's real father."

"She shouldn't have," Irene whispered.

'Yes, she should. I went back to my hotel thinking about how critical she'd always been of you, and about everything she said, and about dawn I figured that if she was on your side, I was behaving like a real ass. I decided I'd get a bit of sleep until a reasonable hour, then come back and beg you to forgive me before I left. Unfortunately, my alarm didn't go off. By the time I woke, I was due on board the ship in twenty minutes. I was wild. I didn't know what to do. I was still hurt and confused and afraid if I missed the ship I'd never get the money together for another ticket. Finally I pulled myself together and dashed for the ship, figuring I'd write and explain it all. But I couldn't. Every time I started to put it on paper, I found myself without words. I wanted to tell you in person how wrong I was. I didn't know if I'd live to get the chance, but I was determined it would be the first thing I'd do when I got back."

'Peter, don't—"

"Let me finish—please. Irene, I've planned this speech for three years. I've revised it in my head a thousand times, but now I can't remember it at all. All I can say is that I was wrong. I don't know and don't want to know whose child your daughter is. I just want the opportunity to try to be a father to her if you'll give me half a—"

"Peter, stop. You're saying too much. Too fast."

He smiled. "For you, perhaps. Not for me. I've thought about almost nothing else for years. It seems like this conversation is long overdue. Just hear me out. You don't have to say anything, but I'm about to burst with what I need to say."

Irene hardly knew how to reply. She just nodded. He paced the room and finally sat back down, leaning forward and putting one hand forward as if to take hers before pulling it back and lacing his long scholar's fingers together. "Irene, we've made a lot of mistakes and I'm beginning to think most of them were mine. Is there a chance for us? No, don't answer. You'd be perfectly justified in never wanting to see or hear from me again. But please just agree to see me from time to time. Give me a chance. There's so much more I need to tell you."

If, a week earlier, even an hour earlier, she'd been told he would ask this, she'd have had her answer ready. No. Absolutely not. In fact, she'd had the answer ready for years. He'd left her twice; she'd never give him another opportunity to hurt her that way. She didn't love him. She'd told herself that so many times she believed it most of the time. They were unsuited—permanently, hopelessly unsuited. She was starting divorce proceedings the next day. That's what she would have said, and meant it. She'd gotten over the hurt and the love. She had Connie to love. She didn't need him.

But hearing him ask, seeing him sitting so very near, watching the once-familiar way his hair fell over his forehead, and remembering his touch—in the presence of all that, she found herself saying, "Peter, I don't know. Perhaps."

He stood again and started scribbling on a pad of paper

he'd pulled from his shirt pocket. "Irene, I won't press you. This is where I'm staying. Call me whenever you have some time."

She glanced at the paper he'd handed her very carefully so their hands didn't touch. Was he as afraid of physical contact as she was at this moment? "The Plaza? *You* are staying at the Plaza?"

He smiled again. "The book enjoyed a modest success—actually an astonishing success for a book of its kind. It's used, I'm told, by most of the theological schools in the country. There's money in divinity," he said with a wry grin. "Who knows what the war may have done to that trend. While I was away, my publisher put it all away for me and there was a generous check waiting for me."

"I'm glad to hear it, but I wasn't questioning your *ability* to stay there. I'm surprised at the inclination."

"'Irene, I've spent part of the last three years in conditions that made my childhood seem like an easy life by comparison. I kept thinking more and more often of the house you lived in—we lived in—when I left, and it became more appealing every day. The colder and dirtier and sicker I got, the more I thought about it. Tall ceilings, sparkling windows, pretty pictures, thick carpet, plenty of hot water. As much as I disliked that house when I lived in it, I came to think of it as the closest I would ever get to heaven."

"This house is even nicer," she said softly.

"So I see."

"Peter . . ." She honestly tried to stop her words, but they kept coming in spite of her. "Why don't you come stay here? It is, after all, your house. Mama and the girls would love to have you here. They kept talking about you all evening and missing you, and Aggie must think you're glad to get her off your hands the way you got her here and abandoned her. It would make her feel very good indeed if you'd stay—for a while."

"And you, Reenee? What do you want?"

The use of his private name nearly undid her. She felt her eyes filling with tears and she turned away before he could see them, but when she spoke the sound of them was in her voice. "I don't know. I don't know what I want anymore."

He didn't reply, and when she finally looked back he was staring at her with a curiously knowing look. "Don't you?"

"No. I've gotten everything I thought I wanted of life. I'm rich, you know. Very, very rich. And I'm important in society. Secure enough that I can afford to be any way I want and nobody can cut me out anymore. I'm *somebody*, and yet . . ."

He waited a minute for her to go on, but when she didn't he said, "I'll do it. I'll come stay, but only until your sisters leave."

All of a sudden she realized that he might be under a misunderstanding. "I'm glad," she said rather primly. "I'll have the maids get a room ready for you."

He grinned. "Don't worry. I wasn't planning on flinging myself back into your bed, Reenee."

"I didn't mean—"

"Of course you did, and you handled it very nicely, but it was unnecessary. I'll go get my things."

She followed him to the door, her legs feeling wobbly. What had she done to herself! Why had she invited him back? She was making a complete fool of herself and courting heartbreak. While he put his coat on, she was trying frantically to think of some way to extricate herself from this utterly impossible situation she'd created. Before she could object, or even grasp what was happening, he'd slipped his arm around her and kissed her lightly, quickly, on the lips. "Be back in an hour," he said as he walked out the door.

She watched out the narrow window as he strode down the walk. And as he turned and waved jauntily, she knew she'd lost. This wasn't a matter of determination or willpower or common sense. It was a matter of the heart.

She'd fallen in love with her husband all over again. No, that wasn't true. She'd never fallen out of love.

36

Irene had feared they'd have to have a never-ending round of heart-to-heart talks, but she never got the opportunity of telling Peter she didn't want to rummage around in her soul for a while. After their first interview, he avoided such things even more assiduously than she did. After the first day, she found her tension easing and let herself start simply enjoying his company.

Nobody could have made himself less obtrusive and more indispensable than Peter. From the moment he and his book-lumpy duffle bag came in the house, the atmosphere changed subtly. He became, without any effort, the head of the family, the central point around which they all revolved. He had a habit of benevolent command that had lain dormant until the war, but now came to full flower. The servants automatically deferred to him, Irene's sisters, now grown women, married, and mothers, seemed to honor him more now than when they were children. Their husbands accepted Peter as a war hero and senior male of the family. They had come to visit for a few days before going back to California. Their partner had not only run the cannery in their absence, but had expanded it, and they were hurrying back to purchase another cannery. They were going to leave their wives and children behind for a few more weeks. Having been forced to learn English in the service, they were well on their way to becoming very prosperous young men, and if missing the front had saved their lives, it had left them curious and they spent hours questioning Peter about the war in Europe. Irene found it interesting that he seemed to tell them a great deal without actually saying much of anything about his own experiences.

Connie, too, accepted Peter immediately. He didn't single her out for any more individual attention than the other children, but he was wonderful with all of them, listening to them with all the courtesy and interest he gave to adults. Connie called him "Papa" and Irene wondered how he felt about it, but she didn't ask—not at first.

Even Olbracht, a year or two Peter's senior, and certainly his equal in experience, came to him for advice. Luckily, Irene was present. "We are enjoying the peace and prosperity of this house and the loving family," he said at the breakfast table one morning a week after their arrival. "But we must get on with our lives."

"What do you have in mind?" Peter asked mildly.

"I gave it much thought while I was in the Russian army and later when I was captured. All my life, I have traveled. Not far, but all the time. I was away from Agnieszka and the children many days and always felt like a visitor in my home. This I don't want again. I would like to be a farmer, and my wife is in agreement."

"I think that's a wonderful idea."

"You know something of the land here in this country. And the laws. How should I go about this? I want to keep cows, not grow crops."

"Dairy farming—well, Wisconsin is known for being a good place," Peter began.

"So is upper New York state," Irene put in.

"That's true," Peter said. "Aggie and Irene would be closer to each other that way. Would you like me to help you look for a place, Olbracht?"

"I would, yes. You are more familiar with the idiom and the currency of this country, and I'd welcome your advice."

"Olbracht! I know just the place!" Irene said excitedly, suddenly remembering the conversation she'd had with Clara the week before. "I have a farm upstate."

"*You* have a farm?" Peter said with amazement. "Whatever for?"

"No, I just have the land. It's not a working farm anymore, but I think it has all the necessary buildings. I bought the land with the idea of building a warehouse on the part we wanted and selling the rest. Back when we entered the war and Bernard Baruch took away our city warehouses. But we never used it and I've been trying to sell it."

"And you'd give it to Olbracht and Aggie?" Peter asked.

Irene had expected them both to respond enthusiastically to this suggestion, but there was a hard edge in Peter's voice and a wary look in Olbracht's eyes. What was the matter with them?

"I had in mind *selling* it to him, actually. I would, for a family member, carry the mortgage—or *we* would, if you agree, Peter. It's yours, too."

"When could we look at it?" Peter asked. The edge was gone.

"Anytime. Tomorrow? We could take the train and make a family day of it."

"I thought you were busy with the designs for the fall show. It's next week, isn't it?" Peter asked.

"Two weeks, but I can work late tonight instead. Oh, let's do it. It would be fun."

Neptune et Cie owned a luxurious private railway coach which she took to St. Louis every spring, but Irene didn't even consider using it for this trip. It was too fancy and, it had always seemed to her, rather lonely. It would be more fun for everybody in the public coach. And it *was* fun. They nearly filled it by themselves. Zofia and her friend Apolonia Jedrychowski and her grown daughter and two grandchildren came along, as did Lillie, Cecilia, all their babies and the nursemaid and her newly hired assistant. Then there were Aggie and Olbracht and their two as well as the cook's assistant, who was in charge of the picnic baskets and drinks. Of course Connie came along as well. Irene still worried incessantly about her health, but she would have been devastated if she'd been left behind. "We make a sort of unruly army all by ourselves, don't we?" Irene said to Peter when they slipped out onto the back platform for a breath of air.

"This is the sort of day I've dreamed of all my life," he said, smiling at her with a warmth and intimacy she'd almost forgotten. They were quiet for a while, watching the glorious fall landscape slide past. "I'm glad you're offering to sell them the land instead of giving it to them," Peter said at last.

"I couldn't have made such a gift to Olbracht. His pride would have been wounded. Oh, I see. That's why you were so sharp with me when I first brought it up."

"You've changed, Reenee. Ten years ago you wouldn't have considered giving up a day's work at your most important season for a family outing, and what's more, you'd have insisted on giving this farm to them. You'd have chained them to the front gatepost if necessary to make them take your generous gift."

She felt her face flushing and started to object, but stopped and thought first. He was quite right. She'd have alienated Olbracht back in those days when her wealth was still new to her and she didn't know how to share it gracefully. She would have tried to force it on him and been hurt and offended when he refused. "I did that to you, didn't I?" she said softly.

"Over and over again. But you meant well. I always knew that." He leaned against the rail of the little balcony at the back of the train, thinking. "No, that's not honest. I didn't know it then. But I do now. Dear Lord, I wonder why we had to put ourselves and each other through so much to learn such obvious, easy things—a smart pair like us?"

After a long silence he said, "Irene, whatever happens to us, I want Connie to go on believing I'm her father."

"You must mind terribly that you're not," Irene said, unable to meet his eyes.

"I suppose I should, and sometimes, at night, I do. But most of the time I don't even remember it. That sounds impossible, even to me, but it's true. When she calls me Papa and looks at me with those eyes that are so trusting and so like yours, I never even think of it."

"That wasn't how you felt the first time you saw her," Irene said, unable to simply accept what he was saying. It seemed too easy to believe.

"No, not then. But it was a surprise and I was a fool. So, I might add, were you. Then. I've learned a lot, Reenee. Having seen so many lives lost, just thrown away, I've come to realize how important and innocent young lives are. In every sense but the biological, Connie is my daughter. She believes it and I am coming to believe it."

Irene was surprised to realize that she did too. Connie should have been his daughter. Both she and Peter wanted it so, and Connie already thought it was. Perhaps it *was* that easy.

Aggie and Olbracht fell in love with the farm and were ready to move in that day. "There aren't even any utilities," Irene said.

"Utilities? After what we've been through, do you think we care about a thing like that?" Olbracht asked, grinning.

Peter took Irene's side, knowing she wasn't quite ready to have Aggie torn away from her again. "We have to handle the paperwork first, Olbracht. The deeds, mortgage, that sort of thing."

So they agreed to come back to the house in the city, but only as long as absolutely necessary. When they all got home that evening, the farm was the only topic of discussion. Irene sat on the floor playing a hectic game of cards with Connie and the older children while Olbracht talked endlessly about cows. After the children went to bed, Peter taking Stefan up at his special request, she rejoined the adults and listened as her three sisters talked about the kitchen of the farmhouse. Finally even Olbracht wore out the subject and gave up for the night. As the adults drifted off one by one, Irene caught Peter's gaze, intense and speculative, on her. She waited until all the rest had gone and said, "What is it? You've looked all evening like you're on the verge of saying something."

"It's just that I never dreamed of seeing you like this. No, I *did* dream it. I just never believed it could be."

"Like what?"

"Tranquil. At peace with yourself. Not that you haven't always been very composed. You were never a fidgeter, but I always sensed you were keeping some sort of tremendous energy at bay with great effort. But tonight—all week, in fact—I've seen you sometimes just sit quietly. Truly relaxed."

"Why shouldn't I be? I have what I wanted. Here we are in a big, beautiful house. My family, all of them still living, are with me. We are well-fed, well-dressed."

"The whole dinner discussion was in Polish," he said.

"Even Connie knows a surprising number of words and seemed to follow everything that was being said. I suppose that's Zofia's influence."

"That's funny. I didn't even notice."

"What a change!"

"Why should that astonish you so? Did you suppose my character was set in concrete?"

"It's always seemed as strong and unassailable as that."

"I think you're insulting me," she said with a smile. "I could say all the same of you. There's never been a more stubborn man than you. And yet you've changed, too."

"Have I? In what way?"

"I'm not sure I can describe it. You seem . . . well, more aware of everything going on around you. I've watched you with the family. Four of them can be talking to you about different things and you seem to keep track of all of it at once. It used to be you would bury your head in a book and seem to lose touch with everything else. But it's more than just that. It all seems so easy. No, that's not it, quite. Not so much something you've gotten as something you've lost, I think."

"Anger?"

She stared at him, thinking. "Yes; I think so. Often before, when we were young, you seemed ready to be angry. At me, usually. But not always."

"I killed a man."

She waited for him to go on, certain this seemingly unrelated remark was the key to something important. "It was what you were sent to do," she finally said gently.

"But I didn't kill him for my country. I killed him for myself. Does that shock and offend you?"

"Oh, Peter," she said softly. "I was at Monsieur's side when he died, and Stefania's. A friend of mine put a gun in his mouth and pulled the trigger. I looked at my brother with half his head blown away. I've been through too much to be shocked or offended anymore. Tell me about it."

He took a cigarette from the dented case and lit it with great care. "There's not that much to it, really. He was a German soldier. We ran across each other by accident during the night. I had just checked on the patrol and was on the way back to my tent. He'd gotten past the line somehow. Maybe lost, maybe on some sort of heroic suicide mission. I never knew. He tackled me and I killed him. But when I did—I don't know yet how to say this, exactly—when I grabbed the throat of that man, that stranger who wanted *me* dead, I was killing an army of my enemies. He was the butcher who beat me, all the people who might have given me a scrap of bread when I was a starving child and didn't. His throat was my mother's; his bulging eyes were Andy Spry's eyes; his face was Neptune's—"

"And me? Was he me?"

"No, but part of him was the me that couldn't own you and possess you. That part of me hated you sometimes. But I killed that jealous, selfish man as well. I knelt on the German soldier's chest. His hands were clawing for me, ripping at my hair, my clothes, trying to gouge my eyes, and I choked out his life. And then I stood up and realized what I'd done. I should have felt a terrible guilt—reasonable, scholarly Dr. Peter Garrick, the brilliant, pious Catholic philosopher. But instead I felt an overwhelming sense of freedom, as if I'd spent my life in a jail and had just walked through the gates."

He leaned forward and tapped the long ash of his cigarette into a porcelain ashtray, then took a short puff and went on. "I didn't kill him because it was my job as a soldier, Irene. I killed him because he dared to try to kill me. As if this tremendous fury had been building up for years and had suddenly found its outlet. He was everybody and everything that's ever threatened me. He became all my devils, and in killing him I'd exorcised them. It seems impossible to me now, sitting in this warm, safe room with you, but I've never had a religious experience that was half as cleansing and purifying as those few hideous, murderous minutes."

He ground out the cigarette and got up calmly to put another small log on the fire. He leaned against the mantel, smiling briefly when he noticed his book displayed there. "Does any of this make any sense to you?"

"Yes, knowing you. Having known you. Did you suppose I could hold it against you? Is that why you waited to tell me?"

"Of course. Can you blame me for wanting a week or two of your company before coming up with a confession that might make me a ghoul in your eyes? But I had to tell you. So," he said briskly, "now you know the worst. You can order me out and I'll understand. I won't like it, but I will understand."

"I wouldn't dream of ordering you anywhere, Peter. I can't pretend I really grasp this, but I can accept it as something that happened and made a difference. A lot of things have happened to both of us, things we didn't expect we might do but that made us better somehow. I had an affair with a man I didn't even love. That's as much against my moral principles as murder, but good came from that, too. My daughter. And having her in my life has enriched and ennobled me." She paused, as if surprised at herself. "Oh, dear, how high-flown that sounds!" She laughed, and so did he.

"I think, Reenee, that is the very first time we've ever been absolutely honest with each other. It's a nice feeling, isn't it? Too bad we didn't try it sooner." He paused and then asked, "Didn't you love him? The man who fathered Connie?"

"Not then. I grew to love him very much as a friend. But that was later. And it doesn't matter anymore. He's gone. Dead, too. Like Teo and Stefania and Monsieur and the rest."

"But we're alive. And Connie's alive. We survived it all, didn't we?"

"'Survived? Just survived? No, we flourished." She stood up and went to stand facing him in front of the fireplace. Without speaking, he put his hand to the side of her face. She put her arms around him and let herself be drawn into the embrace she'd missed so desperately all these years.

"Do I dare say it now, Reenee?" he asked, rubbing his cheek on her hair.

"Please . . ."

"I love you. I've loved you since the day I first saw you. I've never stopped and I never will stop."

"And Connie . . . ?"

"Connie is my daughter. And if I have moments when I remember that she's not entirely mine, neither you nor she will ever know about them. I promise you that."

* * *

When the maid brought Mrs. Garrick's early-morning breakfast tray, she was astonished at the condition the room was in. Had there been a robbery? she wondered with alarm. There were clothes strewn everywhere. The pretty green dress the mistress had worn last night was in a heap on the floor. Her lovely silk underwear was flung over the arm of a chair. And the bed! It was in chaos. Counterpane dragged halfway to the floor, sheets rumpled and askew. The maid paused, balancing the tray and wondering what she should do. "Mrs. Garrick?" she called timidly.

In a minute the mistress appeared from the door of the adjoining bathroom. She was dripping wet, with soapsuds still clinging to her knees, and she wrapped herself hastily in a towel; her long hair was in soggy disarray; her face was flushed and had a wonderfully wanton look. She was so different that the maid wasn't entirely sure it was really Mrs. Garrick.

"Yes, Hobbes? Just set the tray down anywhere," the vision said. And giggled. *Giggled*!

There was another laugh, and a splash echoed from the bathroom. A man's laugh. The master!

Hobbes nearly dropped the tray in her eagerness to get back to the kitchen and report this development. They'd all been placing bets on how long it would take Mr. Garrick to move into Mrs. Garrick's room, and it was just possible Hobbes herself had won the bet!

Aggie and Olbracht moved to their new farm a week after first seeing it, and Lillie and Cecilia began to gather their belongings to go back to California. "This house is going to seem very big and empty when they've gone," Irene said to Peter late one night as they lay in each other's arms. "Do you think we ought to move into someplace smaller? Someplace you pick out?"

"We could," he said, stroking her arm lightly. "Or . . ."

"Or what?"

"Or we could start filling it up again. With more of our own children."

She wriggled into a less comfortable but far more intimate position. "I thought that's what we'd been working on all week."

'Working? Is this work? If so, I like it."

The response to the showing that year was spectacular. But Irene accepted the compliments with a preoccupied air. It just didn't seem to matter as much as it used to, and she found herself listening to herself responding to the compliments and thinking: Who is this woman?

She got home that evening a few minutes after Peter did. He'd been gone for two days visiting his old college and checking up on old friends. "How was everybody?" she asked, turning around so he could unhook the back of her dress.

He started taking the pins out of her hair. "They were fine. Those who were still there. Several had died in the war, of course, and a couple older professors had succumbed to age. I'm glad you've never cut your hair."

She slipped out of her dress and into her dressing gown. "Peter, I want to talk to you. I'm going to ask Chandler if he'd like to buy my half of the business. I'm sure he will, and I'll be sure to ask a reasonable price so we don't have to haggle."

"Then what would you do?" Peter asked, dumping the handful of hairpins in the bowl where she kept them.

It was the last thing she'd expected him to say. "What would I do?" she repeated. "Stay home. Have babies. Be a proper wife."

"Hmmm," he said, taking off his shoes as if they were discussing whether to have carrots or peas with dinner rather than something of such earth-shaking importance. "Is that what you want to do?"

"Of course it is. I've got you back and I intend to keep you forever. I can't take the risk of the business interfering again."

"That's very nice, but not what I asked. Do you *want* to give up being a furrier?"

"Yes."

"Liar."

"I'm not."

"Yes, you are. You'd last a year that way. Maybe a year and a half, then you'd turn into a shrew."

"Peter!"

"You've got the potential," he said, smiling. "Besides, if you do this, you'll wreck the plan I have in mind."

"Plan? What plan?"

"Well, I've got things to do too. I can't go on hanging around here. I'm on the verge of becoming the male equivalent of a shrew myself. I want to go back to teaching and writing. I talked to the head of the college today about it."

"About what?"

"What I'm proposing to you. The way I see it, you've got a business that requires your skills and actual presence from late summer to February or so. Right?"

"Right."

"And I'm in a business that has a fall and spring semester plus summer school. You see? If we live here during your busy time of year, I could do my writing then. And in the late winter, when the spring semester starts, and through the summer, we could live upstate and I could teach while you're thinking out your designs for the next season."

"You could do that?"

"The school wants me back and is willing to agree to those terms."

"And you want to? To live in the city half the year?"

He sat down beside her on the edge of the bed. "It's like I said before, it's amazing how stupid two smart people can be. We've had this problem of wanting two things that exclude each other. And incredibly enough, we've wasted a lot of years thinking only one of us could have his dream. It never occurred to either of us to look for a way both of us could have *most* of what we want. I'd like to live in the country and teach all the time and you'd like to work at your office all the time, but we can't have a marriage that way. But if each of us is willing to bend half the time, we can do it. Of course, it will mean Connie has to attend two different schools each year when the time comes, but children have endured worse fates than that and survived."

"Peter, this is wonderful. I think it really could work! I'd have to turn a great deal more responsibility over to Clara, but she's well able to handle it. More able than I am in a lot of ways. And it would give me a legitimate reason for raising her salary substantially. I've been trying to do that for years and she wouldn't accept. Oh, Peter! It's brilliant of you. Why *didn't* we see this solution before?"

"Because we weren't ready for compromise. Either of us."

"I can't wait to tell Clara."

"Let's have her to dinner tomorrow night, shall we? I haven't seen Clara yet since I've been back."

"Yes . . . no, I've got somewhere I have to go. Never mind, I'll cancel it."

"What is it?"

"A benefit dance for Russian immigrants. Not your ordinary serf-type Russians, but some sort of dispossessed nobility. They're terribly fashionable these days. As far as I'm concerned, they're just cadging their way around the world instead of getting down to the business of taking care of themselves, but I'm expected to rally around sympathetically because I'm still generally believed to be related to the Romanoffs. The point of this dance, as I understand it, is to raise money to purchase a small hotel for them to live in."

"Why cancel? Let's just take Clara to dinner early and all go to this thing."

"You would be willing? You?"

"Am I not invited?" he asked innocently.

"Of course you are, but I never dreamed you'd consent. You never would before."

"Then it's time I started. You're going to have to endure a fair number of boring faculty dinners. It's only fair."

Irene started laughing. "What a surprise it'll be. There isn't a soul left in New York society that believes I ever had a husband. How astonished they'll be when, after all these years, I actually turn up with the handsome Dr. Garrick, the renowned scholar. My darling Peter, you'll be an absolute sensation!"

* * *

They made a party of it, inviting Chandler and Gwen as well as Clara to join them for dinner at home before attending the charity ball. Peter was so good-looking in his new dinner jacket that Irene could hardly keep her eyes or hands off him.

When they explained their plans, Chandler tried very hard not to show how relieved he was at getting Irene out of his hair for half the year, but nobody was fooled. Clara was delighted with her new role and when Irene mentioned that her pay ought to be doubled, Clara surprised them all by saying, "At least!" They toasted everyone's success, exchanged congratulations, and finally got ready to leave. As they put on their coats, Clara said, "Irene, you're wearing the crown sables. I've never seen you in the coat before."

"I've never worn it before."

"Never? But I thought you had it made up quite some time ago."

"I did," Irene answered. How could she explain what a strange disappointment the coat was? It was beautiful and valuable beyond imagining, and it should have meant a great deal to her. For many years of her life she'd imagined having just such a coat. It had symbolized all her aspirations. But, wearing it at last, it was merely another fur coat. No more or less than any other. That thought gave her a quick pang of conscience. Monsieur had left her the pelts, sure his gift had a special significance. And it should have had. Peter was more right than she'd known. She *had* changed.

They piled into Chandler's limousine and Irene cuddled close to Peter. She was happier than she'd ever been in her life, and yet . . . Was there something in her that would be perpetually dissatisfied? Would a vague sense of "unfinished business" always haunt her? She *was* happy with the decisions they'd made. She was truly looking forward to the life they would lead from now on. She honestly craved the leisure that the compromise would require of her. She was content—no, far more than content. She hardly had words for the deep sense of satisfaction that formed the framework of her life now. Peter was happy, having come into his own in very much the same way she had. And Connie was the happiest she'd ever been with the life they had now. She had both a mother and a father who adored her.

So what was nagging away at the back of Irene's mind?

They were a little late arriving, and rather than stopping for drinks or to take off their coats, they simply got in the receiving line to do their social duty right away. Inch by inch, they moved along, and Irene enjoyed herself hugely as she introduced Peter to several people milling about. She was just watching old Mrs. Piper's eyes widen in disbelief when Peter gave her a subtle nudge to indicate the line had moved on.

Irene turned, took a step, and found herself looking at one of the Russian princesses for whom the affair was being given. Irene was suddenly stunned, swamped with memories.

The long rutted driveway with the ice-crusted puddles.

Teo's shoes sucking loose of the mud.

The candles lighted in the middle of the day.

The cold stone of the kitchen floor.

The guest of honor had the same sort of bobbing curls, but instead of being glossy, they were streaked with a few gray hairs and totally inappropriate on a grown woman. The dress was a different color and its ruffled collar and lace cuffs were shabby, much mended—not really much like the ruffles the little girl had worn that day, and yet the similarity in Irene's mind was eerie. All that was missing was the shiny gold ornament at her neck. And the big wooden box that made music.

"No," Irene whispered. Peter looked at her questioningly as the host mumbled an introduction.

She couldn't be the same person. And yet, to Irene, she was—either in fact or in spirit, it didn't matter. To Irene at that moment this raddled Romanoff was the girl in the big house who broke her eggs. She symbolized one of the unhappiest and most important moments of Irene's life.

How dare you talk to your betters that way, you dirty, common girl!

Irene suddenly felt cold in spite of the sables.

Someday I will be rich and I will slap her back!

Without any conscious volition—against reason, against natural inclination, against all the social rules she'd absorbed with such determination—she raised her hand in a gesture that was the culmination of all she'd worked for. This—*this* was the unattained goal, the unfinished business, the ultimate vindication!

But as she reached out, she found she couldn't slap the woman. Rationality reclaimed her, the chilling sense of the past retreated. Instead, she laid her hand to the princess's cheek and knew in that victorious moment that she didn't *need* to slap her anymore. Like Peter killing the German soldier and exorcising his own devils, Irene felt her last demon expire as she felt the soft, useless flesh under her hand. In that moment Irene knew she had won, she had succeeded—and in a way she'd never dreamed. The prize wasn't the money, the position, the employees that toadied, not even the society that lionized her. The prize was love and tranquillity; the things she'd never had the sense to seek, but which had been granted her through sorrow and so many terrible errors. How very, very fortunate she was to have sought the gilt, and to have found the gold in spite of her own foolishness.

A silence had fallen over the room. The importance of the moment electrified the air. People strained to listen to what was transpiring between Irene Garrick and the Russian princess.

"You can't imagine what I've done because of you," Irene said to the uncomprehending woman. She was smiling broadly, and there was a thrilling intensity in her voice that caught and held everyone who heard her. "The things I've acquired, the things I've lost or missed, the people I've helped—because of you.

"Peter," she said, turning back to him, "do you remember what I told you about the girl back in the village who slapped me?"

He smiled and took her hand. "I remember. I understand."

Irene smiled back at him for a long moment and then she slowly took off the sable coat. Peter nodded his approval. Irene touched the soft fur one last time before gently draping it around the woman's shoulders. Chandler, who had been watching all this with perplexity, suddenly interrupted. "No, Irene! That's too much. You can't give a valuable coat like that away to somebody you don't even know!"

'Oh, I know her," Irene said. "I know her. Or someone

like her. And tonight, for the first time, I know who I am. I'm Irina Gieryk, the *crème de la crème*, with or without the coat. I don't need crown sables anymore."

She stepped back, looking at the woman and then at Peter with a smile. For a long moment they stared at each other with a sense of deep satisfaction; then he put his arm around her and they walked away. But Irene stopped and turned after a few steps. "Auction the coat off and use the money to buy that woman and her friends a place to live," she said loudly to Chandler, and after a pause added, "but tell her she still owes me two kopecks for the basket of eggs."

About the Author

Janice Young Brooks is a native Kansas Citian who lives there with her husband and two teenage children. Her Signet novel, *Seventrees*, received the American Association of University Women's prestigous "Thorpe Menn Award" for literary excellence in 1981.